G·A·L·W·A·Y
B·A·Y

GALWAY BAY

GRAND CENTRAL
PUBLISHING

NEW YORK   BOSTON

Grand Central Publishing
Hachette Book Group
237 Park Avenue
New York, NY 10017

Visit our Web site at www.HachetteBookGroup.com.

Printed in the United States of America

First Edition: February 2009
10 9 8 7 6 5 4 3 2 1

Grand Central Publishing is a division of Hachette Book Group, Inc.
The Grand Central Publishing name and logo is a trademark of Hachette Book Group, Inc.

Library of Congress Cataloging-in-Publication Data
Kelly, Mary Pat.
    Galway Bay / Mary Pat Kelly.—1st ed.
        p. cm.
    Summary: "In the bestselling tradition of Frank Delaney, Colleen McCullough, and Maeve Binchy comes a poignant historical family saga set against Ireland's Great Starvation and the building of Chicago."—Provided by the publisher.
    ISBN-13: 978-0-446-57900-1
    ISBN-10: 0-446-57900-9
    1. Ireland—History—Famine, 1845–1852—Fiction. 2. Domestic fiction. I. Title.
PS3561.E39463G35 2009
813'.54—dc22

                                                                        2008017649

Book design by Giorgetta Bell McRee

*For Honora's children
down through the generations*

PROLOGUE

We wouldn't die, and that annoyed them. They'd spent centuries trying to kill us off, one way or another, and here we were, raising seven, eight, nine of a family on nothing but potatoes and buttermilk. But then the blight destroyed the potato. Three times in four years our only food rotted in the ground. Nothing to eat, the healthy crops sent away to feed England. We starved. More than a million died—most of them in the West, which is only a quarter of the country, with Ireland itself just half the size of Illinois. A small place to hold so much suffering. But we didn't all die. Two million of us escaped, one reaching back for the next. Surely one of the great rescues in human history. We saved ourselves, helped only by God and our own strong faith. Now look at us, doing well all over the world. We didn't die.

> —HONORA KEELEY KELLY,
> born 1822. Told to her great-
> granddaughter Agnella Kelly,
> Sister Mary Erigina, born 1889, and
> reported to the author, Honora's
> great-great-granddaughter.

Part One

The Before Times—1839

Chapter 1

Dawn, St. John's Night—June 23, 1839

AH, THE SUN. Rising for me alone—the only one awake to see dawn fire the clouds and watch Galway Bay turn from gray to blue. Thank you, God, for this perfect summer's morning, for the sand of the Silver Strand growing warm under my feet, for the larks and blackbirds tossing their song into the sky and the sharp fresh smell of the sea. Please, Lord, let the weather stay fine for my sister Máire's wedding.

Now, I'd better hurry along the shore to the stream near St. Enda's well and wash my hair or it won't dry in time. Of course, if you'd given me feather-light curls like Máire's instead of this stick-straight mass . . .

I wonder, will the nuns cut it the very first day? Miss Lynch told me they won't shave my head. That's a Protestant lie. My being accepted into the first convent allowed to open in Galway City since Cromwell, two hundred years ago, is a great honor for the whole family, Miss Lynch says. Mam's over the moon. It was a near thing, though. The scene came back to me as I followed the shoreline away from Bearna village into the woods.

❖   ❖   ❖

"Honora Keeley is my best pupil," Miss Lynch told Mother Superior two weeks ago, Mam and I with her in the parlor of the Presentation

Sisters Convent, keeping our eyes down. "She speaks perfect English, has studied Latin, history, literature, geography, and mathematics."

Mother Superior nodded, telling Miss Lynch what a great woman she was to teach the daughters of her tenants, opening the Big House to us. Admirable. Not many landlords would do that.

"Thank you, Mother," Miss Lynch had said to her. "I realize you don't usually consider girls, girls . . ." Then she'd stopped.

Ah, spit it out, I'd thought. Say: Girls like Honora Keeley, too poor and too Irish. Not like you Lynches, who've bobbed and bribed your way through the centuries to stay rich *and* Catholic.

I am a Keeley, an O'Cadhla, Mother Superior, I'd wanted to tell her. We ruled Connemara long before the Lynches and the rest of their Norman relatives set foot in Galway. My Granny Keeley says, "What are Normans anyway? Only Vikings with manners put on them!" But if I'd said anything at all like that, Mam would have collapsed on the spot.

So. I'd spoken up very politely in my best English and said that I was proud to be a fisherman's daughter. My da was born into knowledge of the sea, I told her, and can gauge winds and tides, steer a clear course through Galway Bay, and follow the gulls to a school of herring.

Mother Superior nodded, so I'd gone on to explain how the fishermen along Galway Bay—men of the Claddagh as well as those from Gleninna in Clare and Connemara—went out together, and then we women sold the catch under the Spanish Arch in Galway City. "We're very good bargainers," I'd said, "and also patch the sails and repair the nets."

And why did I think I had a vocation to the religious life? Mother Superior asked me. I told her I'd always felt close to Our Lord and His Blessed Mother. I admired St. Bridget and all the holy women who'd helped St. Patrick bring Christianity to Ireland, studying and teaching and praying in the great abbeys for a thousand years until the English wrecked them all. And now that the nuns were back, I'd be honored to join them. "My granny says that you're standing up to the Sassenach," I'd told her. And then she'd questioned me about my studies and I'd recited prayers in Latin and English and we'd finished up talking about what a great time it was for the Church now that Daniel O'Connell, the Liberator, had made the British government get rid of the last of the penal laws that had outlawed our religion and Catholics could go to school openly, build churches, own land, vote even.

"A new day," Mother Superior had said. And she would be happy to find a place for a girl like me in the Community of the Sisters of the Presentation. I would enter in September and undergo a two-year trial period, she said. I'd be called a novice and wear the black habit, but have a white veil. I'd start my studies immediately. My family could visit four times a year. I would miss them, Mother Superior said, but I'd get the needed grace.

Now less than almost three months until Entrance Day: September 15, 1839—my seventeenth birthday.

✧ ✧ ✧

I stepped through a gap in the hedge, crossed to St. Enda's well and Tobar Geal, the clear, cool, fast-flowing stream beside it. Flowers covered the bank—féithleann (honeysuckle), fraoch gallda (St. Dabeoc's heath), and fearbán (buttercups). I named them to myself in Irish but translated them into English as if reciting for Miss Lynch or Mother Superior.

I pulled up my skirt, knelt on the soft grass, inhaled the lavender scent of the soap Miss Lynch gave Máire and me for Christmas, then undid the three hairpins—careful, mustn't bend them. I leaned over, ducked my loosened hair into the water, and then lathered the soap into bubbles, digging my fingers into my scalp.

"Rua and donn," Mam called my hair. Red and brown. Mixed. Better that way. A redheaded woman brought bad luck to fishermen. If Da met one on the road, he'd go back home and not fish at all. So not red and yet not brown. "Mixed hair," Mam said, "and nothing wrong with that."

"Everyone can't be blond like me," Máire had said. Máire resembled Mam and her family, the Walshes—a tiny waist and curves above and below. "Péarla an Bhrollaigh Bháin," my Snowy-Breasted Pearl, Johnny Leahy, the groom, calls her, she'd told me. "Don't let Da hear him," I said, but she thrust her chest out at me and said, "Some have brains and some have bosoms," then crossed her eyes and I had to laugh.

I take after Granny and Da and the Keeleys—tall and thin with green eyes, "but they see as well as your blue ones," I told Máire.

Lather and rinse, lather and rinse, then a long third rinse. I shook my hair back and forth. Drops of water caught the morning light— rainbows in the air. How close to the scalp will the nuns clip my hair?

Round pebbles turned under my bare feet as I followed the stream's channel out of the woods and down to the sea where my rock waited, a small squat tower on the strand, layered with seaweed, dulsk.

I peeled off a bit and spread it out in the sun. Dulsk tastes best dried where it's picked. Now, I'll sit, eat my dulsk, and enjoy a sweet hour of quiet. Bearna will be stirring soon enough.

The easily found seaweed was gone already, the rocks stripped of winkles and barnacles, the shellfish on the shore taken. The farming people had come down from the hills looking for food for the hungry months, July and August, when the potatoes dug last fall have been eaten and the new crop isn't ready.

Mam tells the women, "Cook those cockles and mussels. Don't eat them raw, they'll kill you."

"Thank God we have fish to sell," she'd say to me. "Once the farmers give their wheat and oats to the landlord for the rent, they're left with only potatoes to eat. Those women never touch a coin. Some are married to poor laborers who work for nothing but the use of a one-room cottage and a scrap of a potato garden. We know how to deal and dicker in the market, get real money. A fisherwoman has a better life than the wife of a farmer or laborer."

Perhaps, but we too depended on the pratties. Our food came from the field the fisher families shared. Money went for rent. And the farm women never know the fear we do when the mist rolls down from the mountains, the Bay dissolves into the sky, and the sea goes wild. Nothing to do but try to pray the boats home safe. Every year, some men lost. The land might be hard, but it didn't kill.

Galway Bay . . . so calm and quiet. But I know your moods. Turn my back and you could be raging and rolling. At least the land stays still. But what farm woman's heart lifts as mine does when our Bearna boats join with the Claddagh fleet and the Clare men? Hundreds of hookers and púcáns move together down Galway Bay, their red sails full of wind, following the Claddagh Admiral's white sail out to the sea. The Bay's empty now, though. No fishing for two days, not on St. John's Night or his feast day tomorrow. So, a good time for Máire's wedding.

Well, I won't be the wife of a fisherman, watching my husband away, praying him home as I had always expected. A bride of Christ, Miss Lynch says.

I wondered, did Miss Lynch pick me because she's still fond of Mam from when Mam was Mary Danny Walsh from Bearna village, working in the Big House and the same age as the landlord's daughter? She might have stayed there, but John Keeley and his mother arrived from Connemara, and Mam fell in love with Da and married him. And when Máire, her first child, was born, she asked Miss Lynch to stand as godmother. Miss Lynch accepted. An honor for us, Mam says.

When Miss Lynch started the free school for girls, Máire and I were in the first class. I was five and Máire seven, creeping up to the attic classroom in Barna House, afraid we'd meet the landlord. Ten of us came from the fisher cottages and ten from the farming townlands, scrubbed clean and ready for the learning. All of us were shy but Máire. She'd been cheeky enough to correct Miss Lynch and ask her to pronounce her name "Mah-ree"—the Irish way.

Most girls left Miss Lynch's school at twelve to mind the younger children, mend the nets, sell the catch, and then at sixteen marry a fisherman's son. But Da and Mam let me stay on to study, except for the days I was needed under the Spanish Arch with Mam and Máire.

It was Máire told me to watch the way Mam looked at the new Presentation Convent and talked about the sisters when we passed it. "Mam wants you to be a nun. She and Miss Lynch have it fixed up between them. Miss Lynch will pay the dowry. You'd better find a fellow fast if you don't want to go into the convent."

But what fellow? Máire'd been courted by every boy in Bearna, but I never felt a pull toward any one of them—a sign the convent was God's will for me. Our Lord hadn't sent me a husband so I could serve Him. Maybe He was sparing me, too. I'd seen the drink take over fellows until they made their wives' lives a misery, and I'd heard my own mam scream through my little brother Hughie's birth, though she said a woman soon forgot the pain. Still . . . Almost three months. The whole summer. No school. I'll be ready by September.

Drowsing in the sun, I heard Mam say, "I'm grateful to God for calling you. . . ." and Da telling me, "Daniel O'Connell won a great victory getting the nuns back. I'm proud of you, Honora—the first fisherman's daughter to become a Holy Sister. . . ." Miss Lynch was saying, "A link is restored. . . ." and Granny Keeley was adding, "Irish nuns are women warriors, equal to any man." And I fell asleep.

The noise of the tide breaking on a rock woke me—Galway Bay, rougher now.

There, on the surface of the water, I saw something moving. A piece of wood? A cask lost from a ship? It's pulling against the tide, floating parallel to the shore. A seal? But the seals live farther out in the colder waters where Galway Bay joins the Atlantic Ocean.

Two eyes stared straight at me. Not dark eyes set in the sleek black head of a seal, but very blue eyes in a man's face. Could it be a sailor fallen from a ship or a fisherman? But sailors and fishermen could not swim.

This one was swimming. His arms were stroking through the water. A flash of feet and legs kicking under the surface, splashing and thrashing. Was he going down?

I ran into the surf. "Are you drowning?" I shouted.

"I am!"

Need something for him to hold on to. The tide pulled at my legs. Here he is. His face. Closer. He's . . . laughing! He dove down into the water, slid up again, then launched himself onto a wave, riding it onto the strand.

He stood, foam swirling around his long legs, hands at his sides— not covering himself. Looking me right in the eye—smiling.

"You're not drowning at all."

"I am," he said. "I am drowning in your beauty. Are you a girl at all, or are you a mermaid?"

"I'm real enough." I can't move. Has he cast some spell on me? Granny says mermen can step out of the sea, but this fellow's human, no question.

Strong, muscled legs. Wide shoulders. The length and breadth of the man. And no clothes needed. Bulky, unnecessary things they seemed. The male part of him was growing before my very eyes.

He saw where I was looking. "You can't be a vision," he said, "or I wouldn't be . . . Please, my clothes are just over there."

Clothes—get them for him now. Miss Lynch could be looking out her window from Barna House just above us. But still I stood, gazing.

An image of the parlor in Presentation Convent came to me: Mother Superior, Miss Lynch, and Mam . . .

But the picture blurred, then faded away.

And all I saw was him.

Chapter 2

"Tell me who you are," he said. "Tell me everything about yourself." He'd dressed himself in dark trousers and a loose linen shirt, and
the two of us were leaning against my rock.

"My father and brothers fish, and my mother and sister and I sell
the catch in Galway City." I pointed to the cluster of whitewashed cottages tucked back along the curve of the shore and told him I lived in
one of those with my mam and da and granny, my older sister, three
younger brothers. "Thirty of us fisher families in the village, Bearna,
it's called—the Gap, in Irish. Though the name's been twisted in English to a Barna." I stopped. This isn't what I want to say.

He knew. "That's the outside. Tell me the inside," he said. "What do
you think, feel? How can I win your heart? Give me some great quest;
send me over the mountains, through the seas. I'll ride my horse,
Champion, to Tír na nOg and back to earn your love."

"Love? You don't even know my name."

"Then start there."

"Honora Keeley."

"Honora. Beautiful. Honora: honor."

So it really does happen. Love at first sight, as in Granny's stories
of Deirdre and Naoise, Grainne and Diarmuid. To look at a face and
know this is the one. Astonishing. True.

"And what are you called?"

"Michael Kelly," he said. "My father was Michael Kelly. My mother's father was Murtaugh Mor Kelly. I come from Gallach Uí Cheallaigh."

"Gallagh of the Kellys," I said, making English of the name. "I'm starting to understand."

"Understand what?"

"That you're a Kelly."

We laughed, as if I'd made the cleverest remark possible. Then he took my hand, and I went silent.

I looked around the rock and up at Barna House—the curtains were still drawn, good. I had to lean across Michael to see our cottages. Quiet. Everyone sleeping still. I let my hand rest in his. Warm.

"You're not . . . I mean, is this some kind of enchantment?" I asked him.

"It is, of course," he said. "Wait, let me fetch my fairy steed."

Steed! He said "steed" and "fetch," so I answered, "Please, my gallant hero."

✦ ✦ ✦

How well he moves, striding along the strand, fairly running up Gentian Hill to the horse standing on the summit. A fairy place, that. Should I stand up now and run away? What if he's about to carry me off to a fairy rath? But I didn't stir as he led the animal down the hill and over to me. Michael had a saddle over his shoulder and a bundle under his arm. I stood up to meet him.

"Easy, easy now." He patted the horse's neck and set down his burdens. "You're fine, Champion," he said, and then to me, "Neither of us has ever been near water that has no limits. To see Galway Bay stretching out toward the sea like this—very exciting for both of us."

"A fine horse," I said.

"She is. And going to stand quiet and polite while I sit down beside Honora Keeley. Her name is Champion."

"Rua," I said. "Red."

"Chestnut," he said. "The color of your hair, all fiery in the sun. Truly, Honora Keeley, it was your lovely hair flowing around you made me think you were a mermaid. Like the one carved in the lintel of Clontuskert Abbey."

"A mermaid? I thought *you* were a merman or a seal," I said.

"Do you want me to be a seal? I would be a seal for you gladly."

"Be a man. A man with a fine horse."

And then I realized: a man with a horse. Oh, Jesus, Mary, and Blessed St. Joseph! A gypsy, a tinker . . . A lifetime of warnings: "Don't wander off, or the gypsies will get you!" "Those tinkers would steal the tooth out of your head and sell it back to you!"

When the painted gypsy caravans drove through Galway City, Mam pulled me close to her. The women in the market whispered, "They beat their wives something awful."

"Turn your face away, Honora, don't stare!" Mam said. "Gypsy women can give you the evil eye."

And now here he was, a man with a horse—a gypsy!

"And where are the others?" Go carefully, Honora.

"Others?" he asked. "Only Champion and me."

"You're not traveling in a pack of wagons?"

"You think I'm a gypsy?"

I didn't care. His eyes were the same blue as the Bay, and his mouth— smiling now.

"I'm not a gypsy, though I believe there are decent enough people among them. A terrible thing to be wandering the roads, and I suppose a bit of thieving here and there is understandable."

"Understandable," I said, "but you aren't one?"

"I'm not, Honora Keeley, though I am without home or hearth at the moment."

"At the moment?"

"I want to tell you my story, but I don't know where to start. Should I begin with my mother?"

"Do," I said. "Mothers are very important."

Then we laughed again. He took my other hand, and I didn't care if he had a mother or not, if he was a gypsy or not.

His horse lifted her head and snorted.

"Is she laughing, too?" I asked.

"Probably. Champion likes this story because both of us were born outside what my old schoolmaster called 'the natural order of things.'"

What did that mean? He'll tell me. We settled ourselves against the warm rock. I turned so I could watch his face as he started the tale. Lovely how his lips form the words. His eyes, rimmed in a deeper blue, hold such light. What thick black hair, and that straight nose. A hero come from the sea. Michael Kelly . . . Well into his story now.

" . . . so Murtaugh Mor—"

"Sorry, Michael. And who is he? I thought you were starting with your mother."

"I am. Here, sit closer so the wind doesn't carry the sound of my words away over Galway Bay to the green hills of Clare."

"I'm fine. I can hear. Start again."

"My mother's father, Murtaugh Mor Kelly, was a huge, big man, and few in Gallagh or indeed in any townland around Ballinasloe would challenge Murtaugh Mor Kelly. Even Colonel Blakeney, the landlord, spoke to him with a certain respect. 'Martin,' he called him, trying to put English on him, though he was 'Murty' to everyone else.

"Now, Kellys had been ruling East Galway for a thousand years when Blakeney's ancestors rode in with Cromwell, burning and pillaging."

"And destroying the abbeys and torturing the poor nuns," I said.

"Strange you should think of that, because abbeys come into it! Amazing that you should mention abbeys!"

"Amazing," I said. More laughter. I moved closer to him, both of us warmed by the sun now.

"The men in my mother's family have been smiths for generations. You've heard the stories of Goibniu?"

"My granny tells them. Goibniu made weapons for the heroes of old and welcomed the valiant into the other world with a great feast in the time before Saint Patrick came to Ireland."

"He did so," Michael said. "And even after Saint Patrick, smiths like Goibniu pounded gold into thin sheets to shape chalice cups for monks, croziers for bishops and abbots, and make great neck torcs, brooches, and pins for the chieftains. The kind of knowledge learned from forging iron and gold makes smiths silent, cautious men who hold tightly to their secrets. And that was my grandfather.

"But my mother was easy with the silence. Though not by nature a closemouthed woman, she was happy enough, she told me, to spend her days cooking and minding my grandda, because marriage had passed her by. No one cared to ask for the hand of Murty Mor's daughter. A quiet man frightens people, especially if he's well-muscled—"

"Like yourself?" I said before I could stop myself. I felt his arm against my side—well-muscled, certainly.

"I'm only puny compared to him," Michael said. "He was a giant who lifted rods of iron with ease and could hammer out a horseshoe with a few strokes. It would take a very brave man to walk into that dark forge to ask Murty Mor Kelly for his daughter. And none had."

"But one did," I said, "because here you are."

"Here I am."

Silence—thickening between us.

"Go on," I said.

"Have you heard of Gallagh Castle?" he asked.

"I'm sorry, I haven't," I said.

"Good. Then I can tell you. Imagine a huge stone fort built on a high hill with terraced slopes so the crowds who come to watch the Kellys race their horses on the Course will have soft seats. The castle's a ruin now, but when dusk falls, ghosts appear, and with them the good people, who you know are fond of fast horses."

"That I do know," I said. "My granny is a great woman for the fairies."

"Ah," he said. "Something else we have in common." We smiled. "A Kelly on his ancestral land has no fear of fairies," he said. "As a boy, when I rode my imaginary horse over the Course, I heard the noise of that other crowd rooting me over the final jump—up and over—and a soft landing on green grass."

"Good to touch down easy," I said.

"Right you are, Honora." He squeezed my hand. "So, you have Gallagh Castle and the racecourse fixed in your head?"

"I do, Michael."

"Now, as I said, the whole place was thought to be fairy country and none in the neighborhood would plow or plant the hillside. Even the Blakeneys stopped trying to force their tenants to till those fields. Nor would horses graze there. Oh, they might lean down for a few mouthfuls of the sweet green grass, but then their heads would come up, their ears would twitch, and off they would trot to the fence by the road to stand there until they were taken away. And the Blakeneys' cows, animals with little intelligence compared to horses, would not graze on these fields either."

"Everyone knows horses are superior," I said, though Champion was the first one I'd ever been this close to. "Look how Champion stands here listening."

"And she's heard the story before," he said. "Now, the most famous of the Kellys of Gallagh was William Boy O'Kelly."

"When?" I asked.

"When what?"

"When did he live?"

"Oh, long before Cromwell, but a few centuries after the first Kellys came down from the North. Their leader was called Maine Mor. His son Ceallaigh gave his name to our family line. Ceallaigh means 'contention,' and true to the name, the Kellys fought. Against the invaders, but also, if the truth be told, among ourselves. Contention. Brothers killing brothers for the title of Taoiseach, Chieftain. Now, you won't hold that against me?" Michael asked.

"My ancestor Queen Maeve knew a thing or two about contention," I said.

"Maeve's your ancestor? Why, her stronghold's not far from us."

"We Keeleys are the descendants of her son Conmac—Conn-na-Mara, Conn-of-the-sea."

"So you and I were connected," he said, "even before . . ."

I could only nod. He leaned closer, still holding my hand.

"Sorry to get between you and your story, Michael. Go on."

He cleared his throat. "So. This chieftain William Boy led the clan during a sliver of peace, the Normans settled and Cromwell not yet arrived. He decided to have a party, the greatest party ever given or heard about in the entire island of Ireland. He invited all the chieftains and princes for many miles around. They came with their wives and children, their warriors and servants, their poets and priests, to Gallagh Castle for this great Christmas feast. In those days, families within the clan owed allegiance to the chieftain, and each one coming to Gallagh had a particular duty. Take the Naughtons—they carried the Kellys' French wine from the port to the castle, an important responsibility," he said.

"And have you a great fondness for drink?" I asked.

"I can take it or I can leave it alone," he said.

"Good," I said. "So. Go on. I suppose the guests brought horses?"

"They did. Splendid horses—some glossy black, others pure white. One's coat was the color of a newly ripened chestnut. Lovely for horses, or women," he said, and brushed the crown of my head with his one finger, soft and swift, yet I felt his touch through my whole body. "A good heavy fall of red brown hair you have—like Champion's tail."

"Champion's tail!"

"Couldn't begin to compare with the thick, lovely mass of your hair, Honora Keeley. Your eyes . . . so clear. Green with flecks of gold and . . ." He stretched his hand toward my face, then dropped his arm back down to his side.

I swallowed. "Go back to the party, Michael," I said, my voice sounding hoarse.

"Oh, right."

"So . . ."

"So the feasting began. They roasted whole sheep in huge fireplaces. And all the guests thanked the cooks kindly."

"Good manners," I said.

"Right," Michael said. "And if someone wasn't mannerly? That person's slice of meat was cut from the far end of the animal, the cold shoulder. William Boy's guests were enjoying themselves so much that he hadn't the heart to send them away when Christmastime passed. They stayed on, and the feasting and the racing and the dancing and the storytelling and the music went on for three seasons, until the first of August—Lughnasa—when the harvest called them home. The openhearted generosity of William Boy O'Kelly is remembered to this day, for even now, when someone wants to warmly welcome you, they extend the Fáilte Uí Cheallaigh, the Welcome of the O'Kellys." He stroked my hand. "A very warm welcome indeed." He let go.

"Your mother, Michael," I said.

"She comes into it now. Years after the party, when our enemies took the land, the Blakeneys pulled down Gallagh Castle and changed our town's name to Castle Blakeney. Still the Kellys remembered and told the old stories.

"And one morning before dawn on Bealtaine, my mother set out to climb the hill to Gallagh Castle. In our part of the world we believe that on Bealtaine, the first day of May, the dew on the grass has great power."

"We believe that, too, Michael."

"Do girls wash their faces in it to improve their complexions? Not that you would need concern yourself about that."

"It is said, Michael Kelly, that roll in the dew that day and your body will glow with great beauty," I said.

"Roll?" he asked. "I suppose no clothes would be worn?"

"I wouldn't think so, Michael Kelly."

"Ah," he said. Then he jumped up and turned away from me.

I stood. "You're not leaving, are you?"

"I'm not. Not at all. But Champion needs a drink of water, and so do I."

"Of course," I said. "There's sweet water in the stream near Saint Enda's well."

Michael took Champion's reins, and we three walked toward the gap that led into the woods.

We passed Barna House—curtains still closed. But the sun's full up. Miss Lynch will be awake soon and looking out her window. We stepped into the clearing around the well.

"Now, your mother on Bealtaine?" I asked after Champion drank from the Tobar Geal and Michael leaned down for a quick swallow of water.

"My mother had terrible trouble with her feet: corns and bunions and swelling ankles and hammertoes, a disaster altogether. A wise old woman told her if she walked up to the ruins of Gallagh Castle at dawn on May Day, the dew would cure her.

"So, up she went to climb the slopes of the course while darkness held the town quiet. At first light she saw the castle. She started up the hill but then stopped. She heard music . . . the sound of pipes. Could they be fairy pipes?"

Michael paused. Champion lifted her head as if to hear better. The oak trees shaded us. Michael walked over and sat on the stone wall surrounding St. Enda's well. He patted the space beside him. I settled myself next to Michael. We smiled at each other. He continued his story.

"Now, all her life my mother enjoyed hearing about the good people and all their doings. She'd marked the raths and fairy trees, abided by all the good people's requirements from a child. She found the same comfort in respecting their rituals that she did in performing the patterns and prayers at wells like this one—all a way to put shape on the wild randomness of life, she told me. But to really hear fairy music . . . This was something she had never expected.

"The music pulled her forward. If following that tune meant leaving her father and the forge and the whole surroundings of Gallach Uí Cheallaigh to live the rest of her life in some fairy rath, well, so be it. . . . And then she saw him. A piper, surely, but rather raggle-taggle for a fairy and much bigger than the good people are said to be. He sat on the big rock near the arched entrance to the ruined castle, sending his music up to the dawn. And that was my father."

"Your father," I said.

"He was playing the sun up out of the shadows, and when it shone full on their faces, he greeted her. 'I'm Michael Kelly,' he said, 'from

Callow Lake,' which was ten miles south, a marshy lake where William Boy's son had settled. 'I'm a piper, as you see,' he said. 'I intended to come here and play a sad lament for the Kellys of old. But I hear joyful tunes in this air, reels and jigs. Powerful how the memories of a great party linger.' And my mother agreed, 'It was a powerful party.' So . . ."

"So, they married, didn't they, your mother and your father?"

"You want me to rush to the end of the story?"

"I only want to know that one thing."

"They married."

"Good," I said. "Go on."

"My father had over five hundred tunes, jigs and reels, laments and marches, music for dancing, for mourning, for war, and for peace. For generations his family were pipers to the O'Kellys of Callow, supported by them. But now with the land lost and times hard, my father traveled the roads, playing where he could. Every place he went he learned a tune or two, sometimes from a tin whistle player or a singer who sounded the notes for him. In the winter, he'd come back to Callow Lake, where Edmond O'Kelly, William Boy's descendant, kept a small cottage for him. He'd entertain Edmond with the stories of his journey. He collected bits on the history and genealogy of the Kellys from the various branches of the family, which interested Edmond. 'And is there a wife in that snug cottage in Callow?' my mother asked him. 'There was,' he told her, 'a fine woman who gave me a son before she died.' 'And you didn't marry again?' my mother asked him. 'I wouldn't afflict the life of a piper's wife on another woman, not when I have to travel so far to play for so little. The snug cottage's gone now, and my son, Patrick, hires out to whatever farmer will have him.'"

"So, you have a brother, Michael," I said.

"I do—twelve years older than me. Very accomplished altogether."

Patches of sun splashed the ground around us now—morning going, the Keeleys getting up. But I couldn't leave, not with Michael's father about to confront his grandfather.

"My mother and Michael Kelly, the piper, walked into the forge, just enough light to see Murtaugh Mor Kelly, bent over the fire. He straightened up, all sweat and grime and strength, the hammer clenched in his fists. Rigid with silence. My father stood his ground, didn't turn away as those who'd wanted my mother's hand before had done, but stated his proposal. 'You're courting the forge,' my grandfather said to him, 'looking for a soft spot to land in your old age.'

"'I have my own trade,' he said, and showed my grandfather his pipes.

"'A wandering piper—ever on the roads, sleeping God knows where, not much better than a beggar—would take away my daughter?'

"'I would not ask any woman to follow my path, though I might invite her to join me on a great occasion, at a gathering where my pipes played a proper role.'

"'A great occasion,' my grandfather said, banging the hammer on the horseshoe before him. 'Few of those in this country these days.'

"'True enough. At least you have a reminder of the old spirit here in Gallagh Castle.'

"'Gallach Uí Cheallaigh,' my grandfather said. 'And it's a ruin.'

"Now they were conversing in English, though my father and mother had spoken in Irish on the slopes of Gallagh Castle."

"Do you have Irish?" I asked. We'd been speaking English.

"I do, Honora," he said, "though not as fluent as I would like. In our part of the country, the Blakeneys made it a condition of keeping the forge that no 'O' be used in our name and no Irish spoken. I think my grandfather lived in great runs of silence because he didn't want to put English on his thoughts. But he daren't speak Irish and risk betrayal. I once heard him curse Queen Elizabeth for forcing the Kelly chieftains to swear they'd bring up their children after the English fashion and have them speak only the English language."

"Miss Lynch said who Elizabeth was angry because the Normans and Old English families who first conquered Ireland had come to speak only Irish and Latin. *'Ipsis Hibernicis Hiberniores*—more Irish than the Irish,' she called them."

"Who is Miss Lynch?" Michael asked.

"My teacher. I'll tell you about her later. Now, please, go on with your story."

"My throat is dry," he said, and he got up from the well and went over to the stream.

I followed him. He knelt down and cupped water into his two hands, then stood up and lifted his hands to my face. I opened my mouth and he tipped the water past my lips. I wanted to kiss the hollow of his hand. Jesus, what's happening to me?

"The story, Michael," I managed to say, sitting down on the well, him taking his place next to me.

"My grandfather had forgotten the horseshoe left in the fire, turning now from red to white. He quickly speared it and dropped it into the trough of water. The hiss of the steam and the smoke rising distracted both men, and my mother spoke up.

"'I want to marry this man,' she said."

"Just like that?" I asked.

"Just like that," Michael said. "Unexpected."

"Well," I said, "didn't Grainne fall in love with Diarmuid the moment she saw the love-spot on his forehead, though she was meant to marry Finn, the chief?"

"I believe that was the case," said Michael.

"And Deirdre, intended for King Conor her whole life, ran off with Naoise the first time they met. Unexpected."

"A surprise for Naoise, and Diarmuid. Both fellows off adventuring and here come these girls and they're in love. . . . Not what a fellow expects," he said.

"I suppose not," I said. "Especially if he's out riding his fine chestnut horse, going who knows where."

He's only passing through. I'll never see him again. . . .

But Michael said, "Those old tales come from somewhere. My mother marrying my father was very unlikely."

"Unlikely," I said. "But it happened."

"It did," he said.

He covered my hand with his. Warm. He stopped speaking. I took a breath.

"Go on. What did your grandfather say to your mother?"

"He said, 'It's late in the day for marriage, Fionnuala.' My mother's name was Fionnuala."

"That's a beautiful name."

"I like a good strong name on a woman—Fionnuala, Honora."

"Ah," I said.

"'There's a time for breeding,' my grandfather said to her, 'and when that time is passed, it's gone.'"

"A hard saying," I said.

Michael nodded. "My father spoke right up and said, 'I have a son and I'm not worrying about getting another. But when your daughter stepped toward me, I felt the loneliness I carry lift as mist does in the warmth of the sun. My son Patrick's mother was a good woman, and she wouldn't begrudge me happiness. Perhaps it was her prayers brought your daughter to me,' my father said, all solemn-like. 'It was my bunions,' my mother said. So . . .'"

"But it wasn't too late for her, because you were born."

"I was, and grew up with her and my grandfather Murtaugh Mor, the blacksmith. My father would spend the winter with us, and sometimes my brother, Patrick, would come. I had a solitary enough childhood, but I could romp around a bit with Patrick."

"I've always had my sister, Máire, and— Oh, dear God, Máire's wedding! How could I forget? I have to go, Michael. Now."

"Wait," he said.

I stopped, then turned back. "I never asked where you were going before you dove into Galway Bay."

"I thought I was off to see the wide world, Honora, carrying my father's pipes and a blacksmith's skill. I'd come to Galway City to get some handy money for the journey."

"What do you mean?"

"Champion and I mean to win the Galway Races."

"The Galway Races? You have to be a gentleman to enter the Galway Races. Michael, you're not a gentleman, are you?"

"I am not!"

"Thank Jesus and his Blessed Mother. My da might let me marry a tinker, but never a gentleman! Oh, I didn't mean to say 'marry.' I mean . . . You must think I'm terrible bold."

"For speaking the truth? Here, let's go and speak to your father right now."

"But what about traveling the world?"

"I don't fancy traveling alone anymore," he said.

"Oh." My voice went very soft. "I'm glad."

We walked together onto the strand toward the cluster of cottages. The neighbors were up, and many seemed to be looking our way, talking to one another, pointing.

"I'll go first and explain. You see, my family thinks I'm going into the convent in September."

"What?" Michael shouted, startling Champion, who pulled away from him. "You—a nun?"

As Michael grabbed for the reins, I started running, my loose hair streaming out behind me. "We'll sort it out later," I yelled over my shoulder to him. "I can't be late for Máire's wedding!"

Chapter 3

Such ructions and upsets—worse than the riptides in Galway Bay itself. "Honora the Good having a wee court with a handsome gypsy laddie. Wonderful!" Máire said, and laughed.

But Da was very angry. "You can be sure the rest of this lad's band is waiting for us to be dancing at the crossroads, so they can sweep into Bearna and rob every house," he said.

"Best of luck to them. They'll find little worth stealing," said Granny.

"He's not a gypsy," I said, "though I wouldn't care if he was."

"Enough," Mam said. "You and I, Honora, will go to Miss Lynch tomorrow, in case she was watching from her window and got the wrong idea."

"In *case*, Mam?" Máire said. "I'm sure she watched every move and motion."

"We were behind the rock, Máire. She couldn't have seen much—"

"*Stop* right there, Honora," Da said. "In less than three months you will join the Holy Sisters and be a credit to us and every fisher family in Bearna."

"But I can't be a nun. Michael Kelly came to me out of the sea this morning—like in one of your stories, Granny!"

"What are you talking about, Honora?" Mam said.

"I fell in love, Mam, like Deirdre did and Grainne and Queen Maeve."

"Honora, whist!" Da said.

"You don't understand, Da! I'm not the girl I was this morning. I'm changed. . . ."

My three brothers rushed into the room, Dennis going right up to Da, nearly as tall as him at only fifteen. "The gypsy's gone," he said.

"We saw him ride away!" said Joseph, thirteen, small like Mam and Máire, bouncing on his toes, swinging his hurley.

Hughie, just six, came over to me. "A mighty horse, Honora!"

"Well, that's done and dusted," Mam said. "Now, could we go to the chapel? The whole parish is waiting for us."

"Not to mention the groom," Máire said. She shooed us out the door toward the chapel, then pulled me back from the others. "Fellows like that mean no harm. A bit of sport with a pretty girl, then on their way."

"Not Michael, Máire. He was serious."

"Did he give you a time and place to meet him?"

"We didn't have a chance. We—"

"Well then"—she shrugged—"a nice memory to take with you to the convent."

"Honora, Máire, hurry!" Mam called to us.

He'll have slipped into the chapel. I'd told him about the wedding. He'll be there among the guests.

He wasn't. All the while Father Gilley was joining this man and this woman, I was sneaking looks from our front for-the-family pew at the congregation behind me. Not a sign of Michael in the rows of fisher families, all the Bearna ones, the Clare and Claddagh people, too, and our Keeley cousins from Connemara come in their hookers and púcáns. Had he found a place among the farming men and their wives who'd walked down from the hills? A surprising number here. There's Rich John Dugan, a man with a lease of thirty acres and a herd of ten cows, and a friend of Da's. But not a glimpse of Michael. Nor was he standing in the back with the cottiers and laborers who never missed any wake or wedding.

Michael was off to see the wide world. A very small world, this one, crammed into Bearna Chapel. What adventure here? Still, when Michael lifted the water to my lips, I . . .

Face front. Quick. Miss Lynch has caught me turning around. Had she seen Michael and me on the strand? I don't care. I'll tell her I've changed my mind. Hadn't Mother Superior said there was a trial period, to make sure? Michael hasn't left. He couldn't have.

The ceremony ended. Máire winked at me as she came down the aisle holding Johnny's arm. She does know about fellows. A bit of sport? I can't believe that—not of Michael.

⬦ ⬦ ⬦

A hundred or so people walked up to Paddy's Cross for the dancing, one half chatting about the wedding, the other half wondering out loud about Honora Keeley and the gypsy. Farmer and fisherman united in gossip.

I'd ducked away from Máire and Johnny and my family, who were talking to Miss Lynch, and was searching the crowd for Michael. Near me I heard Rich John Dugan, say, "A tinker, surely, or where would he get the horse?"

John Joe Clancy, a fisherman, answered, "He probably stole it. The soldiers will be upon us in no time and a disaster altogether."

"That boyo's long gone," Dugan said. "He was seen riding hell for leather along the high road. Good riddance."

Long gone? Please God, no.

Father Gilley rode past me, nodding his head at the "God bless you, Fathers" that came up from the crowd.

Granny Keeley came up next to me. "Sure, look at him on that fine horse—the king! That man would never risk his head to say Mass for people gathered at a secret place the way priests did in the penal days."

"Granny, what if Michael Kelly's gone? What if I never see him again? I'll die."

"You won't."

"I can't go to the convent, as if nothing's happened. I love him. God sent Michael, I'll tell Miss Lynch. Marriage is a holy vocation, too. Wasn't Saint Bridget always matching couples?"

"I did think it a shame that after you spent so much time learning my stories you'd not be telling them to your own children when I'm gone. Never saw you as a nun, Honora, so even without Michael Kelly coming along, I—"

"Don't say 'without Michael Kelly,' Granny, please. I don't want a world without Michael Kelly."

"Honora, catch yourself on. Have some sense."

I heard the music. The fiddler McNamara from Doneen. But also . . . "Granny. Listen . . . the pipes! He's here, I know it! Michael Kelly's here."

And there he was, sitting on a big rock near the crossroads, playing the uilleann pipes. He had the bag tucked under his elbow and was pumping his arm to push the air in and out while his fingers moved up and down the chanter.

"He didn't leave. He didn't."

I started toward him, but Granny stopped me. "Don't make a show of yourself. The neighbors are watching," she said. "Remember, this is Máire's wedding. Don't interrupt the dancing. Wait."

I found Máire and Johnny and told them the piper was Michael Kelly. "He's good, isn't he?" I said.

"And charging nothing," Johnny said. "The fiddler McNamara said this fellow was waiting here at the crossroads, pipes ready."

"He's good-looking," Máire said. "Not that I'll be noticing men anymore."

"Better not, Pearl," said Johnny as he put his arm around her and brought her into the reel.

Da and Mam were right in the middle of the dancers. I'll tell them about Michael when they stop for breath. Granny stood close to me. I didn't dare to even try to catch Michael's eye. He's seen me. I'm sure of it.

After two more sets, Da called for the dancing to stop. He'd jugs of poitín from Connemara to pass around, and the bonfire my brothers and Johnny made from dried whin bushes and fallen tree branches pilfered from Barna Woods was ready to light.

Johnny and Máire threw a burning piece of turf on the mound. It blazed up to great cheers—St. John's Fire, a celebration of the Baptist and of midsummer's night. The jugs went around the circle at the bonfire. I saw Michael walk away into the darkness beyond Paddy's Cross. Granny had moved closer to the flames.

I can't wait any longer. I slipped away. He was leaning against a stone wall, watching Champion graze in a small bit of pasture. I reached my hand out to him. He took it.

"You didn't leave."

"How could I? Champion likes this place," he said, "as much as I do. And the farmer only charged me a few pennies."

"Good."

Michael pointed across to the far hills where other bonfires flamed out against the darkness. "At home we drive the cattle through Saint John's Fire to bring health to the herd."

"Not many herds left around here," I said.

"Some good land, though. Champion and I have been looking today."

"You have?"

"We'd want to lease a good few acres, high up, with a clear view of Galway Bay."

"Michael, I was so afraid you'd left."

"I'm going nowhere, Honora." He tucked me under his arm, holding me as carefully as he had his pipes, and I . . .

"God bless all here." Granny.

"Granny, this is Michael Kelly."

"I know."

"My granny, Mrs. Keeley," I started.

"I'm very glad . . . ," Michael began, but Granny waved him quiet.

She filled her pipe from a small tobacco pouch and tamped it down. Michael took a piece of straw to the bonfire, came back, and lit the pipe for her.

"Thank you," she said to him. "Good tobacco. My son gave Máire a fine wedding." She drew on the pipe. "Her husband Johnny's a fisherman. The right kind of match," she said. She puffed again and then exhaled some smoke. "He'd never allow a daughter of his to marry a smuggler or an outlaw."

"I'm not one of those. You have my word," Michael said.

"You're not a settled man."

"I was and will be again," Michael said. "I'll work hard. Honora will want for nothing."

"There's a price money can't pay," Granny said. "Has Honora told you about our kinswoman Queen Maeve?"

"She mentioned the relationship."

"Did she explain Maeve's bride price?"

"I didn't, Granny," I said.

"Then I will. Fadó," Granny began, and settled herself on a big rock near the wall.

"A long time ago," I whispered to Michael.

Granny pointed to the low wall, and Michael and I sat on it. Granny nodded at us.

"Maeve was a great queen, ruling her kingdom fairly. She felt no need of a husband because under the law in those times a woman's power and position didn't depend on a man."

"The Brehon laws," I put in.

Granny nodded, then went on. "Maeve's soldiers were her thigh companions, and all was well with her. But one day she decided she did want a husband to be at her side—a king as noble as she was herself. So. Maeve set her own bride price. Three requirements—and what was the first one, Honora?"

"She required a man without meanness," I recited, "because she was great in grace and giving, and a stingy man would embarrass her."

"What about that, Michael Kelly? Are you a generous man?" Granny asked.

"I was taught to offer the Fáilte Ui Cheallaigh, the Welcome of the Kellys, to one and all, and never to pass a beggar by."

"Good." Granny went on, "Maeve demanded a man without fear. Why, Honora?"

"Because she liked a bit of contention and wanted a man easy with give and take."

We both looked at Michael.

"I've got that one all right. Didn't I tell you, Honora, Kelly *means* 'contention'? I was reared on give and take."

Granny nodded. "Fine. Now the third one—tell him, Honora."

"Maeve needed a man without jealousy because she liked to have one man in the shadow of the other."

Granny and I waited.

Michael didn't say anything. Then, "Without jealousy," he said. "That might be hard. My father often recited this poem: 'Love comes and goes, but jealousy is bred in the bone.' A monk wrote that verse in the margin of the manuscript of the Book of the Hy Many, the history of the Kellys. I used to think that if even monks feel that way . . ." He took a breath. "I don't envy anyone and I'm not a begrudger, but if another man . . . Maeve had thigh companions, you say?"

"But I wouldn't, Michael," I said. "Other men, I mean. Even Maeve didn't—"

"She did," said Granny.

"But, Granny, *you* said 'without jealousy' means more than

just . . . Well, Miss Lynch says there's symbols in poems and stories and paintings, one thing standing for another. A rose means Our Lady, so the thigh companions are symbolic, and no jealousy means trust and—"

"No jealousy," Granny said to Michael.

"All right. If the thigh companions are symbols and not . . . then I will. I do. I mean I can be a man without jealousy and without . . . what else?"

"Meanness," Granny said.

"No meanness, I agree to that."

"Fear?" I asked.

"No fear. I have that one," Michael said.

"Jealousy?"

"Yes. I mean, no jealousy—at least not on purpose."

"Good. You may speak to my son."

I jumped off the wall and went to Granny, Michael following after.

"Thank you, thank you," I said, and hugged her thin frame.

"I'm grateful," Michael said.

"I'm not saying Honora's father will accept you. There are practical matters to be considered." She stood. Though Granny's as tall as most men, she had to look up at Michael.

"I do have skills," he said to her. "I'm a blacksmith as well as a piper."

"But you're far from your home place," she said.

"Not by choice, but maybe not by chance, either. I planned to go adventuring, but now, well, a tale can take a turn."

"It can," Granny agreed. "Honora herself was headed down another path."

"She mentioned that," Michael said. "I surely wouldn't want to interfere with . . ."

I spoke up. "I'm not going to the convent. Granny agreed. She's glad," I said.

"But your mother's not happy and your father's confused. You must explain to them before Michael meets them," Granny said.

"I will, of course."

"What age are you, Michael?" Granny asked.

"Eighteen."

"Isn't that perfect, Granny? Máire says if a man waits too long to get married, he gets set in his ways."

"Mmm. It's not only time shapes the character. Maeve needed a man well able for a strong woman. So does Honora."

"I know," he said, "and I will try to be worthy of her—a husband without meanness or fear or jealousy."

"I believe you will. Now. I'll tell my son to expect you tomorrow." She left us.

"I should go, too," I said. "I see Mam and Da leaving the bonfire."

Michael took my hand. "Slán abhaile, Honora. Until tomorrow."

"Tomorrow," I said, "and all the days after."

Chapter 4

"Oh, Da, you'd never force me into the convent like evil fathers did in medieval Spain and France," I said to him.

Da was still being very severe with me as the last bit of the short night edged into dawn. Michael would be here in a few hours, and Da kept repeating, "You'll go to the Holy Sisters as arranged."

Standing up now, discussion over. He needed his sleep, he said. Exhausting enough to marry off one daughter without the other one going at him about medieval this and that.

Then Mam told me very sharplike to remember the lovely parlor in the convent. Think of living surrounded by beautiful things. Hadn't she herself found great joy in polishing the wooden tables and glass cases in Barna House and dusting Miss Lynch's books, all the time wishing she could read the English words in them? I'd have books galore at my fingertips and be able to fill myself with knowledge. The Presentation nuns even had their own wee chapel, with Mass every single day, and I'd live under the same roof with Our Lord in my own little room with a real bed, not a pallet of straw on the floor, and I wouldn't work digging for bait and sprats and mending nets or selling fish and being insulted by gentlemen in the market. I'd be teaching children to read and write and do better for themselves. And all the peace and quiet I'd have. Time to think and to pray, dressed in a lovely habit and wearing shoes, and . . . The words cascaded out of my usually quiet mother.

"Mary. Mary," Da said. Puzzled.

She looked at him and stopped talking.

Then he said, "Your mother wants what's best for you," and went on, asking how could I shame my family by losing the run of myself over a gypsy? I could not. Would not. Not his daughter Honora, who'd never given them a moment's worry.

I panicked. I'd never, ever defied my parents in the littlest thing, and now to go against them so completely . . . Shaming the family? Me?

Granny saved me. "Best Honora not go to the convent. They mightn't keep her."

She said I wouldn't be able to obey, that I was a rebel. I said I wasn't a rebel, Máire was the rebel. Then Mam spoke up for me, saying I'd always been a good daughter, that's why she knew I'd see sense, but Granny interrupted her and said she didn't mean I wasn't kind and helpful, but I was a Keeley woman with the blood of Queen Maeve in me and brains besides, and now with learning added to that, well . . . I'd never be able to keep my gob shut and do what I was told. What with giving my opinions and needing to be right, I'd not last the week. The nuns would send me home. And that would be a greater disgrace to the whole family than me changing my mind now.

"But, Granny," I said, "I don't think I'm always right, but if I know the answer, why shouldn't I tell it? Like Máire says, 'Some have bosoms and some have brains,' and I—"

That woke Da up. "What?" he said.

Then Granny looked directly at me: "Ní tha gann call ríomh aois. Sense does not come before age."

And I realized while she was arguing me out of the convent, I was arguing myself back in. So I said no more while Granny went on about my willfulness and added more sayings in Irish until Da said, "All right, all right, Honora won't go to the convent," though he thought I was letting Daniel O'Connell down. Granny said the Liberator had survived worse. Mam said, Well, if I was sure . . . And I said I wanted to marry Michael with all my heart and mind and soul and strength, but Da interrupted me and said not becoming a nun was one thing, but marrying a wandering gypsy piper was quite another, and he was going to sleep now and we'd finish this later.

"Thank you," I whispered to Granny.

"There is truth in what I said," she told me. "Don't be too smart for your own good, Honora."

⬥ ⬥ ⬥

That afternoon, Da sat stern and stiff on his stool by the hearth. Michael stood in front of him, shoulders back.

Máire and Johnny had left their marriage bed for this interview. Máire knew I needed her. And she didn't want to miss anything. My brothers were outside minding Champion, letting their friends pat the finest horse ever brought to Bearna. Granny, at her spinning wheel, fingered the empty spindle—no flax or wool for ages. Mam sat on the other rush stool. Dim—only the barest brush of light could come through the small windows of our cottage. Enlarge them and the rent'd go up.

"Robert Emmet in the dock," Máire said.

"Don't be joking about our patriots, Máire," Da said.

"I wouldn't, Da. I wonder would you ever recite Emmet's famous words for us, Da? I'm sure Michael Kelly here would appreciate hearing . . ."

Distracting Da with Ireland's heroes had shortened many a scolding for Máire, but Da wasn't having it today.

"Now, young man," he began.

But Máire stopped Da again. Could she thank Michael for playing his pipes and asking not a penny? "A generous spirit! Da," she said. "Like your own. You're so openhanded and giving—flaithiúlacht, as Granny would say—a princely wedding . . ."

"The best of poitín," Johnny said. "No harshness in it."

"Because Connemara water's used in the brewing," Da said.

"And you wouldn't have seen anything like the meitheal that built our cottage last week, Michael," Máire said. "So many of the neighbors working together that they finished in three days, all come to show their regard for our da. They would do the same for any daughter of John Keeley. Am I right, Da?"

"You are, Máire," Da said. "The meitheal was mighty, surely. Never were walls raised faster or straw thatched tighter. Whatever our differences, we're a grand people for helping each other." Da relaxed, stuck his legs out.

Good on you, Máire.

But then he looked over at me and straightened up. "Enough of this. We're not here to talk about your cottage, Máire, but to inquire into this young man's line and lineage," Da said. "Now, Michael . . . the horse. I want to know where and how and in what way you obtained that animal. Because as you must know, a lone man on a horse . . . Now, I hold nothing against the traveling people, but a girl from a settled family wouldn't—"

"Da, Michael is not a gypsy! I keep telling you," I said. "His grandfather was a blacksmith in Gallagh."

"Gallagh?" Da said. "Near Aughrim?"

"It is, sir."

"A great battle fought at Aughrim."

"Indeed there was. Not a good day for our side."

"Few enough of those, though I believe it was the French general let us down there," Da said.

If Da starts naming towns remembered for some sad slaughter, he'll put himself in bad humor.

"Da," I said, "Michael was about to tell you about his grandfather, the blacksmith, and the forge he *owned*."

"Owned it?" Da asked Michael.

"He did," Michael said, "though not the land under it, of course."

"Must have been well in with the landlord," Da said.

"Colonel Blakeney was a hard man from a hard family, but he wanted the Bianconi cars to come through our village and a blacksmith was required, so he needed my grandfather."

In Galway City I'd seen the big Bianconi wagons, pulled by six Irish draft horses, that this Italian fellow was sending all over Ireland. Each transport, which we called Bianys, carried twelve passengers as well as cargoes of porter and stout. Bianconi, being of the Faith and great with Daniel O'Connell, hired Catholics as drivers, and they'd sometimes pick up the stray countryman or -woman walking on the road and not charge them. Michael's village had become a stop on one of the Biany routes, he said.

"Colonel Blakeney's agent knocked three cottages into a pub to serve the passengers as they waited while we took care of the horses. Now, Blakeney's agent took most of the Bianconi money meant for my grandfather, but what could we do? Still, we earned our rent. We had grain and oats for the horses, and Grandda had custom from the farmers—always a group of them around the forge.

"A fellow called Jimmy Joe Donnelly was the most horse-mad of all of them. He'd been the Blakeneys' stableman, but now the family lived in London year-round and only came back for the odd week's hunting and used borrowed horses. A horse dealer called by one day and bought the lot, except he didn't want the old stallion, the Red Rogue.

"'He's past it,' the dealer said. 'The last five mares he's covered have produced nothing. Send him to the knackers.'

"But Jimmy Joe said he'd buy the horse himself. The men around the forge laughed, saying Jimmy Joe would be financing the Red Rogue's love life and nothing to show for it.

"But Jimmy Joe bought the horse. If you could have seen him, Mr. Keeley, magnificent: fifteen hands tall, some mix of draft horse and hunter, a bright chestnut color. The Red Rogue held his head high, and was most impressively endowed. Jimmy Joe kept him in the field behind the forge, and the two of us would stand in the evening at the stone wall, watching the old stallion," Michael said.

Da nodded.

Able to tell a tale is Michael Kelly, my hero from the sea, wooing my family with his stories as he had me.

Michael went on, "'We were great men once,' Jimmy Joe would say to me, 'and horses like this were our due. Didn't my great-great-grandfather have the care of the O'Kelly stables? Hundreds of horses: mares, foals, and stallions. I believe Red Rogue is descended from that stock. How could I let him be put down?'"

"He was right there," Da said. "We *were* great men once. The O'Cadhlas had horses, too."

"And so did the Leahys," said Johnny. "Herds of them, cattle, too."

"Go on, Michael, go on," Da said.

I smiled at Michael: Well done, keep talking!

"Now the Rogue took no notice of the Biany horses—they were geldings, beneath his notice. And there were no mares nearby to incite the Rogue."

Da nodded. "Not good to have a mare around a stallion," he said, as if he'd been riding and breeding horses himself for years instead of never having been on the back of one.

"A good stallion needs a willing mare," said Johnny Leahy, and touched Máire's knee. She giggled.

I chanced a quick look at Granny. She winked at me. Michael had Da and Johnny imagining themselves as men mounted and mighty, part of an army that could fight back. Victory to the Irish! They're driving the Normans away! King James is beating King Billy! Here we are, battering Cromwell! The land would still be held by the clans, still shared equally, if every Irishman rode a great stallion like the Red Rogue.

"It happened that I formed a bit of a bond with the Rogue, quite by accident. I'd taken the pipes up to the high field to try out a tune," Michael said.

"Hold there a moment, Michael," Da said. ("Michael"—not "young man"—good!) "I want to hear about this piper father of yours."

"All in good time," Mam said, caught up now. "Get on with your story, Michael."

"I was playing that evening when didn't the Rogue come pounding toward me, ears pricked up, and then he stopped dead, lowered his head to listen. Jimmy Joe came out. 'So the old rascal likes a bit of entertainment,' he said. I asked Jimmy Joe if there was any chance I could take him out for a gallop."

"You're a rider, then, Michael," said Johnny Leahy.

"I am. And yourself?"

"I had to give it up, with the fishing and all."

"True enough," said Da. "Takes away the sea legs. But go on."

"Well, Jimmy Joe said to me, 'The Red Rogue? You must be joking! He'd throw you and stomp you. I don't mind giving the Rogue some comfort in the last years of his life, but I don't want to be responsible for murder.'"

"But you defied him, didn't you!" said Da. "You jumped up on the back of that great horse and—"

Michael shook his head. "I didn't, sir."

"Oh," said Da. "Ah, well . . ."

"One day a team pulled in with a mare in the lead spot. 'What's this?' I asked the driver, because I was worried about stabling a mare near the Rogue. 'That's old Bess, the virgin queen,' the driver said. 'The company bought her to breed, but she's barren. A good strong puller, so we've put her in harness. No stallion will bother with her.'

"Bess had a look of patient endurance that touched me," Michael said, "and I wondered, how many times had she been covered by a stallion with nothing to show for it? And now they'd work her until she dropped and send her off to the knackers. I told Jimmy Joe about Bess. Would he buy her? I hated the thought of Bess dead from dragging some publican's barrels of porter. 'I'm sorry, Michael,' Jimmy Joe told me. 'Hard enough to feed the Red Rogue.'"

"Poor Bess," said Granny.

"And it got worse," Michael went on. "Bess picked up a stone. Grandda removed it, but she was too lame to go on. Blakeney's agent held his gun to her head. 'A bullet to the brain,' he said, 'and then I'll have plenty of horsemeat to sell to the man takes care of the hounds for the foxhunters.'"

We all gasped. Da hit his fist on his knee.

"Is there no hope of justice for anyone in our poor bedeviled country?" Da said. "Is the whole place to be butchered to supply the Sassenach?"

"A disgrace," said Granny. "Never happen in Queen Maeve's time, I can tell you that."

"Oh, Michael," Mam said. "You surely did not let the agent kill her."

"I did not. 'I'll buy her,'" I told the driver. "'I'll give you what the knackers would, here and now, cash.' The words jumped out of my mouth. I expected an argument from my grandfather. He was not a man for grand gestures where money was concerned. But he took a pile of shillings from his iron box and gave them to me. And Bess was mine."

"Fair play to you, Michael," Máire said.

"Aye," said we all. "Aye, fair play to Michael."

"I made a stall for Bess near the forge. Her quiet ways kept the other horses in order. She ignored the stallion in the next field.

"Now, by this time I was nearly sixteen and my mother began to say, 'If you don't spend some time courting the girls instead of worrying about Bess and the Red Rogue, I'll never be a grandmother.'

"'And where would I find a woman compares with you?' I'd say."

"What age are you now?" Da asked.

"Eighteen, sir," Michael said.

"Johnny and Máire are eighteen, Da, the age most people marry and—"

"Honora," said Da, "Michael's speaking."

Michael smiled at me. "The girls of Castle Blakeney were nice enough, but they were always giggling and gossiping and playing one lad against the other. I'd had a picture in my mind of the woman I would love."

"And what was that?" This from Máire.

"She'd look like the mermaid carved near the entrance of Clontuskert Abbey. Do you know the abbey? Cromwell destroyed most of the church, but the graveyard remains, and some arches."

We didn't, but we could imagine it. So many gray stone ruins across Ireland, giving their names to townlands, reminders of times long past.

"A Kelly place, the abbey, with tombstones carved through the centuries. Some of the letters spill off the end of a stone to be taken up on the next line: KE, then LLY. I read them all as a boy. Saints stood in the abbey's archway—Michael, holding sword and shield, crushing the dragon, and Saint Catherine next to him. But my favorite figure was a mermaid. She had long waves of hair and was gazing into a mirror, her tail curved up, pleased with herself. I'd touch that fall of stone hair and know someday, somewhere, I would find her—a girl with the look and spirit of the Clontuskert mermaid. So I couldn't court the Castle Blakeney ones."

Michael looked at me, and I felt as if he'd touched me.

Da said, "The horses, Michael, get on with the horses."

Michael breathed in a gulp of air. "So," he said. "The Rogue began coming to the long stone wall between Jimmy Joe's high field and the forge. He'd neigh and snort and whistle when I played. One night I was in the long acre trying out a tune on the pipes and who comes dancing out to join me but Bess? Well, I knew what would happen when the notes of the tune reached the high field."

"I know, too," said Johnny. "The Rogue!"

"Right you are. I tried to shoo Bess to safety, but she stood her ground, nuzzled my shoulder, and pushed me away toward home. Bess switched her tail and lifted it high. And then Red Rogue appeared, running for all he was worth from the other field. The Rogue gathered himself and flew over the stone wall."

"Right to Bess," said Máire.

"By now I was watching from the corner of the forge. I could see the Rogue blowing and snorting, his head moving, his red body coiled and ready. Bess stood her ground, her head up. Waiting. Then she turned away from the Red Rogue and trotted to the far end of the field where a tall oak grew—our fairy tree."

"That's it?" asked Johnny. "She just left?"

"Not by a long shot," said Máire. "Am I right there, Michael?"

"You are, because the stallion went after her and I could see them no more." Michael paused.

"And then?" Máire asked.

"I left them and went in," Michael said.

"As well you should have," said Mam.

"At dawn I found the Red Rogue, standing still and quiet, the wind lifting his mane, and Bess grazing near him. When she saw me, she whinnied in Rogue's direction, then trotted back to her stall in the forge."

"And is that the end?" asked Da.

"That was the beginning. Jimmy Joe was full of apologies when he heard. 'That rascal jumped the fence into your field. I heard the noise. I hope your mare will be all right.' A month later, I could see Bess was in foal, but would she carry to term? The chorus at the forge didn't think so. Bess seemed well. Her coat gleamed and her eyes were clear, but the size of her distended belly worried Grandda.

" 'You took a chance, Michael,' " he told me. " 'Both she and the foal could die.' "

"I felt terrible. 'I didn't think beyond that moment,' I told him. My mother said nothing.

"During the months we waited, my grandfather weakened. He stopped coming to the forge, slept the day through. The chorus of farmers saw his end coming. Without Grandda, Bess had no chance. 'What a hand he had with difficult births,' they'd tell me. 'A great pity he won't be able to help her. Poor Bess will not survive,' they said."

Da shook his head. Mam closed her eyes and Granny spun her wheel. Máire took Johnny's hand.

"The birth was as bad as predicted: hours and hours of Bess panting and pushing, her eyes rolling, and me saying over and over, 'I'm sorry, girl, I'm sorry.'

"Just before first light, Bess stopped trying. She was lying on her side with her eyes closed when the door to the forge opened and there, leaning on my mother's arm, stood Murty Mor. He crossed to Bess and started whispering into her ear, rubbing his hands on her body, until . . ." Michael paused.

"Until?" Johnny said. "Until, until . . . ?"

"Until two spindly legs appeared, and then two more. Grandda and my mother and I eased the foal out and helped her stand, unsteady on her legs but healthy, a filly with the bright chestnut coat of the Rogue and the deep, dark eyes of her mother."

"Well done, Bess!" said Máire.

"Your grandfather was mighty," said Granny.

"My mother and I helped Murty Mor back to the fire, and two days later he was gone."

"And God rest his soul," said Mam.

"Bess lasted another year, long enough to see her filly grow sound and strong. She liked to watch the foal run. The Rogue's daughter all right. The chorus at the forge was full of admiration. 'If you were a gentleman, Michael Og, you'd have a fine horse to ride with the hunt, or you could enter her in the Galway Races!' And somehow it eased the sadness of Murty Mor's going. 'She's a champion,' I told them, 'and I've named her Champion.'

" 'Sell her,' they said. 'Take her to the Ballinasloe horse fair. You need the money.'

"I asked my mother, but she said we'd manage. I'd taken over the forge and was doing well enough. But then she sickened and died. God rest her. I buried her in Clontuskert Abbey graveyard with my father, grandfather, and all the generations of Kellys. The Blakeneys evicted me from the forge, brought in another blacksmith. So I set off on Champion, and look where she's led me."

"Now," I said into the silence that followed. I didn't have to add, Do you believe that he's not a gypsy or a thief or a highwayman?

"It's a fair tale," Da said. "I'll agree to that. But do you have any living relatives at all?"

"I have a brother, twelve years older than me, a half-brother. Patrick Kelly."

"Well, that's something," Da said. "Where is he?"

"I don't know," Michael answered.

"What will you do with yourself now?"

Da didn't say the words: *with no home, no money, and no land;* but we heard them.

"I intend to enter Champion in the Galway Races, and win," Michael said, sure and firm. "The prize is twenty-five pounds."

Da and Johnny started laughing.

"Michael," Da said, "those races aren't for the likes of us. You arrive with that horse and they'll take her off you and put you in jail."

"I was told in Galway City if I could find a gentleman to sponsor me, Champion could run. I'd planned to use the winnings to support me on my travels. But now . . . I'd buy myself a lease so Honora and I—"

"Dangerous, drawing attention to yourself like that," Da said. "Even if you won, there's no empty land that I know about. Now, if you were a fisherman, I might have been able to help."

"He could learn to be a fisherman, Da," I said. "Couldn't you, Michael?"

"I could try," Michael said, and I let out the breath I didn't know I was holding.

"Have you done any fishing at all?" Da asked.

"My brother and I took some fine salmon from the rivers at home, and never once got caught by the sheriff."

"That's what we call angling," Da said. "More luck than skill. It's skill needed to cast nets, to find the schools of herring. You need a quick mind as well as a strong back."

"He has those, Da," I said. "Please, please."

"A man deserves a chance," Granny said to Da.

"I'll have to ask the Admiral," Da said. "We fish with the men of the Claddagh. You know about the Claddagh?"

"I saw the village coming through Galway City."

"Saw the village, did you? Well, seeing is not believing. The Claddagh existed before Galway City, and the men there hold tight to their right to fish Galway Bay, theirs since time out of mind. Every year a leader of the Claddagh is elected; we call him the Admiral, and he controls the whole fleet. When I came here from Connemara, I was accepted because the Claddagh men knew my seed, breed, and generation. And for all your way with a story, young man, I can't say I know that about you."

"Da, please," I said. "You always say you're a good judge of men."

Da said nothing. And then, "I will give you a go in our boat if the Admiral agrees."

"Thank you, Da!"

"I am a fair swimmer, sir," Michael said.

"I won't mention swimming to the Admiral. We stay *in* the boat. That's the point, lad—stay on top of the water. And that's no mean feat in Galway Bay—tricky currents and pointed rocks waiting under the surface. But a man can support his family, and a young fellow who does well could consider marriage. Honora's dowry is a share in the boat," Da said.

"When can we leave, sir?" Michael stood up.

"Easy now," Da said, but he laughed and clapped Michael on the shoulder and took him out to see the púcán with Johnny.

"I'm so happy," I said to Mam and Máire and Granny, only the three of us in the cottage. "Isn't he wonderful!"

Mam said that he did seem a good lad, and Máire talked about how handsome Michael was, but Granny said nothing. She put a finger in a spoke and spun the empty wheel, sending it circling round.

"What are you thinking, Granny?" I asked.

"A sad story he told," Granny said. "Oh, Michael made a fine tale of it, but mind how quickly he skipped over the eviction. To be robbed of the forge where his grandfather's grandfather pounded iron, put off the land of his ancestors, left with nothing but the shirt on his back and that red horse, who is a danger and a responsibility . . . that's a wound that's slow to heal."

"But, Granny, Michael doesn't seem a sad sort of fellow," Máire said.

"He isn't," I said. "He was on his way adventuring with his pipes to play. Not a care."

"Leaving your home place is a sorrow," Granny said. "Generations lost to memory. One day, no one in Gallagh of the Kellys will remember the blacksmith or the piper or his mother. A sad thing for him, and he feels it, believe me. Feels too much, maybe. A deep loneliness in that fellow."

"Not anymore, Granny. Now Michael will become part of us. A new story will begin: 'Fadó, a young man came over the Silver Strand on a red horse and he became a fisherman, and married Honora Keeley and they lived happily ever after.'"

Granny smiled and spun her wheel. "We can but hope, a stór."

Chapter 5

"THERE, MÁIRE, SEE? That's Da's boat, and the Leahys' . . . Why are they heading in?"

Máire and I stood on the pier, watching the red sails of the two púcáns dip and bend. We'd seen them off hours before dawn that morning, with food for three days of fishing. Here they were, back before sunset of the first day.

"Is that your Johnny steering, Máire?" I asked. "Look how he wraps the sail around the wind."

"He's good at making things swell," Máire said, patting her stomach.

"You're pregnant already?"

"Johnny and I had a bit of an early start."

"An early start? Oh. Does Mam know?"

"I'll tell her when I start showing."

"Máire."

"Don't look at me like that. I'm a married woman now. They're making a ruckus over you and Michael Kelly, but it's really very simple. A fellow and a girl catch each other's eyes, they feel a pull toward one another, a bit of courting to see if they suit, and then . . ." She shrugged.

"Then . . ."

"You'll see. A great feeling altogether, little sister. Better than a wild reel or a gulp of poitín."

"What about love?"

"Well, love comes into it, but when you're pulling your husband's body into yours, you don't parse your feelings like the girls do in Miss Lynch's books. No thinking, Honora. Great altogether. A few words from Father Gilley, and Johnny and I can enjoy ourselves whenever we want and not a farthing to pay to anybody. Though I suppose the wee one I'm carrying will cost us a penny or two."

"Are you glad, Máire?"

"I am, Honora, and so's Johnny. He's sure it's a son and he's already talking about teaching him to hoist the sails."

"The boats are riding high in the water," I said.

"No load of herring there," Máire said.

Da and Johnny brought the two púcáns near the pier. Dennis and Joseph held Michael between them and helped him off our boat.

"Your fellow's changed colors! Would you say he's greeny white or whitey green, Honora?" Máire said.

The boys supported him over to us.

"Here, Michael!" I put my hand out to him.

"Sorry, Honora," he said.

Da came to the rail and looked down at us. "You were brave in the boat, Michael, but you don't have the stomach for it."

Michael straightened up and turned to look at Da. Dennis and Joseph shook their heads at me.

❖ ❖ ❖

"Worst case of seasickness I've ever seen," Da said, walking beside us as the boys helped Michael to the cottage. "You're a decent man, Michael, but you'll never go down to the sea in a ship. You'd best find something else to turn your hand to, or I can't give you permission to marry my daughter."

"Da," I said, "he'll get over it. Take him out again."

"Some men just aren't suited for the sea, Honora. It would be cruel, and unlucky for the rest of us."

"I understand," Michael said.

"Then Michael can hire himself out to Rich John Dugan to work for a cottage and a potato patch."

Máire heard and turned around. "You'd be the wife of a cottier? Miss Lynch's prize pupil, the lowest of the low?"

No one spoke as Da set Michael down on his own stool by the hearth. I gave Michael a cup of cold water. As he sipped at it, his color came back.

"With twenty-five pounds I'm sure I could rent a farm and set up a forge," he said. "I must enter the Galway Races."

"But if you lose, what then?" Da asked. "A share in a boat is all I have for Honora's dowry. It will do you no good."

"I'm going to win."

"Mr. Lynch might sponsor you, Michael," Mam said. "We could ask."

Miss Lynch had been suspiciously understanding about my change of heart. I wondered, had her father really wanted to pay my convent dowry? A two-minute conversation at the door of Barna House and she'd sent me on my way. And now here was Mam offering to arrange for Michael to see Mr. Lynch himself. She understands, after all.

"Please, Mam," I said.

Now Michael looked at Da. "I would never ask for Honora's hand unless I had something to offer her, sir."

"You have everything to offer," I started.

"Whist, Honora. Michael knows how a decent man behaves," Da said. Then to Michael, "If you couldn't support her, I'd have to look elsewhere for Honora's husband."

"Da!"

"I accept that," Michael said.

I don't.

❖ ❖ ❖

"Isn't the carpet lovely?" said Mam as she and Michael and Máire and I waited in the little room off the kitchen where the Honorable Mr. Lynch transacted business. "He meets here with his agent and the merchants from town," Mam explained to Michael.

Papers lay piled every which way on the dark wood desk. A long row of leather-bound ledgers filled a shelf. The rent rolls—hundreds of tenants' names listed, with rent paid and rent owed written next to each. Here's where Mr. Lynch sits turning the pages and telling his agent: Give him another few months, but evict him, and him. Send for the bailiffs to serve the notice, get the drivers to sell off any stock. Then he closes the book. Puts it away.

The Lynches were better landlords than most, but I remembered when they put the family of Mary Doyle, a farming girl in our class, off their land. Miss Lynch explained to Mary that it wouldn't be fair to the tenants who worked hard to pay the rent to allow those who didn't pay to stay on forever. Landlords have debts, too, she'd said. Mary Doyle kept her eyes down, said nothing, and we never saw her again.

"That carpet came from the land of the Turks," Mam was saying, "sent by one of the Lynches' cousins in France."

"Probably smuggled in by the Keeley cousins in Connemara," Máire said.

"Please don't be cheeky with Miss Lynch," I said to Máire.

"She doesn't mind. Gives her a bit of a laugh. She likes me. She's my godmother, after all," Máire said.

"Only because you were born first. I don't see—"

"Girls, please," said Mam. "Molly Counihan can hear you."

"The housekeeper," I said to Michael.

Michael had left Champion with Dennis and Joseph to find fresh water for her and a bit of grass.

"She'll need a proper pasture soon," Michael had said.

Miss Lynch greeted us, her brown hair pulled back as always, her lips tight together in her smooth, plump face. Mam's age, but not a patch on Mam for good looks—what with Mam's blond waves and blue eyes—work-worn though she may be.

"Miss Lynch, will I introduce you to Michael Kelly?" Mam said.

"Good morning," Miss Lynch said.

"Very nice to meet you, Miss Lynch. Honora says you are a fine teacher," Michael said. "Thank you for seeing me."

Miss Lynch nodded. "I've known Honora and Máire since they were born."

"And you're my godmother," Máire said.

"I am," Miss Lynch said. "You see, Michael, Mrs. Keeley was a Walsh when she worked for us. And Walsh was probably originally 'Welsh'—there were retainers from Wales with my family when we Normans came to Ireland with Richard de Clare—Strongbow. Does he know our history, Honora?"

"I've told him some," I said.

"Honora has the dates and doings of your ancestors off by heart, Miss Lynch," Mam said.

❖ ❖ ❖

Oh, I knew the Lynch annals well, saw how their family wound their way through the history of Ireland, starting from when the Norman king of England, Henry II, invaded us in 1171 sent by the only English pope ever to sit in St. Peter's chair, Pope Adrian IV, who had the nerve to say that the people of Ireland—the land of saints and scholars—had gotten too easygoing and needed reform. His Norman kinsmen reformed us right out of our country. Where before the land was held by the tribe, the tuath, everyone with a share, now one Norman lord claimed tens of thousands of acres, with the Irish only tenants to him.

Miss Lynch thought it wonderful that the Normans built stone castles and grand churches, though Granny said, "Who asked them to clutter the place? We had our holy mountains to pray on, high hills for our ceremonies, fairs, and gatherings. We raised plenty of food, hunted in the great forests, had herds of cattle. Much better before they came."

Still the Normans married Irishwomen as the Vikings had done, called themselves Irish and suffered with us when Cromwell came.

Cromwell. The devil let loose among us to butcher our bodies and devour our souls. He massacred women and children and called it God's work. Numbers beyond counting perished. The rest were driven west, no Irishman or -woman allowed east of the River Shannon on pain of death. Thirty thousand were sold into slavery in the West Indies. But even Cromwell couldn't destroy us all.

Two centuries of the Sassenach trying to kill off the Irish papists one way or another, yet we had survived somehow. Miss Lynch said Ireland had near nine million people now. Overpopulation, she called it, and a problem to the British government. But Granny said, "Our victory and thank God for the potato. They'll never beat us as long as we have the pratties." And the Lynches had brought back power.

❖ ❖ ❖

Now Mam and Miss Lynch were waiting for me to perform. Miss Lynch guesses Michael and I want to marry and knows we need some help from the landlord, but we can't ask her directly as if we're equal to her. Must sing for her favor.

"Why not quiz Honora," Máire said to Miss Lynch, "as you did in class?" Máire turned to Michael. "Always quick with the answer."

"All right," Miss Lynch said. "An exercise. Let's see . . . What date did my ancestors build Saint Nicholas' Church?"

"Thirteen twenty," I said.

"Correct. Explicate."

"It was constructed on the foundations of an earlier church operated by the Knights Templar—connections of the Lynches during the Crusades."

"The Crusades," said Mam. "Imagine."

"Name one very important visitor to the church." Miss Lynch turned to Michael. "This may surprise you."

"Christopher Columbus," I said. "Brought by his Irish navigator, Patrick Maguire, to Galway to consult old maps that chronicled the voyage of Saint Brendan in the sixth century. Some say Brendan discovered Amerikay."

"Never heard that," Michael said.

"How many Lynch mayors of Galway City?"

"Eighty-four."

"Name them."

Máire rolled her eyes at me.

"Pierce Lynch," I began, but stopped when the door of the office opened.

Miss Lynch was all aflutter as the Honorable Marcus Lynch entered.

The landlord. We all stood.

"The Keeley sisters, all grown up now," he said. "Not those little girls sneaking up to the attic. Sit, sit."

How short he seems next to Michael. Very old-looking—he must be near seventy. White beard, his fine coat strained by his stomach and his own importance.

Miss Lynch never tired of telling us how lucky we were to be the tenants of such a man. Ninety percent of the land of Ireland was owned by Protestants, she said, and many of them lived in England. "Absentees. Heartless. High rents. Evictions. Some have never even seen their Irish estates," she'd say. "We Lynches stay right here. We travel to London only when Parliament is in session."

So. Marcus Lynch was a member of Parliament, only because Daniel O'Connell fought to get Catholics admitted. The Honorable.

"What is it you want?" he said to us. "I gave you half a crown for your wedding only last week, Máire. And you, Honora. Henrietta told me you've changed your mind. No dowry for the convent after all. Well done."

"Yes, sir," I said. "But now I . . . Well, this is Michael Kelly, and—"

"Never heard of him. Kellys are in East Galway," Mr. Lynch said.

"That's right, sir. I'm from Gallagh, or Castle Blakeney," Michael said.

"And did you have some trouble, young man? We won't have any disturbances on this estate. I'm a fair landlord, I let my daughter teach peasant girls in my own house. Not many would do that. But no treason tolerated here, no Ribbonmen. 'Ribbonmen'—such a gentle name for such a rebellious group. Do they really pin ribbons on their jackets when they blacken their faces and go out to maim a landlord's cattle or terrorize his agent?"

We said nothing.

"Now, I'm a Repealer. I want an end to the Union. Our own Parliament. But I'm a loyal subject of Queen Victoria, and so is Daniel O'Connell. He's completely against violence."

"I'm not a violent man, sir," Michael said.

Mr. Lynch turned to Mam. "Tell me, Mary. Do you know this lad's family?"

Mam, please, for once in your life, lie.

"I could tell you many things about his people, sir. Very hardworking. A widowed mother caring for her father and—"

"So, I won't have to call out the sheriff to arrest this fellow, then?" Mr. Lynch laughed. A great joke.

We stayed silent.

"I suppose you want to marry Honora. Is that it?"

"Yes, sir," Michael said. "I—"

Mr. Lynch interrupted him. "Well, I hope you're not looking to become a tenant on any of my estates. Impossible. Tens of thousands of acres and every inch is occupied. Not my fault you people multiply like rabbits, dividing and subdividing the land until there's not a decent piece on the whole place. And now the Poor Laws! I'm accessed a tax on every tenant who pays less than four pounds rent a year. Half the estate! Impossible! I tell them in Parliament that their laws are ridiculous. 'Let Irish property pay for Irish poverty,' they say, as if we Irish landlords were made of money! Made of debt, more likely. I'm a Tory, and proud of it. The best chance for Ireland is to remove all doubts about our loyalty. Irish agitation makes Parliament uneasy. I'm trying to bring some order to my estates. Fewer tenants, not more."

Bigger plots, so you won't have to pay poor rates.

"And I'm not allowed to sell a single acre until I pay off my mortgages and creditors. Pity. Business fellow told me he could make Barna another Brighton—all that coastline, the pier, the strand. Build bathing lodges and villas. A real seaside resort."

What was he talking about? Thirty fisher cottages on that strand—our homes. But Mr. Lynch was waving his hand.

"Told him I couldn't do it. Land's encumbered. Debts, debts, debts."

Then Michael stood up, tall and broad-shouldered, dwarfing Mr. Lynch. "Sir," he said.

Mr. Lynch stepped back.

"I have a horse," Michael said.

"I'm not in the market for a horse," Mr. Lynch said.

"I don't want to sell her. I plan to run her in the Galway Races."

Mr. Lynch laughed. "Racing's for gentlemen, boy."

"But I understand that if a gentleman enters a horse, he can use anyone as rider," said Michael.

"It's true the Pykes have used tenants as jockeys, though I understand the son will be riding this year. Cousins of ours, but turned Church of Ireland. Wouldn't mind taking them down a few notches. Is this horse any good?"

"Very good," Michael said.

"Might be amusing," Mr. Lynch said.

Please God, let him agree.

"If I sponsor you, and run your horse as my horse, we will split the winnings in half. That's fair."

"Yes, sir."

"And if you lose, I get the horse."

"But, sir—"

"That's the proposition, young man. Take it or leave it. I'm taking a chance, sight unseen."

"But I can show you the horse, sir."

"Not necessary, not necessary. And though I've never been a gambler . . ."

"No, you haven't, Father," Miss Lynch said. Her first words since her father had come into the room. "I don't think—"

"You're too prim, Henrietta," he said to her. "Why shouldn't I have a bit of fun?"

And risk nothing, I thought. What does it cost to enter, a few pounds? If Champion wins, you get that back plus half the prize money. If Champion loses, you get a good horse. No wonder the Lynches are rich.

"If I win, sir, you'll rent me a bit of land?" Michael said.

"If you win and can pay in advance, who knows?"

❖ ❖ ❖

"You made a bad bargain, Michael," I said as we walked. Ahead of us, Máire talked away to Mam. "Mr. Lynch is taking advantage of you," I said.

"He is."

"You're risking Champion for me."

"For us."

"Are you sure?"

"I can't ask an educated woman like you to marry a man without money or land."

"I don't care, Michael. We could wander the roads together."

"That's not a life for you, Honora."

"But if you lose her, we'll have nothing. Why not sell Champion and—"

Michael touched my lips with one finger. "Whist, Honora. I've ridden thousands of imaginary races on the Gallagh course, and I always won. Champion and I can make what I imagined real. We will win." He bent down to me, those blue eyes gazing into mine.

Don't parse. Don't think.

"You will, Michael. You will, of course."

"We'll take the money to buy a lease on the tidiest farm in the county of Galway," he said. "There's empty land somewhere, no matter what Lynch says."

"Will it be near the Bay?"

"It will. I'll put a big window in our cottage so you'll always see Galway Bay, Honora."

"A window? Wonderful."

Michael took my hand. "And there will be books," he said.

"Books," I repeated.

Mam and Máire were far ahead.

"The Irish surely are overdue a victory," I said.

I thought of the words the Norman conquerors had carved on the medieval walls of Galway City: "From the fury of the O'Flahertys, O Lord, deliver us." The chieftains, the wild Irish, might return at any moment. And win.

We walked faster and faster, swinging our joined hands.

"We will win," he said.

"We will."

Chapter 6

THE KNOCK CAME as we were eating our dinner, the whole family listening to Michael tell us how relieved he was to have finally found good pasture for Champion. A week since Mr. Lynch agreed to sponsor Champion, and the horse had been growing scrawny, worrying Michael. Little enough grazing around, and farmers charged cash money for the use of it.

"We went high into the hills," Dennis said.

"It's near Tonnybrocky, up the Ballymoneen Road," Joseph put in.

My brothers had become Michael's assistants, spared by Da from the boats because the fishing was so poor that the Claddagh Admiral had kept the fleet in. Da said the new English trawlers were ruining Galway Bay, destroying the spawning grounds by churning up the bottom. From time out of mind, Da said, Irish fishermen had caught only full-grown fish, leaving the others to grow and breed. "That's why our nets have large holes, but now . . ."

A knock meant trouble. Friends and good news came right in. It was landlords' agents and policemen who beat their fists against the door.

Da eased the door open. A stranger stood there, barefoot, wearing a frieze coat—a small, baldy fellow with a fringe of brown hair and quick blue eyes, about thirty years of age. He looked around to see into the room.

He's hungry. Beggars often came to the door in the hungry months. Whole families, who traveled twenty or thirty miles so as not to embarrass themselves by begging in their own townlands, spent the month of July going door to door, then went home to find work in the harvest.

Mam always gave to beggars and treated them with respect. Any family could slip down very quickly, she said—eviction, the bailiffs battering down your cottage, and that was you finished and on the roads. Happening all the time—what Da feared for me—no land, living in a shelter dug into the side of a hill, a child on the way.

But this fellow was no beggar. "My name is Owen Mulloy, and I've come after thieves," he said, pointing at Michael, Dennis, and Joseph.

"Thieves? Now wait a minute," Michael began, standing up.

"What else is a man who sets his horse to eat the grass of another man's pasture, tell me that?"

"Pasture? An abandoned field," Michael said.

"I admit the pasture's neglected. No use for it. I was a man with an interest in three cows and a horse, but now I have no stock at all."

"A sad and familiar story," Da said. "My sympathies, Mr. Mulloy."

Mulloy nodded. The anger had gone off him—one of those fellows who flares up and sputters, then calms down.

Michael apologized for his mistake, and Mam asked Owen Mulloy to sit down and share our meal. After some toing and froing, Owen Mulloy accepted a prattie, but he wouldn't eat the mussels Mam had added to the potatoes. Too slimy.

"The man who shared the cows with me was evicted," Owen Mulloy said, "even after we sold our stock to pay the rent."

"Bíonn siúlach scéalach," Granny said.

"A traveler has a tale," Owen Mulloy translated. "True enough, though I've come from only two miles away and my story's a very short one, because what happened is not worth telling. The neighbor who shared the stock with me had three daughters. The oldest one wished to marry the son of a farmer near Minclough, a likely lad. They went to the landlord for permission."

"Which landlord?" asked Da.

"The Pykes."

"Which Pykes?"

"The Scoundrel Pykes," Owen Mulloy said. "I'm sure you've heard the tales of the old Major, and they're all true. A devil. He takes a bride's first night. Droit du seigneur, the Pykes call it, but it's rape, a criminal violation, and they're never called to account."

"Too many other landlords doing the same," Granny said.

Mulloy nodded. "My neighbor sent his daughter off with her young man—they left the area entirely. When old Major Pyke found out, he evicted the family in spite of the rent being paid. My neighbor was a tenant at will, as are so many. No protection at all. So," said Mulloy.

"And where did they go?" Da asked.

"Amerikay."

"Oh, the poor, poor souls," said Mam. "Leaving all they loved behind."

Granny crossed herself, as did we all. Exile. Amerikay. The last resort.

"Mr. Mulloy, it was only that Champion needed feeding," Michael started.

Owen Mulloy interrupted him. "I took a good look at your horse as I was coming in. She's a fine animal. I see why you think she deserves the very best of grass. Faugh-a-Ballagh," he said.

"Faugh-a-Ballagh!" I said. "The Irish Brigade's battle cry when they served in the French army and defeated the English at Fontenoy— 'Clear the Way! Faugh-a-Ballagh!'"

"Faugh-a-Ballagh is the name of a racehorse," Mulloy said.

"Oh." Sometimes I *am* too smart for my own good.

"Your horse puts me in mind of his line, the mus-cu-la-ture," Mulloy said, dividing the syllables. "She might make a hunter with the Galway Blazers."

"A hunter?"

"You surely know the Galway Blazers. That gang of gentlemen," said Mulloy, "who get pleasure out of chasing the dogs who are chasing a fox. They like to blow horns and dress up. Like children. Im-ma-tur-ity run riot."

"Why are they called Blazers?" Joseph asked.

"Two reasons are given. One, after they drink in-or-din-ate amounts of whiskey punch, they get to fighting duels, blazing away at each other. Two, they set fire to a hotel out near Birr when they were visiting another hunt. Either one could be true, or both."

"You seem to know a lot about them, Mr. Mulloy," Da said.

"My father looked after the Pykes' stables when I was a boy. I helped out a bit. Whatever else about the landowning gentlemen of Ireland, they love their horses, no question. The gentry might turn a blind eye to the Scoundrel Pykes interfering with the daughters of their tenants, but they wouldn't stand for the Pykes mistreating their horses. The old Major and his son, the young Captain, ride with the Blazers. It's the Pykes and their friends who put on next month's Galway Races on the old course at Parkmore."

"Where I'm entering my horse," Michael said. "I have a sponsor—Mr. Lynch."

"Well," Owen Mulloy said, "very en-ter-pris-ing. The course has walls and fences," he said, thinking aloud. "Steeplechases, you call them, the fashion ever since those two Corkmen raced from church to church. At Parkmore even stable boys can ride."

"As you yourself did?" Michael asked.

"I did," said Mulloy. "Won a few races, until one fall too many stopped me."

"A fall?" I asked.

"Riders fall all the time," Mulloy said.

So Michael could break his neck as well as lose the horse?

Maybe he shouldn't . . .

But before the evening was over, Owen Mulloy had agreed to let Champion graze in his pasture and said he'd help Michael train her for the race. In return, Michael would weed Owen's fields and give him something from the winnings.

"Only two weeks until the race," Owen said. "Hard work ahead. We'll start tomorrow."

"Champion's able for it, and we are, too," Michael said.

❖   ❖   ❖

Michael and Owen laid a course in a pasture enclosed within stone walls built by Owen Mulloy's great-great-grandfather. They rolled whin bushes into bales, piled up rocks, balanced Joseph's hurley on two boulders, and made the walls themselves into jumps.

They worked with Champion through long summer evenings when the sun never thought of setting until ten or eleven. During the day, Michael weeded Owen's barley and oats, and in return Owen gave Michael an old shed to keep Champion in and to bed down himself. He'd been staying with Máire and Johnny, and she was ready for him to leave.

"Enough is enough, Honora," Máire said to me the day Michael left. "Johnny and I have waited too long for our own bed to want to be overheard by Michael in the loft."

Máire liked to hint to me about the joys of marriage. "Now I know why there are so many children running around Bearna," she said to me, "though I sometimes find it hard to believe Mam and Da actually do the same thing Johnny and I do."

"I wouldn't ask them, Máire."

"You'll see, Honora."

"Do you think I'll learn as easily as you did?"

"Has Michael Kelly kissed you yet?"

"He hasn't."

"Do you want him to?"

"I do. From the first moment I saw him coming out of the sea— smiling, tall, with those blue eyes and the male part of him standing so straight and proud . . ."

Máire started laughing. "You'll be fine," she said. "Always a good student." She gave me a quick hug, something she hardly ever did.

"Michael said he's going to buy me some books when he wins the Galway Races, and he says it will give him great pleasure to watch me reading by the fire."

"He's looking forward to watching you read by the fire? Ah, well, to each his own."

⊕　⊕　⊕

A week into the training, I brought Granny up with me. We sat on one wall of the homemade steeplechase course. She was worried.

"I wish Michael Kelly didn't get sick at sea," she said. "Not good to draw attention to himself. What's to keep some red-coated soldier from saying, 'I want that Catholic horse; here's five pounds'?"

"That's not the law anymore, Granny."

"The Sassenach don't let the law get in the way of what they want. Couldn't he find a Connemara pony to ride? They are the smartest animals in the country, and no landlord ever took one off a man."

"Can't run a pony in the Galway Races. And look at Champion! She's mighty, isn't she, Granny?"

Thrilling to watch Michael stretch himself along Champion's neck.

How quickly she had lifted herself up and over, then galloped straight at the next obstacle. A well-matched pair.

After a while Champion and Michael trotted up to us. "What do you think of her, Granny?" Michael asked, patting Champion.

"She's a champion, a curadh, surely," she said.

"Curadh," Michael said. "I don't know that word."

"Curadh is the old word for champion, and the right name for her," Granny said.

Owen Mulloy came up. He'd heard Granny. "Champion suits her."

"Curadh," said Granny.

"Best to use English. Easier for the bettors."

Granny looked Owen Mulloy up and down. He stared right back at her. Da said Owen Mulloy was one of those "boys in the know," with inside information about everything, from a parliamentary election to a marriage agreement—always predicting and analyzing.

Granny had no use for such talk. "Men like to think they put order on things," she'd say. "Control what happens. Women know better." But she only nodded as Michael walked Champion back and forth and Owen outlined his strategy for the race based on his own special knowledge.

"Major Pyke's big dun-colored gelding—called Strongbow, would you believe—will take the lead, no question, followed by the rest of the field, then Michaeleen and her ladyship here. Stay back, Michael. The dun horse is mean and ter-ri-tor-i-al."

"Territorial?" Michael asked.

"He likes plenty of space, fights any horse who comes too close. Forces them to fall going over the jumps. Young Captain Pyke, the son who rides, doesn't mind fouling the other riders. Lay back. Wait. When the rest tangle up in confusion, take Champion over the barrier."

"I understand," Michael said.

Granny had been looking around as Owen spoke. "And how much of this land do you look after?" she asked.

Michael had told me that Owen Mulloy held acres and acres on an old lease and sublet to other tenants.

"All of it, in a manner of speaking. We still operate the old rundale system. Six families work the land together. Three on my lease. The other three rent from the Scoundrel Pykes directly, no leases, year-to-year payments. We all live in a clachán, our cottages close together, and go out to the fields. We share the plowing and the planting, the weeding, the turf cutting, and in happier days the care of the sheep and the cows and the pigs. Each man looks after the landlord's crops and his own potato patch."

"A good system," Granny said. "The way the old Irish lived."

Owen Mulloy nodded. "My father and his father and his father—seven generations of Mulloys did the dividing and shuffling for the whole community. Great crops from these fields then. Ro-ta-tion—change a field from oats to barley to potatoes to pasture. Saving the soil. And always a bit for a son or daughter who wanted to marry and start a family. But now the Scoundrel Pykes have sent agents around to make us stripe the fields, line them up. Every man separate, all tenants at will, easy to evict, pitting tenant against tenant, because who wants to be stuck with the bad land?" Owen said. "They want to force us to break up the clachán, put each cottage in the middle of a field, English style. But who wants to walk a long way over dark fields for a night of music or storytelling at a neighbor's fire? I know a fellow named Francy Coyle out near Shantallow. His landlord set him up in a big square of land, no rent for two years and a cottage in the center. The idea was he'd work harder with no neighbors to chat with. An experiment. Francy couldn't stick the i-so-la-tion. His Maggie got so lonely, Francy had to hire a serving maid so she'd have someone to talk to."

We laughed at that, and Owen Mulloy said that one good thing about agents for the Scoundrel Pykes—they never stayed long.

"We outlast them."

A lovely evening—the light softening, the smell of meadow grass, fuchsia, and whitethorn. I looked up at the sky—pink, reflecting the sun going down beyond Galway Bay below us.

I noticed a group of fields above us, rolling down from a small boreen. Wild-looking, no crops growing on them. "Those are some sad-looking fields, Mr. Mulloy," I said.

"Askeeboy, you call them. They give our townland its name."

"Askeeboy—yellow water," said Granny. "Marshy."

"You're right, missus. Muck and mire. On my lease and the wettest fields for five townlands. Old Major Pyke's kiss-my-foot-how-are-you agent thinks I should find some man foolish enough to take on those fields. In the old way, there'd be a use found for them, in rotation. But not now. Better to let them lie fallow—less rent to pay."

"Must be a great view up there," I said.

"There is that. Galway Bay in all its glory. You can see the sun set into the water in winter. Beautiful in every season."

"Shall we go up and look?" Michael asked.

"Too much of a climb for me," said Granny.

"You two go," said Owen Mulloy. "Mrs. Keeley and I can enjoy a bit of a natter."

"Granny. Call me Granny, Mr. Mulloy."

"And I'm Oweny to you, as I was to my own mother, God rest her."

"God bless all mothers," said Granny.

Friends. Good.

"Come, Honora. Champion would enjoy a slow walk uphill with you on her back," Michael said.

Michael had given most of the children of Bearna a ride on Champion, leading them back and forth in front of the cottages while they waved like squireens, the parents saying, "We were great people once, with horses beyond counting. See how the little ones take to the riding? No fear at all. Horses in their blood!"

But I hadn't had a go yet. Now Michael lifted me. With one motion of those strong arms, he had me in the leather saddle he prized so much—a gift from Jimmy Joe Donnelly, he'd told me. I held on to Champion's mane as Michael led the horse from the pasture. Now I understood why gentlemen and ladies liked to ride—I could see all around me. We came to the top of the hill in no time.

There it was: Galway Bay spread out below us. Mounted on Champion, neither bush nor branch blocked my view of the blue hills of Clare fringed in green across the Bay or the Silver Strand stretching into the waves below us with the wide water leading out to the sea.

I leaned down to touch Michael's hand, closed around Champion's reins. "So beautiful," I said. "I've never seen it like this before."

But he wasn't looking down at the Bay. Not at all. He was measuring the ups and downs of poor, pitiful Askeeboy—water-soaked and abandoned. "It could be drained," he said. "Patrick would know how to save these fields. Look, Honora, at their situation," he said, imitating Owen Mulloy's "sit-u-a-tion." "The fields are in shadow now with the sun going down, but in the morning they'd be first to take the light. Great yields from this farm if it was cared for."

Michael lifted me down from Champion's back, led me up the hill. He stepped into a field. I heard a squelch and saw his foot sink in the mud.

"Patrick would make channels to take the water away. Look, Honora, there's an oak in the middle of the field, a fairy tree."

"Lucky," I said.

"And here, this lane—only a boreen now, but the base for a good road. Mulloy said roads are promised."

"Roads are always promised," I said.

"What do you think, Honora?"

"Think about what?"

"Renting this land when we win the Galway Races."

"I'm no judge of land, Michael, but this seems, well, difficult. I wouldn't want to have the Scoundrel Pykes as landlords."

"I'd lease it from Mulloy, be his subtenant. The Pykes would never know. And these fields are abandoned. We wouldn't benefit from another's hardship. When the road comes, I could set up the forge. This bit of pasture would do for Champion and her foals. I need Patrick, though. . . . Don't know if I could plant these fields without him."

Something in Michael's voice every time he said "Patrick" had kept me from asking straight out about his brother. I looked down and saw Granny and Owen Mulloy sitting on a wall, Granny talking away. A good time to unravel this secret.

"Michael, where is Patrick?"

He didn't answer me for a moment and then finally spoke in a low voice. "I don't know, Honora. You see, Patrick is the kindest and gentlest of men and great with the land, but he can't abide injustice, won't look the other way. It's quite a tale."

A raft of clouds held the last of the sun's fire. We'd be slip-sliding down the steep road to Bearna in the dark if Michael's story was a long one, but this was my chance to hear about the mysterious Patrick, and I wasn't going to let it go.

"Michael, tell me." I sat down on an old wall with Michael beside me, Champion pulling blades of grass from the puddly ground.

"Now, where should I start?" Michael said. "Patrick was accustomed to traveling. At harvesttime he sometimes went as far away as Scotland. Always the hardest-working of all the laborers, despite being the youngest of the spailpins. My mother and father had hoped he'd live with them, but he couldn't settle. Never a boy, really, a man always. My mother said it was the news of my birth that brought him home. March seventeenth it was, his own name day, planting time. He was twelve. I was two months old. My mother says Patrick came straight to me. I turned my face to him. Patrick said to her that I had our father's blue eyes. He smiled at me. I reached out my hand and grabbed Patrick's finger. He touched my cheek and I laughed. 'I always wanted a brother,' Patrick said to my mother."

"Lonely," I said. I took Michael's hand. "Hard to have no home."

"It is," said Michael.

I'll make a home for you, Michael. I will. Up here, or wherever.

"Patrick was glad to be with us," Michael went on. "He found plenty of work on the farms in the parish. At the end of each day, he came to the forge to see me. One evening my mother was in the forge doing the accounts and I was tucked in a corner away from the drafts that came through the door of the shed. I was seven or eight months old. Above me were shelves holding collars and bridles and bits and long bars of iron. In came Patrick, and right over to me. My mother said he usually stopped to wash his hands, but this day he picked me up straight away. No sooner had he taken me in his arms than a Biany wagon hit a rut in the road outside. The barrels of porter fell to the ground and rolled up against the walls of the forge—a hard bang. The walls shook. The age of the wood and the weight of all that clabber hanging on the wall conspired. Everything fell—bits, bridles, iron bars—all crashing down on the pallet where I'd been lying just seconds before."

"You would have been killed!"

"Killed! Killed wouldn't have been the half of it!" he said.

"True, true. Think of your poor mother! Think of me with no you."

"And if I weren't dead at that moment, I would have been maimed or my senses knocked into a cocked hat," Michael said. "Add to that the disgrace of being done in by barrels of porter."

"Don't joke, Michael," I said. "He saved you. Patrick saved you."

"He did—a twelve-year-old hero," Michael said. "When Patrick told me the story himself, he said, 'I was headed to the pump to wash the dirt off my hands and then something made me turn toward the forge. I almost didn't. Almost.' "

Now I took Michael's other hand and held it. "But he did. Patrick did. He came. He saved your life. Michael, when can I meet him? When can I thank him?"

Michael smiled but looked off toward the Bay. "There's more to the story," he said. "So. Patrick stayed with us, working for the farmers in the area, watching me grow. When I was, what, maybe five, he took me with him up to a bit of gravelly ground. We picked the stones out and put manure from the Biany horses on it. Then he taught me to cut the eyes from the seed potatoes and plant them deep into the turned soil. That harvest we had loads and loads of potatoes and never again had to buy them from Jimmy Joe and the others.

" 'He's trying to turn Michael into a farmer,' my grandfather said to my mother. 'Land will break your heart,' he told me. 'It's not yours, ever. You hold it at the landlord's whim.' But Patrick said, 'Every inch of Irish ground belongs to us. What difference does it make if the Sassenach register a deed somewhere? The land belongs to those who work it. The day will come when we take it back, and Michael should learn to tend it rightly until then.' "

"Something of a rebel," I said. "Well, that's no harm. My da's always talking insurrection, too. And he was only, what, seventeen?"

"There's many who talk, but Patrick's a man of action."

"Don't say too much." With not a soul in sight, I whispered.

"The landlords in our part of the country are ruthless, cruel men. The Cnocnacrochádon, the Hill of the Hangman, stands above the crossroads as a reminder of the fathers executed there for stealing to feed their children. Enough to take the heart out of any man, but not Patrick. When I was about nine, and Patrick with us, the wheat crop failed and some of the Blakeney tenants fell behind in their rent. They would be evicted unless they paid up immediately. Patrick got the money for them."

"How?" Softly again.

"He robbed Colonel Blakeney himself, pulled him off his horse on a lonely stretch of road. Held him down and took his purse. Didn't even use a weapon, the story goes. The Colonel couldn't be sure it was Patrick—the man had a scarf tied around his face. Colonel Blakeney needed a blacksmith and Patrick had left. So, our family wasn't punished. But Patrick could never come back. We heard Patrick was hiding in the mountains, a highwayman, it was said. I'm sure he missed bringing the land to life. I've never seen him since. I think my da met Patrick now and then in his wanderings, because sometimes he'd return with more money than he could have made piping for dances at the crossroads." Michael looked down. "Da died about three years after Patrick left, and I thought sure he'd come. He didn't, but we found three big kegs of whiskey at our door and had a wake that's still talked about at Gallagh. The last great wake, they called it. Throngs of

Kellys came from Callow and from Ahascragh. We buried my father in Clontuskert Abbey. . . ."

"With Saint Michael and the mermaid," I said.

He smiled. "And all the Kelly graves. A clatter of pipers played a lament for my da while Mam and Grandda stood stiff and sad. . . . I looked across the fields while they piped and saw a figure on the hillside."

"Patrick," I whispered.

"I believe it was. That was six years ago. Not a word from him since. Rumors," he said, "but nothing more."

"So he doesn't know your grandda and mam died, or about Champion or anything?"

"I think he has ways of getting the news from Gallagh, but now that I've left . . ."

"For all you know, Patrick could be in Amerikay."

"He'd never leave Ireland," Michael said. "Honora, I think I have to tell your da about Patrick. He might not want you to marry a man with such a brother."

"Why? You haven't spoken to Patrick since you were nine. With all the tens of thousands of Kellys, who's to connect you with him?"

"Still."

"Have you ever heard of Martin O'Malley?" I asked Michael. "He's a famous smuggler in the Connemara mountains. Now, there's a real outlaw. He's got an army out there. Martin O'Malley's a cousin of my granny's. Most of her family still lives far out in Connemara. Her nephews were the huge big men at Máire's wedding. They bring cargoes of turf to the pier. Stuck inside are bottles of Spanish wine and jugs of Connemara poitín. Granny calls it 'doing a few favors for Martin O'Malley.' So you see, Michael, the Keeleys aren't as timid and law-abiding as they might appear. Though we'll not tell Da about Patrick Kelly."

❖ ❖ ❖

We met Granny and Owen Mulloy on the road.

"I've just told Owen the story of Macha," she said. "Do you know about her, Michael, the fairy woman who married the Ulsterman? Macha was such a fast runner, her husband bragged that she could beat any horse. The king ordered her to race at the fair, even though she was pregnant. She won, all right, but delivered twins on the course. Macha cursed the Ulstermen so they would experience the pain of childbirth going into battle, except for Cuchulain, who—"

"Ah, Granny," I said. "Shouldn't we be going?"

"A tale for another time," she said.

Michael lifted Granny into the saddle and me behind her. He led us slowly down the path toward the Bay.

"I never realized the hardships the farmers face till Oweny told me," Granny said. "Too much rain, too little rain, the frost comes too soon or not soon enough, and the thaw is too late or too early. This summer was too cool, the last one was too hot. Bugs and hares do damage. And weeds. I thought fishing was a difficult business."

"As to that," Michael said, "Owen Mulloy will never be swept off his boat by the wind or see it capsize in a sudden storm. Or throw up."

"True enough," said Granny. "Still, all that work for crops that have to be sold for rent, with the farmer paying to take them to market!"

"Thank God for the pratties," Michael said.

The flowers of the potato plants shone white in the moonlight as we passed the fields. Bright enough to see our way down to the Bay where the moon lit the water.

Mam and Da came to the door to watch Michael lift Granny and me from Champion's back. Mam half curtsied to Granny. "Riding to the hounds, missus?" she said.

Da nodded to Michael. "Come in for a smoke."

"I'd best get back up the road."

Da asked three times, as was polite, but was relieved when Michael refused. Da wanted to get to his bed. So did I. I'd never kept anything from Da and Mam, but Patrick was a secret to be locked away.

"Good night," we said to Michael.

"Slán abhaile, safe home," said Mam.

Home. Would that be my home up there in the hills?

I heard Granny going on to Da about farming taking more intelligence than meets the eye.

Askeeboy . . . Well, we'd need a better name for our piece of it.

Chapter 7

"SUCH A SLEW OF PEOPLE," Michael said to me as we approached the racecourse. "Protestant, Catholic, and Dissenter, all out for the races."

"The love of horses could unite this country!" Owen Mulloy said as we made our way through the crowd, searching for Mr. Lynch. "The chance of a good wager. A warm afternoon, fiddlers, and poitín—all differences forgotten."

"There's Mr. Lynch," I said. "At the registry booth."

As we got closer, we could hear Mr. Lynch arguing with a race official.

"My good man, I am the Honorable Marcus Lynch, a member of Parliament, and my word is my bond."

"Cash in advance, sir. The stewards require cash."

"And you will get cash from the horse's winnings or his sale price."

"The clerk knows the Lynches owe money for generations," I whispered to Michael.

After a bit, another man came over.

"The chief steward," Owen said.

He shook the Honorable Mr. Marcus Lynch's hand and gave off to the "fool of a clerk," who then filled out a paper.

Mr. Lynch saw us and shouted, "Bring on the horse!"

Not a bother on Champion, calmer than I felt with thousands of men making an unholy racket around us. They pushed and shoved to place bets with the fellows shouting out odds. Very few women— not respectable—but Da hadn't the heart to forbid me coming. He, Dennis and Joseph, Johnny Leahy, and half the fishermen in Bearna were in the crowd somewhere, ready to back Champion with the pennies collected from every family in the townland—three shillings on Champion's nose at thirty to one. A long shot. A lot of money to lose. I'd stopped asking Michael did he really think she'd win after he told me it was bad luck to keep questioning.

"I wonder, will Mr. Lynch put a wager on Champion?" Michael said.

"Only if he can bet on credit," I said.

I looked at the oval track set out in the park. Good green grass, fresh from yesterday's rain. Clear today—a cloudless warm July afternoon.

"Owen Mulloy got it right," Michael said. "See? The gates, the walls, the piles of brush stuck out here in the park are just like his pasture."

"Where is he, Michael?" I said. Owen had disappeared somewhere. "Drink's being sold all over the place. Would he, I mean, is he the type to—"

"Easy, Honora. Look, there's Owen."

Owen was talking to some dodgy-looking lads. He hurried over to us. "Got the word," he said, "from the boys who set up the course. As close to the horse's mouth as you can get." He waited for us to laugh. We did. "Now, Michael, go to the right on the first jump, the wall; then dead center on the second, the gate; take Champion away to the left over the bushes and bring her slightly right of center on walls three and four."

"But you said Strongbow would be crashing and colliding with the other horses," I started. "How can Michael aim Champion—"

Mulloy held up his hand to stop me talking. No mere woman should point out his in-con-sis-ten-cies. Michael winked at me.

"Michael, remember, strat-e-gy!" Owen Mulloy said.

Michael mounted Champion. While the other riders wore jackets and top hats, Michael was in a frieze coat and bareheaded. But none of them were a patch on him for looks or ease on horseback. My gallant hero on his great red steed smiled down at me, those blue, blue eyes so steady and sure, his black hair shining in the sun.

Mr. Lynch walked over to us. "Magnificent animal," he said, patting Champion.

"Well, the girl is," said a voice, "in spite of the hanging red petti-coat."

I turned to see a fat, red-faced man in a shiny top hat, black coat, pants, and boots. He was pointing at me.

"Good morning, Pyke," Mr. Lynch said.

Is this Satan walking up to us? I wondered. I ducked to the other side of Champion.

"Don't go, girl," Pyke said.

Michael heard Pyke call to me and started to dismount, but Owen Mulloy gestured for him to stay put and began talking to Pyke.

"Don't her lines, the horse's, put you in mind of the mare Her Lady-ship brought with her from England?" he asked.

"I see no resemblance whatsoever," Pyke said, looking at Champion.

I slipped away into the crowd.

Major George Scoundrel Pyke, in the flesh. I spat on the ground as Granny did when evil appeared in any form.

I saw Owen guide Michael and Champion to the starting area, then found Da, my brothers, and Owen's neighbors standing on the far edge of the course.

"I never thought I'd be at the Galway Races watching my own horse run," Da said. "An O'Cadhla today, Lord of Connemara."

Owen rushed up to us.

"Is meeting Major Pyke an ill omen?" I asked Mulloy.

"Not at all," he said. "Look your enemy in the eye. Sorry about the old goat's remarks. I would have taken him up on it, but I thought Mr. Lynch would speak for you, him being in with the priests and all."

I didn't say anything.

"Speak of their holinesses, here's Father Gilley, a great sportsman," Owen said. "Good morning, Father." Owen pulled off his hat, as did Da, my brothers, and the other men.

I half curtsied when the priest approached us.

Father Gilley nodded—not on horseback, but still above us.

"Not suggesting you're a betting man, Your Holiness," said Mulloy, "but if you have any friend so inclined, a bit on the horse named Cham-pion would be very ad-van-ta-ge-ous."

"Thank you, uhm . . ."

"Mulloy, sir. Owen Mulloy."

"A parishioner?"

"I am that, sir." Owen lifted his hat even higher, and I bent a little lower as Father Gilley walked away.

"Have to lay the respect on thick with that one, Honora. We might need him if Mr. Lynch tries to wiggle out of our agreement when Champion wins."

"You're confident, Mulloy," Da said.

"I am. And glad to get a word or two with the priest—get him on our side."

"Granny says soft words butter no turnips," I said.

"Jesus, I hope that's not true or the strategy of a lifetime's destroyed. I find the gentry, agents, and priests very open to flattery and nothing too ham-fisted for them. I guess they have such a high opinion of themselves, it blinds them to . . . Oh, they're lining up! Say your prayers, girl!"

Praying, I was. Good St. Bridget, Enda, Patrick, Mac Dara, and you, of course, Our Lady, and Our Lord, too, plus Lugh, Queen Maeve, Macha—and anyone else with a bit of power—hear me. . . . Let Champion win! If she loses . . . I can't think about that.

I had my eyes tight closed when they started, but the sound of ten horses hitting the ground and Owen Mulloy's yelp told me they were off. I heard Da and my brothers roaring.

"Champion Abu!" Dennis shouted.

"Jesus Christ, didn't Michael hear a word I said?" asked Mulloy.

"But, Owen, he's first, he's leading!"

"And here comes that bollocks Strongbow. Look at the way the Major's bollocks of a son, Captain Robert, is riding him! He'll foul Michael just for badness!"

The big ugly dun-colored horse jumped the first wall and started after Champion. Only a few yards before the next gate. . . .

"When he catches her, he'll kill her!" Mulloy said.

Michael leaned forward on Champion's neck and she sped up, gathered herself, and jumped the gate, landing easy on the grass.

"Is that the right place for that jump, Mr. Mulloy? Left, center, or—"

"Who gives a fiddler's fart!" he said. "Go on! Go on, Michael! Come on, Champion, you red banshee! Run!"

Now we were all jumping up and down and screaming—Da, the boys, the fishermen, the farmers, the Claddagh women.

"Curadh, Curadh! Run, run, run!" I shouted.

The other riders let Strongbow and Champion set the pace, waiting for Strongbow to attack our filly, knock her and himself out of the race, leave the field to them.

At the turn, Captain Pyke pulled Strongbow to the right. The horse surged ahead, hitting Champion in the hindquarters.

"Foul!" Mulloy shouted toward the stewards. "Foul, you blind bastards! Did you not see that?"

The push from Strongbow put Champion off her stride, and she faltered and pitched forward. . . .

I closed my eyes. Don't let her fall!

"She's steadied herself!" Mulloy said. "Good on you! Good girl! Now pull away from that ignorant guilpín and the horse he's riding!"

She did. As if thinking, Let's get this over with, Champion flew over the last two jumps and crossed the finish line—first.

"She won, she won! Champion's won!" Mulloy yelled.

Da hugged me and then pumped Mulloy's hand.

"Hoo-ray, hoo-ray, hoo-ray!" Dennis and Joseph shouted.

"Thank you, Saint Bridget," I said, "and all of you up there! Thank you!"

❖   ❖   ❖

Owen Mulloy insisted Father Gilley come for the prize giving and convinced Mr. Lynch—by wrapping a string of "Your Honors" around every word—to let Father Gilley divide the money between Michael and Mr. Lynch, with one sovereign going to the poor of the parish.

"Which we aren't," Michael whispered to me.

And Mr. Lynch agreed. Twelve sovereigns to Michael, twelve for himself, and one for Father Gilley.

Da and the boys, with Johnny and the other Bearna men, went off to collect the sixty shillings they'd won on their bet—a good sum, even when shared among so many.

I saw old Major Pyke laying into his son something awful and Strongbow, huffing and puffing, welts rising on his hide from being whipped.

"You rode a great race, Michael," Owen said. "Did just what I used to do, got in front of the feckers and let the devil take the hindmost!"

"Mr. Mulloy, what about the strat-e-gy?" I said.

"Not much good in the heat of battle."

Da had come up beside me, with Johnny, my brothers, and Owen's neighbors, all congratulating Champion, who neighed and whinnied. A grand celebration.

The Scoundrel Pykes looked over at us.

"You've made enemies there, Michael," Da said. "I'd stay clear of them."

"No need to see them again. Champion's first and last race. Owen and I plan to breed her. We'll train and sell the foals."

Da nodded.

Dennis and Joseph and Johnny crowded close to look at the pile of coins in Michael's two hands.

"Handy money," said Da. "Never saw so much."

"Now then, Owen, take seven of these," Michael said. "One for your fee and six for a year's rent of Askeeboy and the surrounds."

"Askeeboy? Are you sure?"

"Is that a fair rent?"

"More than fair. The agent will be only too delighted. And no need to tell him your name. The Scoundrel Pykes will never know they have a new tenant."

"And we'll share the pastureland?" said Michael.

"It will be an honor to have Champion eat my grass."

"She'll be grazing with her foal soon," Michael said.

"A great partnership, Michael! And you, too, Honora Keeley soon-to-be Kelly."

I looked at Da.

"Mr. Keeley hasn't consented yet, Owen. He's known me only a month," Michael said.

"Mr. Keeley," Owen said, "I've been judging bloodlines my whole life as my father did before me, and this boy's bred from good stock."

Da said nothing, but he patted Champion and smiled at me.

"I wish you God's blessing in Askeeboy, Michael Kelly," Owen said.

"Knocnacuradh," I said.

"What?" Mulloy said.

"The Hill of the Champions," I said.

"Knoc-na-cur-adh," Michael repeated, using the long Irish "ah." "And the best place to watch the sun go down on Galway Bay," he said.

"It is that, whatever you call it," said Owen Mulloy.

Michael set me in front of him on Champion's back, and Da made no objection. We were the happiest people in Ireland, singing and laughing, Da walking with Owen and his neighbors, Dennis and Joseph and Johnny going ahead, shouting, "Faugh-a-Ballagh! Clear the Way!"

We circled above Galway City and crossed the river at Menlough. Many a man would have headed straight for the pubs in Galway City and sent the rest of us on our way. But Owen wanted to gather his wife and children and the neighbors' families for the celebration in Bearna that had surely begun.

"We'll pass the land Michael will take over," Owen said.

"Askeeboy?" Da said.

"Knocnacuradh," I said.

Owen Mulloy was standing in for Michael's own father—making the marriage contract. Da couldn't refuse. Michael had actual money—gold coins, got legitimately with the Honorable Marcus Lynch's support. We need never see the Pykes again. And as for Patrick Kelly, ná habair tada—whatever you say, say nothing. What Da didn't know wouldn't hurt him.

Though late evening, the sun was still high in the sky when we reached Owen's clachán.

"Look, sir, you can see the Bay," Michael said. "We're up so high, Honora could come down and warn you if clouds are gathering."

Da turned and stomped away.

"What did I say?" Michael asked.

"Till the land," Johnny Leahy said. "Play your pipes, ride that red banshee horse, but never pass a remark about the weather to John Keeley. It's unlucky."

I caught up with Da. "He'll learn, Da, he will. Here . . ." I took his hand. "Look here, Da—a fairy fort. Granny would like that. Owen Mulloy said there was an ancient stronghold here—the Ráth of Ún. Gives the whole parish its name, Rahoon. Surely that means it's a lucky place."

Da walked over to the raised circle of ground. He likes to think of the times when the old Irish ruled the whole place—the O'Cadhlas, Lords of Connemara. Great people once.

"And here, Da, a holy well." I showed him a deep hole in the hollow of the hill, with a low stone wall around it. "Saint James' well."

"My grandfather was James," Da said.

"And there'll be a baby James living up here if you'll please say we can marry. Da, I love Michael so much and he's a fine, honorable man. He prays and doesn't drink, well, not all that much, and—"

"Enough, Honora. You may marry, but tell your husband never, ever to make a remark about the weather or speak to me of a rabbit or fox."

"He won't! Thank you, Da! Thank you!"

❖　❖　❖

Whole townlands came out to cheer us as we followed the Bally-moneen Road down from the hills to the coast road and into Bearna. Word had spread—one of our own had won the Galway Races. People from Rusheen, Shanballyduff, Cappagh, Derryloney, Truskey East and Truskey West, Ballybeg, Lachlea, and Corboly stood in the summer dusk and called out to us. "Is it Red Hugh and the Wild Geese come to free us?" I heard. Many shouted, "Faugh-a-Ballagh!" and, "Remember Fontenoy!"—the Irish Brigade's victory cries.

Riding in front of Michael on Champion, his arms circling me, his hands on the reins, I felt like the queen of a conquering army, waving at her liberated subjects. Centuries of tugging the forelock forgotten. A great people altogether. Victory.

❖　❖　❖

At the hooley in our cottage that night, our Bearna neighbors met the people from Askeeboy/Rahoon. Owen's wife, Katie Mulloy, had brought some early potatoes, freshly dug, for Mam to cook.

Katie was a comfortable woman with light brown hair and dark eyes, five years younger than Owen, she said, with two boys—Joe, six, and John Michael, four—and a two-year-old daughter, Annie.

I liked how she smiled at Owen as he explained to a circle of fisher-men that their townland's official name was Rahoon and the parish was called Rahoon. "Which leads to a bit of ob-fus-ca-tion, which is no bad thing. Those we want to find us do."

"He was taught by one of those Latin-type hedge schoolmasters and fell in love with big words," Katie whispered to me as we worked together, mashing the bit of butter from the Dwyers' cow, the last one in the townland, Katie said.

"What's that you're saying, Katie?" a little gingery-haired woman behind us asked. "Couldn't hear."

"I said, 'Isn't this lovely for fisher people and farmers to get together,'" Katie said.

"Squashed together, I'd say." The woman put a hand on Granny's spinning wheel and began to turn it. Granny saw her, stepped over, and stopped the wheel. The woman shrugged and walked away.

"Tessie Ryan," Katie told me. "The raggedy Ryans." Tessie's husband, Neddy, worked around the place for Owen and did duty days for the landlord. Katie said to watch what I said to her because she twisted everything. Neddy Ryan was small, too, and both of them had twitchy noses that Katie said put her in mind of two rabbits. "But their daughter Mary's a lovely girl," Katie said. "Minds my Annie sometimes."

We watched Tessie go up to Michael and heard her ask to see the gold sovereigns. Michael brought them out of the sack he had tied to his waist and laid them in her cupped hands.

Don't, I wanted to say. Don't.

"They're heavy and very cold," Tessie said. "Never held as many as this. My father had a gold coin we pawned with a gombeen man, but we couldn't pay the interest on what we borrowed, so we lost the coin."

Tessie fingered the sovereigns. The good fortune of others made begrudgers of some. This woman is trouble. Another reason to keep the knowledge of Patrick Kelly to myself. What if there's a reward out for his capture?

Mam looked away from Tessie, who still clutched the money. Poor critters, she'd be thinking. No sense of the wide world.

"I left my pipes at Máire's. Let me get them," Michael said as he put the coins back into the bag.

He'll hide the money in Máire's cottage, then carry it up to Owen's shed and bury the money deep and safe.

❖ ❖ ❖

Máire and Johnny led the crowd out onto the hard-packed sand on the strand in front of the cottages for the dancing. Bits of pink-and-purple clouds lingered in the sky, their colors reflected in the Bay. "Great to dance so near the waves," Katie said as Michael piped the first reel. The Bearna people, well used to one another, stepped through the set fast and sure—come together, four hands, two hands,

hands across the back. Máire pulled the Rahoon ones into the dance. Farmers and fishermen mixed, swinging one another's wives and daughters, the strand full of music and motion as the sky eased into night and the Bay disappeared into the dark.

Behind the seawall, I saw a little girl crying. I went over to her. "What is it?" I asked. "Come and join the dancing."

She cried harder.

"What's your name?"

"Mary."

"For Our Lady. That's my sister's name, too, though she says it the Irish way, 'Mah-ree.' . . . Can you say that?"

"Mah-ree," she said through her sniffles.

"Lovely," I said. "Now, won't you tell me what's wrong?"

"I'm afraid of this big water."

"Don't be. The Bay's behaving itself tonight—so quiet and gentle. When the tide's out like this, there's shiny stones at the shoreline. Would you like one?"

She nodded. She took my hand and let me lead her to the water's edge. I picked up a round pink pebble streaked with green and silver and put it in her hand. She rubbed the stone and smiled at me.

"Can I keep it?"

"Of course."

"Don't tell my mother."

"Who's your mother?"

"Tessie Ryan."

"Oh. Well, uhm . . . see the fellow playing the pipes? That's the man I'm to marry."

She looked over at Michael and back to me. "You're lucky."

"I am," I said, and hugged her.

Mary ran over to Katie Mulloy, who held her wee Annie. Mary showed the stone to the little girl, who laughed.

On the strand, Máire and Johnny lifted their arms and clasped hands to make a bridge for the dancers. Dennis and Josie, the girl he was courting, ducked underneath. Mam and Da followed, with dozens of couples coming behind them. Faugh-a-Ballagh! Clear the Way!

The reel ended. Michael sent out the first notes of a jig. Owen Mulloy found Granny. A space was cleared, and the two of them began dancing. Granny kept her shoulders and arms still, stomping her heels and toes, fast and furious. Owen Mulloy was hard-pressed to match her, but keep up he did. The other dancers made a circle around them, clapping and shouting.

It was Owen who cried, "Enough! A recess, Michael, please!"

❖ ❖ ❖

"We're celebrating our wedding before the marriage," Michael said to Owen Mulloy as he drank from the jug Owen had carried down from Askeeboy. I sat between them on the seawall.

"No bad thing to have a quiet ceremony. Major Pyke needn't know," Mulloy said, "stuck away like he is in that big gray stone house at the edge of a cliff up the coast. All the furniture, crystal chandeliers, and carpets in the place come from the other side of the world, paid for on the backs of the likes of us. And Her Ladyship, whose money keeps the whole shebang going, wanders around like a ghost, drugged to the gills with laudanum. The young Captain stays away, off with his regiment. A place to avoid, I'll tell you that."

❖ ❖ ❖

Long after the full moon rose over the water, Michael and Champion led the Mulloys and the Rahoon people up the hill by its light. Máire didn't go home but sat whispering with me at our doorway as the short summer darkness gave way to dawn.

I told Máire why my wedding would be quiet and quick. "Máire, he was disgusting, that old Major, the way he looked at me."

"I know," she said. "Not pleasant to have men's eyes trailing over your body that way."

"But, Máire, I thought you liked the attention."

She shook her head. "Nice when *Johnny* calls me his Snowy-Breasted Pearl. But one of his sisters heard him and told her husband, and now other fellows call me 'Pearl' to my face."

"I didn't know."

"They wouldn't say it in front of the family," she said. "It does give me a kind of power. I can keep men guessing with a bit of banter, a joke. But sometimes I wonder, Who's Máire, and who's the Pearl?"

"Máire, I think I understand. I have someone inside me who's Honora but not Honora, and she says the most outrageous things. But, Máire, I can let both of them speak to Michael."

"And I have released my snowy breasts to Johnny," she said. "Into his hands I commend my—"

"Máire, that's blasphemy!"

But we both started laughing.

Then Johnny shouted from their cottage, "Máire, have you no home to go to?"

"Your Pearl's ready!" she said, then whispered to me, "I hope he is." She winked and was gone.

Chapter 8

Even a quiet wedding costs something, what with the jugs of poitín and the priest's fee. Da didn't want Michael to spend one of the gold coins and take away a father's right and privilege. So we were to wait until the boats went out and Da had a good catch to sell.

The Claddagh Admiral decided the fleet would set out three days after the fifteenth of August. I was up with Da, three hours before first light, helping with the nets and sails.

"See, Da," I said, "I made a packet of oat cakes, and here's your salt and ashes."

"Thank you, Honora."

I wanted to say: Special for you, Da, this last time before my wedding. But that sounded ill-omened. I looked over at the small spirit house Da had built so many years ago as an offering to the winds and said a prayer.

Máire and I stood on the strand with Mam and the other women as the twenty Bearna boats sailed into the still-dark Bay to join the Claddagh men, all of them following the Admiral's white sail just visible against the sky. A fair wind moved the fleet down the center of the Bay.

"Going well," Máire said.

"Johnny's boat's already up with the leaders," I said.

"He likes to be one of the first."

❖ ❖ ❖

Mam and I spent the next day at Knocnacuradh, cleaning the cottage while Michael helped in Owen's fields. The Rahoon people and the Bearna fishermen had joined in the meitheal that built our cottage, set apart from the clachán above the tight circle of cottages on the brow of the hill.

"From up here, we can see Galway Bay," Michael had explained to Owen Mulloy.

Owen had not been pleased. He'd found us tracing out the shape of the rooms with pebbles a week after the Galway Races. "If you don't live in the clachán, there'll be remarks passed, Michael," he'd said.

"What remarks?" I'd asked.

"Well, Honora, you're not a farm wife, things you don't understand."

"What things, Owen?"

But he didn't answer. Unlike him. Then in a rush, "It's Tessie Ryan. She's telling the women you have notions, Honora. Your ed-u-ca-tion, and then . . ." He'd turned to Michael. "Fisherwomen are known to boss their men, Michael. Going back and forth to Galway City—what do they do in town?"

"They sell fish," Michael said. He'd folded his arms and swayed forward and back a bit. I'd not seen his face so set-looking. Angry.

Owen Mulloy didn't notice, talking to me. "Tessie says your granny works spells and your mam brews potions from herbs picked at the full moon."

"Medicine," I'd said, "for women giving birth. My mam's the midwife in our village."

"I told the others that," Owen had said, "but then Tessie started going on about your sister, the one called the Pearl. Some stories she picked up, so . . . better she doesn't visit. . . ."

"Stop right there, Owen," Michael had said. "I'll not live in a place where Honora and her family are not respected. All bargains are off. Come, Honora."

Michael was being im-pet-u-ous, Owen had said. "Put the cottage in the clachán. Prove Tessie Ryan wrong."

But Michael wouldn't listen. "We're off, Mr. Mulloy. Thank you for your help with the race. Keep your fee, but please return the rent money."

"Go, then."

Owen Mulloy's temper had flared. He'd started hopping around, pointing his finger at Michael's chest. Did we feel no gratitude? He was only trying to let us know. Michael'd been breathing heavy. Owen's lucky he's the smaller man, I'd thought, or Michael would punch him.

"Michael," I'd said. "Wait."

"*Wait?*"

"I know you want to bring these fields to life."

"Not if you're misunderstood and insulted."

"What if I want to stay?" I'd asked Michael.

Then Michael had looked at me. "You choose, Honora."

Owen had started sputtering. "You'd let *her* decide? A woman dictating to her husband?"

And that had riled Michael again—the two of them began shouting at each other.

"Michael, Owen, stop! Would you both listen to me? Owen Mulloy, surely you know the story told about the wife of the fellow you're named for—Eoghan, the chieftain?"

"Not the time for a story," Michael had said.

"Always time. Fadó," I'd intoned as the both of them glared at each other.

Better make this quick, I'd thought as I began one of Granny's best tales: "The Cailleach at the Well." The cailleach, or hag, looked after a well deep in the forest, I told them. Very old and wrinkled, she was, with a wart on her nose.

"One day, the seven sons of the chieftain Eoghan came to the well, very thirsty, hot from their hunting. The hag held out a golden cup filled with water. 'You each may have a drink,' she told them, 'but first you must kiss me.'"

And now Michael and Owen were listening, leaning against the old stone wall.

"The brothers refused her. 'Too ugly,' one said, and they rode away. But the youngest, Niall, stayed. He looked into the woman's eyes and saw kindness there, and loneliness. He kissed her rightly on the lips, and she gave her cup to him. He drank.

" 'You will have the Sovereignty of Erin,' she said. 'You will be chieftain.'

" 'I won't,' he said. 'I'm the youngest of seven brothers.'

"Now, among the old Irish," I'd reminded Michael and Owen, "the eldest did not necessarily succeed his father. Any son or nephew might be chosen. Still, Niall felt he had no chance.

"But the cailleach said again, 'You will have the Sovereignty of Erin, and when what I say comes true, you must marry me. Promise me.'

" 'That's a promise I can make,' he thought. No fear of being chieftain, so he agreed to marry her. Not too long after this, Eoghan, the chieftain, died, and who was selected? Only Niall. The night before he was to be inaugurated, Niall found the hag waiting for him in his tent. She'd come to claim what he'd promised. In those days a promise was a promise, and terrible consequences befell a man who broke his word.

"Niall put his head in his hands. No escape. But when he looked up, he saw a beautiful young woman standing before him. 'Where's the other one?' he asked.

" 'I am she,' the woman said. 'I'm under a spell. For twelve hours of every twenty-four I can appear as you see me now. But for the other twelve, I will have the form of the hag. Now, what's it to be?'

" 'What do you mean?'

" 'As your wife, shall I be as you see me now by day, or by night?'

"He thought long and hard. If he picked 'by day,' all the world would see he had a beautiful wife, but then at night she'd be the hag. Why not have her beautiful by night and keep her to himself?"

Owen had interrupted me. "Go for the night!" he'd said. "Who cares what people think? If you've got a gorgeous woman in your bed and no one the wiser . . ." He'd stopped. "Go on, Honora."

"And then Niall thought about the woman. How did she feel? And he said to her what Michael said to me: 'You choose.' And the spell was broken. She could be her true self, lovely all the time. She became queen of Tir Eoghan and the happiest woman in Ireland."

Owen had gotten off the wall and taken my hand. "That's a mighty story, and I take your meaning."

"You do?"

"I'm going to tell Tessie Ryan to shut her gob. And will you be choosing to stay with us, Honora?"

"I will," I'd said. "In our cottage on the high hill."

❖ ❖ ❖

"You choose, Honora," Michael had said, and by all that's sweet and holy, I have chosen well, I thought as Mam and I worked.

"A wonderful view, isn't this, Mam? And Michael says one day we'll have a window."

We set the pot Michael bought in Galway City on the iron hook in the hearth.

"I wouldn't say anything to Tessie Ryan about a window."

"I won't, Mam."

"I noticed there's milkweed down the boreen, and marshy places have irises, which can be useful," Mam told me. "I'll give you a list of healing plants to look for and note the best time to pick them. Some need a full moon, others dawn."

I wouldn't be mentioning *that* to Tessie Ryan, either.

❖ ❖ ❖

Hard to live two miles away from Mam and Da, Granny, Máire, and the boys, I thought as Mam and I started down the hill on the Bally-moneen Road.

"It's an easy way, really," I said, trying to convince her and myself. "Less than an hour's walk. We'll be up and down to each other often, won't we? Michael *could* sleep in the cottage now, but he wants to stay in Owen's shed until we can step over the threshold together."

She agreed. "A man should follow the woman in—that's the luck."

"The lease starts on September twenty-ninth, the feast of Saint Michael the Archangel, Michael's name day. Could we have the wedding then? It's a Monday—lucky. We wouldn't have to worry about taking people from the harvest. Or maybe we could be married on my birthday, September fifteenth, three weeks from now."

Mam had stopped on the road.

"Though that was the day I was supposed to enter the convent. Miss Lynch might take offense, and her father was good to us with Champion," I said. "Mam, are you listening to me? We have to choose a date."

She pointed above. Big black clouds were bullying their way across the blue sky to settle over Galway Bay.

"Run, Honora," Mam said.

The wind hit. Lightning burnt the air and flashed on the stones under our feet. I felt my hair stand up around my head. A driving rain started. Then hailstones fell.

I thought I heard Michael shouting down to us, but we kept running as the path turned to mud.

Protect the boats, dear Lord. Please, keep them safe. Da, Dennis, Joseph, Johnny Leahy—all of the fishermen, please, Blessed Mother, St. Bridget, Mac Dara, hear me.

⊹ ⊹ ⊹

We had to pull and pull against the wind to get the door into our cottage open.

"The Bay has lost the run of itself," Granny said. "Broke over the seawall, washed against the cottages. Nothing to do but kneel in the house and pray."

"They've put in somewhere, surely, Granny," I said.

But we knew Bearna was the only safe harbor for twenty miles.

As fast as it had come up, the storm rained itself out and blew past. Wind still rumpled the Bay, but now we could go out. We ran with the other women across the strand and out onto the pier. Máire was there already.

"I see the sails!" Annie Leahy, Máire's mother-in-law, called out. "They're coming! They're coming! Thanks be to God, they're coming!"

"We'll be mending sails forever," Mam said as the boats got closer and we saw the tears and tatters.

"A kiss with every stitch," said Máire. "I was worried that Johnny might . . . So silly. We'll have a party tonight!" She ran to the pier's edge.

The Bearna fishermen steered their boats up to the pier while the Claddagh men went on, the Bay rocking them along as if nothing whatsoever had happened.

"There aren't enough boats," Mam whispered to me.

"What?"

"Count them. There should be twenty . . . I only see nineteen."

"Do you see ours, Mam? Do you see Da?"

"I do. And the Clancys, and the Folans, and the Dooleys and the Higgins . . . Honora, I don't see the Leahy boat."

Da jumped off our boat, went to Máire, took her in his arms.

The Leahy boat had disappeared in the storm. Johnny, his da, and his brother, Daniel, were gone.

❖ ❖ ❖

"The storm came up so fast," Da told us that night. "No time to do anything but lie down on the deck and hold on. I saw Johnny lowering the sails on the Leahy boat, the better to ride out the storm. He'd gotten them halfway down when this wave—the tallest I've ever seen—carried the boat up, then slammed it under the water."

"The sea," Granny said from her place at the spinning wheel. Mam was with Máire at the Leahys. Michael, my brothers, and I sat on the floor huddled near Da on his stool. Hughie had settled himself on Da's lap, something the six-year-old had not done for ages.

"There was no way to help them," Dennis said.

Joseph only shook his head. My young brothers carrying a man's grief at fifteen and thirteen.

"You did well, boys," Da said. "Brave in a boat, both of you. I was proud of my sons today."

❖ ❖ ❖

The next day, Máire and I walked the shore, searching. We climbed over rocks, following the broken stone teeth along the shore of Galway Bay.

"Máire, a ghrá, his body may never wash up," I said after that first day.

"Johnny did not drown."

"But they saw the boat go down."

"He got to the shore. He's walking along the rocks to me right now, or he's hurt in a cave, or . . ."

"Ah, Máire," I said.

Survivors did climb out of the sea. Sailors from the Armada ship *Concepcion* that wrecked near Ard made it to land. Granny says Da inherited his black hair from one of them. Such tales gave Máire hope as we searched every cave and cove from Bearna to Spiddal.

On the eighth day, a púcán crewed by three of the Ard Keeleys docked at Bearna pier, bringing the bloated corpse of Johnny's brother, Daniel, the youngest of the three on the boat. They hadn't carried the body more than twenty steps before Annie Leahy, his two sisters, his granny, and Máire were upon them. The current had carried Daniel Leahy almost fifty miles to where Galway Bay met the sea. Only his body had washed onto shore. No sign of Johnny and his father.

The wake began that night at the Leahy cottage. The same people who'd shared the joy of Champion's victory only a few weeks before now crowded together in sorrow. Michael and I stood behind Máire, close so she could lean on us, but she stood straight through all the long hours.

Daniel lay wrapped in a sail in the center of the room. Clothing from Johnny and his da would be placed on the floor to represent their bodies.

Annie Leahy put down her husband's old woven belt. Máire spread out Johnny's wedding shirt, smoothing the arms, pulling the collar so the edges were flat.

She stepped back, and the Widow Clooney began the keening. "Three men from one family—so kind, so fearless, so skilled in their fishing, so sure in the ocean, but a wind past describing, strong and destroying . . ." She went on and on, crouched on the floor, eyes closed, head back, sometimes murmuring, sometimes shouting, "An evil pact of the wind and waves defeated the best effort of the Leahy heroes to fight their way back to the women who waited for them. Sons with no issue, a family name disappearing, no children to remember the brave Leahys." She paused and opened her eyes, and screamed over and over—a blood-stopping cry.

Then Mrs. Leahy cried out, "No issue, no son with our name!"

Máire, silent before, wailed now. A sound without form, no words. I knew then she hadn't told her mother-in-law she was pregnant. Annie was a very godly woman, and she wouldn't like to know that Johnny and Máire had hurried their wedding night, but surely now . . .

All had great sympathy for Máire, but hearts broke over Annie's loss.

"Poor Annie Leahy," Mam said after we got home. "To lose her husband and all her sons. The sorrowful Mother herself had an easier time of it—at least Our Lady could hold His body and mourn. But

Annie won't see her sons until after her own funeral when she meets them again in heaven."

✧ ✧ ✧

So. Máire came back to live with us. She didn't want much to do with Annie Leahy, and I didn't know why. Finally she told me.

"After that terrible keening, no more Leahys, I told Annie Leahy I was pregnant. I thought she'd be glad. But then she asked me how many months. I said I'd missed for the first time in May. 'Well before the wedding,' she said. 'Are you sure it's Johnny's?'"

"She was out of her head with grief. She didn't mean it."

"Not so out of her head she didn't ask me how many months and count back in a flash. She always has thought I'm no better than I ought to be."

"You need to help each other, not let anger . . ."

But Máire refused to speak to Annie. Three weeks went by. Máire would not relent, nor would Annie come to her.

"I need a father for this baby and a place to live. I don't want to stay with the family forever, and I can't keep the cottage built at the meitheal—the oldest Leahy girl claimed it," Máire said. "She's getting married, and says Johnny paid the rent for it with money from his father, so it belongs to the Leahys. She wants it as a dowry. And as for Annie Leahy . . ."

"Come live with Michael and me."

"I'll marry. I think there will be men in Bearna and the Claddagh only too glad to offer for the Pearl," she said. "And as much as I'm breaking my heart over Johnny, he wouldn't want our child to be marked and commented on. I need to get a father for the baby before it's born."

She chose one of the Connors—Kevin—and she and Kevin Connor and Da and I went to Father Gilley's to arrange for the wedding.

"Better sooner than later," Máire said.

✧ ✧ ✧

"But, Máire, we don't conclusively know that your husband is dead," Father Gilley said.

We were in Galway City at the parish house. I thought of the awful puffed-up body of young Daniel, his face chewed by fish, his hair the only human-looking part of him. When I had walked the shore with Máire, I'd prayed we'd find Johnny's body to bury. But after seeing poor Daniel, I was glad Johnny's grave was the sea.

"Do you think, Father, that some ship bound for Amerikay picked Johnny up?" Máire said. She'd proposed that from the first.

But Granny had told Máire very kindly that the cousins from Ard said no ships could have sailed into the sea during that storm, and none had been seen in the days before or after. She'd accepted that.

Here was Father Gilley making her hope again.

"So, Father, my Johnny might have been saved?"

"Ah, my child, I doubt that very seriously; however, without conclusive proof of his death, the marriage bond remains in place, and"—this last was to Kevin Connor—"I could not sanctify any union. I'm sorry."

But the look on his face said he wasn't sorry at all. He was pleased, for whatever reason, to apply some version of Church law to Máire. Forcing us to obey made him feel the big man, acting like the Sassenach, who made rules and regulations that had nothing to do with real life, to give themselves another stick to beat us with.

Máire and Mam went to Miss Lynch, hoping she'd speak to Father Gilley, but that was not to be.

"Oh, I couldn't possibly question Father Gilley's judgment," she said.

❖ ❖ ❖

"What odds to be a widow in a parish oversupplied with them," Máire said to me that night. "And me only nineteen. Here's Mam and Da with three sons to raise up and find boat shares and bits of field for them and their families. And there's Kevin Connor, happy to take me and my child, and willing that I call it Leahy. What's to become of me now? Does that fool of a priest want me to go off to Bride's Hotel? That would give him some real sin to preach against."

"Máire," I said, "you would never, ever do that."

"I suppose I never, ever would, but I know how men look at me and I don't want to spend the rest of my life fending off lads who fancy a chance with the widow, or spend my time convincing wives that I have no interest in their husbands."

I thought of Owen Mulloy, worried about the Pearl visiting us.

No one would bother a young woman growing up in her parents' house, or a married woman protected by her husband, but an experienced widow presented great temptation, especially to men convinced that the Pearl would welcome them, and then, ructions.

"Máire, if you lived with Michael and me up in Knocnacuradh, he'd make sure no one bothered you."

"I couldn't go up there with those farm women," she said. "At least now I can go to town with Mam and sell the catch."

Granny was furious at Father Gilley. For thousands of years, the Irish followed the Brehon laws, where marriage was a contract between equal partners. "Ten different legal relationships between a man and woman," she said. Granny told Máire she had Irish tradition on her side. Johnny was gone. The contract broken. "When I was young in Connemara, we got married without priests. Touched our fingers together through a hole in a stone cross. Done and dusted."

Máire asked did Granny know some fellow still following the ancient ways. Granny told her she just might.

❖ ❖ ❖

"For God's sake, Honora, get married," Máire said almost every day of the month that followed.

"It doesn't seem right," I said. My birthday came and went. Father Gilley celebrated the Month's Mind Mass for Johnny and Daniel and their father, but it still seemed too soon to have my wedding.

"He'll pray for Johnny's soul, but won't agree that he's dead. What kind of sense in that?" Máire said to me.

She and I were alone, the rest up digging the potatoes from the garraí Mhurchadha—the fishermen's common field—and Michael gone, too, helping Owen Mulloy.

Three days until St. Michael's Day and the start of the lease. Bad luck for Michael to move in alone. I couldn't leave Máire. Though she didn't look very pregnant, Máire thought the baby might be born as soon as Christmas.

"Granny thinks I should go out to Ard/Carna, far away from all the priests. Says there's surely a spare Keeley second or third cousin out there to marry me," she said. "They know Johnny's gone, for haven't they lost enough of their own?"

"It's a poor enough place, and Máire, you'd be so far away."

"Maybe I'll find a handsome highwayman. There's no law west of Oughterard, no roads, thousands of men out there," she said.

"Oh, Máire!"

She sang:

> *Let me sing of a young highwayman*
> *Dick Brennan was his name . . .*

"Stop it, Máire! Do you want Annie Leahy to hear that her disgraced daughter-in-law is singing?"

> *Brennan on the moor,*
> *Brennan on the moor . . .*

Máire started laughing and crying at once.

"That's what I'll do. I'll have old Martin O'Malley make a match for me with an outlaw or a poitín maker. There's one behind every rock in Connemara."

I would have told her about Patrick Kelly then, but Máire was sobbing. "Where do you think he is, Honora? My laughing Johnny with his sweet mouth. Is he in heaven at all? No body buried, no bones to rise up on the last day. Did the fish he hunted revenge themselves on him? Oh, Johnny! Your wee one inside me." She rubbed the tears from her eyes. "I'll not walk in Bearna with a bowed head, Honora. And you should have your wedding. I know what Johnny would say: 'Máire, for God's sake, shake some sense into your sister—there are plenty of girls would want a fine handsome man like Michael Kelly with a plot of land and a sack of gold. Tell her to marry the fella.' So it's Máire for Connemara, and Honora for Askeeboy," she said.

"Knocnacuradh," I said. "And I won't leave you."

"Get married, or somebody will start telling Michael Kelly that Honora Keeley was for the nuns and she's probably having second thoughts and too timid to tell him, and here's my lovely daughter."

"You don't know Michael," I said.

"Honora, you don't know men."

❖　❖　❖

Father Gilley married us on the Feast of St. Michael, September 29. I was two weeks past seventeen and Michael was eighteen. It was understood in the townlands that with Máire in mourning the wedding would be small, with no dancing afterward, only a feed of pratties and a sip of the poitín brought by the Keeley third cousin who sat next to Máire in the chapel now.

As he performed our ceremony, Father Gilley looked over at Máire and the Connemara man. Máire stared right back at him. She'd make a good highwayman herself.

Father Gilley went on about marriage not being entered into lightly, while Máire looked him up and down. Then he called Michael and me up to the altar.

"Do you take Honora Keeley to be your wife?"

"I do," Michael said.

Father Gilley's voice faded away as Michael took my hand and we pledged ourselves with our eyes—his so blue, the color of Galway Bay on the morning he was sent to me.

"I do," I said.

❖　❖　❖

Only about twenty of us walked down through the village, past the Big House. Miss Lynch and her father were away in Dublin, and most others in the village were still at the harvest. We came to the boreen that turned down to the sea and our cottages when we saw two riders in the distance, coming from farther out the coast, Fubo way.

"Hell and damnation," I heard Mulloy say.

The old Major and his son, Captain Pyke. Our group parted to make way for the big horses. Nothing to stop a gentleman from riding you down. Please, ride by.

But the old Major saw Owen Mulloy and stopped. "Leaving the harvest for a wedding, Mulloy?"

"Crops all in, Your Honors," Owen said.

"Where are the bride and groom?" asked Major Pyke.

Michael and I were within a circle of people, not easily seen.

"Come now, don't be shy. Tessie Ryan, is that you?"

"It is, Your Honor."

"A far way from your home, Tessie. Now, show me the bride and groom."

"There they are, Your Honor." She pointed through the circle.

The old Major walked his big horse over and looked down on us.

"Ah, the peasant jockey and his colleen bawn. Quite lovely, isn't she, Robert?"

The young Captain moved up next to him. His eyes fastened on me. Dear God, let them ride on.

"Too bad old Mr. Lynch is so timid with his tenants. Initiating this girl would be a pleasant duty."

"It would, Father."

I looked down at the ground.

"Oh, Your Honors!" It was Tessie. "These aren't Mr. Lynch's tenants, sir. They're your very own, leasing from Owen Mulloy."

"Really? And what are their names, Tessie?"

Shut up, Tessie!

"Michael Kelly, Your Honor, and Honora Keeley."

"Honora. Now, that's a name I like. And are you honorable, Honora?" the old Major said, and then turned to his son. "Honor Honora by taking her first night. A fine old tradition, droit du seigneur."

"Technically speaking, sir, Michael Kelly is *my* tenant," Mulloy said.

"Now, Mulloy, save your blarney. I've known you too long to be taken in by it. You are trying to deny Honora her chance."

Michael spoke up, cool and polite, but no "sirs" or "Your Honors": "I would take it kindly if we could start on the right foot. I'll be a good tenant and pay my rent on time, but I expect—"

Mulloy broke in: "Michael Kelly will reclaim that marshy ground for you, Major Pyke. He'll set up a forge. A blacksmith's shop on the high road might be just the in-duce-ment Bianconi needs to send his cars out this way. The Mistress would be pleased."

"The Biany cars can go to the devil, and the Mistress is in London," said Major Pyke. "I'm speaking about Honora, Mulloy, Honora and my son. Will he uphold the reputation of the Scoundrel Pykes? Oh, I know what you people call us. . . . Are you ready, Robert, to initiate Honora on her first night and bring luck to the marriage?"

"I am. Come on, girl." And the young Captain rode close to me, leaned down, trying to grab my hand. "Mount up with me. Later, I'll return the favor."

I put my hands behind my back.

"Captain Pyke." It was Da. "My daughter's a virtuous girl, she—"

"Of course she is. That's her appeal."

Michael stepped in front of me, with Da beside him, putting themselves between the Pykes and me.

"Ride on, Captain Pyke," Michael said.

"*You* are ordering *me*?"

I stood still, prayers running through my head. If Da and Michael touched him, they'd be jailed, transported, hanged even. No greater crime than attacking a soldier. Michael was reaching for the horse's reins as Da stepped forward.

"Michael, Da, don't!" I said. Then I heard Máire.

"Good day, Your Honors." She moved around Da and Michael, looked up at young Captain Pyke. She took the hand he'd reached out to me, kissed it, and curtsied.

"Who are you?" he said.

Máire became the Pearl, smiling up at him. "I am the Widow Leahy, sister of the bride."

"The Widow Leahy, you say?"

"I am, sir, but only married a very short time."

"Ah," said the old Major to the Captain, as if we couldn't hear. "Now here's a specimen—look at those breasts. Games to be played there, son. And an innocent, I would say, as virginal as the sister. These people breed like animals, but they know nothing of pleasure. This one could be taught to do many things. What tutorials you would have! I might even join you."

"That would not be necessary, Father," the Captain said. "So, young Widow Leahy, I can't give you your first night, but perhaps a second or a third."

"Perhaps," Máire said.

"Perhaps?" The old Major laughed. "My son will take you or take your sister, as he pleases. Otherwise I'll evict you, Owen Mulloy, and all the other parasites up there with you."

"Máire," I said to her. Dear God, why are you doing this to us!

She turned to me. "It's all right, Honora."

Granny and Mam were beside her. Granny spat on the ground. Mam said, "I'll get Father Gilley."

"Father Gilley, is it?" Máire said. She looked over at the Keeley cousin, but his eyes were on the ground. He didn't want to know.

"Take the bride, Robert. They're trying to cod us. Get the girl," the old Major said.

But Máire took the young Captain's hand again. "Your Honor, can

I mount up there with you now? I can straddle the neck, no problem. Then you could teach me how to move with your horse, going up and down and up and down. I would be a very good rider." The Pearl smiled, and I think I heard the young Captain groan. He reached down and pulled her up so she was sitting in front of him on his horse. Then she leaned back on his chest and whispered something to him. He turned the horse's head, dug his heels in, and started back toward Fubo.

The old Major looked at us and laughed.

We stood in silence, except for Granny. She spoke in Irish, cursing him in a flat, hard tone: "You'll have not a day's luck; you'll have no grandchildren at your hearth, no day without pain, no night without torment."

"What's she saying, Mulloy? What's the old witch saying? Some kind of pagan spell? Tell her she can't affect me."

"My granddaughter is descended from warrior queens. You have no power to disgrace or demean her," Granny said to him in English.

"We'll see about that, you old hag!" He turned his horse and left.

I started weeping. Michael put his arm around me.

But Granny grabbed my shoulders and shook me. "Don't you dare cry. Don't waste your sister's sacrifice. Máire will survive, make no mistake.

"They will not win," she said. "They will not take God's grace from us. No matter what they do, Máire will survive. She is a warrior."

"The Pearl's shameless, no question," said Tessie Ryan, but nobody paid her any mind.

The neighbors came to Mam's cottage. They drank the poitín but said little.

Mam took a burning sod of turf from the fire. "Come, Honora, I'll carry this piece in from Saint John's Fire up with you."

"Thank you, Mam, but Michael and I will go up the hill alone. I think it's better."

⸙   ⸙   ⸙

So. *Siúil, siúil, siúil a rún* . . . Mam's song: Walk, walk, walk, my love . . . She'd made it a lullaby for us. I heard it in my head, then sang a bit to Michael as we climbed up to the cottage. I stepped over our threshold.

My first night. Major Pyke had stolen it, as surely as if he'd actually raped me. How could Michael and I . . .

I put the smoking turf in our fire, and the flame caught and spread. Michael went out to water Champion, then came in carrying his pipes. He sat on his stool by the fire, and I sat next to him on mine. Michael put the bag under his arm and pumped air into it.

"A lament," he said.

The sounds flowed out—a dirge for bodies and hearts broken in so many battles of all kinds, century after century.

Granny had said, Don't waste your sister's sacrifice. Don't let them win. But I felt numb with sorrow.

Michael finished, set down his pipes, and put his arm around me. I rested my head on his shoulder. We watched the flames. I touched Michael's face, solemn and set. My hero from the sea.

"Mo ghrá," he said—my love.

"A stór," I answered—my darling.

We stood up and went to the soft bed Michael had made from hay that still held the scent of summer.

They did not win.

We claimed our own first night.

PART TWO

The Great Starvation

1845~1848

Chapter 9

Six years. June 23, 1845. Six years to the day since Michael swam out of the sea to me. He and I stood in the doorway of our cottage, watching the sun douse our fields, warming the wheat and oats and barley, ripening their green into gold. Knocnacuradh met the dawn rejoicing.

"All growing well, Michael," I said.

He smiled at me. He'd done it. Wrested abundance from the bad land. The struggle had broadened his chest, muscled his back and legs. He'd always had the mighty arms of a blacksmith, and now his whole body held a kind of solid power. A man.

At night I'd run my hands along the length of him, smoothing the knots and knobs from his muscles until he'd reach up, pull me to him, and I'd open myself to his strength. Connecting. The joy of it . . . Dear God, I'm a lucky woman.

Michael put one arm around me, then set a stone into my palm. "Shaped a bit like a heart, don't you think?" he said.

"It is," I said, rubbing my fingers along the edges of the small rock.

"See the green under this pinky color? Connemara marble, it's called."

"Lovely," I said. Michael held my open hand in his, and we watched the sun pick out flecks of light on the stone's surface.

"A gift to mark this day." This day, that morning.

"Thank you, Michael," I said. "A lovely token."

"And tonight after the children go to bed . . ." He kissed my cheek. Our children—tokens of that morning, too. "Of course, we have our living tokens," he said.

"How do you do that?"

"What?"

"Always know what I'm thinking."

"I say what comes into my head," he said.

"And match the words in mine." From the first, and still—reading each other's thoughts.

"The baby," we said together, both hearing Bridget letting me know she was awake and hungry.

"Go on, Michael."

"I've time. Bring her out."

Already bright inside the cottage. That big window lets in every bit of morning light.

"Here, a stór."

Bridget's little face, red with the crying, eased as her bow of a mouth found my nipple. Plenty of milk still, thank God. She'd been born on April 28, when there'd been enough potatoes in the pit, so I could eat and keep her fed. Some flesh on you now, my baby, a help until the new potatoes are ready next month. Easier for you than your big brother Paddy. Our firstborn came during the "hungry months," and I couldn't satisfy the poor wee scrap. Awful. A sturdy lad now, though, thank God, five years old in a few days and the image of Michael— same blue eyes, heavy black hair.

Paddy turned over, burying his face in the thick pallet of fresh hay Michael made for him. Next to Paddy, Jamesy slept on, arms stretched out, taking in the sun's warmth through the glass. Jamesy, two and a half, my Samhain son, born on October 31, when the harvest was gathered and the pratties abundant. A sweet-tempered baby, gaining weight quickly. Very like Mam now with his round face and kind nature, though his eyes were a kind of hazel. Three healthy children. Such a great blessing.

I carried Bridget out to Michael. He brushed his lips over the top of our baby's head. So gentle with her.

Bridget let go of my nipple and looked up at her da.

"No question where she got her eyes," I said, and reached up and touched his cheekbone. "Like yours and Paddy's, the same deep blue rimming a circle of sky."

We looked at our daughter.

"Your eyes, but Máire's hair, blonde and starting to curl," I said.

"Máire," he said. Her suffering was the shadow over us. "Best be off to the fields. See you at midday. The boys can help me shoo the birds away from the potatoes—flocks of them coming around now the plants are in flower."

"They'll enjoy that," I said.

He'd make it a game. They'd be Finn and the Fianna, or the Warriors of the Red Branch. Was there ever such a man for playing with his children as Michael? My da never went racing around with my brothers. Wouldn't. Couldn't. A kind of distance there. Not so Michael and his sons. Giving them the fun he'd missed as a boy.

"We'll come up later. The boys will be delighted to dash around and frighten the poor things."

Michael stepped away, then turned, waved to me, and walked across the hill.

"So, Bridget," I said to my baby. "Shall we seat ourselves on the bench your father made and enjoy this summer's morning?"

Michael had lugged a flat-topped boulder from the high field and set it against the back wall of the cottage at the very spot where I'd first looked down at Galway Bay. Here I settled to feed Bridget, leaning against the cottage wall, my head near the window.

"Your da keeps his promises," I said to Bridget.

Michael bought the glass with the pennies he'd earned doing scut work in a forge in Galway City. A winter of walking the icy roads into town had been rewarded on the day, a year ago now, when Michael and Owen and Joseph and Hughie carried that two-foot-square pane of glass the five miles from Galway City. They'd laughed like fools over how many times they'd almost dropped it and had given all manner of advice to Michael as he'd hammered out the opening in the wall and brought Galway Bay into our cottage.

"A powerful man, your father," I told my baby as she sucked strongly. I sang to Bridget as I watched the distant waves. Some scrambled to reach the land, bunching up together, while others rolled slowly toward the shore.

With these far waters to soothe me, I could bear to remember . . . Máire.

✧ ✧ ✧

Da and Michael had gone up to the Scoundrel Pykes a week after Captain Pyke had ridden away with Máire. But when they asked to see her, the old Major set his dogs on them and threatened arrest and worse if they ever dared trespass again. Then Owen Mulloy heard from the Pykes' coachman—Máire would contact us. Wait. We did.

I'd been stiff with Owen Mulloy and all the Rahoon people up here during that first autumn. I couldn't forget Tessie Ryan: "These are your tenants, Major Pyke, your tenants." And Máire sacrificed because of her. Tessie had come crying and caterwauling to our fire, "I'm so sorry, forgive me," all the while taking in every dab and detail of our cottage. She'd spread the news of our rush stools and iron pot before the tears on her face dried. Only for her bringing little Mary her daughter with her had I let her in at all.

Though Owen Mulloy and the others tried to make us welcome, giving us loads of potatoes and helping Michael dig a pit to store them, they wouldn't stand against Tessie and condemn her. Tessie could easily turn on one of them. Her eye caught every break in behavior and put the worst possible interpretation on it. "Too sick for Mass was Maggie Dolan? Then why did I see her under the fairy tree at Ward's, crouched down like she was putting a piseog on her neighbor's field?"

Then Tuesday the week before Christmas that year, Owen brought a note from Máire. I was to come alone that afternoon, when the work was done and the place quiet.

The sun had already set when I arrived at the Scoundrel Pykes. Dark early this day, the shortest of the year. Hide in the stables, she'd said. I waited an hour, getting colder as the wind knifed through the spaces in the wall. Michael had built a snug, warm place for Champion where every stone fit tight together and room had been left for the forge if the road was ever built.

Finally she came.

"Máire, Máire," I called softly into the dark, and my sister, always so defiant, had collapsed into my arms. "Go on, Máire," I said. "Cry, cry it out."

She stopped at that, pulled away, and stood before me, big-bellied yet somehow smaller, her cloud of curls flat against her face. "They haven't broken me yet, Honora. If I let the tears start running, I'll not be able for them."

"Do they hurt you?" I asked.

"Strike me, do you mean? They wouldn't dare. Not when they're convinced I'd murder them in their beds. Come into the kitchen."

"I couldn't," I said.

"It's all right. That's why I sent for you. The men are away."

Our whole cottage would fit into one corner of this kitchen, I'd thought. The Pyke house, bigger and older than the Lynches', felt like a fortress. Could have roasted a side of beef in the hearth, but no fire blazed there. Only a few clods of turf smoldered under a hanging pot.

We sat in front of the little smokey fire. I told Máire that Mam and Da had gone to Father Gilley and the Lynches, trying to get her rescued.

"But . . ." I stopped.

"But what?" asked Máire.

"They, well, they . . ."

"Turned a blind eye?" she said. "Why not? Landlords have been taking advantage of girls for generations, and it's only that the Scoundrel Pykes claimed me on the public street and put the deed in front of them that any notice at all was taken."

I couldn't tell Máire that Tessie Ryan and her chorus had put it out that Máire went willingly and Father Gilley didn't disbelieve them.

"I'm coming home with you today," she said.

"Máire, I'm so glad. Will there be bother about it?"

"Not at all. The young Captain's off with his regiment, and the old Major will be in Dublin through Christmas and the New Year. And the Mistress—well, come with me to meet the Mistress."

Máire led me through rooms stuffed with chairs and tables muddled together—a real meascán, a mess. Only the dining room with its square table and sideboard seemed in good order.

"Look." Máire pointed to a framed drawing hanging on the wall.

I read the title: "The Irish Frankenstein."

The sketch showed Daniel O'Connell as a mad magician bringing to life a monster labeled "Paddy" with the face of an ape, horns growing from his head, and a clay pipe in his monkey mouth.

"That's from a magazine called *Punch*," Máire said. "The Major points it out to guests and goes on and on about O'Connell awakening the savages—us."

"Us?"

"Us—the Irish—the apes. Honora, old Major Pyke had some professor fellow eating here who went on about how the Irish aren't completely human. They made Thaddy, the stableman, come in from the yard. This professor took out a tape and measured the distance between Thaddy's forehead and his chin. He said it was the wrong amount of inches and that Thaddy was closer to a gorilla than a man."

"That's crazy," I said, and giggled at the thought of such foolishness.

"It's not funny, Honora. That's the kind of talk I have to listen to." And then the laughter spurted out from her, too. "If you could've seen the look on poor Thaddy's face—and the professor going on about inches and quarter inches, angles and planes."

I turned away from the drawing. "And to think, that was in a magazine and people paid money for it." I shook my head. "Ah well, the Bold Dan will turn the tables on them, wait and see."

I followed her through more dark rooms smelling of damp, up a winding stairway, then down a hall into a bedroom lit by a kerosene lamp.

"Mistress, someone's come calling."

Sarah Pyke, the wife of the old Major, the mother of Captain Robert, lay stretched out on a couch, her dress falling over the sides and her head propped up on pillows, snoring.

"Is she sick?" I whispered.

"In a manner of speaking," Máire said quite loud. "She can't hear us—sound asleep."

A tall looking glass took up one corner.

"Have a look at yourself," Máire said.

There I was, all of me. "I never saw my whole self before," I said. "I had no idea I was this tall."

Máire came and stood beside me.

"I tower over you, Máire," I said.

"An illusion," she said. "I'm so pregnant, I look short."

"I'm pregnant, too."

"I can see. You've bosoms at last."

"I do," I said, looking at myself. "Though my waist and hips are still narrow. And my belly hasn't swelled much. I'm only two and a half months."

"Your breasts will get bigger," Máire said. "Mine pull my shoulders down." She stood slumped and flat-footed. Not like herself at all.

I'll rouse her, I thought. I pointed to my breasts. "Michael said he liked them even when they were smaller. He said he could fit one in each of his hands, and then squeeze so gently and . . ."

I rolled my eyes at her in the mirror, and she laughed and said, "Honora, *I'm* the hussy in this family."

And I said, "Michael told me he fancies my brains *and* my bosoms, so there."

I stuck my tongue out at her image in the mirror and she did the same, until we were making funny faces at each other and laughing louder and louder.

"Who's there?" Sarah Pyke—awake. "Have you come from the Palace?" she said to me.

"No, ma'am, from Bearna."

"But," Máire said, "she's brought a message from the court, Mistress."

Sarah Pyke smiled. "I knew it. I knew she'd invite me." She turned to me. "She greets me so graciously when I ride out in the park each morning. The paths are so straight, all paved with crushed white stones."

"And where's that, missus?" I asked.

"The park, of course," she said impatiently. "Hyde Park. That's where I see the young queen. She comes by in her carriage, and every day she tells the coachman to stop. She greets me, and always says the same words: 'Well done, thou good and faithful servant. Having one child, one son, is quite enough. No one would expect you to endure more.'"

"And right she'd be," said Máire.

Sarah Pyke closed her eyes.

"She's away in dreamland," Máire said. "Poor critter."

But Sarah Pyke opened her eyes. "I need more medicine," she said.

"You've had your dose, Mistress," Máire said.

"I need my medicine! Now, girl!" Sarah Pyke sat straight up. "No insolence from you!"

"I'm going, Mistress. That's what I came to say. My time is coming. My child is due."

"I had a child. One—a son," she said.

"You did, surely. Now, a wee nap and you'll feel so much better."

But the woman was trying to stand. "My husband knows I need my medicine. He left a bottle for me so I'd have plenty while he was away. He is away, isn't he?"

"He is, ma'am."

"Good, good. Send me my maid."

"I will. And you understand, don't you? I'm going."

"Go. What do I care? Go."

Máire had her bundle tied up in her room behind the kitchen. "Let's get out of this place. Think of Christmas here!"

"Will the Mistress be all right?" I asked.

"Her maid—somewhere about—is an Englishwoman who's well in with the old Major and happy to keep the Mistress sleeping or silly."

"What about her son?"

"Robert? The soldier laddie? It'll be months before he's back. He wasn't one bit pleased when he found out I was to have Johnny's child. He won't come after me. He'll just find some other girl."

"But, Máire . . ."

"Nothing we can do. Let's go."

❖ ❖ ❖

Máire's baby had been born the next day. She'd held tight to the Mary Bean that protected women during childbirth—that oval, brown bean with a cross inscribed in it by nature that Granny had found on the beach near Ard. Máire found special strength in the Mary Bean, she said, because it came from the sea where her Johnny rested.

She named her baby Johnny Og. A big, healthy fellow.

"Look at his face, let Annie Leahy question you now, Máire," I'd said.

"What?" asked Mam.

"I'm just saying he's the spit of Johnny Leahy."

"I'll just slip over to get Annie now," Mam said.

"I don't want her, Mam," Máire said so fiercely that Granny and Mam stopped and looked at each other.

"Not for a few hours," I said. "Let Máire sleep."

"Best indulge her," Granny said. "We wouldn't want to give the fairy woman a chance to steal into her."

Mam had said nothing. After Joseph's birth, a fairy woman had taken Mam away and Granny had a hard time calling her back from fairyland. Women were most vulnerable the day after giving birth.

"Annie can see him on Christmas Eve at the chapel," I said.

"Father Roche, the new priest, could baptize him after Midnight Mass. Wouldn't that be lovely?" Mam said.

"Father Gilley stays at his parish in Galway City now, so we needn't worry about him," Granny told Máire.

Michael and I had sat with Mam, Da, Dennis, Joseph, Hughie, Granny, and now Máire—the whole family together in the chapel, delighted with the newborn baby in Máire's arms.

I smiled at the Mulloys. Christmas. Peace on earth.

But then who walked out on the altar—only Father Gilley himself. He didn't bother to say *Introibo ad altare Dei* but roared out, "How, on this holiest of nights, do you dare to defile this sanctuary?"

I'd been leaning over, smiling into the baby's face, not really listening. Some sinner was being admonished. Poor soul. I'd glanced up to see Tessie Ryan and Annie Leahy, turned around, staring at our family and shaking their heads.

Then I realized. "It's us, Michael," I'd whispered. "He's going on about us."

"Not us," said Máire. "Me."

"Scandal—giving scandal to the parish—sullying all that's pure with your shamelessness. Dragging your family into your sin. . . ."

Most of our friends and neighbors kept their heads down, their eyes on the floor. Father Gilley had denounced other sinners, but never as he was doing now. Though not a word against that devil the old Major. He feared the Scoundrel Pykes. Landlords.

If Máire had sat there humbly, Father Gilley might have shouted himself around to demanding that she confess her sins and then forgiven her. But Máire interrupted his rant by standing up, holding tight to her child. She looked straight at Father Gilley. He stopped. Máire still had a chance. If she'd sobbed, said, "Oh, Father, I'm sorry, I'm sorry, I was forced. This is Johnny's son, the last bit of Johnny Leahy left in the world. The only place his quick smile, his courage, his ease with nets and sails will be expressed and extended—Johnny's baby." But Máire had said nothing.

I was the one who got up and spoke into the silence. "Father, this is Johnny Leahy's son," thinking I could make Father Gilley see sense.

Then Michael stood with us. Murmurs from the pews: "Johnny's child, of course it was Johnny's child." Annie Leahy got up, trying to see the baby.

Then Tessie spoke. "How do we know that? No one who saw the Pearl climb up on Captain Robert's horse would believe she hadn't met him before—who knows how many times, and—"

I turned to look her in the face. "Tessie Ryan, everyone in this chapel knows what Máire did, she did for me. And she's come back now. She's with us."

Father Gilley pointed toward the door of the chapel. "Get out, you sinful women."

And our whole family had stood together and left the chapel.

Father Gilley, furious that we'd defied him, told the congregation that we would be forbidden the sacraments until we denounced Máire. The Keeleys and Michael and Honora Kelly must be avoided as occasions of sin. Associate with us and they'd be denied the sacraments and reported to the Lynches.

On Christmas Day, the shunning, the seachaint, began. No one in Bearna spoke to the Keeleys. In Rahoon, our neighbors acted as if Knocnacuradh were still empty ground.

After a week of this, Máire said she would go back to the Scoundrel Pykes. "If I'm gone," she'd said, "Father Gilley will leave you alone." We'd all argued with her. But Máire said, what choice had she? She wasn't about to stay in Bearna. Where would she ever get work? "I'll only be five miles away," she'd said, "not gone to Amerikay. The old Major's up in Dublin most of the time, and I'll manage Robert right enough. Remember, he's off with the army a lot." She'd find a way to get messages to us, and I could sneak up to see her.

"But, Máire," I'd said. "He'll, he'll . . . How will you bear it?"

"He mostly talks," Máire had told me, "tells me how he hates his father and how cruel the other boys were to him at boarding school. As for the other, he's quick enough."

We couldn't stop her.

At first, nothing changed.

"Patience," Granny had said. "Patience. Father Gilley will fasten on some others soon enough, and the neighbors will be at our door."

"And we'll slam it in their faces," I said.

"Don't blame them. Can't go against the priest. But it's a long road with no turning."

When Da heard in mid-January that the fishing would begin, he went to the Claddagh Admiral to ask could he go with the fleet.

"Ever notice, John Keeley," the Admiral had said, "that Our Lord picked fishermen for his disciples, and it was Judas, who never set foot in a boat, betrayed him? We'll not turn against you, John Keeley, on a priest's say-so."

So Da sailed out with the fishermen, as he ever had, and not a word more was said. The Bearna fishermen followed the Admiral's lead. When the boats returned, Mam gathered the catch with the other women and sold the fish under the Spanish Arch.

But up in Rahoon, the shunning continued. Farmers needed Father Gilley to say a good word for them to the landlord or the rate collector. Afraid, the lot of them. And yet for Michael and me, the shunning, meant to be our greatest punishment, led to our greatest joy. In that isolation we came to know each other as we never would have in life's ordinary round. During that January and February, when the long nights of bad weather kept us home in our cottage and the hostility of our neighbors left us alone and apart, we two became one. With no fear that a shouted, "God bless all here!" would bring a visitor in through the door, we spent hours making love, amazed at the pleasure we could give each other.

Mam had told me that no harm would come to the baby if Michael and I wished to . . . We did. I'd always been glad enough to be healthy. My legs could walk and run, my arms lift and carry. I was delighted, too, that I'd conceived so quickly, but this other, this, this bliss . . . The ripple and rush I felt as Michael stroked me made me profoundly grateful that our bodies could express and receive such love, and no great study needed. We let ourselves be giddy. We were on an island away from the world, piling up the turf into great blazing fires, boiling up our feed of potatoes, the room so warm we could leave off our clothes entirely. Michael would play the pipes and I'd sit cross-legged in front of him on the bed we'd made from hay and covered with a soft blanket Michael bought in Galway City. The sound wrapped around my bare skin.

And the talking we did . . . I was used to the give-and-take of a large family, where one broke in on the other, splintering sentences, bouncing thought away from meaning. But Michael and I listened to each other, each waiting as the other found words for what we'd never said before, never even thought before, giving shape to dreams and to fears. I'd no idea I was such a worrier—the ifs and buts that flowed out of me. Michael teased them away. We'd live long, happy lives and die on the same day surrounded by our tall, strong sons and clever, beautiful daughters and a slew of lively grandchildren and great-grandchildren. Our bones would lie in one grave in Bearna churchyard, and our souls would soar over Galway Bay, together forevermore. I believed him—my hero, who'd stood with me against Father Gilley and the world. Then Michael took me to that lonely place within where he mourned all that had been taken from him and let me fill it with my love.

Spring came too soon that year, and Michael brought me a bunch of snowdrops, spring's first sign, those white flowers that poke out of the earth on St. Bridget's Day, February 1.

"They put me in mind of old women in frilled caps telling each other, 'Thank God the winter is going,'" I'd said to Michael.

"The worms are waking up, too," Michael had said, "happy as Larry, burrowing through the dirt, not knowing a dirty big blade of a spade will come slashing down into them."

Planting time. Shunning or no shunning, the ground had to be turned and boulders hauled away—hard to do on your own. Michael left the cottage at first light now, up to the fields, probing and pushing the drowned earth. He made channels with pebbles to drain the water. But the ground stayed wet and mucky.

"I can do this," he'd said after he'd used one gold coin to buy seed potatoes. "I watched Patrick often enough."

"When you were nine years old, Michael. And what about setting the potato ridges? One man can't do it—it takes two—one to open the ridge up and the other to lay the seed potatoes in and cover them," I'd said. "Why not ask Owen's help, Michael? He might want an excuse to end the shunning."

Father Roche had gone to Mam and told her if the Keeleys came to the chapel, he'd not refuse them communion. Father Gilley would turn a blind eye.

"We could return to Mass, too," I told Michael. "Then maybe Owen might—"

But Michael said that asking Mulloy would be like turning against Máire. "Think of what she must be suffering for us," he'd said.

Not as much as you might think, I'd wanted to say. I'd gone up a few weeks after Christmas to find Máire settled in and Johnny Og the pet of Mrs. Cooney, the cook. Máire had joked about Father Gilley. "He's gentry himself, Honora. It's his job to keep us monkeys in line. We Keeleys stood up to him rightly, though," she'd said, laughing.

It's Michael, not Máire, whose spirit could break. Such an uneven battle he's fighting with this bad land. If he doesn't plant now, Knocnacuradh will die before it lives.

"Let's ride away on Champion," I'd said to him. "I'll take to the roads with you in a snap of my fingers." But Michael said I didn't understand how much I'd miss Mam and Da and Granny and my brothers and Galway Bay itself, and he wasn't giving up. When Michael made up his mind, he couldn't be budged. A stubborn fellow, for all he seemed easygoing.

During that spring, I'd hear the sound of his pipes from the far field. Sometimes he'd take long rides on Champion, going nowhere in particular.

Then one night in March, we'd heard a step outside the door.

"Michael," I whispered. "Wake up."

He'd heard it, too. He eased himself out of bed, grabbed the spade to use as a weapon, and moved to the door.

"It's me," came the low voice from outside. "It's me, your brother. It's Patrick."

Michael dropped the spade and opened the door, leaving me only seconds to pull the woven blanket over me and cover my full breasts and swollen belly.

The man who stepped through the door put the heart across me— a blade of a face with a narrow nose, a wide mouth, two hazel-colored staring eyes, and close-cropped brown hair. He was almost as tall as Michael, but spare and lean. He carried two jugs of poitín, which he set on the floor.

"Patrick"—Michael stepped forward and stretched out his arms. "Patrick."

But Patrick didn't speak, didn't move. He looked from Michael to me. I wanted to slide down—cover my face as well as my bosom—but I knew I had to hold his cold gaze. If it's a staring contest you want, Mr. Patrick Kelly, I'm well able for you.

But Michael put his two hands on Patrick's shoulders. "Are you trying to scare the wits out of my wife and freeze your little brother's heart, you great bollocks?"

Patrick laughed. The ice covering those eyes cracked, and the two were in each other's arms.

"And here is Honora, Patrick. She's—"

"A Keeley," Patrick said. "John James Keeley's daughter, and her mother is Mary Danny Walsh. A family of fishermen, and it's her sister that got you into the bother you're in."

"Not my sister's fault," I said. "A devil of a landlord—"

"Major George Scoundrel Pyke," Patrick finished, "and his soldier son, Robert. We know them well."

"We—and who is we?" I asked.

Michael laughed. "Better answer, Patrick. She's a woman who won't be put off. Now come in and tell us where you've been and where you're living and—"

"Your granny would know the men I'm with," he said to me.

"The Martin O'Malleys," I whispered.

"I'm naming no names," said Patrick.

A rough bunch, and some wanted. I asked no more questions.

Michael was pouring out nine years of news, though Patrick knew the bones of it. He'd heard about the deaths of Michael's mother and grandfather, the eviction, the loss of the forge. Well-informed. And now?

"Get up and get dressed, Michael," Patrick Kelly said. "I came to lay out the potato ridges with you, and plant your fields."

"It's night," I said.

"There's a full moon," said Patrick.

❖   ❖   ❖

They began that very night, two long moon shadows moving across our land, with me following.

"We'll plant the wheat and barley later. Best to start with the potatoes so you'll be sure to have food. We can set the beds up on that high hill," Patrick said.

"I hadn't intended to go up that far," Michael said. "Hard going to climb up there."

"Which is why that land hasn't been used—that's good. New soil for the pratties works best, I've noticed. So."

Patrick marched Michael and me up the steep slope. At the top, Patrick took a pinch of earth, crumbled it, and sniffed.

"Such a generous plant, the potato. You couldn't get anything else to grow in land like this." They started working; Patrick took the lead. "You," Patrick said to me. "Get a load of pebbles."

I didn't move right away.

"Pebbles, girl."

You might be thirty, I thought, and me seventeen, but I'm a married woman with a baby growing inside me, and I won't have orders barked at me.

Michael winked at me. "Would ever you gather a handful of stones, Honora, a stór, and bring them up to the General and me?"

If Patrick heard, he said nothing.

Plenty of pebbles between larger boulders. I gathered them in my skirt and brought them up to Patrick and Michael.

Patrick had stamped out the shape of the ridges. "Now, the pebbles, if you please." He dropped one at the head of a ridge and started to line the other stones behind the first one. He gestured for Michael and me to do the same.

After an hour, rows of pebbles stuck out in the tufts of grass and weeds, white in the moonlight—a straight line down in the center of each ridge-to-be.

"The potatoes," Patrick said. He stood still and tall above us.

"The pebbles mark the place where we'll plant the seed potatoes," Michael whispered to me.

Patrick started to slice into the earth, cutting a triangle of sod, the scraw, then flipping it over so the point touched the pebble. Michael came behind him, the two brothers working backward along the ridge, Michael becoming almost as deft as his brother. They paused only to carefully tap down the earth.

"Can't break the scraw," said Patrick, "or the rain will wash away the goodness of the soil."

And soil it became, where before only rocks and weeds had covered the ground. Dawn came. The larks sang the sun up, while from the bishop's house below us, a rooster crowed. Michael and Patrick had dug twenty ridges straight and parallel.

We slept the day away. Patrick had insisted on sharing Champion's shed. Michael had tried to explain Champion's birth and the Galway Races, but Patrick had said, "Stop. That's a story for the fire, after we finish."

Patrick didn't appear until nightfall. They began to cut out the eyes from the seed potatoes.

"Lumpers," Patrick said. "The worst."

"Plant a better variety and the landlord will raise the rent for sure," Michael said. "The agent would say if the likes of us can buy pinks, then we can afford to pay more rent."

Patrick began to warn Michael about the work and watching he'd have to do. "Keep the ridges clean of scratch grass, Michael. Yank every bit out. Leave the tiniest bit and it will choke the potato plants before they can grow. Watch out for shepherd's purse. It can drop its seeds in the center of the ridge, and then you're f— Well, it's bad, but of course docks are the worst of all. They put their dirty big roots down and wrap around the pratties."

"Though dock leaves ease the sting of nettles," I said.

Patrick raised an eyebrow at Michael and went right on. He talked about the problems of weather—too hot, too cold, too wet, too dry— Michael listening and nodding. "Keep the blackbirds away. They'll peck the potatoes to pieces looking for worms. And watch for rats." Patrick went on and on.

That night, Patrick and Michael replaced the pebbles with the eyes, slipping each into the earth. When they finished, Michael's back was so stiff and painful, he couldn't raise his arms. No bother to Patrick, though.

"And he's twelve years older," Michael said.

Patrick left after five days. The potatoes were set. He and Michael had laid the drains. Patrick taught Michael how to judge the way the land fell, to determine which field should be left for grass for Champion and which planted for wheat.

"You'll need your neighbors' help in plowing, but I say it will be forthcoming."

I started to tell him the ins and outs of the shunning, but Patrick waved me to silence, shook hands with Michael, and was gone.

The day after Patrick left, Owen Mulloy came to the door and Katie with him, acting as if nothing whatsoever had happened.

"Michael, let's hitch a plow to Champion and see if she can plow as well as she can run."

"Champion's not a plow horse," Michael said.

"None of us are, but she can do her bit," Owen said. "Get her ready for motherhood. Barrier, Sir William Gregory's stallion, likes strong mares, I've heard." And he winked at me.

"Rascal," I said.

"Barrier or me?" said Owen Mulloy. And that was the shunning, over.

A few weeks later, Katie had us in to their house, and I saw a jug of poitín at the side of Owen Mulloy's hearth—very like the one Patrick had left for us. A meeting of the minds. I'd give a lot to have heard that conversation—Owen all words and ges-tic-u-la-tions, and Patrick—still.

That Sunday, we went to the chapel together.

✠   ✠   ✠

And in all these years, the only reference Owen Mulloy has made to Patrick Kelly's first visit was a long ru-min-a-tion on the Ribbonmen and the Molly Maguires and Captain Midnight and all the other men "who take it in their own hands to enforce the old justice"—keep a bailiff from pushing a poor man out, make a drover think twice before he herds a man's cattle off as payment for the rent. Perhaps some of their meth-od-ol-o-gy might be a bit harsh, and all too many of the fellows ended up hanged or transported, but someone had to take a stand against a government that even outlawed the making of whiskey. "So if not for the hard men, we'd be denied uisce beatha—the water of life. Bad cess on a man who'd betray any one of them. Ná habair tada."

And Michael had said, "I hear the boys in the mountains can ease off a little now that we have Daniel O'Connell."

"Well, surely," Mulloy had said. "No one better than the Lib-er-a-tor!"

Six springs ago. Summer now, and I'll be twenty-three in September. Three children, two foals, fine crops, a wide glass window as promised, always a good fire to warm the long winter nights when I tell Michael and the children the stories Granny taught me—Fadó. Six years of trials, true enough, but so many blessings. At twenty-four, Michael, the young hero of the Galway Races, had grown into a man respected for his skill and persistence, a fellow who could be counted on to help a neighbor, pipe a tune, share a laugh. Husband, father, my love. And he loves *me*. Amazing.

CHAPTER 10

WE'LL START DIGGING the pratties tomorrow," Michael said in the first week of October. A cloudy, close sort of day after a summer of decent enough weather. "Owen Mulloy heard rumors in Galway City of poor potato crops in Cork and Kerry, but he says rain's been lashing the fields down there. We'll be fine."

"I'll tell my family to be ready to come up to help us," I said.

"I think I'll take the boys for a ride on Champion. Won't be much time once we start with the harvest."

"Enjoy yourselves," I said.

"Be careful up there," Michael said. "That place . . ."

I dreaded these trips to the Scoundrel Pykes, but it was the only way to see Máire. With the old Major's heavy drinking telling on him, Máire had convinced him that Granny had the cure to restore his health. The mix of milk thistle and herbs had eased his gout and gave us the excuse to go to the Big House. Máire never came down to us.

❖ ❖ ❖

"Come to Nana," Mam said, opening her arms to Bridget, finding such joy in her grandchildren—and a second baby due for Josie and my brother Dennis any day. Mam rocked Bridget, saying what a wide-awake baby she was and big for five months. "*Siúil, siúil, siúil a rún,*" she sang. She'd soothed us with that song.

"We should be on our way," Granny said to me.

After an hour's hard walking along the Botha—the coast road—Granny and I came to the road that led up the cliff to the Pykes' house. The old Major got the government to build this road right up to his door. No sign of a road for us, I told Granny, so no forge, and the anvil and hammer Michael managed to buy lying idle.

"Tessie Ryan's saying that Máire's having Captain Robert's children to get him to marry her! As if Máire has a choice, or—"

"I'll tell you why Tessie's so quick to point the finger."

"I know why, Granny. She's jealous and unhappy and a begrudger."

"She's not married."

I stopped. "What?"

"They never had the fee for the priest. Her mother told me. So Tessie pretends they were married out Moycullen way, where her granny lives. Don't say anything. It's known but never mentioned," she said, striding along, swinging her stick.

"I'll only tell Michael. It will help him have patience with Tessie." I never keep anything from Michael—tell him my every thought. So accustomed to speaking freely, sometimes words popped from my mouth.

Now I said, "Why don't you poison the old Major, Granny?"

"Why not poison all the landlords?" said Granny. "Irishwomen do their cooking."

"True enough," I said.

"I'll not do murder unless it's required. Why risk my immortal soul for the likes of them?"

"I suppose they're not worth going to hell for."

We had reached the top of the cliff. She stopped to take a breath, looking up at the gray stone house. "Some would say we're walking into it right now."

❖ ❖ ❖

"Granny, Granny! Aunt Honey!" Johnny Og Leahy, almost six now and a little pleated man like his father, ran through the kitchen yard to meet us.

When I'd told Paddy these cousins he'd never met called me Aunt Honey, he'd asked, "What's honey?" I'd tasted the sweet stuff once or twice as a child, but there'd been no money to spare for honey for a long time. Máire'd stolen a small jar for me to take to Paddy. The big wide smile that came over his face as he sucked the honey off his finger made Michael and me laugh. "You see why it's a good name for your mam," Michael had said to him. "Sweet." Máire still tried to smuggle bits of food to us, but she had to be careful since the old Major had Winnie Lyons arrested for taking two cabbages.

We followed Johnny Og into the kitchen, where Máire stood at the stove. At her feet were Thomas, her four-year-old, and the littlest boy, two now. She'd named him Daniel O'Connell Pyke. "With his curly hair and puff of a nose, isn't he the image of the Liberator? And it makes the old Major furious!" she'd said. Three beautiful boys—nothing stringy about Máire's children. No hungry mouths up here.

"That's far enough," said the crabbed man at the kitchen table.

"I'm cooking Mr. Jackson's breakfast," Máire said. "He prefers not to have people near him when he eats."

"Who are these women?" the man said.

"My sister, Mrs. Kelly, and my grandmother, Mrs. Keeley. This mannerly fellow is Abner Jackson, Major Pyke's new agent."

"Hm," he said.

Máire ladled something from a pot into a bowl. "Oatmeal, porridge," she said to us. "Mr. Jackson starts his breakfast with oatmeal, and then he has three eggs and a load of rashers. Am I right, Mr. Jackson?"

Again, no reply.

"Mr. Jackson's from the North of Ireland," said Máire. "He spends his words as he spends his money—sparingly. He's always telling me to save my breath to cool my porridge, doesn't understand that I don't eat porridge."

Jackson kept his head down, spooning the thick gruel into his mouth slowly and deliberately.

This one will not be drawn. Máire shouldn't tease him. Granny and I stayed still, and Daniel started to whimper.

"Johnny Og, take your brothers into our room to play." Máire underlined *brothers* and *our*. Johnny Og took Thomas's hand and hoisted Daniel up on his hip. They left us. "Well behaved, aren't they, Mr. Jackson?" Máire said.

He finished the porridge. Máire set a plate of eggs fried in bacon grease in front of him and then a portion of rashers.

"Mr. Jackson likes plenty of fat and meat with every meal. He won't touch a potato, though I tell him he's missing a treat. The new potatoes are sweet and firm," she said as she leaned over, her breasts close to his face.

"Jezebel," he said.

"Jezebel?" said Máire. "And who is she when she's at home?"

Again Jackson said nothing. I looked at Granny. What was Máire doing? Did she want him to explode?

"You need to read the Bible," Jackson said.

"Mr. Jackson wants to convert us. Don't you, Mr. Jackson? He's gotten the Major to bring in missionaries from a Bible society in London. They're building a church and school on the estate. They've promised to educate our children and employ our men, and all we have to do is jump—become Protestant. Isn't that right, Mr. Jackson? I explained to Mr. Jackson that 'jump' is from the Irish word for 'turn.'"

Jackson kept his eyes on his eggs and rashers, cutting and chewing as if he were the only person in the kitchen.

"It's our religion makes us savages," Máire said to us. "That's what's been decided in London. Now this missionary, Reverend Smithson, you call him, will give a beautiful, leather-bound Bible to any person who will jump. But only one man has accepted this lovely gift. Isn't that right, Mr. Jackson?"

Again, no response.

Máire went on. "His name is Packy Bailey—a simple fellow, but so happy and willing. Reverend Smithson told Packy to denounce the pope and all the bishops, and Packy repeated whatever the reverend said.

"'I denounce the whore of Babylon, who sits on the throne of Rome,' he said. Of course, Packy had no notion at all what he meant, but he was proud as can be, throwing his chest out and denouncing this one and denouncing that one, with every tenant and laborer on the estate made to come out to listen to him." Máire shook her head at the scene.

"But then the Reverend Smithson wanted Packy to repeat, 'I denounce the worship of the woman who bore Jesus Christ.' And when he had to say 'the woman who bore Jesus,' something flickered in Packy's mind and he saw behind the words.

" 'Could you be talking about Mary, Our Blessed Mother?' he asked.

"And the Revered Smithson said, 'You have no Blessed Mother. A human woman gave birth to Jesus, and that's that.'

" 'That's what?' Packy asked."

Now Jackson stood up. "That's enough—stop!"

"But my grandmother and my sister are very interested. They would like to hear the rest of the story, Mr. Jackson. As I was saying, Reverend Smithson said to Packy, 'We all have mothers.'

" 'Ah, but Your Honor,' Packy said, 'my mother loved me. She didn't care that I was slower than the others, or, as you tell me, too stupid to know truth from lies. She loved me and told me I had another mother who loved me, too—Mary, the mother of Jesus—and that Mary would speak to her son Jesus for me, and that Mary knew when Jesus was in a good mood and she could get around him and speak up for me. She'd say, "Packy Bailey's a good boy," and to please her, Jesus would let me into heaven.'

"Then with all the workers and tenants listening—and yourself, too, Mr. Jackson—Packy said, 'I like living in that little shed you gave me, and I will gladly clean and sweep for you and say that the pope is from Babylon and the bishop is a sliveen, but I could never speak against Mary, sir. She's our Blessed Mother.'

"And that was the end of Packy's conversion."

"Bailey's a simpleton," Jackson said.

"Simple he is," Máire said, "but not an idiot. And he knows about a mother's love. And so do I, Mr. Jackson, don't forget that. So do I, and so do my sons, the Major's grandsons."

Jackson stood up from the table. "I know your game. You want to provoke me so I'll send you out of here."

"If that would suit you, Mr. Jackson, I could leave now with my mother and sister."

"You go right ahead," a voice croaked. The old Major stood in the doorway—fatter and redder in the face than ever, limping with the gout as he walked toward us.

"But I thought, sir—" Jackson started.

"Don't think so much, Jackson. The Pearl may depart whenever she wants."

Granny and I looked at Máire. She hadn't moved.

"Of course, the two boys will stay here. Keep them handy until Robert makes a proper marriage. Even a bastard's better than no heir at all."

He turned to us. "See, despite what they say about me, I'm a fair man. A very fair man. Of course, you'll never see the children again, Pearl."

"I couldn't," Máire mumbled.

"Speak up, Pearl."

"I couldn't leave them."

"Did you hear that, Jackson? You'll find these papists have an inordinate devotion to their children. Quite inexplicable when they have so many. I don't know how they tell one from the other. Now where are the fruit of my dear son's loins?"

"Boys," Máire called, then moved to the open door at the back of the kitchen. "Johnny Og, bring the boys."

The Major turned to Granny. "You have my powder, old woman?"

"I do."

"Bring it."

Granny packed the powder in a seashell, to add the power of the sea, she'd told him. "The same as before, sir—milk thistle ground fine, with herbs to restore your liver and heal the gout."

"Hear that, Jackson? And who would know better the cure for too much liquor than this dipsomaniac people? Here, you, the sister."

"Me, sir?" I said.

"Me, sir? Don't mock me, girl. Here, taste this."

He held out the shell of powder to me, and I wet my finger and touched the grains and put them on my tongue.

"Milk thistle, sir."

"Always take care with them, Jackson. Don't be fooled by their 'sirs' and 'Your Honors.' They'd kill you soon as look at you. Don't turn your back on them."

Johnny Og led the two younger boys into the kitchen. Thomas ran to Máire. Daniel lurched after Thomas. Máire put her arms around them.

"The older one has the Pyke nose," the Major said.

He did—a big beak sticking out of his face.

"I'm not sure if this youngest one is a Pyke at all," the old Major said. "Have a fling with the pig man, Pearl?"

"Your son well knows that—"

"Stop. Stop," said the Major. "Too much talking around here. Jackson, did you do as I told you?"

"I did, sir. I sent away the other two maids. Stopped this one chattering the day away. She can do the cooking, too, serve Her Ladyship. You're here so rarely."

"Quite right, Jackson. Quite right. Here rarely—and more and more rarely, I hope. We've the new house in London, and Her Ladyship's family's made a place in the country available to help her recuperate. No, we won't be seeing as much of you, dear Pearl, though my son will be home for his annual leave and will expect your services. Quite good services, Jackson. I wish I could offer you a turn, but my son is absurdly possessive about his Pearl of great price."

I kept my head down. Mam wouldn't come up here with us. Afraid she'd pick up a knife, stab him straight through the heart, she'd told me.

Jackson snorted. "Your son has nothing to be concerned about," he said.

"Do you hear that, Pearl? Jackson's impervious to your charms. It's his breeding. Good Ulster stock. He told me Andrew Jackson, who was president of America, is a connection. Jackson—isn't that right?"

"Yes, Your Lordship."

"Tell them. A history lesson is always salutary."

"Andrew Jackson came from Carrickfergus, like I do. An Indian fighter, he was, and defeated the savages and made the land safe for decent farmers," Jackson said.

"And you, Abner, will do the same for me. Clear my land of these swarming good-for-nothings. Wipe it clean. Wide fields and vast pastures to raise cattle and sheep, with good solid men like yourself, Jackson, to tend them. I've been soft and the land has suffered, but deliverance is at hand, as the Reverend Smithson might say, deliverance. This evil people will be chastened—evicted. Big news for you to carry back with you, Honora Kelly. I've let your horse-riding husband hide behind Mulloy long enough. Tell him and all my tenants that rents will be increased. And no more hanging gale. The rent will be paid, and paid when it's due, or they'll be gone. Mr. Jackson fears nothing or no one and doesn't care about outlaws lurking in the mountains, do you, Mr. Jackson?"

"Not at all. Let them try to stop me from doing my duty."

"A good time for courage, with two new regiments coming to Galway City," the old Major said. "Steal food from this house and you'll find yourself in jail, Pearl, or transported to Australia. No more blind eyes turned. Consider yourselves warned."

He dropped his voice on those last words and limped away. Jackson followed him. Thomas and Daniel started crying. Granny went over to them. Johnny Og ran out the back door.

"Good at frightening women and children, aren't they?" I said.

"It's not as bad when Robert is here," Máire said.

"You can't stay here, Máire," I said. "Da will come up with Michael and Dennis and Joseph to face him down. Let Major Scoundrel Pyke and Jackson thunder at four strong men."

Máire stroked Daniel's hair and looked down at Thomas.

"You won't leave us, will you, Mam?" said Thomas. "You wouldn't let him take us?"

"I'll never leave you, boys. You know that," Máire said.

She looked at us, shook her head.

"You'd better go," Máire said.

Granny hugged her and the boys. Máire whispered in my ear, "He hates us. Jackson hates us. Tell Michael to mind himself."

"I will, Máire. But will you be all right?"

"The old Major needs Robert, and Robert needs me."

❖ ❖ ❖

Da and the boys were unloading the catch as Granny and I arrived. Josie Bailey, Dennis's wife, was sorting through the fish. Now there's a true fisherman's daughter—deft and quick and good at selling, ready to go to the market, though she'd soon give birth to their second child. They'd one little girl and Josie wanted another. "Sisters."

Mam came out, holding Bridget. "A fog's coming in," she said. "I've been watching the mist collect on the hills. You'd best stay here tonight, Honora."

"I need to get back, Mam."

"Shall I walk you up, Honora? I'd like to see Paddy and Jamesy. I could sleep up at Knocnacuradh," my brother Hughie said. Twelve now, very smart.

"Isn't there school tomorrow? The master will be expecting you. Mam says you're a great student. *Amo, amas, amat,*" I started.

"*Amatus, amant,*" he finished. "But I could read your book, Honora," he said.

Michael had found an old Latin grammar book for me in Galway City, probably had belonged to some hedge schoolmaster. "It was cheap enough," he'd said. "When the high road comes and I open the forge, we'll buy more."

"You'll all be coming to help dig the pratties tomorrow, and I'll give you a loan of the book," I said to him, our only redhead, another tall Keeley.

"Time for you to sleep, Hughie," Mam said. "Honora, this fog's settling. Stay. You won't be able to see the road."

"If I didn't know every crack and crevice on the path up to Knocnacuradh from the coast road by now, wouldn't I be an amadán and a shame to Hughie the scholar?"

"Amadán means 'idiot' in English," Hughie said.

"Right you be, Hughie," I said. I kissed Mam and put Bridget on my hip.

"Safe journey, Honora," said Mam.

The fog wrapped itself around me, heavy and moist. I'll go along the strand—faster, and the tide's out. I could hear the waves hitting against the fingers of rocks that stretched out into the water, but the fog hid the Bay from me.

Bridget cried out.

I'd squeezed her to me without realizing it. "Sorry, a stór. Mam's baby, Mam's baby girl."

In the deep dark, only the feel of rough ground and ridges under my feet told me I'd found the path. Right foot, left foot, right foot, left foot.

"Jesus, Mary, and Holy Saint Joseph! Protect me!" I shouted. How far have I come?

A flickering light above.

"Honora!" Michael stood on the drumlin, holding a piece of burning turf.

"Honora, there you are. I was getting worried. This is a very peculiar fog. Come in, come in, we have your dinner ready, the boys and I."

At our own fireside we ate sweet, floury new potatoes from the early crop, and I said over and over what good cooks my boys were. I held Bridget in my arms while Michael and the boys told me of the great raid they'd made on the chestnut trees in Barna Woods.

"First tell your mam, Paddy, what's special about those trees."

"They're old, Mam, old, old, old."

"And what's important about that?" Michael said.

"Because . . ." And Paddy chanted, "Ireland was thrice clad and thrice bare."

"Very good, Paddy," I said.

"Thrice," said Jamesy. "Thrice, thrice."

"He doesn't know it means three, Mam."

"I do," James said. "Three, three, three!"

"And what does thrice clad and thrice bare mean?"

"It means," said Paddy, "they cut our trees down three times."

"They?"

"The bad people."

"Shorter than telling him about the Vikings and the Normans and the Sassenach and Cromwell and the rest of them," Michael said.

I nodded. "Same story, different characters," I said.

"Ireland had tall trees everywhere, Mam, but now they only grow around the Big Houses. But, Mam, we got some of our own back on our raid," Paddy said.

"A raid!" said Jamesy.

"We sneaked!" said Paddy.

"Hands and knees," said Jamesy.

"Da, too, Mam, crawling through the woods until we came to the tallest chestnut tree. Then we threw sticks and stones up into the branches," said Paddy.

"I threw, too, Mam."

"Be quiet, Jamesy, I'm telling it," Paddy said. "Stones and sticks—"

"Paddy threw hard," said Jamesy. "Hard."

"I did," said Paddy. "Right, Da?"

"You both did well, and chestnuts fell, and we grabbed them and ran home singing 'The West's Awake.' Come on, boys."

And their high voices joined Michael's deep baritone:

> For often, in O'Connor's van,
> To triumph dashed each Connaught clan,

They stumbled through the verse but were strong on the chorus:

> The West's Awake!
> The West's Awake!

They repeated it while I clapped my hands and Bridget laughed.

"Now," Michael said as he stripped the green covering off the chestnuts. He made a hole and put a bit of line through each of the two nuts. "See," he said, "you swing one against the other. The chestnut in my right hand attacks the chestnut in my left." He cocked his wrists and made the two nuts collide.

The boys cheered. "Let us try, Da, let us try!"

Paddy took one and Jamesy the other.

"Let's watch them," Michael whispered to me. "You can tell a man's character by the way he handles a chestnut."

Paddy swung his chestnut straight at Jamesy's, but Jamesy held his back until Paddy's went by him, then let fly with his. There was a great collision, but neither chestnut shattered.

"Now there's a grand combination for brothers," Michael said. "Jamesy with the brains, and Paddy with the brawn. One man plans the strategy and the other unleashes the mighty blow."

I started laughing. "Michael, Jamesy's not three years old yet, and Paddy's only five."

"All the more reason to start. But here's the most important lesson. Listen to me, you two."

And his sons quieted, looking up at him.

"Stick together, and no man can better you. See my fingers?" He spread them out. "Jamesy, take Da's finger and bend it back."

"I'll not hurt Daidi."

"I'll do it," said Paddy, grabbing Michael's smallest finger and pushing on it.

"Ow," said Michael. He jumped up and ran around the place until he had both boys as well as Bridget and me killing ourselves with the laughing. Then he made a fist. "See, I put my fingers together in a fist. I hold them tight. Now, mo bouchaill, try to bend it."

Paddy couldn't dislodge the finger at all.

"Strong now, because these boyos are together. Together. Do you understand, boys?"

"We do, Da," Paddy said, and Jamesy nodded and nodded, his plump little face jiggling.

"And now to sleep," I said.

We settled them onto the straw pallet to the side of the hearth.

"A story, Da," Paddy said.

"A day of stories," Michael told him. "And work tomorrow."

I tucked Bridget into the rough cradle Michael had made and stretched out on our straw mattress.

Michael had found bogdeal—petrified wood "from when Ireland was clad"—in the forest and tossed it into the fire. The flames turned as blue as the flowers on Gentian Hill, then became the red purple of the fuchsias that would bloom in our lane.

"The flowers of May come in October," I said to Michael.

He took off his trousers and got in next to me. I put the blanket over him.

"Here we are, so warm and cozy—so lucky. And Máire's up there in that prison," I said.

He held me tighter.

"It's as if she's paying for our happiness. I can't bear it."

"Máire's strong," Michael said.

"I'm tired of hearing that. What does that mean? Does she suffer less because she's strong? She's afraid, Michael. Máire was never afraid, but this agent is a hard, dour man. The old Major's let this Jackson bring in missionaries."

"Missionaries? You've lost me, Honora."

"To turn us Protestants. We're heathens, and we shouldn't have decent land. After all the loads of seaweed you carried up on your back for the fields, after the planting and pulling and watching and waiting, this Jackson's yearning to raise the rents and evict us, and all because Johnny Leahy drowned and Father Gilley wouldn't let Máire marry again."

Michael's arm came around me.

"And she's not strong," I went on. "Well, the Pearl's strong, flirting and flouncing, but Máire—Máire's frightened, and so am I."

"Shhh, now, shhh."

"Michael, this Reverend Smithson, he wants to take the Blessed Mother from us, too."

"Now, a stór," said Michael, "they can't evict the Mother of God. Ireland is hers."

"They can if she falls behind in her rent," I said. I took in a long breath. "I'm so worried, Michael. Jackson's a different seed and breed altogether. He hates us. And he knows you are on Mulloy's land. The landlords might not have much use for us, but I've never felt the cold, out-and-out hatred from them that I did from this Jackson. It went across my heart and chilled me to the bone—like the fog. It's an awful fog, Michael."

"Shall we have a sip of poitín, a stór?"

"Poitín?"

"It'll warm you, lift the fear a bit."

"I don't know. I've only ever drunk it at dances, wakes, or weddings. Never just sitting and talking."

"Try it."

"I wouldn't want to be drunk."

"And right you'd be. Drunk's frightening on its own terms, but if you sip in the warmth, it brings a kind of courage. Warriors swear by it."

He reached down behind the bed and brought out the jug of poitín that Patrick kept replenished on his visits.

Patrick Kelly came to us two or three times a year—in the spring, casting a cold eye on Michael's potato beds and fields to make sure they were proper done, at Christmas, and then sometimes in the summer. Came at night, stayed one day, and left at night. He never said where he'd been or where he was going, but he always had a jug of poitín for us.

"Take a sip of this, a stór. A drop of whiskey, the fire flaming in colors, a story, and a good husband can take the fear right out of you."

I took a quick swallow from the jug and then a longer pull, and he was right. I felt the whiskey go down to calm my fluttering stomach.

"Uisce beatha," I said, "the water of life."

"Fadó," said Michael. "There lived a blacksmith, said to be the strongest man in Ireland, and men came from all over to challenge him. Who could hold up the mighty hammer longest? Well, this fellow held it high over his head for days and days and nights and nights, his arm all straight and stiff." Then Michael stopped and brought me to him, whispering to me, and I knew who was the strongest, the best, the most loving man in Ireland—my husband, a ghrá mo chroí, love of my heart.

After we made love, I felt a great energy in me. Why suffer the old Major and Jackson?

"Michael, let's hitch Champion to a wagon, load up our children, go up to Pyke's, get Máire and her boys, and go. Escape."

"Escape where, a stór?"

"Anywhere, get away from the Scoundrel Pykes and Jackson. Be gypsies. You could learn to repair tin pots."

"I could."

"And we could camp out under the stars."

"We could. Of course the winter's coming. Cold," he said.

"And we'd never see Knocnacuradh again."

"We wouldn't, not if we were hiding Máire and her children. Wouldn't you miss Galway Bay and your mam and da and your brothers? Don't despair, Honora. Máire will find a way to get home. My mother used to say, 'It's a long road that has no turning.'"

"That's what Granny says, too—and my mam."

"Do they say, 'What God has for you won't go past you'?"

"They do."

And, 'This too will pass.'"

I laughed. "That, too." I suddenly was very, very sleepy. "This too will pass. Winter will go, spring will come. And the corncrakes will be back."

"They will be," he said. "And the lark, and all the singing birds of heaven." He stroked my head. "They won't destroy us, Honora. There's too many of us."

I closed my eyes.

"Go to sleep now," he said. "Tomorrow we'll start digging the pratties. When the pit is full to overflowing with potatoes, food for the winter and beyond, when the grain is harvested and the rent is paid, we'll have no need to fear any man."

I yawned. "The family will be coming up tomorrow if the fog lifts."

❖   ❖   ❖

But fog still smothered Knocnacuradh and the surrounding townlands that next day—no digging, however much Michael wanted to get started. Nearly ten hundredweights of potatoes to harvest.

Those first twenty ridges he and Patrick had set out had become sixty now. Each had forty plants, and each of those would yield twenty to thirty potatoes apiece. Thousands and thousands and thousands of them. A generous plant, as Patrick said, but in need of care. Michael had fertilized the plants with seaweed, quicklime burned down from oyster shells, and he'd added a bit of Champion's manure. He'd made sure every scraw was tapped down, fitting together perfectly. No black-birds or rats disturbed the ridges of Knocnacuradh.

For some of our neighbors, Michael represented a kind of reaching above that made them uneasy: his skill as a piper, his victory in the Gal-way Races, the breeding of Champion and selling her foals, his dream of a forge. But John Joe Gorman, the Tierneys, the McGuire brothers, and even Neddy Ryan understood what it took to set a ridge and bring forth a ton of potatoes. And no one cut turf in the bog faster or piled it more neatly than Michael. The men of the townland appreciated Michael's skills and looked to him as a leader—an accomplishment for a fellow here only six years.

And this year we'd have our biggest yield ever. But the potatoes were ready *now*. They could go mealy if left in the ground.

The next morning, a fine drizzle broke up the fog.

"Come on, Mam!" said Paddy. The boys stood at the door, eager to start the digging.

"Where's your da?"

"The great giant Finn McCool's off to take his morning piss, Mam."

"Paddy!"

"That's what Da told us." He and Jamesy started to laugh—were still laughing when Da, Granny, Mam, Joseph, and Hughie arrived. Dennis stayed in Bearna with Josie, near her time now.

"God bless all here," Da said.

The other families from the townlands had started toward their fields, too, and called out to us—"Good morning, missus!" and, "God bless—a decent day for it, finally!"

And the sky was clearing. We should get a lot of the potato crop in today.

"I'm running ahead with Joseph," Paddy shouted. "He's giving me a go with his hurley."

At eighteen, Joseph was still five feet nothing. Paddy's nearly up to his shoulder, with the height he gets from the Keeleys and Kellys both—muscled already. A sturdy lad, halfway up the hill, with Jamesy puffing behind. Hughie, good boy that he was, swung Jamesy up on his back and took off after Paddy and Joseph. More like brothers than uncles to my sons.

I walked between Mam and Granny, carrying Bridget. Da and Michael were just ahead, deep in talk of some kind. They get on so well.

Michael's part of the Keeley men now, with his own fine children, his loneliness filled.

I took Granny's hand. "Our own pratties," I said. "And nothing to do with Jackson or the Scoundrel Pykes or anybody but us. Michael says they keep us safe."

"They do," Granny said.

I heard Joseph and Hughie shouting down to us, but I couldn't catch their words. And then Paddy and Jamesy were shrieking, "Da, Da, Da!"

Michael started running.

The boys sounded frightened. I saw Michael reach them, then fall down to the ground. What's he doing?

Where's that awful smell coming from? Has something died up here? The stench seems to rise from the land itself.

Mam and Da and Granny and I were at the ridges now. Paddy ran to me. He lifted up his hands to me, covered in black muck.

"The pratties, Mam," he said. "They're gone!"

Michael and Joseph and Hughie were tearing at the ground.

"Here, Mam, take Bridget," I said, and knelt down next to Michael. "Where are the potatoes?" I said. "Where are they?"

He pulled out a great stinking glob and held it out to me. "Here. This." He shook the filth off his hands, wiped them on the grass, and kept digging.

The stalks of all the plants, green the day before, were black and blasted, with slime instead of potatoes under the ground.

"This can't be!" I said. "How could they all die in one night?"

"Here, Michael, here's a good one," Joseph called, "and another, and another—five solid potatoes up here."

"And a sound ridge over here!" Da shouted. "Look, green patches among the black."

Michael stood up. "Dig the potatoes from the green ones—fast, fast!—before whatever's doing this spreads. Hurry! Hurry!"

Paddy ran to Michael.

Mam knelt next to me. Granny carried Bridget a few steps away. Jamesy came to stand at my shoulder.

"Mam, Mam, listen."

"I can't, Jamesy. I'm digging. Help me."

"Listen, listen!"

"What?" Now I heard it—echoing from glen to glen. . . .

"Keening," Granny said.

Wailing voices came from every hillside—the neighbors—their potatoes dead and dying, too.

The sound stopped us. We were frozen, kneeling in the muck and mire.

Michael recovered first. "Dig! Dig! Dig!" he shouted, heading for the high ridge.

I crawled to another patch and plunged my hand into the foul-smelling mess. I felt a hard lump—a good potato. But when I grabbed it, the potato fell apart in my hand, oozing through my fingers.

"We must dig faster!" Michael yelled. "Get any whole potatoes out! Carry them to the stream, scrub away the muck."

"Michael!" It was our Joseph. "Up here, at the top! They're all sound!"

"Get them out! Get them!" Michael shouted.

Granny took Bridget and Jamesy away. A hard rain started. Rivers of evil-smelling mud flooded the ridges, soaking us through. We dug and dug, gagging on the smell.

We stopped only when the last of the light went.

We carried any whole potatoes to the stream near our cottage to wash them, then rubbed them dry on our clothes and stacked them in the pit. All that we had saved barely covered the bottom.

We staggered into the cottage.

Granny had boiled up some of the early potatoes, dug up last month.

Michael looked into the pot. "Sound! These were sound! And the fields were healthy yesterday. . . . What could have happened? What blight could have hit so fast? How could the potatoes rot overnight?"

"We must eat and sleep," Granny said. "Take one prattie each."

Michael usually eats ten.

We ate. I put Mam, Da, Granny, and the children on the straw pallet, and the rest of us collapsed on the floor. I lay down next to Michael.

"The ridges behind the long acre might be sound," he said.

They weren't. Two days of digging and the pit wasn't half-full. Only the potatoes on the very highest ridges—the ones Michael and Patrick had planted first—had survived the blight.

Not enough. Not near enough.

A wake the next night. We sat up together, my family staying at

Knocnacuradh, Owen and Katie Mulloy and their children joining us. Half of their potatoes were gone, too.

We had talked ourselves into silence now, the night was almost gone, the children asleep. Owen and Michael stood leaning against the wall. Mam and Granny sat on the two rush stools. The rest of us slumped on the floor. I held a sleeping Bridget, and Katie rocked her new baby, James, two months old. Da paced.

Numbers ran through my head: twenty potatoes per day for Michael—five each for the boys and ten for me . . . forty per day. Last year we had pratties enough for ten months. How many? Ten thousand? Twelve thousand? What was in the pit now, a thousand, maybe?

What else can we eat? Nuts from Barna Woods, maybe, winkles from the strand, seaweed from the rocks. There will be catches to sell. But winter fishing's chancy. Bad weather keeps the boats from going out.

I saw Michael looking at me, hearing my thoughts.

"We're panicking," he said. "This is bad, but it could be worse."

"Fields ruined for miles around," Owen Mulloy said, scratching his bald head. "Unheard of. The whole district, the whole country, maybe. I've seen Rusheen, Shanballyduff, Cappagh, Derryloney, Truskey East and West, Ballybeg, Lachlea, Corboly—all the same—more than half the pratties destroyed."

Granny stood. She lifted her head, the green eyes I'd inherited looking at each one of us. "We are going to face this like the people we are. Now, Honora."

"What, Granny?"

"Pray. You lead us."

"Me?"

"You are the woman of the house," she said.

"All right. Hail Mary, full of grace . . ." I stopped. Too formal. "Mary, Our Mother," I started. "Listen, please. You know our needs. Year after year you've given us lovely white potatoes, but now they've turned black and—"

"May I make a suggestion?" It was Owen Mulloy. "Every man-jack in Ireland's praying at the feet of Our Lady, God bless her and keep her, and all sobbing and moaning about the potatoes. It might be as well for us to go straight to the Man Himself."

"Jesus?" I said.

Mulloy shook his head no.

"God, our Father?"

Again, a negative.

"Saint Patrick," he said. "You know his prayer—give us a blast of the Breastplate."

I began, "I bind to myself today the power of God to hold and lead me. Christ be with me, Christ before me, Christ behind me, Christ to the right of me, Christ to the left. In the radiance of the sun." I stopped. I'd lost the words. "Dear and Glorious Saint Patrick, Apostle of Ireland, please help us," I finished.

"Amen," they answered.

"And let us pray," Mam said, "to our patron Saint Enda, who chose our own townland for his holy well, and who loves our green fields and our beautiful Galway Bay."

"Honora," said Granny, "we'll make a vow to Saint Mac Dara."

"What?"

"Ask his help. Promise to visit his island on his feast day in the summer."

"We'll do that," Da said.

"And now the rest of you," said Granny, "repeat after me: Oh, Saint Mac Dara, the fisherman's friend . . ."

We said the words.

"Fill our nets, still the winds, calm the seas," said Granny.

We prayed with Granny.

Then Michael went to the loft and brought down the pipes. He played a lament—the music pushing away thought for just that moment.

Chapter 11

HE BLIGHT OF 1845 has caused a partial failure,' the *Galway Vindicator* says. So will we only 'partially' starve?" Owen Mulloy asked. It was two weeks after the disaster, and Owen quoted from the newspapers he'd gotten from some friend in Galway City. "'A patchwork of destruction, one field black, the next green,'" Owen read. "Scientists are puzzled as to what caused the devastation."

All kinds of explanations were considered in the columns of the *Vindicator*. Was it the heavy rain, that strange shrouding mist, the electricity in the air from lightning? John Finerty, the editor, wrote alarmed editorials.

"The fellow's a Catholic," Owen said, "and the paper supports O'Connell, so we can believe him when he says no one knows what brought the blight."

"Whatever about why it happened," I said. "What's to be done? Any reports on that?"

"Does it say there'll be roadworks, any way to earn money?" Michael asked.

"Loads written about how the Liberator's roaring at them in Parliament," Owen said. "'Ireland's in a state of emergency and the government must act.'" He stopped. "Ah, damn him . . . listen to this: 'Prime Minister Peel responded, "There is such a tendency to exaggeration and inaccuracy in Irish reports that delay in acting upon them is always desirable." ' That old Orange Peel—O'Connell's enemy and Ireland's, too. Exaggeration, is it! Jesus Christ, let him try to survive on pratties turned to muck!"

"But, Owen, the English and the landlords don't eat potatoes," I said. "The blight didn't hurt the grain harvest."

"Crops are being loaded onto ships in Galway City right now," Michael said.

"Going to England," Owen said, "along with cattle, sheep, pigs, and chickens. There's so much food passing through our hands, but none for us. We could starve surrounded by plenty."

"I could sell Champion and Oisín," Michael said.

After selling Champion's first two foals back to Sir William Gregory, he and Owen kept the third, a colt they called Oisín. Here was the horse they'd been waiting for, Champion's spirit, the Red Rogue's speed, Bess's endurance, combined with the strength of Barrier, the stallion sire. Selling him would mean abandoning their dream of a stable of victorious racehorses named for Ireland's heroes, Irishmen taking their heritage back from the Sassenach and landlords. But now . . . Owen was shaking his head.

"Better to hold the colt until the panic is over. We'll get no price for him now anyway. Keep Champion, too—she's an asset. At least we have good grazing for the two of them," he said.

Owen got up to go. "We can't despair," he said. "The sin against the Holy Spirit."

"You're right, Owen," I said. "We've our faith and half a pit of potatoes."

That evening, I sent Paddy out to the pit for five pratties—two for Michael, one for each of the boys and me. My milk still fed Bridget.

"Mam! Mam!" Paddy ran in, screaming. "Mam! Come quick! The pit's full of—shit!"

I ran out with Paddy. That same foul stench—our solid potatoes! I knelt at the edge of the pit.

"Mam!" I heard Jamesy crying for me in the cottage and Bridget wailing. Paddy looked at me. No tears from him, not from my sturdy lad.

"Run for your da. He's with Champion and Oisín in the pasture."

I plunged my hands deep into the pit, clawing through the clabber, desperate to save whole potatoes.

Michael came running. "Honora, what? What?"

"The blight! It's attacked the pit!"

He knelt down next to me, fishing through the muck.

Only half the potatoes were still sound.

It was the same in Rusheen, Shanballyduff, and all the townlands—sound potatoes dissolved into slime.

Thank God we'd stored the potatoes from the high ridge in the loft to use as seed potatoes. They were still sound. But what now?

"Billy Dubh won't take the hammer and anvil in pawn," Michael said, his voice low, the two of us holding on to each other, the children asleep. He'd gone into Galway City that day, three weeks since the failure now. "Won't buy them, either. No market for them, he says."

"Billy's the worst kind of gombeen man—greedy for money and land."

"He'd give me a few shillings for the saddle, but Owen said to wait. Billy's cheating me and I'll never be able to afford another like it. If Oisín is to race, we'll need the saddle."

"At least we still have the three gold coins from the Galway Races," I said. "The potatoes in the pit won't feed us through the winter no matter how careful we are."

"We need some employment," Michael said. "Public roadworks. If the government would only hire us to drain the land or lay railroad tracks . . ."

It was hours before we fell asleep.

Just before dawn, Paddy woke me. "Mam. Mam, he's here."

Patrick Kelly stood at the foot of our bed. He'd come in without a sound or a footfall.

"Patrick, we—" I started, but he held up his hand.

"Quiet, Honora," he said. "Show me the pit, Michael."

❖   ❖   ❖

Michael and I and the children followed Patrick outside.

"Uncle Patrick will help us, won't he, Da?" Paddy said.

"He will," Michael told him.

Patrick looked first at the solid potatoes in the pit, only a quarter of what there should be. Then he asked did Michael have any of the rotten pratties.

"I buried them," Michael said, "near the marsh."

"Dig them up," Patrick said.

At the foot of the hill, Michael uncovered the pile of rotten potatoes, releasing that putrid smell.

The children and I stood together while Patrick Kelly sniffed the diseased bits, rubbed them between his fingers, touched them with his tongue.

"Ugh," said Paddy.

"Ugh, ugh," Jamesy echoed him.

"Now to the ridges," Patrick said. He turned to me. "Honora, take the children in."

"Michael, I can't!" I said.

"Let us come, Da," Paddy said.

"Please, please," said Jamesy.

"Come along, then," Michael said.

"I need silence," Patrick said.

"Whist," I said to the boys as we followed the two men.

Decaying stalks covered most of the ridges Patrick and Michael had laid out so carefully on that moonlit night six years before. Only the highest ones had survived.

"Clear these away," said Patrick. "Burn all the stalks." He held up a plant. "Look," he said to Michael. I moved closer to them. "You can just see the fuzz along the side of the leaf, here, and down the stalk. That's the fungus killed the plant."

"But the ridge above this was sound," Michael said.

"Show me."

Up we went.

Patrick lay flat on the ground, stretching his body into the soil, tasting a bit of dirt.

"The blight's not here," he said. "But why?"

"And this is the worst of the ridges," Michael said. "No sun, the freeze hits here first."

"But sheltered," I said. "Away from the rain."

"Maybe the cold kills the blight," Patrick said. "Maybe that fungus on the plant needs warmth to grow, a soft rain to root it into the soil. The blight's a living thing."

"It came in that fog," I said. "That evil fog."

Patrick started down the hill. Michael took Bridget from me, and I held the boys' hands.

Back at our cottage, Patrick climbed into the loft to inspect the potatoes dug from the good ridges, our seed potatoes. He rolled each one in his hand, smelling it. Michael sat cross-legged in the loft with him. The children and I were below, looking up at them. I kept silent.

It was six months since we'd seen him—before Bridget was born. He hadn't even mentioned the new baby. He doesn't change—lean and quick and not a wrinkle on that knife-edged face of his.

"Sound," Patrick said. "You're right to set them aside for seed potatoes."

❖ ❖ ❖

"But can the blight get to the good pratties even now?" I asked when later, with the children asleep, we three sat at the fire. Michael and I shared one rush stool, and Patrick took the other. "Will a fog come up from the rotten fields and slip in through the cracks in the walls?" I asked.

Michael touched my hand.

"You're too full of imagination," Patrick said to me. "I think the blight's dead for now. We've had a freeze, and nothing lives in frozen soil." He took a piece of turf and put it on the fire in the hearth. "Invite your neighbors over for Samhain."

"What?" I said. "But, Patrick . . ."

"A way of meeting that gives no information to informers," Patrick said. "The countryside is being watched, make no mistake—the landlords and the government are afraid the people will rise. They'll be looking for ringleaders, troublemakers. A Samhain gathering where the old traditions are observed only means the people are standing firm in the face of adversity."

"Or are too feckless to understand what's facing us," I said. "That's what the landlords will think."

"Better yet," said Patrick.

I looked at Michael, but he only shrugged.

❖ ❖ ❖

Michael and Patrick raided the apple orchard at Dangan House and gathered nuts in Barna Woods. Stealing was no bother to Patrick the highwayman. I hope there's no reward out for him. The Ryans were bound to come, and I would put nothing past Tessie, including informing.

"She won't," Michael said to me the night before Samhain. "Their whole potato garden was destroyed. I gave her some of our pratties to see her through the next few weeks. So they need us."

Six Ryans now with the new baby. It was Mary, twelve now, who minded the twins, Henry and Albert, and cuddled the infant, Thaddy.

"Enough dodging and ducking," Patrick said to me when I told him my fears about Tessie. "Time to make ourselves known."

Ourselves?

✤ ✤ ✤

"My brother," was how Michael introduced Patrick to the others. Even my family had never seen him on any of his secret visits. All were here—Ryans, Mulloys, Keeleys, Kellys. Only Dennis and Josie had stayed in Bearna, their second daughter born last week.

"We'll play the usual games," Patrick said, taking charge.

Granny and Mam and I tied the stems of the apples to pieces of hemp frayed from the nets. Michael looped the lines over the rafters of the loft so the apples hung down.

"Line up, children," I said.

"Can we have teams?" asked Joe, at twelve the oldest Mulloy.

"Boys against girls," said his brother, John Michael, ten.

"Fine," said Annie Mulloy, the little one Mary Ryan had looked after. She was eight now, and clever. "Mary and I can beat all of you, and we'll have the most bites of the apples!"

"All right," I said. "Boys."

Paddy and Jamesy and the five-year-old Ryan twins, Albert and Henry, stood next to the older fellows. Paddy called for Hughie to join them.

The children knew calamity had descended, but if the adults could have a party, maybe all was not lost.

For the first time since we'd dug the ruined potatoes, Jamesy smiled.

Then the knock came. Patrick Kelly swung himself up into the loft. Michael opened the door.

"God bless all here!" Billy Dubh, the gombeen man himself, a known informer, watching. "I heard you as I was passing. Didn't expect a Samhain party at such a difficult time," he said, strutting in.

"For the children, Billy," Michael said to him.

"Go on with the games, then, don't let me stop you," Billy said.

I'd woven straw together for a blindfold, and now I tied it over Paddy's eyes and turned him. He walked right into the hanging apple, which hit him a clout on the forehead.

"Ow, ow!" he said, which Jamesy and the Ryan twins found a great joke.

Billy Dubh laughed with them. Everyone else kept silent. Billy looked hard at me, so I started laughing, too. Finally the other adults joined in, Dubh staring at each face.

Just then, Paddy managed a first bite before the apple slipped away. We all cheered.

"My turn," Dubh said. He didn't bother with the blindfold but put his hand on the apple and started chomping until only a core was left.

"He's eaten it all," Jamesy said.

"Now, Billy Dubh—" Michael started.

"It's the girls' go," I said quickly, and blindfolded Annie Mulloy. "Make a show of it," I whispered to her.

Annie nudged the apple away from her and then let it swing back to touch her mouth. She pretended to try to catch it, knocking it away two, three times, until she got a good bite.

"Smart girl you are!" Granny said.

"The old mo-men-tum," said Owen.

"It's far from momentum you were reared, Mulloy," Billy Dubh said. "Have you no poitín at this party? I suppose you've got it hid in the loft. I'll climb up."

"Stop!" said Granny. "No drink in this house, and I'm beginning my story. Sit down, Billy Dubh."

"You'd better," said Tessie Ryan. "She'll turn you into a crow!"

"An improvement," I heard Michael mutter.

Dubh looked over, but Granny had begun. He sat down on the floor.

"Fadó," she said as Mam and I and Katie Mulloy handed around the nuts from Barna Woods. Cracking and crunching accompanied the story as Granny told about the Connemara man who'd passed a graveyard on a Samhain midnight. He saluted a fellow he met at the gates, but when this fellow nodded back at him, didn't the fellow's head fall off? The head shouted curses at the Connemara man as it rolled across the road. Very frightening Granny made the story.

"Horrible!" said Billy Dubh.

"I believe a headless man was seen at the gates of the Rahoon grave-yard only a few years ago," Michael said.

"You're right," said Owen. "Isn't that graveyard on the road you take home?" he asked Billy Dubh.

"He's safe enough until midnight," Granny said, "but after that . . ."

"Getting late," I said.

"I have to be going," Billy Dubh said. "Any of you need to borrow a shilling or two or have something to pawn, come to me. I've also a few hundredweight of potatoes—buy now before the price goes up!"

"Thank you, Billy," Neddy Ryan said.

"God bless all here," Billy Dubh said, and hurried away.

We all laughed.

"Now that was comical," Owen Mulloy said. "That ignorant guilpín running away from the headless man, all the time telling us he was ready to cheat us."

Patrick dropped down from the loft.

"Nothing funny about Dubh," Patrick said. "Dubh is a dangerous man. The soldiers are on alert, expecting trouble. A fellow was arrested in Galway City for singing 'A Nation Once Again' in the street. Dubh could inform on any one of you, for anything."

"What trouble could we cause?" said Neddy Ryan. "Sure, aren't we all frightened to a standstill?"

"But you've nothing to lose. Men are dangerous when they're forced against the wall," Patrick said.

"Nothing to lose!" I said. "Why, we have everything to lose. I've seen the new agent, Jackson. He wants us gone—starved to death or evicted makes no difference to him."

"Honora," Mam said. "The children."

The younger ones had found a place to curl up and sleep. But all the rest of us were awake and listening.

"Someone will help us," Tessie said. "The landlords will let us work for food, or the government—they've helped before."

"The government will do nothing," said Patrick. "When O'Connell tries to push Peel and the Parliament to help us, the English dismiss him. 'Here's the Irish, acting the poor mouth,' they say, and do nothing," he said, chopping off each word. "Half the countries in Europe have the blight. They've lost their potatoes, too. But those governments closed their ports, kept the food in the country, bought grain in Americay—doing what a government *should*—aiding its people in a crisis. But the British do nothing for us."

"They don't fear O'Connell anymore. The government crippled him when they outlawed the monster meetings," Owen Mulloy said.

"Sad but true," Da said.

After years of gathering crowds as large as five hundred thousand people to protest the British policy, the government suddenly forbade any such assemblies. This while tens of thousands were on the roads already, headed for the biggest meeting of all to be held at Clontarf, where Brian Boru defeated the Vikings. Regiments of soldiers were sent out, ready to fire on the crowd if it gathered. Daniel O'Connell got them turned around, averted a slaughter, but he was jailed and came out of prison a different man.

"They've broken the Liberator," Patrick said.

"Now wait," Da said.

But Patrick went right on. "O'Connell still thinks Victoria, 'the darling little queen,' will help Ireland. He tells the Irish to be loyal to the Crown. There's new men called Young Ireland who want a complete break with England—Ireland should be a republic, like America. I've met them: John Mitchel, Thomas Meagher, William Smith O'Brien."

"Physical-force men," said Michael.

"Call them what you will, but they know the facts. England owes Ireland. Mitchel has the figures. In the forty years since the Union, we've paid eight million pounds a year in taxes. What's that, over three hundred million pounds? Add to that the ten percent tithe every one of us pays to the Church of Ireland to support churchmen for the likes of the Scoundrel Pykes. A fortune. All we ask is some of those taxes back. Parliament refuses. The British distract O'Connell with promises of relief and public works while ships leave Galway and Cork and Dublin loaded with *our* grain, *our* cattle, *our* sheep, *our* pigs, and *our* butter! We can't afford to buy what we grow. Now we've lost the potato. What do they care? They've wanted us dead for centuries—Ireland without the Irish. The blight is the weapon they've been waiting for. Britain will look the other way as we starve to death."

Da and Owen stared into the dying fire; Tessie was crying; Neddy had his head in his hands; Granny's eyes were closed; Mam's arm was around Hughie's shoulder; Katie wept, holding her baby, James, close; Joseph sat with his knees under his chin; the Mulloy boys looked up at Patrick; Mary Ryan watched Hughie; Paddy moved over beside Michael and me and stared up at his uncle; the rest of the children slept on.

No one spoke.

I leaned toward Michael, who took my hand and looked up at Patrick from where we sat on the floor.

"And what are we to do, Patrick?" Michael said.

"Stop the shipments of food out of Ireland."

"How?"

It was as if they were the only two in the room.

"Attack the wagons," Patrick said. "A few armed men could do it, put such fear into the likes of Billy Dubh that no man will drive a wagon, no docker will load cargo into a ship. There are some ready to act now"—he looked at Michael—"who aren't afraid—brave men."

I felt Michael start to stand—I held on to his arm.

"Courage won't help men known to the drivers. They'd be betrayed and arrested before they got home," I said.

"Sooner," said Owen Mulloy. "Soldiers are escorting the cargo wagons—I saw them. They'd shoot any raiders down."

All the men were shaking their heads.

"I remember what happened when the British put down the Rebellion of 1798," Da said. "The bodies of our people were hanging from trees in every townland from here to Mayo, two of them brothers of mine. Daniel O'Connell remembers, too. It's why he's so against violence."

"It wouldn't work, Patrick," said Michael.

Mam started talking, very softly. "I remember the time the Claddagh people . . ."

Something in her voice made us all listen.

"I was selling fish with the Claddagh women, and we went against merchants giving short weights—caused a big ruckus, we did, marching through the market, shouting. The soldiers came out, but we threw stones at them. The city council made the traders lower their price. Could we do something like that, Patrick?"

"A demonstration, you mean?" said Patrick.

"Our own monster meeting," I said. "That's a very good idea, Mam.

We could get the whole parish together and march through Galway City to the harbor, to the courthouse."

The heads were coming up. . . . Could we really act without bringing total disaster on ourselves?

"There would have to be discipline," said Da. "No incidents—no violence."

"A peaceful meeting," said Owen, "with permission and priests attending. Father Roche is a decent man. He'd stand with us."

"It would be a start," Patrick said. "Better than nothing."

"Will you march with us, Patrick?" Michael asked him.

"I will," he said. "The time for hiding is over. We have to act before the hunger makes people so weak that"—Patrick looked from one face to the next—"they can only lay down and die."

✥ ✥ ✥

But at the end of the day, it wasn't Patrick who rallied the people of the townlands to march on the port. It was Michael.

"He frightens them," I told Michael after no one in Rusheen would open their doors to Patrick and him. "Go on your own or with Owen Mulloy. You're known and liked."

And no one suspected the piper going from cottage to cottage, playing for a few pratties, was carrying another message: Join together on St. Martin's Day, November 11. Shut the port. And the people said they would.

"Michael makes them want to be brave," Owen told me.

Patrick had gone off. Owen assumed Patrick was recruiting Ribbonmen and outlaws and worried if these hard men would stay peaceful.

"Can't give the soldiers any excuse to arrest us," he said to Michael.

"Patrick knows what he's about," Michael said. Only to me did he confide Patrick's true mission. He'd gone to get the great treasure of the Kelly tribe, their battle standard, the bachall, their cathach—the crozier St. Grellan carried when he and St. Patrick came as missionaries to the Kellys. Michael told me how the two Christian priests found the pagan Kelly queen mourning her stillborn son. St. Patrick prayed for the child's soul. Grellan brought the baby back to life. The Kellys converted and chose Grellan as their guardian saint. His crozier—a hazel rod covered in pure gold—was the emblem that rallied them in times of trouble, and it was also an instrument for discerning the truth: Hold the crozier and lie and the gold staff would grow hot and sear the liar's hand. There was awe in Michael's voice when he told me the story. Patrick had gone to Ahascragh, where a man called Cronelly had the keeping of the crozier. Patrick would bring the battle standard back in time for our march. "Powerful altogether," Michael said.

But as the day approached, Patrick had not returned.

"Saint Martin's Day—we can't change it," Owen said.

✦   ✦   ✦

We went forward without Patrick. And we did it. We shut the port. Thousands from every townland, men and women, marched to the harbor, chanting and shouting: "Save our food! Keep the crop! Shut the port!" We women came first to show the soldiers we intended no violence. Michael, Da, Owen, and my brothers urged the lines of marchers forward from within the crowd.

When the dockers saw themselves surrounded by thousands, they put down the bags of grain, sides of beef, and tubs of butter, stopped herding the pigs and sheep onto the decks. The ships that would carry away the harvest were not loaded. "It's shut!" the dockers shouted at us.

And the people cheered them, standing together.

But when we moved to the courthouse to confront the officials waiting to hear our demands, a regiment of soldiers carrying muskets surrounded us. Surely these men, the Connaught Rangers, Catholics from Galway, most of them, wouldn't attack their aunts and cousins without cause, I thought. But then I saw their mounted officers spur their big horses into the midst of the crowd. These wouldn't hesitate to order the soldiers to shoot.

Father Roche, the young curate, spoke for us to the high sheriff. "Cease export of all food!" he said. We cheered. "The government must enforce fair prices for food, landlords should suspend rent payments, public works must be opened so money can be earned."

The sheriff raised both hands. A committee would be appointed, he said to us, to consider the demands.

Then a shout from the front interrupted him: "No committee—

action!" It was Patrick at last, running at the sheriff, urging all to chant: "Action! Action!"

The sheriff pushed a stout, red-faced man forward.

"Quiet now. Listen. Here's a high official from London," Father Roche shouted, "come to help us." He looked at Patrick. "Please."

Patrick waved the crowd silent.

The man told us the government had found a way to save the diseased potatoes. Seventy thousand circulars had been printed with instructions. The soldiers would pass them out to us.

I took one—English. Few people would be able to read it.

The official began to read out the instructions: "Take a diseased potato, grate it, then strain the gratings through linen cloth, lay them out in the sun or bake them in an oven at one hundred eighty degrees."

Mad entirely. Grate muck? Linen cloths? Ovens? Who had such things?

Howls from the crowd.

Patrick shouted into the official's face: "We'd rather die now, fighting to keep our food, than die later of starvation and fever!"

The crowd took up the cry: "Die fighting! Die fighting! Die fighting!"

I could see that some who'd joined us wore ribbons on their jackets—the hard men, come with Patrick.

"Fight! Fight! Fight!" they chanted.

An officer called out a command. The soldiers lifted their muskets.

"Go home!" Father Roche shouted in Irish. "Go home before there's trouble!" He ran over to the officer, pleading with him to let the people disperse.

But Patrick yelled, "Don't go! Stand against them! Don't go!" He stepped in front of the priest and lifted a long staff into the air—gold, catching the sun, shining. He'd gotten it—Grellan's crozier.

"This holy relic is from the time of Saint Patrick!" He waved it above his head. "A battle standard, full of power! We can't retreat before them. Be defeated by their lies!"

Waving the crozier back and forth, Patrick led the crowd's chant: "Give us our crops! Give us our crops!"

The soldiers took a step forward, and Father Roche shouted, "Listen to the sheriff! He *will* speak for you!"

"You have my word!" the sheriff shouted. "Go home! Go home!"

But Patrick was next to the sheriff. "Take the crozier and swear an oath that you'll present our case," Patrick said. "But if you promise falsely, Grellan's staff will burn your hand."

The sheriff looked at the crozier, then out at the crowd. "I am an officer of Her Majesty, Queen Victoria! I would not lower myself. Arrest this man!" he shouted at the approaching soldiers.

They had Patrick trapped.

Suddenly the skirl of pipes cut through the noise, the first notes of "A Nation Once Again."

Shouts from the crowd: "Look up!"

Michael sat on the city wall at the side of the courthouse, high above us—the piper drawing all eyes, distracting even the soldiers.

And the crowd began to sing as Michael played:

> *When the fire of youth was in my blood . . .*

I heard the sheriff shouting, "Arrest them all!" but the soldiers stopped, confused, as a thousand voices sang:

> *And Ireland, long a province, be*
> *A Nation Once Again!*

On the courthouse steps, Father Roche was pleading with the sheriff. As the song ended, he shouted, "Go home and you won't be arrested! Go home now! Now!"

And we went.

❖   ❖   ❖

"I saw him," I said to Michael when I found him at the city gate. "I saw Patrick. He got away."

It started to rain as the soldiers herded us onto the coast road and the crowd straggled away up to the townlands in the hills.

"We stood up to them," Michael said. "The battle standard has been raised. We won't give up."

"We won't," I said, and Michael and I climbed the muddy path to Knocnacuradh.

Chapter 12

"Paddy, Jamesy, lie down, pretend you're asleep," I said.

"Mam, it's midday!" said Paddy.

"Do as I tell you. Now."

Through the window, I'd seen the squad of ten soldiers turn up the boreen, Billy Dubh leading them. Two weeks since the demonstration, a cold, dull, end of November day. They were not out marching for their health.

"Open up!" said Billy Dubh, pounding and shouting.

I opened the door, holding Bridget on my hip. "Good morning," I said in Irish.

They're looking for Patrick.

"Where is your husband?" Billy Dubh asked in Irish.

"In Galway City," I said, "trying to get work as a blacksmith. But every forge has too many already—"

"Stop speaking that gibberish!" said a tall officer, a thin-shouldered fellow with a heavy muffler wrapped around his neck.

Dubh spoke up. "She's saying her husband's not here," he translated to the officer.

"Lying," the officer said. "You peasants lie as easily as you breathe. Ask her where the pipes are. Tell her we'll tear this hovel apart if she doesn't produce them."

Dear God, it's Michael they want.

"They're arresting all the pipers in the area," Billy Dubh said to me. "And taking the pipes."

All pipers. But did they know Michael was *the* piper who recruited the people, then played at the demonstration?

"Pawned," I said. "He pawned the pipes ages ago."

"She says they're pawned," he told the officers. "Probably true. These people are pawning everything to get food. Now, I wouldn't have given a shilling for Irish pipes. Who could I sell them to? Not like the bagpipes you fellows use—Scottish, as they should be."

This must be the new regiment replacing the Connaught Rangers, who were too soft with us at the demonstration—Protestants all, probably.

"We do like a good marching tune, don't we, lads?" the officer said to the soldiers. He looked straight at me and started to sing:

> *Scarlet Church of all uncleanness*
> *Sink thou to the deep abyss*

He watched me, looking to see if I'd give away that I understood this English.

"You papists are Satan's spawn, you know," the officer said in an even tone. "You prove it with your devilish magic and charms and golden wands."

He meant the crozier. Bridget started to cry.

"Here's a lively one to cheer the wee-un," said a soldier standing behind the officer. He and the others sang:

> *Oh, Orangemen, remember King William*
> *And your fathers who with him did join*
> *And fought for our glorious deliverance*
> *On the green, grassy slopes of the Boyne!*

Bridget clapped.

"There's a bonny wee girl," a young soldier said. "She'll grow up beautiful and marry an Ulsterman."

The officer kept his eyes on me. "Some good-looking women in this place. Too bad they're so dirty," he said.

"Very clean girls at Bride's Hotel," said Billy Dubh. "One or two fit for an officer like yourself. I could arrange a good price, sir, and have your men looked after, too."

"Enough of this," said the officer. "Search the place."

"Mam, Mam!" Paddy called out. "I'm burning up! Bring me water! And Jamesy, too!"

In English!

"So, at least your children know more than gibberish," the officer said.

"The fever," I said in English. "My children have the fever."

Billy Dubh and the soldiers had heard Paddy call out for water and were repeating "fever" to one another.

"Your honor," said Billy Dubh, "I wouldn't want to risk your lordship's good health. I mind now that some pipes were pawned last year, and now I remember it being said they came from this townland, so—"

"Shut you up! We will go for now."

They went off singing:

> *And soon the bright Orange*
> *Put down the Green Rag*
> *Down, down, croppies, lie down!*

Paddy and Jamesy came beside me. "Weren't we great, Mam?" said Paddy. "It was Uncle Patrick told us, if ever soldiers came to the door, we should play as if we were dying of the fever!"

❖ ❖ ❖

"They know, Michael. They do—about the pipes and Patrick. Everything!" The words spilled out on Michael and Owen Mulloy, finally back from Galway City that night, the three of us outside the cottage.

"Only ter-ror-iz-ing," Owen said. "If they knew Patrick Kelly was related to you, they would have taken you away, Honora."

"Me?"

"To get information. Patrick's a wanted man with a price on him, but they don't have his name, only a description of him and of the crozier."

"A dozen pipers in the parish, Honora. No one will give my name," Michael said.

"You're very trusting, Michael," I said.

"Only those who took part in the demonstration could identify the piper. Who will admit that?" Owen said.

"I suppose you're right," I said. "The harvest is gone. The Sassenach beat us. What do they care that we marched and sang? Still, I'm glad you buried your pipes in Champion's shed. Better keep them there."

Michael nodded. "Here, Honora. Look." He dragged a sack forward. "A hundred pounds of oatmeal. Owen bought the same. The traders had a great laugh, telling us the meal we were getting was Irish oats bought by an English firm, taken to Manchester for milling, and then sold back to the Irish market—with a commission taken at each step!"

"When we could have milled our own oats!" I said. "What madness. The two of you must be knackered carrying those heavy sacks, and me keeping you with all my worries. Good night, Owen."

"Better if Owen comes in, Honora. We've some things to explain to you."

The children didn't wake as they usually would have when Michael returned. They were learning to sleep the hunger away.

"Nettle tea, Owen?" I asked as he sat on the rush stool.

"Holy Mother, have we come to that already?" he said.

"There's a sip of poitín left," Michael said.

He got the jug and we sat together near the fire. Plenty of turf. At least we're warm. Thank God.

Owen took a long drink from the jug. "Ah, that's better. Have to resist them some way."

Michael offered the jug to me. I shook my head. "Best have a drop," he said, and I did tip the jug back for a quick swallow. "We had to spend all three gold coins for the meal," he said.

"What!"

"The price was rising as we stood there," Owen said.

"This way, with the pratties in the pit, we'll have food through February if we eat one meal a day," Michael said.

"So we have no money at all."

"The roadworks will surely open in the spring. We've Oisín to sell, Honora. The winter's never killed us yet," Michael said.

"But if prices are going up already—"

"There's an invisible hand going to lower the cost of food," Owen interrupted me.

"What are you talking about?"

Then Owen tried to explain what they'd learned talking to the traders in the market and to the fellows Owen knew in the *Vindicator* office. Because the potato crop was half what it should be, we had to buy other food. A demand, Owen said, that let merchants charge higher prices. Other merchants, seeing the profit to be made, would bring in more food—a bigger supply—and the price would go down. The invisible hand setting things right.

But Irish people don't have cash money, I told Owen. A coin or two hidden, maybe, but no wages. Do they think there are factories lined up along the strand road offering jobs? And who are these "merchants" who will bring in cheap food—the gombeen men? the crooked traders?

"You've got it in one, Honora," Owen said. "The invisible hand doesn't work for Ireland."

"We tried to tell the trader fellows that," Michael said. "Our crops pay the rent. Our food is the potatoes we grow ourselves. No money comes into it."

Public employment had saved us at other bad times, Owen said, but now the government was wary. The invisible hand wouldn't work if the government interfered. Couldn't build a road that benefited one landlord, because that would place another at a disadvantage. Laying tracks for a railroad would help one company over another. Same problem with draining land. Public projects must not aid private enterprise. So nothing really useful could be done.

Insane. I asked Owen Mulloy was all this invisible hand blather only an excuse for the government to abandon us, let us starve?

Then Michael said a newspaper fellow had showed him an article from a London paper that said disasters like war or plagues or fire were sent by God to thin out the populations, get rid of the excess. The blight was a law of nature working as it should.

"Ireland without the Irish," I said, "just as Patrick Kelly told us."

⊕   ⊕   ⊕

December. We were in the heel of the winter now—storms raging, surf pounding. No fishing. Da tried again and again to launch his boat, but the waves pushed it back to shore before he could get into the channel. Many fishermen had already pawned their nets and tackle to buy whatever food was in the market—prices still going up. Da had been able to keep his nets because of the meal we had given him. He shared this food with the Leahys and Baileys. We'd given some of our meal to the Ryans, McGuires, and Dwyers. We couldn't eat while others starved.

No roadworks or employment of any kind. Michael went from forge to forge. "Pay me later," he said, but nothing.

A sad, sore Christmas. Patrick Kelly stayed away. In the chapel, Father Roche preached patience and handed out two-pound sacks of meal to each family. He'd bought them himself. No sign of the Lynches. In Dublin, Molly Counihan said.

After Mass, I walked back to the cottage with Mam and Granny.

"How many months are you, Honora," Mam said to me.

"Three, I think. Michael doesn't know."

"Tell him," Granny said.

I did that night, telling him I'd waited because at first I wasn't sure and then didn't want to worry him.

Michael put his finger on my lips, so gentle. "Whist, Honora, a stór. We'll manage."

By January, the hunger was telling on the children. When I hugged Paddy and Jamesy, I felt every rib. Katie Mulloy was very worried about her baby, James. "My milk is too thin, Honora, and he's so little flesh on his bones."

We ate once a day—in the evening, so the children could sleep through the night—oatmeal, mostly, with two potatoes from the pit shared among us. The boys looked with longing at the seed potatoes stored in the loft, but they understood that those could not be touched. "Only three months, and we'll plant them," Michael promised.

Michael had tried to sell the saddle, but Billy Dubh refused to pay one penny for it. He'd showed Michael the pawned clothes, nets, pots, and bedding that filled his cottage. He'd not take our blanket.

At least the soldiers had not returned. Perhaps the rain and muddy roads were keeping them in the barracks. Or they knew they had nothing to fear from us.

No chance of defiance now. It was hard enough to get through each day. I prayed for the government to forget the invisible hand and help us.

✧ ✧ ✧

February. Michael was first up every morning. He'd go down to the stream, fill the pot with clear, cold water, pour some in the trough for Champion and Oisín, and give them a bit of the hay left from the summer.

Michael and Owen had tried to sell the horses, but no one would pay for them, only take them for nothing.

"Keep them," I'd said. "The grass will be ready soon—Champion and Oisín will have more to eat than we will."

When Michael came in with the water, I'd have the fire going. We were grateful for bog lands and the great racks of turf Michael had lifted last summer. The boys would wake up and then we'd make a game of watching bubbles form on the bottom of the pot, then leap to the surface of the water.

"Boiling," Jamesy would say.

Paddy would drop a handful of nettles into the pot, careful to hold them by the stems so as not to get stung. We'd inhale the steam as it rose up.

"You did well," I'd say to the boys. "Thank God for good smells."

This morning, we sipped nettle tea from the one cup Michael hadn't sold.

A bright day, dry, not cold.

"I think I'll take the children down through Barna Woods to see if there's snowdrops still there from Saint Bridget's Day. Then we'll go to Mam and Granny. . . . Might find some cockles or mussels on the strand."

"Are you able for that much walking?" Michael asked.

"This little fellow inside me is determined. Moving around now."

"I was thinking I'd take out the window," Michael said. "Fill in the space with mud bricks and sell the glass. Might do it today."

He'd proposed this before, but I'd argued to keep the window. "Selling the window is like losing faith, Michael. When I watch the sun go down in Galway Bay, all those wonderful colors remind me that a God who created such beauty couldn't abandon us forever. Don't let's block out that light."

"But if this Jackson sees it . . ."

"He won't. Eight months until the rent's due. Then the harvest will be in, and this nightmare over. If we lose the window . . ."

"We can't lose it," Paddy said, listening to every word. "Nobody else has one. Only us."

"Paddy brags, Da," James said. "He tells the other boys only the Kellys have a window and Champion and uncles who pull fish from the sea. He says that soon the forge will be open and he'll learn to be a blacksmith and strike a mighty blow and—"

"It's not bragging," said Paddy, "it's only saying. And it keeps me from thinking about how hungry I am."

Now Bridget was crying. Neither praying nor bragging nor sunsets could help her little belly. I rocked her. No milk in my breasts.

"Here, boys—Da will let you sip the magic drink from his cup. Nice and slow, now. Feel how warm it is in your tummies."

I dipped my finger in the tea and let Bridget suck on it, then fished out the nettles. I put a pinch of the meal into the pot and stirred it with a stick as it cooked in the nettle water—better than plain water, Granny said.

"Mam heard from Mrs. Anderson, the coast guard captain's wife, that they've a load of American corn stored," I said to Michael. "The woman said it's being held in reserve."

"In reserve for *what*?" Michael said.

"That's what I want to find out," I said. "Michael, wouldn't you eat *one* prattie before you go? It's a long walk into Galway City. What if the roadworks open, and you're too weak to pick up a shovel?"

"Believe me, if there's work going, I'll do it. But I'm afraid we'll only be lining up for nothing again. I can wait until this evening to eat."

❖ ❖ ❖

"The government had ever so much trouble bringing over this Indian corn," Mrs. Anderson was saying.

Mam and I and the children stood listening to her.

"Or maize. It's also called maize," she said.

We were in the shed off the pier where the coast guard men kept their gear. Mrs. Anderson's husband, the captain, had his office here. As she showed us the sacks and sacks of the stored Indian corn, she pointed and smiled as if to say, Sir Robert Peel and the British people will not let you starve. But you won't get this food until we're sure you really are dying.

"The Corn Laws make importing American grain impossibly expensive," Mrs. Anderson said. "High tariffs on foreign grain. Necessary, I suppose, but the laws don't apply to Indian corn. Isn't that lucky?"

Mrs. Anderson went on about how Prime Minister Peel took taxpayers' money to secretly bring this Indian corn from America. It would be sold at low prices to the Irish peasants. We'd learn to eat corn instead of potatoes. Which would be a good thing, didn't we agree?

We said nothing.

Captain Anderson joined us, eager to let us know how much trouble the British government had gone to on our account. "Problem with this stuff," he said, putting his hand on a sack, "it rots if it's not ground at once. In America they have steel mills to grind it up. Stronger than ours. Now, this corn had to be unloaded, dried out in kilns for eight hours, cooled for a few days to prepare it for our mills. Here, look." He opened the top of the sack and took out a handful of the coarse meal, picking out a few pieces. "This is what the corn looks like in its raw form," he said, holding up a puckered kernel.

He handed it to me—hard as the hobs of hell.

" 'Peel's brimstone,' I've heard it called," I said.

He laughed. "You Irish have such humor! The meal would be finer and easier to cook if the corn were ground twice, but the government decided that wasn't necessary," he said. "Mr. Trevelyan—the man in the Treasury who's in charge—says that it wouldn't do to make charity too agreeable." Captain Anderson laughed again, but Mrs. Anderson and Mam and I looked down at the floor.

Captain Anderson wants us to be grateful for the efforts they'd made when our own grain could've been milled right here in Galway.

"And have you tried it, Captain?" I asked.

"Honora," Mam said.

But I wanted to know. "Have you?"

"I haven't had the chance," he said, "but I am sure it's quite nice if it's boiled for the prescribed time—two hours, I believe. Why don't I give you and your daughter a bit, Mrs. Keeley? Sort of an experiment—but don't tell anyone. We're not allowed to release this corn until there's real distress."

"But if you did release some now, people won't be tempted to eat their seed potatoes," I said.

"Ah, but it's other temptations we're concerned about," said Captain Anderson. "Wouldn't want to see the cornmeal sold for whiskey, would we? Can't give the press in London the chance to attack the government for helping the Irish people. The coast guard has to walk a careful line. In the past we were accused of being too softhearted."

❖ ❖ ❖

Later, inside the cottage, Da stopped me from raging against Captain Anderson. At least the man respected Da's knowledge of Galway Bay, asked his advice about currents and tides. Surely that food would be sold soon.

"Indian corn is like crushed-up stone. People won't know what to do with it," I said.

"It was tried years ago—made people sick," Granny said.

"Captain Anderson's a decent man," Da said. But Da was thinking of one thing only.

"We're going out tomorrow, Honora," he said. "The winter storms have passed and there will be fish."

"Finally a catch to sell at the Spanish Arch," Mam said.

"And Michael will be planting in a few weeks," Joseph said.

❖ ❖ ❖

Dusk had fallen by the time the children and I started up the hill to Knocnacuradh. It was more of an effort now to make the climb, all of us weaker. I felt the little life inside me stir—five months. I stopped to shift Bridget to my other hip. Jamesy was beside me, Paddy behind.

"Paddy, come on."

"I don't feel good, Mam."

"I know, I know. It's the hunger, but I'm taking some potatoes down from the loft tonight."

"I'm really sick, Mam," and he stopped and bent over. "It's cutting me, Mam. I feel like there's knives in my stomach."

Now he was on the ground, curled into a ball. I set Bridget down.

"Watch her, Jamesy. What is it, Paddy, what is it?" I asked, kneeling next to him.

"I only took a little, Mam, only a little."

"A little what?"

"From the bag the man gave Nana."

"That corn was too raw to eat!"

"I didn't know. It's hurting me! Mam, it's cutting me!"

"Try to throw up, Paddy." I put my finger down his throat. He gagged, but nothing came up.

"Mam, Mam, what's wrong?" said Jamesy. He started crying.

"It hurts," Paddy kept saying. "It hurts!"

I pushed harder. Paddy's muscles tensed, and finally a stream of yellow meal came out—kernels of corn mixed with blood gushed out of him.

"That's right, bring it up, a stór, good boy. Bring it up."

Bridget began crying, too—a high-pitched whimper—and Jamesy started weeping, tears running down.

"Blood, Mam, look! Blood—Paddy's bleeding!" he wailed.

Finally Paddy stopped retching. He took in a few breaths.

"Can you stand up, Paddy?"

"I can't, Mam."

"Put your arms around my neck. I'll take you on my back."

"I can't reach," Paddy said.

I got down low enough so he could roll himself onto my back. He held on to my neck. When I felt his weight on me, I straightened up very slowly, using Jamesy for balance.

"Jamesy, you carry Bridget."

We moved up the hill, Paddy lying along the length of my back. I stumbled. My stomach hit the ground. I lay flat for a moment.

"Mam, Mam," Jamesy said. "Get up. Get up, please."

Pushing myself up with my hands, I stood. Had the baby felt the bump? I had so little flesh to protect him.

Paddy clung to me.

"Hold on," I said to him, "hold on." Then I could see the cottage above us. "Michael!" I shouted. "Michael!"

"I'm coming, a stór!" Michael shouted. "I'm coming, Honora!"

He ran down for us, and then he had Paddy in his arms and Bridget. I must have fainted because the next thing I knew, I was on the straw mattress near the fire.

"I'm here, a stór. I'm with you. You're safe—safe."

But I wasn't safe. The labor pains started, and then my poor baby was born too soon . . . much, much too soon.

❖ ❖ ❖

Mam held me and whispered, "It's for the best, a stór. He couldn't have lived. He's in heaven."

I put my head on her shoulder and sobbed.

"Let me see him, Mam. Please let me see him."

"You shouldn't," she said, "a stór, you shouldn't."

"I need to, Mam, I need to see him, to tell him I'm sorry . . . I'm so sorry."

It was Michael brought him to me, holding the still little body in the hollow of his hands. A boy.

"Pray to Saint Grellan with me, Michael. He brought a stillborn child to life. Pray, Michael."

"Our son's in heaven, a stór," Michael said.

I touched the small wrinkled face, the tiny ears. Mam kept her arms around my shoulders.

I heard Katie Mulloy say to Michael, "There's a cillín near Saint James' well. We can—"

"You can't! You can't! Don't bury him in the cillín, Michael, not there! Please, not there! Not in unconsecrated ground! Unbaptized babies, strangers, and suicides? Not there!"

"We have to, Honora," Katie Mulloy said. "If Michael tried to bury him in the churchyard, Father Gilley would—"

I closed my eyes. "Please don't."

"Honora," Mam said, "he's with God, whatever the priests say. You must take care of your living children. Let Michael bury your son. It's for the best."

"I'll mark the place, Honora," Michael said.

Mam was telling Paddy and Jamesy that they had a tiny angel brother in heaven and when they said their prayers, he'd be listening. No matter what anyone might say to them, their brother was in heaven.

And then I left them. Some woman lay in our cottage during that next week, but she wasn't me—not Honora Keeley. I was somewhere else. Gone astray, and I had no wish to return.

❖ ❖ ❖

"Listen to me, Fairy Woman! Leave her!" Granny's voice. "Leave her! Come back, Honora." I felt her bony hands on my shoulders, shaking me, then other hands—Michael's—and I was sitting up, leaning against his chest.

He kissed my forehead. "You've had a long, long sleep, Honora, but we need you to wake up now."

"Here, alanna, eat." Mam's voice. She tipped the cup to my lips.

Nettle tea, I thought. But this was broth, fish broth. I tasted a bit of herring, a chunk of lobster. I chewed.

"Good girl, Honora," Michael said. "Your da and the boys brought home a fine catch."

Then Mam again: "I need your help, Honora, to sell the fish under the Spanish Arch. Come, Honora, wake up! We have to sell the catch now or it will rot."

"No fish-curing station after all the times the government promised us one." I didn't realize I was speaking out loud.

"You've come back to us, a stór," Michael said.

❖ ❖ ❖

"Fresh herring! Lobster! A-live-a-live-o!" I called out, holding up the red scaly bodies and the pinching claws of the lobsters, back again under the Spanish Arch, but no banter with the Claddagh women now, no jokes with the customers. Finally we'd had a decent catch, but we had to sell it now, today, or leave piles of fish to rot away in the market. No more time to heal my body or my spirit. We needed this money.

Three women watched us from the edge of the market, children with them, dressed very poorly. They came over to us. The oldest one, the granny probably, whispered, "Please, for the love of Our Lord." The two young women and their children stood behind her.

I looked at Mam. She nodded. I wrapped three lobsters in a sheet of newspaper and gave them to the women.

"Boil them," Mam said in Irish, "in a big pot."

From the look of them, they'd left pots and home far behind. Evicted most likely, and too proud or too afraid to go to the workhouse.

"Thank you," each woman said.

"God bless you."

Where were they sleeping? I wondered. A lean-to in a ditch? Two of the children were Paddy's and Jamesy's ages, and two were even younger. The mothers gripped their little hands so tightly. Strong women. They'll find a way to cook those lobsters.

At the end of the day, it was Mother Columba from the Presentation Convent who bought all the herring and lobster and gave us a penny a pound. Fair enough. How long ago it seemed since I'd gone to her parlor, asking to become a nun—another life.

"A nice fish stew for our students," Mother Columba said. "The government requires that we feed only our pupils and that they eat at school. Can't take food home. The official said the family might sell it. So difficult to deal with men who believe all Irish people are liars and cheats. They watch us. They watch Father Gilley. They watch Captain Anderson of the coast guard. They're suspicious of anyone they think is 'soft for the people.'"

"But who are *they*, Sister?"

"'They' is every official with a little authority, sent over from England. For them it's the chance of a lifetime. They're already asking for bribes from men who want a ticket to work on the roads, and the works are not even open yet."

"Bribing with what?" I said. "What is left?"

"Drink, a jug of poitín. There've been relief committees set up— local men, said to have some sense. But I've heard some landlords on the committee are only putting their tenants on the rolls so the six pennies a day will go to pay the rent."

"Six pennies a day?" I said. "That's all they'll pay?"

"If the works ever get started," said Mother Columba. "The time that's wasted with filling out forms! If you could see the mail we get from all the officials—two or three letters a day from this man Routh. We're required to account for every farthing, show we're following their rules. This Routh controls even the money we collect ourselves, the donations that come from America. We wanted to buy seed and give it to the farmers for planting. The government wouldn't allow it, said we'd be undercutting the seed merchants, interfering with the market. Ridiculous." She shook her head. "We can't waste ourselves in anger. We must pray. Stay sane. It's our only chance."

The four shillings we got from Mother Columba bought us nearly forty pounds of meal, at two farthings a pound with another five percent to the trader, his fee.

"Better buy it now, missus," the trader said. "The price will go up when the roadworks start and there's more money about."

"That doesn't seem fair," I said.

"We're allowed to make a decent profit. It's the law, missus," the little crook told us.

He gave us two bags, and I settled one on my back.

"Can you manage that, a stór?" Mam asked.

"I can, Mam."

The weight reminded me of the length of Paddy on me that night.

And then the fairy woman who'd stolen me away came up beside me: *Your baby is rotting away in the ground,* she said. *Gone to muck and mire, like the pratties. Your other children will die, too. Come away with me now. . . .*

"Honora . . . Honora!"

"What, Mam?"

"I've been calling your name. There's the cillín. We'll stop and say a prayer."

The cillín was only a bit of wasteland down the hill from the well of St. James, far from the graveyards at Bushy Park and Bearna. Nothing marked this enclosure, no stones with names and dates for the little ones who hadn't lived or for those who'd taken their own life.

I walked over to a mound of dirt. A bouquet of snowdrops lay on the top—Michael marking the grave. I knelt down with Mam next to me. No prayer came to me, only *I'm sorry, I'm sorry* going through my head.

Mam stood up and walked over to a boulder nearby. She picked up a pebble and started scratching on the side of the big stone.

"What are you doing, Mam?" I asked.

"I'm drawing a rooster like the one on the gatepost of our own Bearna graveyard," she said. "Your uncle Daniel carved it."

Uncle Daniel, dead before I was born. A young man, but he'd had some life.

"Fadó," she began, still drawing on the rock. "It was the second day after Jesus died and was buried in his tomb. The Roman soldiers who crucified him were cooking their dinner when the captain of the guard remembered that Jesus had said he'd rise up from the dead on the third day. What if his followers stole the body and pretended that he'd come back to life? Better put a stop to that.

"So the captain said, 'Right, boys, go back and put a big stone across the entrance to that fellow's tomb. By the time you get back, the rooster in this pot will be well cooked and you can have your dinner.'

"So they did the job and came back, ready to eat, but the captain kept asking, 'Are you sure? Are you sure the tomb's well barricaded?' Finally one said, 'There's no more chance of that fellow getting out of the tomb than there is of this rooster climbing out of that pot!'

"With that, the rooster jumped up onto the edge of the pot and started crowing: 'Slán Mhic Máire! The Son of Mary is safe!' he said. 'The Son of Mary is safe!'

"And the rooster says those same words every morning," Mam said, "to remind us Mary's Son is safe. And your son is slán too, a nún—safe with Mary. He is, Honora. You must believe that. And you must give him a name."

"I couldn't, Mam," I said.

"I called the little one I lost Johnny, for your father."

I said nothing.

"What's that Kelly saint called, the fellow had the gold crozier?"

"Saint Grellan," I said. "He brought another baby back to life, but not my son."

"Sometimes I think the ones the Lord loves, He takes to Himself quickly. Your baby won't starve or die in agony from the fever. An angel now, watching over the family. You'll find comfort in speaking to him, but you must call him by name. So . . . Grellan?"

I nodded.

"Grellan Kelly," Mam said, scratching the name on the boulder. "Don't listen to the fairy woman, Honora," she said as she finished. "Listen for the rooster's crow."

✧ ✧ ✧

It was March, St. Patrick's Day. Time to plant the eyes cut from the seed potatoes we'd managed to save, the pratties I had denied my children.

"Mam, I got ten from this one, see?" Paddy said. One by one he dropped the eyes into the pot.

"Good boy, Paddy," I said. "Watch yourself with the knife."

"May I have a go, Mam?" Jamesy asked.

"You're minding Bridget, Jamesy."

"But, Mam—"

"Do as I say. Don't be distracting me." I held the seed potato in my left hand as I sliced each eye.

When the roadworks had finally opened two weeks ago, Owen Mulloy and Michael had walked to Galway City before dawn to stand in line with thousands of other men, all waiting eight hours to go in front of the inspector and prove they were paupers because of the potato blight. Men "previously destitute" weren't allowed to work. Michael and Owen each had a letter from Father Roche that certified their "present destitution"—hard for two men who'd always found some way to feed their families.

"An awful process," Michael had said when he'd come home that first night long past dark.

He told me that many of the other men seeking work had no English. One stood there dumb while the clerk hurled questions at him he didn't understand: How many potato ridges did you plant? How many were diseased?

"I tried to translate," Michael had said, "but the clerk shouted, 'No colluding, no colluding!' and waved me away. The poor fellow knelt down before the official and started entreating him in floods of Irish. The official called for the soldiers, and they lifted the man up and carried him away."

And then after all that, Owen and Michael had gotten onto the gang only by giving the last jug of Patrick's poitín to the foreman.

Michael had sat a long time, staring into the fire.

"Come to bed, a stór."

He'd get only two or three hours of sleep before he'd have to walk the five miles back to Galway City, barefoot in the cold rain, to join the work gang.

How sad and defeated Michael had seemed that night. I'd wanted so to comfort him, kiss him, make love. But when he'd pulled me close to him, I'd held myself stiff and tight.

"We can't," I'd told him. "We can't risk another now."

"I know," he'd said, and turned away.

❖ ❖ ❖

But now, hope. Seeing the potatoes planted and growing will strengthen us all. And not a moment too soon. Bad weather had stopped the fishing again. Both the food Owen and Michael had bought in the fall and the meal Mam and I got in February were gone.

We relied on what the pennies Michael earned on the roadworks could buy—Peel's brimstone, the cheapest food sold in the market.

"Bridget's hungry, Mam," Jamesy said, the guardian now of his little sister—a year old next month, but she couldn't pull herself up and stand as the others had at her age and hadn't said a word beyond "Mama." Jamesy crawled with her, worried when she'd collapse after a short distance.

"Nearly cooked," I said to Jamesy.

He only nodded.

I was making a stirabout from the Indian corn. A slow process. I couldn't eat it. The look and smell of the stuff always brought back the awful night I'd lost baby Grellan. Paddy hated it, too, shuddering now as he ate, while Jamesy dug into the pot with a flat stick and I fed Bridget.

"After we dig the pratties, you'll never have to eat this again," I said to the boys.

"Will they be ready by my birthday, Mam?" Paddy asked.

"They'll take a longer time." I took his fingers, named the five months until the harvest. "And by Jamesy's birthday at Samhain, the pit will be full to the top with lovely white potatoes," I said. "But we must get back to work, Paddy. We have to have the eyes ready for your da tonight."

The moon would be near full for the next few days, so Michael could set the beds out at night after he came home from the roads.

"Now, aren't you glad we didn't eat the seed potatoes?" I said to the boys as the pile of eyes grew. "Every eye is a plant, and every plant will be twenty beautiful white potatoes. A generous plant."

Michael came home two hours after nightfall.

"Look what I did, Da!" Paddy pulled him over to see the pot full of eyes.

"Wonderful! Impressive!" Michael said.

"Mam helped, too," Paddy said.

"A good team," Michael said. He set down a sack.

"You got more meal," I said.

"Something better. Seeds for turnips and wheat. The seed merchants came around giving credit. They'll collect the money directly from the foreman before we're paid, with interest put on. What choice? We have to get the seeds and the potatoes in the ground now." He sat down near the fire. "I'll miss Patrick's help."

"Any word?" I said.

"Nothing. If he'd been taken, we'd know," he said.

"Are you talking about Uncle Patrick, Da?" Paddy said.

"Don't worry about your uncle Patrick. You're the man to help me set the potatoes this year."

"Come over to Bridget, Da," Jamesy said, pulling on Michael's hand.

"She's asleep, Jamesy."

"She's not, Mam."

I'm glad now there'd been no buyers for the cradle Michael had made. Jamesy got such pleasure from rocking her in it. Now he helped her sit up and look at Michael. "Go on, Bridget," Jamesy said. "Go on."

"Da," said Bridget. "Da, Da."

"Talking!" Michael said. "Talking!" He lifted Bridget from the cradle. "Bridget, my princess," he said, holding her up in the air. He winced then and set her back down; the strain of holding her up was too much, his back that bad.

"Good lad, Jamesy," I said. "Rest a bit before we start, Michael."

"Too much to do."

We were not the only family planting by moonlight. I saw dark shapes scattered across the hillside—the Mulloys, the Dwyers, the McGuires, the Ryans—all the fathers taking their only free hours to put in their potatoes. No time to sleep.

Michael turned the ground with the spade, and Paddy and I followed, dropping in the eyes, while Jamesy minded Bridget in the cottage.

In five nights, we had the potatoes planted, the seeds for the turnips and wheat sown.

✧ ✧ ✧

Two days later, Michael came home at midday. "No work," he said. "We're let off to do our duty days for the landlord, plant their crops. A week without pay."

The Scoundrel Pykes sometimes claimed as many as a hundred duty days a year, Katie Mulloy had told me, and never would feed the workers, let alone pay them.

Because we were subtenants and paid Owen Mulloy, Michael had been spared during the last six years. But the foreman on the road-works listened to no such explanations.

I was worried. I didn't like to think of Michael near Jackson and the old Major. But he assured me he and Mulloy would be in the fields far away from the house, two more bent backs, sowing the seed like the other tenants.

I hadn't been up to see Máire since that fall day before the failure. She'd sent down a note at Christmas with Thaddy Quinn, telling me to stay away. She'd let me know when it was safe to come back—give Thaddy the old Major's medicine. Nothing since then.

❖   ❖   ❖

"Did you see Máire?" I asked Michael late that night, the children long asleep.

"I did," he said.

"What did she say?"

"Nothing," he said.

"Nothing? What do you mean?"

"Thaddy Quinn came out to us in the fields. Jackson caught Máire giving food to the cottier women—only bits and pieces left over from the Major's dinner, but Jackson accused Máire of stealing and wanted her arrested. Captain Pyke stopped him, but now she can't leave the house. We were to hide in the stables and Máire would try to come out to us. We waited until long after dark. Finally Máire slipped out the door and started toward the stables. Then, out of nowhere, there's Jackson. He grabbed Máire and pushed her down. I started out to help her, but Owen and Thaddy pulled me back. 'Don't go out there,' Thaddy said. And I didn't. I hid in the stable while Máire lay on the ground. Your sister, Honora—who sacrificed herself for you, for us—there at Jackson's feet, and him cursing at her. I wanted to knock Jackson down and kick the life out of him. But I didn't move, Honora. What manner of a man have I become?" He slumped down, his head in his hands.

"A really brave man knows when to show some sense," I said, stroking his head. "Do you think Máire would want you arrested? She understood. She got up, went inside, and tended to her children. And it was our children you were thinking of when you didn't move, Michael.

I'm thankful Jackson didn't discover you together. He'd say you were plotting some outrage and get you both hanged."

He knew I was right. More troops in Galway City. The government saw each desperate attempt to get food, whether it was stealing a sheep, stopping a meal wagon, or poaching a salmon from the landlord's river, as an act of treason. Rebels one and all, no matter how weak, and in league with the outlaw Ribbonmen in the mountains. The Sassenach still feared the fury of the O'Flahertys.

Chapter 13

Spring brought field greens to eat. I mixed in birds' eggs with the corn mush. We survived, watched the green shoots of the potato plants rise, and prayed the harvest of 1846 would take away our hunger.

Summer came. The boats went out. So much herring we couldn't sell it all. We gave the fish to all our neighbors. Mam could buy a few sacks of meal and still put money away toward the rent. Michael said our wheat crop would bring enough for our rent. After all, we won't have to worry about food—we'd have the pratties. A terrible winter, the worst in memory, and the blight the fiercest enemy ever sent against the Irish, but we had survived.

And now, Granny told the family, we will fulfill our vow and join the pilgrimage to St. Mac Dara's Island, to thank him as we promised. We'll go on his feast day, July 16—the bad times surely over.

At first, Michael said he couldn't come with us. I asked why. The new Whig government had closed the roadworks. Mulloy told us these fellows got elected by promising to stop helping the rebellious Irish. Peel had been too soft.

"You'll not miss any pay," I'd said to Michael.

But he'd said the land needed attention and so did Champion, in foal again. Two months since she'd gone to Barrier. Sir William Gregory had let Owen and Michael put off the payment of Barrier's fee.

Champion wouldn't deliver until March, but it was well to keep an eye on her in the early stages.

"Is it the boat trip?" I'd asked him. "No one ever died of seasickness yet. The Bay's meant to be calm, and it's not like we're headed for Amerikay. We'll leave at first light and be at Ard by midday, and then it's only three miles to the island.

"You have to go," I'd said. "It's you I want to thank Mac Dara for, Michael. Working so hard for us, pushing your body. You could have ridden away that first morning, gone off adventuring on Champion, but instead you married me. Brought life to the land, fathered three children, and saved us this winter."

He kissed me and said he'd come with us, surely.

⟡　⟡　⟡

We were a grand proud family sailing down the center of Galway Bay in Da's púcán. We had a beautiful summer morning and a following wind for our trip to Mac Dara's Island.

A tall sailing ship moved through the channel ahead of us. The passengers were tenants from the Gore estate, going to Canada. Da told us they'd given up their land for the price of their passage rather than being evicted with nothing—a stark enough choice.

The people being sent away stood at the ship's rails, staring at the green hillsides along the Bay.

Da said that the sorry-looking vessel, its sails patched and riding low in the water, was an old slaver that hauled timber from Canada now. Stones had always been used as the ballast needed for the return voyage, but now Irish exiles provided the weight, Da explained. Lots of these old slave ships were back in service now, Dennis said, cramming passengers into the cargo space. A good few sank in the middle of the ocean.

How thin my brothers were. Dennis, at twenty-one, had an old man's sunken face. Josie held their wee girls, both so frail. Joseph was nineteen, but he had a young boy's slight body. Hughie, almost thirteen, seemed all bones. Had lack of food stunted them for good and all?

The hillsides bordering the Bay were bright with green and the white flower of potato plants. Surely the pratties will put us right—not long now.

✧ ✧ ✧

The hungry winter had marked the Keeley cousins at Ard. The huge big men who'd come to Máire's wedding were gaunt now but determined to make the annual pilgrimage to the island as was done for a thousand years. We'd come from Bearna to join them a good few times. Always great fun. There'd be dancing and curragh races after the devotions. Máire and I had shocked them all by winning the girls' race twice—powerful rowers when we pulled together.

I prayed for Máire as we climbed up to the ancient chapel on the island—only small, but lovely—built of gold-colored rocks and set between the sea and sky. Michael had recovered himself after the boat trip, breathing in the sweet, fresh air, carrying Bridget as we followed our boys, who ran ahead, delighted with all these new cousins.

I'd explained to Michael that Mac Dara, the patron of fishermen, was never called by his given name, Sionnach—Fox—because the animal was so unlucky for the fishermen, it couldn't even be referred to. "Always Mac Dara—Son of Dara."

And now on the summit we knelt near his chapel and thanked our saint for helping us survive. "Please bless every family. Bring Máire home. Let the pratties be healthy and abundant," I prayed.

I showed Michael how to make the sacred pátrún, walking around the fallen stone huts where Mac Dara's monks had lived: three times in the direction of the sun, two hundred people circling and praying.

The Ard Keeleys provided the feast—a dizzying amount of food— lobsters, oysters and mussels, wild strawberries, dulsk.

"Easy now," Granny cautioned Paddy and Jamesy. "If you eat too fast or too much you'll get sick." The boys took a good long time, chewing and swallowing, grinning at me as they ate. Thank you, God.

We sat together on the strand to watch crews race their curraghs in the Atlantic waters around the island. Still strong rowers in Ard/ Carna despite the hard winter.

And then the dancing began. Four of the Ard Keeleys were great lilters. They made such powerful music, we hardly missed the fiddle and pipes—pawned, of course, but, "Sure we'll get them back when the pratties are dug." Jamesy and Paddy got a great laugh at Michael whirling me around in the reel.

Michael and I collapsed next to one of the turf fires, all of them bright flares against the night sky and the dark sea.

"Come with me," Granny said. She was standing above us.

She led Michael and me to the far shore of the island, where slabs of stones met the water.

A white-haired man with a long beard stood with two younger fellows.

"Martin O'Malley," Granny said. "With a message for you, Michael."

The famous smuggler. Here. What . . . ?

"Someone's waiting to meet you," Martin O'Malley told Michael. "He's at Ballynahinch." Then to me he said, "There'll be a curragh waiting for you here at first light. Take it and follow me. Now, go back to the dancing." Not another word from him.

"The family will take your children to Ard," Granny said. "We'll wait for you there."

The last reel finished. The dancers slept. As the sky lightened, Michael and I walked with quick, quiet steps to the shore. Martin O'Malley had launched his curragh. It bounced in the waves, held steady by the two young men—his sons?—at the oars. We pushed the second boat to the water's edge, then jumped in.

Michael wedged himself in the bottom of the boat as I gripped the oars: thumbs on the edge, right wrist over left. It was years since I'd rowed, but my muscles remembered. A thrust out, oars above the water, then the quick plunge down and we were launched into the glistening tide, rushing over the sea, following the other curragh.

The sun was full up when Martin O'Malley waved at us and turned his boat toward Aran. I rowed into the inlet and up onto the small strand.

"Where are we?" Michael asked, a little shaky but sound enough.

"I hope on the coast near the river that goes into Ballynahinch Lake. We're to meet him on the island with Grace O'Malley's tower. We'll have to carry the curragh to the river. . . ."

"I'll give you a hand." Patrick stood on a rock above us.

❖ ❖ ❖

The river ran fast enough to lift our curragh over the rapids. Patrick and Michael held tight to the sides of the curragh as I steered us into Ballynahinch Lake and rowed toward the island where the square keep Donal O'Flaherty built for his wife three hundred years ago stood covered in ivy.

"This island was a crannog," said Patrick as he and Michael pulled the curragh up onto the island's shore. "Thousands of years ago, people settled here because it was a handy place to defend. Still is."

We followed Patrick through the doorway of the castle. I saw the date, 1546, the year Donal married the pirate queen who'd one day lead two hundred ships against the English and confront Queen Elizabeth in her own London palace. But she'd come here as a sixteen-year-old bride. Grainne, in Irish, Grainne Ní Maille—my granny's name, her clan and mine.

Now Patrick Kelly hid here, fighting his own campaign against the Sassenach. I sniffed the air. Financing his war in the traditional way by distilling poitín.

"Impressive," said Michael, walking across the dirt floor to a forty-gallon tin tub set inside Grace O'Malley's old fireplace. A big wooden barrel of mash was nearby.

"So this is where the whiskey comes from," I said.

"It is," Patrick said.

He and Michael examined every bit of the still, explaining to me how the mixture of sprouted barley was dried and crushed and mixed with hot water, then stored, filtered through branches of evergreen and oak set in the bottom of the cask, then forced through a long copper wire—a worm, they said. On and on, the two of them went—throwing words like "wart" and "singling" and "doubling the run"—until I said, "That's enough!"

"And would you like a sample?" said Patrick.

We drank Patrick's poitín and ate slices of cold salmon on thick brown bread. "Baked in the ovens of Ballynahinch House," he said. "The cook is friendly to us."

Us?

"And the salmon?"

"Caught in the landlord's river, but Thomas Martin turns a blind eye. After all, his father was Martin O'Malley's partner in the smuggling."

"But it's not smuggling you're doing now," Michael said.

Patrick said nothing.

We sat eating salmon and brown bread, chewing and chewing and chewing—the joy of it.

"Not smuggling," Patrick said. "It's better you don't know too much, but our fellows have put the fear of God in a good few landlords, agents, and bailiffs and feed a fair number of people, too. But now it's time for me to go."

"A shame to leave such a place," Michael said.

"The sheriff's put a price of twenty pounds on my head. Too tempting for informers. Happened after Ballinglass. You remember the place, Michael?"

"I do. On the Mount Bellow Road," Michael said. "Da played for a wedding there. He took me—a tidy little place."

"It is," said Patrick. "The people had drained the bog and set themselves up rightly near the river Shaven—sturdy cottages with vegetable gardens. Like everyone else, they lost half their potatoes, but the other crops had come in. They'd paid their rent, eaten Indian corn, and survived."

"As we all did," I said, thinking they were lucky with the vegetable gardens.

"Four months ago, I passed through—Friday, the thirteenth of March it was," Patrick went on. "The people were planting seed potatoes, and I'd stopped to help. I was asleep in a shed when I heard this racket. When I stepped out I saw the bailiffs coming with soldiers. The whole village was to be cleared, all tenants evicted. This troop of Red Coats on big horses rode into the center of the village. A force to be reckoned with, no question. The might of the British Empire. They'd fought Napoleon to a standstill and were defeating the tribesmen of India at that very moment. And who were they off to subdue this morning? Women. Women and little children and old men. And the great military objective? To force the people of Ballinglass off the land. Why? Because that's what the landlord, Mrs. Gerard, wanted. The rent was *paid*. Remember that: *paid*. But she didn't want rent, she wanted them gone.

"A crew of men began tumbling the houses. They had this battering ram, a massive tree trunk, tied around with chains attached to a team of horses so the men could swing it forward. These cottages were built of stone—strong. Didn't fall easily. They battered the walls of that first cottage over and over before it finally collapsed.

"An old man went up to the officer in charge. 'Please, Captain,' he said, and began telling him that many families in Ballinglass had sons in the British army, that his own boy was a soldier in India. He turned to the soldiers and begged them to stop the battering-ram boys from destroying the homes where their comrades were born. 'We paid the rent,' he kept repeating.

"The captain turned his horse away, but the man held on to his boot. Then the captain kicked the man. He fell. Another soldier got off his horse and started kicking him, too. The Red Coats were laughing.

"I had carried Grellan's crozier out with me, and I ran into the center of the soldiers, slashing at them with it. They left the old man and rushed at me. Luck was with me and I was able to get on that first fellow's horse and ride away.

"Only misfortune for the people of Ballinglass. All evicted, their cottages pulled down, driven from the townland. And worst of all, many of those soldier sons of theirs were killed fighting in India at the very time the British army was evicting their families."

"Those poor people," I said.

"At least you tried to help, Patrick," Michael said.

"Did them little good and gave myself away. Too close to Gallagh, Michael. Grellan's crozier was recognized, and so was I, my name was given to the soldiers. Watch yourselves."

"But there are so many Kellys. Unless—do they know you're Michael's brother?" I asked.

"It won't matter. If they come, tell them the truth—I've gone to Amerikay."

"Amerikay," Michael repeated. "You, gone from Ireland. Hard to take it in."

"Not going forever, Michael. There's men and money in Amerikay will be the saving of Ireland. There'll be Irishmen grasping Grellan's crozier and swearing an oath to fight for the freedom of their native land."

Patrick unwrapped a long, narrow bundle, and there it was: the bachall, the battle standard of the Kellys.

A shaft of sun came through the ivy-shrouded window slits, bright on the crozier, making the red gold staff shine—a fire in this dim place. Circles and spirals twined together along the shaft, with the head of some mythic animal on the top. We had made this—we Irish.

"We *were* a great and mighty people," I said to Michael.

"And will be again," Patrick said. "The Wild Geese will return."

I remembered Granny's stories of the Wild Geese, the Irish soldiers defeated by William of Orange, who joined the armies of Europe. Sometimes she'd point to a formation of geese flying over Galway Bay. "Na geana fiadhaine." She'd say, as Patrick had, "They will return."

Michael took Grellan's crozier from Patrick. He tightened his fist around it until the muscles in his arms knotted, hearing warrior songs in his head.

Patrick needs to fight, so let Patrick go gather an army and come back. But let us have our victory in Knocnacuradh. Who's the braver— the man who dies for Ireland or the man who lives for Ireland?

"Let me see the crozier," I said to Michael.

But as he passed it to me, Patrick reached out and took the staff. "A geis against women touching Grellan's crozier," he said, and wrapped it up again.

"A geis . . . ," I started, and then stopped. Patrick was going and taking the crozier with him. Michael was staying, choosing me, us, life.

"Where in Amerikay?" Michael was asking Patrick.

Patrick looked at me. "Walk down to the shore with me," he said to Michael.

"Oh, for feck's sake, Patrick. Anything you say to me, you can say to Honora. I'll tell her anyway."

"It's only to protect her."

"Don't tell me, then," I said.

"Chicago," Patrick said.

"Never heard of it," I said.

"In the middle of Amerikay. Lots of work there, and fewer Englishmen than in New York and Boston."

"Chicago," Michael said. "Chicago," memorizing the strange name.

Michael put out his hand and Patrick took it, then Michael put his hand on his brother's shoulder.

"God bless. Safe journey, Patrick," Michael said, and hugged him.

Patrick stood with his arms at his sides, finally lifted them, embraced Michael, then stepped away.

"I'll be back," he said. "I know where to find you—on your neat, bright farm where the fields take the sun."

"I'll have the forge up when you come back," said Michael.

"You will," said Patrick.

I heard footsteps outside the castle doorway.

"My transport," Patrick said. "Stay in here until we're gone."

I put out my hand, but Patrick didn't take it. Instead he kissed me on my cheek, and I could see that Michael was pleased at the gesture.

"A sister for you at last," Michael said.

"A sister," said Patrick.

Patrick pulled a small package from his pocket and handed it to me. "Here are seeds from the Aran potatoes. The blight never came out there—healthy."

"Seeds? Potatoes don't have seeds," I said.

"They do. The early fruit has seeds. Keep them through the winter and plant them."

At the doorway, Patrick turned and tossed a small bag to Michael, who caught it in one hand.

"What's this, Patrick?" he asked, but Patrick was gone. Michael opened the bag and poured three gold sovereigns into my hand.

"But Patrick will need this money. I'll go after him. We can't take . . ." he said.

"We can and be grateful," I said. "Sit down here and let the man leave. Too late to start back now. We'll sleep the night in Grace O'Malley's castle."

⬦   ⬦   ⬦

I woke to darkness around me and no Michael. "Michael," I called. "Michael?" I found him standing on the edge of the island, staring across the lake to the farther shore. "Shhh," he said to me. "Look."

A herd of Connemara ponies drank from the lake. The stallion stood over his mares and foals, head up, sniffing the wind, white in the moonlight. Michael turned to me.

"I'll miss Patrick. Even when I didn't see him I knew he was out there somewhere—tending a field, cooking up a jug, talking revolution, somewhere. And then when he did appear we would talk about our father, the piper, my grandfather Murty Mor, and my mother. The only one left who knew them. Will I ever see him again?"

"He said he'd be back, Michael. You heard him."

Michael pointed to the stallion. "Do you think that horse, given the expanse of Amerikay, would come back? He'll be off, and who could blame him? Some crave freedom more than anything, more than . . ." Michael stopped. He stared at the herd.

I took his hand. "That stallion and his herd look sleek enough now with a month of summer's grass inside them. But they'll be skin and bones in the winter, not like Champion with her snug, mud-walled stable and a big foolish fellow bringing her hay and watching over her," I said.

"But Champion might prefer that savage fellow to Gregory's tame stallion."

"I don't hear Champion complaining," I said.

I pulled his head down and kissed him. We went back to the castle. We made love where Grace O'Malley had lain, and I became a pirate queen myself, wild, not holding back. We'd survived.

Chapter 14

*P*ut your candle down, Paddy—there, on top of the well so Saint Enda can see it," I said. "He'll keep the flame burning as a sign of his protection."

Hundreds and hundreds of people, from every townland, filled the tree-shadowed clearing around Tobar Enda this last Sunday in July, 1846—more than on any Garland Sunday in memory.

St. Garlick Sunday, Dubh Crom Sunday—strange names. Granny made sure to tell Paddy and Jamesy that it was Lughnasa we were celebrating, really—August 1, the beginning of the harvest—and the Irish people had been coming together on this day at wells and lakes, rivers and streams, on hilltops and mountainsides, since long before Christ was born.

Granny had stayed with us during the two weeks following the trip to Mac Dara's Island and spent hours telling her tales to Paddy, Jamesy, and little Bridget. Paddy interrupted one of her stories about the good people and their ways to ask her if the fairy woman who'd taken their mam for that week after their baby brother died would ever come back. Granny had told them straight out to stop worrying. The fairies didn't dare attack a woman who was brave in a boat, and I was that. She'd smiled at me, ready to make a saga of *my trip*, the journey to Grace O'Malley's castle, but I'd had to tell her, "Ná habair tada." She'd agreed.

"Leave the candle, Paddy. Now."

The line bunched and stopped. Coughs came from behind us. Michael waited with Jamesy, holding Bridget. Mam and Da, Granny, and my brothers had finished the ritual, tipping over their lit candles, making a wax puddle, then anchoring the candles in the spilt wax. The stone lip of the well and the surrounding rocks held a votive army that would keep away all harm and let the pratties stay healthy. Please God.

But now Paddy whispered to me that he wanted to keep his candle, take it home.

Scold him, give him a good shake—I could almost hear the thoughts of the mothers behind me: Don't let a six-year-old defy you.

But it wasn't defiance I saw in Paddy's face.

"Please, Mam, please," asking me the way I was begging Our Lord. "Please, please!" He turned to Michael. "I need it, Da, I do."

Michael looked at me. "Wouldn't you think, Honora, that Saint Enda could see the candle burning up in Knocnacuradh?"

"I would."

"You may bring it home, Paddy," Michael said.

"Oh, thank you, Da, thank you!"

I took Paddy's hand and we walked together over to Mam and Da and Granny, who were standing with Miss Lynch.

"Good evening, Miss Lynch," I said.

"Your boy, Honora. Father Gilley would not approve. The candles are not to be taken."

"I know, Miss Lynch, but Paddy wants to guard his light."

Michael said, "What harm?"

"Objections were raised to giving out the candles," Miss Lynch said. "Mightn't the people try to sell them? But my brother, Nicholas, told the others on the relief committee that the people would be too afraid of offending their saint."

Her brother, Nicholas. I'd heard he'd returned from his travels, married with a young son, though his family stayed in Dublin. He was taking over for his father.

"After all, they had funds left over," she went on.

"Funds left over, Miss Lynch?" asked Michael.

"Why, yes. The new government ordered that all types of emergency relief works be ended, the food depots closed. Nicholas said that Sir John Russell—he's the new prime minister . . ."

"We know the name, Miss Lynch," Michael said, "but why no relief if there's money left? I don't understand."

"Sir John Russell—my brother says his nickname is 'the Widow's Mite' because he's practically a dwarf and married to Lord Ribblesdale's widow—is a Whig and was a friend of O'Connell, but his government has turned against the Irish."

"The money, Miss Lynch," said Da.

She explained that because the relief committee had been required to *sell* the cornmeal, it had made a profit of six hundred pounds, which now couldn't be spent on any kind of help for the people for fear we'd become dependent on charity. But Father Gilley had taken two pounds for the candles.

"Six hundred pounds left over," Michael said, shaking his head.

There'd been so many weeks when Michael hadn't been paid for his work on the roads, and now to find there'd been money all the time.

"Miss Lynch?" Michael started.

I knew that tone. Michael doesn't rile easily, but once he . . . Will he start thundering at Miss Lynch? But Michael caught himself on, stopped.

Miss Lynch was going on to Mam, "We've prayed for a bountiful harvest, and I'm sure Our Lord will hear our prayers."

✧ ✧ ✧

Michael and the children and I trudged along the Bay and up the hill to Knocnacuradh alone. No céili in Bearna on this Lughnasa.

"Why is Miss Lynch still fat, Mam?" Paddy asked me.

Michael laughed. "A good question, Honora. She has the only round face in six townlands."

"We'll all be plumped out soon enough," I said. "There's bilberries to eat when we get home. You were right not to go for her, Michael. She's no idea what our life is. Won't let herself see."

"Six hundred pounds," Michael said.

It began to rain.

"See, Mam?" said Paddy. "All those candles at the well will surely go out, but Saint Enda will see mine and make our pratties grow."

"Good man, Paddy," Michael said to him. "God helps him who helps himself."

That night I asked Michael, "Was it right to give in to Paddy?"

"When I saw him standing there, so determined, I thought, That's Honora as a child. So sure of herself, and—"

"Me? I was a docile little girl."

Michael laughed and kissed me.

✥   ✥   ✥

Even though I blew out the candle when Paddy went to sleep and lit it first thing in the morning, after seven days only the smallest stub of wax remained.

"I think that boyo's given its all," Michael said to Paddy.

"It's burning," he said.

A blue flame did cling to a bit of wick, a pinpoint of light in the dark of the cottage.

Another dull day, no sun since last Sunday. And the pratties?

"Green, Honora, and growing," Michael said, reading my thoughts.

"Should we walk up and look?" I said. "It's a soft rain, and a run would help these lads sleep."

"Can I bring the candle, Da?"

"Good idea. Maybe you could hold it up to heaven and let the last of it burn out, and then, then . . ." Michael looked at me.

"We'll plant the stub in the ground," I said. "It will grow into a tall candle."

"By harvesttime?" Paddy asked.

"Could be," Michael said.

Paddy'd been counting off the months. The early potatoes would be ready soon and the full crop next month.

Paddy ran ahead with Michael. I carried Bridget, and Jamesy held my hand as we stepped out into the drizzle.

We'd only just started up toward the ridges when the rain stopped. Good, I thought. Good. But then . . .

"Michael! Look, the fog!"

Only wisps of it floated down at first. Cold fingers of fog touched my face and prickled my nose. It was getting heavier, solid now, winding itself around each of us, separating one from the other.

Holding tight to Bridget, I pulled Jamesy close and reached out for Michael. Paddy stepped between us. We stood still, the five of us, not able to see beyond ourselves.

"It went out! The fog killed my candle!" Paddy cried.

And then the stench came, mixing with the fog, choking us.

Michael started running, with Paddy after him. I ran, too, Bridget on my hip, Jamesy coming behind me.

Michael and Paddy disappeared into this evil mist. I caught up with them at the first potato ridge. Michael bent over the plants, which were shrouded in fog. I knelt down, trying to see, still holding Bridget, Jamesy next to me. Paddy stood apart.

"Michael, are they—"

"Black," he said. "All black." He got up, ran to the next ridges.

Please God, let some be sound. Please, please . . .

"These are blighted, too," Michael shouted back to us. The fog muffled his voice as he reached the higher ridges. "Dead . . . This one, too . . . dead, dead, dead . . ." Fainter and fainter . . .

I sat down in the damp and ruined field, holding Bridget against my shoulder, Jamesy on my lap.

Paddy stayed rigid and apart. "I didn't mean it," he whispered to me. "I should have left the candle at the well. I didn't mean it, I'm sorry, I didn't mean it."

I turned him to me, took his face in my hand, and said, "Paddy, you're a fine, sturdy lad and God loves you. You did nothing wrong."

"But why, Mam? Did I make Saint Enda angry? Why did God do this to us?"

"God didn't send the blight," I said.

Michael returned. "Honora, they're all gone. All. Every ridge. Nothing. No potatoes at all. Worse than last year."

"I'm sorry, Da. I'm sorry," Paddy said between hiccuping cries. "I shouldn't have asked for the candle."

Michael knelt down and took Paddy in his arms.

"He thinks God's punishing him," I said.

Jamesy and Bridget were wailing now. Michael looked at me. Tears filled his own blue eyes, so like Paddy's. He blinked them away and put his hands on Paddy's shoulders.

"You did nothing, and neither did God. The old blight is a fierce enemy, and it got our pratties again, but an Irish hero doesn't cry when the enemy attacks. He fights back. He protects his family."

Paddy's chest was heaving, but he'd stopped sobbing.

"Would Cuchulain give up, or Finn McCool? Would they? . . . Answer me."

"They wouldn't," Paddy said.

Jamesy sobbed softly, but he was listening.

"And are you a soldier, Paddy?"

"I am," he said.

"Me too," said Jamesy.

"And we've Mam and Bridget as our warrior queens," Michael said.

"You do indeed," I said.

Michael stood up. I moved over to him. He put his arm around me, pulling Bridget and me into his chest. Paddy and Jamesy stood between us, holding our legs, Paddy's face in my skirt.

Through the fog, I heard shouts going from glen to glen. Then the keening started—in Rusheen, Shanballyduff, Cappagh, and all the townlands around us. I stood silent, leaning against Michael. He held the children and me to him. As the sorrowful sounds and evil-smelling fog wrapped themselves around us, I prayed.

✥ ✥ ✥

November—the eve of Samhain. Ghosts walked the roads—not the souls of the dead, but real people dying.

A week now since Mary Ryan had come for me in the early morning. "Hurry, Mrs. Kelly, come quick."

A good, reliable girl, Mary. I'd left the children with her the few times there'd been a catch to sell in Galway City during this storm-cursed autumn of no fishing. She'd bring the twins and baby Thaddy, and the children would play together. I'd feed them whatever we were eating—stirabout or a bit of turnips—and give her something to take to Tessie. "When the roadworks open, your da will get work and you can share with us," I'd tell her. She was a proud little thing.

But the roadworks hadn't opened. No help of any kind came from the government. Our three gold coins were gone, with the guts of the winter ahead of us.

Michael and I had run with Mary to the Ryans' cottage. We'd found Tessie rocking her poor wee baby Thaddy—only a swollen belly and four sticks of arms and legs. The twins, Henry and Albert, sat near a sputtering fire, holding hands.

"He stopped crying." Tessie looked up at us. "I thought he was asleep."

But baby Thaddy was dead.

"Is he . . . ?" Mary asked me.

I only nodded.

She started weeping. I held her. Tessie began to scream—not keening, howling.

Something was slamming into the outside wall of the cottage. Michael went out to see. "Neddy is tumbling the cottage so they'll take them into the workhouse," he said when he came back.

Hours before Tessie finally laid the little corpse on a straw pallet.

Michael had tried to stop Neddy, reminding him that the workhouse was worse than prison—husband and wife separated, children kept from their mothers, useless labor demanded of the inmates, meals of spoiled food, a terrible risk of disease. Entering the workhouse was a shame against a family for generations. Michael told Neddy he should wait—there was talk that the landlords would have to give employment.

But Neddy had hacked at the walls like a man demented. Complete destitution was required in order to enter the workhouse. The Ryans must erase themselves from the estate, become "homeless paupers." An official would come later to confirm that Neddy had destroyed their cottage.

I offered to keep the children. Maybe Neddy and Tessie could go . . . I didn't say "begging," but Tessie knew what I meant. Tessie wouldn't hear of it, nor would she leave Mary. She needed Mary. The twins obeyed only her. And Mary wouldn't leave her little brothers.

Neddy said that he could carry the body of baby Thaddy to the workhouse to prove their need.

And then Albert had called out, "Paddy!" and there was my son in the doorway, staring at the little body.

The Ryans went that very day. "We'll eat tonight," Tessie said.

Paddy lay awake that night. Michael sat with him, stroking his back and telling him that soldiers fought even harder after a comrade fell in battle. He must be very brave in honor of Thaddy. Paddy nodded and finally fell asleep.

✧ ✧ ✧

Now on this Samhain's eve, a week later, Paddy seemed bent on tormenting Jamesy. "I remember when we ate three times every day,"

Paddy was telling him. "I could have as many pratties as I wanted, and Mam would say to me, 'Go on, have another, my sturdy lad.'"

"You're lying, Paddy, lying! Isn't he, Mam? Three times? He's lying!"

"We did, Jamesy," I said. "You remember the apples, don't you, and the nuts we had last Samhain? And the great feast on Mac Dara's Island?"

"I do, Mam."

"We'll have food like that again."

"But I remember Uncle Patrick better than you do, and Oisín," Paddy said.

"I remember Oisín," Jamesy said.

"Of course you do." Michael and Owen Mulloy had gotten two pounds from the Biany people for the colt. A favor, really—Oisín wasn't a draft horse. Bred to race. And the money'd not bought enough.

"But I remember Oisín being born. You don't mind that, Jamesy. That was in the before times and—"

"You two stop this," I said. "Now, Jamesy, sit with Bridget and give her a sip of the nettle tea. Take some yourself. It warms your belly."

"It doesn't," Mam," he said. "It goes through me and makes my bum ache something awful."

"Come, Paddy," I said. "We'll look for Da."

We walked out in front of the cottage and stood on the drumlin.

"Paddy, why are you taunting Jamesy? Why won't you let him have his part of remembering?"

"Mam, he's too little to really remember. But I'm not. I know what it feels like to have a full belly. And when I say he doesn't, then he says he does, and he makes up the memory and his belly feels full too for a bit. . . . You see?"

"I see, a stór."

We stood looking down the hill for Michael. The roadworks had finally opened two days ago, but Michael was so weak that I was afraid he'd collapse climbing the hill.

If only the work had begun right away in August after the failure, when he'd been stronger. Those first three months . . . If not for Patrick's coins, would any of us be alive?

High food prices took that money so quickly. No cheap Indian corn this year, though the coast guard depot was piled high with it. Captain Anderson told Da that Trevelyan said Peel had been wrong to sell it for so little last year and interfere with trade, so the corn was being held. "For what?" Da had asked. The captain didn't know.

I saw him. "Michael! Michael!"

Michael was carrying something. I hugged Michael and took the bag. He'd been able to trade the saddle for one week's food. We'd have to eat very little every day. Paddy held Michael's hand and we pulled him inside, where it was warm. At least we had turf.

I cooked an inch of the meal into a porridge, stirring it in boiling water, while Michael went out to Champion, carrying our one tin cup.

Michael came back in, gave me the cup, and I poured the contents into the meal.

"Is that Champion's blood, Mam?"

"It will give you strength, Paddy."

How many times could Michael nick the vein in Champion's neck without harming her?

I held Bridget up, took some of the gruel on my finger, and put it between her lips. "Take it, take it." She shook her head and pulled away from me. I held her mouth open and coated her tongue with the stuff, then gave her a sip of water.

Jamesy watched, afraid. "Why won't she eat, Mam?"

"She's trying, Jamesy. She'll eat it. You eat yours, a stór, very slowly."

"Eat, Bridget," Paddy said, "or your stomach will blow up like Thaddy Ryan."

"Thaddy? Thaddy?" Bridget had been asking for him, and for Mary, too. "Mary? Sing?"

Mary had a sweet voice and had often sung "The Singing Bird" to Bridget.

But now Jamesy tried: "*I have heard the blackbird pipe its tune*"—a clear lovely voice.

Bridget smiled.

Jamesy's round little face was thin now, skin pulled tight around those soft hazel eyes. Paddy's, too, all sharp cheekbones, his blue eyes hard pebbles. And Bridget's blond hair was limp, her eyes sometimes vague and staring.

They need to eat. With hardly enough meal here for one person, I'm trying to feed five. Michael's spent twelve hours breaking stones on the road—he can't survive on this muck.

Paddy put his stick into the pot and took out a bit of meal. "I can hardly feel it in my stomach," he said.

"There was talk on the roads today," said Michael. "A sheep stealing up in the mountains."

"Talk of men arrested and hanged, too, I would think."

Michael nodded, putting his stick into the mixture. He pulled a little out and sucked the mush from the stick.

I settled the children down, and they finally slept. Michael and I sat on the floor near the fire.

"Another troop of soldiers has come to town. Forty or fifty guard every meal wagon that goes out. But people are so desperate they still attack the wagons. The soldiers killed a woman today for cutting a corner of a meal sack, trying to catch some in her hands to bring home. Nothing seems to move them," he said.

"You wouldn't believe what it's like in town, Honora. Crowds of starving people are wandering the streets. Why are they not beating down the doors of the Great Southern Hotel?"

"Because they're afraid of the soldiers," I said.

"Today I saw a woman and her four children in front of the hotel's windows, looking into the dining room, watching travelers eat enormous meals, standing there silent. Finally the little boy threw a pebble at the window, not to break it, but to get a traveler's attention. The manager of the hotel came out and shouted, 'Get away from here, get away!' and the next thing a troop of soldiers rode up. 'Croppies lie down!' That's what they shouted, Honora. 'Croppies lie down!' We're dying. They know, Honora, and they don't care."

I held him to me.

"We won't be paid for two weeks because there's no small silver coins," he said. "Some men come to the works too weak to stand. Widows, Honora, are allowed on the crew now because they are head of their family. They can't lift the hammers to break rocks. The foreman says now we'll be paid according to the number of rocks broken, not by the day. If your pile's not high enough, no pay at all. While we were breaking the last of the rocks in the dark freezing cold, who comes riding by but the Galway Blazers on their way to a hunt. To see them laughing and calling to each other . . . they didn't even look at us."

"I wonder how the Ryans are managing in the workhouse."

"Owen Mulloy saw Neddy breaking stones in the yard, and spoke to him. Neddy said he was very lucky to get in. Long lines of people, hundreds, maybe thousands, are clamoring to get into that hell and being turned away."

"Food in hell," I said. "Michael, should I go to Máire? She might find some way to give us something."

"Don't, Honora. Don't."

"Why not?"

"Mulloy said that Jackson's waiting for any excuse to evict us all. Any. You go to Máire, she gives you a piece of bread, he'll call it stealing and you'll both be arrested." He leaned close and whispered to me, "There are dead bodies in the streets, Honora."

I pulled him closer.

"And you, a stór, the baby? I'm so worried," Michael said.

"This fellow's a fighter. How could he not be, conceived in the Pirate Queen's castle?" I said.

"I wish I hadn't . . . Not fair to you," he started.

"Whist, Michael. Lie down, a ghrá."

We fell asleep holding on to each other.

Chapter 15

THE WEEK before Christmas brought snow. Hardly a flake most winters, and now this steady fall for three days. A veil of white over the window blocked out the weak winter sun. At least the darkness inside the cottage, day and night, keeps the children sleeping longer—until the hunger wakes them.

Jamesy whimpered. I knelt next to him. He's shivering. I touched his forehead. Not hot, not fever.

Black fever—typhus—had hit Cappagh, only four miles distant. Three families had been struck and every single one of them dead in two weeks, God rest their souls. A terrible, painful death, Granny says. At the end you were out of your head, your limbs swollen and black, and the neighbors were terrified to come near, pushing food and water through the door and praying the fever wouldn't spread.

Granny's remedies didn't help the sick. Starving bodies can't fight off scurvy or dysentery let alone typhus or yellow fever or, God forbid, cholera. Cases had been reported out near Moycullen.

"Mam," Paddy said, "I have to go." Half-asleep.

"Here, a stór." I helped him to the bucket in the corner, held him as he squatted.

"It burns, Mam."

Loose and watery, but no clots of blood. Good. I wiped him with a piece of newsprint. "Try to go back to sleep."

I settled Paddy next to Jamesy on the straw pallet by the fire and covered them with empty meal sacks. The woven blanket was gone, traded for a few pounds of Peel's brimstone. Bridget's cradle will be next. She coughed—a dry, harsh sound. They're getting weaker every day. So many children are sick throughout the parish.

We'd all been so healthy growing up. Even the English visitors who'd come to our classroom remarked how hale and hearty Irish children looked. Surprised, they said to Miss Lynch right in front of us, "When they only eat potatoes," as though they were annoyed at us.

There was great strength in the potato, but little nourishment in corn mush. And now that last sack of meal's near finished.

Plenty of food filled the market, for those with money. The servants from the Big Houses were buying the Christmas goose right now.

"Mam." Paddy again. "I'm too hungry to sleep."

"I've Granny's tea made." Granny's recipe was bark and melted snow boiled together—bitter tasting, but soothing on the stomach.

I put more turf on the fire, filled our tin cup with the tea, and handed it to Paddy. Jamesy awake now, and Bridget was coughing again.

I picked her up from the cradle and sat the two boys down on each side of me, close to the fire. I took the tea from Paddy and tipped a bit of it into Bridget's mouth and gave the cup to Jamesy.

"Is it near time for Da to come home?" Paddy asked.

"A while yet, Paddy."

"Best get on with the story, Mam," Jamesy said, passing the cup back to Paddy.

"Do you remember where we stopped?" I asked them.

"Queen Maeve was leading her army off to capture the Big Brown Bull," Paddy said.

"Driving her chariot," Jamesy added. "You forgot that, Paddy."

"Who cares about the chariot?"

"It's important, isn't it, Mam?"

"It is, Jamesy."

Bridget took some more tea, smiling at me. My brave wee girl.

"Whist, you two. Now, fadó," I started. Thanks be to God, "Maeve's Cattle Raid" is a long tale and has plenty of fighting.

⟡ ⟡ ⟡

"Five pounds of cornmeal, Honora," Michael said as he came in covered with snow, his feet frozen. Those strips of sacking wrapped around them do no good.

Paddy and Jamesy pulled him over to the fire.

I poured a measure of meal into the pot. "You'll have to be patient. You know it has to cook a good long time. Here, let's get to work on your da's poor feet," I said to them.

Bridget and I started on Michael's right foot, the boys on the left, trying to rub life into his stiff blue toes.

"Do they hurt very much, Da?" Jamesy asked.

"A bit of pain's good, Jamesy. Means the feeling's coming back."

"A miracle frostbite hasn't taken them," I said.

"I stamp my feet as I work." He winked at the boys. "The foreman thinks I'm dancing. Makes him very angry."

"Show us, Da," Paddy said.

And didn't Michael get up as soon as his feet were any way warm and start shuffling around the place, the boys leaping in front of him, distracted until the stirabout was ready.

"Eat slowly. Very slowly," I said.

❖   ❖   ❖

"Surely there'll be no work on the roads today," I said to Michael the next morning. The storm was worse.

"I have to appear or I'll lose my place. We'll move rocks around until the overseer is sure no progress can be made. He'll send us away, but I might get a penny or two."

"Please don't go, Michael."

But he bent his head down and stepped out into the wind-driven snow.

I pushed the door closed and went back to the fire, staring at the flames, grateful for my sleeping children's even breathing, some food in their stomachs. I felt the baby in my womb move, still alive. Thank God.

A blast of wind as the door opened. Michael was back, showing some sense, staying home. He said nothing to me but picked up the spade and started out again.

"Wait, Michael, what is it?"

He only shook his head, his lips tight.

"Michael, tell me."

"Something terrible, Honora." He turned to leave.

"I'm going with you."

"Don't," he said.

"I am." Paddy woke up. "Watch the others," I said to him.

I wrapped an empty sack around me and followed Michael into the storm. Hard to move. I sank into the soft snow, my legs and feet going numb. I held Michael's arm.

He helped me over the gap in our stone wall. We followed our lane toward the crossroads.

He pointed to a mound of snow in the ditch. I saw a hand and arm sticking out of the drift. Michael used the spade to carefully clear away the snow. A man's body. He turned it over—Neddy Ryan!

I knelt down. Under Neddy I saw Tessie's body, covering the three children. Alive?

"Mary, Henry, Albert?" I shouted.

Michael lifted up Tessie. The two boys were curled around Mary like kittens around a mother cat—stiff with death.

"No. No," I said. I crouched down close to Mary. Snow fell onto her closed eyes, onto her cheek. I brushed the flakes away. Some kind of a growth on her face. Hair. Clumps of it across her chin. A rusty color. Michael was kneeling beside me. "Look. What is it?"

"Oh, God. A fellow on the roadworks was talking about this. I didn't want to believe him."

"What?"

The wind had died down, so I could hear every word Michael said in a low, flat voice. "In the final stages of starvation, this hair grows on children's faces. The fellow had seen it. 'Like fur,' he said. It comes as the body starts digesting its own organs, trying to stay alive."

No. No. I saw the same hair on Albert's and Henry's faces. I turned my head into Michael's shoulder. I can't take this in.

Michael held me to him for a moment, but then he pulled back. "Listen."

Sharp barks. Howling. The wild dogs were foraging—a pack of them in the hills beyond the old glen, so vicious they'd fought off all efforts to hunt them down.

"We have to bury the bodies," Michael said. "The dogs."

I nodded.

Michael stood up and helped me to my feet.

"But how can we? The ground's frozen," I said.

"We can cover them with rocks from their cottage."

I followed Michael the short distance to where the Ryans' cottage had been. Michael knocked the snow away from a heap of stones, all that was left of the tumbled walls. He pulled out five big rocks and started back. I managed to carry two smaller stones.

We went back and forth, building a cairn over their bodies. Michael carefully fit stone upon stone, leaving no spaces. I filled in any cracks with pebbles.

We stood up, and Michael took my hand. "God rest their souls," he said.

Tessie and Neddy, the raggedy Ryans, foolish and feckless. I imagined Tessie in the workhouse, trying to use gossip and chat to wheedle food for Albert and Henry, urging Mary to "sing a song for Matron." Poor sweet Mary singing, "I have seen the lark at break of day." The workhouse officials probably considered them nothing but whingeing beggars.

"Trying to get home," Michael said. "Not being fed in the workhouse, so coming to us and the Mulloys. Caught by the storm, sheltering in the ditch, not knowing where they were. Fell asleep and never woke up."

"Fools. They were always fools," I said.

"Honora, that's a wild cruel thing to say."

"We're not like them, Michael. We won't let our children die. We'll find some way."

"We will, a stór," he said. "But Neddy tried. He—"

"Brought it on themselves. The two of them. They—" My voice was getting higher, shriller.

"Hold on, Honora. You sound like the foreman on the roadworks. He says the Irish are to blame for their own suffering. Lazy beggars with our hands out, not grateful to the British government."

Michael's right. I'm seeing the Ryans as the British see us. We're scum to them—to the officials, the landlords, the townspeople. They look at the fur on children's faces and say, "See? Animals. Little monkeys."

"We are doomed," I said.

"Honora." Michael reached for me.

"Don't touch me! They're dead! And soon we will be, too. Dead! All of us. Paddy and Jamesy and Bridget and I will be curled up under your dead body." I was pounding on his chest. "Do something! Do something!"

"Stop it, Honora! We will not die! Champion. I'll kill Champion. I'll do it right now! I'll hack her leg off! The meat will feed us! Our children will not starve."

He pushed me away, picked up a rock from the cairn, and started toward Champion's shed.

I stood for a moment and then ran after him. "Kill her!" I shouted. "Kill her! I'll roast her legs! I'll slice up her tongue! We'll eat, eat, eat! Do it, Michael! Do it!"

I caught up with him in the mud-walled shed. The smell of Champion—sweat and manure. Manure that once fertilized our fields.

Champion looked at us with those big, quiet eyes.

Michael raised the jagged stone.

What were we doing? "Michael, stop!" I grabbed his arm. "Stop!" I hit his shoulder. "Stop!"

Finally he turned to me. We held each other for a long, long time in that small, dark place, listening to Champion's breath.

"You great amadán," I said. "You'll butcher Champion, will you? With no knife, no ax, and no heart for it?" I patted the horse's head. "And how would I cook her, anyway? We'd need a hearth like William Boy O'Kelly's."

Michael dropped the stone. "She only eats hay, and even you haven't found a way to make a meal of hay."

"Champion's foal will be born near the same time as our own baby. How could we . . . Come," I said. "The children will be awake and wondering."

"We won't tell them about the Ryans," he said.

"We won't."

Outside, we passed the sad cairn again. The snow had stopped and the fields stretched before us. All white. No sound. The dogs silent.

Suddenly Michael broke away from me and started running across the long acre. What now?

Then I saw him fall flat onto the snow. I ran toward him.

"Michael!"

He stood up, holding a white hare by the ears, the creature kicking and squirming. Michael would not let go. He walked across the field toward me. When he reached the wall he lifted the rabbit and swung its head down against the stones. Blood spurted out—a thump, snow-muffled, another thump, and the rabbit was dead.

I was down on the ground, scrabbling for a sharp stone, something to scrape the skin off the rabbit. We wouldn't need the giant fireplace of the O'Kellys. Our own hearth and our own pot would do for this miracle.

Michael came toward me. Blood dripped from the rabbit like a trail of holly berries in the snow.

"Our children will not die," he said.

Was it you, Mary, who sent that hare out from his burrow? Thank you, thank you. Forgive me, Neddy, forgive me, Tessie, in heaven now, safe from all harm, at last.

⟡　⟡　⟡

Christmas morning we walked down to Mass at Bearna Chapel under a blue sky, the snow melting.

Father Roche read the Christmas gospel in Irish, then repeated, "She wrapped him in swaddling clothes and laid him in the manger because there was no room for them in the inn."

I looked over at Michael. His eyes were closed, listening to Father Roche, or sleeping.

Jesus had been born in such a poor place, Father Roche said, because God, his Father, loved the poor. A comfort to remember that in these hard times, he told us.

Too late to comfort the Ryans. Michael and I had decided to tell no one they were dead until spring, when we could bury them properly.

Michael *is* asleep. Spending himself for us, and never a complaint. He'd said the rabbit stew gave him strength to break twice as many rocks on the roads. Four extra pennies, a few more pounds of corn-meal. We'd given it to Mam. She'd cook a stirabout for our Christmas dinner. He'd had Paddy and Jamesy bring their chestnut battlers. "We'll take on Hughie," he'd said. You're keeping our bodies and our spirits alive, a stór.

Now Father Roche was talking about these kind English gentle-men—Quakers, you call them—who'd been so appalled at the hor-rors they'd seen in Ireland that they were raising money to open soup kitchens for us. And they'd promised Father that Catholics would not have to give up their faith to receive this charity. Not like Reverend

Smithson and the other Protestant "helpers" who gave only to those who jumped, turned Protestant.

Father Roche finished his sermon talking of the three Wise Men and the gifts they brought for the baby. Some good people in the world. I started to think of how after the Wise Men left an angel told Joseph to take Mary and Jesus and flee to Egypt, run from the evil. Flee. The image of the Holy Family escaping stayed with me through the end of Mass.

❖   ❖   ❖

As we ate Mam's attempt at Christmas dinner, Da said he hated the idea of lining up for soup—one station to serve an area twenty miles square. A huge cauldron would be set up over an open fire at the end of Barna pier. Eight ounces of soup would be given each adult, six for children, to be eaten then and there. The officials wouldn't let us take the soup away, afraid we'd sell it for whiskey. Thousands of people would be drinking soup from the same cups, standing out in the rain and cold. "The government means to take our self-respect away," Da said. "And the Quakers have to follow the regulations."

"They can't take what we won't give," said Granny, sucking on her empty pipe.

Granny had gotten so thin. The skin of her face was pulled tight against her cheekbones.

I noticed that Dennis's two little ones sat close to her. Granny fed them from her stirabout, not taking any herself, only sucking the empty pipe. When I offered her some of mine, she shook her head.

"I'm fine, Honora," she said.

"I met the Claddagh Admiral in Galway City when I was going to the roadworks," Dennis was saying. "Worse storms in January. Only for my Josie and Mam and Granny turning every scrap of seaweed and winkles and Indian corn into food, we'd all be gone."

I took Dennis aside. "Granny's giving her food to your little girls," I said softly.

He didn't answer me.

I went up to Da and whispered to him, "Granny's not eating."

"We know, Honora."

"You know? Then why don't you do something?"

"Do what? No one can stop your granny from doing what she's decided to do."

Michael was talking to Joseph and Dennis. "If the seas would calm," I heard Joseph say.

"We'd have to provision the boats, get our nets and tackle and sails back from the gombeen men. Instead of soup, give us money to redeem our nets," Da said.

"No sense," Michael said. "No sense in any of this. The roadworks are a disaster. Money wasted. Men collapsing from hunger and the strain of useless labor, and all the time the land lies neglected. Landlords won't give seed on credit, and we'll all be too worn down to plant in the spring. What good does it do the landlords to have the land lie fallow? It's their land, their crops! No sense."

"Perfect sense for the landlords, the Sassenach," I said.

"What do you mean, Honora?" Da said.

"They want us gone, hell or Connaught, all over again. We took the bad lands of Connaught and made something of them. Now they're taking them back. At least Cromwell was honest, told us plain. Killed us quick. False promises lure people like the Ryans to the workhouse and . . ." My voice was climbing.

"Honora." Michael stopped me.

Paddy had turned from where he and Hughie were swinging the chestnuts at each other. "The Ryans, Mam? What about the Ryans?"

"Your mam's giving off about the government."

"Again?" Paddy said.

And the whole family laughed.

I stepped past Dennis, past Granny, past the children, and went out.

The Christmas sun was setting into the Bay, leaving a bank of bloodred clouds behind. A new year was coming, 1847. A black old year it will be. Black '47.

"Honora."

Michael crossed the strand to me and put his arm around my shoulders. We stood together looking at Galway Bay, the wide way that led to the sea and to Amerikay. Escape—is that our only hope? Take the child and flee, the angel told St. Joseph, and the children left behind were slaughtered, Holy Innocents. We cannot stay. We'll die if we do.

"We must flee to Amerikay, Michael," I said. "You have to get word to Patrick, in that place Chicago. He said there was work there. He will have earned money. He could send us our fare."

Michael turned me to him. "Honora, a stór, how would I find him? And even if by some miracle we got passage, how could a child born in April travel during this sailing season? You're upset because of the Ryans, but Honora, I'm not Neddy. I will not let our children die. I have the potato seeds Patrick gave me. Champion's foal is due in the spring. We can sell it. We can't give up. And could you really leave your family, Knocnacuradh, Galway Bay?"

I didn't answer.

"Come, Honora. We should go in." He took my face in his hands and kissed me.

Michael, I wanted to say, we're none of us safe. The Ryans died first because they had nothing at all to fall back on, but now we've spent all our gold coins. If the roadworks are stopped or the soup kitchens don't open, then even your strength and spirit won't protect us.

Some of the neighbors came that night. Not like Christmases past—with Michael's pipes hidden and every fiddle pawned.

Then Mam started to lilt. Josie joined her. We danced that Christmas night, waiting for Black '47 to begin. For one moment we were as we had been. But the lilting and the dancing didn't stop my heart from beating Amerikay. Amerikay.

Chapter 16

We moved a few steps forward, not far now from the end of Barna pier where the cauldron of soup hung over the open fire. Paddy tugged at my hand, but Jamesy stopped.

"My legs won't work," he said.

Michael heard and picked him up, holding Jamesy in one arm, Bridget in the other.

"Hard on the little ones," a woman I didn't know said to me. Her children stood near her. A boy of about twelve carried a little fellow Jamesy's size, and two girls of nine or ten held their mother's hands. "Have you come from far away?" she asked me.

"Up the hill, near Saint James' well," I said. "An hour's walk. My son usually doesn't complain, but the line's very slow today."

"Tired, the poor wee fellow," she said. "Aren't we all? We walked five hours from Oughterard. There's a government soup shop nearer, but the stuff they give's only water with a little rice and a few peas. Goes right through you. Made my children sick. And you have to pay two farthings a cup for it." She shook her head.

"The sisters put a bit of meat into the soup," I said.

The Sisters of Mercy had started distributing soup in February, using money from the Quakers and the Church. But it was the English official sitting in the heated shed built for him near the end of the pier who was in charge. As Da had said, the government controlled all relief. Set the rules. No soup given to anyone not registered. None could be taken away.

Thousands lined up every day to go through the torturous process. Hundreds never reached the soup cauldron—sent away when the official closed distribution at sunset. The sisters had asked the relief committee to allow them to give the whole of a family's ration to one member. So much more efficient, and the family could eat it at their own fire. Only sense. Save the old, the children, and the sick from making the long journey, keep disease from spreading. The government said no.

Sister Mary Agnes told us the official said the government did not intend to make charity agreeable. No matter how many died, she said, the government acted as if the whole terrible calamity were some kind of Irish trick to get food from them. That's why most places in the country still didn't have soup kitchens, in spite of a law in Parliament.

Sister's right, I thought as I looked at the official standing in the doorway of the shed. A small, plump young fellow, sent over from England. Probably his first job, his salary paid from charitable donations and the little bit of money given by Parliament.

"Name and townland," he said to Michael.

"Michael Kelly, Askeeboy." He set Jamesy down.

The man knew us, saw us every day, but liked to make a show of finding Michael's name on the roll and always said, "Michael Kelly, *pauper*," then, "Not working on the roads?"

"The works have been closed, sir," Michael said.

As the official well knew. "Three children," he said. "Where are they?"

"Here," Michael said, touching Jamesy and Paddy on the shoulder and holding Bridget out for the official to see.

The man made three checkmarks. "And another one in your woman's belly. You people have no self-control."

Keep quiet, Michael.

The fellow went on. "Yesterday one of you thought he'd fool me. Didn't tell me his child had died. Trying to get the extra portion. I caught him, though." The man laughed.

I kept my eyes down, but I could feel Michael tense his shoulders. "Don't," I murmured. A flash of anger and the fellow would take our names off the roll or have one of the company of soldiers guarding the pier arrest Michael—soldiers out here to keep order in a crowd of people too weak to do more than shuffle forward.

At the cauldron, Sister Mary Agnes filled two large tin cans for Michael and me and smaller ones for the children. She'd heard the official. "Sorry," she whispered. Three other sisters worked with her.

A few dozen people stood hunched against the wind, eating the soup. All of us were aware of those in line watching, waiting for us to finish. I sat Bridget down and started to spoon the soup in her little mouth while Michael tried to keep the boys from gulping down their portion. Sometimes they ate so fast, they vomited their one meal of the day.

"Hurry up!" the official shouted at us.

"Here, a stór, eat, please." I tried to get Bridget to take the last spoonful. She turned away. A bad sign when children couldn't eat. The Dwyers' youngest stopped eating the week before she died.

I rinsed the tin cans in a pot of water and gave them back to Sister Mary Agnes. The official was questioning the Oughterard woman, so Sister could speak to me without the official hearing.

"Still no letter," she said to me.

The Sisters of Mercy had a convent in Chicago, and I had written to Patrick Kelly there. Michael, behind me, heard Sister. He hadn't wanted me to send the letter. Not good to bring attention to Patrick. Sister Mary Agnes said she'd enclose the letter inside one she wrote to the Mother Superior. "Do you think the British read the sisters' mail?" I'd asked him. He'd shrugged. Stranger things had happened.

Now Michael said to me, "Come along, Honora."

The official was watching.

As we walked to Mam's cottage with the children, I said to him, "No harm will come to Patrick. Sister Mary Agnes asked the Superior in Chicago to give the letter to the priest at Saint Patrick's Church. He'll know every Irishman in Chicago. Gives Patrick a way to send money to us."

For our fare, I thought, but didn't say. The baby inside me held on to life somehow, a strong fellow. He'd be born in mid-April—old enough to travel by July. We could sail then, if Patrick Kelly responds. I'd convinced Michael to go somehow and . . .

"Honora," Michael said, "your mother."

Mam was running across the strand toward us. Granny. She'd been feeding her soup to Dennis and Josie's little ones. When the official caught her at it, she told him, "It's my soup. I can do what I wish."

He'd said to her, "This is the queen's soup. If you don't need it, I'll take you off the rolls."

Granny had begun reciting an Irish phrase at him in a low, sing-song tone. "Spells," an old man standing nearby told the official, who said, "Pagan nonsense," but didn't bother her again. Now Granny was too weak to leave the cottage.

But Mam was shouting, "They're going out! The boats!"

Fishing for the first time since last fall. A whole season had been lost to the most severe winter storms in a generation, but now, here was the Claddagh fleet following the Admiral's white sail.

I saw that Da and my brothers were pushing our boat out through the surf. "But they have no nets," I said to Mam—standing next to me now. "Nor food."

"The Quakers gave money to redeem the nets and buy supplies," Mam said as our boat took its place in the procession. "The schools of herring have arrived. God is with us, Honora."

And Michael smiled at me. I could hear his thoughts: We won't have to leave. We will survive.

❖ ❖ ❖

Inside the cottage, Granny lay on a straw bed near the fire.

"Oh, Granny," Mam said, "the boats are out, thank God."

"Mac Dara," Granny said, "answering our prayers."

Prayer and fasting—our only weapons. My brave granny, did you offer yourself for us?

Michael and I knelt down next to her.

Mam came over, holding a tin can. "Some spring greens boiled up, Granny. Please try to eat them."

Granny closed her eyes.

Mam looked at me and shook her head.

Granny couldn't eat . . . the final days. I'd watched a man force soup down his father. The food so shocked the starving old man's system, he'd died.

"Granny, sip the broth," I said, shaking her gently. "There's herring coming. Please, Granny, please."

She opened her eyes, filmed over now, their green color dulled—

that hunger stare. I'd seen that same blankness in the eyes of the women waiting for the soup, crouched against the seawall holding skeletal children, all resistance gone, their unseeing gazes fixed on the Bay.

Please God, not Granny. She took a small sip from the cup in my hand.

"Honora," she said.

"I'm here, Granny," I said.

"Michael?"

"Here."

"And John's with us," she said. "Good."

"Granny, Da and the boys are out fishing, remember?"

"Didn't you tell me that five minutes ago? It's my John, my own husband, John Keeley, who's standing at the door."

Her husband dead how long, fifty years?

"The best of men," she said. She sat up and spoke into the empty space. "Hold there a moment, John. Honora . . ." Her eyes cleared— bright now, holding mine. "Your husband," she started, and stopped.

"Michael," I said.

"Who else? Come closer, Michael. You're a good, kind man, and strong, but I understand what you don't say. I know the loneliness of a lifetime spent away from your people and place."

"I've made a new . . . ," Michael began.

Granny waved her hand at him. "You have done well with Honora."

"Granny," he said, "I love her."

"As my John loved me, but I could be a torment to him. I was glad when my son found Mary Walsh, a gentle, soft woman. But it's hardness that's needed now. Honora's good in a fight. She'll stand with you, Michael."

Michael smiled at her. "She's my thigh companion."

Granny nodded. "Fadó," she began, but faltered and looked over at the door. "Jesus Christ, John Keeley, could you not wait a bit? I'm telling a story!" She gathered her breath. "Fadó." But her body sagged. "You finish, Honora. You tell the stories," she said.

"I will, Granny. I promise."

Granny closed her eyes and let her spirit leave the body that could no longer contain it.

❖ ❖ ❖

There'd been no wakes held in Bearna for more than a year. Hardly time to do more than dig a grave and say a quick prayer with so many dying. Whole families lay in pits or in ditches under cairns, like the Ryans.

But they came for Granny. All the fishing families from Bearna, even the Claddagh Admiral, crowded in the cottage where Mam had laid out Granny's body.

"Why?" Paddy asked me as I sat against the wall in the corner with Jamesy and Bridget near me.

"Why what?"

"Why are all these people here? What did Granny do?"

"She told stories," I said, "and she was very wise."

My brother Dennis had sobbed to me, "She saved my children."

As the night went on, the neighbors told stories about the fierce Connemara woman who had come with her son so many years before, and Da had actually laughed, happy in remembering.

I heard other kinds of talk, too. Owen Mulloy was speaking with John Joe Clancy, Joseph with our Walsh cousins: "Amerikay . . . escape." No need to beg the landlords for the fare. The uncles and sons who'd gone out last year to lay rails and dig canals were turning the dollars they earned into bank drafts for their family's passage, then mailing them to the Sisters of Mercy or to Presentation Convent or any safe place where a letter would be held. The ones who'd gone ahead were saving the ones left behind. The American letter—the rescue had begun. But no letter from Patrick Kelly, no answer to our appeal.

Michael turned away from two men to come over to me.

"Go talk to Hughie, Paddy," I said. "Take Jamesy."

They went across the room.

"What are the men saying?" I asked Michael.

"A dangerous business," he said. "What good is a bank draft if the bank manager calls the landlord when you try to cash it? Those two were telling me that Pat Shea was made to wait in the bank while the manager sent for the landlord's agent, who took the money off him. Said he owed rent. Another fellow was on the ship when the sheriff came. He hadn't paid for a sack of corn. Took his ticket. Put him off."

Owen Mulloy came up to us. "Sorry for your trouble," he said to me.

"She was a mighty woman." And then, not even pretending he hadn't heard, he said, "Get a priest to take the drafts to the bank. There are ways."

The cheapest passage was to Canada. Two pounds for adults, one for children, and then food for the journey—another twenty-five pounds. Nine adults, nine children after my baby's born, so fifty-one pounds would see Mam and Da, Dennis and Josie, my brothers, Máire, and the children, all of us away. Michael could ride Champion to the Scoundrel Pykes, give them the horse in exchange for Máire and her children. I remembered the ship we'd seen going to Mac Dara's Island, how sorry we'd felt for those stone-faced people. But they were the lucky ones. They had escaped, as we must.

I knelt in front of Granny's body, so peaceful by the fire. Oh, Granny, send us a miracle. Let an American letter from Patrick Kelly arrive soon.

❖ ❖ ❖

Da and Joseph and Dennis and Hughie carried Granny's coffin the short distance to Bearna graveyard. Paddy's and Jamesy's hands were in mine while Michael carried Bridget. Jamesy stopped, pointed to the rooster carved in the post at the gate.

"Why is that there, Mam?" he said.

"I'll tell you later," I whispered.

"Grainne Keeley Ní O'Malley laid to rest." A new curate said the blessing. Father Roche had died of black fever caught from giving last rites to the dying. "Eternal rest grant to her, O Lord. Eternal rest."

The bottom of the coffin opened and Granny's body dropped into the grave. Eternal rest, and the coffin used again and again. Slán, Granny, slán. No keening, no crying, no tears left.

"We are doing our best for you, Granny," I said.

At least we knew where she lay. At least she was close to Galway Bay. At least we could kneel and say an Ave here for her—for you, Granny. At least we gave her that much. There'd been whispers of a mass grave up near Paddy's Cross—ten fever victims, the families able to do no more than lay them in a pit. And stories of families very close to death, huddled together while the father barricaded the door of the cottage from the inside, making it their tomb.

"The rooster, Mam." Jamesy stood at the gate, tracing the outline of the rooster as Michael had done with his mermaid at Clontuskert Abbey, claiming it.

While the others were still shoveling dirt onto Granny's coffinless body, I told Jamesy about the soldiers who crucified Jesus and how the rooster jumped from the pot to say, "Slán Mhic Máire!" The Son of Mary is safe. "Jesus didn't really die. And neither did Granny or any of the other poor people that have gone into the ground. They will all live again."

"Really, Mam?"

"Really, Jamesy. Granny is safe."

"With Jesus."

"That's right, Jamesy."

"But those fellows would have been better if it was a hen came alive in the pot," said Paddy. "They'd've had eggs."

❖   ❖   ❖

A week had passed since Granny's funeral, near the middle of March. Michael and I sat up late whispering by the fire while the boys and Bridget slept—a sweet breathing sleep, not the passed-out stupor of hunger. Da's catch had fed us. Not enough fish to take to the market, so we'd all eaten herring stewed with spring greens. With that and the Sisters of Mercy soup, the children had regained some strength, and so had Michael. A few days of food couldn't fill out the hollows in his cheeks, but the glaze of exhaustion was gone from his eyes. He's only twenty-six, I thought, yet those days spent breaking stones in useless work have taken a toll. But now, settled against his chest with his arms around me, the fire warming us and the pains in my stomach eased, I felt supported and could let out the words I'd been holding back.

"Michael, I'm so frightened. I think of poor little Grellan. To lose another . . ."

Michael stroked my hair. "I know. I know."

"If only we could leave," I said. "If only Patrick would send our fare before the starvation and disease kill us."

"Spring is coming," Michael said. "The ground is soft. I have the turnip seeds to plant."

A Quaker man had come to the soup line and given away a load of seeds. The government had bought them to distribute but had given up the idea when seed merchants complained about unfair competition. The Quakers had purchased the supply and given away the seeds. Good people, the Quakers. Others had good intentions toward us, too. The Americans sent ships loaded with food. Even some British people contributed money to help us. But the British government, controlling even the money raised by private charities, took those funds meant for us and squandered them on high salaries to their officials and useless schemes. Those with good intentions seemed to have no power, and the powerful had no good intentions. We had to get out some way.

"The winter didn't kill us, a stór," Michael said.

"But so many died. Paddy was asking me if heaven would be big enough for all the dead people. Two more of the Dwyer children last week, Michael. Little Francie Lonergan's gone, and Bridey, too. Two families in Truskey . . ."

Michael held me closer. "There's food pouring into the market in Galway City," he said. "Indian corn and rice."

"What good is that if we have no money? Only the ones with American letters can buy food. Why doesn't Patrick write us?"

"Maybe he didn't get your letter," Michael said.

"But he must know we're starving," I said. "Didn't Mulloy tell us every town and city in Amerikay's collecting money for us?"

"Every politician who wants an Irish vote is speaking out against the British," he said. "Patrick's working for the Cause. I doubt if he's much money."

"He should sell Grellan's crozier."

"Honora!"

I'd gone too far. "I'm sorry," I said.

"We've survived the worst, a stór," Michael said.

"Sometimes"—I turned to say this right into his ear—"I wonder why people don't run into Galway Bay . . . float away."

"Honora!" He twisted me around to him. "Never, ever even think that!"

"Why? Because of hell? Hell's now, Michael."

"We will live, Honora, and our children will live. We won't die to please them. Jesus, Honora, if your granny could hear you. It's because you're so close to your time, a stór. Now sleep, Honora."

He eased me down on the straw and stroked my face until I did let go of my worries and slept.

❖   ❖   ❖

I awoke late to find Michael feeding Bridget and the boys the last bits of herring. He smiled at me. "Good morning, Honora."

"Good morning," I said.

The boys were sipping nettle tea from our cup.

"Da told us a soldier story, Mam, and this is mead we're drinking, like Finn and his men," Jamesy said.

"Good."

"Mam," Jamesy went on, "Paddy said he ate eggs for breakfast in the before times. Every day, he says. He's lying, isn't he?"

"Every day I can remember," said Paddy, looking at me in a straight, cold way that reminded me of his uncle Patrick.

"I don't know anywhere they eat eggs every day, except maybe the Big House."

"Or at the bishop's. That rooster crows so mightily," Michael said. "He must be keeping those hens happy enough."

"Those hens are lucky to be alive," I said. "It's a tribute to the respect people have for the bishop that they haven't been stolen and eaten long ago."

"A tribute to that great monster of a wolfhound who guards the henhouse," Michael said.

"The doggie likes me," Jamesy said.

"It's true, Michael," I said. "Jamesy has a way with that animal."

We'd met the dog a month ago as he trotted alongside the bishop on the strand. Angus, you called him, and he had a way of pulling his lips back from his teeth that said: I'll bite you in half with one snap of my jaw. He frightened every child in five townlands. Mrs. Riley, the bishop's housekeeper, doted on the brute and cared for that dog as if he were a big baby. If we had half the food she gave that monster . . .

"Mam," said Jamesy, "tell Da."

"When we met the dog, Jamesy held out his hand and said, 'Here, doggie, here,' and the creature wagged his tail like a mad thing. The bishop insisted that Jamesy step up and pet the big head, and Jamesy did it! Very brave altogether."

"Well, isn't he a Kelly?" said Michael. "And isn't the Enfield a kind of hound? An Enfield guarded the body of Thaddy O'Kelly when he was slain fighting for Brian Boru against the Vikings. I've told you boys that story."

"What good does standing over a dead body do anybody?" Paddy asked. "I'd rather have a horse. Champion would have reared up and kicked those Vikings right in the head, then pulled Thaddy O'Kelly up by his cloak with her teeth, so he could mount her and ride away to fight some more. Right, Da?"

"Champion would have done that, surely," Michael said, "but having a hound on your side is a good thing."

"Can we have a dog someday?" asked Jamesy.

"Someday," Michael said.

Wild dogs were taking over the empty townlands—not even the hungriest dared hunt them—though the bodies of the Ryans were safe enough. The animals preferred the freshly dead. Typhus in Clarenbridge, cholera in Bushy Park—too close.

"No dogs," I said.

"Is the baby alive inside you?" Paddy asked suddenly.

I looked at Michael. "He is, Paddy."

"If I had an egg, I'd give it to you, Mam. I wouldn't even take a taste. It would be all for you, Mam, so that this baby wouldn't . . . you know, like the other one. I would, Mam, I'd give it to you," Paddy said.

"I know, alanna."

"Me too," said Jamesy. "Me too."

"Brave boys you are. Now come with me to water Champion and let your mam have a lie-in," Michael said. "Come now, Bridget. Let Da see you walk."

Almost two now, and Bridget still not steady on her feet.

"Can I ride Champion?" I heard Paddy ask as Michael shut the door.

I did fall back asleep. When I awoke, alone, it was almost midday. Where were they? We'd miss the soup if we didn't hurry.

"Michael? . . . Michael?"

"Here, Honora." He came in, shepherding Bridget. "She ran up to the lane. Good girl you are," he said to her. Bridget smiled at me.

"Where are the boys?"

"Aren't they here? I sent them back up hours ago."

"I haven't seen them. Where are they?"

"I'll try the Mulloys," he said, and went out.

"Paddy! Jamesy! . . . Paddy! Jamesy!" I shouted from in front of the cottage, holding on to Bridget.

Michael came running. "Not at Mulloy's," he said.

"They shouldn't go off like this." The dogs in the hills attacked sheep. Would they go after two small boys?

Then we heard them—running steps, panting breath, heads down—not a word, going right past us and into the cottage.

"It didn't break! It didn't break!" Paddy said. He opened his hands. A big brown hen's egg was cupped in his palm. "Here, Mam, here!"

"A raid, Da!" Jamesy said. "We got it on a raid! Tell them, Paddy, tell them!"

"I will. But first, Mam, take the egg. We didn't steal it, Mam, truly. Like Finn and Cuchulain, Da—we raided the enemy! We were the Irish Legion! Faugh-a-Ballagh!" Paddy said. "We started out very polite. We went to the bishop's door and when the housekeeper answered, I said, 'Good morning, missus'—in English. But she wasn't a bit nice, said, 'What do you want? Stay back!' Said, 'Don't be bringing sickness in here and don't ask me for any food. We have none to spare. Go away.'

"But I stood there and said, 'Missus, my brother wants to see your dog. We met the bishop and he said Jamesy could come and pet Angus.' "

"Then I said, 'Doggie, doggie,' " Jamesy told us, "and I looked at her like this." He smiled up at us—that baby smile of his that wasn't to be resisted. I didn't realize he knew its effect. A charmer.

"His father's son," I said to Michael.

Paddy went on, "Then she said we should stay in the yard and she'd bring Angus around to us, and to wait down at the wall. So I sat Jamesy on the wall and told him to tell the housekeeper I had to pee and was off in the trees."

"Pee, pee, pee," said Jamesy, and he grabbed Michael's hand and swung it until he had Michael laughing.

"Listen!" Paddy said. "I hid behind the hedge. The housekeeper brought the dog out on a leash—"

"Let me tell this!" Jamesy said. "I patted him and said, 'Doggie, doggie, doggie.' "

"And I," Paddy said, "crawled right into the henhouse, Da! I reached under a fat red hen and took the egg. Then I ran away from the henhouse and yelled, 'Missus? Would you send my little brother to me? I messed myself, missus,' though I didn't, Mam, really, I didn't."

"Pee, pee, pee," Jamesy said. "Da, I was so, *so* brave. Tell them, Paddy."

"He was, truly, Da. You were brave, Jamesy. He jumped from the wall by himself and walked past the dog, who was snapping and growling now—but Jamesy? Not a bother on him."

"Not a bother," said Jamesy.

"He walked right to me, slow and sure—I took his hand and then we ran and ran. So," said Paddy.

"So," I said. "What brave boys we have, Michael. My sturdy lads, come over to me."

I set the egg down carefully and hugged them to me, one on each side of me. If they'd been caught, if the dog had attacked them . . .

Michael stood over us, rubbing the boys' heads and saying, "Faugh-a-Ballagh! Hoo-rah! You didn't let fear stop you, boys. That's the thing. Fingers into a fist."

"Will you eat it, Mam? Cook it and eat it now," said Paddy, against my shoulder. "All for you, Mam. Right, Da?"

"All and only for Mam. Take it, Honora," Michael said.

And so I did, cracking the egg into a bit of meal and mixing it, cooking them together. I offered some to Paddy and Jamesy.

"Taste it just," I said to the boys.

But they clamped their lips shut until I had eaten it all.

"We will win," Michael said. "With sons like this, Honora, we will win."

❖   ❖   ❖

In mid-April, the gombeen men reclaimed Da's nets. The Quakers could no longer give money to fishermen, forbidden by government order—direct payments created dependency.

The roadworks reopened, at least. A few pennies earned and the weather easier on Michael. The boys helped him plant the turnip seeds. No potatoes to sow. Michael did put the seeds Patrick gave us last summer into the ground, though Owen Mulloy doubted potatoes would grow from them.

I waited for our child to be born and thought about Amerikay. Michael fed us with Champion's blood mixed with dandelion stems and sorrel and the soup Sister Mary Agnes smuggled to him during those last days when I wasn't able to walk down the hill to the pier. No letter from Patrick.

"I'm going to check Champion," Michael said on a rainy April night. "Her time is close, too."

The next day, my pains began. Mam was there, pressing the Mary

Bean into one hand while I held the Connemara marble stone Michael had given me in the other. "Hold on, a stór. Hold on, Honora."

I felt a deep cramping inside me, then pain much more intense than with the other three births. I couldn't help myself—I screamed and screamed.

"That's right, Honora. Yell," Mam said.

Mam and Michael were bending over me. Paddy, Jamesy, and Bridget stood in the corner, staring at me, afraid.

"Michael, take them out," I said. "Go on, children—help Da with Champion."

"The horse is in labor, too," Michael said to Mam.

"Go. Take the children," Mam said.

They left us.

"Here we are, Mam, the two of us," I said.

"We are. Shall I sing to you, Honora, a stór?"

"Do."

And so she did. "*Siúil, siúil, siúil a rún . . .*" Mam and I alone, but Granny here, too, and I saw St. Bridget herself standing behind her. Hour after hour the pain ripped through me. Finally Mam said, "Push, push," and I clutched the Mary Bean, heaving and breathing and straining, and he came out of me, born. A long, scrawny bit of a thing, silent—no strong cry, only a whimper—but alive.

"Honora." A whisper in my ear—Michael. "A stór mo chroí, our son needs you."

I heard a chorus of, "Mam, Mam, Mam"—my children. I opened my eyes. Mam put the bundle of bones into my arms, and then he was at my breast. I felt him sucking and licking. But there was nothing there—nothing for him.

"I can't, Mam. I've no milk. Baptize him now, Mam, now. Save him from the cillín."

And she did, dripping the water on his pale forehead. "I baptize you," she started. "Will you name him Michael? It'd be strength for him—Michael the archangel."

"Not Michael," I said.

If he dies . . . I won't put Michael's name . . . And he will die. I have no milk. And the Lynches with a herd of cows.

"Mam, Mam," I said. "We'll give him a Lynch name. Stephen, after that young soldier. Then, Mam, listen to me: Take him to Miss Lynch." I tried to sit up. "She has no child, Mam. Tell her to take Stephen, feed him, and she can keep him. The Lynches have herds of cows. Plenty of milk. Give him to her. Try, Mam. Go. Now."

"Honora, easy. You're raving."

"Please, Mam. Call him Stephen," I said. "We will have a Michael. This one is Stephen."

And Mam slowly repeated the name. "Stephen. I baptize you Stephen, in the name of the Father, the Son, and the Holy Spirit. There now, he's God's child now."

"He's cold, Mam."

"Hold him close, Honora."

"I'm sorry, Stephen. Sorry." Poor little thing, sucking nothing, not even crying, no strength for it. Lord, why did You let him live to die? "Take him to Miss Lynch, Mam. Take him."

"Honora," Mam said, "listen to me. Miss Lynch has gone away. And you would never give up your baby."

"I would, Mam. So he can live."

And then Michael was kneeling by me, holding the tin can. "Milk," he said. He stuck my finger in the frothy liquid.

Milk, it was milk. I put my finger into Stephen's mouth. He sucked the milk from it. I dipped my finger again, and again he took the milk. Mam ripped a piece from her blouse.

"Soak it," she said.

I did. Stephen sucked milk from the cloth until the little body was warm and he mewed. A small sound, but something. His lips went like mad, taking every bit of the milk we could give to him until the can was empty, and then he howled. Thanks be to God, he howled.

"He won't die," I said.

"He won't," said Michael.

"You told Miss Lynch. She gave you milk from the cows for Stephen."

"Not the cows, Mam." It was Paddy, speaking up, pushing to be next to Michael.

"Not the cows," said Jamesy.

"I'm telling her," said Paddy. "You be quiet."

"I won't be quiet. I can tell."

But it was Bridget told me. "Horsey, Mam, horsey."

"What? What does she mean? . . . Michael? Mam?"

They started laughing, then told me. Champion had given birth, and our Stephen's first meal was Champion's milk.

"Mare's milk?"

"Stephen drank it," Michael said.

"He did, surely," said Mam.

❖   ❖   ❖

I went in and out of dreams the first night of Stephen's life. I thought Miss Lynch had come to claim Stephen, then she turned into Máire. She took Stephen, put him at her own snowy breast—the Pearl. I even heard her children saying, "Aunt Honey, Aunt Honey." I'd gone astray.

"Honora. Would you ever wake up and hold this rackety child? He's sucking me dry. Honora!" Her face was close to mine. Máire, flesh spilling out of her blouse, real and warm and here. "They've left, the Pykes are gone and Jackson with them. I'm free, Honora. Free."

❖   ❖   ❖

We ate that night from the basket of food Máire had brought— loaves of wheaten bread, a frikin of butter, a sack of oatmeal, and another of Indian corn.

"We would've brought more," she said, "but I had baby Gracie and Daniel. Johnny Og and Thomas carried the basket between them. They did a great job. Michael," she said, "reach down in the bottom."

He pulled some small hard balls from the basket, misshapen and gnarled but full of eyes. Seed potatoes ready to plant, dozens and dozens of them.

Michael lifted one up, turning it carefully in his hand. "Look at the number of eyes. Ten, at least. With these and the seeds Patrick gave us, the whole of the townland will be planted. The land won't fail us again."

Máire didn't tell her story that first night. Too tired. The children slept together in a huddle and only grinned at one another. Our brothers and Da came up the hill to see Máire the next night—a grand reunion. "If only Granny were here," Máire said. But her sadness at Granny's death was balanced by her joy. Máire exclaimed at Hughie, grown as tall as Dennis, and wasn't Joseph the image of Uncle Dan Walsh? She told Dennis she longed to meet Josie and their two little girls, but for now she had best stay quietly at Knocnacuradh. Mam smiled. Máire's homecoming had smoothed some of the lines from her face, and she'd washed her blond hair into curls. Even Da, gaunt now, his black Spanish hair gray, seemed young again, happy. During the next week, we said nothing about Máire's return to anyone outside the family. The new baby excused the comings and goings. Mam told Katie Mulloy I was sick and to keep the neighbors away. When seed potatoes were found in cottage doorways, the neighbors whispered: Mrs. Molly Maguire, the Quakers, and thanked God. Men suddenly felt strong enough to turn the earth and plant the pratties.

Finally, the night came for Máire to tell her story. Máire had both her baby Gracie and Stephen fed. Mam and Da, the children, my brothers, Josie, all of us gathered together—a bit of the before times. Fadó . . .

"After the second time the potatoes failed," Máire said, "I kept my head down. We had food and I could still slip a bit to the stableman or one of the laborers. But then about the time you came, Michael, Jackson got bolder. He started telling the old Major what to do, no more pretending, giving orders, 'Evict! Evict!' Jackson convinced him getting rid of the tenants would make the estate profitable. Jackson kept quoting that boyo in the Treasury, Trevelyan. I mind him sitting at the table, reading from the London papers in that slow, dour way of his. The words would put the heart across you: 'God is doing what man couldn't.'"

"Doing what?" Da said.

"Killing us. Clearing the land of us." Máire mimicked Jackson's flat north of Ireland accent, and we heard the mad hatred under the words.

"'We must thank Providence, sir,' Jackson would say. 'As Mr. Trevelyan said, "God is doing what man couldn't." The Lord God of Hosts is sweeping from Ireland the mendacious, the rebellious, the immoral, the slothful, the violent.' That was Jackson's dinner table chat," Máire said, "how we'd all be carried down into the deepest and hottest regions of hell."

Mam crossed herself. Da shook his head. Joseph, Dennis, and Hughie looked down. Michael took my hand. Hard for the children to hear this, though I suppose Máire's sons knew this rant only too well.

"Well, at first," Máire went on, "the Master was taken aback. Pleasure is the Pykes' only religion, and neither the old Major nor the Mistress wanted to think much about fire and brimstone. The old Major told Jackson he'd been spending too much time with Reverend Smithson and the church mission people. But little by little, Jackson took control. He started watching me: 'I'll catch you stealing, and then it's Australia for you, and none to save you,' he'd say.

" 'Say what you like,' I'd tell Jackson, trying not to let him see my fear: 'Robert Pyke's left me with another wee Pyke in my belly and two walking and talking, so I'm protected.' "

"And you were eating," I said.

"I was, Honora, and aware of it, truly. But how would me not eating help you or any of the others who were starving?"

"Go on, Máire," Da said.

"You were a holy martyr for your sister, and neither she nor anyone in the family will forget it," Mam said.

"I wonder," said Máire.

"You saved our baby," Michael said, staring at me.

"And I'm so thankful. Go on, Máire," I said.

"Well," Máire said, giving me a "we're not finished yet" look, "Gracie was born in February. The old Major and Mistress planned to leave for London. They feared catching some disease, with fever all around us. Jackson was going with them to get them settled and attend to the old Major's business affairs. So I was packing for the Mistress and telling her that I'd take care of the house and things while they were gone, thinking that I could finally get food to you. I dosed the Mistress with medicine and I went to bed in my room behind the kitchen. And then here was Robert Pyke yelling, 'Wake up, Máire! Wake up now!' Standing over the bed in uniform, his greatcoat still smelling of horses and the outdoors. 'What are you doing here?' I asked him. All he said was, 'Get up!' The baby began crying. So I started feeding her, and then I saw the old Major standing in the door. He said to Robert, 'Look at her. A sow with her piglets.'

"Robert said, 'My father wants to see the children.' I didn't understand. I said to him, 'Your father has seen the children every day of their lives.' Then the old Major said to me, 'I don't look carefully at the servants' children. I want to look now. Names, ages,' he said. They lined up like little soldiers: 'Here's Johnny Og, seven; Thomas, five; Daniel, three; and Gracie, two months,' I told him."

I looked over at Máire's boys—no expression on their faces, bodies fed but spirits bruised, I thought. Afraid.

Máire was saying that both men were drunk. "Robert's humoring him, I told myself. He's afraid of his father, truth be told. Robert pointed to Johnny Og and said, 'He's not mine.' And the old Major said, 'Of course not—look at the protruding jaw, the apelike slant of the cheekbones, the nose turning up.'" Máire took off the old Major's accent, the drawling tone, the slurred words. "But then he called Thomas to him. 'Plenty of good Anglo-Saxon in him, that nose—like your mother's,' he told Robert. He said the reason he'd married the Mistress was to get some of her solid plodding blood. Rather than doing what most Galway tribesmen did—marry cousins or in-laws—he'd snared a real Englishwoman with a great deal of money, and that's what Robert would do one day. But, just in case, they would take Thomas with them. They wouldn't take Daniel—too much of the Celt in him. 'See the red tone of the skin?' the old Major said, and he asked Robert if he was sure Daniel was his.

"And then I spoke up. 'He knows the boys are his sons and your grandsons, and this baby Grace his daughter,' I said. And what did the scoundrel say but was I sure of that? Maybe the wee baby was Robert's sister and her half-brothers' aunt! The old Major told Robert that we'd . . . that I'd . . ."

"The dirty scoundrel," Da said.

"That's what Robert called him. And the old Major laughed and said he was only having a bit of fun. But they would only take one child, and Thomas would be the one. I was to be turned out. The old Major said if they left me in the house, I'd be passing out food before the carriage got to Spiddal. They would have to get rid of me. I begged, God forgive me. I told Robert how I loved him and couldn't I go as a servant to London. Anything to be with my son. I cried, and that pleased the old Major no end—'The proud Pearl a whingeing pauper like all the others in this cursed country,' he said. I was to get Thomas ready and bring him to the library, but thank God and His Blessed Mother the old Major and Robert got drunker and fell asleep. So I packed up what I could fit into the turf basket and got out."

"Oh, Máire, weren't you afraid?" I said.

"Terrified. But the boys helped, and Jackson lives in the village with the Smithsons, so he wasn't in the house. We made our way down the road in the dark and hid among the rocks on that empty stretch of strand near Furbo until later in the morning. Johnny Og kept watch and told me when the Pykes' carriage passed by. I was worried they might look for Thomas in Bearna though I doubted if the mistress would let them stop to search and risk being contaminated."

"No one came," Da said.

"Good," Máire said. "Still better I came to Knocnacurdh."

"But won't Jackson come looking for you?" I asked.

"He'll not be back for months and months, and by that time I'll be in New York."

"Máire!"

She reached down into the waistband of her skirt and pulled out a handkerchief. She opened it to show us a big pile of gold sovereigns. No one said anything. I don't care if she stole the money. I only hope there's enough for us to go with her and that Michael will agree to leave.

"I didn't steal it," she said. "Robert passed it to me. He didn't want his children to starve to death. And that's more than you can say for other landlords who have fathered many a child."

"When?" I said.

"When what?" Máire said.

"When are you leaving?"

"As soon as we can find a ship."

We. Amerikay.

Chapter 17

"Hat's the *Cushlamacree*," I said to Máire, pointing down at the three-masted ship moving along Galway Bay below us. "Going to Amerikay."

It was the middle of May now, a month since Máire'd come home. The Scoundrel Pykes and Jackson hadn't returned. Many of the landlords had left. Owen Mulloy had said that the landlords were leaving management of their estates to their agents. "Off to London or Dublin where they won't see their tenant's dead bodies lying on the road. Offends their sen-si-bil-i-ty," he told us.

The Mulloys and the other neighbors had welcomed Máire very kindly. Shunning and judging belonged to another time.

The two of us sat on the boulder near the cottage, nursing our babies, as if Máire'd never been away. My milk was flowing now because of the food Michael had bought with some of Máire's money. Plenty of Indian corn, rice, and peas in the market, and cheap, Michael said. Lucky for us, but most people had no money or the means to get it.

Why didn't the relief committees just buy up loads of food and give it away? Priests could hand it out, or the police, or even the soldiers. Enough of them around the place. We'd been able to give food to Mam and the Mulloys and our neighbors, but for how long?

A fresh breeze filled the tiered white sails, pushing the big vessel forward.

"Please God, we'll be on our way soon," I said to Máire. "I wish Mam and Da and the boys would stay up here at Knocnacuradh, away from the fever, until we can sort out our passage, decide what ship and when we're going." I held Stephen up to her. "Stephen's put on weight. By the middle of June he'll be able for the journey."

But Máire was shaking her head. "Catch yourself on, Honora. There'll be no journey. You and I are the only ones want to go to Amerikay. Mam and Da don't, and neither does Michael."

"That's not true. Michael's considering it. He needs a bit more convincing, but . . ."

"A bit more? You're driving him mad, holding those advertisements from the *Vindicator* up in front of his face, showing him drawings of ships, asking him which one he likes."

"But they're all different. That one, below us in the Bay, the *Cushla-macree*, has room for three hundred, but the *Erin Queen* is smaller."

"Michael doesn't care, Honora. He doesn't want to go on *any* ship."

"What if I tell him we'd leave from Liverpool on an American ship? They're faster and safer, but cost more. I suppose we shouldn't spend all of your eighty pounds of money on the passage. Should have something when we land in Amerikay."

"Stop it, Honora. You're whistling in the dark. Michael won't leave Ireland, not while there's any hope things will get better. Neither will Mam and Da, and a lovely day like this makes me want to stay, too." A drizzly morning had become a sunny afternoon. "To see the yellow whin bushes blooming against the green of the fields, feel the sun . . . Oh, look, Honora, a rainbow."

A faint arc—blue, green, yellow, and pink—stretched across the sky over Galway Bay.

"A rainbow all right," I said. "But see where it is? Out to the west with the *Cushlamachree* sailing under it, going to Amerikay."

"Mam! Auntie Máire!"

Paddy came running up with the rest of the pack behind him. Food had revived my children, who were happy to play with these new cousins. Michael came chasing after the boys, carrying Bridget on his back.

"The Giant! The Giant!" Johnny Og shouted as they all tried to hide around Máire and me.

"Amadáns," Máire said. "You'll scare Gracie and Stephen."

But she was laughing and so was I as the boys flung themselves down and started rolling around on the grass. Only Thomas stood apart. Michael put Bridget down next to me.

"Been a long time since we rollicked around," Michael said. "Thank you, Máire."

"Nice for my lads," Máire said. "Not much fun where we've been."

"Uncle Michael let us help him weed the fields, Mam," Johnny Og was telling Máire. "Paddy and I have our own potato patch to take care of."

"So?" said Jamesy. "Daniel and I are Da's special helpers, aren't we, Daniel?"

Máire's youngest boy nodded. Three and a half but not much of a talker. Jamesy will teach him.

"Thomas did *nothing*," Paddy told me. "Said his da was a lord and he didn't have to work."

"Is that so?" Máire said. "Would you like a royal clout on your bottom, Sir Thomas?" She reached for him with one hand while cradling Gracie in the other arm—awkward. Thomas ducked away. But I had Stephen tucked close and could grab Thomas. He looked at me. That beak of a nose takes up his whole face, poor little fellow. He's only five years old.

"Now, Thomas, there's lords and there's lords," I said. "Tonight I'll tell you the story about Silken Thomas Fitzgerald, a Norman lord like the Pykes, who worked very hard for Ireland. Would you like that?"

He nodded.

"And you'll help in the fields tomorrow," Máire said to him.

"But why, Mam, if the blight's going to come and kill all the potatoes?"

Now Máire did clout Thomas. Jamesy started to cry, and Daniel bawled along with him.

Michael clapped his hands. "Enough!" he shouted. "The cold winter killed the blight, and there'll be mounds of pratties *if* we take care of our fields. Now," he said, picking up Bridget, "I'm off to bring water to Champion and her foal. Who wants to come?"

Off they all went, Thomas included.

"I'm sorry, Honora," Máire said. "He's no manners. A Pyke in that way."

"He only put words to what we're all dreading."

"Michael seems very sure the blight won't return."

"He does," I said.

"He won't go to Amerikay, Honora, unless you force him to. Should you?"

"I don't know. Do you think I want to leave? I love every blade of grass in our fields, every wave on Galway Bay, but if the potatoes do fail . . . Maybe your money would sustain us, but how could we eat while our neighbors starved to death? Then there's all manner of sickness and the fever. . . . Oh, Máire, I prayed so hard that an American letter from Patrick would deliver us, and then you came to save us once again. But now . . ." Stephen started crying. I'll be weeping next. I stood up and jiggled him in my arms. "Whist, whist, it's all right."

"Ask him would he like a sip of the good stuff—Auntie Máire's milk."

I laughed, as she knew I would, and we walked into the cottage together.

❖ ❖ ❖

That night after the children were asleep, Máire and Michael and I sat by the fire. "Michael," I said, "Máire says you don't want to go to Amerikay but won't tell me straight out."

"Jesus, Honora," Máire said, "you don't have to blurt it out like that. Michael will think I'm talking about him behind his back."

"Honora and I talked about this at Christmas," Michael said to Máire. "Of course I want to stay. But if we have to leave, we have to leave. Your money, Máire, makes it possible. Still, by a kind of miracle, the fields are planted. We're not sick. Maybe if we have just a bit more faith, hold on a little longer . . . Think of it, Honora. If we go, we'll never see Ireland again. Hard to imagine."

"Patrick went," I said.

"He's coming back."

"That's right, to free us."

"What are you talking about?" Máire asked.

We'd no chance to answer, because Owen Mulloy came in through the door. "He's dead. Daniel O'Connell is dead." He held up the *Galway Vindicator*. Heavy black lines divided the columns. In bold type the headline read: THE LIBERATOR IS DEAD. "He died of a broken heart, and your Young Ireland fellows bear a share of the blame," Owen said to Michael, "going against the fellow who did more for Ireland than any other."

"No one doubts his achievements, Owen," Michael said.

But Mulloy was launched. "Monster meetings, millions jammed together in peace and protest, and yet these jumped-up fellows preach violence."

"What's he going on about?" Máire whispered to me. "Everyone loved the bold Daniel O'Connell."

"Young Ireland are fellows who thought Daniel O'Connell should be stronger," I said, "be willing to take up arms, organize a secret army, use physical force—friends of Patrick Kelly, Michael's brother."

Owen heard me. "Insurrection never got us anywhere but hanging from trees," he said.

"Whatever about Young Ireland," said Michael, "the Parliament letting Ireland starve was what really killed Daniel O'Connell. Young Ireland is right. Ireland must be independent."

"What does it matter," I said, "if the country's free and all of us are dead?"

"If Ireland were free, we wouldn't be dying," Michael said. "Patrick said that at the start. Other countries lost their potatoes and closed their ports. They don't have corpses piling up in ditches like we do."

"But that's my point," Owen said. "By breaking with our Liberator, Young Ireland bollixed up the Cause! Daniel O'Connell had millions with him, and we were organized. Repeal collectors, Repeal police. It's all gone now. The O'Connells were chieftains, and whatever about Young Ireland, they're only gentlemen, fond of rhe-tor-ic. They call for physical force . . . *how*?" Owen Mulloy was away on a rant—his old self, stacking syllable onto syllable, aroused. And then he wept.

Daniel O'Connell was dead—our uncrowned king. As Owen Mulloy held up the *Vindicator*, it was the drawings of the passenger ships to Amerikay on the back pages that I studied through my own tears.

⊕ ⊕ ⊕

June, then July, with no sign of blight. Michael was sure the potatoes were sound. Owen Mulloy had agreed. "Seven generations of my family have tilled these fields," Owen had said. "They lived through many a hard winter. And now *we* have faced the worst and survived."

Michael had nodded.

Survived—only because of Máire's money, I thought, but all I said was, "Too bad so few were able to plant."

Máire had made me stop nagging Michael about Amerikay. Granny had said I couldn't understand what it meant for Michael to leave his home place. Now he had made another. How could I ask him to leave? I tried to stop thinking of Amerikay. I remembered Granny's saying, "Is glas iad na cnoaic bhfad uibh"—Faraway hills are greener. Maybe, but we can't survive another winter like Black '47. If the pratties fail . . . "They won't," Michael told me again and again.

Máire had moved back to Bearna, into her old cottage. Her Leahy sister-in-law and her family had left for Canada. Máire'd given Da money to redeem his nets so he and my brothers could fish again. No more soup on the Bearna pier. The sisters were told to move distribution closer to Galway City to serve the desperate people flooding in from Mayo and Connemara.

Every day that passed with no blight cheered Michael and Owen Mulloy, and now today they'd taken Champion to be covered by Sir William Gregory's stallion. Her foal, Macha—Granny would have liked that name—was thriving on summer grass. She'd be sold in the fall at Ballinasloe for a good price, Michael assured me.

I'd come down to Bearna with the children. Mam and Máire and I collected mussels and seaweed, and Mam made a soup for us. The fishing boats hadn't gone out today—storms threatening.

"I've saved some for Michael and Owen," Mam said.

"They should be home from Gregory's soon," I said.

"I'll go watch for them," Paddy said. "Come on, Johnny Og."

Best friends now, the two oldest. Both seven, with Johnny Og six months older, but Paddy the leader. Jamesy nearly five and Daniel almost four, followed loyally, with Thomas—Silken Thomas, little Lord Pyke, soon to turn six—still not sure where he belonged. Bridget, only two years three months old, acted the little mother to Stephen and Gracie, who was a lovely baby.

"Mam!" Paddy shouted at me from the doorway. "Da's coming, and Mr. Mulloy, with Champion!"

I went out to meet them.

Something was wrong.

Always before when Champion had been covered by Barrier at Coole Park, she would come back prancing and dancing, with Michael and Owen preening themselves—horsemen, breeders. Now all three walked with their heads down, shoulders slumped.

"What?" I said. "She wouldn't let him?"

"We didn't ask," Michael said.

"Why? What happened? Come inside."

They left Paddy in charge of Champion, and Michael and Owen sat down to their soup, eating in silence.

Finally Mulloy said, "We're fecked altogether. Pardon my language, but there's no hope for us now."

"What do you mean?" I asked.

"It's Sir William Gregory," said Michael.

Michael and Owen Mulloy had always said Barrier's owner was a decent enough fellow for a landlord. Young, just thirty, he would come out to pass the time of day with them and watch Barrier do the job. What had happened? It seemed the groom on Gregory's estate told Michael and Owen that Sir William Gregory, as a member of Parliament, had proposed and helped pass the Quarter Acre, or Gregory Clause, an attachment to the new Poor Laws. From now on, no tenant who occupied more than a quarter acre of land would be eligible for relief. It didn't matter how many acres a lease entitled a tenant to rent or what at-will arrangements had been made. All but a quarter acre must be given up in order to receive any help at all.

"A quarter acre?" said Da. "That would barely cover a cottage."

"That's right," said Mulloy. "A quarter acre means no potato ridges, no meadows for grazing, no fields tilled and full of oats and barley and wheat. So, no crops to sell to pay the rent. If we do have another failure, in order to work on the roads, get soup, receive seeds or charity from any source, a tenant must surrender forever claims on all land but a quarter acre. They don't want rent. They want us gone. Gone."

"When?" I said.

"When what?" said Mulloy.

"When does it take effect?"

"Now. It's been passed into law."

"Maybe we won't need relief," Da said.

I looked at Michael, silent.

"This new law also says any relief must be paid from rates collected from the Irish landlords," Owen said. "Not likely. And the worst of it is, the rate collectors have started to come to fellows like me, anyone renting more than four acres. I can't pay their rates."

"Fecked," I said.

"Honora," said Mam.

"Fecked is the least of it," said Máire.

"We're leaving," said Owen Mulloy. "We're going to Amerikay. I'm going up now to talk to Katie. We have no choice. We'll go the cheap way—first to Liverpool and then to Canada."

"A heart-scalding choice, Owen," Mam said.

"Not a choice, missus," Owen said. "Necessity."

Michael stood up, apart from us.

Da asked Owen how he would get his fare.

"Rich John Dugan's offered to buy my lease many times, always hungry for land. The price of our passage would be in it, and he's always said he'd keep Michael on as a subtenant." Owen looked at Michael, who said nothing. "Michael thinks I'm being hasty, but if there's blight?" He shrugged. "I couldn't face signing my land away for a sup of soup."

I moved over to Michael, touched his arm. "Perhaps it's time for all of us to go." I turned to Da. "You and Mam, Máire and her children, Dennis, Josie, their girls, Joseph, and Hughie. Máire's got enough for our passage now, but she won't have it if we keep spending her money. We'd be together in Amerikay."

Dennis nodded. "My thoughts have been heading west, Da," he said.

"Mine too, Da," Joseph said, and Hughie nodded.

"We three read Joe Danny's letter. Plenty of work for fishermen in Amerikay, he says, and a fine way of living. No soldiers, no landlords," Dennis said.

"The Lynches have always been good," Mam said.

I remembered Marcus Lynch talking about seaside villas, and making Bearna like Brighton, a resort. Mad talk, but the Lynches were still off traveling the capitals of Europe, according to Molly Counihan. Who knows what they'll do when they return.

"Nothing's certain, Mam," Dennis said, and then to Michael, "So many are escaping, doing desperate things to get their fares. Why not go when we have the chance?"

Michael finally spoke. "There will be no blight, Dennis. And Owen, I believe we've survived the worst. We won't need government relief. Think of what would happen if we all were to leave. How could Ireland ever become a nation once again?"

Owen and my brothers exchanged looks but didn't answer.

"Michael," I said, "Rich John might want other tenants at Knocnacuradh. What then? Please, a stór, think—"

"Honora, whist," Da said. "You heard your husband. He's right. Your mam and I won't be leaving, either. I do understand why you boys want to go, and I won't try to stop you. Better for Máire to have her brothers to travel with."

"I won't be going, Da," Máire said.

"What?" I said.

"If we were all going, that would be one thing. But I don't want to leave you, Mam, and Da. If the worst is over, then . . ." She shrugged. "I'd still give passage money for you," she said to Dennis, Joseph, and Hughie.

"We'd send part of our wages back to you," Dennis said. "Good to have American letters coming."

"And Owen," Máire said to him, "how much would you get from Rich John?"

"Fifteen pounds."

"I can give you that. Sign the lease over to Michael and Honora."

"Máire!" I said.

"You shouldn't, Máire," Michael said.

"Oh, you'll pay me back. I want loads of pratties."

"You'll have that," Michael said, "and a share of every harvest."

Owen smiled at Máire. "There's our tidy cottage on the land, too, Máire."

"True enough, Owen," she said. "Who knows? I might find some lad looking for a widow with a few fields."

"You're one woman doesn't need a farm to make a match," Owen said.

❖ ❖ ❖

"The lease." Owen Mulloy handed the sheet of parchment to Michael. A week since Owen's decision, and now the family was ready to leave. We'd kept vigil through the night, sitting up with them in their cottage—all of us, the children, too, hearing Owen's stories of the seven generations of Mulloys who'd farmed this land. A name for these gatherings now—the American Wake.

Michael passed the document to me. In flowing script and legal language, the first Pyke landlord promised Owen Mulloy's great-grandfather tenure on Askeeboy through that Mulloy's lifetime and that of all his surviving sons, their issue, and the issue of their issue, dated 1730.

"See that cod-i-cil, Honora?" Owen asked. "I name Michael Kelly my heir to this lease." Owen's friend at the *Vindicator* had arranged for a Catholic solicitor to amend the lease. "All done with con-fi-den-ti-al-i-ty," Owen said.

The man would keep the Mulloy departure secret, just in case some representative of the Scoundrel Pykes would try to take Owen's fare from him for the rent, though the solicitor told Owen rumor had it that the Dublin company now managing the Pykes' estate wasn't bothering with tracking down tenants. New laws allowed landlords to sell their estates without paying off debts, as had been required. "The company will put parts of the estate on the market," the solicitor told Owen.

But what would that mean to us? In the solicitor's opinion, we would be protected. "Contractual obligation should be assumed by the new owner," Owen quoted to us. "That's why my father treasured his lease. It gives us some acknowledgment of our lawful right to Askeeboy." But the solicitor had warned Owen that the laws were changing all the time. Owen shook his head. "Not lacking in gall, our conquerors. They stole our land, then graciously allowed us to pay for the privilege of cul-ti-vat-ing it for them. Ah well, you'll care for it, Michael."

"I'll hold it for you, Owen, until the day comes when the Mulloys return," Michael said.

Owen nodded and started to speak. Then he, the greatest talker for ten townlands, went silent.

Katie Mulloy looked at me. She'd spent the week trying to change Owen's mind. "I said to him, 'If the pratties are sound and the harvest is good . . . ' But he's fixed on Amerikay and wouldn't listen to me. Which is Owen all over."

Katie rocked her youngest, James, almost two years old now. He'd survived because the food Máire's money bought in April had kept Katie's milk flowing. I held Stephen, while Paddy and Jamesy sat with the older Mulloy boys.

Joe Mulloy, fourteen, did not want to leave. John Michael, twelve, was excited about Amerikay. Annie Mulloy, nearly ten, hugged Bridget. "You and Gracie are my only sisters," she said.

At dawn, Owen took Michael out for one more tour of the fields. After the children had fallen asleep, Katie and I talked.

"I was Katie Johnny Sheridan from Minclone when I married Owen twenty-five years ago," she said. "I'd first seen him riding the old Major's horse out along the high road near Ballymoneen. I would walk down to the well or across to pick bilberries—put myself in his path. You know how it is."

"I know," I said.

She let memory carry her back and smiled at me. How old was Katie? In her forties only, her small face puckered and pinched now, but still the same eager dark eyes. And when Katie smiled, I saw traces of the girl she'd been.

"Owen was a bit ridiculous," she said. "Too young for the big English words he tried to wrap his tongue around. But I admired his ambition, and oh, Honora, he was always a good-looker, and so gentle with the horses. I couldn't love a man who was cruel to animals. Wasn't he a grand fellow for plans, Honora? He really believed that he and your Michael would raise racehorses and win great prizes. Owen said their jockeys would wear blue for the Blessed Mother and I'd be dressed in silks and satins. Instead . . ."

"Instead," I repeated.

"Well, thanks be to God we're alive, and many, many, many can't say that."

"True enough, Katie," I said.

"And Owen says there's plenty of land and horses in Amerikay. He wants to go to Ken-tuck-y. You mind it, Honora?"

"In the southern part, I think, Katie."

"Good. Warm weather. The shipping agent says it's only a few days' walk from Quebec, Canada. That's where the ship comes in. *Emigrant*— that's the name of our ship—*Emigrant*. Owen likes that—emigrants on the *Emigrant*. It's meant to leave Liverpool in one week. Doesn't give us much time, though Owen says four days' walking will get us to Dublin and there's steamer ships crossing the Irish Sea every hour. Imagine, Honora, every hour. I'd wait all day at the crossroads in hopes of seeing Owen and come back again the next morning if he hadn't passed. Every hour. *Emigrant*—mind that name, Honora, in case, you know . . ."

"I do," I said.

"I suppose the *Vindicator* will print the story if we sink in the middle of the ocean. That'd please Owen." Katie paused. "Honora, do you wonder why we are alive? So many have been taken, not only families like the Ryans, without much to fall back on, but substantial people—farmers with long leases and the rent paid, and they've died. But we survived. The white hare, a few forgotten turnips, an extra helping of soup—little things. Was it luck, do you think, or grace, or one of that other crowd taking a hand?"

"Fairies, Katie?"

"Why not? Better to believe in them than in what the Reverend Smithson preaches—that God is punishing us. Honora, I was ready to send Annie to that school of his. Copper-colored fuzz had started on her cheeks. I thought better a Protestant child than a dead one. But then your father caught the herring, and we were saved. But why us, Honora, and not the Ryans or the Lonergans or the Clancys?"

"I've stopped asking, Katie. I just thank God. I pray we'll be together again."

"In heaven, Honora?"

"In Amerikay."

❖ ❖ ❖

We walked with the Mulloys to Bearna, where they would meet my brothers, collect their children, and start the one-hundred-mile journey to Dublin on foot. Katie had her pot and Owen had used the few extra shillings Máire gave him to buy clothes for the children from a pawn-broker in Galway City who didn't know him.

Maybe the Pykes' agents were far away, but there were so many stories of landlords taking fares for rent, better no one knew they were leaving.

We said good-bye to my brothers. Was it only two years ago Hughie was our scholar, the smartest boy in Master Murphy's school, and Joseph the best hurler for twenty townlands? The quickness of his compact body was gone, now. And would Hughie's tall, thin form ever fill out? I'd cared for them both when they were small—my baby brothers. I'd not see them again.

Jamesy wouldn't let go of Hughie's arm, and Paddy held Joseph's leg.

"Easy now," Joseph said to Paddy, freeing himself gently. "Here." Joseph took his hurley from the bundle Mam had given her three sons. The meal sack also held a stone from Bearna strand, a piece of turf, and a dozen cornmeal cakes. "I scored many a goal with this stick and plenty more left in it."

"But you were going to teach me how to bounce the sleen high and then turn and catch it," Paddy said, indignant, speaking not as a seven-year-old, but man-to-man.

"Sure, when we get rich in Amerikay, we'll come back and you and I will play for Galway against the world," Joseph said to Paddy.

"You'd better."

"We'll send your fare, Honora," Dennis whispered to me. "We'll be together." The oldest boy, a father himself, Da's right hand.

He hugged Mam. Dennis and Josie held up their little girls to her. She kissed each one, silent. Then Máire threw her arms around Hughie and started sobbing. He stood straight, his arms at his sides. Impassive.

"Máire," Mam said. "Máire, please."

"You can't," I whispered to Máire. "No tears. We don't cry anymore."

She looked at me, then took a breath and let go of Hughie. He stepped away from her.

All of us went very quiet and let young Annie, baby James Mulloy, Gracie, and my Bridget do the weeping for us. Máire's boys only stared.

Owen put his hand out to Máire. "Thank you," he said to her. "You have saved us."

Máire took Owen's hand and shook it.

So the Keeley boys and the Mulloys set off for Dublin on that last Sunday in July, Garland Sunday. We prayed with them at Tobar Enda—no candles now, no priest leading the prayers, no crowds of friends and neighbors praying together, circling the well. Silence.

And they were gone.

❖   ❖   ❖

The weather stayed warm and dry. Two weeks later we dug the early potatoes. Healthy.

"If only Owen had waited," Michael said.

"But in the first failure, the early crop was sound, too, and the main crop blighted," I said. "Still . . ."

"Still, still, still! We'll eat tonight, and all belonging to us will, too!" Michael said.

❖   ❖   ❖

I cooked a great feed for Mam and Da, Máire and her children, and for the first time since the potatoes had turned to pus in the pits two years before, we had stomachs full of pratties and a bit of hope.

"If only our boys and the Mulloys had waited," Mam said. Now it was

Michael who said that we couldn't be sure all the potatoes were sound until the main harvest next month, and Da said why not dig them up now and Michael explained that the rest of the crop had to grow more. He said that some of what we were eating came from the seeds Patrick had given him, which surprised him. Michael hadn't thought potatoes could grow from seeds.

While they talked, Máire came up to me. "Step outside," she whispered.

I followed her out. We stood looking down at the Bay, the last clouds of sunset still red in the west.

"The fever has come to Bearna," Máire said. The old coast guard warehouse near her cottage had been turned into a fever hospital and workhouse combined. She could smell the dead and dying. "Every night," she whispered, "Andy John O'Leary drives a cartload of bodies and dumps them into a trench near Bearna graveyard. It's horrible, Honora."

"Dear God, Máire."

"Mam and Da won't talk about it. She says to pray for their souls. Johnny's mother's gone and three Connollys and . . . Jesus, Honora, the whole place is dying around us! Even the songbirds are gone—hardly a lark left. Flown away."

"Eaten," I said.

"Oh," she said.

"You haven't seen the half of it," I said. "Up in the hills the people are all gone, cottages tumbled—some with all the families dead inside. Paddy and I went after robins' eggs up near Cappagh and we saw a pack of wild dogs tearing something apart. 'A sheep,' I said to Paddy, but he'd seen. 'A boy, Mam,' he'd said to me, just like that. 'A boy.' "

"Oh, dear God . . ." Máire started sobbing.

"Stop that! You didn't weep in front of the Pykes. You can't here."

"But it's so horrible! Have you no feelings left, Honora? Jesus Christ!"

"Máire, how dare you . . . ," I started, but I stopped. I put my arms around my big sister. "We can't cry, Máire, we just can't. Plenty of weeping and wailing in the beginning. We keened for the potatoes and mourned every death, but now, after two years, we've learned. If you cry, you die. Hold the grief inside you. Bury it."

"I didn't know," said Máire. "I truly didn't. Even after I came back, during those first months up here with you and Michael, I didn't understand. Jesus Christ, Honora, I can't bear it."

"You can. You will. What choice?" I said.

"Amerikay," Máire said. "I've changed my mind."

"Amerikay," I repeated. "But you gave your money to the boys and to Owen Mulloy. A kind and generous gesture, still . . ."

"Honora, Robert gave me a diamond necklace that his mother will never miss. I have to be careful who I sell it to, but we could get our fares."

"Too late. Michael will never agree. He's convinced the potatoes are sound and the harvest will be good. And now he has the lease."

"I only wanted to help, Honora."

"I know."

❖ ❖ ❖

The weather stayed fine, and three weeks later Michael had us all up on the ridges—Mam and Da, Máire and the children—digging into the sweet soil.

"No stench," he said, "and no fog." He held up a large prattie. "White potatoes! No blight!"

Paddy yelled, "No blight!" and the others took up the chant:

"No blight! No blight!"

We filled the new pit Michael had dug to the top with potatoes from our ridges.

Three days later, the pratties were all sound. Mam and Da carried a load down to Bearna. We could supply them and ourselves, the townland, anyone who came to our door in need.

❖ ❖ ❖

Mid-October. The wheat, oats, and barley ripened into a bountiful harvest.

"The crop will pay the rent," said Michael. "If we can find men to help us bring it in."

Michael and I talked late that night, glad for the warmth of the fire, stretched out on new hay.

"Of course," Michael said, "the best would be if the new company forgot about us entirely. Jackson dealt with Owen Mulloy—there'd be only his name on the rent rolls. But if an agent does come, I have the Mulloy lease."

"I'm worried, Michael. There's a lot of strangers about now, marking and measuring."

"By the time anyone figures out exactly who owns what, we'll have the crops sold. If the worse comes to the worst and we're discovered, we'll pay the rent."

"But they might want to collect Mulloy's back rent from us."

"They couldn't ask that."

"And what about the poor rate?"

"Oh, for Jesus' sake, Honora, what else are you going to worry about? Do you think they're going to track us down for the pennies that would be in it for them? The land's come back, that's the great thing. I know this harvest won't restore us completely, but it will keep us going until next year. I might not have to sell Macha. She's the best of Champion's foals. And we have a lease for fifteen acres of good land."

Michael kissed me, but I wouldn't be distracted.

"I don't know," I said. "We're being watched. I feel it. We're getting back on our feet. Someone will try to knock us down. If only the boys would write from Americay or if your brother Patrick . . ."

Michael got up from beside me and stepped over the sleeping children. He stood at the glass window, looking out into the dark.

Let him stand there. Maybe I am going on too much, but I'm only trying to tell Michael the true situation. The land's back, is it? For how long? Why wouldn't he at least consider going to Amerikay? I closed my eyes and started to breathe evenly. Let him think I'm sound asleep. After a few minutes, I opened my eyes a bit to see if he had turned and was staring at me, sorry and sorrowful. But I saw only his back. Tense. Still those same broad shoulders. He'll fill out now with the pratties.

What are you thinking, Michael, a stór? That I'm a hard, hectoring woman and you should never have stopped for that swim in Galway Bay? And if you hadn't, would I be a nun studying in a library in Rome right now? Who knows. We hadn't had a real fight since the blight struck. It takes a full stomach to risk an argument. I giggled. He turned then.

"You think it's funny?" he started in a soft voice, so as not to wake the children, but I heard the anger under the words.

I got up and went to stand near him, but I didn't say anything. Nor did he. I waited. Finally he spoke.

"We can't all leave," he said. "A man has a right to live in his own country, to feed his children, to follow his faith." He stopped.

"And even play a bit of music?" I said. "And make love to his wife? And run his horses?"

"Yes, all that," Michael said, "in the land of his birth."

"I don't *want* to go," I said. "But . . ."

He turned to me. "Honora, your heart beats 'Amerikay, Amerikay.' "

"Only because I want us to live."

"We will live," he said. "The land has come back."

"But, Michael, the soil might be healthy, but the very air is clogged with cholera and fever," I said.

"There's no disease in Knocnacuradh, and there won't be," he said, and looked back out the window.

"But . . . ," I started, and stopped myself.

Why keep arguing for the worst of the worst? I pretended reason was talking, but it was fear making the argument, saying, "Run. Run. Go!" I am willful. I do want my way. Granny was right, and Michael knows it. He thinks I don't trust him, that I don't believe he can keep us safe. That's not true. It's only . . . only what?

I touched Michael's shoulder. "I suppose we're safe enough in Knocnacuradh, away from the sick and fevered," I said.

We'd kept alive on Peel's brimstone and nettles and a sup of soup stretched and scraped. We had lived. We will live. I put my arm around Michael's waist. We looked out our fine glass window together.

"Down there in the dark is Galway Bay. We can't see it, but it is there," he said. "When I ran along the strand and dived into the sea that summer morning eight years ago, I had no idea what lay ahead of me. I'd left all I'd ever known. I found you. We made a life. We have four children. We've suffered and survived. Don't ask me to leave!"

I stood staring out, too, imagining the *Cushlamachree* sailing down the Bay under the rainbow, across the ocean to Amerikay. The image faded.

Now Michael turned to me.

"Don't be afraid, Honora. I'm with you."

"My hero from the sea," I whispered. "And I'm with you. Here, on this high Hill of the Champions."

"Faugh-a-Ballagh," Michael said, and kissed me.

Chapter 18

"WELL BEGUN is half-done!" Michael said to the ragtag crew he'd gathered to reap our fields the second week of October, 1847.

Paddy and Jamesy took up the chant: "Well begun, half-done! Well begun, half-done!"

Our workers—five of them, one scrawnier than the next—belonged to the government's new category, "the able-bodied unemployed," two from Galway, one from the far reaches of Mayo, one from Connemara, and the other from Sligo. Women and children had been turned out from the workhouse to make room for these men—the only group eligible for relief now. Insane.

They'd been only too glad to leave the workhouse for even the tiny wages we pledged to pay—pledged because the money would come only when the crop was sold.

Michael had done a deal with Billy Dubh, who was here now, walking the fields, praising the fine heavy ears of wheat and the golden oats, making ticks in his little book. Michael showed him the lease Owen had left him. He said, "Fine, fine," not too bothered about legalities. With Jackson gone, Billy was only too happy to forget the Scoundrel Pykes' faraway agent in the Dublin company. He'd take the whole crop, no problem, and sell it—at a profit. Ná habair tada. And if someone came looking for the rent, we'd have to pay it, but we'd still have potatoes to eat.

The men began to harvest the wheat. They moved slowly at first but went faster as the motions of cutting and carrying and tying up sheaves came back to them—hard labor, but not senseless like work on the roads had been. Máire and I brought potatoes out to them at midday. The men stared at the piles we set in front of them.

"How many can we have?" said the youngest, the Connemara man.

"We have a good few in the pit," I said. "Eat up."

"It's just my wife and baby are in a scalpeen out on the Moycullen Road, and I'd like to take half of what I'm allowed to them."

Each one made the same request.

"You have to eat," I said, "or you won't have strength to work."

Michael said each man could have five potatoes to eat and fifteen to take home. Well, that delighted them. They fell on the potatoes, and as they ate, each man told us why he had no pratties of his own. Two had no seed potatoes to plant, two had been evicted, and the oldest man, from Mayo, admitted that he'd simply despaired of the land and had left, sure that the blight was waiting to ambush him all over again.

"What would we have done without you, Máire, and the seed potatoes you brought?" I said as we walked back to the cottage.

That afternoon, Paddy and Jamesy as well as Máire's Johnny Og and Daniel and even Silken Thomas—his nickname now—worked along with the men. Máire and I took Stephen and Gracie and Bridget down to Bearna. "They can play on the strand, well away from the fever hospital," Máire'd said. Máire and I sat talking on the rocks of the strand as we had as girls while Bridget played with Gracie and Stephen.

"Bridget's a real little mother," Máire said. "We could do with more daughters."

"We've enough children," I started, but stopped when I saw Mam hurrying toward us. "Máire, she's waving a letter!"

I picked up Stephen and Bridget and she grabbed Gracie and we ran to Mam. The American letter—finally.

Mam hadn't even opened it. Sister Mary Agnes had brought it to her. The envelope said: "To Michael and Honora Kelly, Askeeboy."

Patrick Kelly, at last, or word from Owen Mulloy, our brothers? I gripped it in my fist. A bank draft? Our passage?

"Open it!" Mam and Máire said together.

Inside the envelope was nothing but two written pages, each signed at the bottom, "O. Mulloy."

"It's from Owen Mulloy, and it's a letter, only . . ." I scanned it quickly. I looked up. "Mam, come, let's go inside."

"Honora, what?"

"Tell us," Máire said.

Stephen and Gracie started crying, sensing something.

"Inside," I said.

I made Mam sit down by the fire. "Where's Da?" I said.

"He rowed into Claddagh."

"Now, Mam, Owen's letter has very bad news."

"The boys," she said.

I nodded.

"Oh, God help us, not all of them—please God, not all of them."

"Dennis," I said.

Máire put her arm around Mam.

"Holy Mary, Mother of God," said Mam. "Poor Josie, the poor girl."

"Josie's gone, too, Mam," I said.

"And the babies, the little ones?"

"He's not sure," I said.

"Not sure? What about Joseph and Hughie?"

"Owen's not sure about them either."

"I don't understand," she said.

"Read the letter to us, Honora," Máire said.

But I couldn't. Owen Mulloy described a horrific journey. Mam didn't need to hear the details of five hundred passengers crammed belowdecks, whole families made to sleep on rough plank beds six feet long by six feet wide, stacked one upon the other, a terrible passage beyond imagining: "A benighted hole full of dirt and depravity, with only ten wooden buckets to contain all the . . ." Owen had crossed out "shit" and had written "waste."

He wrote of wild seas, terrible winds, people screaming with fear, vomit and waste ankle-deep, a forty-day crossing with water for only thirty days and most of it fouled because the storage barrels had once been used for vinegar and wine. What chance for any of them when the fever attacked? Dennis had tended the sick ones before falling ill himself. Owen wrote: "Nothing we could do for him. Josie begged the sailors for pure water to give Dennis, but they are heartless men. He endured days and days of awful suffering and his brothers never left his side. His death was a release. We buried him at sea. Forty others have met the same fate."

"What does he say, Honora?" Mam asked.

"Dennis went quickly, Mam. Josie and the boys were with him. A peaceful death."

"Thank God for that. My poor boy. I dread telling your father. We thought they were safe."

"A grave in the deep for Dennis, the same as for my Johnny," said Máire.

"But what about Josie and little Katie and Mary?" Mam asked.

I couldn't tell her what Owen Mulloy wrote about the place they landed, Grosse Île: "The sick were stretched out on the ground and left to die."

Instead, I said to Mam that Owen had lost track of them during the time they were kept in quarantine. He and his family went on to Quebec. He'd heard that Josie had died, but there'd been no news of Joseph, Hughie, or the little girls. "There's a good chance they're alive," I said.

"Please God," Mam said. She took our hands in hers. "Pray, girls. Pray hard."

We did, until Mam told me to go home before darkness fell.

"Stay here with Mam. I'll keep your boys," I told Máire. A slow, sad walk up to Knocnacuradh. I was carrying Stephen, matching my steps to Bridget's pace. I prayed for Dennis's and Josie's souls, asking God to please spare the others. Right foot, left foot. It was after sundown when we reached the cottage.

"Good girl, Bridget," I said as I opened the door for her.

Two and a half and not a complaint from her on the long way home. Such a help to me, Bridget sang little tunes of her own making to Stephen, lulling him to sleep. So young, but I depended on her as Mam had depended on me when Dennis was born. Oh, Dennis, Dennis . . .

"Da! Da!" Bridget screamed.

Michael lay stretched out on the floor.

"Michael? . . . Michael?" I squatted to touch his face. Warm.

He opened one eye and winked at me.

Then with a rush the boys attacked from the dark corner where they'd been hiding.

"We've killed Finn McCool!" yelled Paddy.

He and Jamesy, Johnny Og, Thomas, and Daniel ran round and round Michael, screaming and jumping.

"I'm Cuchulain!" Paddy said. "I'm in the battle rage!"

"I'm Finn!" said Johnny Og. "And here's my salmon leap!" He jumped up a foot or more.

"I'm Silken Thomas, the Earl of Kildare!" said Thomas, stomping his left foot on the ground, then his right. "And I've fringe on my armor and helmet."

"I'm Red Hugh O'Neill!" said Daniel. "I have a magic sword which you can't see!" He swung the weapon over his head.

Jamesy ran to me. "I'm William Boy O'Kelly and I want you to come to my party! Bridget, too, and Stephen, and everybody!"

"No party until we finish the fighting," said Paddy.

"It looks like you've finished off this boyo," I said, pointing to Michael.

"We killed the Giant, Aunt Honey," said Johnny Og.

"Don't be so sure," Michael said, reaching out to catch Johnny Og's ankle.

Battle cries, laughter—the troops rescued their comrade, then dashed away.

"I'm with Da!" Bridget said as she lay down next to him.

"That will even up the sides," Michael said.

Stephen wriggled in my arms, and I put him down. He crawled up to Michael and threw himself on his chest.

"Are you for me or against me, Stephen?" Michael said, getting his breath back.

"Truce!" I said. "Truce! This is a magic white flag I'm waving, and you're all to lay down your arms. In fact, you're to lay down your whole bodies. We start early tomorrow with the harvesters."

When they're asleep, I'll tell Michael the hard news and show him Owen's letter.

"But, Mam," Paddy started, "Da's been telling us stories, like the before times. Great stories—the Irish Brigade, the warriors of the Red Branch. Even Thomas wants to be with the Irish now that he can be an earl. Can't we hear about another war?"

"Our warrior queen has spoken, boys," said Michael. "Come now, the pratties are boiled. Eat a few to sleep on."

They needed no second telling. During the meal, Jamesy—acting William Boy O'Kelly—ordered Michael to pipe a tune.

"I have no pipes," Michael said.

Still buried. Too dangerous to try to pawn or sell them.

"Da! We're all pretending—can't you?" Jamesy said.

"I can, of course!" said Michael, and whistled a bit of a tune while Jamesy nodded and kept time. "Would you like to learn the tin whistle?" Michael asked him.

"I would, Da," he said.

Michael looked at me.

"I think we can spare a few pennies from the harvest money," I said.

"Thank you, Mam," Jamesy said.

"All right now," I said. "Eat up and go to sleep. We're all tired, even the Giant."

But the children wouldn't settle, and when they did lie down to sleep, the laughing and poking and grunting continued. Three weeks of food had restored them. Finally, they slept. I handed Owen Mulloy's letter to Michael, putting my finger to my lips as I did.

He hunched over the fire for light and read it. After a long time, he looked up. His eyes were wet—the only tears he'd shed during the whole of this ordeal.

"To have gotten so close—to be there, to see it . . ."

Michael had read the facts I'd kept from Mam: The *Emigrant* had anchored in the river, Owen said, with a load of other ships with Irish people aboard. Passengers were not allowed ashore. Owen wrote:

> *The authorities were afraid of fever. We'd little food or water left. Finally the sickest, Josie and the two little girls among them, were taken off and put into a tent hospital—no bed, laid on the grass floor. It was so crowded, some of the sick were left in the open. Terrible cold weather. Ice in the river. They put the rest of us on the other side of the island, with a troop of British soldiers to keep the sick and the well apart. We had to buy our own food. The doctor who ran the island sold milk from his own cows at double the price charged in Quebec City. Joseph and Hughie sneaked across to find Josie and the children. When the steamer came to take us to Quebec, there was no sign of the boys. We've been in Quebec for three weeks, and I've heard from a priest that Josie died and her children were being cared for by a French family. I hope the boys are alive, but I'm not sure.*

Then Michael read the last bit of Owen's letter out, whispering the words:

I'm writing to tell you to stay home. Remember these names: the Vir-ginius, the Agnes, the Larch. These are the coffin ships, and dozens more as bad. Thousands buried at sea, and on that island. God knows how many of us will survive this winter. Michael, they say there was a fellow here in Quebec with a golden staff last year. I name no names. He had quite a bit of bother, but is said to be in good form now and working for the Cause. The United States is meant to be better than here. I'll write again when we get there. Hoping you and all are well. I am yours very truly, Owen Mulloy.

"Patrick," Michael said. "Alive. Some one thing to thank God for."

I nodded. Now, I thought, he'll say, Wasn't it good that we didn't go with them? It could be us dead of fever and buried at sea, or on that hell island, our children orphaned or lost. And there will be nothing I can answer except, You're right.

But he said nothing.

"I love you, Michael Kelly," I said.

"Oh," he said. "Good. But why, exactly, at this moment?"

"For playing with the boys. Children need to laugh. And for crying for Dennis and Josie . . . and for not saying, 'I told you so!' and for so many things."

I sat beside him at the fire. We listened to the up and down breathing of the seven children—easy and sweet. No sickness.

We lay down on our bed of straw. I stretched out my legs and arms. I'd never thought to thank God for space to sleep in, and yet since a child I'd hated being cramped. I liked to fling my arm out and not hit anyone with it. Even though I might put my back against Michael, I wanted room. I couldn't bear sleeping crowded together in a wooden box surrounded by strangers.

When I'd watched the *Cushlamachree* sailing down the Bay, she'd seemed so wide and so high. Were those ships really only floating tombs? Coffin ships, Mulloy called them, carrying our people to graves in the cruel sea or to hostile land. No escape, then, no Amerikay. And yet the Mulloys survived the crossing and tens of thousands with them. A risk, a terrible risk. And now we'd the pratties and a good harvest. I couldn't settle, thinking of Dennis and Josie, God rest them, Joseph, Hughie, the little girls . . . and Patrick Kelly.

"What do you think Mulloy meant by Patrick's 'a bit of bother'?"

"Sounds like jail," Michael said. "But out now. We'll hear from him one day. That's Patrick's way. There will be a letter."

✧ ✧ ✧

Máire didn't come up to help with the harvest. Mam needed her, full of grief Mam was, with not even a wake to ease the pain of these deaths. Nor would she be able to visit Dennis's and Josie's graves in Bearna churchyard.

At noon, the harvesters made fires and produced pots to boil their potatoes right there in the field. They'd managed to hold on to the pots, through evictions or the quarter acre exile.

"One more day," Michael told the men. "One more day if the weather holds."

Which it did. By sunset the next day, Michael and his crew had harvested all the fields and had the sheaves tied up and ready for loading. Pleased with themselves, and rightly, the men sat together enjoying the last bit of the October sun. Michael got each one to tell his story. First they spoke only of the woes and injustices they'd suffered, but then they began to talk about their families and the before times in their own townlands. They conjured up other harvests, grand fairs, green hills, and clear lakes. A bit of joking, some give-and-take, men restored to themselves for a few moments—the harvest gathered and the potatoes whole.

"Here comes Billy Dubh," Michael said, standing up. "I see the wagons. He's even brought a troop of soldiers to guard the crops."

Guard. As if anyone around had strength enough for stealing.

Billy Dubh climbed down from his seat next to the driver on the lead cart. He walked over to Michael slowly, shaking his head. "God bless all here," he started as his eyes went spying and prying around the field. "A fine bit of work's been done, I can see that. A fine bit, and nothing I would like more than to pay you the price agreed on, but sad to say we are all under the same laws, and when the government speaks, what chance do men such as myself have but—"

"What are you talking about?" Michael asked him.

A voice said, "The poor rates. Under all this fool's blather is the hard fact of an obligation your landlord contracted, and I am taking his crops to meet it." A man had ridden up behind the wagons. Jackson.

"You," I said.

"Who?" Michael said to me.

"It's Jackson," I said. "The agent for the Scoundrel Pykes."

"Former agent," said Billy Dubh. "Mr. Jackson has taken a more lucrative position in the Imperial Civil Service, collector of poor rates, parish of Rahoon, barony of Moycullen, County Galway. I have been invited to assist Mr. Jackson since I can offer a familiarity with where the men under the said obligation hold land and have crops."

"Be quiet, you fool," Jackson said. He turned to Michael.

"Is it because we hold the lease?" Michael asked.

"Your landlord is liable, and Major Pyke is in arrears for hundreds of pounds. We are taking this crop." He raised his voice and shouted at the harvesters, "A shilling for every man helps with the loading."

A shilling? We'd promised them six.

The harvesters stood still. The Mayo man looked at Michael. A shilling might be all they could hope for from three days of work.

"Go on," Michael said. "What choice?"

"Let's go in," I said, and reached for Michael's hand.

"I'll stand here," he said.

I stopped. "Then I will, too."

We watched the men load up the wheat, the haycocks, the oats, the barley—five wagons full.

The soldiers had dismounted and stood with the stocks of their muskets on the ground. Any pause in the rhythm of loading, and Jackson would shout, "Troop!" and the soldiers would pound their muskets on the earth.

I'd left Bridget watching a sleeping Stephen inside the cottage, and the boys were playing behind Champion's shed. Please God, let them stay there. If Jackson sees our horses, he'll take them, too.

Billy Dubh walked over to the side of the field where the harvesters had piled their boiling pots. "A few more pence here," he said to Jackson, pointing at the pots.

"Take them," Jackson said.

The Mayo man heard. "Excuse me for speaking, Your Honor, but those pots belong to us, sir."

"And whose tenants are you?"

"No one's now, sir. Cleared all of us, we signed away our land for the relief."

"The price for these will go to pay for the charity advanced you."
Jackson nodded to Billy Dubh. "Take them."

"Touch these pots and I'll have these men unload the carts," Michael said.

"You'll what?" Jackson laughed. He got off his horse and gestured toward the soldiers. "They'll arrest you. You're violating the law!"

Michael walked past Jackson and Billy Dubh to a wagon and reached for a sheaf.

"Stop that man!" Jackson said to the sergeant of the troop.

The sergeant didn't move.

"You heard me. I have the authority. My instructions are 'to use force to the very edge of the law and beyond' to collect the rates—the words of Sir Charles Woods, chancellor of Exchequer himself. Shoot that man!"

"I'll not kill a man who's not attacking me," the sergeant said.

"You fool. They'll be attacking all of us soon enough if you show any weakness." Jackson pointed at Michael. "Strike him, then, knock him down!"

The sergeant stepped forward.

"Please," I said.

"Hoo-rah! Hoo-rah!" I heard.

I turned to see Paddy riding toward us on Champion's bare back, waving Joseph's hurley in the air. The other four boys ran beside him, shouting, "Hoo-rah! Hoo-rah!" with the foal Macha following along behind.

The soldiers lifted their muskets into firing position, aiming at the clatter of children hurtling at them.

I ran in front of their guns. "They're children! They're playing!"

Michael whistled to Champion, and she slowed to a trot and then stopped. Johnny Og, Thomas, Daniel, and Jamesy stood still, staring at Michael, who walked over to them.

The charge had spooked Jackson's horse. He struggled to hold on as the animal reared, pulling on the reins in Jackson's hand, jerking his arm. "Down! Down!" Jackson yelled.

I turned from the soldiers to go to the boys and saw the Mayo man head down, shaking, terrified. I couldn't help him. I had to get to the boys. But then he raised his head, caught my eye, and winked. He turned his face so Jackson and the soldiers couldn't see him bent over with the laughing.

I took a breath.

I shouted at the boys, "You played a good joke on the soldiers."

The soldiers are the danger—not Jackson, not Billy Dubh.

I turned to the sergeant. "High spirits. They, uhm, wanted to show off for your soldiers. You might have a fair few recruits among my boys," I said. "I'm sure there are Irishmen among you. Do you think these lads might have a future?"

The sergeant relaxed. "Muskets down!" he shouted, and the men lowered their guns. "Are you asking me to be the recruiting sergeant?"

"With me as Mrs. McGrath?" I replied.

"As for that, ma'am, Mrs. McGrath's son didn't fare that well if you mind the song."

"That's right," I said. "He came home with two sticks for legs, did poor Ted."

"It happens," said the sergeant.

"And where are you from?"

"Tipperary, missus."

"You're a long way from home."

"I am. Longer than I can say right now."

Jackson shouted, "Enough, Sergeant! Do your duty."

"We don't murder children, sir."

"No impudence! This man's horse belongs to the queen. I order you to take possession."

"Well, sir, we have the crops and I think that will do rightly. Move out, men."

"The horse! I want the horse," said Jackson. He pulled his animal over to where Michael stood with Paddy and Champion. "Get off, you little bastard."

Paddy clung to Champion, his arms around her neck.

"Jackson, Jackson!" It was Thomas. "Over here! It's me! You're confused—*I'm* the bastard, and my brother here. You remember us?"

Jackson turned away from Michael, left Paddy and Champion.

Thomas walked over to him. I imagined Jackson thinking: He *is* the old Major's grandson. What advantage can I get from this?

Michael whispered into Paddy's ear.

Paddy and Champion took off galloping at full speed right at the stone wall that separated this field from the long meadow.

"Stop him!" I said to Michael.

Michael took my hand. "He's all right."

Champion gathered herself and cleared the wall as easily as she'd taken the jumps at the Galway Races. Paddy leaned forward, holding on to her mane, not a bother on him. The foal Macha jumped the wall and went after them.

"Hoo-rah!" I heard from the boys—and the harvesters—and maybe even one or two of the soldiers.

"Chase him," Jackson said to the sergeant.

"Outside my orders, sir."

"Then I'll go," said Jackson. He turned to mount, but the horse bolted and ran, heading back to Galway City.

So.

Jackson and Billy Dubh got on the lead wagon, and the soldiers escorted our crops away to pay the old Major's poor rates.

The harvesters filled their boiling pots with pratties and walked off toward their scalpeen shelters.

A bit of our own back anyway, they said to us. Heartening to see brave lads.

Michael clapped each of the boys on the shoulder. "You did well. Faugh-a-Ballagh! Clear the Way! The motto of the Irish Brigade that beat England and the name of a great racehorse. You won the war and the race today."

The boys shouted, "Faugh-a-Ballagh! Hoo-rah!"

Michael smiled at me.

"Michael, we've got to find Paddy," I said.

"I don't think he's gone too far," Michael said, and he whistled.

Sure enough, the sound brought Paddy and Champion trotting back, the foal trailing behind.

"I didn't know you could ride like that, alanna," I said to Paddy.

"I didn't either," he said.

"Bring the children down to Bearna, to your mother's. Jackson might come back for Champion," Michael said. He mounted Champion. She neighed at her foal, who trotted up beside her.

Michael urged Champion over the wall, with baby Macha jumping alongside them. All were away.

"Our da is great altogether," Jamesy said.

"He is that," I said.

But now what?

Chapter 19

I took the children to Bearna to stay with Mam and Máire and went home to wait for Michael. I paced and peered out into the darkness that whole long night.

At the crease of first light, I hurried down our lane to the crossroads. I walked a mile out and then a mile back along each of the four roads all day. No neighbor came near me.

Finally, near sunset, Michael appeared, striding toward me on the Moycullen Road. I ran to meet him. He gathered me in his arms.

"I was so worried," I said.

"I went a fair way," he said, and we walked up to the cottage, his arm around me. "I couldn't risk trying to sell Champion and Macha," he said. "Anyone who could afford to buy a horse would inform sooner or later."

"So what did you do?"

"Remember the stallion and his herd of Connemara ponies in Ballynahinch?"

"Of course."

"Champion and Macha are with them now," he said.

"How did you ever find them?"

"It was Champion led me to the herd. She's a wonder," he said as we walked into the cottage.

He stretched out near the fire as I set the pot of pratties before him.

"You must be wrecked—riding out thirty miles and walking back."

"I didn't walk," Michael said. "I was picked up by a Biany coach. They've extended the route to Clifden because, the driver told me, the famine is over."

"But it's not."

"The government says it is. Soup kitchens are closed for good. The roadworks won't reopen. The only relief is the workhouse, paid for by Irish landlords."

"For God's sake, Michael, how can they say such a thing? No blight, maybe, but most people had no seed potatoes to plant."

"I know."

"Why aren't you angry?"

"I am very angry, Honora."

"Jackson stole our crops and that sliveen of a gombeen man led him to us, probably arranged the whole thing from the beginning."

"Probably."

"And you've lost Champion and her foal."

"For now," Michael said.

"How will you whistle her back from a herd of wild horses? I'm surprised the Connemara people haven't eaten the whole lot of them by now. They don't have the fine feeling for animals that you have."

"Honora, I thought you understood. Champion's—"

"Gone! Everything's gone—we're worse off than we were before. It is *your* work and *your* sweat they took. Don't you feel humiliated? Don't you want to shout and stomp and strike back?"

"Of course," Michael said. "But, Honora, we weren't humiliated. We didn't let them crush us completely."

"I'd say it was a close thing."

"We saved the boiling pots," he said.

"So?"

"Champion escaped."

"Hmm."

"And our own Silken Thomas became a patriot."

"All very nice. And not one of those victories worth a farthing! Soft words won't butter turnips and neither will small triumphs. Goddamn it, Michael, we're fecked!"

"Not quite. I have a position."

248 Mary Pat Kelly

"I am the Bianconi assistant blacksmith. At your service, madam, earning two shillings a day."

"Michael Kelly, why didn't you tell me! How could you tease me, let me go on and on at you?"

"I am telling you, Honora. And if Jackson hadn't come, and if I hadn't taken that nice ride and met the driver, who remembered my grandfather . . ."

"I love you, Michael."

I kissed my hero from the sea. Thank you, God. Thank you.

✦ ✦ ✦

Before we fell asleep on the straw bed, Michael made a tale of his adventure, and I felt as if we were back leaning against the warm rock near Galway Bay and I was hearing about his mother and the May morning dew, about his father the piper, and Murtaugh Mor, the huge blacksmith.

For all your lovely long body and broad chest, Michael, a stór, it's your way with a story that wooed me and won me and keeps me loving you still.

Michael made me see his journey through the Connemara mountains. I could picture Champion nuzzling Michael's shoulder before she ran off to join the white stallion, her foal Macha behind her.

"I've never told our children the story of Macha's race," I said. "So many of Granny's tales to tell them. Fadó. I promised her."

Michael kissed me.

"We're all alone," he said.

I looked at him. "We can't. The food's brought back my . . . well . . ." I stopped.

"You're right, not a time for risks." He pulled me to him. "Nice to sleep close together," he said.

"It is," I said, settling against his shoulder.

"I do want another child," I whispered. "A son to call Michael Kelly. But not yet."

"We'd best have another daughter," he said. "Nice for Bridget to have a sister."

"True," I said. "A sister's a treasure, no question." And we slept.

⟡ ⟡ ⟡

Finally Black '47 ended and 1848 began. Better for us, but still bad for most. With the pratties and Michael's two shillings a day, we were among the fortunate. Few enough of us.

Michael returned from the forge every night with news of eviction after eviction, tenants ejected into the teeth of winter with no hope of any kind of relief. We whispered these conversations after the children went to sleep.

"People have some chance at survival when they can get down on their hunkers in their own home place, but when they're put out on the roads disease gets them, and the cold and rain become a sentence of death," Michael said.

But because the British government said the famine was over, there was no relief.

One night, a week after the New Year, Michael came home very angry. "A delay today with the coach and this official from London and some others waited in the forge. I had to listen to him go on and on about how the British people had been too generous to the Irish—a mistake. We must be healthy enough now. Some tenants were shooting at their landlords. Should have left us hungry and weak. He told the others that he'd seen battalions of soldiers on the road from Dublin. 'A taste of the steel, that's what's needed,' he said, 'not a mouthful of free soup!'

"At first I said nothing while these men in their great heavy coats and beaver hats insulted the Irish people. Called us paupers! As if we were a different species—not human." He imitated the English accent: " 'The footpaths better be cleared of the paupers' bodies or fever will infect the town!' one man said. And then the official answered, 'They're not dying fast enough.' Well, I couldn't let that pass. I pointed my hammer at him. 'Not dying fast enough?' I shook the hammer, but he wasn't bothered. He looked at the other men. 'This fellow doesn't understand,' he said to them. And then he started to instruct me, Honora, saying that wars and plagues and famine were nature's way of reducing surplus population. He told me that the famous Nassau Senior, professor of economics at Oxford and an adviser to the government, is troubled that only a million of us have died. 'That's scarcely enough to do much good,' this Nassau said."

"Oh, God," I said.

"Then the official told me, 'Ireland will now be turned over to those who can make it pay. The land cleared and a great influx of capital, that's what Ireland needs. Your country will look back on this blight as a great blessing!'

"I took a step toward him, ready to lift the hammer up and strike that evil man, but the boss shouted at me, 'We've got horses waiting for their shoes!' I stopped. The head blacksmith is a good enough fellow, and I respect the agent, Mrs. Carrigan."

"Hard on you to stay quiet, Michael, but you have to."

"I know. But, Honora, I've started to hear about these new Confederation Clubs that Young Ireland has started—Patrick's friends—John Mitchel, Thomas Meagher, William Smith O'Brien. They're giving speeches around the country, calling for the people to rise up."

"Young Ireland would be better passing out food," I said.

Night after night, Michael came home with what he'd seen and heard. More and more he talked about the Confederation Clubs and Young Ireland. With two shillings a day and the potatoes in the pit, he could lift his head and see the dimensions of our disaster.

"We're a people on the edge of extinction," he said, "and no one seems bothered about it."

❖   ❖   ❖

February came, and the snowdrops. Last year, I'd cut up the stems and made a soup with them. Now I took the children to pick a bunch of flowers for Mam. We put them in the tin can left from the soup line and went to Bearna. Michael's two shillings a day had helped Da redeem his nets, and he was out with the fleet. Bearna was shaking itself awake, though the fever hospital near Máire's cottage still spread its stench over the village and the wagonloads of corpses came out through the gates every night.

We were helping one another. Máire and Mam took a share of Da's catch to Mother Columba at Presentation Convent and to Sister Mary Agnes at the Sisters of Mercy. The nuns fed thousands every day with no help at all from the government. Aid still came from America, from the Quakers and other kind souls. And Michael couldn't pass a beggar in Galway but that he gave them a penny.

As we walked into the cottage, I saw Mam sitting, hands folded, looking into the fire. Praying for some news of Joseph and Hughie, and Dennis's girls.

We'd heard nothing, though many American letters were coming now. The Clancys, the Wards, the Muldowneys, all received their passage money—the sailing season begun and the rescue under way again, the ones who'd escaped reaching back for those left behind. But nothing from our brothers or Patrick Kelly. I'd put Amerikay away from me. "I'd be betraying Michael," I'd told Máire. "He'd know if I were still dreaming of going."

"Here, Mam, a bit of spring for you." I handed her the flowers.

"Thank you. Take some to Máire. She's got her cottage looking very neat and tidy, Honora."

"It's nice for you to have her and her children near," I said to Mam.

"It is," Mam said. "Johnny Og went out in the boat with your da."

"My ones are playing on the strand with the other children," I said.

Families were slowly recovering—wages from Boston and New York sent fishing boats out from Bearna. We were the lucky ones, surely, though I never forgot that Michael had gotten his job at the forge because the last two blacksmiths took the fever and died.

"Wrong to rejoice with misfortune all around us," Mam said. "Dennis and Josie and a dozen of our neighbors lost. It'd be such a comfort to know Joseph and Hughie were safe."

"They're good lads and you're powerful with your prayers. We'll be hearing from them."

❖ ❖ ❖

March brought a craze for sowing potatoes I couldn't believe.

I walked up to the ridges where Michael was laying out our seed potatoes on Sunday, the only day he didn't work at the forge—and let Father Gilley try to say anything.

The ground had taken a long time to thaw, but Michael hadn't begrudged the freeze.

"Cold kills the blight," he said. "It did last year. Look at the hillside."

In the distance we could see figures everywhere, bending over their rows, setting potatoes into the beds. In Rusheen, Shanballyduff, Cappagh and every townland—all planting.

"Where did they find the seed potatoes?" I said.

"We are a resilient people, Honora. Anyone who survived this far must have a singular talent for finding a way. And also there are fewer . . .

He stopped but I finished his sentence. "Fewer people looking for seed potatoes?"

He nodded. "Another good harvest will make all the difference. Men who couldn't sow potatoes last year are doing it now. That's what I told the Confederation fellow from Dublin."

"So they're around again?"

"They are. Mitchel's got his own paper now, *United Irishman*. He wrote that we should take to the streets like the French did."

"The French?"

"Crowds in Paris drove their king out, one two three, Mitchel says. He's asking why the West is asleep."

"Tell him the West is hungry."

"The West will wake, Honora. Remember how the boys sang that during the chestnut raid? Ah, but that was the day poor little Grellan . . . God rest his soul." He stopped.

"Amen," I said.

Only two years ago—a lifetime of sorrow lived in such a short time.

But now because of Michael's labor and sound potatoes we would survive. Please God.

"Shall I do the sums, Michael?"

"Do them."

"You've earned twelve shillings a week for twelve weeks so that's seven pounds two shillings. Subtract the three pounds we gave Da to redeem his and the other fishermen's nets and the money for seed, which left three pounds."

"Good," Michael said.

"Then there's the pennies you spent for the tin whistle."

"Jamesy's taken to it."

"He has," I said.

"I've given a shilling or two to Mother Columba," he said.

"That's all right—I've allowed for that and the pennies you hand out to beggars."

"It's very hard to pass them by."

"We have two pounds, five shillings now. We'll need to buy food during the summer, hungry months when the pratties are finished. But this money and your pay should be enough to see us through."

"We'll have enough to help your family and the neighbors," Michael said.

"We will. And if the fishing goes well, if we all stay healthy, if . . ."

"Bad luck to line up too many 'ifs,' Honora. I'm working at a decent wage. What more can we ask?"

"We should be able to save twelve pounds by Saint Michael's Day," I said. "In case the agent does come for the rent."

"A good harvest and no blight will see us right," Michael said. "Look at our neighbors." He pointed to the fields.

"More courage needed to find and plant these potatoes than to rush through the streets of Paris," I said.

❖ ❖ ❖

Two weeks later, Michael brought the *Galway Vindicator* home from the forge.

"Listen to this, Honora. Smith O'Brien says that as a direct descendant of Brian Boru he has the right to create an armed National Guard. Thousands are signing up to join this force. And read this—" He pointed to the headline: IRISH BRIGADE FORMING IN AMERICA. "That's it, Honora. That's what Patrick's been doing. That's why we haven't heard from him—he's recruited Irishmen to come home and stand with us. Imagine thousands of armed men landed on the shores of Galway Bay, joining with this new National Guard. Smith O'Brien says the Irish fellows serving in the British army and in the police won't fire on their own people. They'll join us—all together, men again—taking back our country at the very moment the British thought they'd destroyed us. And Patrick there, raising Grellan's crozier. Jackson will run away, Honora, and so will the English officials, foremen, and food traders. Beware the risen people." He started to sing.

That chainless wave and lovely land
Freedom and nationhood demand

Paddy and Jamesy ran over. The boys listened with eyes wide and heads back and clapped their hands as Michael gave out the final verse in his strong, clear voice.

> *But, hark! a voice like thunder spake*
> *The West's awake, the West's awake*
> *Sing, Oh! hurrah! let England quake*
> *We'll watch till death for Erin's sake!*

The boys and Bridget laughed. Stephen said, "Da! Da!"

Till death. We've clawed our way back to life, and now he has to take on death?

"Hoo-rah! Hoo-rah!" the boys shouted.

My sons—only seven and five—unafraid, looking up at their da. A glorious thing if the exiles did return—the Wild Geese come back at last, with muskets on their shoulders and money in their pockets to chase away all those who'd profited from our misery, to claim the land that holds so many unmarked graves now. Would it console the dead to rest in the soil of their own nation?

✧   ✧   ✧

But at the end of March, the British arrested John Mitchel for sedition. He was found guilty by a jury packed with government supporters, condemned by the words in the *United Irishman* that stirred Michael. In May Mitchel left Ireland, transported for fourteen years. Meagher and Smith O'Brien would be next. But Young Ireland would not be silent.

"They're traveling the country, speaking to great crowds of people. The rising will come *before* the leaders can be jailed," Michael said. It was early June now.

The children slept as we talked in low tones by the fire.

"I thought Young Ireland was going to wait until after the harvest." Michael shrugged.

"What about Patrick and the fellows from America?"

"They could be on the seas now," he said.

"Could be? Doesn't Smith O'Brien know? What about the English? Surely they are watching. Michael, they'll arrest the lot of you. And Patrick's still a wanted man." I sat straight up. "Michael, you haven't told the fellows at the Confederation meetings about Patrick, have you, haven't said he's your brother?"

"Not in so many words."

"Michael, Patrick's a danger to us. You can't talk—"

"There's only a few fellows know I'm related to the man who raised Grellan's crozier at the demonstration."

"Michael, you know there's bound to be at least one informer among you."

"Not these men, Honora. And besides, what will it matter if they know? After the revolution Patrick will be a hero."

Michael soothed me with stories of all the countries that were chasing out kings and tyrants, and that now was Ireland's chance and why couldn't I have some faith?

But I thought of the soldiers who'd come that winter morning, singing their song, "Croppies, lie down," and Jackson, a bad enemy waiting his chance to strike at us.

Michael slept, dreaming a brave man's dream, and I lay awake worrying.

❖   ❖   ❖

"The Church has taken against Young Ireland," he said to me a few days later.

"That's bad," I said.

"Orders from Rome. The British will recognize the Vatican for the first time since Henry the Eighth, if the Irish behave."

"Where are you getting this?"

"The fellows at the Confederation Club," he said.

"So we're to be done in by history again," I said.

Paddy and Jamesy were awake and listening. Paddy stood up and said, "Until Ireland takes her place among the nations of the earth, let no man write my epitaph," and Jamesy followed with: "The Harp is new-strung and shall be heard!"

"Very nice," I said, and looked at Michael.

"Da taught us!"

"I see."

"And listen, Mam." Jamesy took out the tin whistle Michael had bought him and started to play "A Nation Once Again."

"You see, Mam," said Paddy, "Jamesy will march beside me playing that tune when we fight the Sassenach."

Stephen, walking and talking now, shouted, "Hoo-rah!"

Brave words. Michael was planting the old hope in their young hearts. Freedom. A Nation Once Again. Our language, our songs, our stories, ourselves. A government that wouldn't let its people starve to death while sending away the harvest to feed England. Jamesy and Paddy would remember these nights no matter what happened to Young Ireland. And they'd tell their sons, bury the seed deep within them, then tap down the scraws to protect the dream. Good. We needed that hope to survive, but . . .

"Kellys Abu," I said. "But remember, boys, glory comes from living for Ireland, not from dying for Ireland. Am I right, Michael?"

"You are, Honora," he said.

But the boys only looked at me. The Warriors of the Red Branch *fought*. "You're dead!" they'd shout when they thrust their imaginary swords at one another.

"Da," Paddy said, "let's sing the one about the minstrel boy who fell in battle but his harp kept playing."

"Not now, Paddy," Michael said. "Time to go to sleep."

And dream.

❖   ❖   ❖

A week later, Michael came home very late. "Are the children asleep? Sound asleep?"

"They are," I said.

He pulled me close to the fire and then down onto the ground. He whispered, "I met a man today knows Patrick, in Amerikay. This fellow, Thomas D'Arcy McGee, edits a newspaper in Boston. He's come to Galway with another fellow called Terence MacManus to help organize the uprising."

"And he's actually seen Patrick?"

"Better than that. He brought a letter." Michael waved a folded piece of paper at me. "Patrick's in Chicago."

Our American letter at last, and I could see there was something pinned to the corner.

"D'Arcy McGee said Patrick's still wanted and can't risk the mail, but when he heard McGee was coming to Galway . . ."

"Michael, I'm so glad. He's alive."

"Here, Honora—" Michael passed me a piece of paper. "A bank draft for twenty-five pounds."

I looked at the document—"Pay to Michael Kelly." Any bank.

"Dear God, a fortune! Is it safe to take it to the bank?"

"Mrs. Carrigan, the agent at Bianconi's, will change it for me. Honora, we have the rent for certain."

"The rent?" I said. "But, Michael, now we have enough for our fares, and for Mam and Da's, too. Máire has money. She wants to go now. So many dying still, Michael—the O'Driscolls and the Connellys out at Tonnybrocky, and the Manions in Minclone . . . What good if we survive and our neighbors don't? Thank God. Amerikay . . . thank you, Patrick."

Michael was shaking his head. "We can't desert our people, Honora. Patrick sent the money so we'd be able to *stay*. He says: 'We need you in Galway, Michael. A trusted man on the scene.'"

"On the scene?" I repeated.

"The uprising. McGee's off to meet with the Molly Maguires in Sligo, and—"

"But, Michael, we'll never have this much money at once again— enough to get to Chicago." Arguing my case, all my resolutions gone— Amerikay.

"Patrick says Chicago's no place for women and children. He writes, 'We're fighting so Irish people can live in Ireland and not be driven out of their homes.' There are plans for tenants like us to buy our land, Honora. And we have the lease. If only Owen had waited."

"Let me see the letter."

First, an apology for not finding a way to get money to us sooner.

I didn't learn about the Great Starvation until last year.

Didn't learn about it? Where had he been? Ah, here:

I wandered deep into the wilds of Amerikay, in a place I have no words to describe. After a year I came to Chicago, a rough place where Irishmen were digging a great canal. Hard, dangerous work that killed many a man. But hardship made the fellows who survived tough and unafraid—a new breed of Irishmen who haven't forgotten their home-land and are ready to right the wrongs committed against her.

I looked up at Michael.

He took the letter and repeated Patrick's words: "A new breed of Irishman—*that's* the army he's recruiting."

"He doesn't say that."

"How could he? But McGee told me. And I'm to prepare the way in Galway, a trusted man for leaders like D'Arcy McGee to contact, and then when the Irish Brigade lands I'll have men ready to meet them."

"Michael, most have barely recovered from the starving, and so many are sick. There's fever everywhere. . . ."

But Michael wasn't listening. "D'Arcy McGee says the Irishmen in the British army gather to hear Smith O'Brien and cheer him when he speaks."

In his mind, Michael was riding with the Irish Brigade, Patrick on one side, Paddy and Jamesy on the other, banners flying, St. Grellan's crozier held high. Faugh-a-Ballagh! Clear the Way! Kellys Abu!

I said no more.

❖ ❖ ❖

The fine weather of June became days and days of rain through all of July, keeping the children inside—a good chance to start them studying. The schoolmaster who'd taught my brothers had died. The starvation had destroyed the last of the old hedge schools everywhere, and Miss Lynch, afraid of disease, would never hold classes in the Big House again. But I could teach my sons, strong enough now to concentrate, even though with the last of our pratties gone we were eating meal again. But we'd enough, and soon the early potatoes would be ready and the main crop was growing well.

Using the *Vindicator* as a text, the boys learned to read. Smith O'Brien kept the news interesting. Paddy and Jamesy pounced on every new word they recognized in the newspaper columns. Paddy had filled out into a big eight-year-old, and though Jamesy, six in three months, was slight, his round baby face had come back. They connected their da and the mysterious uncle Patrick with the stories in the newspaper of the growing rebellion and shouted, "Faugh-a-Ballagh!" to each other.

Michael had found pieces of slate for the boys and gave one to Bridget. Paddy and Jamesy drew their letters on it in Irish and English with the edge of a charred stick, while Bridget made jagged lines and asked me, "What does it say, Mam? What does it say?"

Bridget looks more and more like Máire, only with Michael's eyes. Three now, with an old head on her, I thought, and a little mother to Stephen.

Another drizzly morning. An awful July. Stephen pulled at Bridget's slate. "Play, Bridget, play!"

"Now, Stephen, let her be. Come to Mam, a rún." I made a sling for him with my skirt and rocked him back and forth while I sang Mam's song to him: "*Siúil, siúil, siúil a rún . . .*" Stephen smiled up at me. Poor fellow—a hard old time of it you've had. A year and three months, not a baby anymore. We hardly noticed you growing. And where'd you get that red hair?

"Oh, Mam," Paddy said. "I smell Stephen."

"Ugh," Jamesy said.

I lifted him and checked his diaper—a piece of meal sack. Nothing. The smell came from outside, through the open door. Could the stench of the auxiliary fever hospital reach all the way up here?

"Bridget, take Stephen." I walked over to the window. Fog covered the Bay. Fog.

"It's not," I said. "Not, not, not!" I heard my voice going higher and higher until I was screaming, "Not! Not! Not!"

"Mam? . . . Mam! What's the matter?" cried Jamesy.

Paddy knew. He took the slate he held and slammed it to the floor. "The pratties," he said.

⟡　⟡　⟡

I wouldn't go up to the ridges until Michael came home from the forge.

"Ruin on every hillside, all the way to Galway City," he said. "Men sitting on the stone walls, heads down, doing nothing . . . not even trying to dig."

We walked up to the beds—all blasted, stalks bent and rotten, and that smell, wrapping itself around us, choking us in the same way the fungus had strangled the plants.

"Thank God you're working, Michael. And thank God for our American letter. Life and death now."

He didn't answer, but walked away, climbing high up to the topmost ridge. He stood there a long time and then came down to me.

"How much, Honora? How much do you have saved?"

"With Patrick's money—thirty-five pounds," I said.

"Will it be enough for an American ship?"

"Michael . . . do you mean it?"

He nodded.

"Mam and Da will come. And Máire. She can sell that jewelry."

"We'll write to this church in Chicago called Saint Patrick's. McGee said the priests there know all the Irish. They'll pass the word, get to Patrick."

"Yes. Yes. Sister Mary Agnes will send it for us. But, Michael," I had to ask him, "what about the uprising?"

"There'll be no uprising. The blight's beaten us. A worse enemy than the British army ever could be. People know what's coming. Starvation. I dread to think of the winter. Martial law and no aid from the government for the rebel Irish, you can be sure of that. I couldn't ask you to endure that again, Honora, I have to decide what's best for my family. Patrick will understand. He'll help us when we arrive. We only have to get there."

"But food for the journey?"

"There's meal and corn in Galway City."

"The price will go up now, Michael, with the failure—they won't wait to raise it."

"I'll get it. Somehow, I'll get it."

"The soldiers will be on alert. They're watching and they might be watching *you!*"

"I'll be careful."

"I'll ask the Lynches. I'll beg them, I'll do anything."

"Beggars," he said. "They've made us beggars. The West awake? What a fool I am."

"No, Michael! You've kept us alive so we can escape, we can go! Amerikay! Say it, Michael, say Amerikay!"

He wouldn't.

I shook him. "Say it!" I pounded on his chest. "Say Amerikay."

"Amerikay," he said.

"Chicago."

"Chicago," he repeated.

"I don't care how hard the life is there—we'll survive. We're strong,

Michael. Didn't Patrick say that those who survive hardship there become tough and unafraid? We won't die, Michael. And we'll come back here someday—or our children will or *their* children will. They'll come back to Galway Bay. They will, Michael—riding in the Irish Brigade! Say it again . . . Chicago."

"Chicago."

❖ ❖ ❖

An uprising did occur during the last days of July, but as Michael predicted, the failure of the potatoes ended any hope of a people's army marching to triumph. Smith O'Brien and a few others had surrounded the police station at Mullinahone, still convinced an early victory would raise the countryside. The police agreed to surrender to Smith O'Brien if he would return with a larger force to save the police the humiliation of being defeated by so few. Smith O'Brien agreed, but the police ran away, raised the alarm. At the nearby town of Ballingarry, forty-six armed police advanced on the Young Ireland men and the two hundred local people who were with them. The rebels threw stones at the police, who then barricaded themselves in a two-story house belonging to the Widow McCormack. Smith O'Brien wouldn't attack for fear of burning down the poor woman's home. The police fired on the rebels, who scattered. In the following days Smith O'Brien and Meagher and others were arrested. The government threatened to hang them, but according to the *Vindicator*, the rebels would be transported as Mitchel had been.

"A sad day for Ireland," Da said to me when I went to see him after the failed rising. I found him walking on the strand.

"Michael said the blight defeated them, Da, not the British," I said.

"Right enough," he said.

"We're going, Da," I said. "Will you please come with us to Amerikay?"

He shook his head. I waited. He stared at the Bay—high tide, the waves breaking close to us. "I'm too old, a stór. Your mam and I will finish our days here by Galway Bay. If your brothers write, the letter will come to Bearna. Your mam will never leave while there's that chance." He turned and started back toward the cottage. He stopped at the door. "When I brought her into this house all those years ago, I promised her that it would always be our home. Níl aon teinteán mar do teinteán féin," he said.

"There's no fireside like your own fireside," I translated aloud.

"It's only the truth," he said.

"Oh, Da, I know. . . . How can we leave you? How?"

"You have to go. They've left the young no choice. When?"

"As soon as we can, Da."

"Don't leave it past August. Autumn storms are bad enough in the Bay, but to cross the ocean during that time of year would be very dangerous."

"You're the man knows," I said.

"I do. This place, Chicago—is it on the sea?"

"It's not, Da."

"Too bad. I know how you love Galway Bay, Honora. A comfort for you to find a bit of water to remind you of it."

Chapter 20

August now and no doubt remained. Blight had killed the entire potato crop of 1848. Fields, planted at such sacrifice, were black and blasted. For the third time in four years we'd lost our food, though once again the other crops and livestock left our ports for England. But panic, not protest, made people rush the carts.

Michael had insisted on telling the Bianconi agent, Mrs. Carrigan, that he was going, though I was afraid Jackson would find out and devise some reason to take our money. "I must give her time to find someone else," Michael said.

"Time to find someone else?" I said. "Twenty or thirty blacksmiths will be on her doorstep the moment you go."

"Still, she was very good to cash the bank draft from Patrick for us and said nothing. We've only two weeks. Mrs. Carrigan will keep our secret."

Máire was ready. She had sold the diamond necklace for twenty gold sovereigns to the woman who managed Bride's Hotel. Fifty-five pounds between us. We'd walk to Dublin. Take a boat to Liverpool. Find an American ship. Thank God Máire and her children were going with us.

"I have to," Máire had said. "Save you and Michael Kelly from being cheated in Amerikay."

Finally, the two weeks passed. We were leaving the day after tomorrow, on August 15—Our Lady's Feast—a lucky day.

I was with Máire at her cottage in Bearna. The children were at Mam's.

"I wish we had a bit more money," she said.

"We have enough for our fare and food. Michael says that Patrick will meet us."

"We should ask Miss Lynch for a few pounds," Máire said.

"But she might tell."

"She won't. Besides, we'll be gone in two days."

We went to Barna House for the last time.

❖ ❖ ❖

Máire and I stood outside talking to Miss Lynch through the back door. "My goodness, what is going to happen?" Miss Lynch said to us. "Ireland can expect no help from England, none at all. Shocking, horrible things the English say about the Irish. They think we're all rebels and beggars and that England should cut off all aid."

We let her natter on. Her travels had aged her. She'd told us how the capitals of Europe had disappointed her. "Rabble in the streets, destroying the great cathedrals!"

Máire interrupted her. "We're going, Miss Lynch," she said.

I was still worried about telling her the truth. "But what harm?" Máire'd said. The Lynches were Mam and Da's landlords, not ours. Da paid his rent last year and would again, and old Mr. Lynch had always allowed a bit of leeway. "She *is* my godmother," Máire had said, "and you were her favorite student, so . . . ." So. Máire said straight out that we needed her help.

"You mean money?" she asked.

"We do, Miss Lynch," Máire said. Very direct.

She looked beyond us at the Bay. "But won't you find it hard to leave?"

We didn't bother to answer.

"We may be going, too, you know," she said. "The new laws. Nicholas has had offers. . . ." She stopped. Ná habair tada, for her, too. "I have very little money of my own. A token, maybe? I could give you a book or a comb. . . ."

"We're walking to Dublin, Miss Lynch," I said. "Then we're taking a steamer to Liverpool and the ship across the ocean from there. We're only taking what we can carry. We have eight children with us."

"Our hands will be too full for books," said Máire.

"On our way here from Dublin, the roads were clogged with people leaving," Miss Lynch said. "Not paupers, oh no, but families with wagonloads of furniture and trunks. The big farmers are going, shopkeepers, lawyers, doctors . . . The joke in London is that pretty soon it'll be harder to find a Celt on the banks of the Shannon than a red Indian on the banks of the Hudson. Oh, they think themselves great wits in London!"

Máire and I kept our eyes down.

"Are you sure you'll even get a ship in Liverpool with all that are going?" she asked.

"We need to look over the ships, find an American one. Money will make the difference. Please, Miss Lynch."

She still stared at the Bay.

"I'm sure Our Lord will bless your generosity," I said.

"Our Lady, too," Máire said.

"I'd like to bring the memory of your goodness with me," I said. "I'd like to be able to tell our children so they can tell their children that there was kindness in Ireland, that our landlord cared about us, that our teacher had compassion for us."

"All right," Miss Lynch said. "Yes, I will. You know, the only thing they really fear in London is that the Irish in America will pass on to their children a hatred for the British."

Máire and I said nothing.

I did want to take good memories of her with me to erase the anger I felt toward the Lynches. Be kind, Miss Lynch, please.

"How much?" she asked.

"How much?" I said.

"How much do you want?" No fluttering tone now, a merchant's daughter after all. A member of a merchant tribe, making us name a sum.

I wanted to say, Keep your money. How can I put a price on what you meant to me and I to you?

"Ten pounds," Máire said.

"Ten pounds! A fortune!" Miss Lynch took a step back into the house. "Oh dear," she said, "I would never have that much in cash! Never!" Then, "Three pounds?"

"Five," Máire said.

Miss Lynch nodded and went inside.

"Oh, Máire, you were wonderful!"

"Shh . . . Act disappointed," Máire said.

But when Miss Lynch came back with the money I showed my gratitude.

"Thank you, Miss Lynch, thank you. This means so much, you'll never know. May God bless you."

Máire said, "Good-bye, Miss Lynch."

"Safe journey, girls," she said, then turned, walked through the door, and shut it behind her.

"She's sad, Máire."

"Maybe."

"Well, she was very generous."

"She knows," Máire said. "Knows a great crime has been committed, but as long as the victims are dead or gone, she'll be able to forget. Now she can say, 'I helped. Remember the Keeley girls? I gave them five pounds! A fortune!' So, sixty pounds between us."

"Good," I said. "Watch—we'll convince Da to come along."

"This fellow Patrick Kelly. Might he be a match for me?" Máire asked.

I laughed and told her that Michael had told me once that the only woman Patrick loved was the dark Rosaleen—Ireland herself.

"Is he any way good-looking?" Máire asked.

"He's Michael's brother, isn't he? Handsome enough, but he's not easygoing like Michael. A coiled-up kind of fellow, doesn't have Michael's blue eyes, his smile . . ."

That evening, I walked out to meet Michael for a quiet word before he came home to the children. We couldn't talk about going to Amerikay in front of them. Ná habair tada, say nothing. Billy Dubh, the gombeen man, was sidling through the townlands seeking whom he could devour. The new laws that made selling land easier created an opportunity for Billy Dubh. A word to the wise to one of the insurance companies or banks eager to buy up bankrupt estates meant a nice fee for him. The vultures circled, and the gombeen man was waving them down.

But we're escaping. Thank God. They won't pick our bones.

Now Michael climbed the hill to me—something of his old high stride back, his black hair thick again. Hard to see those lines around his blue eyes. Twenty-seven's not old. He'll grow young again in Amerikay, I thought as we walked through the gap between the stone walls he and Patrick had repaired that first spring.

"Mrs. Carrigan said she'd give me two shillings extra tomorrow—my last day."

"Look, Michael, our turnips and cabbages are coming up. The Dwyers and the Tierneys and the Widow Dolan, all the neighbors, will be glad of them through the winter."

"Leaving them something, at least." He glanced up at the ridges of dead potatoes and shook his head.

"Come into Champion's shed," I said. "We can talk inside."

"I can't, Honora," he said. "Too many memories of Champion and the foals born there, the dreams Owen and I had. And the fields . . . Our life's blood put into them, and now . . ."

"Now what?"

"Gone. What's that Mangan piece? I learned it in the hedge school from Master Murphy:

> *Solomon! where is thy throne?*
> *It is gone in the wind; Babylon!*
> *Where is thy might?*
> *It is gone in the wind.*

"Master Murphy told us Mangan was talking about Ireland, about the great royal enclosures—Tara—gone in the wind. And now all our efforts gone in the wind."

"Irish poets are certainly great ones for grief. But we won't mourn now. We'll wait until we get to Amerikay, Michael. Dig up the pipes. In Chicago you'll play a long lament, almost a pleasure to cry when your stomach's full and there's work."

Michael nodded and nearly smiled. "True enough," he said.

"Then you'll strike up a dance tune. Wait until our Chicago neighbors hear a real Galway piper. I'll be carrying Granny's stories in my head. We'll have great gatherings altogether and soften up that hard old place."

"I'll play marches for the Irish Brigade."

"You will. Faugh-a-Ballagh!" I said.

"All right, Honora," he said. "I know you're trying to make me look forward, not back. I'll try. And Patrick will be there. When do you think he'll get the letter?"

"Sister Mary Agnes posted it last Thursday. She addressed the outer envelope to the pastor and put our letter inside. It should be safe enough. I wrote that we'd arrive in Chicago by September and would ask at Saint Patrick's Church for news of him."

He nodded.

"We're alive, Michael. You've kept us alive," I said to him. "*You.* You did it."

He shrugged.

"And now, I wonder, Michael Joseph Kelly, if you'd care to follow me. The children are occupied and we'll be well settled in Chicago in nine months, so . . ."

"So?"

I led Michael into the shed. When he saw the bed of grass and weeds in the center, surrounded by yellow whin bushes, purple fuchsia, honeysuckle, and buttercups, he smiled at me. I loosened my hair and let it fall around me and stepped close to him.

"I washed it this morning," I said.

"In the stream near Enda's well?" he said, and kissed me on the top of my head. "A stór."

I took his face in my hands. "A ghrá, we will have a son called Michael Joseph Kelly. He'll be born in Chicago, but conceived here at Knocnacuradh—the Hill of the Champions. Lie down," I said, and Michael eased himself onto the bed. I held up a handful of grass to him. "From the long meadow."

Michael inhaled its scent. "It smells sweet," he said. "Our children never ate grass, Honora. We always fed them something. They never ate grass."

"They didn't. Cabbage leaves and turnip tops, snowdrops and sorrel, but never grass."

"I've seen the mouths of children stained green in Galway City."

"And you gave them a few pence, I hope."

"I did."

"You're an honorable man. Come here to me, my hero from the sea. We're alive."

I leaned down and kissed him, then lay down beside him on the grass. He opened his arms to me. We made love in the small close space that still smelled of horses and hay, and I thanked God for my husband, Michael Joseph Kelly.

As we walked to the cottage, he said, "We made something out of nothing at Knocnacuradh."

"We did, Michael."

"It's not the end, Honora. Patrick said in his letter that our people don't forget their country or the ones left behind."

"How could they?" I said. "They're Irish."

"Patrick remembered us."

"He did, surely," I said. We stood looking down at the Bay.

"We'll have the pipes," he said.

"We will."

"I can teach Jamesy the tunes my father taught me."

"You can."

"You tell them your granny's stories."

"Fadó," I said. A new story. "You and Patrick could find a piece of land to farm."

"He'll never settle. D'Arcy McGee told me Patrick travels one end of America to the other for the Cause. Once he was the one who longed for nothing so much as his own green fields while I yearned to wander."

We stood watching the sun go down on Galway Bay.

"I wonder where you'd be, Michael, if you hadn't gone swimming in the Bay that summer morning," I said.

He put his arm around me. "The fortunate day."

I reached into the band of my skirt and took out the stone he'd given me three years before, held it out to him on my palm—green and pink flecks of silver caught the last of the light.

He touched it.

"A talisman," I said.

"A piece of Ireland to bring with us," he said.

Jamesy came bursting out the cottage door.

"Mam, Paddy's opened up the sack of meal."

I turned to Michael. "That's food for the journey." I called up to Jamesy, "I'm coming," then said to Michael, "We'll bring living, breathing bits of Ireland with us, and they're hungry."

I started up to the cottage, but he stood still.

"Are you going to dig up the pipes?"

"In the morning," he said. "I'm a bit tired."

And he was asleep before the children that night.

I looked at my sleeping husband. We'll make another Knocnacu-radh, I promised him. You will be happier once we're on our way. Michael, aren't you the fellow rode off to who knows where on his big red horse?

A chance to start again—an adventure—Faugh-a-Ballagh!

❖ ❖ ❖

The next morning, I shook Michael awake at dawn. He usually gets up at first light. Not like him to sleep on.

"Michael, wake up, a stór. Can't be late on your last day at the forge."

He opened his eyes, then closed them.

"If I knew making love would wear you out like this, I'd have thought twice," I said.

He didn't answer.

"Michael. . . . Michael! Wake up!" I touched his forehead—hot. "Paddy! . . . Paddy!"

"What is it, Mam?" Paddy said.

"Paddy, go get some water for Da—cold water from the stream."

Paddy came over, looking down on Michael.

"Hurry, Paddy, run."

Paddy grabbed a tin can left from the soup kitchen and went.

Now Jamesy woke up. "What is it, Mam?"

"Go back to sleep."

But he sat up. He watched me put my hand on Michael's forehead. "Is Da sick, Mam?"

"I'm fine, Jamesy," Michael said. "Go back to sleep." Then to me he said, "Take me to the shed, Honora. Now."

"I won't. You've just a touch of something."

Paddy ran in with the water. I held it up to Michael's lips and he drank a bit, then coughed . . . and couldn't stop coughing.

"Da! What is it?" Paddy said.

"Stay back, Paddy," Michael said. "Da's not feeling great. I'll have a lie-down in the shed. Now, Honora."

"Michael, I'll send the children to my mother's. You're not—"

"Now, Honora."

Oh, dear God, please, not this, please!

"You must, Honora, you must. Remember John Joe Foley—three days in the shed and he recovered."

Michael started to stand up as if he would go by himself.

"Wait, Michael, we'll help you."

Paddy and I held him up between us and with slow, uneven steps walked into the shed, then eased him down on the bed of grass where we'd made love only yesterday. Yesterday?

"Paddy, take the others down to Bearna and send Aunt Máire up to me."

"Go, Honora," Michael said. "Go with them."

"I'm not leaving."

"Give me water and let me sleep. Come back tomorrow."

"I'm not leaving. Paddy, go. You carry Stephen. Go. Now."

"Mam, I don't want to leave Da either!"

"You heard your mother, Paddy." Michael's voice cracked as he spoke, but Paddy obeyed him.

A few moments later, they were standing at the door of the shed. Paddy held Stephen. Jamesy and Bridget were crying.

"Da? . . . Da! . . . Da!" they said through their sobbing.

"Go on! Da needs to sleep. Go to Aunt Máire," I said.

⬧ ⬧ ⬧

I sat there with Michael, holding the wet edge of my skirt on his forehead while he slept. Such ragged breathing and a bad odor when he exhaled.

Then Máire stood at the door.

"Come out of there, Honora."

"I won't."

"Come out. Think of your children."

"Go away, Máire."

Michael must've heard, because he spoke, his voice weaker now. "Go, a stór. Go, my love, please."

"I won't." I dipped my skirt into the water and put it on his burning forehead. Was there a yellow color to his skin? I couldn't tell in the dim light of the shed. Yellow fever kills quicker than the black. Not yellow, please, or cholera. Cholera in Galway City. If it's cholera . . .

"I'm hungry," he said.

"Good, Michael. That's good."

"A prattie mashed with some onions would do me grand," he whispered.

"Máire will go. There are onions growing at the side of the marshy field," I called out to her.

"Ah, she won't find them," Michael said. "You go. Máire will stay." He held my hand. "I think I'm better. I wouldn't want to eat if I was really bad."

"Go on, Honora," Máire said. "Take the blurt off him while he has an appetite."

"I'll be quick," I said.

I hurried into the cottage. Thank God I had some of the seed potatoes we meant to leave with Da. I put them in the pot over the fire to boil, then ran out. I climbed over the stone wall, went through the marshy field, and found the few onions left there. I pulled them all and ran back to the cottage.

The potatoes were cooked now. I peeled away the skin and using our one spoon mashed them with the onions into a tin can and went back out to Michael.

Máire stood in front of the closed door of the shed. I made to pass her, but she wouldn't move. "You're not going in."

I reached over her shoulder and shoved the door. Stuck.

"Michael's latched the door from inside," she said.

I took the handle and rattled it. "Michael! Open the door! . . . Michael!"

"Let him sleep, Honora. Nothing you can do. The fever will break or not. He'll survive or not. Nothing you can do."

She put her arms around my shoulders, but I shrugged them off.

"Michael! . . . Michael!" I screamed.

But there was no answer.

I ran to the back of the shed.

"He's trying to keep you safe, Honora," Máire said.

I didn't answer her. Michael had left a small opening in the back to let in air and light for Champion. I stretched up to look through this slit, but the opening was too high. There, one of the stones piled up in the gap in the wall—that'll do. I dragged it over and stood on it.

"Now I can see you, Michael, and I can hear you breathing. I'm here, Michael. I won't leave you, a stór."

Máire came around to me. She'd tied a rope around the can of pratties and onions. I lowered the food down next to Michael through the opening. The can hit the ground.

Food and water in his reach and me here standing vigil. I'll watch. And Michael will awaken. He'll eat and drink and stand up and come out of the shed and we'll go to Amerikay.

I stood on the stone leaning against the mud-walled shed, looking down at Michael. As the day went, less light came through the small window until shadows covered Michael.

Máire came to me, put her arms around my waist, and made me step down. She sat me on the ground, my back against the wall of the shed, and stood on the rock.

"Breathing," Máire said to me as the sun set on Galway Bay and darkness came.

After a while, I got up. "You rest," I said, and stepped up onto the rock. I couldn't see him, but I could hear him grabbing for breath.

The moon rose. The stars came out. A full moon, and not a cloud on it.

Now Michael breathed in spurts. Long moments of silence, but then he'd struggle for air. He's battling.

"Fight, my love, fight!" I said into the opening.

"Honora." His voice stronger—stronger, surely.

"I'm here, Michael! What?"

"Honora, I see her. Champion. Honora . . . Paddy's riding her . . . they're on the course. . . . Look at the people, Honora. . . . A piper . . . it's my father . . . my mother's next to him . . . Murtaugh Mor's holding the great hammer. . . . All of them watching . . . they're cheering our son, Honora! . . . There you are . . . Jamesy, Bridget, and Stephen with you. . . . How could you be at Gallach Ui Cheallaigh? . . . Wait, we're together on the Silver Strand. . . . I'm swimming in Galway Bay. . . . Honora, there's a mermaid swimming with me . . . the mermaid from Clontuskert Abbey. . . . She's pointing to the shore . . . and there you are. . . . How beautiful you are. . . . Honora, you're waving at me . . . the children, too. . . .

"I'm coming, Michael!" I got off the stone and ran to the door. I kicked at it, then I pushed with my shoulder until the door splintered and I was in. "I'm here, Michael. I'm here." I took him in my arms. "I'm here."

He opened his eyes but was still seeing those pictures in his mind. And then he looked at me.

"A stór, a ghrá mo chroí," I said. "Always and forever, a ghrá mo chroí, love of my heart."

"Did I pay the bride price, Honora?"

"You did. And more."

"Tell the children—tell them their da loved them. Take them to Patrick. He'll help you. Chicago. Don't let them die."

"Michael! Fight, fight!"

"Patrick. Chicago," he whispered. "Promise me."

"I promise, but, Michael, you'll be with us, you'll—"

"Good-bye, Honora. Safe home. Slán abhaile." Michael closed his eyes. "A ghrá mo chroí," only a whisper, then silence.

"Michael! Michael, not yet. Michael, please, not yet. Come back, Michael!"

But he lay so still. I knew then. I shook him. Bent down onto his chest, listening for a heartbeat. But I knew.

"Ah! Ah! Ah!" I started wailing.

And then Máire was there with me.

"Come out of here. You need to keen for him right and proper, out where the wind can carry the sound through the glens," she said. "Come, a stór, come. Your Michael's not in this small, dark place. He's outside, Honora. His soul will pass over Galway Bay. He's escaped. He's free. Come. Let's watch for him."

Máire pulled me out into the night and brought me to the rock seat Michael made for me so I could watch the Bay. She sat me down and her next to me. I keened into the darkness.

"My love, my heart, my hero from the sea," I chanted.

"Kind and strong and brave . . ." Máire sent the words out.

"My husband—without fear, without meanness, without jealousy . . . Pride of the Kellys . . . Michael, Michael, Michael . . . I can't, Máire! Without him, I can't . . ." I covered my face with my hands.

"Honora! Honora, look! The moon's rising. It's full. See the way it shines on the Bay?"

I lifted my head and looked down. The full moon shone down on Galway Bay. A path of light rippled along the dark waters, moving as if someone were walking on top of the waves—Michael crossing Galway Bay, stepping into the starry heavens.

"Michael," I whispered. "Slán abhaile, my love—safe home."

Then, a wind, easy, soft, touched my face. I felt him. Not gone.

Here, truly here . . . before me, behind me, below me, above me, on my right, on my left . . . St. Patrick's prayer . . . in the light of the sun, in the radiance of the moon . . . in the splendor of the fire . . . in the swiftness of the lightning . . . in the depth of the sea . . . with me. With me always.

CHAPTER 21

$\mathcal{D}$A AND THREE MEN from Bearna came later that day. They battered down the shed. I watched all the walls fall on Michael, the thatched roof collapse over him . . . his grave. And no one said, "It must be done this way." No one had to explain. Cover the fever dead where they lay. Had to be done. No time to send for a priest. Quick and quiet when fever kills.

"Sorry for your troubles . . . Sorry for your troubles," the men said. "Sorry . . . sorry . . . sorry . . ."

Máire stood with me.

"Michael buried his pipes under the floor of the shed. Now they're resting with him," I said to Máire. "But he'll be all alone up here, forever."

"He's his own fields stretching out around him—more than my Johnny has," Máire said.

Da brought the children and Mam to the cairn made by the stones of the shed. We stood together, Paddy and Jamesy close to me. I held Stephen in my arms; Bridget clutched my hand. Stephen said, "Da? . . . Da?" while Bridget kept asking, "Where's my da?"

"Do you have a few words, a prayer, Honora?" Da asked.

They all looked at me.

I took a breath. "Michael Kelly was a man without meanness, without fear, without jealousy . . . Husband . . . father . . . piper . . . blacksmith . . . farmer . . . horseman . . . Much loved . . . Very, very . . . much . . . loved. . . . Full of love himself . . . and honor . . . He will dwell in perpetual light. . . . He has found eternal rest. . . . Safe. Slán. Amen."

"Amen," they answered.

Jamesy tugged at my skirt. He held up his tin whistle to me. "Will I, Mam? I only know the one tune." Jamesy played the song his da had taught him, the notes shaky but there:

> *A Nation Once Again*
> *A Nation Once Again*
> *And Ireland long a province be*
> *A Nation Once Again.*

"Very good," I said to Jamesy. "Your da would have liked that."

A nation . . . Can a country of unmarked graves ever be a nation? Michael, your bones will dissolve into this earth, to mix with so many others.

But not your spirit. You crossed Galway Bay on a path of light—your spirit before me, behind me, above me, below me. Our children will rise in the strength of your spirit. I will bring them to Chicago, Michael. I swear it.

⟡ ⟡ ⟡

Billy Dubh, the gombeen man, knocked at the door as soon as we got back to the cottage. Watching for us.

"Sorry for your troubles, missus," he started. "Very sorry," trying to push his way in through the half-opened door, that weasel face, those peering eyes.

I started to close the door on him, but Mam came over and let him in.

"You're very welcome, Billy Dubh," she said.

"God bless all here," he said.

Mam looked at me. Don't antagonize him.

"Well now, missus, a difficult day," he said. "A widow left on her own. But thank God there is the workhouse. It's a refuge—a refuge. Those who clung to their land died wishing they had signed away their claim and taken the help."

Nothing about Amerikay . . . So, not as well-informed as he thinks, or else he knew what we'd planned and thought I wouldn't be going now. How could I?

Máire spoke up. "Don't worry about Honora. She has family."

"Ah, well, all the more reason for her to sign this paper. Choices, then—if not the workhouse, her family. But why have the worry of land and rent and poor rates, with agents and soldiers coming around to bother her," he said to Máire. Then to me, "I can spare you that worry."

"Eviction?" Da said.

"But she has a lease," Máire said. "Very legal. Show him, Honora."

Michael had kept it behind a stone near our hearth. He planned to make the lease over to the Dwyers after his last day at work. I handed the parchment to Billy Dubh.

"Ah, a shame, really," he said, shaking his head, a false face of sorrow on him. "I've seen too many of these. They count for nothing when property's been sold." He smiled at us as he tore the lease in two. "There's new management now. Serious businessmen. Better to go quietly now than to wait to be ejected. I will give you two pounds."

"And if we tumble the cottage?" I asked.

"Two pounds total, missus."

"Then I'll wait for the bailiff. Good-bye, sir."

"Let me think," Billy Dubh said. "In view of your sad loss I will make an exception. If you leave right now, I will give you three pounds and I won't ask you to tumble your cottage."

"Done," I said. I pointed to the pot hanging on a hook over the fire. "That is not included."

"Take it. I learned my lesson." He laughed. "Wouldn't want the Irish Brigade attacking me."

"Thank you," I said.

I picked up the pot and walked over to the glass window. A clear day, and the sun shining on Galway Bay. I heaved the pot through the window, shattering the glass.

"Honora!" Mam said.

No one else spoke.

Billy Dubh blew out his plump cheeks and took a long breath. His face was red. I knew he wanted to hit me.

But he didn't. "Wasteful," was all he said.

"You're getting your fee," I said. "I'm not going to let you sell the glass from the window my husband gave me."

✧ ✧ ✧

So. We moved to Bearna. September came. The fifteenth, my birthday, and a month since Michael died. The Feast of Our Lady of Sorrows. I am twenty-six years old.

"Happy birthday, Honora," Mam said to me.

She and Máire sat together by the fire.

"Thank you, Mam." A comfort to be with Mam. She's so calm. Reassuring for the children to live with her and Da—for me, too.

Máire had said right away she wasn't all that set on Amerikay and wasn't it a good thing we didn't pay for the tickets because now we had money to see us through the winter, and Mam said thank God for the good fishing and the Lynches not pressing for the rent.

They assumed I wouldn't want to go now. Do I? I don't know. Michael, I said to him in my mind, at least now I can walk the Silver Strand and stop at the big rock where we sat that first morning—climb up to Knocnacuradh and say an Ave for you at your sad grave.

Mam gave me the porridge she'd made from the meal Máire and I'd brought from Galway City.

Strange. I have more money than I'd ever before in my life. Fifty-three gold sovereigns tucked behind a rock near the hearthstone. Ah, Michael, you were right about the Bianconi people. Goodhearted. Mrs. Carrigan gave me ten pounds from Mr. Bianconi himself. He'd never forgotten Murty Mor, the big blacksmith, she told me. A nice woman. "Are you a widow?" I'd asked. Rude, really, but the words had come out of my mouth.

"Not a widow," Mrs. Carrigan had said, "though my husband travels so much for Mr. Bianconi, I feel like one."

Not a widow. But we were, the Keeley girls, both of us widows now and back where we had started—Bearna/Freeport, in a fisherman's cottage.

On the way back from town we'd stopped at Galway Harbor. A tall sailing ship was anchored in the Bay—the *Cushlamacree* getting ready for its last Atlantic crossing of the season. We'd stared at it a long time. "Over and done with," Máire'd said. Is it?

After the first spoonful of porridge, my stomach turned over. Nauseated every morning now.

Mam looked at me. "Are you . . . ?"

"I think so," I said.

Máire shook her head. "You should have had more sense, Honora."

"Máire," Mam began.

"I think I'll go out to the children now," I said.

"Good. Some fresh air for you," Mam said.

Mam's worried because I'm so silent, mourning without tears, and if I'm pregnant . . . How could I travel now? I can't lose this baby— Michael Joseph Kelly.

September light—still some heat left in the sun at midday. I crossed to the strand to where the children played. Bridget was helping Stephen and Gracie dig deep holes in the sand, while Paddy, Jamesy, Thomas, and Daniel challenged the waves—running forward to just where the surf hit the sand and then backing away.

Johnny Og worked with Da, tying up the púcán in the Gap where the stream emptied into the Bay.

No other Bearna children played on the strand—sleeping, probably, waiting for whatever food their mothers could give them. One meal a day. Ours ate twice a day and still had a bit of heft on them.

Yesterday, I'd found Jamesy and Bridget walking along the strand road toward Galway. They said they were off to meet their da. Wouldn't he be coming home now after his time in heaven? Every night Stephen asked, "Da? . . . Da?" looking at me, puzzled.

"They can't believe he's gone forever," Paddy had said to me.

"Boys," I shouted, "watch yourselves. The water's very cold."

"Mam, look!" Jamesy pointed at the sailing ship moving through the channel, following the Bay to the sea, gone now, the *Cushlamacree*.

Not many more will be going. Sensible captains feared the North Atlantic when winter closed in—storms and cold weather, slow going. Da said he'd seen púcáns that went out too far, too late, come back covered in ice.

Can't wait much longer. Should we take passage on the next ship going, Michael?

"Come on, children. Let's go in."

Máire and her children stayed with us that night. A nest of Keeleys. Clear, easy breathing—no coughing. Thank God.

✥　✥　✥

Voices and pounding woke me. I saw Da holding the door half-open. "Who are you? What do you want?" Da asked.

A paper was thrust through the opening.

"Notice to quit," the voice said. That abrupt tone, the burred Ulster vowels—Jackson. "You are evicted." He pushed Da away and stomped into the cottage. Almost as tall as Da, but a thick body and years younger.

"A mistake, sir," Da said. "The Lynches promised no evictions. I've paid my rent on time for thirty years."

Then I was up standing next to Da, and Mam with us.

"The Lynches are no longer your landlords," Jackson said. "Lord Campbell owns this property now, and he's set the rent to the proper amount. You are in arrears."

"How much?" I asked.

Jackson looked at me. "It's too late. Lord Campbell is clearing the whole seashore. Great plans he has."

"Plans?" asked Da. "What do you mean?"

"None of your business, old man," Jackson said.

And suddenly Da *was* old—his shoulders bowed, not a huge big Keeley fisherman—staring at Jackson. "Plans?" Da said again, confused.

"Bathing houses," Jackson said. "Seaside villas. No concern of yours."

I remembered the men who'd come to Marcus Lynch. Another Brighton, they'd said. And as soon as the Lynches could sell their land, they had, with no thought at all of us.

"Leave now, and I'll allow you to take your possessions," Jackson said. "The law permits Lord Campbell to confiscate them, but he wants to be generous."

"Generous?" I said.

Jackson didn't seem to know me. "Very generous. Much more than he should do for you idolaters."

Máire came over to us. "Jackson."

He recognized Máire soon enough. "Mr. Jackson to you, harlot."

Da moved closer to Máire. He lifted his head. "This is my daughter," Da said.

"Unfortunate for you."

Then Jackson walked over to the children, awake now, sitting up.

"Are the little bastards here, too?" he said.

The boys stared at him. Gracie started to cry. Bridget leaned over to her, patting her shoulder.

"No attack this time?" Jackson asked the boys. "I wouldn't try it. Very different troopers with me tonight."

Now I could hear the noises outside. Through the open door I saw squads of soldiers—two or three at each of the thirty cottages. They were shouting: "Hurry up now! Go! Get out!"

I turned to Jackson. "And where are we to go?"

"To hell or Connaught. Oh, I forgot!" he said. "You are in Connaught. Well, then, hell seems to be your destination."

Mam was putting odds and ends into the boiling pot: her few spoons, Granny's wooden cross from the penal days, and a crucifix carved from the same wood used for the beams in the roof the meitheal had raised thirty years before. Everything else had been pawned.

I had hidden my money behind a loose stone in the wall near the hearth. Fifty-three pounds. I have to get it, and I can't let Jackson see me—he'll take it.

I looked at Máire. She stood silent before Jackson. Her twenty gold coins were hidden in her cottage, unless the soldiers had stolen them already. I took a half step toward the hearth.

Jackson was taunting Máire, his face close to hers.

"Thought you'd escaped, didn't you? Got clean away with your children and the stolen goods."

"I stole nothing."

"That's not what old Major Pyke told me. A large sum of money is missing, and jewelry. I'm placing you under arrest."

"You? Don't make me laugh," Máire said.

"By what authority?" Da said.

"The ignorance of you people!" Jackson said. He took Máire's arm. "I charge you under the Crime and Outrage Act. As a Protestant, I'm commissioned to bear arms and enforce the queen's law to protect property."

"Remember I am the mother of Major Pyke's grandsons!" Máire said.

"I'll be taking the oldest bastard. Might get something for him. If not?" Jackson shrugged.

I took another step toward the hearth and my money. Paddy, Jamesy, and Bridget moved between Mam and Da. Stay there. Hide my movements.

Máire's children sobbed; even Johnny Og was crying. Máire picked up Gracie, rocking her.

Jackson stepped past Máire to grab Thomas. He knocked into Gracie, who started screaming—a high-pitched wail.

"Get rid of that squalling brat, unless you want her to go to Australia with you!" Jackson pulled at Gracie.

"Don't touch her!" Bridget shouted.

Jackson couldn't see where the voice came from.

"Don't hurt her!" Bridget yelled at him. She walked toward Máire. "Come on, Gracie, come to me. Bridey will play with you."

Máire looked at me and I nodded. She put Gracie down and the little girl tottered over to Bridget.

I saw that in order to hold Thomas, Jackson had let go of Máire.

"The battle rage, Paddy!" I said. "Now!"

Paddy understood. "Hoo-rah!" Head down, he charged Jackson, hitting him directly in the groin.

Jackson doubled over, releasing Thomas, who started kicking him.

Johnny Og and Daniel ran at Jackson, too, their fists pounding Jackson's legs. Paddy jumped on his back, and Jackson bent over. Jamesy spat in his face.

Now to the corner. I loosened the rock, pulled out the sack of sovereigns, and tucked it into the waist of my skirt.

While Jackson tried to shake off Paddy, Máire ran out the door.

"The Gap!" I yelled to Máire.

Jackson had Paddy on the floor, his boot pulled back, ready to kick my son.

"Don't!" I screamed.

Da moved between Jackson and Paddy. He'll tell him they're only children. He'll apologize to Jackson. He'll . . . But instead, Da punched Jackson hard on the jaw.

Jackson went down.

"Run!" I said.

"Run!" Da shouted.

And we were out the door, running down the strand. We stopped behind a rock near the Gap. I could see where Da had tied his púcán.

A squad of soldiers was herding the twenty fisher families—almost two hundred people—toward Bearna pier. "Move! Move!" they shouted. Directly above us at the Clancy cottage, one soldier held a torch while another pulled at Mary Clancy, who clung to the doorposts of her cottage. Finally he broke her hold, pushed her to the ground, and pointed his musket at her face. She slowly stood up and moved to join the crowd walking onto the pier.

Children screamed and cried.

Then Jimmy Joe Egan grabbed the arm of a soldier. I could hear him talking in Irish.

The soldier took the stock of his musket and smashed Jimmy Joe in the jaw. "Speak English, you papist baboon!"

The soldiers are drunk. Dear God, help us. Holy Mother . . .

Máire came running from her cottage past us.

"Mam and Da, boys! Come on! Don't look! Come on!" I shouted.

I carried Stephen. Mam had Gracie. Paddy and Jamesy, each holding one of Bridget's hands, ran with Daniel and Thomas to the Gap and Da's boat. Johnny Og and Da were there.

Máire stood next to it, panting. "Hurry, hurry!" she said.

I gave Stephen to Mam. Máire and Johnny Og and I helped Da push the púcán into the stream that went into the Bay.

"Get in! Get in!" I shouted.

Johnny Og took Gracie from Mam and jumped into the boat.

Paddy and Jamesy climbed over the side and landed on the bottom.

I helped Mam in and swung first Bridget and then Stephen in after her.

Da was hoisting the sail.

Thomas pushed Daniel into the boat, then climbed in himself.

"Good boy, Thomas," Máire said. "Don't look back. The Pykes are nothing to you."

Da had the sail up.

Máire and I gave the boat a final push and jumped in.

"We're overloaded," I said to Da, but he didn't turn.

"I don't see Jackson," Máire said.

"Da knocked him out," I told her.

Da said nothing. He took the tiller. The púcán's red sail filled with wind. We started moving.

Da steered us toward the deep channel in the center of Galway Bay. So dark . . . How would he see to avoid the rocks?

We pulled opposite Bearna pier. Our neighbors stood in line as if waiting for the soup. They faced their own cottages, where soldiers holding torches walked along the narrow spaces between the houses.

Then one soldier touched his torch to a thatched roof. The other soldiers did the same. With a *whoosh,* all thirty cottages caught fire.

The glare from the flames brightened the dark sky and turned the water around us orange. I could feel the heat.

"Jackson!" Mam said. "Jackson's in our cottage!"

To hell or Connaught.

"The soldiers will find him, Mary," Da said.

"Or not," Máire said. "Jackson's a great believer in Providence."

Da didn't look at the shore.

"Where are we going, Da?" I asked.

"To Ard, Honora. To Carna."

We sailed away from the light of the Bearna fire into the black night. How will Da even know if we're in the channel?

Clouds covered the moon. Full again, a month since I'd seen Michael's path on the water . . . full . . . But shadowed and shuttered, no use to us.

The wind picked up, driving us forward, blowing hard. The púcán pitched in the waves—overloaded . . . badly overloaded . . .

Dear God, St. Bridget, Blessed Mother, Mac Dara, Michael . . . Help us.

And then the clouds, so thick around the moon, began to blow apart . . .

Christ above me, Christ before me, Christ on the right, Christ on the left . . . the radiance of the moon . . . the radiance of the moon . . .

Radiant. Emerging from the clouds. Shining on us.

Slowly the dark waters took the light and a way opened up before us.

The jagged top of Carrigmor, the great rock that had wrecked so many ships, rose up before us, visible now in the moonlight. Da jerked the tiller to the left and we missed the rock, though we came so close that I could have touched it.

Da set the púcán on the bright path along the center of Galway Bay to the Atlantic Ocean.

At sunrise, we arrived in Ard/Carna.

❖ ❖ ❖

A week now since that morning. The Keeleys had welcomed us, feeding us from the little they had themselves. They said, "Of course you have a place here!" But how could we impose on them? Black '47 had brought death and evictions to the Ard Keeleys. The Sean Mors, the whole family, had died of fever. The blight had destroyed all potatoes here, too. Our cousins could only hope the fishing would sustain them this year. Two families had left for Amerikay in the spring, but no word had come from them.

"Don't know if they're living or dead," said Sean Og, the leader since his cousin Sean Mor's death. "Terrible journey," he'd said to me.

A terrible journey. But one I would make.

I knew I had to go. The path of moonlight Michael sent had brought us to the sea and pointed the way toward Amerikay. I'd find a ship somehow. Even if Máire, Mam, and Da stayed, the children and I must escape. Michael wanted us to live.

I walked with Sean Og on the strand and told him my plan. I would row out into the sea and intercept a sailing ship.

"Impossible," he said. "Mad entirely."

Wait for the spring season, book passage with the Clifden shipping agent, he told me. But I knew in a way I couldn't explain that another winter of starving would kill my sons and Bridget.

I pointed out toward Mac Dara's Island. "Don't the ships slow down near the island where Galway Bay and the Atlantic meet?" I asked.

He admitted they did. The captains needed to gauge the wind and tides as the ships moved from coastal waters into the sea. But the lookout might not see the curragh, and even if he did, the captain would never take us aboard. Jimmy Jimmy Hughie's son had been refused. Others had tried, and the big ships had nearly run them over.

"I'm determined, Sean Og," I said.

Máire, coming across the strand to us, heard me.

"Determined to do what?" she asked.

Sean told her, shrugging his shoulders, shaking his head. Beside himself.

Máire put her two hands on my shoulders.

"Don't say anything, Máire. I'm going. I have to."

"Then I'll go with you, Honora."

"Oh, Máire!" I hugged her.

"Honora's a fierce woman when her mind's made up," Máire said to Sean Og. "You may as well help us."

Sean Og admitted he knew when the big ships were coming—

signals came from up the coast. Old contacts from his smuggling days.

But we'd have only a few hours' notice. Get ready.

✧ ✧ ✧

"I can't, Honora," Da said. And Mam nodded.

"But, Da," I started.

Mam took my hand. "You must go. We must stay," she said. "Try to understand."

"I'm back where I began, Honora," Da said. "Perhaps that's what Our Lord intends."

"And me with him," Mam said.

I stopped trying to persuade them and set my face toward Amerikay.

When I explained to the boys that we were going to Amerikay, they only nodded. They'd said little since we'd left Bearna. Jamesy had cried and cried because he'd dropped his tin whistle running from the cottage, but Paddy showed no emotion.

"I promised your da we'd go to Chicago," I said. "Uncle Patrick's waiting for us there."

"Is it a far way?" Jamesy asked.

"Clear across the sea," Paddy said.

"And when will we come home?" Jamesy again.

"We can't come home," Paddy said to him. "We have no home."

"We do too. Don't we, Mam. We have Bearna and Knocnacuradh—"

"Burned down," Paddy said, "and Knocnacuradh's tumbled and Da's buried . . . gone."

"He's not! He's not. He's with us! You said so, Mam."

"I did, Jamesy."

"Then where is he?" Paddy said.

"You won't see him, but you'll know he's with you, and he wants us to go to Amerikay."

"Mam," Paddy said to me, as if I were the child and he'd caught me in a lie.

That night, Sean Og's brother Tommy Joe took Paddy and Jamesy to Ballynahinch Lake to try for a salmon—Tommy Joe was willing to risk being arrested for poaching in order to feed us well before our journey.

When they returned from Ballynahinch at dawn, Paddy threw himself in my arms.

"Two lucky buachaill you have here, Honora," Tommy Joe told me. "We caught a big salmon, and they saw a great sight altogether, didn't we, boys? A herd of Connemara ponies, very rare these days to see them—they stay well away from people."

"You were right, Mam. Da is with us!" Paddy said. "He sent Champion to us!"

"He did, Mam!" Jamesy said. "Champion and Macha with her."

"As to that," said Tommy Joe, "a mare and her foal did leave the herd and run forward toward us. A chestnut, she was, bigger than a pony, and so was her little one—a filly, I think."

I looked at the boys and smiled. "Your da is watching over you," I said.

"But he's here, Mam, in Connemara. How can we leave him behind?" Paddy asked.

Michael's blue eyes looked at me from Paddy's face. "He'll travel with us, Paddy. I promise."

❖ ❖ ❖

The next evening, Sean Og took me aside. "The signal's come, Honora. There's a bonfire to the north relays the news. A ship will reach Mac Dara's Island soon after dawn," he said.

"You're sure?"

He didn't bother to answer—hadn't the Keeleys been smugglers for generations?

"And it will slow for the tide?"

"Unless the captain's an ejit."

So.

"At least let me row you out to wait for the ship," Sean Og said.

"You can't, Sean Og. The captain must see two women stranded in the ocean, alone. Doesn't the law of the sea say sailors must rescue the shipwrecked?" I said. "If they saw a big strong fellow, they'd not feel any sympathy for us at all."

"You'll be in danger," he said. "If the curragh turns over, two minutes in the freezing water will kill you. It's far from big and strong I am now, but I can row you out."

"And so can we, Sean Og. Don't you remember how Máire and I won all the races? Beat the girls from Ard every time!"

He finally agreed.

We would have to wait for first light to set out, then row quickly, but we should cover the three miles in time.

✧ ✧ ✧

Sean Og and his family and many of the Ard Keeleys sat up with us through the night—another American Wake.

Da didn't want to take the eleven sovereigns I gave him. "You'll need it to get through the winter and to help the other Keeleys," I said to him. Máire and I had plenty—sixty-two pounds. Sean Og had said that thirty was the most we'd have to pay for our passage. I told Da I'd try to send more after we found Patrick Kelly in Chicago.

We woke the children. They were sleepy, confused.

"Don't cry," I heard Paddy tell the others.

"We'll write you, Mam," I said. "We'll send the letters to Sister Mary Agnes. She'll get them to you somehow. And we'll find our brothers, Mam."

She said, "You will. Of course."

Mam hugged each of the children and kissed Máire and me.

Da patted the children's heads, then held my hand. "You're a strong woman, Honora. Remember your granny. Here." He slipped Granny's cross from the penal days up my sleeve.

"Oh, Da."

"Take it for you and Máire. Be sure you tell your children and grandchildren the stories Granny taught you."

"I will, Da."

Da took Máire's hands. "You were always a good, kind girl, Máire, and I'm sorry for all you've suffered."

Máire clung to him.

"Better go," Sean Og whispered to me.

"Máire," I said. "Máire, it's time."

She stepped away from Da, nodded, and picked up Gracie. I carried Stephen, and Mam helped us settle the children in the curragh. Then Da and Sean Og pushed us out from the shallow water.

We gripped the oars, set them in the water, and started to pull.

"Slán," Mam and Da and Sean Og called from the shore. "Slán."

And then we were out of the harbor and couldn't hear them or see them anymore.

"Come on, Máire," I said. And we set out.

❖ ❖ ❖

"Pull! For Jesus' sake, pull, Máire, pull!" Máire had finally gotten the rhythm—left wrist over right wrist—but she wasn't dipping her oar deep enough. The curragh hardly moved, and we needed to get into the open water *now*.

I could see the topsail on the horizon, the ship rising out of the milky pre-dawn sky, pushing against the waves, not too far away.

We need to get closer so the lookout will see us. But if we're too near, the bow will smash the curragh.

"Stay still," I said to our children, who lay in the bottom.

Too many of us for the curragh. If we tip over into the sea, we're dead.

"Máire," I yelled. "Bend down, put your back into it, come on! The Keeley girls passing those Ard ones, clean strokes—not a splash as we fly! Come on, Máire! Show them—show your boys!" Can't let the ship pass us by before we reach it.

"C'mon, Mam!" said Johnny Og. "You're as good as Aunt Honey!"

"I am!" said Máire, and her next stroke matched mine, and so did the next and the next—until we were sliding over the waves.

"Hold on to each other!" I yelled to the children.

Máire and I were bending and pulling as one, feet braced against the bottom, bending and pulling again and again. . . .

"Hoo-rah!" Máire yelled.

"Hoo-rah!" I echoed. "Come on, children, help us mark the time: Hoo-rah!"

"Hoo-rah! Hoo-rah! Hoo-rah!"

We were there, at the edge of the ship's path.

"Quick!" I said. "Hide the oars. Put them under you, children."

Now—now or never . . .

The ship rose so tall above us, the sails like round towers. Will they see us?

We waved. We shouted. We couldn't stand—can't overturn the curragh, can't freeze to death.

"Help! Help! Help!"

Very little wind. The ship was nearly stopped still.

"Help! Help! Help!"

A sailor leaned over the railing. "Are you in trouble?"

"We are!" Máire said. "My husband was swept overboard! We've lost our oars!"

"Where are you bound?" the sailor yelled.

"Amerikay!" Máire answered. "We were to meet our ship at Westport!"

We waited while the sailor fetched another man, the captain.

"We can't help you!" the captain shouted down to us.

"Then we'll die!" I answered him. "We were almost swamped during the night! We won't survive!"

"I can't!"

"We have money! We can pay!" I shouted.

"Thirty pounds!" yelled Máire. "Thirty pounds! Show him, Honora! Hold up the sovereigns!"

I had them ready and held up my hands, the palms piled with gold coins.

Could the captain see the glint of gold in this first light? He looked at us for a long time. And then, compassion? The law of the sea? The sovereigns? For whatever reason, he told the sailor to lower the cargo net. I put the coins away.

"Come on, Paddy, Johnny Og, Thomas," I shouted to them.

The net swung back and forth just above us.

"Grab it, Paddy, Johnny Og. Easy, easy now." If they fall into the sea . . .

I set Stephen and Bridget into the net, and Máire put Gracie next to them. While we held the net steady, the boys pulled themselves in. Finally, Máire and I grabbed the edges.

"Mam! Mam! Mam!" the children shouted.

I brought the net to me, checked the sailcloth pocket tied around my waist. It contained the Mary Bean, Granny's cross, Michael's stone, and a sack with the money—all we had. Then I tumbled into the net, Máire behind me.

As the sailors hauled the cargo net up slowly, careful not to smash us against the side of the ship, I watched the empty curragh bobbing in the waves.

Then we were aboard, the sailors helping us out of the net.

"Welcome to the *Superior*," the captain said. "Bound from Derry for New Orleans."

"Amerikay?" I asked.

"Indeed. The southern route—only sensible way at this time of year."

"We are going to Chicago," I said.

"That's a fair distance from New Orleans," he said, "but closer than you are here."

I gave him sovereigns from the sack in the pocket under my skirt.

I looked up at the tall sails. This ship's very like the *Cushlamacree*, and I am standing at the rail as I had so often imagined, but I'd always seen Michael here beside me. "Your da's traveling with us," I'd told the boys. "His spirit."

The ship moved farther out into the Atlantic. Behind me the blue waters of Galway Bay disappeared into the gray sea.

I've seen you every day of my life, Galway Bay. Michael came to me out of your waves. But I will never see you again. Not in this life. Perhaps in the life hereafter. Please God.

But our children will live, Michael, a stór. We've saved them.

Slan, a ghrá.

Amerikay.

PART THREE

Amerikay

Chapter 22

*N*ot a coffin ship, the *Superior*. Thank God. Enough food, even if it is mostly porridge, and the water's not foul," Maggie Doherty said to Máire and me.

In the three days since the sailors hoisted us aboard, this small, fair-haired Derry woman and her husband, Charlie, had helped us settle into the routine of the ship. It was Maggie found us an empty bunk among the rows of these open plank boxes—one stacked on top of the other—that filled the very bottom compartment of the ship where we steerage passengers were confined.

"Dark down here, and of course there's the stink, but we've ten buckets for the waste of a hundred people, and that sees us right. The men are allowed up to empty the buckets every day," Maggie had told us. "And there's no fever. Thank God."

It had been a struggle to fit the ten of us into the six-foot-square bunk, but we'd put Gracie and Stephen and Bridget between Máire and me, and the boys stacked themselves at our feet somehow and slept despite the yelps and groans of, "You kicked me!" and, "Move over!" that went on through the night. How did the men manage? One box per family, no matter how many. Some were too seasick to get up. Ah, Michael, this crossing would have been a misery for you, though you'd still have made a game of it for the boys: The warriors of the Red Branch hunker down in their stronghold. I miss you, a stór.

We stood with Maggie waiting our turn at the cooking fire above deck, while her twelve-year-old daughter watched the children down below. It's cold today, but no ice on the deck yet. I pulled in great lungfuls of air and walked over to the railing. The gray ocean, so vast, so open, was a relief after our cramped quarters.

"Jesus Christ, Honora, come away from there!" Maggie called to me from the end of a line of women huddled against the ship's center cabin. "You'll fall over."

"I can't bear to look out at the sea," she said as I rejoined Máire and her.

"We're fisherman's daughters," Máire said to her. "We learned to be brave in a boat."

"Nice for you. I prefer the river Foyle. Land's always in sight. Some of these"—she nodded at the women ahead—"never saw any expanse of water at all, let alone this wide and wild ocean. Terrified," Maggie said as we watched two women pick up their pots and hurry below. Quick smiles, but no chat. "Protestants," Maggie whispered as she dipped her pot in a water barrel, then added meal from her sack.

Máire and I had our own supply—ten pounds of oatmeal for each adult every week and five pounds for every child, a fair ration. I filled the pot Maggie had found for us.

"Is it because there are Protestant travelers with us that the *Superior* is better than most?" I asked Maggie as we stood by the fire.

She had told us that though all the passengers came from the north of Ireland, half of them were Catholic like the Dohertys, and the rest were Protestants, "evicted the same as we were, a good few of them."

Máire had told Maggie she didn't know there was such a thing as a poor Protestant. We still hadn't figured out a way to tell one from the other. All spoke with the same flat accent.

"The names will tell you," Maggie had assured us. "Won't find any Patricks or Bridgets among them. They'll be called Sarah and Rebecca, George and Harold, with last names like Johnson, Carson, Smith, Jones, Jackson."

Jackson—no one like him among the passengers. Not one person had called us "papist idolaters." Still, you couldn't go up to people and say, "What's your name?"

Now Maggie looked around. We were the only ones left at the fire. She gestured us closer. "It's true enough that the owner and the captain are Protestant and they might treat their own better, but the real reason this isn't a coffin ship is because of the catastrophe," she said in a low voice. Then while our pots boiled she told us the story. "This man from Derry, McAllister, owns the *Superior* and four or five others. Well, a year back another of his ships was coming from Sligo with a load of passengers. It was to pick up more in Derry, go on to Liverpool, then cross to Amerikay. On the journey up the Irish coast, a terrible storm hit. The sailors feared the water washing over the decks would flood below and sink the ship, so they tied canvas sheets across the openings to the lower deck as a barrier against the sea. With so many belowdecks, the passengers couldn't breathe. A hundred were dead when the ship arrived in Derry ten days later. They'd clawed holes in the canvas trying to get air. The sailors had clubbed them back." She dropped her voice even more. "Scottish sailors, and all the Irish passengers, Protestant *or* Catholic, scum to them. There was a trial. The captain and crew were found guilty of murder. A very black mark against the McAllisters."

"Awful," Máire said.

"God rest them," I said.

Maggie nodded. "Tragic. After that, the company had to be more careful. They took fewer passengers. We've more space and better supplies because of those poor souls," she said. "There now, our porridge is cooked."

We picked up our pots and went below.

We ate in our bunks as well as slept there, and I kept thinking of those doomed people suffocating in a dark hole as I fed Stephen his porridge. Maggie had found us two spoons, so the children ate in turn or with their fingers.

"Excuse me." The woman from the bunk below us was standing there. Like most of the women aboard, she traveled with her family. Though five young girls, one only twelve years old, they were going out on their own, hoping to find jobs as servants in the Big Houses of Amerikay. They were frightened but determined. Their people had borrowed money from some gombeen man for their fares, gambling that the wages the girls sent back would enable them to survive the winter and pay back the loan. A heavy burden. This woman had a husband, a quiet fellow, neither tall nor short, with sandy hair, as well as two sons, sixteen or seventeen, and an older daughter who favored the mother—both had brown hair, pulled tight back, brown eyes—shy. But Catholic? Protestant? I didn't know. She handed me a covering made from pieces of fabric sewn together. "A quilt," she said. "You're welcome to use it."

"Thank you," I said. "That's very kind."

Stephen reached for the bright colors, took the quilt, and rubbed it against his cheek.

"I'd say he's claimed it," the woman said.

"For the journey," I said. "I'll be sure to return it."

"My mother made it," she said.

"Is she . . ."

"She's living, but wouldn't leave our home place, Ballymena."

"My mam and da stayed, too, in Connemara."

"Where's that?" she asked.

"West of Galway City," I said.

"Oh," she said. "Can't place it."

Must be a Protestant if she doesn't know Galway City, but then Maggie had never heard of Connemara and had only a vague notion of Galway City. And to me, Derry meant Doire Columcille—St. Columba's Oak Grove—a holy place from ancient times that later became King Billy's battleground. I'd no idea what it was like now, and as far as Ballymena . . .

"We're near Belfast," the woman offered.

"Oh," I said. Protestant, surely. "I'm Honora Kelly."

"Pleased to meet you, Mrs. Kelly."

"Please call me Honora."

"Honora," she said. She hit the "H" hard, not breathing it out, saying "Ha-Nora," not "Ah-Nora."

"I'm Sarah Johnson."

That confirmed it. "Thank you for the quilt, Mrs. Johnson."

"Sarah," she said. She told me her family was going to cousins in Amerikay who'd been there for generations and had fought in the American Revolution. "None in our family are fond of England," she said.

"But aren't you a Protestant?"

"We're Presbyterians," she said.

"Presbyterians," I said. "And is that something different?"

❖   ❖   ❖

That evening, Sarah brought Mr. Wilson, her pastor, over to our bunk. "We're Protestants all right," he told me, "but we protest the corruption of the Catholic Church *and* the Church of England." A touch of Jackson here? Not really—a young man, thin and bookish-looking. "The rule of Rome gets between man and God. Every community should rule itself with the power shared out so that no one man has total control. No priests for us. The presbytery, laymen, choose a minister, and he's answerable to them. Do you know the Constitution of the United States?"

"I'm sorry to say, sir, it's not something I've come across," I said.

"Well," he said, "the principles in the Constitution of the United States come right from the Presbyterian Church. And you know"—he lowered his voice—"we've always been for an Ireland that would be free and independent."

"The United Irishmen; I know them, sir—Wolfe Tone, and—"

"That's right. And I believe someday the Harp will be new-strung."

"I would agree with that, sir."

Sarah was relieved after he left. "You never know what kind of prattle those ministers will come up with, but we keep them well in hand. And sure, isn't it all the same God anyway?"

"It is, Sarah," I said.

After that, Sarah joined Maggie, Máire, and me in the cooking line. One day I said, "Faraway hills are greener," in Irish: Is glas ial no cnaic bhfad uihh. Maggie didn't understand me at first, but when she put Donegal Irish on the phrase, didn't Sarah get every word? Not very different from the Scots Gaelic she spoke, she told us.

⊹ ⊹ ⊹

For three weeks the sea behaved. A steady wind filled the sails, moving us along rightly. Then with no warning, the winds switched direction, tearing into the ship, swatting it around, bending us toward the sea while we huddled in our bunks, praying and pleading.

As the storm battered us, voices cried out, "God save us, God save us!"

Mr. Wilson prayed the loudest. "Lord Jesus," he said, "you stilled the water. Calm the sea, we pray."

"Amen," from all of us. "Amen."

When the sailors lashed the canvas across the opening to the upper decks, the Derry ones, who knew only too well the facts of the other tragedy, shouted out protests until the captain himself yelled through the covered hatch, "Would yese be flooded and drown? Stay quiet and don't take so many breaths—ye'll be fine!"

Don't take so many breaths? With children crying all around us?

The ship pitched and wheeled and would have thrown us from our bunk but for the weight and length of the big boys crisscrossed over our legs, holding us down.

"Holy Saint Columcille," said Maggie Doherty.

"Pray for us," we answered.

"Blessed Saint Bridget," I heard.

"Pray for us," we said.

"Amen," Sarah Johnson answered.

Family after family called out saints whose names I'd never heard of—local monks and nuns, holy men and women who'd lived in their area: Comgall and Colman, Fintan and Fergal, Davnet and Declan.

I gave them Mac Dara, St. Enda, and his sister Fanchea, then the Kellys' Grellan.

The Presbyterians joined in, saying, "Pray for us," after every name, even after Mr. Wilson reprimanded them: "Save your breath! Don't call on pagans!"

No one paid him the least mind. Not enough breath to argue, only to murmur, "Pray for us, pray for us." The sound comforted and quieted the children and calmed our fear.

After ten hours of this, even the hardiest were seasick beyond anything felt before. Vomit streamed down from the bunks onto the deck, mixing with the seawater flooding in through every crack and crevice.

"We're going over!" someone shouted, and a few passengers jumped from their bunks, trying to climb up the steps, push back the canvas, get on the upper deck.

"Get back!" Charlie Doherty shouted.

A panicked rush could trample dozens.

Máire held Gracie at one end of the bunk. I cradled Stephen at the other. The children twined themselves around us—all sobbing, even Paddy.

Máire and I sang Mam's lullaby to them.

Finally, the storm eased. The sailors raised the canvas sides. We sucked in the air.

"Thank God. Thank God," from all sides.

✠ ✠ ✠

The next day the sea calmed, the sun shone. The captain let us all on deck. We congratulated one another on surviving, praised God and all His saints, and agreed that we Irish were a wild, brave people altogether. No thought of Catholic and Protestant.

We'd left the North Atlantic, the captain told us. On the southern route now.

The good weather held, and two weeks after the storm, Maggie's husband, Charlie, came to tell us he'd heard from the captain we'd arrive in four days.

Charlie, a small man with gingery hair, prided himself on being in the know. He referred often to his brother Peter in New Orleans, who had a job waiting for him. "Plenty of work in Amerikay," he said.

We'd been at sea thirty-six days. It would be a forty-day crossing— that pleased Sarah Johnson. "We're like Noah," she said to Charlie, "and soon we'll be seeing a bird with an olive branch. Land nearby."

✠ ✠ ✠

"We arrive tomorrow," the captain announced. That night, all the passengers filled the top deck, as the sun pulled us west toward our new home. Birds flew through the sunset, soaring and swooping.

Both Patrick Donnelly, one of the Donegal boys, and Sam, Sarah Johnson's oldest, brought out their fiddles and began to play a reel. It was impossible to *sit* and listen during a reel.

No one called out: "The Walls of Limerick," "The Siege of Ennis." Why give offense? Who knew what names they gave to their dances? Tonight, on the fortieth day of our voyage, with the deck steady and the night warm, I'd gladly dance "The Battle of the Boyne" reel.

"They can move, for all that they're Protestants," Máire said as we watched. "Tomorrow. Tomorrow we'll be walking on the shores of Amerikay." She got up and joined the dance.

I sat to the side, holding Stephen and Gracie until Bridget came to take their hands and bring them into the circle of children who were leaping and skipping—sea legs sturdy and land in sight.

The sets came together and bunched, and one of the Greencastle men called: "Swing your partner, take her home."

Máire fit her foot against a sailor's and whirled away.

The adults danced the patterns, but the children ducked and dived, not caring about steps. Paddy and Jamesy clasped their hands and made a bridge for the other children to run underneath.

Michael would have piped a glorious tune on such a night.

The bright stars and half-moon cast speckles of light onto the dark waves. October 31, 1848—Samhain Eve, the night this world and the next meet and mix. I looked up at the sky. Do you see us, Michael, crossing the last of the wide ocean, so far from our home? We've survived the passage that killed Dennis and so many others—buried at sea, the waters behind me a graveyard. Is it a lament you'd be playing, as well as a dance tune, if you were here, a stór? A lament, a dance tune, and then you'd strike up a marching song to give us courage. Faugh-a-Ballagh!

✧ ✧ ✧

Soon after sunrise, the sailors' shouts—"Land, land!"—woke us, and by midafternoon we were in the river, only hours from the port of New Orleans.

"Very lucky," Charlie Doherty said, "to enter Amerikay on the Mississippi."

Storms often drove ships bound for New York into the rocky shores of the North Atlantic. Here, the *Superior* followed the river's curve into a crescent-shaped harbor. "Easy," said Charlie as the sailors dropped anchor with all of us passengers on the deck, watching.

As soon as the ship stopped, a great blanket of heat dropped over us, as if the steam from a thousand boiling pots clogged the air.

"Hot," said Máire.

"Hard to breathe," I said.

"Humidity," Charlie Doherty said. "It's the humidity"—only he pronounced it "cue-midity." "Tropical. New Orleans has the same climate as the Amazon Basin."

Maggie Doherty nodded. "Charlie's brother Peter wrote that we'd get used to it. Though the thought of summer . . ."

The first of November today, the new year—a good omen, that. No sickness on board, no quarantine. We'd be off the ship that very day, Charlie told us.

I returned Sarah Johnson's quilt and said good-bye to her as the family departed.

Finally, our turn came. I carried Stephen, took Bridget's hand. Máire held Gracie in her arms. We followed Johnny Og, Paddy, Jamesy, Daniel, and Thomas down the gangplank and boarded a wooden boat about the size of a curragh. Two sailors would row us to the dock.

"You're red as anything," Máire said to me as we settled into the boat. "Are you sick?"

"The heat," I said. "Very warm."

The sailors, young Derry fellows, moved us through the harbor with quick strokes of their oars. The movement of the boat stirred the air, but my skin had turned slick and clammy.

"Mam," said Jamesy, "look." He held up his arm to show me the water dripping down. "Am I melting away altogether, Mam?"

"Sweat, lad," said the older sailor. "You'll sweat plenty in Amerikay."

"Jesus, Honora! Look at the size of this harbor," Máire said. "There must be fifty sailing ships!"

Massive vessels, most taller than the *Superior,* crowded together, one hull almost scraping against the next, topsails near touching. The two sailors edged the dinghy into the narrow spaces between these monsters.

Johnny Og and Paddy tried to stand up to look around.

"Sit down, sit down!" I said.

But the younger sailor said, "No harm. Let them greet America on their feet—toe-to-toe. A tough enough place, and it smells out fear and worry. Look it in the eye, boys."

Máire held Gracie, and Daniel stayed close to her. I had Stephen with me and Jamesy and Bridget. Thomas sat alone on the seat, looking backward, staring at the *Superior.* He'd enjoyed himself on the ship, no question. Thomas had refused to stay belowdecks. Máire had found him one afternoon in the captain's cabin, entertaining the captain's wife with tales of balls and hunts and all the goings-on of the Scoundrel Pykes, shocking her to the core of her Presbyterian heart, avid though she was for every detail.

"Sodom and Gomorrah," she kept saying, "Sodom and Gomorrah."

Didn't he take the hand of the captain's wife—at seven years old— "Thank you for your hospitality."

"Where does he get it?" Máire kept asking. "Where? There was no gallantry at the Scoundrel Pykes, I can tell you that," she said.

I touched the package of sovereigns under my skirt. Safe. We were closer now to the crowds of people on the docks.

"What are those smells?" Máire asked the young sailor.

Not ocean smells, not fish . . . Something else pushing at us through the hot, heavy air.

Máire breathed in. "Nice."

"Coffee and cinnamon," the sailor said, rowing us right up to the wharf. "See those heaps of yellow fruit? Bananas, ma'am."

"Bananas?"

"Loads of cargo from Mexico, Cuba, Costa Rica, Puerto Rico, all the Spanish places," said the sailor. "Spain and France fought over New Orleans for years and years. Old Napoleon won it, then turned around, sold it to the Americans, but it's still French—though different from France."

"You've sailed to France?" said Johnny Og.

He'd become a pet of the sailors, climbing in the ropes, helping with the sails. Máire had encouraged him: "The sea's in your blood."

"All over the world, lad."

"We're going to Chicago," Paddy said to the young sailor.

"Chicago's a thousand miles up the river. Very late in the season to travel that far north, missus," he said to me.

"Cold up there already," the older one said. "They say the wind never stops blowing in Chicago."

"I could do with a cool breeze."

"You'll have to find a steamboat, a paddle wheeler, to take you up the river, and do it quick."

Paddle wheeler? Steamboat?

"Look there," he said, pointing over to a big white five-storied boat. "The *River Queen*," he said. "It'll take you to a port on the Illinois River where you transfer to a canal boat, but if the canal's frozen already—"

"Don't be rushing away from New Orleans," the younger sailor said to Máire. All kinds of attractions." He winked at her, and she smiled at him. "Coffee and a *beignet*, among others."

"What's beignet?" Máire asked.

"A kind of doughnut, ma'am."

"What's a doughnut?" I asked.

They helped us up onto the wharf. I tried to walk, but the planks of the pier rocked like the deck of the *Superior*. I couldn't balance myself—my feet didn't know where to put themselves.

Stephen squirmed in my arms. "Down. Down." The sun brightened his red hair, but the heat didn't seem to bother him. I set Stephen down. He took off, heading along the long wharf toward the dockyard. Bridget went after him. Then Johnny Og, Daniel, Paddy, and Jamesy started running. Paddy shouted, "Wait for us, Stephen!"

Máire balanced Gracie on her hip and turned to Thomas. "Your arm, sir," she said, and put her hand on his wrist. They walked down the dock.

I stepped forward on my right foot, and the left one followed.

So, Michael, our children go before us except for this wee one inside me—our youngest, Michael Joseph Kelly, who will be born in Chicago. Amerikay.

Chapter 23

A CRUSH OF SAILORS and dockers, passengers and peddlers, swept us along the pier. I caught Stephen. Bridget grabbed my skirt. Máire had Gracie, but the boys had lost themselves in the crowd.

"There they are!" said Máire.

They had joined a circle of people watching two boys perform—one about ten years old, the other eight, maybe. The older one sang:

> *Gonna bend down, turn around,*
> *Pick a bale of cotton*
> *Gonna bend down, turn around,*
> *Pick a bale of hay!*

The younger boy made the song into a dance—bending down, taking something from the ground that he put into an imaginary pile.

Our boys wiggled their way to the front and began keeping time with the dancing boy, tapping their toes, then beating and brushing their bare feet on the wooden planks of the wharf.

"Look at our fellows," Máire said to me. "Not a bother on them."

The American boys had tight black curls and brown faces.

A man and woman passing stopped next to me. "Masters should not allow their slaves to caper around like this," the woman said.

"Too many of these pickaninnies running around New Orleans," the man replied, and they walked away, complaining to each other.

Slaves? These little boys?

"All right, move on now, this is a working pier! Get out of here, you monkeys! Come on, you black bastards."

That accent—Irish.

A tall, thickset man, all muscle and might, pushed his way through the crowd and stood over the boys, swinging a club at them.

"For Jesus' sake, man, you'll break their heads open!" Máire shouted.

"What I'm intending to do, missus!"

The two boys tried to escape into the crowd, but the man caught the little dancer by the arm and dangled him in the air as the older one ran away. "No heathen shows on my wharf." He dropped the boy to the ground, but still held him.

"Leave him alone!" I said in Irish.

"Who's that speaking?" he asked.

"It's me speaking! Mrs. Michael Kelly. A big fellow like you shouldn't torture a little boy. Haven't we enough of that in our own poor country without—"

"And what poor country would you be talking about, missus? My country is this one!" He stamped his foot on the wharf. "And my job is to keep these crews working." He pointed his club back at the ships, where groups of dockers unloaded and loaded cargo, carrying sacks up and down the gangplanks. "Irishmen," the man said. "Working, missus. Not loafing around like these children of Satan."

"You sound like some old Protestant preacher," I said to him. "Did you take the soup?"

That got him. He let go of the boy, who put his head down and ran.

"Who are you to call me a souper? I held on to my faith!" the man said.

The crowd dispersed. Only Máire and I and our children faced the giant man.

"I'm as good a Catholic as you or anybody else," he said. "I put money on the plate at Saint Patrick's every Sunday. Don't speak about what you don't understand, missus. No good comes from taking a soft hand with slaves, whatever age. That's the way of this place. You'll learn. And what about these strong, healthy boys of yours? They should be laboring, not standing, wasting their time watching foolishness." He pushed his club against Johnny Og's shoulder, then tapped Paddy and Thomas. "A few days working and you'll forget about two little darkies. You'd see what it takes to make your way in this country." He moved off, swinging his club at the dockers now. "Back to work!"

"Mam," said Paddy, "what's a bad man like that doing in Ameri-kay?"

"Just another fence to jump, Paddy," I said.

"I wish Da were here. That fellow scares me," Jamesy said.

I spread my fingers out and then gathered them into a fist. "What did your da teach you? Stand together and you won't be frightened."

Paddy and Jamesy made fists.

"C'mon, you lot," said Máire.

Wagons lined the road near the dock, crowded with men—Irish from the look of them, but not from the *Superior*.

A fellow came up to us. "You got husbands looking for work, la-dies?" Another Irishman, skinny, but swinging the same kind of club the other bullyboy had.

"We're widows," I said.

"Widows, is it? Maybe we could make arrangements. Lots of lonely men out in the camps. I could manage the both of you."

"If your wagons are going in the direction of Chicago, we could come along, do your washing and cooking on the journey. Earn our way," I said.

Máire grabbed my arm.

"We have children, but they don't take up much room," I said.

"Honora, come on." Máire dragged me away from the wagon and pushed me, with the children, into a byway alongside the wharf. "For Jesus' sake, Honora! Sometimes you're too much of an ejit to be true! Cooking, washing, giving us a ride to Chicago? Catch yourself on! He wants us to be whores."

"Oh," I said.

"Oh!" she imitated me. "Manage us? Believe me, if I sink into deg-radation, I'm taking the full whack of the wages of sin and not giving any part of it to some dirty sliveen!"

"You don't want to go where they're going," said a woman, brown-faced like the little boys, a red scarf tied around her head. "Some of those men'll dig canals in swamps full of mosquitoes. They'll get bit all over, catch the fever, and drop down dead. Some will lay rails for twelve, fifteen hours a day. Half of them'll die, too. Masters not about to set slaves to such dangerous labors. Won't risk valuable property. They work us to death, too, but over time and on their own plantations. Those Irish not worth nothin' to nobody," she said.

"Each one has a family at home," I said.

"You Irish, too?" she asked.

"We are," Máire said. "Who are you?"

"I've been following you since you helped my boys," the woman said. "Lorenzo, Christophe, *venez vite.*"

The two musicians stepped out from a doorway.

"*Mes fils,*" the woman said. She pointed to the taller boy. "Lorenzo," she said, then, "Christophe."

They came over to us.

Jamesy reached out and touched the tight black curls on the littler boy's head.

Paddy licked his finger and rubbed it on the cheek of the taller boy, then held it in front of his eyes.

Neither Lorenzo nor Christophe moved.

I grabbed Paddy's hand. "I'm sorry, missus," I said to the woman.

"Mam," Paddy said, "I only wanted to see if the brown came off."

"It don't," the woman said.

"Forgive my sons' bad manners," I said. "Everything's so new and . . ."

She waved me silent. "Where are you headed?"

"Chicago," I said.

"Chicago? A far way."

"I'm hungry," Jamesy said. "Are we going to eat in Amerikay, Mam?"

"Lorenzo! Christophe! *Les bananes!*"

The two little boys ducked away, then were back in a moment with a bunch of the curved yellow yokes we'd seen on the pier.

The woman broke one off from the bunch and handed it to Paddy, then gave one each to Johnny Og, Thomas, Daniel, Jamesy, and Bridget, while the smaller boy, Christophe, handed two each to Máire and me. "For the babies," he said.

"Bananas," said the woman.

We all nodded and smiled at her.

"Bananas. And what in the name of all that's sweet and holy do we do with them?" asked Máire.

Paddy looked at Lorenzo and then put the end of the banana in his mouth and bit down. "Oh," he said, and pulled it out, looking at the teeth marks.

Lorenzo and Christophe bent over with laughter, pointing at Paddy.

"*Garçons!*" the woman said, and that one word stopped the hilarity. "Lorenzo," she said.

"*Pardón*, Mama." Lorenzo took the banana and pulled away the yellow skin, revealing a curve of white.

Paddy and the other boys peeled theirs, then held the spearlike fruit in front of them.

"Now," the woman said. "Eat."

Paddy took a slow bite and chewed. Johnny Og, Jamesy, Thomas, and Daniel did the same. Then the woman peeled Bridget's and she bit the top. Soon they all were burying their teeth in the bananas and laughing.

"Good, Mam," Jamesy said.

Máire and I peeled our bananas. She looked at the curve in her hand, then at me, and started giggling.

The woman caught the look and smiled.

"Don't say *anything*, Máire," I said as I took a bite of the softest, sweetest prattie ever grown.

"Banana!" I said, and laughed.

"Banana!" said Paddy.

"Banana!" said Jamesy.

"Banana!" said Johnny Og, and then:

"Banana!" said Bridget.

Máire fed a bit to Gracie.

"Different," I said. "But I like it. Bananas."

With that, Stephen reached over and grabbed a piece of my banana and shoved the whole of it into his mouth.

We all laughed.

"Thank you so much," I said to the woman. "We've eaten mostly porridge for six weeks. I'm Honora Kelly."

"I'm M'am Jacques."

"I'm Máire Leahy," Máire said.

Banana.

❖ ❖ ❖

I could see that during our short time in New Orleans, we would meet more different kinds of people, eat a wider variety of food, and see a greater range of trees, plants, flowers, and buildings than would have come our way during a lifetime in Galway. Dizzying. Exhilarating.

Oh, Michael, is this the wider world you sought when you went adventuring?

❖   ❖   ❖

"This place beats Tír na nOg," Máire said to me as M'am Jacques led us through streets of three-storied yellow and pink and blue houses.

"Le Vieux Carré," she told us. "The French Quarter."

M'am Jacques took us to the place she lived—a convent, would you believe—where a woman called Sister Henriette Delille and two other nuns cared for sick, abandoned slaves and gave religious instruction to slave children. Against the law to teach slaves any other subjects, forbidden for them to learn to read and write, she said, though the nuns were allowed to maintain a school for free children of color.

She herself was a "free woman of color" and had begun her own order, the Sisters of the Holy Family, when the white convents had refused her admission. She explained all this to Máire and me while she fed our children their first meal in Amerikay.

"Only biscuits and milk, I'm afraid," Sister Henriette said.

Only? The children could barely eat for grinning while they chewed those warm biscuits covered with butter and strawberry jam. My four had never tasted such food nor had they drank milk since the before times. Thomas nodded to Máire as he gobbled up biscuit after biscuit, the little lord giving his approval.

"Delicious," Máire said, sipping her coffee, something not even the Scoundrel Pykes drank.

That night, Máire and I sat with Sister Henriette and M'am Jacques on the porch of their small wooden house.

"No porches in Ireland," I said.

"Or swings, either," Máire said as we rocked back and forth, holding Gracie and Stephen while the other children slept inside. "A lovely scent, that," she said.

"Night-blooming jasmine," Sister told her.

"Nice to be warm," Máire said.

We'd both been surprised when M'am Jacques told us that Sister Henriette owned her. "She inherited me and my sons when her own sister died." M'am Jacques went on about the Delille family. "All the girls are beautiful," she said, "speaking three and four languages, playing piano, painting pictures. Wasn't their granddaddy a French nobleman and their grandmother the daughter of an African chief?"

Then Sister Henriette said to M'am Jacques, "Hush now," and told us she'd gladly free M'am Jacques, but if she did, M'am Jacques would have to leave New Orleans. Recently freed slaves weren't allowed to live in the city. "Slavery's our country's great sin," she said. "I pray every day America will repent and make amends."

"Best you go to the Irish church, Saint Patrick's, for Sunday Mass tomorrow," Sister Henriette said, though she supposed we could go to the French church, St. Louis's Cathedral, or the Spanish one. She explained that she and the sisters and M'am Jacques attended St. Augustine's, a colored church, and while that congregation would welcome us, our being there could cause trouble with the white authorities. I said that St. Patrick's would suit us. The Dohertys from the *Superior* would surely be there, and Charlie's brother could help us buy our tickets for Chicago.

Sister Henriette had heard about Chicago from French missionary priests. "The frontier," she said. "On the prairie." I'd wanted to hear more, but Máire stood up and said she needed to sleep.

We thanked Sister Henriette. I told her no words could express what her unquestioning kindness meant to us.

"It's our vocation," she said.

The next morning, Lorenzo led us to St. Patrick's.

"See who's in the side pew?" Máire said as we walked into the fine stone church with its tall tower.

Maggie and Charlie Doherty sat with a couple—probably Charlie's brother and his wife—and a row of combed and curried children.

Our ones looked every bit as presentable. They'd each had a bath. "Never so clean in my *life*," Jamesy said. Sister Henriette dressed them from the clothes donated to the nuns by the rich families of New Orleans. She'd even found shoes that fit for each one and skirts and blouses for Máire and me. It was M'am Jacques pulled out the red silk shawl with fringes and wrapped it around Máire's shoulders.

"Doing all right for ourselves in Amerikay," Máire whispered to me as we shepherded the children into a pew.

We held Gracie and Stephen in our laps. The children had so much to see and hear that they kept very quiet during the long Mass. Father wore shiny green vestments, a choir sang, and all around us were life-size statues and colored glass windows. Three huge paintings rose above a high altar, carved from marble, which was covered with flowers and gold candlesticks.

"Better than any church in Ireland," Charlie's brother Peter Doherty said as we stood visiting after Mass, part of the crowd of people who all seemed to know one another. The parish. Peter told us the best architect in New Orleans had been responsible for the magnificence. "James Gallier," he'd said. "Though he was a Gallagher when he left Donegal. He gets more work for himself as a Frenchman." Peter told me the paintings alone cost one thousand dollars—a hundred just for the paint, five years' wages for a working man.

"Beautiful," I'd said, then asked him the names of the saints portrayed. The picture showed two women dressed in elegant gowns and fur-collared cloaks, kneeling before a richly dressed bishop in front of a pillared church. Was this the pope in Rome? Peter Doherty laughed at me. Didn't I recognize St. Patrick himself baptizing Eithne and Fidelma, the daughters of Art O'Leary, the high king? I'd sense enough not to tell him Fidelma and Eithne should be wearing homespun and that any chapel in St. Patrick's time would have been small and wattle-made. Being Irish was a different proposition in Amerikay.

Charlie had told Peter we were headed for Chicago, and Peter agreed to help us change our money into dollars. He said our thirty-two pounds would be worth one hundred dollars, enough for tickets all the way to Chicago. Peter Doherty worked on the docks and was very knowledgeable about shipping. He told us the *River Queen* left tomorrow, Monday, and said we'd better be aboard if we wanted to reach the Illinois and Michigan Canal before the ice closed it.

"Tomorrow?" Máire asked. "So soon?" She'd been talking to Maggie and Peter's wife, Annie.

Annie Doherty invited us to their house for a meal. They lived a fair distance from St. Patrick's, which surprised me.

"The Irish started coming to New Orleans quite a while ago," Peter Doherty told me. "Our pastor, Father Mullin, fought in the War of 1812."

The new arrivals lived in a neighborhood called the Channel. The Dohertys brought us to a cheerful muddle of wooden cottages painted blue or pink or yellow or green. All had porches, with children playing on them.

The Dohertys served us tea and a feed of pratties. I noticed that their children, born in New Orleans, drew out their words as M'am Jacques did, a lovely soft tone in their voices, which delighted Jamesy.

Our ones went off with the young Dohertys while we chatted in their neat cottage. Peter had already found a place for Charlie on the docks. Maggie had hoped to earn money doing laundry or cooking and cleaning in one of the Big Houses. But Annie said slaves did all that kind of work. Rent was cheap enough, though, and the mild winters helped. "Don't have to spend a lot to keep warm," she said.

Peter Doherty collected all the children and led the group of us to the bottom of their street. "The Mississippi," he said proudly. "The fourth-longest river in the world—not a Sassenach river can touch it." He pointed up the river and told us the *River Queen* would take five days to steam up first the Mississippi and then the Illinois River to a place called LaSalle, where we'd change to a canal boat for a day and a night. "You'll be in Chicago a week from today."

"Do you know anyone in Chicago?" Máire asked Annie.

Annie said she didn't. "It's a rough place, so they say."

"New Orleans is lovely," Máire said.

"You won't find me disagreeing with that," Annie said.

Peter Doherty walked us back to Sister Henriette's house. He'd looked surprised at where we were staying but lifted his hat to Sister Henriette and said he'd see us tomorrow to sort out the money and tickets.

"We'll give Sister some of our dollars," I said to Máire as we climbed the porch steps.

She nodded and started to say something, but then M'am Jacques was there, saying, "*Venez, venez.*"

And we were off—following M'am Jacques to a large open space where slaves came to pray, sing, and dance. It was called Congo Square. "Here we continue the traditions of our ancestors," she said.

Drums and drums and more drums—men, women, and children danced together as if they were moving to the pounding beat of one great heart.

Lorenzo and Christophe folded our boys into one of the lines of dancers. When the children had all tired themselves out, M'am Jacques brought us delicious bits of meat roasted over one of the many open fires. "This tastes better even than bananas and biscuits," Jamesy said.

As we were leaving, M'am Jacques pointed out a very tall, beautiful woman dressed in white. "That is Sister Henriette's cousin Marie Laveau," she said. "She knows the rituals of our African religion. I will ask her to bless you."

M'am Jacques lined us up in front of Marie Laveau, who then laid her hand on each of the children's heads. They stood very still as she bent down and spoke a few soft words to each one. Máire and I held Gracie and Stephen out to her for the blessing.

Then Marie Laveau grasped my shoulders and looked into my eyes. "*Soyez forte*," she said to me. Then in English, "Be strong." She moved to Máire and held her in the same way. "*Soyez sage*," she said to Máire. "Be wise. Be careful."

❖ ❖ ❖

Exhausted, all of us. We came back to Sister Henriette's and put the children to bed.

"We should sleep, too. We have a lot to do tomorrow. The *River Queen* leaves at sundown," I said to Máire.

"I need to talk to you," Máire said. "Come to the porch. Sit down," she said, motioning to the swing.

We sat together for a moment, moving back and forth, surrounded by the warm, sweet-smelling night.

Then she said, "Honora, we should stay in New Orleans. We'd be fools to leave."

"Máire, we have to go to Chicago. I promised Michael. Patrick Kelly's waiting for us."

"Michael's dead, Honora, and for all you know, Patrick Kelly is, too."

"Mam," I heard.

I turned to see Paddy. "What are you doing out here? You need your sleep." I stood up from the swing and went over to him. "We're leaving tomorrow."

"No, Mam," Paddy said. "We like this place. We want to stay. Aunt Máire said we could."

"What?" I looked at Máire.

She came over to me. "The boys talked to me, Honora. Surely we all have a say in where we settle."

"We're going to Chicago," I said.

"What? You think you can issue an order and I'll obey, no question? I won't," Máire said. "And you should listen to your sons."

"Paddy?" I said to him.

Now Johnny Og, Thomas, Daniel, and Jamesy stood with him.

"We'll earn money by dancing with Lorenzo and Christophe, while Thomas collects from the crowd," Paddy said.

I tried to make all the practical arguments: We were two women with eight children and another soon to be born, and we had little money. We'd found great kindness here, but Sister Henriette and the Dohertys were struggling themselves. They might help travelers for a few days, but we couldn't expect them to take us on indefinitely. But neither Máire nor the boys would listen.

"We've been practicing, Mam," Jamesy said.

"You too, Jamesy?" I said.

"We could get Jamesy a whistle, Aunt Honey," Daniel said.

"New Orleans is quite a good city," Thomas said.

"You've an uprising on your hands, Honora," Máire said.

"And you're the leader?"

"You've got us this far. We have a hundred dollars—enough for a good start."

"And then what, Máire? You heard Annie Doherty. Slave women do the housework here."

"There are other ways to earn wages. New Orleans seems a place appreciates beautiful women," Máire said, pulling her red shawl around her.

"Dear God, Máire. Surely you don't want to play the Pearl in Amerikay. You have a chance to begin again."

Máire started shouting at me. Who was I to judge her after all she'd done for me?

"Please, Máire. The boys . . . ," I said.

But the five of them stood there with their arms folded—little men. And Johnny Og's, what? almost nine, Paddy's eight, Thomas is seven, Jamesy's six, and Daniel's five years old.

The Warriors of the Red Branch—arrayed against me.

Sister Henriette and M'am Jacques heard the ruckus and came out to the porch.

"Boys!" Sister Henriette said. "This is not good. You must show respect."

Sister Henriette spoke to us in the most general terms of the side of New Orleans we hadn't seen. She made vague references to *demimonde*, all the time looking at Máire. Then M'am Jacques said that white boys and colored boys did not perform together on the streets of New Orleans.

But Máire kept shaking her head. Finally she said, "All right. Divide the money. I'll stay with my children. You leave with yours."

Bedlam. "No, no, no!" from the boys. They wouldn't be divided.

And Paddy said, "The fingers and the fist, Mam!" and they all clenched their small fists and lifted them into the air.

Then Sister Henriette said to me, "Chicago *is* a long journey. Are you certain?"

"I am, Sister. Surely you understand. I made a solemn vow to my husband that I'd take our children to his brother, Patrick, in Chicago. I believe that Michael won't rest in peace until we're safe with his brother."

I turned to the boys. "Don't ask me to go against your da. Paddy, there's not a single person in New Orleans ever knew him. Uncle Patrick does. Don't you remember when he came and helped put in the pratties, stood up against the Sassenach? He's your father's brother, boys."

"Like us, Paddy," Jamesy said to him.

"I guess we can't stay here if our da's brother is waiting for us in Chicago," Paddy said. He looked at Johnny Og. "I have to go."

Johnny Og nodded. "You do." He turned to Máire. "Is there anyone in Amerikay remembers my da?"

Máire shook her head.

"I remember him, Johnny Og—the best fisherman in Bearna," I said. "Your uncle Michael played his pipes at your mam and da's wedding." I turned to Máire. "Please. If we separate, we lose so much."

"We can't let them go on their own, Mam," Johnny Og said. "Aunt Honey's not a good talker like you. Somebody'll cheat them."

"Johnny Og's right, Máire," I said.

Máire turned to Johnny Og. "So, you want to go?"

"I do," Johnny Og said.

"Me too, Mam," Daniel said.

Máire turned to Thomas and asked, "What about you?"

"I like New Orleans," he said, "but—I'd miss Paddy and Jamesy."

"Dear God in heaven," Máire said. "Some uprising." Then she laughed. "All right. I'll go with you to Chicago. We'll find Patrick Kelly. But don't be surprised if I come back here someday."

❖ ❖ ❖

Máire and I went with Peter Doherty the next morning. We spent sixty dollars for third-class fares on the *River Queen*—ten each for Máire and me, five dollars for every child. Four dollars apiece for passage on the canal boat, no charge for the children. So, sixty-eight dollars. Food for the trip cost five dollars. With the ten given to Sister Henriette, we had seventeen dollars left from all our money. Peter wouldn't take anything for his trouble.

"You'll need every penny," he said, and waved good-bye to us as the *River Queen*'s paddle began turning and the steamboat started up the Mississippi. It would travel day and night.

No waiting around in Amerikay.

❖ ❖ ❖

Máire and the children dozed, leaning against sacks of sugar and coffee, as we moved north through the darkness. Other passengers crowded the bottom deck of the *River Queen*—mostly families, but some single men and women, too, all asleep. Not me. A young fellow from Sligo seemed to need a listening ear. He was heading out to the west of Amerikay to find work on the cattle and sheep ranches. He would travel by steamboat to St. Louis, then by wagon train for another thousand miles to a place they called Bent's Fort on the Santa Fe Trail, he told me.

"Think of it—me, who never went more than a day's walk from my own townland when I was home in Ireland, going two thousand miles across Amerikay to become a cowboy!" he said.

"You're very brave," I said, "going off on your own into nothing."

"Me, brave, missus? I'm a man on my own. You and your sister, women alone with eight children—that's what I would call brave." He dropped his voice. "See those others?" He nodded toward five families sitting together with trunks piled around them. "Swedes and Norwegians," he said. "Farmers going beyond Saint Louis to the empty country. Good luck to them." Better supplied than the Irish families, he said, who were more like us, taking on Amerikay with a bundle of clothes.

And a few hidden dollars, some tokens. I felt for Granny's cross, the stone Michael'd given me, and the Mary Bean. Finally, the young fellow closed his eyes. I slept.

Johnny Og got up at first light and woke us all at dawn, full of the wonders of the steamboat. He'd found the pilothouse, the smokestacks, the engines, and the greatest prize of all—the paddle wheel.

"Come see it, Paddy!"

"I won't," Paddy said, huffing still. "Are you sure Da wouldn't want us to make a fortune singing and dancing with Lorenzo and Christophe?" he'd asked just before we boarded the boat.

But when Jamesy, Thomas, and Daniel jumped to their feet and went off after Johnny Og, Paddy frowned at me and said, "I'd better watch out for them," and took off running.

"They'll come back when their stomachs are growling," I said to Máire. "We've chicken, and Sister Henriette gave us biscuits. So kind. Generous! . . . Máire?"

She didn't answer. Asleep, or pretending to be. She'd been very silent since we'd left. "I've given in, but I won't pretend to be happy," she'd said.

"Máire, are you sure you're not hungry?"

No answer.

Stephen and the girls still slept, and I closed my eyes as the sun rose over the Mississippi.

"Wake up, Mam!" Paddy, excited now, stood in front of me with the other boys around him.

Midday. I'd slept longer than I thought.

"Listen to this, Mam, listen." Paddy dropped his voice and cupped his hands around his mouth. "By the mark, twain!" he boomed. "That's what the man says who drops the line over the side of the boat: 'By the mark, twain!'"

"He measures the water, makes sure it's deep enough," Johnny Og added. "Ah, Mam," he said to Máire, "could we live here on this boat, go back and forth, up and down the river?"

I looked over at Máire. "His father's son," I said. "Brave in a boat."

Máire didn't reply to me but smiled at Johnny Og. "Stay on the boat, is it? That sounds a lovely idea."

"Oh, Mam, you would like the rooms above us."

"I would?"

"You would, Mam," Thomas said. "Ladies, real ladies eating and drinking at long tables with china and silver, like at home."

Home. Poor Silken Thomas. The Big House was never your home.

"And card games, Mam, and music," he went on, "the same as the places my da was going to take us to in London."

"Robert told great stories about the gambling houses in London, fortunes made and lost on the turn of a card," Máire said to me.

"The rents of Irish tenants wagered and lost," I said.

"Beautiful carpets, Mam," Thomas went on, "and drapes and lamps and—"

"Honora," she said, "pass me one of those biscuits. I'm peckish." Máire bit through the crust into the soft center. "Eat up now, boys," she said. "We'll go for a wee tramp around the boat."

Máire settled the red silk shawl around her and started up the steps to the upper deck, with Johnny Og and Thomas on either side. "Coming, Honora?"

"Go on," I said. "We'll stay here."

⬦ ⬦ ⬦

A few hours later, we came to a wharf. "Natchez, Mississippi—this is Natchez, Mississippi," a voice called out. A bell rang.

After an hour, we cast off. The big wheel started turning. No new passengers. Bridget, Gracie, and Stephen let me sing them to sleep as the engines throbbed and the paddle wheels churned through the river. I slept.

Máire and the boys came back in the middle of the night.

"Wonders," she said. "Miracles and wonders up above." She eased down next to me, smiling and talking. "Oh, Honora, those rooms! Saloons, they call them—lounges with crystal chandeliers, red walls gilded with gold. And the people! Dressed like I've never seen before! Wouldn't poor addled Mistress Pyke cross her eyes in jealousy to see the satin and silk of the ladies there, the shiny boots of the gentlemen? And didn't some man come over and tip his hat and ask me if the boys and I didn't want a closer look? He took my arm and brought us into the midst of it all! And here's the best part. The gentleman said there are saloons in Chicago, lots and lots of them, and guess who owns them? The Irish! And he said Chicago had something of the spirit of New Orleans. So. Isn't it a good thing Sister found this red-fringed shawl for me among all the charitable garments?" She smiled, leaned back, closed her eyes, and slept. Máire never could sulk for long.

❖   ❖   ❖

Three days later, the last of the Irish left the boat at a place called Memphis. Two more days—more room now down among the cargo and the children comfortable enough. The boys ran all over the *River Queen* while Bridget and I played games with Stephen and Gracie in the corridor near us. Máire and Thomas "promenaded"—her word—on the upper deck. She found the kitchen, made friends with the cooks, and brought us bread and slices of ham to eat when we'd finished our New Orleans food.

The *River Queen* turned into the Illinois River. We'd been traveling nearly two months. Very weary, all of us.

❖   ❖   ❖

LaSalle, Illinois. Dawn. The children stumbled like newborn foals down the gangplank of the *River Queen* and onto the pier to board the canal boat. The Sligs fellow waved good-bye to us.

"Your fares are paid all the way to Chicago," Peter Doherty had repeated over and over. "Don't let some villain come up and try to convince you different. Terrible altogether, how they prey on travelers. They'll tell you your ticket is no good because it shows one horse pulling the canal boat instead of two. Or they'll say, 'Your ticket has a horse, and that's donkeys pulling this barge. Buy another.' Ignore them," he'd said. "Speak up for yourself."

But the boatman took my ticket, no bother.

LaSalle, Illinois. LaSalle . . . The French had owned this territory once, Sister Henriette told us. Amerikay now.

The canal boat *General Fry*, a stump of a thing—long, but wide and narrow-bottomed—could barely fit between the stone walls of the canal.

"Come on, missus! Step lively there, boys. A cold wind's sweeping down from Chicago. Clumps of ice in the canal if we don't hurry. Temperatures drop overnight. You've left it late enough. We're one of the last boats going."

The fellow shouting wore a blue uniform and waved the shiny horn he held in one hand at us, urging us forward. "Come on! Let's go!" The two big horses who would pull the boat along the tow path moved in their harnesses, impatient, too: Come on. Move.

We followed the other passengers into the cabin at the center of the boat, where big glass windows looked out at the deck, and settled ourselves on a lovely plush sofa.

I was exhausted, but the baby inside me was wide awake and kicking. Still, I closed my eyes and was falling asleep when a loud sound startled me wide awake.

"Holy Sweet Jesus!" Máire said.

Another blast!

"There, Mam, on the deck," Jamesy said. "The boatman's blowing his horn."

"We're off!" said Johnny Og, running out of the cabin and across the deck to the rail.

"See, Mam?" said Paddy. "The horses have started pulling."

Twenty-four hours, a hundred miles at a steady pace, and we'd arrive in Chicago. Stephen, the girls, Máire, and I fell asleep, lulled by the canal boat's easy motion. But the boys, including five-year-old Daniel, stayed out on the deck with the boatman.

"Mam, Mam!" Paddy called to me. "Come out and see!"

The sun was high in the sky. The boys have forgiven me for taking them from New Orleans. Give them food, sleep, and a big engine to look at and there's not a bother on them, I thought as I joined the boys on deck.

What beautiful colors the leaves of the trees on the canal bank had turned. I'd never seen such a mass of red and gold. "What are those trees?" I asked the boatman.

"Maples," he told me. "The last of them. Bare boughs in Chicago." He stood next to the gate on the deck. "Maples, oak, birch grow along the canal route, but out beyond on the prairie there's hardly a tree or bush." He pointed to the open space I could just glimpse through the trees. "No wood, no fuel. Farmers build their houses from sods."

"Sods?"

"Pieces of ground, cut up and piled one on the other."

"Like skalps," I said.

"Pardon?"

"Shelters built in ditches with pieces of turf," I said.

"Oh," he said, not interested. "The sod houses out on the prairie will be gone soon enough. The farmers will build frame houses with lumber brought to them by the boats of this fine Illinois and Michigan Canal. We pick up their crops, bring them to Chicago, carry everything they need back to them. The canal's only been open six months, and change is coming already. We'd never have finished the I and M Canal but for the wild Irishmen. They could dig, I'll say that for them. No brains, but plenty of brawn, and willing to risk life and limb to make a dollar. But they don't put the same value on human life that we do, I guess because there are so many of them."

"I'm Irish," I said, "and—"

"And you have how many children?" he interrupted me. "Ten?"

I walked away from the man to the boat rail. What an ignorant guilpín. Our boys hadn't heard him, thank God. Too busy waving at the children on the bank. Are these the farm children who'd be moving from their mud houses into wooden homes?

The boatman followed me, going on and on about how the Irish workers died because they wouldn't wear proper clothes, and they drank rotgut whiskey. . . .

I tried to close my ears. Too tired to argue with him.

But then a fellow who'd been standing there quiet, drawing in a notebook, spoke up. He was German, he said, named Carl Culmann, an engineer surveying public works in Amerikay. Nowhere had he come across the level of craft as he'd seen in the canal, he told the boatman. Very skilled workmen, to fit the stones in so carefully. The walls had to hold back millions of gallons of water. He turned to me. "I compliment your countrymen, madam."

"Thank you, sir," I said. I turned my back on the boatman and went into the cabin.

❖ ❖ ❖

At dawn, the boatman called out, "Summit!" The children and Máire slept on, but the older, plump man next to me, a farmer coming to Chicago to sell his harvest, wanted to talk. Why do I get the chatty fellows?

The *General Fry* was for passengers, the farmer told me. Other boats carried cargo—tons and tons of it. The wheat he was selling would be loaded onto a steamer in Chicago, go across the Great Lakes to Buffalo, out the St. Lawrence River, and then to Europe.

"All by water," the farmer said. "Think of it—a waterway from the Gulf of Mexico all the way to Canada and the Atlantic. The dream of centuries, this Illinois and Michigan Canal! Our congressman, a young lawyer called Abe Lincoln, gave a big speech the day the first cargo arrived in Buffalo. He said what the old-time French explorers could only imagine we Americans had done. Watch Chicago grow now!" he said. "How many people living there now?" he asked the boatman who came into the cabin.

"I'd say at least fifteen to twenty thousand."

"Twenty years ago," the farmer said, "population was less than a thousand. But it's a shame, really. Life in a city is no good."

"Why do you say that?" I asked.

"Why? Because Chicago's a barren place, full of brutes and criminals. Even the Indians say it stinks—that's what Chicago means in their language: bad smell." He paused, expecting me to laugh. Then, "You're Irish," he said.

"I am."

"I have a question for you. Why won't you paddys start farms on the prairie?" the farmer asked. "Acres and acres of land going cheap, yet you people crowd together in shantytowns."

"Well . . . ," I started.

But he was off telling me how just a few miles west of Chicago grass grew six feet tall and the soil was so rich a dry stick would grow in it. "The land's flat," he said. "Easy to plow. I can stand in my field and watch the sun go down below the horizon and there's nothing between me and it—not a hill or a mound, only the grass and wildflowers. There for the taking. Yet the Irish won't farm! They stay jammed in Chicago. Why?"

"Money's needed to buy even cheap land, and then there's the seed," I said. "And the plows and shovels, the chickens, calves, and pigs, and . . ."

I remembered the families of Swedes and Norwegians on the *River Queen*. I was sure those still-faced men had money belts wrapped around their waists full of the profits made from selling their land at home, something to help them start again in Amerikay. Our fellows had only their own strong backs, and what they earned went back to Ireland to pay the rent and bring out another family member.

✥ ✥ ✥

Five loud, long notes on the trumpet. "Bridgeport," said the boatman. "Last stop."

"Bridgeport?" I said. "Where's Chicago?"

"The boat stops here. This is the end."

"But . . . I don't understand," I said. I looked out—no buildings or streets, only an empty wharf.

"The center of the city is a few miles north, but the canal ends here," the farmer said to me.

"We have to find Saint Patrick's Church in Chicago. How do we get there?"

"You can pay a small boat to take you up the river, or hire a wagon, or walk," he said.

"Walk? And how far is it?"

"Four, five miles."

Walk? Not walk, I thought. The children had traveled two months with hardly a whinge or whine, but to ask them to go five more miles on foot?

"Please, we have to get to Chicago," I said.

"Bridgeport is where you people live," the boatman said. "It's where the digging for the canal began. You'll find someone. You have no choice anyway, missus. Off you go."

The boatman made Máire and the children stand up—still half-asleep, all of them. I picked up Stephen, took Bridget's hand. Máire carried Gracie. We stood on the deck.

"But, sir . . . ," I began.

The boatman pushed me, put his hand between my shoulders and shoved me down the gangplank—I could hardly keep hold of Stephen. Bridget started crying, grabbing on to my skirt, tripping on the ramp.

Máire still stood on the deck, clutching the red silk shawl to her. "This is Chicago?" she said. "Where are the pink buildings? Where are the church spires? Where are the saloons!"

The wharf was empty. I saw a few small wooden houses in the distance. Not one person about, no streets. Only a path of mud.

I suppose I had expected that somehow Patrick Kelly would have been watching for us and would be here to meet us, or that I could ask a docker where Patrick Kelly with the golden staff lived.

But we were alone in this bleak place.

"Sunday morning," the farmer said, standing beside me. "Early. Your people probably had a big time last night—sleeping off the whiskey. Well, good luck to you." And he was gone.

Máire picked up Gracie and walked down the gangplank. The boys stomped after her.

We had eaten all the food we'd brought. We'd landed—alone and hungry, and nowhere to get out of the cold.

Máire pulled her red shawl around her and stared straight at me. "Now what, Honora?"

"I . . . I don't know."

"A godforsaken freezing place," said Máire.

The odor alone would keep God away. The smell seemed to come from the river that curved away from the canal.

A foul wind blew tears into my eyes. I was dizzy and shivering, sharp cramps in my stomach. The baby. Michael, where are you?

And then I was weeping, and the children and Máire along with me—bawling and sobbing.

The Sassenach had not been able to break me. Starvation? Disease? I'd stood up to them. Even when Michael died, I'd held on. I'd keep my promise to escape with our children to Amerikay. But now . . . nothing. I had no sense of Michael's presence, nor of God's. Where are You, Lord? I've done my part. Máire is right, You have forsaken this place, and us, too.

I want to be home. I want to stand in the sun on the Silver Strand of Galway Bay. I want to be young again. I want my husband, my mother. I want—

"Christ on his cross, what's all this caterwauling?"

I turned. Ah, shite. Here he comes, Chicago's version of that New Orleans bullyboy, slapping the same kind of club into his palm.

"Is it against the law for two mothers and eight children to weep when they've reached the end of their endurance?" I asked him. "Well, then take us to jail! Please! We'd welcome a cell out of the wind."

He turned to Máire. "What's she on about?"

Máire sniffed up her tears. "She's given up at last, thank God. And now, if you'll tell us where this boat turns around, we'll be heading back."

"To Ireland?" he asked. "I wouldn't advise it, missus."

"Not Ireland, you big sliveen! New Orleans!" Máire said.

"Who are you calling a sliveen?" he asked.

"I don't see anybody else standing around out here in the cold!"

"Máire, please!" I said.

"Don't you 'Máire, please' me! You're the one so sure we'd find Patrick Kelly. Patrick Kelly? He's probably dead and buried with his golden staff beside him! Why did I let you talk me into this—"

"Is that Patrick Kelly the Galway man you're talking about?"

"It is. Do you know him?" I asked.

"And he has a golden staff?"

"He has! Where is he? Thanks be to God! Where is he?"

"He should be in that cell you're so anxious to get into."

"What do you mean?"

"He's wanted," said Máire. "I knew it! Now can we go back to New Orleans?"

"Máire, please."

The boys forgot about weeping, listening and watching this big man.

"Patrick Kelly is an agitator," he said.

"Agitator?" asked Máire. "Is that some stripe of a murderer?"

"Look, girls, there's some call Patrick Kelly a hero, but the Illinois and Michigan Canal pays me to walk this wharf, to see that the cargo is loaded and unloaded with no bother. Patrick Kelly puts himself between the men and the bosses. Gloves."

"Gloves?" I said.

"Gloves. A notion that the company should give out gloves to the men. Jesus! What class of Irishman needs gloves? So you lose a finger or two—frozen off or cut off—don't we have five of them on each hand? I'm from Ballina. Mayo men don't whine for gloves. Some very weak people from counties like Limerick and Donegal."

"If you are a true Irishman, you'll find a place for us to shelter and something to eat," Máire said. "I am no kin nor connection to Patrick Kelly. My name's Máire Leahy." She smiled at him.

"Tim John Tunney, at your service."

"Isn't there a saloon somewhere?" Máire asked him.

"A saloon?"

"You know, with carpets and crystal chandeliers? And a chair for a lady to rest on. I was told that Chicago had saloons, and that the Irish owned them."

"True enough." He laughed. "Though we call them bars, or taverns. And you're right—McCormicks and Garveys and Donlons and Keefes own them, but as for crystal chandeliers and carpets—"

"Mr. Tunney," I said, "I have some money. Please tell us where we can find our children a shelter for the night." I felt the tears starting up again. I couldn't hold back. Every breath became a sob. Stop, Honora. If you cry, you die. But I couldn't control myself.

"Ah now, missus," the man said to me. "No need to cry. And keep your money. You'll need it. Let's see . . . I'll take you to Mass, that'd be a start. Near time now."

"Mass? At Saint Patrick's Church?" I asked. "That was where we'd sent the letter." Maybe Patrick himself would be there.

"Saint Patrick's is miles and miles away," said Tim John. "I'm going to take you to Saint Bridget's. We'll kill two birds with one stone, as they say here, because Saint Bridget's parish holds its Sunday Mass in James McKenna's Scanlon House—a saloon."

⒞HAPTER 24

⒧cKenna's Tavern," said Tim John Tunney, "and Saint Bridget's Church." Carrying Stephen, he herded us into a narrow wooden building. "Now, up to the fire," he said.

I staggered, then gripped Paddy's shoulder to steady myself.

"Come on there, boys, get your mother into this chair."

Paddy put his arm around my waist and helped me to sit down. "Mam," Paddy said into my ear, "don't let this one die."

I clutched my stomach and closed my eyes.

"Oh, Honora," Máire said. "The baby?"

"Tim John." A woman's voice. "Take these children into the kitchen. I'll see to her." She lifted up my legs, set them on a stool. "Here, missus." Her hand tipped a tin cup against my lips. Cool water. "Straight from Lake Michigan," she said.

"She's weary," Máire said. "We've come a long way."

"You can relax, girls," the woman said. "You're among your own."

She gave me more water. I drank it down, not as dizzy now, and the cramping eased. I opened my eyes.

"Better," I said. "Thank you."

"No bother. Glad to help," the woman said, her small face close to mine. I felt kindness from her. She had gray hair, blue eyes, and was smiling at me. "Rest yourself, dear. I'm Lizzie McKenna, and you're very welcome to McKenna's Scanlon House Tavern," she said.

"Thank you, Mrs. McKenna."

"Lizzie," she said.

"I'm Honora. Honora Kelly."

Máire was kneeling next to me. "You've your color back, Honora," she said, and stood up. "I'm Máire Leahy," she said to Lizzie McKenna. "We're sisters."

"Then I'll be leaving you in good hands, Honora. Have to finish my cleaning. Father Donohue's good enough to ignore the smell of drink, but if the bar's not rubbed down right, the nice linen cloth he brings will stick to the whiskey spills." She hurried away.

"Are you all right?" Máire asked me.

"I am."

"Good." She looked around the dim room, lit only by the fire and a few lanterns. The small windows framed a gray, sunless sky. "A bit different than the church we went to last Sunday," she said.

"Máire, please."

"I'm only saying . . . I'd best see to the children."

❖ ❖ ❖

More than a hundred people crowded around the tall, middle-aged priest who celebrated the Holy Sacrifice on top of the bar. There were family groups, knots of girls, and a line of men who stood in the back of the tavern. Everyone wore dark clothes—heavy woolen jackets on the men, shawls on the women. Not the place for our bright New Orleans cottons.

Máire had our children sitting on the floor near the fire. Jamesy held on to one of my feet and Paddy the other.

Before communion, Lizzie said to me, "Stay where you are," then brought Father Donohue over to me.

"*Corpus Christi*," he said as he placed the host on my tongue. "*Viaticum*, bread of travelers," he added, then smiled. "Fáilte."

Well now, this priest's a human being, and very easy with his people, I saw, when after Mass he stayed on in the tavern, talking, even joking as he went from group to group.

"Here he is, finally," Lizzie said as she brought the priest to us.

After Lizzie introduced Máire and me to him, he said, "We're glad to have you at Saint Bridget's parish."

"Father Donohue's a Tipperary man," Lizzie said. "We used to have only French priests in Chicago, but now even our bishop's Irish." She put one hand on her hip and looked up at the priest. "But with a name like Quarter, he could pass for French. Is that why he got the job, do you think, Father?"

"Now, Lizzie," he said, and winked at her, which made Máire laugh.

"Father's not devoted to his own dignity like Father Gilley, or that overbearing priest in New Orleans," she whispered to me.

"Let me know if I can help you in any way," Father Donohue said. "I come to Saint Bridget's on Sundays, but I'm assigned to Saint Patrick's."

"Saint Patrick's," I repeated. "That's where we sent the letter to my husband's brother, Patrick Kelly."

"A lot of Patrick Kellys in Chicago," Father said. "A lot of letters."

"It was the Sisters of Mercy in Galway sent the letter to their convent here, to be brought to Saint Patrick's."

"Galway, you say? Is it Patrick Kelly who has Saint Grellan's crozier you want?"

"It is," I said. "It is."

"I believe we are holding a letter for Patrick."

"Holding? So he hasn't received it?"

"Patrick Kelly's not been in Chicago since midsummer," Father Donohue said.

"But you know him?" I asked.

"We all know Patrick Kelly," Lizzie said, "though as to where he is and when he'll be back, no one could say, I'd wager."

"He'll return sooner or later," Father Donohue said.

But we need him now, tonight. Where are we to go?

❖ ❖ ❖

After Father Donahue left, McKenna's changed back into a tavern. A tall man with a mustache—Lizzie's husband, I suppose—presided over the bar. I'd never been in a public house or shebeen before, and this fellow's control of the drinkers impressed me. He responded to raised fingers, nods, and quiet requests but ignored shouts, moving along with the jug, pouring whiskey into small glasses, picking up coins, having a word with each customer—a kind of ritual here, too.

The women stayed around the fire. I stood up to give my chair to a frail old woman just as Lizzie bustled up, followed by two lads carrying a stack of stools that they arranged around the hearth.

"The only day you ladies come into our tavern. May as well be comfortable," she said, sitting me back down. Lizzie pointed to each of about twenty women, telling us their names and the county each was from in Ireland.

I nodded and smiled. "We're from Bearna," I said. "Galway."

They all shook their heads at that, no Galway people among them, though the woman next to me said she'd heard Galway Bay was lovely.

Máire chatted away to a group across from me, her shawl a flare of red against the dark clothes of the others.

Lizzie and her lads came back, carrying trays of white china mugs of tea. "Sip away, ladies," she said, and sat beside me.

"The children—" I started.

But Lizzie pointed to the far corner where our bunch had joined a circle of children. "Amusing each other," she said. "That's my husband, James McKenna, behind the bar. He'll keep an eye on them."

As Sunday morning became afternoon, we stayed tucked up in McKenna's, out of the wind. The wood fire didn't burn with flashes of purple and scarlet as bogdeal did, nor give off the steady heat of turf. Lizzie McKenna had to prod the logs to keep the flames licking at them, but the fire managed to warm us while she and the other women, adding their bits and pieces, told me about Bridgeport. It was the canal commissioners, they said, changed the name of their village from Hardscrabble.

"As if the tough times of hardscrabbling have ended, which they haven't," a heavyset woman said.

"Not as brutal as when the men were digging the canal," another one said. "Fellows froze to death sleeping in those raggedy dormitory tents set up along the route. No regular wages, either."

"The company stopping and starting work," another told me.

"Lucky for you, though, Lizzie," said the heavyset woman, Mrs. McCarthy. She turned to me. "James McKenna and his friend Michael Scanlon were two of the earliest laborers. When the canal committee ran out of cash, they paid them with plots of land."

"Still," Lizzie said to her, "took us a long time and a lot of odd jobs to earn the money to build the tavern."

But there was work, all the women agreed. Thank God. The canal boats were loaded and unloaded in Bridgeport, and when the ice closed the I&M Canal, men worked in the quarry, the lime kilns, and the packinghouses.

"Packinghouse?" I asked Lizzie.

"Where the fellows kill and cut up the cattle," she said. "Hough's is the biggest. Of course, they operate only in the winter—the meat rots in warm weather."

"Your boys could get jobs at Hough's," one woman said.

"My oldest, Paddy, is only eight," I said.

"My sons started at six," the woman—Mrs. Kenny, I think—said. "Had to," she went on, "after my husband, Dan, was killed in the lumber camp."

"Your boys have got a good size on them," Lizzie said. "They can clean the blood from the drains or burn the entrails. And Hough gives his workers the cattle's stomachs, which are all right to eat, if you stew them long enough. Got us through some hard times, I can tell you that."

"Hough's throws the hearts and livers into the river," another said. "Boys dive for them—handy."

"Oh," I said. We'd done worse to survive the Great Starvation, but wasn't this Amerikay?

Máire hadn't been listening, laughing with the women on each side of her.

Tim John walked over, carrying a glass of whiskey. He offered it to Máire.

All the women went silent. Every man at the bar watched, some elbowing one another.

"Kind of you," Máire said, reaching up for the glass. She paused. "I'll wait until you bring the others."

"Others?" Tim John asked.

"Surely you're buying a round of drink for all of us ladies."

"I . . . I . . . ," Tim John sputtered.

Lizzie let out a snort of laughter, and then we were all roaring.

"Good on you, Máire," an older woman said. And then to Tim John, "We'll wait; have a glass on you at Christmas."

He shrugged his big shoulders and walked back to the bar.

"Now," the woman, a Mrs. Flanigan, said, "it's me for the stove. Twenty boarders will be looking for their Sunday dinner."

The other women stood up and called to their children. I got up, too, and went with them to the corner, where all the little ones sat on the plank floor, watching two older boys throw a short-handled knife into a target drawn on the wood. These children, like those in New Orleans, had pulled our ones into their circle. Bridget kept Stephen close to her on one side, with Gracie on the other. My helper.

"The children here are well behaved," I said to Lizzie, who came up next to me.

"They'd better be, or their mothers would give them a good whack. The Hardscrabble lads can be wild enough, though, given the chance. Especially that Hickory Gang. Good you have a swarm to stand together." She pointed to Paddy. "Able to land a punch or two, I'd say."

As the other mothers collected their children, only our ones remained.

"Where are we going to sleep, Mam?" Jamesy asked me.

I turned to Lizzie. "We do have some money."

"How much, if you don't mind my asking?"

"Seventeen dollars."

"Warm clothes and two weeks' room and board will take that, I'd say. We'd better find you somewhere."

"Couldn't we just stay here tonight? In the morning . . ."

But Lizzie was shaking her head. "McKenna and I live behind the tavern, but children shouldn't really . . ." She shrugged.

Since the families had left, the atmosphere in McKenna's had changed. More men crowded the bar, louder voices, even a shoving match McKenna ended by whacking a great stick on the bar. Were Máire and I the only women in the place?

I started toward Máire, then stopped. She wasn't alone. Four fellows sat on the low stools near her, talking away.

"Missus." I turned. James McKenna stood next to me. "Feeling well again?" he asked me.

"I am," I said, "and very grateful to you."

McKenna cleared his throat. "Your sister's in good form," he said.

Not drinking, though. No glass in her hand. Máire said something, and the men sitting with her laughed.

"We don't—" James McKenna started. "That is, women aren't . . ." He stopped. "You explain," he said to Lizzie, and went back to the bar.

Lizzie led me to a quiet spot. "You see, Honora, calling Hardscrabble 'Bridgeport' doesn't change the facts. We're still a separate village outside the city limits, and the muckety-mucks in Chicago want to keep the wild Irish out."

From the Fury of the O'Flahertys deliver us, I thought.

"Now," Lizzie went on, "McKenna wants Bridgeport incorporated into Chicago so he can run for alderman, be on the city council. The tavern needs to be respectable, and there's a certain type of woman . . ."

"My sister's not a certain type of woman."

"I'm sure not, and she put Tim John in his place, no bother. I'm not judging. Sometimes girls, to stay alive, or mothers, to save their children, have to sell what they can. There's places for that. Ma Conley's at the Sands for one, and—"

"We're going, Mrs. McKenna. Now. I don't know where, but you can't— My sister Máire's a good woman and a great strength to me." I started to walk away.

"Easy now, Honora," Lizzie said. "I know that. It's only McKenna." She sighed. "No one sees sin like a reformed sinner." Lizzie leaned close. "When we first came here, oh my, it must be twenty years ago, Chicago was a wild, free, and easy place. We had great times at the old Sauganash Hotel—that's downtown where the river goes into Lake Michigan. Nobody minded who was who. A Frenchman ran it—Beaubien, a great fiddler. What dances we had! Soldiers came down from Fort Dearborn, fur traders came and, of course, the Potawatomis."

"The what?"

"Potawatomis . . . the Indians. Thousands of them camped then around the city, trading their furs with the French and later the Americans. And I danced with one and all. The Indian men didn't like the reels, but they could waltz the feet off you, whirl you high in the air! It was the Indian *women* who were powerful at reels. You should have seen them do 'The Walls of Limerick'! And McKenna stepping lively with all the rest. We're Donegal people and fast on our feet. And believe me, we women took a drop, same as the men.

"But Chicago has changed since then. A flood of easterners in charge now, trying to put manners on the place," she said. "Some of them even wanted to change Chicago's name! It's an Indian word— you know what it means?"

"Well . . . ," I started.

She waved her hand. "We don't mind. I'd rather be the smelly place than 'New' York or 'New' Hampshire or 'New' Bedford named after English cities, or be saddled with French—Vincennes, Terre Haute . . . Chicago is a good name, and Bridgeport will be part of it whether the Yankees like it or not. Only . . . I'm sorry if I insulted your sister," Lizzie said. "Now, we need to sort out where you're staying."

We walked over to the fire. The fellows sitting with Máire stood up. Lizzie slagged them a bit, then sent them away.

"Now," she said, "I'm thinking Molly Flanigan might take you in." Boardinghouses in Bridgeport were for working men, Lizzie said. No women or children. The men didn't want to have to mind their manners. "But Molly Flanigan owes Patrick Kelly. You met her today—about my age, but looks older. A widow."

"So are we," Máire said.

"But not for long, I hope," Lizzie said. "Best to get husbands. Chicago can be hard on lone women."

"I will never—" I started, but Máire was up and ready to go.

❖ ❖ ❖

The wind tore at us as we followed Lizzie down an empty road. No one about, though candlelight showed through the small windows of wooden cottages with peaked roofs and smoke trailed up toward the low sky from the chimneys.

"Not a style of house we have at home," Máire said to Lizzie.

"Yankees call them shanties, and us the shanty Irish. Supposed to be an insult, but these wee houses can be cozy enough," she said.

"We'll be glad for any shelter," I said as we turned onto another dirt road.

"Hickory Street," Lizzie said. "Those paths go down to the canal, and see beyond, the open space? The prairie. A Potawatomi family lives right there, at the edge of the prairie."

"I don't see—"

"Their huts are near to the ground," she said. "Rounded. Can you make out the white of the birch bark?"

We walked farther down Hickory Street until we came to a three-story building at the end of the street. The children shivered in their New Orleans clothes.

"Let's get into Molly's kitchen," Lizzie said. "Always warm with that big stove of hers."

We found Molly Flanigan washing up after the dinner she'd served her boarders, and in minutes she had the children eating near the iron stove, which did give off great heat. Molly was the woman who'd told Máire, "Good on you." She had soft brown eyes behind her spectacles—doing well to have spectacles. She chatted away to us, Lizzie nodding and adding comments. Molly's sons were grown and gone, she told us, one out west and the other a sailor on the boats that crossed Lake Michigan going up to Buffalo.

"Good boys, both of them," Lizzie said, "once they straightened themselves out."

Molly's two daughters had married—one lived in St. Patrick's parish and the other farther north in a neighborhood called Goose Island.

"The Irish have spread out all over Chicago," Lizzie told us. "Don't stay jammed together in one place. Kilgubbin and Wolf Point, all those places, are part of Chicago."

All was friendly until Lizzie said we wanted to move into the boardinghouse. Molly said that she just never took families, and there was no space anyway—twenty boarders and only eight rooms, two and three to a room already. Though she did have an attic she used for storage. . . .

"Honora's dead husband's brother is Patrick Kelly," Lizzie said, jumping into the flow of Molly's words.

"Is he. Well then . . ." There'd be little enough space, but she'd take us for a month.

I looked at Máire. She nodded. We'd survived that box on the *Superior.*

"The, uhm, cost?"

"Would six dollars a week do you? Meals, too," she said. "I could make it five if you'd help with the wash."

"We would, of course."

"I usually ask for two weeks in advance."

"But we have to get warm clothes for the children. We'd have no money left," I said.

"I couldn't charge you less," Molly said. "Food and firewood's shockingly expensive. You could stay a day or two until . . ."

Until what? Patrick Kelly showed up? Couldn't depend on that. Ten dollars paid in advance and more rent due in two weeks. Clothes to buy.

"Those jobs, Lizzie, at the packinghouse? Could you help our boys get in there?" I asked.

Lizzie looked at the children. "McKenna could fix up the three older boys, surely."

"But . . ." Máire started, then stopped.

"Well," Molly said, "if your boys will be working, there's no worries. We're sorted. I won't take the advance."

⟡ ⟡ ⟡

Lizzie stayed to help us push the bags and parcels against one wall of the low-ceilinged room. "Fellows leave things with me. A few do come back," Molly said. The straw mattresses Molly brought out covered most of the floor. I'd sleep with Bridget and Stephen on one with Máire and Gracie on another. Paddy and Jamesy would share, and Johnny Og, Thomas, and Daniel would take the last mattress. The children fell on their beds, clothes and all.

Lizzie said she'd best get back to McKenna. "Thank you, thank you," we said to her as she left.

Máire and I started to lie down, too, but Molly gestured us out to the kitchen.

"A good time to talk. My boarders are out on Sunday night. Here, sit down," she said. "I love these wee chairs—brought them from Ireland. I'm from Roscommon, Croghan near Frenchpark."

"Croghan—but that's Maeve's stronghold!"

"Maeve? I don't mind her," Molly said.

"Ireland's queen in ancient times. She—"

"Honora," Máire interrupted. "Molly was telling us about her chairs."

"But if Molly lived where Maeve did, she should know . . ." I turned to Molly. "Fadó," I said.

Molly shook her head. "I've lost my Irish. Never had much, really. Landlords very set against the language in our parts. Sore on the people altogether. My Tom couldn't tug the forelock, so we left. Fortunate, really. Got out before the bad times." She stroked one of the carved wooden chairs. "Those coming over now arrive with nothing," she said.

"We've our lives," I said, "and a close thing it was."

Molly nodded.

"It's a miracle any of us survived Black '47," I said, and would have gone on, but Máire nudged my foot with hers.

"The iron stove gives off great heat," Máire said.

"A fine house, and only for Patrick Kelly I wouldn't have it."

Molly said her husband, Tom, was killed while working on the canal. They'd been buying this house and lot from the canal company, and when Tom died the company tried to put her out and keep the payments she and her husband had made.

"Patrick Kelly forced the company to forgive the mortgage and give me a bit of money," she said. "He told them the men would take it very badly if the bosses evicted a widow. What if something happened to them? Would their wives be treated badly? If the company wanted the canal finished on time, it better do right by me." Molly leaned back in her chair. "Now," she said, "there's those like James McKenna want us all law-abiding, to show the Yankees taking over Chicago that we're not the savages they think we are. But I say we need men like Patrick Kelly to keep the Yankees from rolling over us altogether. When Patrick lifts up that golden staff, every Irishman stands straighter! Laboring in the quarry, the docks, the packinghouses—soul-destroying work, all of it, and easy to lose all sense of yourself. We've Mass, music, and the tavern, but we need Patrick Kelly. I hope he comes back soon."

⟡ ⟡ ⟡

"Jesus Christ, Honora," Máire whispered to me as we lay down on our straw mats among our sleeping children. "Don't be going on about Ireland to these people. Why should Molly Flanigan give a fiddler's fart about Maeve or the Irish language? She's a snug house and money coming in. That's what we need."

"I'm surprised that they don't ask us more questions about conditions at home," I said.

"I'm sure their own people write them plenty. We've no good news to bring."

"You entertained the women well enough."

"Told them tales of the *River Queen* and New Orleans."

"And those fellows?"

"Told me the way of the place. They might have gotten better jobs for the boys than slaughtering cattle."

"It's only until Patrick Kelly—"

"Don't say Patrick Kelly to me—the fellow sounds a madman."

"I—"

"Go to sleep, Honora."

We're here, Michael. I spoke to him in my mind as I closed my eyes. I can't feel you near me, but I know you're pleased that we reached Chicago. And Patrick's respected here. Send him to us, Michael. Please, a stór.

❖ ❖ ❖

Two days later, we got our boys ready to join the march of men heading out to work at first light. We dressed them in the used trousers and shirts we'd bought from the rag-and-bone man, Sheehy, and then cut down, with Molly's help. She'd given us newspapers to stuff into the much too big work boots. We'd spent six dollars outfitting the boys and then another four on the old sweaters and shawls we wrapped around the younger children. Cold in that attic room. Seven dollars left. The boys' wages would have to pay for our room and board.

I combed Paddy's hair with Molly's wide-toothed comb, pulling out the knots and tangles. A month of food's made his hair grow. "You'll need a proper haircut soon," I said to him. Hair on his head, not on his face, thank God.

"Mam, you're hurting me!" Paddy said.

"Sorry, a stór. Now you look powerful. You're a wild brave boy, Paddy, off to do a man's work. Your da would be proud of you." I kissed him on the top of the head.

Máire gathered Johnny Og and Thomas to her, one in each arm, kissing their faces.

"Oh, Mam!" Johnny Og said. "Stop!"

Thomas wiped away the wet spots Máire's kisses had left on his cheek.

"Our boys should be going to school, not setting off to wade through blood and cow guts," I said to Máire as we stood in Molly Flanigan's front doorway, watching our three join the stream of workers.

Paddy walked with slow, deliberate steps, looking straight ahead, some dead man's jacket hanging off him.

"We shouldn't have let them," Máire said. "They're only children."

"They haven't been children for a long time, Máire."

❖ ❖ ❖

It was dark already when Máire and I stepped outside as the laboring army tramped home. White dust—from the lime kiln, I suppose—covered some. Dirt streaked the faces of the quarry men.

Paddy, Johnny Og, and Thomas trailed behind a knot of packing-house workers. As the boys came closer, I saw dark splotches on their clothes.

I couldn't wait. I rushed up to Paddy and took his hand.

He pulled it away. "I'm covered in blood, Mam."

Máire and I half carried our exhausted little boys up the steps to our room, where we'd filled a three-foot-high laundry tub full of hot, soapy water. Jamesy'd been told to keep the other children in the kitchen, but he and Daniel and the little ones stood on the top landing as the older boys trudged up the stairs.

"Paddy, I saved you some of my bread!" Jamesy called out to him.

And Daniel shouted, "We found a place to play the Red Branch Warriors, Johnny Og! You can be the general, Thomas!"

"Go back in the kitchen with Molly," I told them. "Shut the door. Your brothers will be ready soon."

Thomas made for the big round tub, pulling off his shirt and trousers. The first one in, he ducked his head under the water. Máire handed him a bar of the brown soap Molly used for laundry. He rubbed it into his hair and dived down again.

"I'll get you out of these clothes, Paddy," I said.

"Thanks, Mam," said Paddy. "I'm too tired to lift my arm."

I picked at the dried blood that closed the buttonholes of his shirt and pried each one loose. Clots of blood in his hair, streaks of it on his face.

Johnny Og told Máire he could undress himself. He couldn't. Máire helped him take off the trousers and boots. "Shit all over them," she said to me, then to Thomas, "Come on, get out."

He did, wrapping himself in one of the three burlap bags Molly had given us.

Paddy and Johnny Og stepped in the warm water together.

"Thomas got it dirty," Paddy said to me.

"Don't worry, a stór. I'll get clean water for the rinse."

Máire and I washed the boys' hair with the brown soap, then I heated water in Molly's kettle and poured it over their heads.

"We're first tomorrow," Paddy said. "Thomas can wait." He flicked some of the dirty water over at Thomas, who sat on the floor, still wrapped in the burlap bag.

Around us we heard the shouts and laughter of the boarders and their footsteps on the stairs.

"They don't bother with baths," Molly had told us. "A pitcher of water over their heads, a quick rub with a scrap of rag, then into their tavern duds, a bit of dinner, and they're out."

Once a week she washed their work clothes, charging each one ten cents. Máire and I would be helping her scrub them now.

Molly had told me the first days would be the hardest for our boys. "Your fellows, the cleaners, don't stand on slotted wooden floors like the others do. They're down in the muck and mire," she'd explained. "But they'll get used to it."

As soon as the three were clean and wrapped in their bags, the little ones came running in.

"You worked, Paddy!" said Jamesy.

"I did."

"How was it, Johnny Og?" asked Daniel.

"Hard, but we did it."

"Disgusting. Awful," said Thomas. "One hour in there, I went out and threw up!"

"But you went back to work, didn't you, Thomas?" Máire said.

We couldn't pay Molly with only two wage packets.

"I told the foreman I couldn't bear the smell, and he said would I like to take my complaint to Mr. Hough, and I said I would and all the men laughed. They said it'd be a good joke on the boss—so they took me up to Mr. Hough."

"And?" I asked.

"And I told him to please give me a rag to tie around my nose or I couldn't work."

"Not a bad idea," Máire said.

I thought of Patrick Kelly and the gloves. "And what did he say?"

"He didn't say anything. But the fellow who brought me up said, 'Stop talking smart to Mr. Hough, or you'll feel my boot in your ass.'"

Thomas imitated an accent I didn't know. Kerry? The children laughed at Thomas, but Paddy and Johnny Og shook their heads at each other.

"Then I told Mr. Hough, 'My brother and cousin and I have to make money to help our mothers, two widows.' And I told him about running from Bearna and the *Superior* and New Orleans and the *River Queen*, and how we spent all our money to get to Chicago because Patrick Kelly, our uncle, was supposed to help us, but he wasn't here, and where was he? And Mr. Hough said, 'Wherever he is, let him stay there,' and that it was no fault of mine that he was our connection, and didn't he himself have people in his own family he'd rather not talk about? Then he said I told a good story, surely, and would I do the captain of the *Superior*'s voice again. And so I did, and then I took off M'am Jacques, and I even showed him the dance we did with Lorenzo and Christophe. So."

"So?"

"So, he made me the messenger boy. Don't have to go back to the slaughtering floor. I'll carry orders to the foremen and even the letters to Chicago!"

"Oh, Thomas!" Máire hugged him. "Good for you!"

Bridget and Gracie brought Stephen to him, who grabbed him around his leg and jumped up and down. Daniel and Jamesy clapped their hands.

But Paddy and Johnny Og stood in their burlap bags, shivering, saying nothing.

"Lie down now, boys. I'll bring your supper to you. Put on your New Orleans clothes and get under the covers."

"Thomas didn't tell us what happened until now," said Paddy. "He walked all the way home and said nothing."

"Silken Thomas," I said. "It's his nature to keep secrets." I sat next to Paddy on the straw mattress. "Can you stand it, Paddy?"

He looked at me. "They beat the cattle to death. The hammer breaks the skull, brains pour out, and then the men hack at the bodies with axes. The cattle bellow something awful. Some of the fellows laugh when blood spurts over them. Johnny Og and I couldn't laugh. We didn't cry, Mam. Neither of us."

My sturdy lad. He knew—you cry, you die.

"I'll get your dinner, Paddy."

But he was asleep when I brought the food to him.

❖ ❖ ❖

The next evening the boys stayed awake for dinner. Molly served beef with potatoes and cabbage. "The butchers at the packinghouse see me right," she said. We ate at a long table in her parlor, the thirty of us. The boarders came from all over Ireland, but the fellows didn't talk about their home places. They compared complaints, setting the miseries of Hough's against the hardships of Stearn's Quarry or the brickyard.

Paddy, Johnny Og, and Thomas took in every word.

"You think your back aches? Mine's so bad, when I go to bed and fall asleep, the pain wakes me in an hour," the man from Mayo would begin.

"At least you fall asleep! I spend all night awake, and when I get out of bed in the morning, I feel like I haven't even been in it!" the Donegal fellow answered.

"You can get out of bed?" said the Clare man. "I have to roll off my pallet and then wait until the pain eases enough to pull myself up."

"Backs, backs," said a boy from Cork. "Everyone has back pain. How'd you like feet to be your agony? Since I got frostbite last year on the canal, my toes burn and prickle until every step is torture!"

"Feet? At least you can sit and get off your feet! My fingers have swollen bigger than sausages—I can hardly lift the hammer," said the Clare man.

"Lift it? Try swinging it down when the muscles in your shoulders ache. Ever since I broke it, my arm's never really mended."

This last came from Barney McGurk, a Tyrone man who sat across from us.

The competition ended when one man would say, "But sure, we're alive and working, and what more can we ask?"

After his third day at work, Paddy whispered to Barney McGurk that he got so much blood in his hair, his mam thought he was a redhead. Barney repeated it to the whole table. The remark got a great laugh. Paddy smiled at me. My sturdy lad.

Saturday made four days working. The boys ran home this night, delighted with themselves, and piled four silver dollars on the table.

"We'll get six dollars for working the full six-day week," Paddy said.

I added one more dollar for the rent, and Máire and I spent until near midnight Saturday doing the wash with Molly. We'd also helped her clean and cook during the week while minding our children. Busy. Molly said she'd lower the rent another dollar next week. And we still had six dollars.

✥ ✥ ✥

All of the boarders went to Mass. "Strong in their faith," I said to Molly as we walked to McKenna's.

"And there are the girls," Molly said. "Watch what goes on."

After Mass, we women sat together at the fire again. Father Donohue came by to say he had no news of Patrick Kelly. Then he left.

"Now," Molly said. "Keep your eyes on the young ones. It'd be closer for the girls who work as maids on Michigan Avenue and live in those mansions to go to Saint Mary's or Saint Patrick's," she said.

"But there are more bachelors in Bridgeport," Lizzie, who'd joined us, explained.

A small blonde stopped Big Joe Quinn, one of Molly's boarders, as he headed back from the privy. Soon they were talking away in a corner.

As we watched two other girls waylay lads, I couldn't resist saying, "Respectable?" very quietly to Lizzie. How could James McKenna judge Máire, with all this courting breaking out all over? And to think I'd almost chastised Máire. She would have raged at me.

Lizzie understood me but said, "No parents around to arrange the marriages. Girls have to take matters into their own hands."

"My boarders get picked off quickly," Molly said. "The girls coming from Ireland now waste no time—a husband, a place to live, and every extra penny going back to Ireland to bring out their sisters and brothers, their parents."

"Some young girls on our ship. I hope they find husbands," I said.

"A man needs a wife. A woman needs a husband. Only way to survive in this country," Molly said.

"You've no husband, Molly," Máire said, "and you're doing rightly."

"Because of Tom's hard work and the help of Patrick Kelly," she said.

"Now there's a fellow'll never settle. Not that women haven't tried," Lizzie said. She and Molly laughed.

"So is this Patrick Kelly good-looking?" Máire asked. "I've not met him, and Honora never said."

"A fine-featured fellow," Molly said, "if you look beyond the odd clothes."

"You might be one who could tame him, Máire," Lizzie said.

"Holy Sweet Jesus," Máire said. "I'll never marry again. Last thing I need's some man thinks he can order me around."

"True enough," Molly said. "I've grown accustomed to following my own counsel. Couldn't change my ways. Now, Lizzie here doesn't mind listening to James plot and plan."

"Ah well, it gives him pleasure," said Lizzie. "What harm?"

"What about yourself, Honora? You really should," Lizzie said.

"What? Marry again? I couldn't," I said. "My Michael's only dead a few months. I would never—"

"I'm not talking about tomorrow, but you need help—all those children. You're still young, at least. What age are you, if you don't mind my asking?"

"I'm twenty-six."

"What day?"

"September fifteenth."

"The Feast of Our Lady of Sorrows," Lizzie said.

"That's right, the Sorrowful Mother, my patron," I said.

"Well, you're a joyful mother today, Honora," Lizzie said. "You and Máire, with three sons working."

"We are," I said.

"And how old are you, Máire?" Molly asked.

"I'm twenty-eight, though I suppose you thought me younger."

We were laughing when Bridget started tugging on my arm.

"Mam, Kevin Sweeny is teasing me, and Jamesy won't make him stop!"

"Calm down now, Bridget," I said, all the while glad to hear her rushing the words out. She'd been so slow to talk and even slower to walk. Food cured so much. No matter the hardships, we had food, thank God. "All right. Time to go, anyway." I walked over to the children's circle. "Come on, Paddy, we're leaving," I said.

"It's my turn next with the knife," he said.

"You can have a go next week."

"I want to play now, Mam."

"You heard me, Paddy. Get up."

I picked up Stephen. Bridget helped Gracie up. Jamesy and Daniel stood with me, but Johnny Og and Thomas stayed down on the floor with Paddy. All three looked up at me.

"Now, boys," I said.

They didn't move. An older lad, one of the Manions, handed Paddy the knife. Paddy took it.

"Paddy—" I started.

"You're going, Honora?" It was Máire. She looked at me and then at the boys on the floor.

"I am, but the boys—"

"Want to stay a bit longer?" she interrupted me. "That suits me. I'll bring them along soon. Gracie, mind Aunt Honey. Be a good boy, Daniel." She turned and went back to the fire.

I left.

❖ ❖ ❖

"How dare you, Máire!" I said to her when she came home with the boys hours later. "You cut the legs from under me in front of my own son, took my authority."

"You've no authority, Honora," Máire said.

The children were asleep, and we had a moment for a whisper of talk in the hallway.

"What do you mean, no authority? Paddy's eight years old and I'm his mother."

"And he brings home the money for our rent and food. They're good boys, but don't pick fights we can't win, not in front of the congregation of Saint Bridget's of McKenna's Scanlon House and the Hickory Gang."

"I don't care who—"

Máire interrupted me. "The young fellow throwing the knife's the leader of the Hickory Gang. The boys' new friends," she said. "We have to go careful, Honora. We're two lone women with six sons. Good boys, but if we challenge them too directly, they'll defy us."

"They wouldn't," I said.

"You saw what happened. Remember our brothers? Da had to put manners on them at a certain age."

"Our brothers. If only they were here." Molly said people found relatives by putting ads in newspapers all over Amerikay and even in Canada. Expensive, that. "Of course, our fellows have an uncle. Patrick Kelly," I said.

"As far as *he* goes . . . ," Máire started.

Molly came out of her room and down the hall in her nightdress, a blanket wrapped around her.

"Would you ever quiet down, girls, the fellows need their sleep."

"I'm sorry, Molly. I didn't realize we'd raised our voices," I said.

"Now, I wasn't listening," Molly said, "but I couldn't help hearing and—"

"You couldn't?" Máire said.

"I could not," Molly replied, annoyed.

Dear God, can't have Molly taking offense.

"I'm sorry," I said again. "Good night. Come on, Máire."

I took her arm, but Molly stopped me, putting her hand on my shoulder.

"Easy now, I'm only trying to help. I saw your boys at McKenna's—"

"Our sons are good boys," I started.

"Whist, Honora," Molly said. "Children grow up fast in America. Mine learned the way of the place while my husband and I were still scratching our heads. My sons ran with the Hickory Gang—many a night I didn't know where they were. At home there'd been a whole web of people watching over them, but here?" She shrugged. "No grannies and aunts and uncles, no schoolmasters."

"No fathers, even, for our lot," Máire said.

"There's that," Molly said. She looked at me and held up her hand. "I'll not start telling you two to find husbands again, but—"

"School," I said. "A strong schoolmaster can be an important influence. If Jamesy and Daniel could go, maybe we could do lessons with Paddy and Johnny Og and Thomas at night."

"Jamesy and Daniel could try Bridgeport School," Molly said.

Máire said, "We couldn't afford—"

"Bridgeport School is free," Molly said.

"Free?" I said.

"Taxes," Molly said. "I pay them. McKennas do. Anybody owns a house, though not many of our children go there."

"Why not?" asked Máire.

Molly started to explain how the poorest families needed their children to work or take care of the younger ones. No time for school. Better-off people in Bridgeport preferred to send their boys to St. Patrick's, where the brothers taught, and the girls to St. Xavier's, the school that the Sisters of Mercy had started. "Better to pay fees at a

Catholic school than put up with the teachers at the public school," she said.

I didn't hear the warning, only the word *free*. Tomorrow. I'll go tomorrow. Máire can watch the little ones. Not the packinghouse for Jamesy and Daniel. School. A chance.

Chapter 25

BRIDGEPORT SCHOOL stood on the corner of Bridge Street and Archer Road, beyond our square-mile world of Molly's, McKenna's, Hough's, Stearn's Quarry, the canal, and Bubbly Creek—the south branch of the Chicago River.

"Why do they call it Bubbly Creek?" I'd asked Molly.

"Remember I told you the packinghouse tosses parts of animals into the river here?"

"I do—hearts and livers, and the boys dive for them," I said, shuddering.

"The bits not worth fishing out send up bubbles as they dissolve," she said. "That's why it never freezes.

"Follow Bubbly Creek to Archer Road," Molly had said, "and don't be frightened if you see cattle being driven to the packinghouses."

Molly must think me very skittish. Afraid of cows. Then I turned onto Archer Road, and just like that I was smack in the middle of a mass of cattle. More than I'd ever seen in all my life.

"Jesus, Mary, and Joseph! Help me!" I shouted.

They came at me—shoulder to shoulder, hooves tromping and tramping. Hundreds of steers filled the wide road, stretching back as far as the open prairie beyond Bridgeport.

I ran into the doorway of a tavern, standing as far back from the street as I could.

Men on horseback rode alongside the herd.

One passed close to me. He waved his wide-brimmed, battered hat at me. "Morning!" he shouted over the stomping and snorting.

Who are these fearless fellows? I wondered. Cowboys! Of course—the fellow on the *River Queen*, off to be a cowboy.

"Don't worry," he shouted again. "Stock pens just ahead. Get 'em past soon enough! Don't be afraid. They're all tuckered out."

I saw now that the cattle were only plodding along—heads down, obedient, knackered after their long journey. Still huge, each of them. How Mr. Lynch or Rich John Dugan would have goggled at their size. These big fellows could trample those cowboys and destroy half the saloons on Archer Road. Instead, they let themselves be led to the slaughter.

Paddy had seen one steer go wild. The killing blow had only stunned the big animal. He'd charged out of Hough's with all the butchers chasing him. "Took a volley of musket balls to bring him down," Paddy said.

The frozen ground crumbled under the pounding hooves. Clouds of dirt and dung blew toward me, settling into my hair and onto the shawl Molly had lent me. A right mess I am to meet the schoolmaster. And late, too.

"Move these fellows along!" I shouted at a cowboy.

Molly had told us that the stockyards and slaughterhouses were to move out of Bridgeport beyond Archer Road onto the other side of Healey Slough, to the town of Lake. Can't be too soon for me.

❖ ❖ ❖

No one stopped me as I walked into the Bridgeport School and down an empty hall to a door marked "Principal, Mr. Jeremiah Lewis." Teachers and students all in class, I thought as I knocked. After a few moments, I knocked again.

A fat fellow, his eyes squeezed between his cheeks, pulled open the door. "What do you want?" he said.

"I'm Mrs. Michael Kelly, and I'm here to enroll my son and nephew in your school."

"Kelly," he said. "Irish. Catholic, I suppose."

"Catholics, surely."

"All right. Come in." He sat down behind a big desk. I started to sit on the chair in front of it, but he held up his hand. "No need. This won't take long. We have requirements for entrance." He closed his pale blue eyes and sniffed as if there were a bad smell in the room. "Your children must speak English," he said.

"They do," I said.

"Some of you people tried to enroll children who could speak only some peasant patois."

"Is that the Irish *language* you're referring to? What do you call French or German?"

He leaned over his desk toward me. "Americans speak English. Period. End of sentence."

"But surely, sir, students with other languages bring a great advantage to your school."

"No foreign tongues here. You people have overrun our country. The least you can do is conform to our ways. Or get out. Go back."

I could only stare at him.

He flicked his eyes over my patched skirt, down to the wooden clogs Sheehy'd traded me for my New Orleans shoes.

"Our students must be properly dressed and wear shoes, Mrs. Kelly . . . shoes. I've had children come to school barefoot. What is wrong with the parents? No shame."

"No money for shoes, I'd say."

"We also require three dollars from each student for paper, pencils, and the use of the books."

"Six dollars?" I said. "Isn't this a free school?"

"It is. You couldn't expect us to pay for your children's supplies as well? If you can't afford—"

"I have it right here." I reached into my waistband, pulled out the oilskin pouch, and put our last six silver dollars on his desk. "Please write down their names: James Kelly and Daniel O'Connell Leahy," I said. Máire'd decided her boys would not be Pykes in Amerikay.

✧   ✧   ✧

I passed the two new scholars on the way back to Molly's. They were sliding along on the frozen surface of the canal with a load of Bridgeport children, most with feet wrapped in burlap, all laughing and shouting. Shoes or no shoes, our young ones are able for you, Mr. Puffed-up-Toad Lewis.

I went up the long flight to our attic room. Bridget played some game with Stephen and Gracie on one straw mattress. Máire lay stretched out on another, her eyes closed.

"Aunt Máire's sleeping?" I said to Bridget.

"Thinking," Máire said. "Come here." I sat next to her. "We have to find a better place to live. I sent the boys out because they were driving Molly mad, running up and down the stairs. But the weather's getting colder every day. To think of months spent shoved in here together all day . . ."

"Máire, Jamesy and Daniel will be going to school," I said.

"You got them in? Good on you, Honora."

"Except . . . ," I said, and told her how I'd had to give over our last six dollars. And we had to buy them school clothes somehow.

I thought she'd get angry, but instead she lay back down. "That decides it. I'm going to work," she said.

"Of course. And I will, too. Molly says there's day jobs cleaning and doing laundry at the Big Houses," I said.

"You can't work with the baby coming. Besides, who would mind the children? And I don't fancy being a servant. Low wages. And employers with wandering hands—I had enough of that at the Scoundrel Pykes." She sat up, looked over at the children. "Out in the hall," she said to me.

We stood on the landing. "A fellow who saw me at McKenna's called by this afternoon. He offered me a place. Good money."

I waited.

"At Ma Conley's in the Sands."

"But that's a brothel, Máire! The nerve of the fellow. What'd you do? Hit him with Molly's broom?"

"I said I'd think about it."

"But you can't. You wouldn't!"

"Why not? He said in a month I'd have enough to rent a flat. He told me that a woman as, well, good-looking as me would have her own special clients. I'd be in charge of myself. I could get our boys out of the packinghouse, put them *all* in school, wear decent clothes instead of rags from Sheehy's. There's a flat with five rooms going to be available at 2703 Hickory. The McLaughlins are moving farther south. We could move by Christmas."

"You don't want to do this, Máire," I said.

"I don't, Honora," Máire near whispered to me. "I do like to tease you and play the floozy a bit, but to really . . ." She stopped.

I put my arms around her. "You sacrificed yourself once. You don't have to do it again. I'll go back and get the six dollars. Promise me you'll forget about Ma Conley's. Something will happen. Mam always said, 'God's help is closer than the door.'"

"Mam," Máire said. "Are she and Da even alive? We don't know."

"Máire, Máire . . ." I hugged her. "Please, please, don't you despair. You can't."

"I feel so hemmed in, Honora. To come all this way, leave everything, for this?"

"Is it New Orleans? I suppose we could think of some way—"

"Catch yourself on, Honora. We're stuck here."

"I'll get the six dollars back."

"But I want the boys to go to school. I want—"

We heard the front door bang, the boarders on the stairs.

"Listen to that, Máire. Each of those fellows escaped with as little as we had. And now they're earning good wages and sending money home. So will we."

"They do earn good wages, don't they?" She fluffed out her blond curls. "I'll be back," she said, and walked down the stairs.

❖ ❖ ❖

"No need to worry about money for school clothes—all done and dusted. The boarders will take up a collection for the boys. Thank the Pearl," Máire said. "She asked the fellows and gave them nothing more than a smile."

"Thank you, Máire. Thank you, Pearl," I said.

❖ ❖ ❖

Barney McGurk made a speech as he handed us the money in Molly's kitchen the next evening. "Now the teachers can't pass remarks."

Barney came from people who'd scratched a living from the mountains of Tyrone for generations. He'd left years before the Great Starvation. His wages had probably kept his family at home alive. A quiet fellow, older than the others, no chat or banter. Was it his flinty home place or Amerikay that taught him silence? Pleasant-looking, a long face, a grizzle of graying hair, brown eyes.

"A secret there," Máire had said.

But words spilled out of Barney tonight as he gave us the four dollars that had been collected. He told Jamesy and Daniel that the teachers would say bad things about the Catholic Church. "You won't be treated as well as the Protestant boys, the Americans," he told Jamesy and Daniel. They nodded, though they had no notion what he meant. "I served in the American army, fighting in Mexico, all of us dressed in the same uniform, and we Catholics got singled out for punishment. Americans are Englishmen. They hate our faith. Don't forget it. Be on your guard."

"But, Barney, a school is different, surely," I said. "And even if the principal's ignorant, surely the teachers will be glad of children so hungry for learning."

"I hope so, missus," Barney said, "but get these boys ready-made trousers, and buy them in Chicago itself."

✛ ✛ ✛

Molly agreed to watch the little ones and told us not to be frightened of the city. So the next day, with Thomas as our guide, we set out for Chicago.

"Mr. Hough's clerk said I could take the day to help my mother and auntie," Thomas told us.

He wore a jacket and trousers that had belonged to one of Mr. Hough's sons, a gift from Mrs. Hough. "She says I'm charming, Mam," Thomas had told us. He'd met her while taking the messages. "I've learned the whole city," he claimed.

It was the first week in December, and the wind sliced at us something fierce. Jamesy and Daniel plodded along, shielding their faces with my skirts. Four miles to Chicago proper, but Thomas shortened the distance by cutting across patches of prairie, going through tall grass, dried now into brittle stalks. We turned onto a wide road where the mud had frozen into ridges frosted with ice.

"We're lucky," Thomas said. "When the mud's soft it covers my ankles along here."

Then, just like that, Chicago sprang up on us.

"Wabash Street," Thomas said. "The center of Chicago."

Total confusion.

Slews of people, men mostly, knocked against one another on narrow plank sidewalks raised a few inches above streets that teemed with horses and wagons and carriages of all kinds and descriptions. Stumble and you'd be crushed. One street was more crowded than the next; Thomas named them for us: State Street, Lake Street, Michigan Avenue. Some were called after American presidents, he said: Washington, Jackson, Adams.

"This is Dearborn, for Fort Dearborn—where Chicago started," Thomas said.

Barney McGurk had told us that an Irishman had commanded the fort when Indians wiped it out about thirty years before. Not a long time in Ireland, but forever ago in Chicago.

The stink of manure mixed with the smell of smoke rising from a forest of chimneys. A storm of noise. The wagon drivers shouted at crowds trying to cross in front of them, then whipped their horses— *crack!* Wheels screeched, then yells of outrage . . . A constant *bang, bang* as we passed building crews, one after another, with only a few paces separating each site. It seemed as if they'd started building the city this morning and were determined to finish it by tonight.

"An awful mess of a place," I said to Máire.

But Máire was smiling. She'd worn her red shawl, though there was no warmth in it and she would have been better to borrow a blanket from Molly, but she'd insisted. And now, didn't she open out her arms. Wind filled the silk.

"See my wings," Máire said. "Will I fly right over it all, boys?"

Jamesy and Daniel laughed.

"Mam," said Thomas. "Stop."

Máire whirled around. A fellow passing stopped and tipped his hat to her. She smiled at him. "A mad place," Máire said. "I love it."

Thomas jigged ahead, turning back every few steps to shout out, "That's Saint Mary's Church, the brick building. That hotel's the Tremont House. That's the courthouse . . . there's Collins'—they make boats." Knowledgeable already. "That's Rice's Theatre."

Jamesy stopped before the barnlike building. "What's a theater, Mam?" he said.

"Where they act out stories," I said.

"Is it lovely to see?"

"I don't know, Jamesy. I've never been inside a theater, though I walked past one in Galway City."

"Was I ever in Galway City?" Jamesy asked.

"You weren't. None of you children were."

"Hurry, Thomas," Máire said. "I want to see the shops, the saloons."

Thomas and Daniel and Máire went ahead, but Jamesy wouldn't move.

"What's that say, Mam?" He pointed at a poster that hung on the side of the theater.

I read the broadside aloud to him: "Extraordinary Novelty! Mr. Murdock in Schiller's great *Tragedy of the Robbers . . . The Farce of the Artful Dodger:* Mr. McVicker—Tim Dodger, Mr. Rice—Harding." I went on, "Songs! 'We're all a-Dodging'—Mr. McVicker, 'Heigh-Ho for a Husband!'—Miss H. Matthews."

"A whole building for singing and pretending," said Jamesy.

"Theater's closed now," said a fellow who was taking posters down from the walls opposite. "You could try Mooney's Museum—Tom Thumb the midget's playing there—or go see the Virginia Minstrels— you know, white fellows who wear black on their faces and sing colored songs, though most of them are Irish fellows singing Irish songs. You wouldn't know about that. Just got off the boat, am I right? Lots of people get that stunned look their first time seeing Chicago." He smiled at Jamesy. "You should learn to be a carpenter—always good work in Chicago for a boy who can hammer a nail."

"Seems like it," I said.

"Chicago's got a quick way of building—a balloon frame, you call it—no beams or braces, you just nail up the frame. Of course, first you have to drive posts through the sand and hard clay, and . . ."

Máire was waving for me to catch up with her. Jamesy stared at the poster.

"Thank you, Mr. . . . ?"

"O'Leary," he said.

"Come, Jamesy," I said.

"I can read a few words, Mam!" he said, pointing to the poster.

"You'll read it all soon!" Thank God he'll be at school right in Bridgeport. To take on this place every day . . .

Thomas, Máire, and Daniel stood in front of a wooden single-story building with a sign: "Croaker's Dry Goods."

"Finally!" said Thomas.

But Jamesy had stopped in front of the shop next to Croaker's. "Mam! Mam, look!"

Behind a large glass window was a display of musical instruments: fiddles, trumpets, concertinas, flutes, and also, there in the corner, a set of pipes. Bagpipes, not the Irish uilleann pipes like the ones that lay buried with Michael at Knocnacuradh. But still . . .

"Mam!" he said again. "Pipes. Different, but pipes."

"I see, Jamesy."

"When Da played the pipes, he'd let me put my fingers over his. Remember how he taught me to play the whistle?"

"I do," I said. Jamesy tugged me toward the door. "Jamesy, we can't buy anything at this store."

"Only to see, Mam, please!"

"Please let him, Aunt Honey," said Daniel.

Thomas and Máire stood at the door of Croaker's, arms folded, tapping their toes—so alike, I had to laugh.

"All right, Jamesy. Five minutes. Máire," I called out to her, "come in with us."

Máire shook her head first but then walked back to us. Thomas went into Croaker's.

Warm in the music store—a potbellied stove heated the place, and two kerosene lanterns on the counter shed a dim light. A small, neat man came toward us.

"*Guten Morgen,*" he said. Here's a man kept his language. "May I help you?" he asked.

"We're only having a look," I said.

He smiled at the boys. "You play music?"

"A little," Jamesy spoke up. "I learned from my da. He's a piper."

"You are Scottish, then?"

"We're not that, surely," Máire said.

"Irish," I said.

"Of course! I should have known. My wife is Irish. We German and Irish are the most people in Chicago!" he said.

"Let's get together and have a go at the Yankees," Máire said.

He looked confused. "I don't understand. My English is only on the top. You understand?"

We nodded.

"My wife speaks for me. You Irish are lucky having English."

"We had a perfectly good language of our own," I said. "I wish the English had kept their language and let us keep our country."

"I know your history and a bit about your language," he said. "I was a professor at Tübingen University. My name is Edward Lang."

"A professor? And you left?" Máire said.

"Did your pratties die, too?" Jamesy asked.

"It was not potatoes, but politics sent me to Chicago," he said.

"I'm sorry for your troubles, sir," I said.

"Well, you've bought yourself a fine store," said Máire.

"Oh, I'm only a clerk, not the owner. Though I do like working with music."

"We'll be going," I said. "Thank you for your time."

"Tell your wife two Galway women send greetings," Máire said.

But Jamesy was away. I found him standing in the back of the store, staring up at the violins and trumpets on the shelves.

The professor came up to us. "Perhaps there is an instrument—"

"Come, Jamesy," I said. Then, to the professor, "Really. We have to buy him clothes for school."

"Moment, moment," the professor said, and he walked through a curtain.

"Thomas is waiting," Máire said. "We should go."

The professor came back holding a long, narrow box. "Here." He opened the box and took out a tin whistle.

"Oh, Mam!" said Jamesy. "Please, please, can I have it?"

"Jamesy, a stór, we can't. We—"

"I would charge you only ten cents," Professor Lang said.

Jamesy looked at me. "Please, Mam. I'll feel close to Da when I'm playing it," he said.

Michael's musical talent blooming in his son. I looked over at Máire.

Máire shrugged. "Maybe he can play on a corner, collect pennies in a hat. Except he has no hat."

"I will," said Jamesy. "Like Lorenzo and Christophe."

"I could dance," said Daniel.

"You'll see, Mam. We'll make loads of money!" Jamesy said.

"Very American already, your boys," said the professor.

❖　❖　❖

Jamesy blew into the tin whistle as we left the shop and walked into the noisy street—"A Na-tion Once A-gain" part of the clamor now.

Jamesy took the whistle from his mouth and grinned at me. "I'll have the tune for the teacher, and Daniel can sing the words."

"Hurry. Thomas will be cross," Máire said, gesturing us into the store.

Thomas had said Croaker's Dry Goods carried already made clothes—no sewing. "Gets them from New York," he'd said.

Two young fellows were talking to Thomas, clerks, I suppose.

"Of course, real gentlemen only wear suits made by tailors," Thomas said to them. "But these boys need the clothes now."

Mr. Croaker himself brought out pants and jackets and shoes, telling us that he bought all his stock in the East. "I'm a Yankee myself, come from Boston. Now there's a city!" Croaker was short and square, a bald bullet-head with round eyeglasses.

He had no time for bargaining, though Máire tried.

"*One price*" was all he said. No pleasure at all in buying and selling in this dark, cold place, not inviting like the music store. Nothing to see—the bolts of fabric and boxes of clothes sat piled on shelves behind dusty curtains.

"You need a woman's touch in here, Mr. Croaker," Máire said.

"I have asked my wife for her advice, but she has no interest in business."

"A woman clerk would transform the place," Máire said.

"No store in Chicago employs women," Croaker told her.

"All the best shops in London do. Makes it easier for women customers. I myself had such a sales position," Máire said.

"You did? But you're . . . you're Irish," he said.

"Isn't that lucky? Aren't we the best talkers in the world?"

"Don't try to blarney me," he said.

Blarney?

"I could start Monday morning."

"Now, now," he said. "I can't afford to pay another clerk."

"A percentage, Mr. Croaker. Twenty percent of all I sell. What do you have to lose?"

"Give her a chance," said one of the young fellows.

"Five percent," he said.

"Ten," she said.

"Done," he said. "You have children. Who will see to them? Will I be able to depend on you?"

"Ah, that's the beauty of having a sister. She'll care for the children."

"I'll give you a week's trial. What's your name?"

"Máire Leahy. Mrs. Leahy. My sister is Honora Kelly. Mrs. Kelly."

I nodded to him.

✤   ✤   ✤

"Now," said Máire. "Take that, Ma Conley!" She snapped her fingers. "Doing all right for ourselves in America!" She did a quick jig step as we walked down Lake Street with Jamesy blowing on his whistle. Máire's never defeated for long.

"We are, Máire, we are," I said. "You are a wonder, and you, too, Thomas, knowing your way around this wild place."

"Aren't Daniel and I wonders, Mam?" Jamesy said, waving the tin whistle.

"You are. Strutting along, fearing nothing, while your mother's frightened out of her wits."

"You are, Mam?" Alarmed.

"She's joking," Máire said, and Jamesy started again to play random notes as we moved through the crowd.

A wagon loaded with unsteady towers of casks stopped near us. The team of horses following crashed into it. The casks fell out and rolled in our direction.

"Watch out!" I screamed, and pushed the boys back.

But Thomas went forward, grabbed a cask, and ran off.

Many of the men passing—some very well dressed—did the same. The driver shouted curses at them, but they only laughed at him, walking away with the casks under their arms.

"Isn't that Mr. Croaker's clerk?" I asked Máire.

She was laughing too hard to answer me. "Thomas thinks fast, no question."

"But he *stole*, Máire."

"Seems the custom here. I do like Chicago, Honora." She hooked her arm through mine and shooed Jamesy and Daniel forward.

We found Thomas waiting around the corner. He'd pried off the top of the cask.

"Only whiskey," he said. "I hoped it might be nails. Whiskey's so cheap, hardly worth carrying home."

"You shouldn't have taken it, Thomas," I said.

"Somebody would have. Why not us?"

"He's a point, Honora," Máire said. "And we'll have a nice drop for Christmas."

"We should go back," I said. The sun was setting. Wouldn't want to be on these streets in the dark. Bleak and barren Bridgeport seemed a sanctuary—contained, safe.

"We'll go home along Michigan Avenue," Thomas said. "You can see the mansions and the Lake."

We turned down a side street onto a broad avenue lined with grand big houses.

"Any one of these would put Barna House to shame!" Máire said.

I heard Máire exclaiming, but I couldn't listen.

The Lake . . . I stopped still.

Jamesy tugged at my hand. "Come, Mam."

Máire and Daniel and Thomas were ahead of us, but I stepped off the walk and onto the beach.

Lake Michigan? A sea, surely, stretching out under the heavy sky, going way beyond the smoke of the city. No farther shore, no limits at all. Only blue gray water touched with reflected light as the sun set into the prairie behind me.

Jamesy ran up to me. We stood watching the waves breaking on the sand.

"Here's a big one, Jamesy," I said. "Listen to the roar, the boom." I lifted him up. "Close your eyes halfway and look only at the water. See—Galway Bay."

And Michael. Above me, below me, to the left of me, to my right. Near. Finally I felt his presence.

I hugged Jamesy to me.

"Honora, I'm freezing, come on!" Máire shouted from the street.

Máire chattered all the way home.

✥   ✥   ✥

Molly said the boarders were longing to see the new clothes. We dressed Jamesy and Daniel and went to Molly's big table for our dinner. The fellows made a great fuss over the boys. "Our scholars," they called them.

Jamesy played a few notes on his tin whistle, and the Clare fellow said he'd teach him plenty of tunes.

Paddy smiled at Jamesy and patted his shoulder. "Well done, Jamesy."

"You look powerful, Daniel," Johnny Og said.

Bridget and Gracie smiled up at their big brothers, and Stephen clapped his hands.

A happy bunch we were, climbing up to our attic room.

Jamesy kept the whistle clenched in his fist as he slept.

Stephen and Bridget wriggled close to me on the straw mattress. I closed my eyes and saw Lake Michigan—Galway Bay.

CHAPTER 26

CHRISTMAS EVE CAME. Daniel and Jamesy and the girls played in our room while I was downstairs, standing at Molly's kitchen window, holding Stephen. It was dark out now. Where were Máire and the boys?

Hours and hours ago, the three older boys had left to meet Máire at Croaker's store—a half day for them at the packinghouse, and delighted to go downtown to help Máire do the shopping.

"Our first Christmas in Amerikay will be a great celebration altogether," Máire had said. "We'll eat rashers from a proper butcher, not the packinghouse scraps. I'll buy milk, potatoes, tobacco, and two doneen pipes. Sweets for the children, a Christmas tree!"

"That'll cost a lot," I'd said.

"I'll be getting a lot," she'd told me. "Mr. Croaker owes me at least twenty dollars."

Máire had passed that first week's trial and worked two weeks more, selling loads and loads, she'd said, but she hadn't been paid yet. Mr. Croaker's clerks got their wages once a month. "He says it teaches us discipline," Máire'd explained. So not a penny yet, though Máire had received a length of brown wool to make into a skirt and jacket. "Mr. Croaker insists on a good appearance." Neither of us had the least notion about sewing, but Molly's friend Kitty Gorman earned her living as a seamstress. She'd stitched up a lovely outfit for Máire and said not to worry. Pay her when Máire got paid. Today.

You'd think Máire would have rushed home. Not that much shopping to do. I hope she hasn't gone flaithiúlacht with the money. We should be saving. If we could put away five dollars a month, maybe in a year we could move into our own flat. Harder and harder to keep the boys contained and quiet.

Well, today and tomorrow we'll have the boardinghouse to ourselves. Molly's family was gathering at her daughter's place near St. Patrick's, and the boarders had scattered into homes throughout the Irish neighborhoods, invited by families who wouldn't want to see a fellow alone on Christmas.

Molly had said we'd be very welcome at her daughter's but was relieved when I'd said we'd be grand here on our own. "You can let the boys run up and down the stairs to their hearts' content," she'd said.

"I know they're a bit of a handful, Molly," I'd answered, "but to see them healthy and high-spirited after . . ." She'd said she understood, she did, but Molly hadn't seen the frail little ghosts standing in line for soup or slumped against the seawalls. The bodies . . . Thank you, Lord, for my children's lives. Now, where are they?

I carried Stephen over to the chair near the stove and sat down. "I'm a big boy," he'd say, twenty months now. He'd squirm away from me when I cuddled him. But today he wanted only to lie in my arms. Sick, my poor baby, his hazel eyes glazed, his red hair damp with sweat. Fever? "Only croup," Molly'd said. "Children get it in winter here. Gone by spring."

I took the cup of water I'd set on the table and brought it to his lips. "Here, a rún, drink a little water." Michael's fever had made him so thirsty, alone in the shed. Keeping hold of Stephen, I reached down, took a log from the wood box, and put it into the stove. The box was only half-full.

Molly had told me to send Paddy, Johnny Og, and Thomas to the lumberyard. The supply of wood she'd ordered was ready. But Paddy had said, "We'll pick it up on the way home," eager to get downtown. I should have insisted. Paddy's a good boy, working so hard, and not as cheeky to me anymore as he'd been in McKenna's. Let them go their own way, Máire'd said. What choice? She was very motherly to me. "You care for the children, Honora, let that wee life inside you grow. The boys and I are earning powerful money."

Now Máire added her work stories to the dinner table talk. She didn't complain, not even about the four-mile walk downtown. She often managed a lift from a delivery wagon, and one night a fancy carriage dropped her off at McKenna's. Máire liked to repeat the conversations she'd had with the traders and businessmen she met at Croaker's. "Railroads," she'd said. "It's railroads will be the making of us. Chicago'll be the center of Amerikay with railroads going north, south, east, and west. It's our geography."

The fellows had laughed, said that Máire was being taken in by Chicago big talk. Barely twenty miles of track had been laid. Who needed railroads with the canal and lake boats?

It must be freezing upstairs. I stood up, put Stephen on my hip, and went to the landing. "Jamesy, Bridget, Daniel, Gracie! Come down to the stove!"

Jamesy had told me he and Daniel and the girls were "practicing"—I'd heard bits of music and the sound of running feet overhead all afternoon. Good to see Jamesy cheerful. I'd expected him to come home from school brimming with chat about his lessons and the other children, but he and Daniel said very little. They didn't want me to take them to school or pick them up. "We're not babies." He'd asked me would he go to the packinghouse next year when he was seven. Paddy told him, "You won't."

It's me that has to find some work after the baby's born. Though I'm grateful for these days. I only have to do the boarders' wash, help clean the house, and amuse the children. And it's Bridget keeps Gracie and Stephen happy. Only three and full of ideas like "Pretend we're on a boat on the river." A good one, that, because I can be a passenger dozing.

"Children," I called up to them again.

They came bouncing down the stairs.

"How's Stephen, Mam?" Bridget asked.

"Sleeping."

Jamesy touched Stephen's forehead. "Hot, Mam."

"Croup," I said.

I gave them the last of the milk to drink. Jamesy and Daniel pulled Molly's chairs close to the stove. We sat in a circle.

"What games were you playing?" I asked.

"Can't tell, Mam," Jamesy said. "You'll see."

"We're going to—" Bridget started.

"Don't!" Daniel said to her. "It's a surprise."

Gracie was beside me now, patting Stephen's shoulder. Only two months older, but always so tender with "the baby."

"He'll be fine," I said. "Sit with Bridget close to the stove. Light the lantern, Jamesy."

He'd learned to stick a piece of straw through the stove's grate and carefully bring the flame to the lantern's wick.

"Put another log on, Daniel," I said. "Watch yourself."

"Not much wood left, Aunt Honey," Daniel said.

"We'll have loads when your mam and the boys get home," I said.

"I wish they were here now," Jamesy said.

"So do I."

Stephen slept, his breath whistling in his chest.

Then the children and I nodded off, too.

It was the snow woke us. Hard pellets hit the outside walls of the house, beating against the wooden slats.

Jamesy and Daniel rushed to the window. Jamesy lifted Daniel up to look out for a moment, then let him down.

"A blizzard, Mam," Jamesy said.

The boarders had told us about these storms. Like nothing known in Ireland, they'd said. Here, the winds blew across the prairies to meet the gales coming off the Lake and together battered the clouds until sharp pieces of ice fell from the heavens—a different species altogether from the snowflakes at home.

"Like musket balls, coming from all directions. Slice your face open," Barney McGurk had said.

"It comes up fast," they'd all agreed.

In those blizzard stories people got disoriented, went in circles, were frozen within yards of shelter. Máire and the boys are out there somewhere.

"Piles of snow already, Mam," Jamesy said.

The boys had been hoping for a really big snowfall. Great fun, their pals had told them. Fun.

"I'm cold, Mam," Bridget said.

"I know, a stór. Come, all of you, move closer together. The heat of our bodies will help."

Wind pushed through chinks in the wall and the spaces around the window frames.

"There's no heat in my body," Daniel said.

"Come anyway."

"Get close to Stephen, Daniel," Jamesy said. "He's warm."

I touched Stephen's forehead—hotter now, a fever, no question.

I took Bridget and Gracie on my lap, Stephen between them, and the boys sat against my legs.

So little wood in the box! Two small logs and a few sticks. Behind the stove's open grate, one last tongue of flame licked at a stump of a log—almost gone, black with only a thread of red.

"Blow," I said to Jamesy and Daniel. "Blow on the fire."

We knelt together, *whoosh*ing at the embers, trying to bring back the fire. Bridget and Gracie pursed their small lips, blending their breath with ours.

Stephen opened his eyes, looked at Bridget.

She'd put her little hands on each side of his face. "A game, Stephen, blow!" She pressed out a bit of breath.

The embers caught fire. Flames.

"Look, Mam," said Jamesy. "We did it!"

"Daniel," I said, "put two more sticks in."

"The fire's dancing," Jamesy said.

Bridget and Gracie kept blowing at the fire, bright and crackling now but giving off very little heat. Another gust of wind chilled the room.

Jamesy and Daniel crawled closer to the stove. Where are they?

❖ ❖ ❖

"Mam, Mam!" Jamesy pulled on my skirt. "Somebody."

Them, surely. Footsteps pounded on the stairs.

Paddy burst into the kitchen first, his face red, the skin around his lips white. He held his hands over the top of the stove. "I'm frozen. My fingers, my toes." Barefoot, his boots left down at the door, toes blue.

"Get up, girls." I helped them off my lap. "Here—" I handed Stephen to Jamesy and knelt down, rubbing the blue toes. "Help me, Bridget."

She sat on the floor, her little hands slapping at Paddy's other foot.

"Can you feel that, Paddy?"

"Mam, I can't."

I tried to get the blood flowing, kneading his blue skin, remembering the nights I'd stroked life into Michael's poor feet when he'd come from the roadworks.

Máire and Johnny Og and Thomas came into the kitchen and went right to the stove. Máire pressed her back against the big iron oven, and Johnny Og put his hands next to Paddy's. Thomas bent over, took off his shoes, and stuck his bare feet toward my hands.

"Next," he said.

"Not much warmer in here than out there," Máire said.

"Mam, Mam!" Daniel and Gracie wrapped their arms around Máire's legs.

"What happened? Where have you been?" I asked.

"We had a few problems."

"Problems?"

"He wouldn't pay her, Mam," Paddy said.

"Oh, Máire!" I stopped.

"Keep on, Mam, please," Paddy said. "I'm starting to feel my toes."

"Here, Thomas." Daniel bent over and began rubbing his brother's bare feet.

"I knew how many sales I've made. I told him my commission should be twenty dollars, but Mr. Croaker had figured his sums different. He said I'd earned ten."

"Well, ten isn't terrible," I said.

"It's terrible if you're owed twenty. But I couldn't prove it. He had the accounts all written down. Lies," she said. "So I said I'd take ten dollars. But he said he had to deduct the cost of the brown wool cloth."

"Oh no!"

"He had the neck to hand me five dollars and say, 'Merry Christmas!' And I said . . . well, I said some things to him."

"Aunt Máire knows some powerful curses, Mam," Paddy said.

"'Take five dollars or take nothing,' he said to me."

"I said we'd destroy the store, Mam," Paddy said. "We'd break the mirrors, throw the clothes on the floor. But Aunt Máire said not to do it."

"Only because we'd all end up in jail," Máire said. "I can tell you, I quit as soon as I had the five dollars in my hand. We did have enough to buy the food, and we got a Christmas tree!"

"You spent money on a Christmas tree?!"

"We didn't, Aunt Honey," Johnny Og said. "Professor Lang gave it to us. He said the music store wouldn't open again until after New Year's so we might as well have it."

"He was decent, Mam. Gave us glasses of wine."

"Máire! You sat drinking wine?"

"It was clear then. The snow didn't start until we were on our way home. Then the blizzard swept right over us. Couldn't see a thing. We got lost. I thought we were going to die."

"We were scared, Aunt Honey," Johnny Og said.

"Not me," Thomas said.

"You were too," Paddy said.

"Let's just thank God you're home safe. Now . . ."

"The ice burned my face, Mam," Paddy said. "How can ice feel like fire?"

"Talking about fire, let's get *our* fire started. Bring up the wood. We'll build a big fire, get nice and warm."

"Oh, the wood," Máire said.

"The wood," I repeated. "Molly's wood for the stove?"

"By the time we found our way to the lumberyard, it was closed," Máire said.

"We tried, Mam, we did," Paddy said.

"Dear God," I said.

"Hold on now, Honora. Molly always has plenty of wood."

"She doesn't! Look! Look at the wood box!"

Máire leaned over to see the two logs, a few sticks. "Oh."

"Oh? *Oh?* My Stephen's burning up, it's cold in here already! If we can't keep the stove going . . ." I stopped, seeing the children's faces.

"I'm sorry, Mam," Paddy said. "I thought—"

"I don't care what you thought. You should have gotten the wood when I told you! And you, Máire. To loll around drinking wine when we're waiting here for you, worried, and now . . ."

Stephen started crying, a frightening clogged-up kind of weeping. He pushed at Jamesy and lifted his arms up to me. I picked him up and walked back and forth.

"He's sick, Máire. Molly says croup, but . . ." I rocked him and sang. He quieted.

"We should cook now," Máire said, "while the stove's hot. Have our Christmas dinner right now."

She'd brought rashers and plenty of pratties. I kissed Stephen's forehead and gave him to Bridget.

"Quick, the skillet." Máire and I started frying rashers and sent the two big boys out to fill the pot with snow to boil up the pratties.

"The snow's burying us!" Paddy said when he and Johnny Og swung the pot onto the stove.

While we cooked, the big boys set the four-foot pine tree onto Molly's kitchen table, then tied the tiny candles Professor Lang had given them on its branches.

The room smelled of pine and frying bacon. Johnny Og and Paddy lit the candles. The other children clapped their hands.

"Oh, Mam, isn't it beautiful?" said Jamesy.

"It is, a stór," I said. And we'll break it up and burn it before this night's over, I thought.

We sat, two on each of Molly's chairs, in a circle close to the stove. The children took strips of bacon in their hands, glad for the heat. Thomas rolled his potato under his feet.

Stephen ate some of the potato I'd mashed with hot water. Máire hadn't been able to get milk. He was too quiet, his eyes dull, each breath rattling his small chest.

"The wood won't last through the night," Máire whispered into my ear.

"I know that."

"Where can we go to get more in this storm?" Máire said. "McKenna's is closed."

Lizzie and James always spent Christmas Eve with Father Donohue at St. Patrick's, then went to Midnight Mass. They would have to stay over.

"I don't think we can even get across to O'Neill's in this," Máire said.

"We'll be very careful, use the bark from this last log. . . . And there's the Christmas tree," I whispered to her.

Outside, the storm battered the sides of the house.

"We'll burn Molly's chairs if we have to," she whispered back.

"Her chairs from Ireland? Jesus, Máire, we'd have to move out!"

"We'd be alive," she said.

"We can't let the children sleep," I said.

In the blizzard stories, the travelers who lay down in the snow to sleep never woke up again.

Already I could see the children's eyes were closing. Paddy's head had dropped down.

"Mam . . ." Jamesy pulled on my hand. "Is Stephen too sick to be in our play?"

"Your play?"

"Teacher did it at school, Mam," he said. "You know, Mary and Joseph and Jesus, the shepherds and the angels? Daniel and I couldn't have a part, so we're doing it ourselves. We've practiced."

It'll keep them moving. "Go on, then, Jamesy," I said.

"Jamesy . . ." Daniel was standing next to us. "The big boys won't be in the play. They want to go to sleep."

"They can't," I said. "Máire, tell the boys they have to be in the play. Everybody up now, move. Do what Jamesy tells you."

Bridget was Mary; Daniel, Joseph; and Gracie, the Christmas angel. The big boys were reluctant shepherds.

"Kneel down and smile at baby Jesus," Jamesy ordered them.

Stephen lay across Bridget's lap, his eyes half-opened. The rest knelt around them as Jamesy played the tin whistle—his own little tune.

"At school they sing things called Christmas carols. Do we know any, Mam?" Jamesy asked me.

"We know dozens," said Máire, and she sang.

> Full many a bird did wake and fly
> To the manger bed with a wandering cry
> On Christmas day in the morning
> Curoo, curoo, curoo . . .

"Oh, that's lovely, Aunt Máire," Jamesy said. He's so like Michael—generous with praise.

"You know this song, Johnny Og—sing!" Máire said.

"So do you, Paddy," I said. "Sing." Would he remember it from the before times?

Somehow the words came to the boys:

> The shepherds knelt upon the hay
> And angels sang the night away
> On Christmas day in the morning
> Curoo, curoo, curoo . . .

"Wonderful!" I said, clapping. "Wonderful." Then I told them how in Ireland, in the before times, every family put a lit candle in their window to guide Mary and Joseph to their door.

"And would they come?" Jamesy asked.

Paddy and Thomas laughed.

"They would, Jamesy. Surprised many a scoffing boy."

Máire brought out boiled sweets, one for each child, but they shivered as they sucked on the candy. Very little heat came from the stove.

"I bought pipes and tobacco," Máire was saying. "And we have the whiskey."

"No whiskey," I said. "We have to keep our wits about us. We'll break up the Christmas tree."

"But it's so pretty, Mam."

"We have to. Paddy, help me with the tree."

I walked over to the table, past the window. I looked out. Still snowing. The flakes hit the window. Darkness beyond. But something . . . What? A blur of light out on the prairie—low, moving along close to the ground. I scratched at the frost on the inside of the window.

"What are you doing, Mam?" Paddy asked.

"Here, tell me what you see."

He stood on his toes, his eyes just above the windowsill. He turned to me. "Mam!" With a face full of wonder, my child of the before times looked up at me. "Is it true? Are Mary and Joseph coming to our door?"

I pressed my face against the window. "A lantern, Paddy," I said. "A man's carrying it. He's leading a horse."

"So not them, Mam."

"Some poor traveler, surely, Paddy. Máire!"

She came over to me and looked out. "Now, there's someone worse off than we are."

"I'll step down with a candle to light his way to us."

"Jesus, Honora! He could be a robber, a murderer. Quick, blow out the Christmas tree candles. He'll pass us by."

"He might be lost," I said. "Paddy, come with Mam. Bring two candles from the tree. Bridget, mind Stephen."

At the sound of his name, Stephen turned his head to me. A fit of coughing. Croup, please God.

Paddy and I carried two lit candles down the splintery stairs. I opened the front door the smallest crack.

I closed my lips against the cold air. Inhale and my insides will freeze.

"How many inches do you think, Mam?"

"I don't know, Paddy."

Inches. Always part of the blizzard story—twelve inches, eighteen inches, thirty inches, fifty inches, burying houses and animals and people.

"There, Mam, there! The light's closer now."

"I'll stand out and hold the candle."

"Not you, Mam. Me."

Paddy put his feet into the wet boots he'd left at the door and stepped into the night. He sank into a mound of snow, then climbed out holding the candle high, calling, "Here! Here we are! Here!"

The horse struggled through the deep snow, but the man seemed to be walking on top of the drifts. He lifted his head and waved to Paddy.

"An Indian, Mam," Paddy shouted back to me, and moved toward the fellow, who had his back to me.

I could see the man pulling on the harness and halter, clumsy, with something tied to his feet. Very close now.

He turned. Long hair, and dressed in leather trousers with fringes, a fur collar on his jacket, but not an Indian, not with that beard. He held the lantern up to his face—hazel eyes, brown and green and yellow. He stepped close to me.

We stared at each other.

"Nollaig Shona Dhuit, Honora," he said. "Happy Christmas."

"Patrick Kelly—oh, dear Jesus, Mary, and Holy Saint Joseph!"

"Uncle Patrick?" Paddy said.

"Oh, Patrick, Patrick! We've been waiting . . . I didn't think . . ."

"Let me get unloaded and in first before you shower me with questions. Michael!" he shouted up the stairs. "Michael, come down to me. Help me carry up these yokes. They're furs," he said to me.

"We'll be glad for them this night," I said. "Ah, Patrick, Michael's . . . well, he's . . ."

"Asleep already? I'll wake him up. Come on, Paddy. Heave. I've been trapping up in the North Woods. Lucky I stopped by Saint Patrick's. Got your letter. Father Donohue told me you were at Molly's. Good choice."

As he talked, Patrick carried the huge pack up the stairs, Paddy helping him.

Dear God, he's read the letter Michael had written and thinks he's alive. Father Donohue hadn't told Patrick we were alone. Why would he? He'd assume Patrick knew.

Máire held Stephen, standing in the kitchen doorway, the children gathered around.

"Merry Christmas," Patrick said to her. "I'm Michael's brother, Patrick." Then "Michael! . . . Michael!" he shouted. "Get up, you lazy bollocks!"

Máire only stared as Patrick dumped the pack of furs on the kitchen floor.

"Patrick, Michael's not here," I started.

"What? Gone out to lay track for the railroad? We'll get him back. I know a blacksmith here needs a good man like Michael."

"Uncle Patrick," Paddy said, "our da is dead."

"What? . . . Honora?"

"It's true, Patrick," I said. "Michael died."

"Don't say that!"

I reached out to touch his arm, but he stepped back.

"It was fever killed him," I said. "He'd worked so hard and was weak from the hunger. We should have left sooner, gotten out."

Patrick only stared at me.

"Sit down, Patrick," I said, and steered him to the chair by the stove.

"Get that whiskey, Thomas," Máire said.

Thomas brought the cask. I dipped a tin cup into it and gave it to Patrick.

"When?" Patrick asked after he'd drained the cup.

"August."

I took the cup and started to fill it, but Patrick shook his head. "No more," he said.

The children stood close to the stove, shoulders hunched, shivering, saying nothing. Did Jamesy remember Patrick?

"The children are cold," Patrick said.

He opened the grate of the stove—mostly ashes smoldered there. Patrick put the last log from the wood box into the stove, took a stick, and poked the ashes until a flame caught the sticks and the log started burning.

"Open the packs," he said to me. "Spread out the skins. Cover the children. I'll be back."

He walked out the door and down the steps.

"Well," said Máire, handing Stephen back to me. "That's an abrupt fellow.

"Lie down in a circle," she said to the children after we'd covered every inch of floor with the hides. I found a soft white fur—rabbit—and wrapped Stephen up. I held him close as the other children took their places. They made a wheel, their seven little faces the rim, their legs the spokes. The children sank deep into the furs and smiled at us from the soft, warm bed. Máire covered them with the skins of animals I couldn't name.

The candles on the Christmas tree sputtered out.

"Can we go to sleep now, Mam?"

"You can, Jamesy."

"I'm roasting under all these covers," Paddy said.

"Is it Christmas yet?" Daniel asked.

"It will be when you wake up," Máire told him.

I sat down by the stove, holding Stephen. Máire lifted up a long black pelt of something and put it around me. Stephen slept, sucking in air with little jolts that jerked his body. Máire touched his forehead.

"Still warm," she said.

I nodded.

She stood looking down at me. "He's a strong little boy, Honora."

"He is," I said.

She leaned over and sniffed his breath. "No foul smell, like . . ."

"Croup. Molly says it's croup."

"That Patrick Kelly is—" she started, but I put my fingers to my lips.

"We'll talk tomorrow," I said. "Go to sleep, Máire."

"Well, at least Molly's chairs survived," she said as she crawled into the circle of children.

❖ ❖ ❖

Sometime in the middle of the night, Patrick came in with an armload of split logs. He dumped some into the wood box and put two into the stove. The fire flared up again, real heat coming from it at last.

"Where did you get . . . ," I stopped. Why ask?

Stephen started a whimpering cry that put the heart across me.

"Sick?" Patrick asked.

I nodded. "Croup. Children don't die of croup." No fever, please God, please.

Patrick bent over me and looked closely at Stephen in my arms, then removed a small packet from a pouch at his waist. He dipped his fingers into the packet and held them up to my nose—some kind of ointment, a smell like the Christmas tree. I nodded and unwrapped Stephen. Patrick rubbed the salve on Stephen's chest and tucked the rabbit skin back around him.

"Thank you," I said to Patrick as I stroked Stephen's head.

He said nothing, only stood over me, watching Stephen's chest rise and fall.

After a long time, Stephen's shuddery breaths eased. He opened his eyes, looked up at Patrick.

"His eyes," Patrick said.

"Clearer, I think."

"The color of my father's," he said.

"Like Jamesy's," I said. "And your own."

"He's better."

"He is."

Stephen began to squirm on my lap.

"Quiet now, Stephen. Go to sleep."

"Water?" said Patrick.

"Please. The bucket's in the corner and the cup's next to it."

Patrick brought the cup to me.

Stephen took a swallow. "Sing, Mam," he said, and I began Mam's lullaby.

"Michael's youngest son," Patrick said. "What age is he?"

"A year and eight months, and our last child will be born in the spring," I whispered.

"Jesus Christ, Honora. You traveled all that way with a load of children, in such a condition?"

"We would have died if we stayed at home," I said. "I promised Michael I'd bring them to you. And I had Máire's help."

Patrick nodded. Then, "He was the best brother a man could have," he said. He took a fur robe to the far corner of the kitchen and rolled himself up into it.

Thank you, Michael. I know it was you sent him. I leaned back in Molly's chair, held Stephen close to me, and slept.

Chapter 27

I WOKE BEFORE DAWN. Sweat covered Stephen, but his forehead felt cool, thank God. He opened his eyes, said, "Mam, Mam," and touched my face. I dried him off and tucked him between Bridget and Gracie in the wheel of children.

"Go back to sleep." I sat and stroked his forehead until he slept.

Patrick Kelly was gone.

I went to the kitchen window. Pink light brushed the snow as the sun rose out of the Lake. Many, many inches buried Bridgeport—no heaps of rubbish, just hills and valleys now—beautiful. The wind threw sprays of snow into the light—diamond sparks lifted above the frozen surface. Christmas morning.

Has Patrick Kelly helped us only to disappear as he'd done so many times in Ireland? I wondered. But then I saw him, seeming to walk on top of the snow, almost at the door. I wrapped the pelt around me and hurried down the stairs.

When I opened the door he was bent over, removing something from his feet.

"Snowshoes," he said, holding up a round wooden frame with a handle, crisscrossed with a kind of netting. "Indian invention. How's the baby?" he asked.

"Better."

"An Ojibwa cure."

"Ojibwa?"

"The Indian tribe I've been trapping with up north. You're dressed in one of our prizes—a bear skin."

"Very warm," I said. "Come in. They're all asleep upstairs." I walked in the door and up a few steps, Patrick following.

"Wait," he said. "Sit down a moment."

Drawing the pelt around me, I eased myself onto a step. He sat down two steps below me and set a full sack on the step between us.

"What's this?"

"Eggs. Rashers. A jug of milk."

"Thank you, Patrick. And thank you for the wood."

He shrugged off his fur jacket and leaned his shoulder against the step. He'd been working hard somewhere—muscles under the buckskin shirt he wore, some heft on that lean frame of his. Outlandish clothing, though, not only tight leggings of yellow leather with fringe along the sides but soft shoes beaded in different colors and designs. He saw me looking at his feet.

"Moccasins," he said, lifting one foot. He pointed to the flower designs on his shirt. "Porcupine quills, dyed," he said.

"You'd get some queer old looks in Galway," I said.

"You would, too," he said, "wrapped in the skin of a she-bear."

"No bears in Ireland now," I said, "though there must have been once, or where did the MacMahons get their name?"

"Son of the Bear," he said.

I nodded.

"So hard to believe Michael's dead. I can't take it in, Honora," he said. "I thought all of you were safe in Ireland and that the money I sent would see you through."

"If we'd left as soon as we got the money from you, Michael would be alive. But you made him part of the uprising—your man in Galway. He wouldn't go."

"And it's my fault you stayed?" he said.

"Well . . ."

He pushed himself up to my step, sat next to me. "You blame *me* for Michael's death," he said.

I put my hand over my eyes.

"Answer me, Honora." He took my hand away, made me look at him.

"All right. I do. Maybe I'm wrong, but I do. You should have sent money earlier. . . ."

"How? I was on the run, Honora. Hiding all that first year. I didn't even know the pratties had failed until—"

"Why didn't you? Everybody else in Amerikay knew. If we'd gotten that money right away, it would have made all the difference. He looked to you, Patrick! And then when we could leave, you had to enlist him in your revolution. He worked so hard, Patrick, so hard—walking ten miles barefoot through the snow and ice to break stones for twelve, fourteen hours—no real food to eat, getting thinner and thinner. And I couldn't help him. I couldn't do anything. Even the good things—the harvest, blacksmithing—turned wrong. If he hadn't had to work at the forge in Galway City where the fever was, maybe he'd be alive now. I had to watch him die. Alone in that shed. I couldn't save him, Patrick. And you, you were gone. Gone."

He still had my hand. "Honora, is it yourself you blame?"

I pulled my hand away.

"You said you couldn't save him."

"We'd survived so much—Black '47, baby Grellan's death and Granny's, my brothers gone, Jackson . . . But in the end, in the end . . ."

"Don't blame yourself, Honora. Or me. You know who murdered Michael and a million more. They've been trying to destroy us for centuries and will go on killing Irish people until we take our country back. Michael has not died in vain, Honora. I promise you that. We will avenge his death and all the others."

"Too late, Patrick. The Sassenach have won. The Irish are dead or gone from the land forever."

"That's wrong, Honora. The battle's only begun. We're gathering our strength here in America. They didn't take America into account."

I sagged down. "Oh, but Patrick, it takes so much to survive in Amerikay. What's left over for Ireland? Seems most of the Irish have to forget Ireland in order to make their way here."

"You're wrong there, Honora. You'll see."

"Jesus Christ," Máire called down. "What are you two doing there? Come up."

I put my hands down on the steps to push myself up. Patrick took my arm and helped. I wrapped the bear skin tight around me.

"You look like some prehistoric queen of Ireland," he said. "Banba or Eriu, or the great Maeve herself."

I nodded. A truce. "Nollaig Mhaith Chugat . . . a good Christmas to you, Patrick. I'm glad you're here. I'm sure it was Michael sent you to us. Maybe there's truth in not being able to believe he's dead. I feel Michael's with us, somehow. I am carrying his child. A son, Patrick, I'm sure. We'll name him Michael Kelly. A comfort for us both."

He nodded but said nothing, then followed me up the stairs.

The kitchen was warm. Sun was coming through the window. Máire and I cooked the eggs and rashers while the children sat at Molly's table staring at Patrick, not saying a word.

Thomas spoke first. "We had this breakfast every day at my father's house," he said to Patrick as I put the food on his plate.

"So did we," Paddy said.

"You did not. You were poor," Thomas said.

Máire turned from the stove. "Poor? I'll give you poor. Sure we were all poor, and take that sneer out of your voice, Thomas, or I'll shake it out of you."

Stephen clapped his hands. He always got a great laugh from Máire's scoldings. He's well.

"We won't be poor anymore now that you're here, Uncle Patrick, will we?" said Paddy.

"You won't be poor, Paddy, because you have a strong back and a good pair of hands. How do you find Hough's?"

"It's all right," Paddy said.

"He hates it," said Jamesy. "Hates the blood and the shit and watching the men beat the cows to death."

"But I go, Uncle Patrick, I go every morning, and Johnny Og goes with me. We didn't whinge and whine to get out of the hard work like Thomas did so he could run around the city like a monkey on a string," Paddy said.

"Where did you get such an expression?" I asked him.

"Barney McGurk says it."

"Teacher showed us a picture of a monkey in school, Uncle Patrick," Jamesy said. "Brought Daniel to the front of the class to show how his face was like a monkey's."

"You never told me that," I started.

"For Jesus' sake!" Máire said, and banged the skillet on the top of the stove. "What happened, Daniel?"

"Teacher took a ruler and put it up against me and said I had a monkey face because I was Irish."

That set the other children laughing. "Monkey face!" they repeated. "Monkey face!"

"Stop it, stop it!" I said. "This is nothing to laugh at."

But the big boys chanted, "Monkey face, monkey face!"

"Stop it!"

But they wouldn't.

Patrick brought his fist down hard on the table. The plates rattled. Silence.

"You listen when your mother speaks. And you always do what she tells you. And as for that teacher, he's an ignorant guilpín. There are no apes or gorillas or monkeys in this house. Only some bad-mannered children."

The children gaped at him. I looked over at Máire. Should Patrick really speak so harshly to the boys?

"Honora?" Patrick said.

All the children turned to me.

"Your uncle Patrick's right," I said.

❖   ❖   ❖

"Boys can get out of hand," Patrick Kelly said to Máire and me as we sat in the kitchen after our young fellows, wrapped in furs, had run out to join the Bridgeport children rampaging in the snow. Father Donohue hadn't been able to get through the snow. No Christmas Mass at McKenna's.

The small Christmas tree was on the floor now, with Bridget, Gracie, and Stephen on their stomachs under it, looking up into the branches.

"This is where the bird that sang to baby Jesus lives," we heard Bridget tell them.

"*Curoo, curoo*," they sang.

"A good imagination, that one," I said to Patrick as the three sang.

He smiled. Almost pleasant when he smiles.

Máire brought out the doneen pipes and sweet Tip-Top tobacco she'd bought as our gifts. One drag started me coughing.

"Don't waste it," Máire said, and passed the pipe to Patrick. "Her condition," she said.

"He knows," I said.

"You've done well enough for yourselves to get here," Patrick said. "Two women, eight children."

"True enough," Máire said. "Did you tell him, Honora, how Jackson burned the cottages over our heads in Bearna?"

"I didn't."

"We escaped in Da's púcán," she said. "Sailed through the night down Galway Bay to Ard near Carna in Connemara, Granny's home place."

"Your parents?"

"They stayed, Patrick," I said. "We've heard nothing."

"Ard near Carna. I'll look into it," he said. "Go on."

Máire told him how we'd rowed the curragh out to the *Superior* and were taken aboard.

"Brave in a boat, Honora," he said to me.

Máire went on with her story of our voyage, the time in New Orleans, the journey up the Mississippi, our arrival here—the disappointment. "I could have stayed in New Orleans. Opportunities there. But Honora insisted on Chicago. And Patrick Kelly."

"I promised Michael," I said to Patrick. "His dying words: 'Take the children to Patrick in Chicago.'"

Patrick shook his head, drew on the pipe, and breathed out the smoke. "Good on you both," he said. "Now. First, I'll get Johnny Og and Paddy out of Hough's," he said. "I'll have a word with Phil Slattery, the blacksmith. He can take Paddy on as a helper at the forge."

"What about my Johnny Og?" Máire said.

"Michael Gibson has a boatworks," Patrick said. "Johnny Og's father was a fisherman, wasn't he? Michael's a good fellow."

"All right," said Máire. "No need to worry about Thomas. He's set, and my job is—" She stopped. "I liked it until . . ."

"Her boss cheated her," I said. "Croaker."

"One of those men from back east. A Yankee. Can't expect to be treated fairly by them," Patrick said.

"How was I to know?" Máire said. "I sold to the *best* people in Chicago—Cyrus McCormick himself."

"McCormick's a thief and a bigot. Lectures his workers on the evils of Catholicism, brags about how his ancestors fought with King Billy in the North of Ireland to destroy the papists. Typical of the *best* people in Chicago."

"Oh," Máire said.

"Now, the school," Patrick said. "Can't pull them out. No place else to send them yet, though the bishop plans for every parish to have its own school."

"The bishop, is it?" Máire said to Patrick. "Listen to him, Honora. As if the bishop would sit sipping tea with such a savage-looking fellow!"

"Bishop Quarter and I prefer whiskey," Patrick said.

I laughed at that.

Máire flared up. "You think he's funny?," she said to me. "Who is he to come in and lay down the law to us? Took him long enough to get here."

"Don't attack Patrick, Máire. I already have," I said. And then to Patrick, "We do need our own schools. To think of that teacher ridiculing Daniel in front of the whole class—the Irish ape-man? I thought we'd left that behind us."

"There's plenty who insult us in America. The difference is, we fight back. I'll have a word with the teacher," Patrick said. "He'll not bother Jamesy and Daniel again. Now, about dinner—"

"Excuse me, Patrick," Máire said. "Your questions have been asked and answered. Your orders received. I have some questions for you, like where have you been? What have you been doing? Have you a wife, family?"

Patrick stood up. "I'll call the children in. As I was trying to say, we're invited to the neighbors for dinner."

"Which neighbors?"

"The Potawatomis—friends of mine."

"Jesus Christ," said Máire.

Patrick walked to the door and turned. "Honora will tell you what my work is, and no, I haven't a wife and never will. Wouldn't be fair to the woman." He left to collect the children.

⟡   ⟡   ⟡

We wrapped ourselves in the furs. Patrick sat us all on a long sled—a toboggan. Another Indian invention, he said. He'd borrowed this one from the Potawatomis. He pulled us over the snow and through Bridgeport; his snowshoes kept him on top of the drifts.

"This is fun, Mam," Jamesy said as we glided over the canal and crossed Healey's Slough, frozen solid now. In no time at all, we reached a large round structure covered in birch bark with three smaller domed huts around it.

"Wigwams," Patrick said.

"Like the beehive huts the Irish monks built in ancient times," I said to him.

"Warmer," he said.

A man, two women, and a group of children waited at the entrance, all smiling, gesturing us in.

"I'd introduce you, but I don't know the name of the older wife," Patrick said.

"The older wife?" I asked.

"I think she's from the Kankakee tribe. The younger wife is Catherine Chevalier, and she's Potawatomi."

"Two wives?"

"Both good Catholics," Patrick said.

A fire burned at the center of the big round room. The ground was covered in furs. Our host was Chief Alexander Robinson, a spare man, older than Patrick. Che-Che-Pin-Quaw—"Blinking Eyes"—was his Indian name, the man said. His father was a Scotsman, his mother a member of the Green Bay Ottawa tribe, he told us. Though he had long hair, Chief Robinson dressed in the trousers and jacket of any Chicago businessman. But the women—with their shiny black hair and dark eyes, wearing white tunics, embroidered like Patrick's shirt, over leggings—had an unfamiliar beauty. Amerikay in the before times.

❖ ❖ ❖

They served us a Christmas feast. The food was delicious and new to us. "Turkey," Patrick said, and yellow potatoes, and something he called cranberries.

Patrick Kelly seemed a different fellow here, joking with Chief Robinson, complimenting the women in their own language as we settled on the fur-covered floor near the fire.

Chicago, Chief Robinson said, was settled by men like him—fellows of mixed ancestry and their Indian wives and families. I remembered Lizzie's stories of those early days—only twenty years before.

"Tell them about Billy Caldwell," Patrick said. "A fellow from County Armagh, and an Indian chief."

The boys had maneuvered themselves near Patrick. The Robinson children moved near their father. A story was coming. Get a good place. Fadó here, too.

"Billy Caldwell's father was an officer with the British army in Canada, his mother was a member of the Mohawk tribe. Billy was an educated man. He knew Latin as well as English, French, and five or six Indian languages. He was called the Sauganash—the Englishman—but his tribal name was Tall Tree. He became a chief of the Potawatomis, always dressed in buckskin, like your uncle here."

Patrick patted Paddy's head. Jamesy moved over to get a pat—then the others, even Thomas, jostled closer—almost like puppies. Patrick gave each one a quick cuff.

I thought of Michael, playing the Giant with them. How the boys had enjoyed that rough-and-tumble. Their da gone, they'd had none of this physical male back-and-forth. Is there a kind of animal need to tussle with the pack leader, be accepted by him?

The boys sat cross-legged, imitating Patrick. They leaned against him, and Patrick put his arms around them as we listened to Alexander Robinson. Here's the brother who would put a lonely little boy on his shoulders and go galloping around the course at Gallagh Hill. A man other men follow.

The beard suits him, outlines his jaw, shows the high cheekbones. No wrinkles at all—young-looking for a fellow near forty.

Patrick looked right at me, as if he'd sensed my eyes on him, and winked. Jesus Christ. Winked. I nodded at him. He rubbed Jamesy's head.

Chief Robinson had a precise way of telling a story. He said that he and Billy Caldwell had helped organize the first election in Chicago, when twenty-eight people voted, and started St. Mary's, the first Catholic church. Billy Caldwell was married to the daughter of a Potawatomi chief.

I remembered Lizzie McKenna's stories of those early days. "Wasn't the tavern where they all danced called the Sauganash?" I asked Chief Robinson.

"Named for Billy. Shows you the regard he was held in." But then fellows came in from the East. Those Yankee traders cheated the Indians, gave them whiskey for their furs. Later they sold them the stuff on credit and claimed Indian land as payment. The Yankees were determined to push out the Indians completely. The U.S. government went along with them, making all these treaties for Indian land. The settlers made Chicago officially a town in 1833, Robinson said.

But he and Billy Caldwell had signed the Treaty of Chicago in 1833 as representatives of their tribes. "No choice, otherwise the Indians would get nothing," Robinson said, and described the great war dance two years later when the Indians got their final treaty payment and had to leave—thousands of Potawatomis dressed for battle, pounding drums and stomping around the Sauganash Hotel. "Billy and I wanted to paint our faces, put on our feathers, and join them. Give the Yankees one last scare." Chief Robinson said Billy stayed for a while but then went west to Iowa with the Indians. "Died there seven years ago. Sixty years old."

"Billy Caldwell, the Sauganash. A man I admire," Patrick said to the boys. "Fellows like him made Chicago. Tell that to those Yankee teachers in Bridgeport School."

"Billy Caldwell sounds like you, Uncle Patrick," Paddy said.

Alexander Robinson laughed.

✤ ✤ ✤

It was late on Christmas evening when Patrick carried Bridget and Gracie up into the boardinghouse. I held Stephen, his forehead cool, breathing easily, asleep in my arms. Máire helped Paddy and Jamesy, Johnny Og, Daniel, and Thomas struggle up the stairs.

We settled them in our room on the straw pallets, well fed and warm, under the furs.

"Fine sons you have," Patrick said to Máire and me as we sat again at Molly's table. "I see bits of Michael in both Paddy and Jamesy. And nothing of the Pykes in your two, Máire."

"Thank God for small favors," she said.

Good, she's warmed to him a bit. I don't see much of a chance of a match between the two, as Molly'd said, though it would be handy.

"So now, what's this about you and the O-O-O . . . ?" Máire asked.

"Ojibwa?"

She nodded.

"I was with them for a year," he said, "in the North Woods."

"What was it like?" Máire said.

Patrick turned to me. "You know the stories of the Fianna, the Warriors of the Red Branch—the old Irish?"

"I do."

"The Ojibwa live as they did—hunting, fishing, moving from place to place in the great North Woods. Beautiful country, one clear lake joined to the next. What Ireland must have been. No towns or Big Houses. No Sassenach. Clans, families living together. Strange to say, but among the Indians I felt truly Irish for the first time in my life, because I was free."

"Free," I said.

"I often thought of Michael and wished he . . ." Patrick stopped. "Sorry," he said. "So many things I wanted to tell him about America. Tonight . . . at times I forget."

"I know, Patrick."

We sat in silence for a bit, then Máire said, "But, Patrick, tell me, how does running around with Indians help Ireland?"

We heard footsteps on the stairs. Molly came in the door, followed by the returning boarders. The roads were passable now. Everyone home. They surrounded Patrick, laughing and patting his shoulder.

"Will you have a look at this fellow?"

"Thought you'd never come back!"

"Hough will be surprised!"

"The bosses will be glad the canal is closed for the winter, that's all I can say!"

Molly hugged Patrick. And Patrick kissed her on the cheek. She tugged on his beard. "Don't like that," she said. "There's a fine-featured man under all that." Molly drew me away from the circle of men. "So, Honora, he's come at last."

"He has," I said.

Máire began telling the boarders how we'd almost frozen "all because that tightfisted hoor of a gombeen man cheated me."

She was ready to polish the knots and knobs of her struggle with Croaker, but the lads said let's get James McKenna to open the tavern for one to welcome Patrick home, and off they went.

"Thank you for my sweet Tip-Top tobacco," Molly said to Máire as we sat smoking together.

I brought the smoke in and out slowly and started coughing.

"She's not able for it," Máire said.

"Her condition," said Molly, taking the pipe away and tamping out the burning tobacco. "I'll save this. So. Tell me about what Patrick's been up to."

"He won't say," I said.

"Probably talking revolution to the boys in the lumber camps and lining up the Indians to sail to Ireland with them—take on the Sassenach."

"Your boarders seem to have a lot of time for Patrick Kelly," Máire said.

"They do surely. He led the big strike. Bosses cut the wages, just like that. Men were dying already from twelve hours of digging and hauling rock, standing up to their knees in water. And those tents—sleep too far from the stove, you'd not wake up.

"Patrick Kelly was working out near Summit, eight miles south of us. Payday comes and the money's short. Foreman says, 'Too bad.' What could the men do? The next day, Patrick lines up the fellows and they throw their shovels down. No work until wages are right. Then Patrick lifted up that golden staff of his and started along the canal. 'Put down your shovels, put them down!' he said. And they did. Patrick walked the whole eight miles, stopping the work as he went. By the time he got to Lock Number One at Bridgeport, who was waiting for him but the canal commissioner, Mr. Archer himself. Patrick Kelly went toe-to-toe with him, stood there a good hour or more talking, and then Archer stomped away mad. 'What did he say?' I asked Patrick. 'They don't believe we'll stick together. They sent out a cart with whiskey—a drink for every man goes back to work.' Patrick walked the eight miles back, that staff held high above his head. Not a man took the whiskey and went back to work. Three more days and three more meetings and the commissioners gave in. They paid the fellows what they were owed, didn't cut wages. The lads never forgot Patrick, nor did the bosses. Got to be any time the men were being treated unfairly, they'd ask Patrick to have a word with any of the bosses. Oh, he and Hough had many a go-round, but even Hough respects Patrick Kelly."

✧ ✧ ✧

Hours later I heard the boarders come home, and the next morning I found Patrick sitting at Molly's kitchen table, waiting for Paddy, Johnny Og, and Thomas.

"Saint Stephen's Day," I said to him. "In Ireland we'd still be celebrating Christmas—in the before times, at least."

"The before times," he repeated.

The boys came in, heavy-footed and sleepy.

"Come on, you lot," Patrick said. As they left, I heard Patrick saying, "First to Hough's to tell him you're quitting."

"But I don't want to leave," Thomas said.

"Then don't," Patrick said, and they were gone.

❖ ❖ ❖

"A real forge, Mam! And I struck a mighty blow," Paddy said. "Like Da. And see me?" He spread open his arms. "Only soot, Mam," he said, showing me his black shirt, his streaked face. "No blood. And there's horses, Mam! One's the same color as Champion."

Johnny Og was over the moon, too. At the boatworks, Michael Gibson had let him rig a sail. "He said I have a knack for it, and I told him my da was a fisherman, though I never met him. 'Cause he's dead."

"Say 'deceased,' Johnny Og," Máire said. Lizzie McKenna had told us to say our husbands were "deceased"—more respectable.

Patrick came to Molly's after dinner. We were in the kitchen with Molly, washing the dishes, the children in our room.

"I sold the furs," Patrick said. "Sit down."

We sat at the table as he set ten twenty-dollar gold pieces in front of us.

"My," said Molly.

"There, Molly," said Patrick. "That should pay their room and board for a year."

"Ten months, anyway," she said.

"Now wait," Máire started.

"Thank you, Patrick," I said. "You're very kind."

"Wait now," Máire said. "We can't keep living all of us in one room. We need our own flat. There's one for rent across Hickory Street, 2703, three bedrooms, a kitchen, and a parlor. Thirty dollars a month."

"Reasonable enough," said Molly, "though you'd have to buy food and wood."

"You're better staying here, Honora," Patrick said.

Máire kicked me under the table.

"We're not, Patrick, and Molly would agree."

"Well," she said, "some of the boarders do think small children can be noisy, and I've never had women here before because some are awful flirts. Not that I'm accusing, but having you here"—she looked at Máire—"makes it hard to say no to others."

I could see Máire drawing herself up to answer Molly.

"You're right, Molly, it's time to move," I said.

"The decision's yours and Máire's," Patrick said.

"It is," Máire said.

"You'll need beds and kitchen things," said Molly. "And will the boys' wages pay for wood and food, things for the baby—doctors, medicine . . ." She stopped.

"I'll get a job," said Máire. "And, of course, you, Patrick, you could get a fine job somewhere."

Patrick and Molly started laughing together.

"Dear God," Molly said. "Businessmen in Chicago may have to negotiate with Patrick Kelly, but they'd draw the line at hiring him."

Patrick nodded. "I have my own work, Máire."

"As you keep saying, but—"

"We'll manage, Patrick," I said. "After the baby, I was thinking I could do some teaching at home, hold Irish classes, maybe. When I speak to Paddy and Jamesy in Irish, they answer me in English. Surely other children are losing our language, too."

"I wouldn't count on that as a moneymaker, Honora," Molly said.

"Well, then maybe I could write letters for the boarders."

"Now that's a good idea." Molly nodded.

"If you think you can bring in enough money." Patrick shrugged.

"We can," Máire said.

"Your decision," he said again, looking at me. "The hag at the well and the O'Neill brothers."

I was surprised. "You know that story?"

"Michael told me, to let me understand the woman he'd married. So."

Molly and Máire chattered about blankets as Patrick put on his big jacket and walked out. I followed him down the stairs.

"What is it, Honora?" he said when we came to the front door.

Only two nights ago I'd opened the door to this fellow, only yesterday morning I'd sat here in that bear skin, blaming him for Michael's death. Now . . . I have to ask him.

"Patrick," I said, "the crozier—Saint Grellan's . . . uhm . . . Molly said you used it to rally the men for the strike."

"I did."

"I was wondering. Where is it?"

"At Saint Patrick's. Father Donohue wanted it on the altar for Midnight Mass. Holy relics are hard to come by in America, let alone in Chicago. I'm taking it back today."

"Oh. Well, I was thinking, the crozier's so valuable and, like you say, rare, especially here, being gold and all. And getting by is a worry, even with your money. It's so easy to fall behind and, I mean, wouldn't you get a fortune of money for the crozier—thousands, even?"

"You think I should sell it?"

"Only to the right person, of course. The bishop, say, and give the cozier its own altar at Saint Patrick's."

"The bishop couldn't pay a penny for it. The Church here doesn't have money. And Father Donohue was nervous about even taking the loan of it. 'What if the church burned down?' he said to me."

"But surely someone would buy it."

"Who? There's no Royal Irish Academy here, no National Museum. Oh, there are those who would take it for the gold, melt it down—"

"That would be a sin and a sacrilege!"

"It would be," Patrick said, and walked out.

I followed him out into the cold night. He turned and gave me that hard stare of his.

"I thought you understood, Honora. I need it for the work. When I ride into a mining camp in Colorado or sit around the fire with the men who cut timber in the North Woods or meet with fellows digging for coal in Pennsylvania . . . After we talk about Ireland and what she needs and how they can help her, I pass the crozier from one to the next. Each one holds it and takes the oath. No informers or traitors would dare take the oath because the crozier would burn the flesh off their hands."

"An oath to do what?"

"To fight back." He held up one finger. "Sooner than you think, Honora. The soft underbelly of the British Empire is only a few days' ride north of us."

"I don't understand."

"Canada," he said. "Mostly French and Irish and Indians up there, and all of them hate the Sassenach. There are Ojibwa tribes on both sides of the border ready to join us."

Barney McGurk was walking toward us. "Patrick, I was looking for you at McKenna's. You put Hough in his place today, reminded him that we Irishmen must be respected." He turned to me. "Should have been there, Honora."

"Ask Barney, Honora," Patrick said. Then to him, "You fought to get Texas for America less than two years ago. And who led the troops? Irishmen like James Shields and Thomas Sweeny. Am I right, Barney?"

"True enough, Patrick. But we paid a price."

"Always a price," Patrick said as he turned away from us onto the dark street.

"Where are you going?" I asked.

"Things to do," Patrick said.

"Of course, Patrick," said Barney. "Ná habair tada."

"But you're not leaving, are you?" I asked Patrick. "We're grateful, and it's good to have you here. You won't just go?!"

"I'll be back," he said.

"But when?"

"I'll be back," he said, and was gone.

"That's Patrick Kelly for you," Barney said as we went up the stairs.

❖   ❖   ❖

When Paddy asked me the next day, "Where is he?" I told him: "He'll be back."

"Abrupt fellow," Máire said.

Three days later, we moved.

"Sure it's far from a parlor we were reared!" Máire said as we hung Granny's penal cross over the fireplace.

The parlor windows faced two ways. One looked east toward Lake Michigan and the sunrise and the other west to the prairie, so the room was always sunny. Did you arrange the views, Michael, a stór? We bought a used horsehair sofa and a big easy chair and set them in front of the fireplace.

All the boys slept in one bedroom, but each had his own small bed. Bridget, Stephen, and I had a double bed in the other room, Gracie and Máire in the third. With all we bought, we were still able to pay three months' rent and have twenty dollars. I was grateful.

❖   ❖   ❖

Three months later on Easter morning, Father Donohue brought the first letter from Patrick to us. I opened it right away, not waiting until after Mass. News of our brothers, maybe, or Patrick telling us when he'd be back.

Instead, Patrick wrote that Mam and Da were dead. He'd met a fellow newly come from Ard/Carna. The fever got Mam and Da soon after Christmas, Patrick wrote us. He was very sorry for our troubles.

"What?" Máire whispered to me as Father Donohue started the entrance prayer. I handed her the letter. "No!" she said. I took her hand. Paddy looked over at us.

Mam. Da. We would never see them again.

Father Donohue was preaching now. Resurrection. Death defeated. Eternal life. Together in heaven. Please God.

In our new parlor, Máire and I keened for our parents.

"We're all very sad, Mam. Stephen, too," Jamesy told me.

But, I wondered, did they really remember? So much of home seemed to be fading from them.

❖ ❖ ❖

Michael Joseph Kelly was born in May of that year, 1849. I clutched the Mary Bean, but the pains of childbirth lasted only a few hours as I pushed Michael into life. Lizzie held my shoulders and prayed away to St. Bridget. Michael was a fine heathy fellow—eight pounds. He gave one short cry and then smiled—truly, he smiled. He fastened onto my nipple. My breasts were full of milk for him. Michael Kelly. Our son, a stór, born in Amerikay.

Each dawn I nursed Michael in the parlor, sitting in my easy chair, a small fire taking the chill from a Chicago early summer morning. Baby Michael and I would watch the sun coming out of the Lake and into the window, and then I'd look out the back at the prairie to see the new grass and spring-gold willows, the froth of apple blossoms and one stand of furled maple buds stretching up to the warmth.

Catherine Robinson had shown me where wild blackberries grew and pointed out the old apple trees. She and the other Potawatomis had left in late April, their land taken for a glue factory. I missed her, and our ones missed the Indian children.

Spring would have turned the fields at home every shade of green. I thought of how our land at Knocnacuradh took the light first. I closed my eyes and escaped into the past, lulled by the soft, steady pull of Michael Joseph Kelly at my breast.

Baby Michael lost my nipple and started crying.

"Whist, whist," I said, "there, now . . . grab on now, mo buachaill." I sang Mam's lullaby to him. "A long, long way from our home place, a rún," I whispered to the baby. "I wish you could see Galway Bay, my American boy." He never would. "We'll go to Lake Michigan, and I'll show you waves like the ones at home."

A trumpet sounded—the first canal boat of the day arriving. Men hurried toward the dock, ready to unload the boat, to send those tons of wheat off to the grain elevators. The packinghouse closed at this time of year, so the men were glad to have work on the boats, in the brickyard, or the quarry. No slack season in Paddy's blacksmith shop or at the boatyard, and Thomas still needed at Hough's. Jamesy and Daniel were doing well at school. Patrick's word with the teacher had certainly . . .

"Mam!" It was Jamesy. "Thomas is taking my socks!"

"I'm not, Aunt Honey! They're mine!"

"They're not!"

"Paddy hit me, Aunt Honey!"

"Daniel hit me, Mam!" Paddy said.

"Honora?" Máire's voice. "Would you put the coffee on? Can't be late at the Shop today—inventory."

The Shop. Patrick had helped her get a job at a much bigger place than Croaker's. Máire was full of ideas on how to make it better, conspiring with a young clerk named Marshall Field.

I put Michael on my hip and started toward the kitchen. You'd think Patrick would want to see the new baby. "I'll be back." When?

"Where do you think Uncle Patrick is?" Jamesy asked me at least once a week.

"He could be anywhere," I told him.

"Uncle Patrick's on a secret mission," Paddy had told Máire and me.

"Your uncle's a wild man," Máire had said to him. "Let him stay where he is."

"He'll be back," I'd say. "Patrick has a way of showing up when you least expect it."

"Mam!" Bridget now. "These boys!"

"Yes, Bridget."

Part Four

The Wars

1861~1866

CHAPTER 28

*A*PRIL 12, 1861. I looked at the date I'd written on the fair copy of the letter I'd done for one of Molly's boarders. April 12—one month until Michael's birthday. He'll be twelve in May.

So.

We'd been in Chicago twelve and a half years. In any Irish village we'd still be blow-ins, but here we were considered one of the founding families of Bridgeport. "I remember when a Potawatomi family lived across Bubbly Creek, when we picked wild apples and blueberries, and the open prairie came right up to the canal," I'd say to the newcomers flooding into Bridgeport. Hard for them to imagine there'd ever been empty space here, now that new rolling mills, packinghouses, and factories butted up against the quickly built wooden houses and flats that filled street after street. Never called Hardscrabble anymore.

"We'll be incorporated into Chicago within the next two years. Guaranteed," James McKenna said.

Plenty of work for everyone, and all our fellows doing well. Paddy, at only twenty, was a full partner in Slattery's, the busiest forge in Bridgeport, and Johnny Og near ran Gibson's Boat Works. Years ago, probably on the Christmas Jamesy was eleven, Patrick Kelly had gotten him taken on as an apprentice to the carpenter who built sets at McVicker's, the theater that replaced Rice's. And didn't the musicians in the orchestra take to Jamesy after they heard him play his tin whistle? They taught him other instruments, and now, at eighteen, he plays flute and all manner of horns in the orchestra and couldn't be happier. That same year, Patrick brought Daniel to Mr. Rosa, the barrel maker, and he's still there. Good work, well paid, making more at seventeen than older men do in the packinghouses.

Patrick Kelly comes to see us for a week every Christmas. "The General," Máire calls him, "here to inspect us and sort us out."

"Doing his duty for Michael's children," I said to her. "A brother's love."

Because of the good-paying jobs Patrick arranged for the older boys, the younger children had been able to stay in school—students, and not at the Bridgeport School. All four went into downtown Chicago every day. Bridget, sixteen, and Gracie, thirteen, were St. Xavier's girls.

One Christmas, Patrick had taken Máire and me to meet the principal, Mother Mary Francis de Sales. Surprising, how easy he was with this stern-looking woman. Patrick told us later that a botched dental operation had left her with that forbidding look. "Knew her in the early days when the Sisters of Mercy first came to Chicago," he said. Mother told us she'd never forget how Patrick would leave a load of potatoes or cabbage at the convent door. Happy to give scholarships to his nieces, she said, and now both Bridget and Gracie were at the top of their class.

Father Dunne at St. Patrick's had been glad to have Stephen and Michael in the parish school. "Pay what you can," he'd said. Both boys were earning good grades, and young Michael had been chosen for the choir. He'd inherited his father's singing voice as well as Michael's blue eyes, height, and breadth. Stephen, just turned fourteen, was "Red" to his classmates. A gift for friendship, that fellow has. Hadn't the men at the firehouse made him a kind of mascot, even taking him on the fire runs? I wondered, did Patrick Kelly have a word there, too? I know he rescued Thomas from bother over his gambling debts at Mike McDonald's. Now Thomas only played poker backstage at McVicker's with Jamesy and the actors. No credit issued there. Patrick told Thomas if he gave three-quarters of his pay as Hough's clerk to Máire, he could wager the rest. Thomas called himself Pyke now. Máire'd shrugged. He was nineteen. Let him be who he pleased.

The way Patrick Kelly, in his fringed leggings and moccasins, managed to move the levers of Chicago amazed me. Lizzie McKenna said that Patrick was a throwback to Billy Caldwell, the Irish-Indian Chicago pioneer. "We are a frontier town, after all."

"Patrick Kelly's got clout," James McKenna had explained to me—a Chicago word for a kind of power that didn't depend on money or education or position in the world but was a measure of the force a man had inside him. "Patrick Kelly gets things done. Fellows listen to him," he said. "He's a good friend, a bad enemy, and that's known."

I knew that Patrick had a hand in organizing the big march on City Hall in the mid-fifties when the Know Nothings took over Chicago. An awful year. A group called Americans on Guard had elected this fellow Levi Boone as mayor. He wanted to get rid of the Irish, build a wall around Amerikay to keep all immigrants out. Chicago passed a law saying only the native-born could be policemen and that naturalized citizens couldn't vote in city elections until they'd resided in Chicago for twenty-five years. Amerikay was turning on us. But when Boone and the others tried to close the saloons and beer halls, they went too far. That united Irish and German. Patrick raised up Grellan's crozier, led the demonstrations, and negotiated the settlement, too. The businessmen in Chicago saw sense. The *Chicago Tribune* might call us degraded drunkards and insult our Catholic religion, but the merchants needed our money and the manufacturers our muscles, Patrick said. And right he was.

But what I appreciated most about Patrick was the way he made Michael live for my children. He gave them something of their father. Every Christmas evening—after we'd made our annual visit to Professor Lang and his family, eating the German cakes Sligo-born Ellen Lang baked and admiring their giant Christmas tree—we would gather around the fire in our own parlor. Patrick, Máire, and I sipped whiskey, and the children drank sweetened tea thick with milk while Patrick told us stories. Not old Irish tales, but his memories of their father as a boy.

"Uncle Patrick, tell us 'Saving the Baby Da,'" Jamesy would say, or Paddy might ask for "Racing on the Course." Bridget liked to hear "My Granny Kelly," and Stephen wanted tales of the big blacksmith Murty Mor. The Christmas he was four, young Michael told Patrick that he remembered his da from when he was a big boy in Ireland. Patrick invented memories of Johnny Leahy for Johnny Og, and on Christmas night two years ago he'd told Thomas, Daniel, and Gracie that he'd discovered Robert Pyke had died in an accident in India, trying to rescue soldiers who'd fallen into a raging river. "Very convincing," Máire said to him later, "though I don't believe a word of it. Still, better a dead hero for a father than a living scoundrel. Thank you, Patrick."

Then long after the others went to their beds, Patrick and I shared our own Christmas ritual: We talked politics, Irish politics, hurling history at each other until dawn.

Only physical force could liberate Ireland, Patrick maintained, while I argued for a mass movement and monster meetings, done peacefully, with support from the Irish in America.

"The British only understand violence. We need an army," Patrick would say.

"You can't ask people who've barely survived starvation to risk themselves, when even writing rebellion receives a death sentence," I'd answer.

On and on. Patrick didn't waver. He believed in the principles of Young Ireland. Barney McGurk hinted to me that Patrick Kelly had a hand in helping the condemned leaders of the 1848 uprising—Mitchel, Meagher, and MacManus—to escape from Australia. Patrick told me himself he'd met those fellows in America and had gone with them on their speaking tours of the country. He'd brought John Mitchel to Chicago and taken the whole bunch of us down to hear him speak at the new St. Patrick's Parish Hall. Mitchel called for armed rebellion in Ireland and got great cheers from a crowd of men who'd be safe in their beds within the hour. Nice to see Patrick Kelly that added time, however.

Máire, though in no way interested in "the wild man" for herself, was still curious about his women. "Surely there are some," she'd said to me. And when she'd said to him, "I know you've an Indian princess devoted to you up there in the North Woods," he'd answered, "And why should an Indian woman accept a neglectful husband?"

I'd said to Máire that Roisin Dubh, the Dark Rosaleen—Ireland—was the only woman had captured Patrick Kelly. But then she'd said that surely a fellow so, so male got a bit of "this and that" somewhere, if I took her meaning. Everyone needed "this and that," except maybe "Saint Honora," she'd told me.

And I'd said that I'd had plenty of "this and that" with Michael, thank you very much, and would treasure those memories forever. She'd said she herself preferred present realities to distant memories. If a gentleman buyer, visiting from out of town, wanted to take her to dinner a time or two and then invited her to his room in the Tremont House, well . . .

"All right, Máire, enough," I'd said.

"Oh, never the married ones," she'd told me, "but young men often appreciate an older woman," trying to shock me, but I'd set her back on her heels all right.

The look on Máire's face when I said to her, "Really, all you're doing is following the Brehon laws of ancient Ireland. That code set out ten lawful relationships between a man and woman for the purpose of 'this and that.' The union of an older woman and a younger man was one of those—no dowry exchanged, nothing long-lasting expected— an education for the fellow and some fun for the woman." That had stopped her. She'd looked so surprised, I started laughing. "I'm not Saint Honora or a nun, either. Michael was the love of my life and now I'm happy to raise our children," I'd told her.

Máire wasn't the only one curious about Patrick Kelly and women. Over the years, any number of widows and single girls intercepted him after Christmas Mass at St. Patrick's—talking away to him, smiling up into his eyes—very forward altogether.

"Rude," I'd said to Máire last Christmas as we'd watched Katie McGee going on to Patrick on the church steps, touching his arm. "Embarrassing for Patrick." But Máire had said that he seemed to enjoy Katie, and maybe he would marry a young woman, have children—after all, a man's never past it.

"Patrick's fifty-one," I'd said. "Very fit and good-looking, I'll give him that," Máire'd said. "Ah well, maybe he is wed to Ireland, as you say."

"He is," I'd said.

I remembered how Patrick had moved away from Katie and stood, watching people make visits to the side altar where Father Dunne had set Grellan's crozier, another Christmas tradition. Families knelt together at the rail. Fathers pointed at the golden staff, whispering to their children. Then, heads bowed, they'd pray, "God save Ireland. Grant her freedom."

Máire had teased Patrick at that Christmas dinner about Katie's attentions. Other Irish revolutionaries had wives, she'd said. Hadn't Meagher married the daughter of a very rich New York Yankee family? The woman was maybe a little long in the tooth, but now money was no problem for him. If Patrick got a fine suit of clothes and started orating, maybe an heiress would fall for him and then we'd all be on the pig's back.

He'd laughed then, but later that night he'd told me how the wives of the Young Ireland men had suffered when their husbands were in jail. Many of the women had no proper home, little money. Even now, the men were always gone, in danger from British agents even in America. Mrs. Mitchel and her children moved from pillar to post—Paris, then New York, Tennessee, Virginia. And there were the struggles within the revolutionary groups—not a life you'd wish on a wife. Patrick had gone quiet then.

That was last Christmas.

✧ ✧ ✧

"Honora! Honora!" Máire called to me from the parlor doorway.

"Máire, what is it?"

"I've been standing here watching you stare down at the letter, not writing a word. Gone astray. Off with the fairies."

"Sorry, Máire."

"And me late for the Shop. Still, Mr. Potter Palmer mightn't even notice. All the fellows do now is ask each other, 'Will there be war?' On and on. Mr. Palmer's wife's a southerner, though he's all for Abe Lincoln. I'd better hurry, though Marshall will make up an excuse for me if anyone asks."

Since that first Christmas when Patrick had arranged for Máire's job, she'd made herself an essential part of the grand emporium she called the Shop.

She walked over to the window. "We need new curtains. You can see the wear on these in the spring sunshine. How old are they?"

"Let's see," I said. "We bought them the Christmas Patrick came from the gold fields. Remember? He brought all the boys jackknives, even the little ones, and rag dolls for Gracie and Bridget. Bridget wasn't in school yet, so 1850."

"You have to go through all that? Can't you say we've had them ten years? You sound like the old ones at home, counting backward and forward from the summer the donkey kicked a hole in the shed. And not even knowing their own true age because they can't name the year they were born."

"I know our ages all right, Máire. I'm thirty-eight and you're forty."

"And both of us sticking it well," she said, pulling me over to the large looking glass she'd purchased from the Shop at half its usual price. Máire pinched her cheeks, then brushed her upper lashes with her finger. "A tiny bit of bacon grease makes them darker. You should try it. And rub some of that cream I bought into your skin. Helps with wrinkles, though we've not too many."

Her face was smooth—only a few tiny lines around her blue eyes. So like Mam.

Máire threw back her shoulders. "Bosoms still standing up straight, thank God." She looked over at my image. "You've some curves now, Honora, but a girl's figure still, and those high cheekbones and greeny gold eyes—lovely. Only for that stick-straight hair . . . Ah well. I've a strand or two of gray, but my curls hide it." She smiled at herself and at me. "Molly says that new boarder thought I was Johnny Og's sister, not his mother."

"You could be," I said.

"The widows," she said, and laughed. "Not that we couldn't have married again. But, of course, you're so—"

"Don't start, Máire," I said. "Don't start."

She liked to tease me about Barney McGurk. He'd only proposed to me out of politeness because he spent so much time in our kitchen. Too afraid to ask Máire. And there had been fellows who'd come to me for the letter writing and would start to ramble on about needing a good wife and not minding about the children. Easy enough to discourage them. I loved Michael and always would. There'd never be another man for me. Máire knew that.

"Why don't *you* find a husband? Still time," I said.

Which was true enough. Women in their thirties and even early forties in Bridgeport still gave birth, often to the babies of second marriages. Fellows died young. What was a woman to do? And a man who lost a wife needed a mother for his children.

Máire settled a feathered hat on her head. "A woman's worth more than a dowry," she said. "Jesus, see the time on my new wind-up wall clock? I'll miss the Archer Road horsecar." And she was off to downtown Chicago.

Quiet in the house with all of them gone. I went back to the letter.

This fellow'd sent news about the war, too. He'd wanted me to assure his mother there wouldn't be one, and if there was, he wouldn't be fighting. Didn't bear thinking about.

Bridgeport had supported Stephen Douglas for president. We were Democrats, after all, and hoped he'd find a way to keep North and South from fighting. But the southern members of the party had opposed Douglas and put up their own candidate against him.

President Lincoln was elected. The southern states left the Union. Bad times coming.

Slavery. What had Sister Henriette called it, "the great sin" of America? I thought of M'am Jacques. She'd been sold away from her own mother as a child, she told me. A terrible evil, no question. I agree with the abolitionists. I only wish they weren't so hateful about Catholics. Patrick Kelly said Abraham Lincoln would use force if necessary to keep the South. "Divide America in two and England will march in and take over the whole place. That's why we need Canada to rebel against the Crown and join us," Patrick had told me.

Patrick said that the southern slave owners were like landlords in Ireland. Both groups made worlds of their own on big estates and really believed there were people put on this earth to serve them. Their property, not people.

The woman receiving the letter would have only one concern: Let my son be safe. Every mother's prayer.

I wonder, does Patrick Kelly understand how much I want ordinary happiness for my boys—to marry, have children, do decent work, be healthy? During the Great Starvation, such a life seemed unattainable. Now it was within our grasp. But Patrick didn't value the ordinary. His life had a different purpose. One Christmas evening—ten years ago?—he'd tried to explain himself to me.

❖ ❖ ❖

"I was spared so I could serve the Cause," he'd said. "I should be dead."

Then he'd told me the story. He began with his voyage to America. Martin O'Malley had arranged passage for Patrick soon after he'd left Michael and me on Grace O'Malley's island in Ballynahinch Lake. But the vessel was a coffin ship, Patrick told me, an old slaver, and the captain and crew were former Blackbirders. Nasty fellows. One of the sailors tried to attack a young Irish girl and Patrick fought the fellow— killed him. Self-defense, Patrick said, but he was put in irons and sent to jail when the ship docked in Quebec. Some of the passengers testified for Patrick at the trial, said he saved the girl's honor. The British judge had laughed at that. Honor? Most of the prostitutes in Montreal were Irish, the judge had said. Maybe the girl had been looking for business, and Patrick was only jealous. Condemned to death, and they didn't even know he was wanted in Ireland.

"Missed a trick there," Patrick'd said, "though I suppose they couldn't hang me twice."

He'd escaped. One of the prison guards was from Kerry. The father of the girl he'd saved gave him a horse, "along with some food and Grellan's crozier—they'd gotten it off the ship," Patrick had said.

Irish farmers in the Canadian wilderness aided him, but he was a wanted man. Posters out with a sketch of him on them, rewards offered. Patrick had to keep moving. He traded the horse for food and went on foot, trying to get across the border to the United States. Winter caught him alone in a wild forest without food or shelter. He'd come to the end of his strength and was sick with fever when the Ojibwa found him.

There was an Irishman called Martin Lynch with the tribe. They'd been trapping in Canada and now were headed south to Wisconsin for the winter—1847. Black '47, and him cut off from any news of Ireland and dying to boot. "Only for Martin Lynch asking the chief to hold a medewien healing service for me, I would be dead," he'd told me.

"Medewien?" I'd asked him.

"Whites call the priests 'medicine men,' but no one outside the tribes really understands who they are. These men form a secret society. They learn rituals and herbal cures," Patrick had said. He'd explained to me that the priests memorized the lore, laws, and stories of their people.

"As the Irish poets of ancient times did," I'd said.

"That's right," Patrick had said. "Those at the highest levels of initiation led the ceremonies to honor the Manitou."

"What is the Manitou?" I'd asked.

"That's their word for God, but he's not like the Christian God. Doesn't hand out rewards and punishments. The Ojibwa believe God's in everyone and everything—animals and trees, flowers and rocks, the sky, the wind—a very spiritual people altogether."

The ceremony that had cured him took seven days, he'd told me. The priests had shot at him with magic seashells.

"Shot at you?" I'd asked.

"To kill me, symboliclike. Then I came back to life, cured," Patrick had said.

But he'd been weak enough all through that first winter at the village he called Waaswaaganing, which meant, he'd said, "the place you fish with torches." He'd been very eloquent, describing the lakes and pine forests and the clever ways the Ojibwa knew to live off the land, but the strange part of the tale, Patrick had said, concerned the Ojibwa's attitude toward Grellan's crozier. It seems the chief medewien priest, a fellow called Bald Eagle, Migizi, was quite fascinated with the spirals and zigzags incised in the gold. Patrick told him the staff had belonged to a great medicine man and that Patrick's clan, the Kellys, had carried it into battle. Patrick had even explained its truth-compelling properties.

This Bald Eagle insisted Patrick go with him on a kind of sacred journey. Patrick had said they'd traveled east for days, portaging between rivers and then walking through dense forest—the start of spring, buds on the trees. They'd come to a clearing in the woods and a huge cave. Patrick had said a dolmen was guarding the entrance.

"You've lost me there," I'd said. "A dolmen? You mean like the giant stone structures at home?"

"Not 'like'—identical," he'd answered. "A huge boulder, many tons, balanced on slender pillars. Dolmen. I know it sounds impossible, but I saw it."

"Well, maybe in ancient times the Indians had similar—"

"I told you—not similar, the *same*, and next to the dolmen there was an ogham stone."

"You mean something like an ogham stone?"

"Not like, not similar, *the same*. Carved with Celtic crosses and zigzag lines—the exact symbols that are on Grellan's crozier! That's what Migizi wanted me to see."

"Well, maybe Irish people came from Canada," I'd said. "They could have. . . ."

But Patrick had told me that the place was ancient. Migizi said the structures had been there since the beginning of Ojibwa history. Besides, what Irishman stumbling off a coffin ship in Canada and walking down into what must have been New Hampshire would decide to spend a year or two carving stones?

"But who, then?" I'd asked.

"I don't know! I've heard that Saint Brendan sailed west to Tír na nOg."

"And Columbus came to Galway to look at navigation charts in the old monastic manuscripts. So you think Irishmen were here before Columbus?"

"I did, standing there looking at the dolmen. I did. How's that for a revelation? The Irish discovered America!"

And if that wasn't strange enough, they'd found a family of runaway slaves hiding in the cave, waiting to cross over into Canada. That night, Patrick had stood under the dolmen, lifted up the crozier, and pledged himself to Ireland. No ordinary happiness for him. Patrick Kelly said that he now knew with certainty that he had a special destiny.

❖ ❖ ❖

Ah well, eight months before I'd see him again. A long time. I do look forward to seeing Patrick. What harm?

Better get moving—almost noon by Máire's clock. Must shop at Piper's store. The food this crowd goes through. I wish we'd rented a patch of land west in Brighton, put in cabbages the way the Healys and Malones do. I'll stop to ask Molly how she's fixed—near sixty and she'd hardly changed. Lizzie McKenna, too, younger since her sons came home, back from their wanderings and helping James with the tavern. Then I'll report to Father Kelly at St. Bridget's. "Call me Father Tom," he'd told us. Imagine Father Gilley saying that. Different, the priests in Chicago.

I'd do a few hours' work at the parish office, entering this week's weddings and baptisms in the record book. Thank you, Miss Lynch, for my neat handwriting. Twenty-five cents from Father, another quarter from this fellow when he picks up the letter. And I'd two more men coming tonight wanting me to write home for them, and Mrs. Gilligan asked for help with her naturalization papers. Máire says don't I get bored not leaving Bridgeport, but she doesn't know the half of what goes on. If I didn't move rightly, I could spend my whole day chatting to the neighbors. I don't envy her downtown Chicago, I thought as I left 2703 and set out along Hickory Street.

Not that it wasn't nice to go to McVicker's Theatre with Jamesy once in a while for the plays and music. Wouldn't have missed little Mary McVicker in *Uncle Tom's Cabin*. She's all grown up now. The

McVickers were very friendly with Edwin Booth, who appeared at the theater often. Edwin Booth, "The finest actor in America," Jamesy says. And we'd all gone downtown to watch the men lift up the Tremont House. The city had put in underground sewers that raised the streets above the buildings. Nothing to do but raise the buildings. The entrance to the Tremont was four feet below street level. Two hundred Irishmen used logs and chains and their strong backs to wrench that huge building off its foundation and bring it up inch by inch to meet the street. Impressive. But that was Chicago for you, running to catch up with itself. Frenzied. Thank God they hadn't figured a way to build on top of Lake Michigan. Though the railroad tracks went out over the water now, I still had my swath of strand to stand upon and the wide blue waters to watch.

"Gone to Galway Bay," Máire would tell the boys if they came home on a Saturday afternoon and couldn't find me. I'd taken Stephen and Michael to play on the sand as little fellows and used to get the whole bunch to go there on a summer Sunday for a good stretch of the legs after Mass.

No longer. Busy. All of them too busy.

❖ ❖ ❖

Mrs. Cooley, Father Kelly's housekeeper, let me into the rectory. Very grand we were getting at St. Bridget's. When our new brick church is finished, we'll be the equal of any parish in the city. Some are going too far—the money spent on Holy Family Church—but then that's a Jesuit parish. We'd built our pastor a comfortable but modest priest's house with a separate room for the parish office, where I worked.

"Thank you, Mrs. Cooley," I said to her, a Kerry woman, a widow, and a friend of Lizzie McKenna's, but stern Mrs. Cooley would never waltz with a Potawatomi brave as Lizzie had done. Though I'd say Father Kelly might have enjoyed saying Mass on the bar in McKenna's Tavern.

"Didn't see your sister at the mission last week," Mrs. Cooley said to me as she let me into the office.

"She works downtown, you know," I said.

"At night?"

Mrs. Cooley went on about how we all had a duty to attend the annual three-day series of sermons and services presided over by one special band of Order priests that moved from parish to parish, shocking sinners into repentance with terrifying descriptions of hell and the Last Judgment. "Woe to" priests, Máire called them—"Woe to you who . . ." they'd roar, and then list all possible transgressions. "Examine your conscience!" Father Allen had commanded last week, looking straight at a row of women. "Ask yourself, 'Have I sinned in my thoughts? In my words? Am I condemning myself to hell?' You pray for your husbands and your sons and neglect your own souls! If *you* are not in the state of grace, God will not hear your prayers!" Unsettling, that. Bridgeport mothers hadn't bothered too much about mortal sins—who had time to commit any? But thoughts? Words? There were long lines at the confession booths after that sermon. On Sunday, Father Tom had joked about all the halos in the congregation and said such a lot of saints would surely be generous. The second collection would be for the building fund.

"Here you are, Mrs. Kelly." Father Tom handed me a pile of marriage applications. Would I go through them and schedule dates for the weddings? Father Tom was about thirty, I'd say, born in Ireland but educated and ordained in America. "A lot of these, Mrs. Kelly. I suppose it's the threat of war makes couples want to act quickly."

"Surely some way will be found to avoid war," I said.

"I pray for peace, Mrs. Kelly, but if the worst comes, America will find Irishmen ready and able for the battle. Our actions will silence those who question our patriotism and insult our religion.

"Now . . ." Father Kelly shuffled through the letters—most of which I'd helped the couples write—and set a few on the side. "Problems here," he said. "Impediments."

"Pardon me? I don't understand."

"This man"—he pointed to the letter—"wants to marry his dead wife's sister."

"And that's forbidden?"

"Affinity. Too closely related, against canon law."

"Oh." Canon law?

"They could get a dispensation from the bishop, but Bishop Duggan's not the easiest man to deal with."

I had to ask: "Could a man marry his brother's widow?"

"Not without a dispensation from the impediment," he said. "Forbidden."

"Forbidden?" My voice sounded strange and there was a ringing in my ears.

Father turned to me, concerned. "Are you feeling well, Mrs. Kelly?"

"I'm fine, Father. A bit dizzy."

"Shall I call Mrs. Cooley?"

"No! I mean, I'm fine, really. Warm in here, I think. I'd best get on with these."

He left the office. In that instant I realized how important Patrick Kelly had become to me. My body was saying what my mind wouldn't admit. Too closely related, and what I felt for Patrick was not sisterly. Look at the way I'd spent all morning thinking of him. What have I done?

I entered the names in Father's book with possible dates and hurried away.

Impediment. The word came back as I walked along Hickory Street. Impediment. Left foot, right foot.

✤ ✤ ✤

Bridget had Gracie, Stephen, and Michael bent over their homework and the dinner ready when I came in. She could run the whole household. She'll graduate with high honors unless she lets some lad distract her. I was her age, sixteen, when Michael came to me from the sea.

Michael . . . In my mind all the time, I believed he somehow read my thoughts. He knew I'd always been faithful to our love, but now, to have these feelings about Patrick, his own brother, when the Church itself forbade any such relationship. Of course, I've never done anything, but be honest, Honora, all those thoughts. Sins every one. Drive those thoughts away. Keep busy. Keep your mind occupied. Remember, the mission priest said, thoughts can send you to hell.

I concentrated on the children and on dinner. Máire wasn't home, nor were the boys. "We'll wait," I said to Bridget.

Eight o'clock and they still hadn't appeared. We ate. Nine o'clock came and went. Where were they?

At half-past nine Paddy marched into the kitchen, the other boys behind him. "It's war, Mam. We're all enlisting."

They stood together, the five of them. Men. God help me. My sons.

Paddy looked at me with his father's eyes—sky blue, rimmed in violet. He folded his arms. They were thick with muscles from striking the mighty blow at Slattery's forge. Twenty-one years old in June. At eighteen, Jamesy was as tall as Paddy, but leaner, with only a trace left of his round baby face. He was still able to use his "puppy dog face" to convince me of anything. Very serious now, his brother's second in command.

Daniel O'Connell Leahy seemed so young at seventeen. His curls and good humor drew the girls. Solemn tonight. Johnny Og was at Paddy's side—the oldest, twenty-one already, and the shortest, but the steadiest of the lot, the most sensible. And Silken Thomas, nineteen, a gentleman in his fawn trousers and a broadcloth coat, his beak of a nose in the air, but one with them now.

"The secessionists fired on Fort Sumter, Mam. President Lincoln's declared war and we're joining the Irish Brigade," Paddy said. "It's Da's dream come true, Mam."

"The Shields Guards, the Emmet Guards, and the Montgomery Guards are combining," Johnny Og said. "They volunteered every man."

I knew about these groups he mentioned. They were Irish military clubs that paraded through Chicago on St. Patrick's Day and on the Fourth of July. The men wore green jackets with brass buttons, carried rifles, and waved flags embroidered in gold with harps and shamrocks and "Erin Go Bragh"—"Ireland Forever"—and we all cheered them. A great proud moment. March like that in Ireland and the Sassenach would arrest the whole lot. But it was one thing to act fierce on Michigan Avenue and quite another to fight an actual war.

"You're not enlisting," I said.

"You don't understand," said Paddy. "We must rally for the honor of the old land, for the defense of the new. That's what Colonel Mulligan told us at McKenna's. He's leading the brigade."

"He is?" I said.

Though only thirty, James Mulligan was one of the most prominent lawyers in the city and a true Catholic gentleman. He was the first graduate of the University of St. Mary of the Lake and editor of the *Western Tablet,* our Catholic newspaper. A leader of the temperance movement, he'd recently married Marion Nugent, a St. Xavier's girl from a good family. It was James Mulligan I held up to the boys as an example of what they could become.

"Surely you want us to listen to Colonel Mulligan," Jamesy said.

"Not if he's calling you to war," I said.

As I was speaking Máire arrived. She pushed her way through the boys and said, "I don't care if Saint Patrick himself rides down Hickory Street on a white horse. You're not going." She turned to me. "The clerks at the Shop are the same, ready to become an army. Impossible to get through the streets—bands of fellows roaming around shouting how they'll teach those secessionists a lesson."

"We will, Mam," Johnny Og said. "Johnny Reb will learn how Irishmen can fight. Chicago's not the only place brigades are forming. There's Irish units in New York and Michigan and Boston and—"

"No," I said. "No. No."

"The war's only meant to last three months, Mam," Jamesy said. "That's the length of our enlistment, and as soon as we settle the secessionists, we'll sail to Ireland. Free the slaves and the Irish, too."

I kept shaking my head.

"Have you forgotten Lorenzo and Christophe and M'am Jacques?" Paddy asked me. "America's our country. It needs us."

"And we'll have fine uniforms, Mam," Thomas said to Máire.

"A musket apiece," Daniel said, "and a long knife."

"Stop it!" Máire said. "Jesus Christ on his cross, none of you has the slightest idea about soldiering. Didn't I listen often enough to your own father, Thomas and Daniel, telling the old Major how he'd thrown troops against the enemy? Thrown. Cannon fodder, they called the men. Dressed them up in lovely uniforms all right, but cloth won't stop bullets."

"Ah now, Mam." Johnny Og patted her shoulder. "Our officers won't be like the Pykes. Colonel Mulligan and—"

"So you've the whole thing done and dusted," I said. "Well, think again. If your uncle Patrick were here, he'd talk some sense into you."

"But Uncle Patrick is coming, Mam. Colonel Mulligan said so in his speech."

"He did, Mam," Jamesy said. "He told us that Patrick Kelly will bring the golden staff to the meeting so we can swear a true oath on the relic of our ancestors. He's an officer in the Irish Brigade."

"Well, that puts the tin hat on it," Máire said.

✧ ✧ ✧

Patrick will stop them, I told myself as I stood looking at the Lake the next afternoon. He'll tell them they're too young, tell them something. He'll act for Michael. He's their uncle. A member of the family.

I turned away from the dazzle of sunlight on the Lake and headed back to Bridgeport.

A figure came across the strand. "Honora." Patrick Kelly. "Bridget told me I'd find you here," he said when he reached me.

"Patrick. You must talk to the boys. We can't let them get into this war. Paddy, Jamesy, Johnny Og, Thomas, and Daniel are going to Kane's Brewery tonight to enlist."

"It's the Fontenoy Barracks now, Honora."

"Call it what you will. Máire and I won't let our boys . . ."

He stepped close to me. "You can't stop them, Honora," he said. "They're not boys, they're grown men. Irishmen. Warriors, ready to fight for a just cause. When the call comes, only a coward turns away."

"But, Patrick . . ."

"Finally, finally we have our chance," he said. "We've fine officers. Mike Corcoran in New York is a Fenian."

Patrick had told me about the new group of Irish revolutionaries that had begun in New York and took their name from the warriors who followed the legendary Irish chieftain Finn, the Fianna. Many members of the Brotherhood had been born in America, and now they'd all gather together in the Union army, some with the highest ranks, Patrick said.

"James Mulligan will establish a brigade in Chicago," Patrick said. "We have Tom Sweeny in Saint Louis. Young Ireland's with us. Thomas Meagher's raising a regiment with D'Arcy McGee's brother, James, who was an officer in the Papal Guard. There's men joining who've served in the French army, the Spanish army, the Austrian army. It's as if the Wild Geese from all over the world are coming to America, forming a giant 'V' in the sky. Irishmen are banding together to win victory here, in Canada, and then in Ireland herself—A Nation Once Again. If only Michael were here to see it."

"Michael wouldn't want our sons to go to war."

"He'd know there's no choice. If the secessionists destroy the Union, there will be endless wars. Other countries will attack. Britain's already taken the side of the South. The British burnt Washington in 1812, their warships are on Lake Champlain. Why not invade, reclaim North America? British generals are planning it right now, Honora, believe me. And then all hope will be gone. America's our last chance."

"Patrick, if my boys die, politics won't console me."

"It's not politics, Honora. It's survival. And the war won't last long. The North has the men, the factories, the money."

I turned away from him. The sun was going down, moving toward the prairie and night. No way to stop it—like war.

Then Patrick was next to me at the water's edge. I started talking. Not planning the words, I told him about Granny's dying, little Mary Ryan frozen in the ditch, the bodies in the road torn apart by dogs. The horrors I'd kept buried within me spilled out. Patrick had to understand.

"So many mornings at Knocnacuradh I'd wonder, how will I feed them? Now Paddy and Jamesy have grown to be fine, strong young men. They should be finding girls to love, not risking death."

"But think, Honora, they'll be part of the first army of Irishmen to fight for ourselves in three hundred years. We're not serving a foreign cause. We're defending our new land, freeing our homeland."

"But, Patrick, the Irish in the southern states will be fighting, too. My sons could be killed by another boy who survived the Great Starvation, the son of a mother who fed him on nettle tea and somehow brought him alive to Amerikay. It doesn't bear thinking about. I'm for the Union. I want the slaves freed, Ireland saved. But my boys drank horse's blood to survive. To shoot bullets into healthy bodies? Death is my enemy. I can't make death an ally. I've fought against it too long."

He turned me to him and put his arms around me. I let my cheek rest on the smooth leather of his shirt. I started to cry. He held me tighter.

"You've had a terrible hard time," he said. "You've been so strong. Be strong now. You have no choice, a stór. Your sons will go whether you approve or not. Even I couldn't stop them." He patted my back. "You're a warrior, too, Honora. Like Maeve herself. Remember the demonstration in Galway City? How brave you were?" Patrick took me by the shoulders and held me away from him. "Your sons need your strength. Give them your blessing. Michael would want you to."

"Would he?" I took a step back.

Patrick kept a grip on my shoulders. "He would, Honora. He'd march with us, holding Grellan's crozier high, shouting, 'Kelly Abu!—Clear the Way! Hoo-rah!' Michael was a soldier for Ireland. He fell in a brutal war. The Sassenach murdered him and a million more using starvation as their weapon. Here's our chance to begin to avenge those deaths."

"By having more die?"

"Michael Kelly's sons survived because of America. Would you have them stand by and watch this country destroyed?"

"I'm a mother, Patrick. I want my sons safe. Slán."

"Then support them with your love, your faith. A great comfort for them, for me, to know we're protected by your prayers." Patrick put his hand on my cheek.

"My prayers?" I said. I pulled away from him and ran out from behind the rocks toward the road. Patrick called out to me, but I didn't turn. My prayers. Will God even listen to my prayers?

I was on 12th Street now, passing Holy Family, the Jesuit church. I stopped. A huge hulk of a building, stone walls and tall towers—Saturday afternoon. Confession, and the priests here don't know me. I climbed the wide steps into the church—dark.

The enclosed flame in the tabernacle lamp hanging over the main altar drew me forward. Jesus was here. His priest would absolve me, put me in a state of grace, purify my prayers.

Three or four women waited in the pew near the confessional box—strangers to me. Good. My turn came. I knelt in the enclosed space. The shutter over the grill slid back.

"Bless me, Father, for I have sinned," I whispered. What to say? "Father, I have feelings for a man and, I think about him and . . ."

"Are you married?" Impatient.

"Yes. Well, no."

"Which is it, woman?"

"I'm a widow, Father."

"Children?"

"I have five."

"And the man. Is he married?"

"He isn't, Father."

"Not a priest, I hope."

"Oh, dear God, no, Father."

"That's something. Still, a widow with five children has no business having impure thoughts. Marry the fellow. That'll end the nonsense."

"That's not . . . You see, Father, I . . . Please, Father, couldn't I just say my act of contrition now?"

"Not that simple, missus. A good confession requires honesty, not lies and evasions. Making a bad confession is a mortal sin. You're endangering your immortal soul, right now, right here!"

Why hadn't I gone to Holy Name? One priest there's so deaf, Máire says, he gives out the penance—three Hail Marys—before you even finish telling your sins. I want forgiveness, so I can pray for my sons without guilt, and here's this fellow piling new sins on me.

"Answer me, please," the priest said.

"There's no question of marriage, Father. The man doesn't know how I feel."

What are you doing, kneeling in this dark box trying to answer a fool's questions? asked a voice in my head. Granny. *Catch yourself on, Honora. What real wrong have you done?* I need absolution, Granny. I can't risk being on God's bad side. Not now, when my boys need my prayers. *You're not a child, Honora, you—*

"It's no good going silent, missus. Answer me," the priest said.

"Father, as to marriage, there's an impediment."

"Impediment? And where'd you get a word like that? A canon lawyer, are you?"

"No, Father. You see . . ." Just say it. "This man's my brother-in-law. My, uhm, deceased husband's brother."

"A de jure impediment then. A relationship forbidden because of affinity. Some might say such a marriage would violate natural law, as well as the canons. Do you understand?"

"I—"

"He is part of your family circle, regarded as such by your children, your neighbors."

"We don't see him all that much. . . ." But I couldn't deny that Patrick Kelly was woven into our lives beyond the actual amount of time he spent with us. Still, I'd never seen him as my brother, and if this impediment was so serious, how could Father Tom arrange a dispensation? I had to ask. "Isn't there a dispensation, Father?"

"Dispensation? Who are you to be throwing around such words? Obey the Church's law. Stop being a scandal to your children and your neighbors."

"But I haven't done . . . No one knows."

"They always know. Now, have you come for absolution or to argue yourself into hell?"

"Absolution, Father, please."

"Remember, a firm purpose of amendment is a necessary condition for forgiveness. Avoid the man. Put him out of your mind. Thinking of him is a near occasion of sin. Dwelling on those thoughts is a sin in and of itself. Embrace your widowed state. The purpose of marriage is the procreation of children, not sexual congress—real or imagined. For a woman of your age . . ."

I bowed my head as his words lashed me, silencing even Granny. So angry. Surely he'd heard worse.

"Now, say a good act of contrition." As I prayed, he finally let go the Latin words: "*Absolvo te.*"

What I wanted—*those* words, not his. The sacrament. Forgiven. Cleansed. He gave me a whole rosary for a penance, the most I'd ever received. Better say it in this church now.

A rack of vigil lights stood before Our Lady's altar. I found a penny in my purse and put it in the slot.

Hail Mary, full of grace, I prayed, looking up at the serene white statue. Grace. Please, Blessed Mother, keep me in the state of grace. Take our boys under your protection. Please. Let me name them for you: Paddy Kelly, Jamesy Kelly, Johnny Og Leahy, Daniel Leahy, Thomas Leahy Pyke. Remember, too, Most Gracious Virgin, all the Bridgeport fellows enlisting right now, and the Irish boys in Chicago and New York and Boston, the Dohertys in New Orleans, the Mulloys wherever they are. All these young men, so eager for war—wrap your mantle around them. Peace. Ask your Son for peace, Blessed Mother. Our Lady of Sorrows, my patron, you stood at the cross so bravely. Help me. Help all mothers to be strong for our sons. Amen.

I didn't mention Patrick Kelly. I could pray for him later at St. Bridget's.

❖   ❖   ❖

The boys didn't come home for supper. We waited. Bridget, Gracie, Stephen, and Michael finally went to bed. Midnight by Máire's clock.

"And Patrick went to the meeting?" she asked me again and again. "And he knows we don't want the boys to enlist?"

"I told him," I said.

Daniel and James and Thomas came clattering up the stairs first. They stopped when they saw us in the parlor.

Máire hurried over to Daniel. "You didn't enlist, did you?" she asked him.

"I didn't, Mam."

"And you, Thomas?"

"Me either, Mam."

"Oh, thank God," she said, and hugged each of them.

I looked at Jamesy.

"Uncle Patrick wouldn't let us, Mam," Jamesy said. "Not until Paddy and Johnny Og finish their three months."

"What?" said Máire. "What do you mean?"

But none of the three boys answered her. The door opened. Paddy and Johnny Og came in.

"I'm not a coward, Mam," Johnny Og said to Máire.

Paddy came over to me. "I had to join, Mam. Couldn't stay back, let other fellows fight. Have to stand up against bullies. It's the right thing. I know it. When I held the crozier and I pledged myself for the glory of the old land, for the defense of the new, I felt so strong, Mam. So did all the other fellows." A head taller than me, this oldest child, my firstborn. I had to tilt my head back to look into his eyes. He does need his mother's blessing, my prayers.

"I understand, Paddy. Your da would be very proud of you."

"I know that, Mam. That's why . . ." He stopped. Then he leaned down and put his arms around me. "I love you, Mam. Give me your blessing."

"You have it, Paddy," I said. "My sturdy lad." I kissed his cheek. "My prayers go with you."

Máire said nothing.

"Where is your uncle Patrick?" I asked.

"Gone," said Paddy. "Gone to rally the Irish units in Detroit, Buffalo, New York City, Boston. But he will be with us when we go into battle."

Máire walked into her room and slammed the door behind her.

Chapter 29

*M*áire had moved her children out the week after the boys joined the Irish Brigade. We told the children we'd been hoping another set of rooms would become available in the building. They had. About time for more space, we'd said. Máire had gotten a raise and I would have letters galore to write, so we could afford to live separately. Besides, eleven people in four rooms—ridiculous. Not a word about the ten dollars Máire'd given the McGintys downstairs to encourage them to leave sooner than they'd planned. I'd smiled and carried clothes and boxes to the flat below, and Bridget and Gracie and I had scrubbed the floors and washed the walls while Máire was at the Shop.

The lives of our children, Máire's and mine, had remained intertwined. I doubt they even noticed that Máire's not spoken to me once in the month since that night the boys enlisted. She'd come into the bedroom after the others were asleep.

"Get up."

I'd followed her up to the attic of 2703 Hickory. This crawl space, which provided storage for the four families, was where Máire and I went for private talks.

"How could you betray me?" she started.

I tried to explain Patrick Kelly's argument. The boys would go anyway. Better to accept their decision. Our support, our prayers, would encourage and even protect them. And it was a just cause and—

She'd cut me off. She told me the men downtown said the war was a business opportunity. There'd be army contracts for meat and uniforms and blankets, not to mention arms and ammunition.

"It's about money!" she'd screamed at me. "The rich will get richer and the sons of the poor will die."

She'd started in again about the Pykes and the British army.

"This army will be different," I said. I told her how Patrick Kelly said the Brigade would get good training and equipment, fine leaders. She'd gone wild. How dare I mention Patrick Kelly's name? I'd taken his side against her because I had a grá for him—mooning over my own brother-in-law. Disgusting.

I stood up and started down the ladder. But she grabbed me, shouting about all we'd been through together, after all she'd sacrificed.

Then the top-floor tenants—the Sullivans—pounded on the ceiling, shaking the attic floor.

"Keep your voice down, Máire. The neighbors," I said.

"The neighbors? The neighbors?" Máire still shouting. "Can't disturb the neighbors? Afraid they'll learn the truth about Saint Honora? Honora the Righteous? That she's sold out her sister and her own sons to please a man?"

"I didn't."

"I'm moving out," Máire said to me, her voice low and hard.

And I'd said, "Go on."

❖   ❖   ❖

We still had meals together. Máire helped Johnny Og assemble his uniform as I helped Paddy. We made their trousers and bought blue jackets for them. Máire was cheerful enough in front of the children but never even looked at me.

All June, and through July, Paddy and Johnny Og trained at the new Camp Douglas on the south shore of the Lake near 33rd Street, waiting for orders that would make the twelve hundred men of the Irish Brigade an official part of the federal army. They ate dinner at home and slept in their own beds, thank God.

Maybe if the Brigade didn't go into battle, Máire would forgive me. A chance. Each state was required to supply a certain quota of men,

Paddy told me. Governor Yates of Illinois had not called on the Brigade because enough other fellows had volunteered. Don't need the Irish. Keep them out. Paddy was afraid the Irish Brigade would miss the war entirely.

But then Colonel Mulligan went to Washington, to President Lincoln himself, according to Paddy, and convinced the War Department to accept the Irish Brigade as the 23rd Illinois Volunteers. Great joy in Bridgeport.

"We'll show them," said Barney McGurk, James McKenna, and the other men. "Irishmen are the greatest fighters in the world. Revenge for Skibbereen!"

Now they were leaving. Máire put a good face on it, standing with us and all of Bridgeport, to cheer the Brigade. A warm, sunny July 14. The boys would march down Archer Road and then to a downtown railroad station. They'd go by train to Quincy, Illinois, then on to St. Louis. "We'll be fighting in Missouri," Paddy had told me.

"Here they come!" some shouted. Off to war, twelve hundred strong, singing an Irish song:

> And now I'm bound for the Army camp
> Come Heaven then pray guide me
> And send me back home again
> To the girl I left behind me.

Jamesy and Daniel stood on one side of me, arms folded, wishing they, too, were bound for the Army camp. Thomas, next to them, joked with Máire, glad enough to be on the sidelines. Stephen and Michael and the latest version of the Hickory Gang ran alongside the Brigade.

"Here's Colonel Mulligan, Mam," Jamesy shouted to me over the noise as the Brigade approached our position on the street.

Colonel Mulligan passed close to us, striding along with his men, not mounted on some great horse. Didn't need to lord it over them—a real leader. He marched with his head high, shoulders back, elegant in his green jacket, the brass buttons gleaming in the sun. A fine-featured man, no question, serious with straight-ahead-looking eyes. Colonel Mulligan, sure to be General Mulligan, and then after the war Senator Mulligan—even President Mulligan. Could there be an Irish Catholic president? "Not impossible," James McKenna said, "after we help save the Union."

Now came the flags, the Stars and Stripes and the Brigade's own large banner. Beautiful. Clusters of green shamrocks were embroidered around the gold Harp of Tara. Grand big letters spelled out the mottoes: Faugh-a-Ballagh, Clear the Way; Erin Go Bragh, Ireland forever. Stirring.

I glanced at Máire. She had her head turned, talking to Thomas. But Bridget and Gracie were jumping up to see over the crowd.

"Jamesy, who's that carrying the Brigade's flag?" Bridget asked.

The tall young standard-bearer held the banner high and straight, letting it snap in the breeze.

"The colonel's brother-in-law, James Nugent," Jamesy said.

As if hearing his name, the young man turned his head. Bridget and Gracie clapped their hands, waved at the fellow, bouncing up and down. The fellow smiled at them. Now there's a handsome lad—blue eyes, white teeth, blond hair showing under his cap.

Máire was watching the girls. I caught her eye, ready to share a silent comment on their excitement. She only stared at me, her face still, then turned back to Thomas.

"Johnny Og and Paddy are coming!" Stephen and Michael said, rushing up to us.

There they were—our sons. I wanted to reach over, take Máire's hand. Hold on to her. My big sister. I didn't dare.

"Paddy! Johnny Og!" our young ones shouted.

Johnny Og and Paddy saw us. They didn't wave, couldn't probably. Not military. But they did nod and smile.

A young woman stepped into the street and touched Paddy's sleeve. He squeezed her hand. Bridey Kelly, from Roscommon, the girl Jamesy said Paddy was courting. Lovely-looking tall girl, matching Paddy's step for a brief distance, then dropping back into the crowd.

Paddy's sweetheart. All were together—mothers, wives, sweethearts. Waving. Cheering. Terrified. Slán abhaile. Safe home.

❖ ❖ ❖

Our Holy Hour began by accident. I'd gone into St. Bridget's for a visit one afternoon and found Bridey Kelly lighting a candle.

"Let's pray for Paddy together," I said, and we whispered the rosary. Comforting. We added trimmings—a Hail Mary, Our Father, Glory

Be, for all of the Irish Brigade, and then all the Union soldiers and the secessionist army, too. Some mother's son, each one.

The next day, Bridey brought her mother. I met Molly on the street and invited her in. By mid-August, a crowd of us gathered every day. The Holy Hour, we called it. When Father Tom offered to preside over our prayers, I thanked him very much but said we wouldn't dream of taking his time.

The truth is, we prefer to be on our own. We take the decades in turn; one woman begins, "Hail Mary," the rest of us answer, "Holy Mary, Mother of God, pray for us sinners now and at the hour of our death." Informal, one nods to the next. After the rosary, each of us adds something we choose ourselves.

I might say St. Bridget's prayer in Irish. One day, Molly Flanigan taught us a Mayo hymn. Each woman had a favorite saint, a special prayer. I was reminded of the passengers on the *Superior*. So many Irish saints. Good to get them all working for us. Then we'd call the roll of the men off fighting, drawing divine protection around each name, trying to ease one another's fears. At the end, we'd share whatever news we had.

Letters from the soldiers began to arrive at the post office downtown. At first we all went down every day. Then we set up a rotation— two women collected all the letters. Most came with postage due. One day I gave money to a mother crying at the postal counter because she didn't have money to redeem her son's letters. After that, we asked James McKenna and the other tavern owners to set up a fund so no wife or mother would be denied her letter. Often the letters would be read aloud at the Holy Hour.

But neither Paddy nor Johnny Og had written.

One afternoon in late August as we walked home from the Holy Hour along Hickory Street, Molly said why didn't I ask Máire to collect the letters at the post office when she finished at the Shop. It was understood that Máire's work kept her from the Holy Hour, and we made sure to mention Johnny Og in every prayer.

I told Molly that Máire often worked late, and the post office would be closed, and . . .

Molly knew I was only making excuses. "Are you two feuding?" she asked. "Is that why she moved?"

"Not at all," I said. "We were all crowded together. . . ."

"Honora," Molly said as we stopped in front of our door. "Grudges can destroy families. Resentment passes from generation to generation, and nobody knowing what started it all."

"I know what started it. Máire didn't want our sons to enlist. And neither did I at first, but then Patrick Kelly explained—save the Union, free the slaves, capture Canada, liberate Ireland—the Cause. Máire thinks none of it's worth dying for."

"Young men don't expect to die," Molly said.

But they had. Hundreds killed in the surprise defeat at Bull Run, the battle fought the week after the Brigade marched away. The New York Irish Regiment led by Patrick's friend Meagher, part of the 69th, suffered many casualties.

"Máire will never let Thomas and Daniel join. Never."

Molly's son, who had worked on the Lake boats, was in a Michigan regiment. No word from the one out west. About half her boarders had enlisted. Barney McGurk had tried. "And him sixty," Molly said. Barney thought there'd be many more men called. Conscription would come. Lizzie McKenna's sons were already serving.

"I'll have to be going, Honora," Molly said. "Find a way to make it up with Máire." But then she turned back to me. "Tell me, Honora," she said. "Not meaning to be rude nor inquiring, but your husband passed away how many years ago?"

"Thirteen years in August."

"A long time," she said.

"Doesn't seem like it."

"And if you don't mind me asking, was your husband a jealous-type fellow?"

"He was not," I said. What put that in her mind? Had Máire said something to her about Patrick Kelly and me? Máire wouldn't, would she? I started talking fast, telling Molly how Granny'd asked Michael could he pay the bride price: no meanness, no fear, no jealousy. "He agreed," I said. "So, not jealous."

"Great wisdom in those old stories," Molly said. "Good night now, Honora. See you tomorrow at the Holy Hour."

❖ ❖ ❖

Does Molly know about the letter from Patrick Kelly that had come by messenger? The boy told me that my husband had paid extra for delivery. "A lucky woman, missus," he'd said.

"Not my husband," I'd started, then stopped. Had that boy set people speculating?

In the letter, Patrick wrote that he had been in St. Louis with his friend Captain Tom Sweeny. They were guarding an arsenal full of weapons and ammunition to keep it safe for the Union. Lots of secessionists there, even among the Irish, he said. Patrick had been inducted into the unit by Sweeny as a kind of scout. "So I'm an unofficial official member of the U.S. Army. The Brigade is coming to Missouri. When they arrive, I'll join them." He'd signed, "Yours respectfully, Patrick Kelly."

I hadn't read out the letter at the Holy Hour.

❖ ❖ ❖

Then, glorious news came. Barney McGurk pounded on our door on a Tuesday morning with the early edition of the *Chicago Times*. The headline read: IRISH BRIGADE CAPTURES LEXINGTON. MISSOURI RIVER TOWN TAKEN. September 9, 1861, the date on the story read. The Brigade's first battle was a total victory.

"They did it!" Barney kept repeating. "They did it! They won control of the Missouri River and the upper Mississippi for the Union, and not a shot fired. The defenders ran away!"

I ran down to tell Máire. "Gone to work," Gracie told me.

Stephen and Michael and the Hickory Gang built a huge bonfire that night, and Bridgeport celebrated the victory. I found Máire in the circle of people and stood next to her. Molly and Lizzie were watching us. Máire smiled and clapped, and we walked into 2703 together.

"They won, Máire," I said. "Please, let's talk."

Silence. We climbed the stairs. She shut her door.

Then the next day's newspapers reported that an army of Missouri secessionists under a General Price was marching toward Lexington. Two days later, twenty thousand Missouri enemy troops commanded by Price surrounded the Brigade, cutting them off.

The first siege of the war. No food, low on water, the Brigade waited for reinforcements. A week, ten days went by. Our Holy Hours lasted into the night. "Storm heaven," Lizzie McKenna said. "All we can do." The newspapers warned the Brigade would be overrun and massacred by the enemy.

I made dinner for both families, and we ate together during that week of waiting. Máire and I were polite to each other—pretending, even, during this crisis. The boys were so full of speculation, I don't think they really noticed.

On Wednesday, September 18, the *Chicago Times* said: THE LATEST BY TELEGRAPH: PRICE SURROUNDS LEXINGTON AND SUMMONS MULLIGAN TO SURRENDER, WHICH HE REFUSES TO DO.

That night, Máire came into St. Bridget's as I was leaving.

"Máire." I held out my hand to her, but she walked past me down the aisle and knelt next to Molly.

On Friday, September 20, the Confederates broke through the Brigade's defenses. They soaked round bales of hemp in water and pushed them up the hill, shooting at our boys from behind rolling shields that damped out any return fire.

September 21, 1861. Colonel Mulligan surrendered. No massacre. Some casualties, but no definite numbers. "Light," the newspapers Barney carried said. Our boys weren't even taken prisoner—where would the Confederates put them? Paroled, Barney said. "They promise not to fight anymore." Thank God. Thank God.

Dawn when Barney brought the news. I ran down and knocked on Máire's door, while he woke Bridget and the boys.

"Máire, please." I pounded harder. "They're safe! Slán, Máire, please! A surrender yesterday. It's in the papers."

But she wouldn't open the door.

I pulled on the knob, shaking the frame. "I'll shout and scream until the neighbors call the police!"

Nothing.

"Máire, please! Answer me."

The door opened. Máire stood there in her business shirtwaist and skirt. "It's how I handled the Pykes," she said. "Silence."

"Oh, Máire, such great news! The boys are coming home."

"Never would have gone in the first place," she said, "if you'd stood firm with me."

"I'm sorry. I am. The war is over for Johnny Og and Paddy. They're not allowed to fight anymore. Couldn't we start talking again?"

"I've things stored up in my head to tell you, Honora, that you won't like hearing. What do you have to say to that?"

"I say a fight is better than loneliness, Máire."

And she laughed. Parole.

Barney sat with us in the kitchen that evening. The whole crowd of us—Jamesy, Daniel, Thomas, Bridget and Gracie, Stephen and Michael—stayed up all night.

"I'm glad, Mam," Bridget said when she saw Máire and me talking together.

We hadn't fooled them.

Barney explained to the others that "paroled" meant the soldiers could be let go if they promised not to fight anymore. The Brigade agreed. The secessionists sent them home.

"Home?" Bridget asked Barney. "Just like that? When the day before they were going to kill them, every one?"

"I don't understand," Gracie said. "If the enemy would let them go free, why didn't Colonel Mulligan surrender sooner?"

"Because he would've lost the battle," Barney said.

"He lost anyway!" I said.

"But the colonel thought he could win—reinforcements were coming," he said.

"Oh, bother the reinforcements!" Máire said. "What is this? Change partners and dance?"

❖ ❖ ❖

We waited. The newspaper reported only that the paroled soldiers had to make their own way back to Chicago. No list of casualties. "Light" casualties meant one hundred had died or been wounded in the fighting before the surrender, a high number for us. Some had to be from Bridgeport, but no names were reported. Colonel Mulligan wasn't paroled. He would remain a prisoner with General Price until he could be exchanged for a Confederate officer. His young wife, Marion, had watched the battle from a nearby hotel. She'd been allowed to join him in captivity, which seemed strange to me.

No word from Paddy and Johnny Og, or Patrick Kelly. Dear God, could they have been wounded or worse? We didn't know.

Again the Holy Hour stretched into the evening. I lit candles for the boys, and Patrick Kelly, too. I'd put him out of my heart, but I could hope the fellow survived.

September became October. Boys straggled back—Lizzie McKenna's youngest son and Molly's son. Neither had seen Johnny Og or Paddy. The boys were closemouthed about the great battle of Lexington. All they would say was, "It was hard going—lucky to be out of it."

You'd think Lexington—a defeat, after all—would have put the other boys off the idea of war, but not at all. Jamesy, Daniel, and every male in Bridgeport were determined to avenge the Brigade. Remember Lexington! Battles lost stir them more than battles won, I thought. The truce between Máire and me held.

Mid-October, a month after the surrender, I was outside hanging the wash on a Saturday. Jamesy had taken all the young ones to McVicker's. I preferred to be at home in case any news came.

Two men on horseback were riding across the last stretch of prairie toward Bubbly Creek. Cowboys, probably. When they crossed the canal bridge, I could see them: a man in buckskins—Patrick Kelly—and with him a skinny boy, bent over his horse's neck, his face hidden. But I knew him.

"Paddy! Paddy!" I ran and reached them as they came off the bridge. "Oh, Paddy!"

He slid off the horse into my arms.

"Paddy, Paddy . . ." As I hugged him close to me, I could feel every rib. My sturdy lad, so bony. An old man's face, hollow-cheeked, covered with bristly whiskers—dirty. Standing still in my arms.

"You're home. You're whole. Thank God. Are you hurt?"

"Only very tired," Patrick Kelly said from atop his horse. "He did well, Honora. Michael would've been proud. He was very brave."

"Johnny Og? Where's Johnny Og?" I looked out over the canal, but I could see no other rider.

Patrick got off his horse, lifted a rolled buffalo robe from behind his saddle, and laid it carefully on the ground.

"Johnny Og," Paddy said.

"Dear God."

For the first time since he was a tiny boy in the before times, Paddy wept.

❖   ❖   ❖

I waited outside our building for Máire to come home from work. She started running when she saw me walking toward her. She knew as soon as she saw my face. Patrick and Paddy had carried Johnny Og's body up to her parlor and set the buffalo robe in front of Máire's fireplace. I led Máire into the room.

"He's there, Máire," I said.

She went down on her knees and started to pull the covering away.

"Wait, Máire," Patrick said. I knelt next to her, put my arms around her. "Johnny Og was wounded on the last day of the siege," Patrick went on. "He was put on a steamboat the Sisters of Mercy had turned into a hospital and was taken to Saint Louis."

"I was in Saint Louis, too, Aunt Máire," Paddy said, "but I didn't know where Johnny Og was. All of us from the Brigade got separated. We had to get home on our own, but I couldn't leave without Johnny Og. It was Uncle Patrick found me and took me to him."

"He was alive when we got there, Máire," Patrick said, "but his wounds were infected. He had fever."

"And he knew us, Aunt Máire, but he thought the hospital boat was the *River Queen* and we were coming up the river from New Orleans, that we were only just arriving in Chicago."

"A priest from Saint Louis heard his confession," Patrick said.

"Not much to confess," Máire said. "He never put a foot wrong."

"He didn't, Aunt Máire," Paddy said. "The best of all of us, and we never . . ." He stopped. "He sent you his love. The last word he said was 'Mathair'—Mother."

"Mother," Máire repeated. "I wish I'd been a better mother to him."

"You were the best mother ever, Máire. The best," I said.

"His body will not . . . ," Patrick started.

"Unwrap him, Patrick," Máire said.

Patrick got down and untied the buffalo robe. Johnny Og's whole body, even his face, was wrapped in bands of white linen.

"Johnny Og," Máire said over and over. "Johnny Og."

She kissed the wrapped head of her eldest child, the baby she'd held that Christmas Eve in Bearna. Johnny Og.

"Wrap him up, Patrick," Máire said. "Better the other children don't see him when they come home."

We helped her up.

"A proper wake, Honora. He needs a proper wake," Máire said.

"He will have that," Patrick Kelly said. "His brothers-in-arms will wish to honor him."

I expected Máire to spit the words back at him—brothers-in-arms—honor? But she only nodded.

"And a military funeral," Patrick said.

Máire nodded again. "Johnny Og was always a good little soldier. I couldn't have survived the Big House without him. He knew the old Major hated him, and he learned to keep his head down. Never a whine or a whinge."

"A brave man," Patrick said.

"He'd be twenty-two at Christmas. Not much more than a boy," Máire said.

❖ ❖ ❖

The wake began on Saturday afternoon. Máire and I were together in her Bridgeport parlor, as we'd been in the cottage at Bearna. A body this time. But such a poor, battered body.

"He was next to me, Mam. Right next to me. He had just moved there, just stepped into the spot," Paddy had whispered to me his first night at home. He'd said nothing more since then.

And now, at the wake, Paddy was greeting the young soldiers in uniform, and the older men, their fathers and uncles. "The Brigade's a family," one man said to me as he followed Paddy to the kitchen to join Jamesy and the others.

Máire and I sat with the women, keeping watch—close enough to touch the coffin.

I wish we had a keener like Widow Clooney from home to put words on this awful sadness.

"My first born," Máire said to each person as more and more people entered.

Michael Gibson from the boatyard took Máire's hand. "A great worker, he was. He had a true feel for the bones of a boat. A good son. He would have liked to sail the world. But he said the ocean had taken his father and he couldn't worry his mother by going to sea. Killed on dry land."

"A good son," Máire repeated. "A very good son."

No sign of Patrick Kelly since he'd arrived two days ago, though Mr. McGillicuddy had simply appeared with the coffin and said Patrick Kelly had paid for it.

"Here's Uncle Patrick, Mam," Jamesy said. "And look who he's brought with him—Alderman Comiskey and Mr. Onahan. Here, in our house—shows how important Johnny Og was."

I went to tell Máire. Lizzie McKenna and Molly Flanigan, sitting next to her, looked over.

"Well," Lizzie said, "first time those two have been at Bridgeport, I'd say, and dressed so lovely."

"A real tribute to your Johnny Og, Máire," Molly said.

"Of course, Patrick Kelly's still in his buckskins. He should have a uniform," Lizzie said.

"He's his beard trimmed and his hair cut," Molly said.

"I believe he's a scout," I said.

Lizzie looked at me.

Máire stood up and we walked over to receive the men. Patrick presented them to Máire and then went out to the kitchen.

John Comiskey was a Chicago alderman from Holy Family parish. He also acted as the Brigade's fund-raiser and treasurer. William Onahan was the publisher of the *Western Tablet,* the man who started the Catholic Library and Literary Association—well-spoken, a friend of the bishop's. Men of great dignity and achievement, and they're younger than I am, I thought. Early thirties, I'd say. John Comiskey was a tall, well-built fellow with a prominent nose. William Onahan only reached Comiskey's shoulders, a tidy fellow with thinning hair, gold spectacles. John Comiskey took Máire's hand.

"I'm sorry for your trouble, Mrs. Leahy. A brave lad, taken from us too soon."

"No more Leahys," she'd said to me last night. "My Johnny was kind and easygoing, brave in a boat, and his son Johnny Og like him—no more Leahys, for all that Daniel and Gracie carry the name."

But now as John Comiskey patted her shoulder he remarked on the many Leahy families in Chicago.

"Really?" Máire focused on him. "Are any from Galway?"

"They could be," he said.

"I must meet them," Máire said.

"A great clan, the Leahys," William Onahan said.

A little boy stood behind John Comiskey.

"And who's this wee fellow?" Máire asked.

"My son Charlie," Alderman Comiskey said. "He's only two, and shy. My wife's visiting another bereaved mother from the Brigade, so he's with me."

"Only a minute since my Johnny Og was that size," Máire said.

"Charlie." She knelt down to him. "Hello, Charlie."

He smiled at her.

"Honora, where's Bridget or Gracie?" Máire said. "They should take Charlie up to your place—play with him."

I took Charlie by the hand. I couldn't see Bridget or Gracie, but I found Michael out on the landing, tossing a ball up and catching it.

"Michael, this is Charlie," I said.

"Hi," he said, still tossing the ball.

Little Charlie was watching him. "Ball," he said. "Ball."

"It's a base ball," Michael told him.

"Base ball," Charlie Comiskey said.

I went back to John Comiskey.

"Could my Michael take Charlie outside to play?" I asked.

"I'd appreciate that," John Comiskey said.

"Stay close to the house," I said to Michael.

My youngest, and he's taller than many of the men here. Only a minute, Máire had said, before they're grown and gone. Young Michael is always agreeable, as Johnny Og had been. No complaints from Johnny Og. He needed no petting or cajoling. As a boy, he'd taken care of his younger brothers. Solid. He would have been a wonderful father.

Máire had rejoined the women. She sat straight, contained. No tears. She thanked the Bridgeport neighbors as they said to her, "Sorry for your troubles. A good lad. A fine boy."

Now Patrick Kelly brought Paddy and the men out from the kitchen. They stood in front of the coffin, an honor guard formed of the Irish Brigade in uniform jackets and work trousers, the older men wearing Sunday shirts and pants, and John Comiskey and William Onahan dressed in their gentlemen's suits. How many? Thirty, forty, more, massed around Johnny Og's pine coffin, shoulders squared, heads high. Patrick Kelly, somehow military in spite of his buckskins, placed a scrap of green cloth on the top of Johnny Og's plain box.

"This fragment comes from the flag of the Irish Brigade," Patrick said, "which was cut in pieces before the surrender. The enemy did not capture our flag. The banner of the Irish Brigade was not taken. Corporal Johnny Og Leahy joins a tradition of courage stretching back to Fontenoy and beyond. He will be spoken of down through the centuries. An Irish hero. In his name, let us defend our new land, then free our native land. Faugh-a-Ballagh!"

"Faugh-a-Ballagh!" the men shouted. "Hoo-rah!"

I saw the look on Jamesy's and Daniel's faces as they joined in, "Hoo-rah!"

Patrick lifted Grellan's crozier and held it over the coffin, blessing Johnny Og and all of them. Jamesy took his whistle from his pocket. The high, clear notes of "A Nation Once Again" sounded. The men sang the anthem, and the women joined them.

I looked over at Máire. She was nodding her head.

Now Father Kelly spoke. "Corporal Johnny Og Leahy is in heaven, reunited with his Heavenly Father and his earthly father. I believe, as do many of you, that Ireland's our heaven and we will see it again when we die. Johnny Og Leahy, who gave his life for the honor of the old land, for the defense of the new, is there now. Remember what the cock crows: Slán Mhic Máire. Now, Johnny Og, son of Máire, you too are safe. Safe at home."

I had to go outside. I took my shawl off the hook, wrapped it around me, and slipped out.

I walked down toward the edge of the canal. Indian summer, I'd learned to call this bit of time before the winter grabbed Chicago by the throat.

War. Such a short word to cover so much. All those boys inside were shouting to "get into the war, avenge Johnny Og." They hadn't seen his body when Patrick unwrapped the buffalo robe.

At least we could bury Johnny Og. Annie McCafferty didn't know where her son's body was. Neither did Kitty Gorman or Mary Malone. Paddy had told me dead soldiers were piled into trenches and their bodies covered over with dirt. "Like in Ireland," he'd said, "during the Great Starvation."

We'd saved our children at such cost. To lose them now? What sense?

"Honora." Patrick came up behind me.

I stopped, looked up at Patrick. "I do thank you, Patrick. Paddy told me how you helped him."

Patrick shrugged. "I wish I'd been able to get there sooner," he said. "I was fighting at Wilson Creek in Missouri with Tom Sweeny. Sweeny's quite a man, Honora. He lost his right arm in the Mexican War. He rides into battle with the reins of his horse in his teeth so he can hold his saber. All Irishmen are showing such courage—the Sixty-ninth at Bull Run, the Brigade at Lexington, and many more."

"I keep thinking that Johnny Og was wounded on September twentieth, only one day before the surrender. One day, Patrick. Why didn't Mulligan surrender sooner?"

"James Mulligan expected the relief at any moment. General Frémont might have hurried a bit if he'd known one million dollars confiscated from the Bank of Lexington was buried under Mulligan's tent."

"He'd come for money, but not for lives? Not for Johnny Og?"

"Plenty of Johnny Ogs, Honora."

Night was falling, shrouding the prairie.

"At least Paddy's done his ninety days and he's finished," I said.

"His time will be extended. Soldiers will be kept as long as they're needed."

"But the parole. The Brigade can't fight again!"

Patrick kicked at the ground. "As soon as Mulligan is released, he'll go straight to Washington and have the Brigade reinstated."

"But he can't! That was part of the parole! Here, look."

I carried Paddy's parole, folded up and tucked inside my blouse. A talisman—he was out of the war. In it, Corporal Paddy Kelly pledged his word of honor not to take up arms against the Confederate states or give aid or comfort to the government of the United States or any of its armies.

"Given at Lexington, September twenty-fifth, 1861," I read. So," I said, "he can't fight. None of the lads can—see? Pledges his word of honor."

"Look again, Honora. It says 'until he shall have been exchanged or otherwise released.' They parole our troops and we parole theirs. Everyone goes home and joins up again. Eventually there will be prisoner-of-war camps, enemies captured can be removed from the field and—"

"Removed from the field? You make it sound like a hurling match."

"Too bad it's not," he said. "The Ojibwa settle their quarrels by playing lacrosse."

"And the old Irish sent one champion to fight another. Single combat."

He nodded. "Listen, Honora, I have to leave now and I'll . . ."

"I won't let Paddy go back to war, and the others aren't enlisting," I said, interrupting him.

"Honora, I told you before, you won't be able to stop them. They're pledging themselves up there, swearing on Johnny Og's coffin."

"Do you think Máire would let Thomas and Daniel . . . ? Please keep your guns and drums away from us."

"You'll see," Patrick said. "Máire will want Johnny Og's death to have some meaning, as the boys of the Brigade do."

"But death isn't real to them."

"We all die, Honora. These boys have warrior blood in them. Victory here and freedom for Ireland—they'll change history."

"History? Now they're dying for history? September twentieth, 1861—Johnny Og Leahy is wounded. October twelfth—he dies, at age twenty-one. Write it down. That's history. I'm sick of history."

"You can't escape history," said Patrick. "You're Irish."

"Mam!" Michael ran up to me, with Charlie Comiskey following. "It's too dark to see the ball—we're going in."

"I'm coming with you, Michael."

"Good. Come on, Uncle Patrick," he said, taking his hand. "I have a good plan for getting those Rebs who killed Johnny Og."

I picked up Charlie Comiskey, and I pulled Michael to me. "Uncle Patrick has to go, Michael. He's going on a long trip and we won't be seeing him."

"Till Christmas?" said Michael. "That's not too long."

"I may not be able to come for Christmas," Patrick said.

Just as well, I thought.

"He's trying to make the war shorter," I said.

"Not too short, Uncle Patrick," Michael said. "I'll be thirteen next year and I could—"

"Michael!"

"Your mother's cold, Michael. Go in with her. Honora, I've spoken to John Comiskey. He's a job for you, sorting out the Brigade's correspondence when Colonel Mulligan returns. The Union army's captured some high-ranking Confederates. They'll be exchanged for Mulligan soon. The office is downtown. You'll need the money, Honora. Prices will rise. War does that. And I don't know where I'll be."

"Thank you. Good-bye, Patrick," I said. "I'll be praying for you."

"Do that, Honora."

Chapter 30

Colonel Mulligan returned to Chicago on November 1, Samhain, and I received a note from him. He had meetings in Springfield and Washington but expected to be back in two weeks. My job as his secretary would start then. It couldn't come soon enough. The cost of food went up every day.

Máire had not gone back to the Shop. After being so brave through Johnny Og's funeral, she'd collapsed, sleeping most of the day, sitting up with a jug of whiskey into the night. In the three weeks since we'd buried Johnny Og, she'd left the house only on Sundays to visit his grave at Calvary Cemetery, up north beyond the city limits on Lake Michigan.

A long, cold, bleak trip it was. A train took us to Howard Street, then we hired one of the waiting hacks that provided transport for funerals during the week and visitors on Sunday.

Full winter now, the sky low and leaden over the gray lake, a chilly wind blowing.

We'd stand at the mound over Johnny Og, Máire wrapped in a black shawl. The Snowy-Breasted Pearl had become a grieving mother. "At least I've tucked his body into a snug grave," she'd said to me last Sunday.

I'd put my arm around her. "Why not come to the Holy Hour, Máire?"

She'd looked surprised. "I'm done with all that, Honora."

"What?"

"I'm ignoring God. Otherwise I'll start hating Him. This way's better. Let's go home now."

Later, I'd settled Máire by the fire and drunk a whiskey with her.

"Go home, Honora. I'm fine."

I'd stirred the fire and left. She'd wanted me gone so she could drain the jug and maybe sleep. "Every night the same, Auntie Honey," Gracie had told me. "She'll only eat a potato or two."

Gracie and Thomas and Daniel had their dinner upstairs with us now. Máire wouldn't come. "I'm not hungry."

"Leave her alone," Molly Flanigan had told me, and Lizzie said the same. "Give her time, and if she finds comfort in the whiskey, what harm?"

Johnny Og's army wages paid Máire's rent for two months. But money was running out, and she wouldn't, couldn't, return to the Shop.

Paddy was drinking heavy, too. In McKenna's every night until the early hours. He hadn't gone back to Slattery's.

"Why?" he had said. "I'll be reenlisting, and then there'll be the bounty, Mam."

Twenty-five dollars bounty was paid on enlistment. Most families in Bridgeport were struggling. Good jobs were getting scarce. The big companies that got army contracts for meat and beans and flour and boots drove the smaller places out of business. Hough's was gone, Thomas out of a job. The new packinghouses paid low wages—fellows hired by the day, fired for no reason. The bosses didn't want Irish workers. They preferred the new people coming in from all over Europe, who couldn't speak English and had a harder time standing up for themselves. Even Daniel's barrel factory suffered, their prices undercut by new factories.

A bonus of twenty-five dollars right away and regular army pay would support a family, no problem. At the Holy Hour, mothers who hadn't spent Sunday afternoons at Calvary Cemetery thanked God their sons had reenlisted, and prayed for a swift victory.

Paddy was only waiting for Colonel Mulligan to give the word. Jamesy, Thomas, and Daniel planned to join him. And Máire and I could not stop them.

Bridget and Gracie had wanted to give up school to work and bring in money.

"Work and do what?" I'd said. "Be a maid in the house of one of your classmates from Saint Xavier's? Graduate. Then you can become teachers."

I couldn't charge mothers to write letters to their soldier sons or ask Father Kelly to pay me. He'd stopped construction on the church. Every collection went into a fund for widows and orphans. So I was very relieved on the day in mid-November when Paddy escorted me to the Brigade's office downtown, and glad too that he was beside me in the chaos. Chicago was gorging on the business brought by war. Buildings burst out of the mud. Trains arrived from every direction. Crowds and more crowds.

"These are the offices of the lawyers and traders and insurance brokers. They're the ones grease the wheels of Chicago," Paddy said as we climbed the stairs of the brick building on Lake Street.

He knocked on a door on the third floor. Gold letters spelled out lines of names on frosted glass: first, Arrington, Fitch & Mulligan, Attorneys-at-Law; then, *Western Tablet,* William Onahan, Publisher, James Mulligan, Editor; and then on the bottom line, John Comiskey, Alderman 10th Ward, Treasurer, Shields Guards/Irish Brigade.

"Come in," a voice called.

The three men, sitting together at a long wooden table, stood immediately, putting their cigars on a dish in the center of the table.

Paddy saluted. "Corporal Kelly reporting, Colonel, sir." He clicked his heels.

"At ease. At ease, please," Colonel James Mulligan said. I noticed again his dark, intense eyes, that disciplined mustache. A very serious man.

Paddy clasped his hands behind him, stood with his feet apart.

Colonel Mulligan spoke very kindly to me, beautiful manners altogether, saying how proud I must be of Corporal Kelly and asking me to express his sympathy to Corporal Leahy's mother. Then he asked if I'd had any news from Patrick Kelly, which led Mr. Onahan and Alderman Comiskey to praise Patrick's efforts as what Colonel Mulligan called "our builder of morale." I thanked Mr. Onahan and the alderman for coming to Johnny Og's wake and funeral.

"We must honor the fallen," Colonel Mulligan said. Then he explained my first assignment: Letters of condolence must be sent to the families of all one hundred Irish Brigade members killed or wounded at Lexington. Colonel Mulligan would write a sample letter, which I would then copy onto the Brigade's stationery. He handed me a sheet of heavy white paper with "The Irish Brigade" engraved in Gaelic-style letters at the top. On the left, shamrocks surrounded a harp set above a banner that read, "Erin Go Bragh" and "Remember Lexington and Fontenoy."

Colonel Mulligan said the bodies of many of the Brigade soldiers were buried in Missouri. Unmarked graves, I thought. He wanted the letters to be a kind of memorial for the families, something they could treasure. Father Kelly had confirmed what Patrick Kelly had told them, that I wrote a lovely hand. How quickly could I do one hundred letters? I asked the colonel if I could work at home and bring the letters to him to be signed. He said yes and that I should take them to his house.

"I'll have them for you tomorrow afternoon," I said, thinking Bridget and Gracie could help me. Alderman Comiskey wondered if ten dollars would be acceptable. Very acceptable, I said. Colonel Mulligan then said that he couldn't ask me to write my sister's letter. He'd do it, and I could use it as the model for the others.

He sat down at the table, took a sheet of stationery, and began to write—stopping and starting, tapping his finger on the desk.

As he worked on the letter, I looked over the list he'd given me:

Company A: Patrick Carey, John W. Smith, J. J. Armstrong, John Kelly, John Foley.

Company B: Michael Grenahan, Frank Curran, William Mulligan, F. Cummings, Patrick Fitzgerald, Edward Conlee, McCarthy, no first name, John Delaney, John Gallagher.

All dead.

Patrick Mooney, Edward Hanlon, David Shea, Anthony McBreagh, John McLaughlin, Thomas O'Meara, John McCloy, James Roche, Patrick McMann . . . Dead.

I noted the different spellings—Kelley with an "e" and without. Conry and Conroy, Conlee, and Connelly—they'd put English on their names to accommodate America.

I looked at Paddy, whole and healthy, and thought of Johnny Og and Máire.

❖　❖　❖

"Máire, here, I've something for you. Let me in, please." An age until she opened her front door. She took the letter and walked into the kitchen to read it. I followed her.

Cold in here. That fire's burnt down to ashes. Máire's hair looks greasy—unkempt. She had a black shawl wrapped around her. I wonder where her red silk is.

Máire set the letter on the table, pushed it one way, then another. She finally opened it. Máire read the letter twice. Then she ran her fingers over the paper, rubbing the heading. The harp—Erin Go Bragh—Remember Lexington.

"Would you like to hear it?" she asked me.

"I would."

She read:

Dear Mrs. Leahy,

Your son died for a glorious cause and I know you do not begrudge him his destiny. I pray that in return for your sacrifice, Our Lord will bless you with the grace to carry this cross. He asked the same courage of His own mother. As she saw the resurrection, so too will you see John live again in our victory, here and in our beloved Ireland. John Leahy's name is added to the roll of the brave. He will be remembered.

Your obedient servant,
James A. Mulligan, Colonel of the Irish Brigade,
23rd Illinois Volunteers.

"Added to the roll of the brave," Máire repeated. "He will be remembered. My son. My Johnny Og. More than his father got." She smiled at me. The first smile in a month.

"More, surely," I said.

"And that tidy grave. We must put up a headstone—green marble with 'Irish Brigade' on it and the shamrocks and harp for all to see."

"We will," I said.

"Do you believe what Father Kelly said? Is my Johnny Og safe at home?"

I looked at her and took her hand. "He is, Máire. Johnny Og's meeting his father at long last."

She nodded and squeezed my hand. "Johnny would be proud to have a son who struck a blow for freedom. Do you think he knows?"

"He does, Máire. Michael is with them, too."

"In heaven," she said. "With Mam and Da and Granny. A great gathering. I suppose if I'm going to believe in heaven, I've got to let God back in. I have missed going to Mass. Couldn't trust you to bring me back the news from the church steps." Máire stood up and looked around the kitchen. "Best start a meal for the boys. Look at the state of that fire. Have you some wood I could borrow, Honora?"

"I have, Máire."

"Though why I say borrow . . . You'll not be getting it back."

"No bother."

"Remember Christmas Eve, when we were going to burn Molly's chairs and then Patrick Kelly came?"

"I remember," I said.

"A good fellow, Patrick Kelly. Bringing Johnny Og home. Johnny Og had such an old head on him, and now he'll not live to comb gray hairs," she said. "I thought we'd escaped death."

"I know."

She paced back and forth, stopped at her looking glass. "Jesus," she said, "I'm a mess! I look like the dog's dinner. Honora, you wouldn't have a bit of stew you could heat up for me, would you? I'm very hungry all of a sudden."

"I would, Máire."

"I've come back, Honora," she said. "The fairy woman had me tied and tethered somewhere. Colonel Mulligan's words worked a charm against her. She's let me go. I might sleep tonight."

"Maybe without the poitín?"

"Maybe," she said. "Is Colonel Mulligan right? Will I get the grace to be strong?"

"You've always had courage, Máire."

"I have," she said. "I must think of the others. Imagine if a woman had only one child and lost . . . Could you hurry with the stew?"

"Come upstairs," I said.

And she did. We ate together that night for the first time in the month since Johnny Og's funeral. Then Gracie and Bridget and Máire too, thank God, worked on the colonel's letters with me. Máire said writing words to console other mothers and the wives of the men who'd served with Johnny Og would help her.

"Excellent penmanship, Máire," I said.

"Thank you, Miss Lynch," she answered.

We added our own bits to each letter: He was a credit to the Cunninghams, a hero of the proud clan of O'Mara, in the tradition of the Fitzgeralds, the O'Donnells . . . Born to be warriors, I thought, and devil a thing we can do about it. We didn't finish until midnight.

"I'll sleep tonight," Máire said, "and I think I'll go in to the Shop in the morning."

❖ ❖ ❖

Bridget and I delivered the letters to the Mulligan house the next morning. I'd asked Máire to come, but she was eager to get back to the Shop. Bridget hadn't wanted to go, either.

"You can miss school one day."

"But I have nothing to wear. What if James Nugent is there?"

"You're not going to a ball," I said. "Wear your uniform skirt and coat from Saint Xavier's with that blouse I gave you for Christmas."

The Mulligans lived on the North Side, not far from Holy Name Cathedral across from Lake Michigan.

Bridget and I stood looking up at the gray stone building with its long second-floor balcony.

"It'd be lovely to step out there and have your tea with the sun coming up over the Lake," I said.

"I'm sure the Mulligans drink coffee, Mam."

Marion herself answered the door and hugged Bridget, looking none the worse for her month as a prisoner. I said she looked well, and she told us General Price had been a gentleman, for all that he's a secessionist. Marion said she remembered Bridget from St. Xavier's— wasn't Bridget a freshman the year Marion graduated? A junior now! How quickly time goes. . . .

She brought us into the parlor, and soon she and Bridget were chatting away. Bowed windows looked out across to the Lake. A small fire burned in the grate, and two horsehair chairs were drawn up to each side of the hearth.

Was this where James Mulligan and his wife sat at night? Him smoking his pipe and she sewing or reading? Not too many evenings at home for the colonel now. But later in life, they would enjoy each other's company here.

Would James Mulligan live to comb gray hairs? So eager to lead men into battle and have this girl, Marion—a mother already with another on the way—follow him.

An older woman came into the room, followed by a young maid carrying a large tray with cups and saucers and a silver tea service.

"Put that on the table, Biddy," the woman said. The girl set down her burden.

"Ladies," said the older woman. "What a pleasant surprise. My son-in-law, Colonel Mulligan, is such a one for surprises. Biddy, bring more cups. I'm Alice Grant Nugent—Marion's mother."

Mrs. Nugent sat down, regarding the two of us the way Miss Lynch had looked me over at Barna House—ready to inquire and instruct.

When had we come to Chicago and how? I was a widow? Dreadful. Oh, yes, she'd heard that the conditions were awful in Ireland. But she'd never understood: Why hadn't the people simply eaten fish? She didn't expect an answer.

Now, her family, the Grants—"we Scotch-Irish"—had been in the country for many, many generations. A cousin of hers, Ulysses S. Grant, was a very important officer in the Union army. "He'll be a general soon," she told us. And where do we live? Bridgeport? Oh. Was it true conditions had improved there?

"You're from Bridgeport, aren't you, Biddy?" said Mrs. Nugent to the maid as she brought the teapot to her.

"I am, Mrs. Nugent." And then she turned to me. "I know you, Mrs. Kelly and Bridget. I'm Mary Gleason's youngest."

"Bridget Mary, isn't it?" I said.

Mrs. Nugent smiled and poured tea into my cup and then Bridget's. "Nice for you to meet friends, Biddy," she said.

"I get to Bridgeport for the Saturday night céili and Sunday Mass at Saint Bridget's. Late Mass," Biddy said, and laughed.

"Must never neglect our souls," Mrs. Nugent said. "We go to the cathedral. Bishop Duggan is a dear friend of ours."

"I tried Holy Name once," said Biddy. "But there's better-looking fellows at Saint Bridget's. Though there's a right few at Saint Patrick's. Lots of railroad men live in the boardinghouse near the parish. Sometimes I go to Mass at both places."

"How devout of you, Biddy," Mrs. Nugent said. "Thank you. That will be all."

Biddy winked at us as she left.

We all sat with our knees and lips pressed together, and then Marion started laughing. Bridget and I joined in.

Mrs. Nugent said to Marion, "What? What is it?"

"Biddy and her Masses," Marion managed to say.

Alice Nugent turned to us. "You see, ladies, I'm a convert to your faith, and I sometimes don't understand these things."

Marion and Bridget laughed harder.

"Someone's having a good time." A young man came into the room. "I heard the noise and wondered."

Marion looked up and smiled at him. "My brother, James," she said.

Bridget stopped giggling. I heard her say, "Oh," very softly.

Oh, indeed. James Nugent stood in the double door of the parlor, his head almost touching the frame above. Golden hair, a color you didn't see on boys very often, unruly, as if he'd tried to flatten the curls down but they wouldn't obey. Very white teeth and a lovely smile. He had Marion's blue eyes, her straight nose. But where her chin was round and her cheeks plump, his face had angles enough to stop him being pretty. He walked over and kissed his mother's cheek.

"What's the joke, Mama?" he said.

"Joke? What do you mean?" said Mrs. Nugent.

He turned and smiled right at Bridget. "What a lovely surprise on a winter's day," James Nugent said.

Marion introduced us.

"Ah, Corporal Kelly's family, and connected to Patrick Kelly, too, I understand. I'm very sorry about your nephew, Mrs. Kelly, and your cousin, Miss Kelly."

"I'm Bridget," she said.

"Bridget was my granny Nugent's name, my father's mother who came from Ireland. I remember she had a reed cross she called Saint Bridget's cross."

"Croiseog Bhríde," I said in Irish.

"Granny spoke Irish," Marion said, "but we never learned it."

"Why would you?" said Mrs. Nugent.

"I know 'Faugh-a-Ballagh,'" said James Nugent. "That's Irish."

"Clear the Way," said Marion. "I know that one."

"And do you know the history behind it?" I asked.

James Nugent answered: "In 1745, the Irish Brigade fighting for the

French beat the British at Fontenoy. Faugh-a-Ballagh was their battle cry."

"I was courted with stories of Irish heroes," said Marion.

"Weren't we all?" I said.

A nice girl, this, in spite of the mother.

I watched Mrs. Nugent's face as her son charmed my daughter, Bridget, a girl from Bridgeport. Not one bit pleased.

Bridget's a very beautiful young woman. I hadn't quite realized. Blond curls, blue eyes, and Walsh curves, sitting there so calm and composed in her St. Xavier's uniform, at ease in this room. She was telling James Nugent other phrases in Irish she remembered.

" 'Nollaig Shona Dhuit' means 'Happy Christmas,' " she said.

He tried to say it, and they laughed.

"The Brigade will have its Christmas dance in a few weeks. I would be honored if you would accompany me," he said.

"Now, James . . . ," Mrs. Nugent began as Colonel Mulligan came in.

"I'm leaving this afternoon for Washington," Colonel Mulligan said. "Trying to get the War Department to reinstate the Brigade. Glad to get these sent." He sat down and began to sign the letters. "A beautiful job, Mrs. Kelly."

"Bridget wrote a good few. She studies at Saint Xavier's, you know—soon to graduate. Top of her class. Your brother-in-law kindly invited my daughter to attend the Brigade's ball," I said.

"Not formally," said Mrs. Nugent.

"Mother." James Nugent winked at Bridget. "I'll send you a note."

"And please give your sister my condolences," Colonel Mulligan said.

"Your letter meant a great deal to her. She wrote some of these letters. She said she was very glad to help other mothers."

"Yes. That will be important. I'm sorry I have to leave. I'd like to thank her."

"She works in Mr. Potter Palmer's store downtown—his best saleswoman."

I saw Mrs. Nugent open her mouth, but Marion nudged her in the ribs.

"We'll be going now, Colonel. I'll take the letters to the post office. Good afternoon."

✥   ✥   ✥

"Oh, Mam, how could you? You were bragging about me in front of Marion Mulligan and the colonel," Bridget said. "What will James Nugent think!"

We walked along LaSalle.

"Let's hope he thinks for himself and doesn't let his snob of a mother, Alice, boss him. If he hasn't the courage to stand up to her, he's no good to you. Puts me in mind of the story a Claddagh woman told me about a mother who didn't like the girl her son loved," I said. "Would you like to hear it, Bridget?"

"Mam, I'm in no mood for a story. I'll never be able to look James Nugent in the face again."

"Now, Bridget, a story shortens a journey." She didn't say no, so I began. "Fadó, a long time ago, a Claddagh fellow loved a girl and his mother took against her. The mother spread terrible gossip about the girl. Said she was no better than a whore, and on and on. The fellow believed the slander and broke off with the girl. Then he found out it was all lies. He went to the girl to apologize, but she would have nothing to do with him. He haunted her father's cottage, but she wouldn't see him. One day he caught the girl coming down to the strand. He begged her to take him back. 'Marry me. Marry me.' He said he was furious with his mother. Now, these two loved each other with a kind of passion that can be a curse. And so the girl said, 'I will marry you.' He was over the moon. 'I will marry you,' she went on, 'when you bring me your mother's heart in your own two hands.' And the boy did it. He cut out his mother's heart and offered it, all dripping with blood, to the girl. 'From my own two hands,' he said. And you see that heart and those hands on the Claddagh wedding ring."

"Oh, Mam, that's a horrible story!"

"Maybe, but there's something to it. Mothers can be very possessive of their sons." Mothers and sons—Johnny Og's last word was "Mathair." I'd cut out my own heart to save my sons. If Mrs. Nugent didn't want her son involved with a Bridgeport girl, at least Bridget was warned.

✥   ✥   ✥

Máire came home from the Shop more like herself than before the war had started.

"You won't believe it!" she told me.

She'd been called to Mr. Potter Palmer's office, and who was there? Only Colonel James Mulligan himself, wanting to thank her in person before he left for Washington. Mr. Potter Palmer had been very impressed. A collection had already been taken up among the clerks as a contribution toward a stone for Johnny Og's grave, she'd told Colonel Mulligan. And then the two men had asked her would she consider a more active way to honor her son's memory? It seemed women's clubs all over the country were coming together in the United States Sanitary Commission, to help improve conditions at hospitals and army camps.

"Think about it, Honora," Máire said. "It was fever killed Johnny Og. Maybe with better medicine, he'd have survived."

The women were going to try to keep close track of the wounded and get information to their families.

"I could have gone to him if I'd known where he was," she said.

"Máire, this all sounds wonderful. And you'll be so good at it."

"I will," she said. "Most of the others are Protestant society women, but I'm well able for them. Don't I deal with them every day in the Shop?" Máire's eyes filled. "Johnny Og would be pleased."

"He would," I said.

Máire's new sense of purpose cheered us all, though Bridget had received no note from James Nugent and tried to hide her disappointment. For two weeks, she'd gone to the post office every day—nothing.

Máire noticed Bridget moping about the place and asked me what was wrong with her. "It's nothing, really, compared to your real sorrow," I said to her, but she made me tell. Máire said lovesickness was a relief—normal, at least. She had a long talk with Bridget. Whatever she said, Bridget wrote James Nugent a note wishing him a happy Christmas and inviting him to visit the family sometime. Máire got Thomas to take it: "He'll talk his way past the mother," she said.

Now they'll think Bridget's a bold piece, I thought, but said nothing.

Thomas came back full of his conversation with James Nugent. It seems Mrs. Nugent told her son that Bridget Kelly was engaged to a Bridgeport boy in the Brigade, claimed her maid had told her. An officer mustn't turn the head of the sweetheart of one of his own men. Well, Thomas had set him straight. So.

Bridget was sure she'd never see or hear from James Nugent. The humiliation, the shame . . .

"Do the washing," I told her. "Take your mind off James Nugent."

The next day, Saturday, Bridget set the washtub up in the yard. It was cold, but the sun was out and there was a breeze from the west. I said if she could get the clothes rinsed and up on the line by noon, they'd dry and not go all icy.

I walked over to the window to see how she was getting on when I saw the young man come striding along: black trousers, green jacket, brass buttons shining in the sun—and those golden curls . . . James Nugent himself.

I smiled. He wasn't carrying his mother's heart. But this was Amerikay, after all.

Chapter 31

THE CHRISTMAS OF 1861 came and went with no sign of Patrick Kelly—disappointing for us all. Though I was a bit relieved. No near occasion of sin.

Paddy and the Irish Brigade stayed in Chicago. Jamesy and Máire's boys had not enlisted. No fighting. Both armies in winter quarters. For the first time in my life, I hoped for a late spring.

I'd started going into the office every day and was glad that the work I did for Colonel Mulligan demanded such concentration. Kept my thoughts from going astray. I looked after the mail, sorting through the sack of letters Mickey Gilleran, our messenger boy, brought from the post office and giving each man his letters. Colonel Mulligan received the most. At first he had dictated the replies to me, word by word, a slow process. Then one day he said, "You know what I mean. Finish it." The results pleased him, and now I read his letters and drafted the answers for routine matters. Not that Colonel Mulligan wasn't a powerful man for words, but his brain raced ahead of his pen, and I recopied even secret communications to the War Department in Washington. Soon Alderman Comiskey and Mr. Onahan were asking for my help, too. Very busy, I was. Good.

"We're both of us women in the know," Máire said to me on this late March morning as we rode the horsecar downtown together.

Máire had moved up through the ranks to become an official with the United States Sanitary Commission. "Hygiene," she'd say. "It's hygiene that will save lives. More soldiers die from filth than from wounds," she told anyone who would listen. Máire never forgot that her own Johnny Og might have been saved.

Today, she was going on about Camp Douglas. The Union army compound now contained a stockade for Confederate prisoners that was a disgrace, she said. Built so quickly, without drains or sewers, the place had been bad enough for regular soldiers, but now almost ten thousand sick men in rags were crowded into a space meant for half that number.

It was General Grant, Mrs. Nugent's cousin, who'd filled Camp Douglas when he captured two forts in Tennessee called Fort Henry and Fort Donelson. No thought of any kind of parole. Unconditional surrender were the only terms he offered. "The gloves are off now," Colonel Mulligan had said. Surprising, too, because General Buckner, the Confederate general Grant had beaten, had been his best friend at West Point. "Simon Buckner sent Grant money for his fare home from California when Grant had to resign from the army because of drunkenness," the colonel said. The three men in the office had shaken their heads. Buckner was married to a Chicago girl.

In Chicago, a friend was a friend. Certain rules applied. "Defeat the fellow, but don't rub his nose in it," Mr. Comiskey had said. "Might need him again one day."

The Confederate prisoners had arrived near the end of February, at the same time Colonel Mulligan finally got orders from Washington. He could reassemble the Irish Brigade, except—I flinched, remembering the colonel's reaction—the Brigade was assigned to guard Camp Douglas, with Colonel Mulligan as commandant, right on the Lake at 33rd and Cottage Grove. Freezing out there with the March wind blowing in from the water and not a tree or bush to stop it. Paddy says there's no heat at all inside the barracks. Prisoners' fingers and toes get frostbite and have to be amputated. Some don't survive the operation. "Poor devils," Paddy had said to me. He hates guarding that prison. What awful duty for the proud Irish Brigade. And no way to get the orders changed.

"It's hell, pure and simple," Paddy had said.

Every day, the colonel sends another letter to some general or politician or government official, demanding the Irish Brigade be sent to the field "as a legally constituted combat force." Paddy says it plainer:

"Let us fight and get the damn war over." I was only glad that he ate supper at home and slept in his own bed. However awful the place, it wasn't a battlefield.

Máire kept giving out about Camp Douglas, but we were almost downtown, so I interrupted her to say that the colonel was trying to make conditions better. But he'd been given little money to run the camp, and whenever he made any improvements or allowed the prisoners to have visitors, the *Chicago Tribune* attacked him as a Copperhead, the name for fellows soft on the South, secessionist sympathizers. Irishmen are Democrats, the paper said, untrustworthy. Didn't the colonel realize the prisoners were only waiting for a chance to escape and set Chicago on fire? the newspaper said. They are the enemy. No treatment is too harsh.

"A lot of powerful people in the government agree with the *Tribune*," I said.

"And doesn't the *Tribune* remember that our boys are in southern prisons? Those camps are even worse," Máire said. "We've complained, written letters, but if our side is as bad as theirs . . . Jesus, Mary, and Joseph, isn't war the most demented activity ever invented?"

❖ ❖ ❖

I came into the office and went over to a table in the corner I used as my desk. Here I was out of the fray. Men were often meeting with the colonel or Alderman Comiskey or Mr. Onahan, or all three, dozens every day. Some of them were contributors to the Brigade, others were suppliers bidding for contracts to supply the camp. Then there were all manner of fellows looking to have a word on one thing or another, who then stayed to discuss war strategy, the incompetence in Washington.

Such a conference was going on now. From the look of the two fellows speaking to Alderman Comiskey, I'd say it was Chicago politics they were discussing. Fellow aldermen. I wonder, will James McKenna ever see Bridgeport part of Chicago and himself on the city council? "Next year," he'd said. "In 1863 we'll be incorporated into Chicago."

I started opening the mail. All week I'd been reading sad pleas for information from the families of prisoners. Many, many Irish. The letters would begin: *I address you as a fellow Irishman, knowing your devotion to Ireland which we share. I implore you . . .* Their sons had fought with the 10th Tennessee Infantry, the Rebel Sons of Erin at Fort Donelson or Fort Henry. No word since. Killed? Captured? *Please God, captured, and with you in Camp Douglas.* The names—John O'Neill, Patrick O'Donnell, Anthony O'Brien, Murphys, McCarthys—were the same ones listed on the roster of the Irish Brigade. These southern boys weren't fighting in support of slavery or secession, the letters would try to explain, but *because we live here in the Confederate part of Tennessee. Such a fever for war, and my son's no coward, but an Irishman ready to prove himself. And don't the Fenians say we'll all get together to liberate Ireland after the war?*

If we'd stayed in New Orleans, Paddy could be in the Confederate army, fighting against the Irish Brigade. What I'd feared had happened. Irish boys, saved from the Great Starvation at such cost, were marching off to murder one another.

Then I opened a letter from today's pile: *My very dear and Respected Commander and Founder of the illustrious Irish Brigade,* I read. *I understand Your Honor must be inundated with imprecations from fellow Irishmen anxious and anguished. We who have been swept up into this cataclysm . . .* Sounds like Owen Mulloy, I thought, following the big words across the page. Owen Mulloy? I turned the page over: *Yours with immense gratitude, Eugene Mulloy.*

Dear God. Could it be?

"Colonel Mulligan!" I shouted. "What is American for 'Owen'?"

"Eugene, I believe."

Owen Mulloy! Our Knocnacuradh neighbors! Nearly fifteen years since they'd left. Not a word from them, and now . . . Owen wrote that his son James, seventeen, one of the 10th Tennessee Rebel Sons of Erin, had been reported missing, presumed dead after the February 8 battle. Over a month now, but his wife in her great faith hoped against hope: Could it be possible his boy was with the colonel?

James, of course, the baby, about two years old when they left. James, who'd only just survived—Katie's milk had been thin. The food Máire'd brought revived her, saved him. James.

"Colonel!" I shouted at him, waving the letter, trying to explain. The men were startled. I rushed across the room.

The quiet Mrs. Kelly had lost the run of herself. I grabbed his arm, and the colonel was so shocked that he let me propel him out of the office, down to the street, and into his carriage.

⟡   ⟡   ⟡

We drove south on Cottage Grove, with me urging his horse to go faster. Please God, let James Mulloy be there, alive. No way to know. No real muster rolls. All the prisoners in Camp Douglas were enlisted men. No officers. The Confederate sergeants had charge of the units of men.

When we finally reached the place, I jumped from the carriage and ran to the gate. "Open up!" I shouted at the sentry.

Colonel Mulligan came up next to me. He took my arm. "Mrs. Kelly," he said, "there are ten thousand desperate men inside this stockade, many of them sick with dysentery and fever. Three died yesterday. You can't go in there and risk yourself."

"Think of my sister's son—your own soldier—dying from a wound that needn't have killed him. My neighbor's boy might be in there, sick and suffering. I have to try to save him. You're the commander, Colonel Mulligan. Order that fellow to open the gate."

He did.

Long rows of prisoners' barracks filled the enclosure. The colonel said we couldn't go into the barracks alone; one of the inmate trustees would have to take us; talking on and on, when Owen and Katie's son might be shut up in one of those forty or fifty sheds.

"Paddy Kelly!" I shouted. "Paddy, it's your mother calling you!"

A Bridgeport fellow named Willie Doherty heard me. He was standing on the wall above us. "Mrs. Kelly? What?"

"Bring my Paddy to me *now.*"

Paddy was not pleased to see me. He saluted Colonel Mulligan and said to me very sternly that I shouldn't be here.

"I'm looking for James Mulloy, Owen and Katie's son. Take me to the Tennessee Irish boys."

"The Rebel Sons? They're wild men," he said.

But I kept moving toward the barracks. Then I saw, nailed on one door, a scrap of dirty cloth with a harp drawn on it. "Faugh-a-Ballagh" and "Rebel Sons of Erin" were written on this frayed banner.

A group of soldiers stood near the door, cooking something on a stick over a bonfire. Scarecrows, with long beards. One held out the stick to me. "A bit of rat, lady?" he said.

The others shushed him but wouldn't let us through. "You can't go in there, missus," one said.

I pushed past them.

A coffin ship. In the dim light, I could just make out plank bunks built one on top of the other, four high, with three or four men on each slab. The stench, the sound of coughing, and a kind of groaning pushed against me.

"James Mulloy! James Owen Mulloy, call out to me!"

Fellows sat up in their bunks to stare at us.

"James, James Mulloy," said Paddy.

"Here I am. Here!"

Alive. Thank God, alive. I ran down an aisle and over to the bunk.

He was struggling to stand, his bedmates helping him to swing his legs out, get his feet on the ground.

"James, alanna, James," I said, and reached for him.

James Mulloy pulled back. "Don't touch me, missus. I'm covered with lice." He used the edge of the bunk to stand up.

He looks like Owen Mulloy. The same nose, those deep-set blue eyes. But, oh, he's skin and bones. He smiled. Dear God, Katie's smile.

"I'm Honora Kelly. Your neighbor from home."

"Home? From Nashville?" he asked.

"Home," I said. "Ireland."

"Galway Bay?" asked James Mulloy.

"Yes, yes," I said. "Your father is Owen, your mother's Katie."

"You do know me," he said.

"I remember the Mulloys," said Paddy, excited, "I do."

Colonel Mulligan stood beside us now.

"Colonel Mulligan," I said, "this boy's sick."

"The hospital is overcrowded," he said.

"A death sentence, to be put in that place," Paddy said.

"I volunteer to take him home and nurse him."

"Mrs. Kelly . . ."

"Parole him, Colonel. To me."

One of the Confederate soldiers took James Mulloy's arm and bellowed at him, "You're pledged to the Confederate States of America. You'll stay here with your comrades."

James bent over, coughing out a stream of blood.

"Fever!" I shouted. "This fellow's got the fever!" I put my arm around James Mulloy and started walking. "Stand back! Get away! Fever! Fever!"

That cleared the way. The Confederate soldier let go of James Mulloy and I was able to get him down the aisle and out the door,

Paddy walking behind me. The colonel argued with the Confederate soldiers as we made our escape.

James Mulloy and I left the stockade, crossed through the army camp and out to Cottage Grove where the colonel's carriage waited. I helped James into the back.

"Mam—you can't!" Paddy was behind me.

"Get up on the box, Paddy!"

"Mam!"

"Jesus Christ, Paddy! Some blacksmith you'd be if you couldn't drive a team of two horses."

"But it's—"

"A *parole d'honneur*, Paddy. Move!"

❖ ❖ ❖

Máire was home, thank God. "We'll put him in Johnny Og's bed," she said. We undressed and washed him. No fever, but that racking cough and the blood that he brought up worried us.

"Get Patrick Kelly's salve," Máire said.

Patrick kept us supplied with Indian remedies. I watched Máire rub James Mulloy's sunken chest with the same tenderness she would have given to Johnny Og. My big sister has a generous heart.

Máire found a willing assistant in Gracie, and as the days passed, James recovered. Food and sleep and hygiene worked their cure.

I posted James Mulloy's letter to Owen and Katie as soon as he could write. What a joy to add my note.

A miracle.

But now the matter of the parole. Colonel Mulligan couldn't flaunt the law quite so blatantly. What if the *Tribune* found out? I knew that the War Department allowed Confederate soldiers to enlist in the Union army if they paid a thousand-dollar bond.

"And betray my friends?" James Mulloy said. "No way to get that kind of money anyway."

Then Colonel Mulligan came up with his brilliant and surprising scheme. Remember, Colonel James Mulligan sympathized with the Fenians. He denied that the British had any right to Ireland whatsoever, but if seeming to suspend his principles could help a fellow Irishman, well . . . Here was the plan:

Because James Mulloy had been born in Ireland, the British considered him a subject of the empire. The Sassenach refused to recognize the status of naturalized American citizens. Máire and I had gotten our papers soon after arriving in Chicago, eager to be Americans, as were all Irish people, but Great Britain said we still belonged to them. Made it easier to call all Fenians traitors, the colonel explained.

Now he said, "Let's use the Sassenach to our advantage."

As a British subject, James Mulloy, though fighting with the Confederate army, was not, strictly speaking, a rebel against the United States. Could he be paroled into the custody of the British consul and then handed over to us?

Colonel Mulligan pulled out law books and military codes and decided the idea was worth a try.

The next day, Máire and I were waiting in the office of the secretary to the British consul in Chicago. We had the proposal Colonel Mulligan had framed in the very best legal language and letters from both Alderman Comiskey and William Onahan. The colonel had decided that we should meet this fellow on our own—more sympathetic and fewer questions.

After nearly an hour, the secretary swanned in—narrow face, jutting chin, and that drawling voice typical of the tribe of English civil servants that had mismanaged our misery during the Great Starvation. He would deal with our case. The consul was much too busy. He took the colonel's document, leaned back in his chair, and started reading.

Patrick Kelly had predicted that the British would favor the South, and events proved him right. The *Chicago Times* reported that Secretary Seward told the British prime minister we'd invade Canada if they didn't stop aiding the rebels, but the British kept building ships for the Confederates, as well as raising money for the South, and transporting Confederate officials on their ships. What had Patrick said? They want a weak America, get some of those colonies back.

The secretary put down the document. "You expect *me* to claim this fellow as our citizen and then parole him to you? On what grounds? You have no standing—"

"I'm an officer of the Sanitary Commission," Máire interrupted him. "I'm sure you've heard of it." She started to list all the important women in Chicago who belonged.

But the secretary stopped Máire with this question: "Why would two enemies of Great Britain like Mulligan and Comiskey appeal to us? And why for a soldier in the army of the enemy?"

"To save a life," I said.

He only laughed.

"Does this argument help?" Máire put the small leather bag on the table. "Twenty-five silver dollars, to cover any, uhm, fees."

Alderman Comiskey had contributed ten dollars, the colonel and Mr. Onahan five, and we'd made up the rest. The fellow only stared at us.

"I believe," I said, "that Alderman Comiskey mentions in his letter the business dealings of British citizens here—imports, land speculation, investments. The city council decides so many issues—licenses, tax levies, zoning—and the alderman is a very respected member."

The secretary picked up the bag of money, felt the weight of it in his hand.

"Colonel Mulligan prepared a letter granting the parole," I said, passing the letter over the desk to him.

The fellow put down the money pouch, dipped the quill pen on his desk into the inkwell, and signed the letter. Then he took the pouch and stood. "I'll never understand you people," he said.

"An Irish solution to an Irish problem," Máire said as we laughed our way down Lake Street.

"A Chicago solution," I said.

Máire stuck her hip out. "I don't understand you people," she drawled.

"And never will," I said.

❖ ❖ ❖

Two weeks later, James felt well enough to tell us his story. The whole family gathered to listen, James Nugent with us, a frequent visitor now.

"When we left Ireland," James Mulloy began, "I was only two years old, so I'm not sure what I really remember and what's been told me. I do remember the ship—the darkness and me crying—and then the island. My da's told me about the Keeley brothers who sailed with us."

"What did he say?" Máire asked.

"Only that two of the brothers lived, but the third one died, and his wife with him."

"And the children?" I asked.

"I don't think he knows what happened to them. We were in Quebec a very short time, then walked for weeks and weeks through the woods, until we came to Saratoga Springs in New York."

"You walked?" I said. "But isn't that a far way?"

"Unimaginably ex-ten-sive, according to my father," James said, making Gracie and Bridget laugh.

"Brave of you," I said.

"There were other families with us. A kind of network of Irish settlements and farms scattered throughout the North Woods. We found help with them."

"Your father wrote to us about my husband's brother—Patrick Kelly. Did he ever say anything to you?"

"Is he the man with the golden staff? There were stories told about him in our family. In fact, there was an Irishman came to Nashville before the war started, recruiting Irishmen to the federal side. They said he carried some kind of relic. Would that be him?"

"That's Uncle Patrick."

"We stayed away from the fellow," James Mulloy said. "But then . . ."

He stopped and looked at Paddy, in uniform, and at James Nugent, with his lieutenant's bars. They only shrugged their shoulders. We weren't fighting the war in this parlor. Still, better to stay in the past.

"But why did you settle in Saratoga?"

"The racetrack, of course. Da found a job as a stable hand, then became a trainer. My brothers worked with him. We won a fair number of races."

"You would," I said.

"We moved to Tennessee, near Nashville, where Da started to breed horses." He smiled Katie's smile. "Da used to say, 'Someday I will have a great horse, and I will name him Askeeboy and we'll race on the grandest tracks of the country. And my old friend Michael Kelly will read about it in the papers and one day he'll come to us. He'll stand in the doorway with Honora and Paddy and Jamesy and Bridget.' He didn't know about you, Stephen, or Michael."

"Probably forgot me," said Máire.

"He talked about you, the most beautiful woman in five parishes, the Snowy-Breasted Pearl, he called you, and sang a song about you."

"Ah," said Máire. "Owen always was a grand man."

✤ ✤ ✤

All through April and May, James Mulloy was with us. One night early in his stay, some rowdies came pounding at the door, shouting that we were hiding an enemy soldier. The boys went down and there was a bit of a punch-up.

Then Paddy told these fellows that James Mulloy was a cousin of ours, in a Tennessee regiment loyal to the Union. Paddy's unit had escorted the prisoners to Camp Douglas. James was on sick leave. Any other questions? No? Then Paddy asked them: Why weren't *they* in the army?

We had no more trouble. Even our close friends preferred to believe Paddy's explanation.

But the battles had started up again. Conscription was expected. A year of war and no end in sight. Rage was building against "the enemy"—best to keep James Mulloy's identity quiet.

Molly Flanigan said to me after one Holy Hour, "I saw Gracie and that lad out walking. I hope he's a *distant* cousin." I told her James Mulloy was a Kelly relation, no connection to Gracie.

"How's your prisoner?" Colonel Mulligan would ask me. He never spoke to me of hating the "sessechs"—war was a job of work to be done, and done quickly.

Colonel Mulligan had gone to Washington, determined to get the Brigade a new assignment.

✤ ✤ ✤

It was the first day of June. I got up before first light to enjoy that early morning time I considered my own, when I heard voices from the parlor.

Paddy was talking to James Mulloy. They must have sat up all night, drinking whiskey and solving the problems of the world. They didn't hear me walking in my bare feet over the plank floor, automatically avoiding the creaks. I stopped in the hallway.

"So," James Mulloy was saying, "would you explain to your mother why I have to go back to camp?"

"She'll not understand."

"Darby Lee and I enlisted together in Nashville," James Mulloy said.

"He's eighteen. He was in the Saint Patrick's Club. Darby Lee. Hard to believe he's dead. How many from the Tenth have died?"

"Near twenty, I'd say."

"All fever?"

"Dysentery, too. Listen to me, James. If you go back, you'll catch some disease yourself. I'd rather put you on a train headed south," Paddy said.

"You couldn't do that to your family and Colonel Mulligan. You'd be Copperheads for sure then. You might even get arrested."

"But the camp's worse now than when you first came. Some fellows like to bully the prisoners. One guard's brother was shot dead at Erin's Hollow fighting your regiment. He says he's going to kill one of you before he leaves—an eye for an eye."

"He should go gunning for that Yankee general McClernand. He sent those poor bastards running up the hill into our guns. What can you do when the enemy charges except fire at him?" James Mulloy said.

"I know. Same at Lexington. All the noise and smoke and men rushing at you. You just shoot."

"I didn't even aim," said James. "I couldn't see."

"We couldn't either," said Paddy.

"Then the woods caught fire."

"What?"

"At Erin's Hollow, the Yankees carried their wounded into a stand of trees. There must have been shells near the trees, and what with the dry weather and the heat, the woods exploded into flames. You could hear the wounded screaming. Our colonel McGavock called a cease-fire and sent a bunch of us down to help the Yankees. We rescued some, but . . . it was terrible. This Yankee soldier and I saw a boy with half his face burned away, carried him out. The soldier, an Irish fellow, was from Galena, Illinois. Once we got the wounded out to the field hospitals, we all stood around talking, both sides. Mostly about stupid orders from dumb officers. But what can you do?"

"Nothing," said Paddy. "Only keep your head down and fight like hell."

I backed down the hall, then walked back to the door, making plenty of noise.

"Well, you boys are up early. Who's for coffee and a bowl of porridge? James Mulloy, I've work for you to do today. Paddy, tell the colonel our prisoner's gainfully employed."

"I will, Mam."

James tried to talk but I wouldn't let him. I kept going on and on about how I needed his help until Paddy whispered to James, "Surrender." They ate their breakfast together.

This reprieve will end soon, I thought. The colonel was sure the Brigade would be ordered to Virginia any day—big battles there. Paddy and James Nugent would go.

And now Thomas had surprised us by enlisting in the Irish Brigade. "In honor of my brother John," he said.

Jamesy and Daniel told Máire and me that they planned to join the new Irish Legion and march away under their own harp and shamrock banners.

James Mulloy would be exchanged into the fight.

Patrick Kelly was out on some battlefield somewhere.

Seven of them.

And Stephen and Michael only waiting.

Mrs. McGrath's song went through my mind—her son Ted forced into the British army came back from the wars with two wooden legs:

> *"Oh, Teddy, me boy," the widow cried,*
> *"Your two fine legs were your Mammy's pride!*
> *Those stumps of trees won't do at all;*
> *Why didn't you run from the cannonball?"*

Run away, I wanted to shout at Paddy and James Mulloy—at all of them. Run away, all of you. But I knew they wouldn't.

Chapter 32

Christmas was less than a month away, 1863 was almost over, and the boys had been fighting in the South for more than a year.

They had marched away singing. Paddy and Thomas left in mid-June with the Irish Brigade, the 23rd Illinois, shouting out that same promise to come safely "home again, to the girl I left behind me." Jamesy and Daniel, in the new Irish Legion, got an even more glorious send-off in August, because it was Father Dennis Dunne, pastor at St. Patrick's, who'd organized this second unit, the 90th Illinois.

Father Dunne had said the highest of High Masses for them at St. Patrick's. Stephen had been an altar boy. He'd swung the gold censer with great energy, sending up such clouds of incense that Máire whispered to me, "He'll choke the life out of them before they get to the fighting!" The nine hundred members of the Irish Legion were blessed by Father Dunne, Father Tom Kelly, and a dozen other priests. Michael had sung a solo with the choir. At the end of the ceremony, the pipes sounded their call. It was Jamesy played "The Minstrel Boy to the War Is Gone," and every man in the Irish Legion sang the words. They roared out the final chorus:

> *Thy songs were made for the pure and free,*
> *They shall never sound in slavery!*

President Lincoln finally freed the slaves. James McKenna had said the president would wait until *after* the election, worried about votes. But he hadn't. "Now our cause is truly noble," Father Kelly told us in his last sermon before he'd gone off to be chaplain for the Irish Legion at their camp in Tennessee.

There'd been celebrations among the colored people in the neighborhood south of us. We'd gone over to see the bonfires, hear the singing. I thought of Congo Square, of M'am Jacques and her children, of Sister Henriette, how happy they must be. I'd come to know a woman from this neighborhood. I'd met Mrs. Williams on my walks along the Lake, and she'd told me that most of the colored families living in their community had been free for a while, but there were some escaped slaves among them who were certainly relieved. Her sons are serving in a colored unit of the army.

In the year and a half the Brigade and Legion had been in the field, they'd been spared from the worst of the fighting. Not at Antietam, Chancellorsville, Shiloh, or Gettysburg. Even Barney McGurk, who'd expected high casualties, was shaken by Gettysburg—fifty thousand killed and wounded or missing in only three days of fighting. During those same bloody days at the start of July 1863, Jamesy and Daniel fought under General Grant to break the long siege of Vicksburg. "One of the greatest artillery attacks on a city in history," Barney said. "Grant had five hundred cannons blasting at them day and night." The surrender came on the fourth of July. Huge bonfires in Bridgeport that night.

But the letter we received from Jamesy and Daniel two weeks later said nothing about the actual battles. They were only glad that the Union controlled the Mississippi River, because now the mail would get through. They'd finally get their pay.

Many mothers in Bridgeport were trying to feed their families on soldiers' wages that never arrived. Food prices rose every day. Thank God for Máire's salary and the money Alderman Comiskey paid me.

Not as much to do at the office with Colonel Mulligan gone, but I still went in every day, eager for news of the Irish Brigade. They were part of the defense of Washington, D.C., and had fought in a good few battles, though you wouldn't know it from Paddy's letters or the short postscripts Thomas scribbled on them. The boys wrote about the camp, the food, and the fellows they were meeting from other places.

Wives and mothers of the men serving in the Irish Brigade and in other units, too, came to the office every day. "We'll be a city of widows and orphans when this is over," I heard Alderman Comiskey say to Mr. Onahan, as casualties climbed.

Sometimes the women came to me at home. They knew I worked for Alderman Comiskey. Would I write them a letter to take to him? Go with them? They got tongue-tied, they said, when it came to asking for charity. "Not charity," I'd tell them. "What you deserve."

Last week, Mrs. O'Brien, whose husband was in the Brigade, had asked if Alderman Comiskey could help her twelve-year-old son, Mickey, get a job. She appreciated the bit of money she'd received already, but she had five younger children, and even when her husband's army pay arrived, it wasn't enough. And she believed that working might stop her Mickey from talking on and on about joining the army.

Stephen had been doing his homework in the parlor during Mrs. O'Brien's visit. At sixteen, he stood nearly six feet tall, hair as red as ever. He'd asked me how Alderman Comiskey got people jobs. I'd explained the clout—that word again—a man like John Comiskey had as an alderman, city councilman, and a member of every Irish organization in Chicago. Favors, given and gotten, I'd said. Votes come into it—at election time, people remembered who'd helped them.

Stephen had said he'd like a job helping people, and maybe he'd try for politics. But then he'd said he couldn't do that. He'd be letting down the men at the firehouse. They'd promised him that in two years when he was eighteen he could become a full-fledged fireman. So. I needn't worry about him joining the army. Uncle Patrick had told him it was his duty to stay in Chicago in case the prisoners at Camp Douglas escaped and set the city on fire—a fireman's special mission. The men at the firehouse had said Patrick was spot on, Stephen said to me.

I told Stephen that perhaps he could be a fireman for a while and then run for alderman. Bridgeport had finally been incorporated in Chicago. Who knows, he might be elected mayor. "A mayor from Bridgeport," Stephen said. "Now that would be something." But then he shook his head. He wanted to be a policeman, too, and own a tavern. No time for all the things he wanted to do. "My son," Stephen had said then.

"Your son? What son?" Surely Stephen would never . . .

He'd laughed. "The look on your face, Mam!" he'd said. "I'm talking about the son Nelly Lang and I will have after we're married."

I knew he and the professor's daughter were great friends. Bridget told me Stephen went to dances at Nelly's parish, St. Michael's, and brought her to parties at St. Bridget's. But now Stephen told me that they intended to marry in eight years, when he was twenty-four. They would have lots of children. His oldest son could become mayor of Chicago. Why not? "Done and dusted," I said. Very American, our Stephen. A Chicago man.

Will the other boys live to marry, have children? Pray. Nothing to do but pray, I thought as I came into the kitchen and started to cook.

❖ ❖ ❖

"Out eating the altar rails, Honora?" Máire said as she passed the pratties to Bridget. We took our evening meals together, only six of us around the table now. Bridget spooned some potatoes onto her plate. Eighteen now, she'll graduate in June, become a teacher or Mrs. James Nugent or both. So lovely, she's like Máire, blond curls, a woman's figure. Gracie, taking the bowl from her, was a Keeley, no question, with her height and straight chestnut hair. At sixteen, she's as tall as I am. Strange things, resemblances. Stephen's the image of my brother Hughie, the uncle he'll never see, and young Michael has his father's eyes and hair. Doing blacksmith work, too, after school, to keep Paddy's place at Slattery's. I'm grateful for his wages. Please God we can afford to keep him in school. Paddy would want him to finish. Paddy . . . Where is he right now? I wonder.

"All right to have more potatoes?" Stephen asked.

"Go ahead," I said.

Potatoes had become our mainstay again, the cheapest food.

"Which one tonight?" Máire was asking me. "Holy Family?"

"I don't go there on Saturday. Too crowded. Confession." All I needed was to run into that canon-law-spouting Jesuit coming out of the confessional. "I made the Stations at Saint Bridget's after the Holy Hour," I said.

Father Kelly had installed the Way of the Cross last year. The fourteen pictures, set along the side walls of the church, brought to mind moments in Jesus's journey to crucifixion in "Stations." I liked to move from one to the next, stopping to pray where Jesus fell the first time, or met his mother, or had his face wiped by Veronica. Father Kelly said we should unite our sufferings with the sufferings of Christ, but it was the

Mother of Jesus I pleaded with: You walked this path of sorrow. Protect our sons. Strengthen their mothers.

I made the Stations in seven different churches each week, which bewildered Máire.

"Why not make the Stations at Saint Bridget's every day instead of running from church to church?" she asked me.

All the young ones stopped eating and waited for my answer.

"I suppose I feel more like I'm on a pilgrimage, going to Lough Derg or somewhere. Harder this way. And I've a reason for each church. Sundays I go to Holy Name Cathedral. It's Colonel Mulligan's parish, and so a good place to pray for the Brigade. The Stations of the Cross there are carved from white stone. Lovely. Monday I visit Saint Patrick's because it's connected with the Irish Legion. Father Dunne displays their flag at the same side altar where Patrick Kelly sets up Saint Grellan's staff at Christmas. The Stations are only framed pictures, but the statues of Saint Patrick, Saint Columcille, and Saint Bridget are beautiful—which helps."

"Helps what, Mam?" Bridget asked.

"Prayer," I said.

"So where do you go on Tuesday, Aunt Honey?" Gracie asked.

"Saint Mary's," I said. "It's near the office, and I couldn't leave Chicago's oldest church out. Then Wednesday I do Holy Family."

"'Do' it?" Stephen asked. "What do you mean?"

"Make the Stations, light candles."

"And Thursday?" This from Michael.

"Saint James—have to, with all the fellows named James I'm praying for, and it's close. And then Immaculate Conception on Friday. Not too far away, and the pastor there was in the field with the Irish Brigade."

"And how do the decorations there compare to, say, Holy Name?" Máire said.

"Hard to say. Immaculate Conception's new, but it does have a stained-glass window and . . ."

Máire started laughing.

"What? What's funny?" I asked.

"You are," Máire said.

Bridget and Gracie were giggling. Stephen and Michael screwed up their faces, but the laughter burst out.

"If you could hear yourself," Máire said. "A mad woman."

"Think of it, Mam," Bridget said. "You also go to Mass every day and the Holy Hour."

"You must spend a fortune lighting candles," Máire said.

"To tell you the truth, I put in three pennies for the nine of them."

"Nine?" asked Michael.

"Paddy, Jamesy, Thomas, Daniel, James Nugent, James Mulloy, Colonel Mulligan, and Patrick Kelly. And"—I looked at Máire—"I light one for Johnny Og, that he may rest in peace."

No one said anything for a time.

"That's good, Honora," Máire said.

"Thanks for including James Mulloy," Gracie said. She'd announced that their wedding would take place as soon as the war ended.

"Still, that's a lot of miles to cover," Máire said.

"Helps me sleep," I said.

The others nodded. We could contain our fear for the men during the day, but not through the long, wakeful nights. Often I'd hear Michael or Stephen or Bridget in the kitchen after midnight and come out to have a cup of tea with them. "Bad dreams" is all they'd say, not wanting to give shape to the dread.

"A boy at school said the odds are against us," Michael told me one of these nights in the kitchen. "Mathematics—eight fighting, two will die." The fellow had figured out that with twenty-five to thirty percent casualties in the battles, and more lost to disease, six men alive was the best we could hope for. That was only the average, Michael explained to me—more of the eight might live.

Or die, we'd both thought but didn't say.

"One has died already—Johnny Og," I said.

"One isn't enough," Michael said, and started crying.

I'd held him close. We survived starvation. We escaped to America, I told him, defying all odds and numbers. Our faith saved us. I didn't usually speak of those awful days to the children, but that night I told Michael something of what we had endured. I told him, too, the story of his own beginnings in Knocnacuradh—life defeating death.

Now, dinner was over. "We're going out, Mam," Stephen said, standing up from the table, and Michael with him.

"Don't be too late," I said. "We need to be at Mass early, so crowded on Sunday."

"But we only have to go to the one, Mam, right?" Michael said.

Laughter all around.

The girls went down to Máire's—schoolwork, they said, but really to share their letters. James Nugent's came regularly. When James Mulloy was exchanged in September, he rejoined the Rebel Sons of Erin, which made it difficult for him to write to Gracie directly. His parents in Nashville forwarded his letters to us. Owen wrote so formally, as if we didn't know each other. Careful. Someone in the post office could open and read the letter as possible enemy communication. I'd thought Owen was only dramatizing himself, but then soldiers had shut down the *Chicago Times* because Mr. Storey disagreed with President Lincoln in his editorials, though the president let the paper reopen. It was impossible to think of Owen and Katie Mulloy as the enemy, yet that was this war all over. Mrs. Lincoln herself had four brothers and three brothers-in-law in the Confederate army. Family feuds are always the most bitter. No quarter given on either side now.

Máire and I settled ourselves by the fire. She poured herself a tot of whiskey and offered one to me, knowing I'd refuse. I'd promised not to drink until the boys were home.

"Suit yourself," she said. She held up her glass and toasted me. "Here's to being spiritual, each of us in her own way." She took a long sip. "I'll give you a dollar for candles. Wouldn't want you to get caught cheating God."

"He wouldn't care."

"But some old one kneeling in the pew watching might." She took another sip. "Prayer is all well and good, but don't be going demented on me."

"I wish I'd known some of these devotions and practices at the start of the war, before Johnny Og . . ." I stopped. Had to be careful with Máire. Sometimes she wanted to talk about Johnny Og. Sometimes she didn't. I'd even hesitated to tell her I lit a candle for him every day.

"Honora, do you really think if you'd visited enough churches, the secessionist soldier wouldn't have shot Johnny Og?" Máire said. Not angry, only asking, leaning toward me.

"It's not that simple."

"Certainly isn't," she said.

"I only know I have to pray, hard and often."

How could I explain the doubts I felt? Never during the worst of the Great Starvation or even that awful time after Michael died had I lost a sense of God's presence, questioned His love. Now . . . Thoughts of Patrick Kelly crept into my mind. God forgive me. Michael, forgive me.

What a relief it would be to pour all this out to Máire. She'll say what a part of me does: Catch yourself on, Honora.

I was about to tell her when we heard someone at the downstairs door, knocking, calling out, "Mrs. Kelly, Mrs. Kelly."

"Late for a visitor," she said.

"Better go see," I said. We went down the stairs. "What is it?" I called out through the front door.

"I'm Captain Peter Casey," the man said. "From the Irish Legion."

I pulled the door open. A man in uniform—tall, fine-featured, but very thin, stricken-looking. Oh no.

"I recruited your boys," he said. "James the Piper and Danny O, we call them."

"Please," I said. "What's happened?"

"A terrible battle with the Legion in the thick of it this Wednesday, the twenty-fifth of November. Your sons . . ." He stopped.

"Not dead? No, please! Not dead?" I said.

"They're missing."

"Missing?" Máire said. "What does 'missing' mean?"

"Anything," Peter Casey said. "They could be dead or in a field hospital somewhere or taken prisoner. Or . . . they could have deserted. They weren't accounted for after the battle of Mission Ridge."

"You were there?" I said.

"No, I've been home on medical leave. My sergeant was in the battle. Mike Clark's his name. He just left my house. He's the one told me. He cleared the battlefield afterwards. He knows your fellows well. Didn't find their bodies. They're not among our wounded and didn't come back to camp."

Máire and I clutched hands.

"Surely you know more," I said.

"A cold night to stand out here," Peter Casey said. "Being in the southern heat makes me feel the cold."

"Come in," I said. "Come upstairs. A cup of tea?" I said.

"A glass of whiskey?" said Máire.

"I wouldn't say no to a drop—a time like this."

Peter Casey talked on and on, telling us we should be proud to be mothers of such great lads. He told us the name of the battle place, Mission Ridge, near Chattanooga on the Chickamauga River. "Chickamauga—River of Blood. And it was," he said. Dear God.

✥ ✥ ✥

During the following week, the *Chicago Times* printed story after story describing the fighting. In the three days of the Chattanooga battle, eight hundred Union soldiers were killed, four hundred Confederates were killed. The combined total of wounded was seven thousand. But the paper gave no names, no casualty lists. Other Irish families had received letters: "I am fine, I'll survive." But nothing for us.

"Wait and pray," Father Kelly told me. As chaplain of the Irish Legion during Vicksburg, he'd seen the chaos that follows a battle firsthand. What he'd thought were dead bodies would lift their heads, call out to him, ask for the last rites. Some miraculously recovered, while others . . . "No record keeping in the fog of war," he'd said. One thing I could be sure of, he told me—our brave boys would never desert. A comfort for me and Máire, he said. As if we cared—better living deserters than dead heroes.

I went into the office every morning but spent most of my time watching out the window. Newspaper messenger boys picked up telegrams from the reporters covering the war over at the telegraph office across the street. They always came to Mr. Comiskey if there were any stories about the Brigade or Legion. But no reports came.

✥ ✥ ✥

Then it was Christmas Eve—a month and no news. I spent the day writing addresses on the food baskets that would be delivered to soldiers' widows, mourning mothers. So many of them. Alderman Comiskey and Mr. Onahan spoke to me with quiet voices, as if I were sick. They think the boys are dead, I thought. They gave me a ham to take home and a bonus—twenty-five dollars added to my wages, "to make your Christmas a little brighter," Mr. Onahan said.

But Máire and I had agreed not to have our usual Christmas celebration. The children understood. How could we, with the boys missing? Or dead. I doubled all my prayers, but to what end?

Jamesy is dead. Admit it, Honora. You'd have heard something by now. Jamesy and Daniel are dead. If he were alive . . . That voice, the fairy woman come back, whispering to me as I started home from downtown.

I'll walk home along the Lake. Cold there, but the wind's force and the noise of the waves might drive her voice from my head.

I stepped over a brittle bank of dirty snow and moved closer to the water, whitecaps rushing toward the shore.

But the fairy woman's voice kept after me until I thought: If Jamesy is dead, then I want to die, too, plunge into the icy Lake.

I started keening into the wind, no words, howling.

For Jesus' sake, Honora, what's wrong with you? Not the fairy woman's whisper. This new voice roared at me, louder than the wind and waves.

Granny. Granny, I'm so frightened. If Jamesy's dead . . .

Ná bí ag caint, Honora. Don't be talking nonsense. Keep those words out of your head.

How? I try to pray. I'm afraid God's turned a deaf ear to all my prayers and pleading. Oh, Granny, Michael was the love of my life, the father of my children. To even consider another man, especially one forbidden by the Church. I want to be good so God will answer my prayers, keep my boy safe, but . . .

You're making God very small, a stór. Look out at this grand expanse of water. Do you think the Creator of all that's worried about your faults and failings? God's mercy is wide, Honora. Now go. You've a crowd of children waiting for their dinner. Get busy and you'll keep the fairy woman away.

And I didn't hear that voice as I walked as fast as I could back to Bridgeport, holding the ham close against me.

Máire opened her door as I passed. "I've been watching for you, Honora. Come in. The others are up in your house."

I sat down at her kitchen table.

"We made a mistake," she said. "We need to get a Christmas tree, presents. Cook a big dinner."

"But how can we? We agreed to wait until we knew the boys were—"

"We have to," she said. "Gracie and Bridget told me they feel like we've gone into mourning, given up hope. Can't do that. If we despair, the fairy woman will come creeping in." Máire took my hand. "After Johnny Og died, I almost let her take me over entirely. But I had this little sister kept tugging on me, wouldn't let me go." She patted my knee.

"Thank you, Máire," I said, and covered her hand with mine.

"And now I'm going to pull *you* back, Honora. Listen to me. I've been sitting here all afternoon thinking about Johnny Leahy and

Johnny Og—fishermen, both of them. I remembered a story Johnny Leahy told me right before our wedding. Fadó," Máire said, and winked at me. "Johnny was out fishing where Galway Bay meets the sea. They'd caught nothing, no fish, all day. When the sun sank beneath the waves, some boats turned back to shore, empty. But Johnny and his da stayed on. A slip of a moon rose, then disappeared. Complete darkness and still they waited. Then, long after most would have given up, the mearbhall—a kind of glow—started up from the deep, lighting up the sea. And suddenly all manner of fish—whiting and herring and great creatures Johnny couldn't put a name to—came swimming up through the mearbhall and into the nets. The glow lasted until the morning star appeared. At the dawning of the day, they saw they'd netted a great catch.

"Mearbhalls come, Johnny told me, only on the darkest night. But no fisherman is able to say when or where. A gift, he said, like life itself." Máire paused. "When Johnny Leahy died, I thought I'd never be happy again. One reason I stepped in for you, Honora. Might as well be miserable at the Scoundrel Pykes as anywhere, I thought."

"I know why you saved me, Máire," I said.

"Quiet now, Honora. Let me get to the point of my story. When Johnny Og was born, I was happy. And when that fool Father Gilley tried to shame me, something reared up inside. 'Johnny Og's my mearbhall, you old fool!' I wanted to shout at him. Now, I hated old Major Pyke and had little use for Robert. Hard years those were, but I had Daniel and Gracie for joy, and Thomas, too. He could make me laugh! And then Johnny Og was taken. Only darkness around me. But you brought Colonel Mulligan's letter. Johnny Og would be remembered—a mearbhall. And so's working to help other soldiers. Those four upstairs are children, for all their size and years, and their mothers are going to give them Christmas—a mearbhall."

"And their dinner," I said, lifting up the ham. "Granny told me to feed them."

❖   ❖   ❖

Every store in Bridgeport was closed this late on a Christmas Eve, but we walked to Brighton Park and didn't we see a light shining from the window of John Larney's store. He had one last scraggly tree left.

We bought it, and I got a new pen for each of my children and Gracie. Máire had her gifts already bought.

My almost grown sons and daughter and their cousin Gracie became children again when we tied candles onto the little tree. Bridget and Gracie teased Stephen about being baby Jesus that first Christmas Eve in Chicago. Máire sang her carol, and Michael harmonized with her. "Remember Jamesy and the tin whistle and what a treat it will be to hear him play the pipes," I said.

"We'll all have to learn to call Daniel Danny O," Máire said.

We opened the presents, each one delighted. Thank you, thank you.

We were all trying so hard to be happy, and no one disagreed when I said we wouldn't attend Midnight Mass, but would go at noon tomorrow, with ham and pratties afterward.

Just as well to stay home. A storm was coming. The snow started at midnight.

❖   ❖   ❖

Full morning when I woke up, after my first full night's sleep for ages. I could have slept on but for the pounding and shouting at the ground-floor door.

Could it be news? Not on Christmas morning. Probably only Molly wanting to borrow sugar. I went down.

When I opened the door, the glare of sun on snow blinded me for a moment. I saw the outline of three men in uniform. And then . . .

"Mam."

"Jamesy!" I grabbed him and rested my head on his shoulder.

"Aunt Honey."

I looked up. "Daniel. Oh, Daniel."

And Patrick Kelly.

It was my joy undid me. My knees buckled and it took the three of them to help me up the stairs to Máire's door.

Gracie raced up to get Bridget and the boys. Such a reunion!

Of course, we wanted the story then and there, but all three were tired and hungry and dirty. Jamesy said the tale deserved a good telling and could they wait, and Patrick said food and a bed first. I'd said Máire had space for him and she'd looked a question at me but said, "I do, of course."

We ate eggs and rashers in Máire's kitchen. I had to tell Stephen and Michael to stop pounding the boys on their backs. "Let them eat!" Bridget and Gracie kept patting the boys' arms.

"Now to bed, Daniel," Máire said. "I'll be sitting by your bed, watching you sleep."

Patrick took Thomas's room and we went upstairs.

Bliss to sit in my own kitchen and listen to my soldier son snoring in the next room. Thank you, Lord. A mearbhaill.

I did turn Jamesy out of bed in time for Mass. Have to show our gratitude. Granny was right, God. I'd made You too small. Jamesy and Daniel dressed in their own clothes. The pants and shirts they'd arrived in were beyond repair, though each had a heavy sheepskin jacket. Patrick wore a uniform that looked brand new. When had Patrick traded his buckskin for this?

We paraded up the middle aisle of St. Bridget's. Máire, in a new hat and coat, leaned on Daniel's arm.

A few women—newcomers—frowned at her feathers and fur collar. But our Bridgeport neighbors, well used to Máire now, admired her spirit and spunk and her war work. She'd arrived that first morning in a red silk shawl and never sailed under false colors. And weren't we all the same, really, the women said to one another. Mothers. She had lost one son, but the other had been restored to her—a victory for the Holy Hour. Blessed be the name of the Lord.

The rest of us followed Máire and Daniel, walking in a cluster around Jamesy, smiling. I caught Molly Flanigan's eye, saw Lizzie, heads turning all along the aisle. Some young fellow stood up to look past us to our honor guard—Patrick Kelly, holding St. Grellan's staff on his shoulder. Kellys Abu. Ireland Boys Hurrah. We took up the whole side pew, right in front of the crèche. There was one special addition to the usual figures of Mary, Joseph, the Christ Child, shepherds, Wise Men, and assorted animals. St. Bridget stood next to Mary. She'd been Our Lady's midwife, so Irish tradition said. Traveling back through the centuries. Why not? All a miracle anyway. And such a lovely statue of St. Bridget.

After we'd finished Christmas dinner later that afternoon, guests crowded into the parlor—James and Lizzie McKenna, Barney McGurk, Molly and two older fellows from the boardinghouse, no young men left there. Michael fit a few boys from the Hickory Gang in the corner, and Stephen had brought Nelly and the Langs.

"Now," James McKenna said, quieting the chat. He raised his mug of whiskey punch, and we all did the same. "To the heroes. Sláinte."

Jamesy frowned at Patrick, but he nodded and drank from his mug and Jamesy and Daniel did the same. I allowed myself a sip.

"To the fallen members of the Irish Legion," Patrick said.

I saw Jamesy nod. "The real heroes," he said, and took a long drink.

"We were only lucky," Daniel said after we all had drunk the toast.

"So. Now tell us, Daniel. The story," Barney McGurk said.

I sat next to Jamesy on the sofa, Máire and Daniel with us. Patrick stood against the wall near the kitchen.

"Uncle Patrick, will you?"

But Patrick shook his head.

"Go on, Jamesy," I said. "Fadó."

"All right. Fadó—if Daniel helps."

"He will," said Máire.

"After the siege was broken and Vicksburg taken . . . ," Jamesy started.

"Good tactics," Barney interrupted.

"Well, we'd won, but the Legion moved to relieve the fellows surrounded at Chattanooga. Anyway, there was a lot of back-and-forth fighting, and then we had to take this ridge—Mission Ridge, Missionary Ridge, I've heard it called both."

"Tell them how you piped us into battle," Daniel said.

"I did give out a few blasts of 'The Minstrel Boy,' " Jamesy said, then glanced over at Michael and the Hickory Gang fellows. "But really, I was scared. I mean, the Rebs had dug in up above. We had to climb this steep grade, with the enemy shooting us. The first line of us was to fire and fall back. But there was no safe place to fall back. We decided the only way to stop those guns was to get up that hill and knock them out. So we charged. Went after the enemy to save ourselves. Daniel and I stayed together, but there was no real order to any of it, only fellows running and shouting. Daniel, tell the next part."

"It got crazier," said Daniel, "the nearer we got to the top. Rebs were coming at us with bayonets, so much smoke and mess that a fellow from your own side might shoot you by mistake. Jamesy had his pipes tied to his back. We wanted to find some rocks, set ourselves up. We only had a few cartridges left."

"After a while," Jamesy said, "most of the firing stopped, but we could still hear shots. So we thought we'd wait. Dark by then. All of a sudden, a Johnny Reb is coming straight at us, his gun pointed right at my chest."

"We lifted our guns," Daniel said.

"And we would have fired, Mam," said Jamesy. "We were ready and he was aiming at us; we couldn't see if there were more behind him. I thought of Johnny Gilroy and Frankie McGee, two fellows who'd been hit, and—"

"We heard this god-awful yell and then a blast of gunfire," Daniel said.

"And then, 'Cease fire!' And there he was, in his buckskins, standing in front of us," said Jamesy. "'You can't shoot the neighbors!' he said. 'What would people think?' Uncle Patrick! And the Reb was James Mulloy!"

The boys started laughing, and Stephen and Michael joined in, and then the boys from the Hickory Gang and James McKenna and Barney, all of them slapping one another on the back—the greatest joke ever.

Not a woman in the place joined in the hilarity. Gracie whispered, "James Mulloy."

Jamesy saw my face. "It was funny, Mam, to have Uncle Patrick pop up like that, saying, 'You can't shoot the neighbors!'" he said. "And to think, if he hadn't, James Mulloy might have killed me, or me him, or maybe both of us, all three. How strange would that have been?"

"All right now," James McKenna said. "Order! Order! Tell us, Patrick, how did you happen to spring up like some pooka?"

Patrick had been standing near the kitchen, not saying anything. I'd hardly spoken to him except to thank him and to say he looked well. He did—clean-shaved and erect. The uniform suited him. "Captain Kelly, Brevet," Jamesy had said, which means a commission given on the battlefield. He never changes—his eyes sharp and bright. Fifty-three years old, but moving like a young man, while James McKenna and Barney, not much older, seem old and frail.

"I was with Grant on Orchard Knob," Patrick said. "Observing—liaison for Tom Sweeny, who's a general now."

"And a Fenian," Daniel said.

"From above," Patrick continued, "I could see both sides, the Confederates dug in above, the Union soldiers waiting to charge. Along the top of the ridge I saw a green flag with harps and shamrocks—the Rebel Sons of Erin; and directly below, a similar flag—the banner of the Irish Legion."

Heads shaking in the room. "Ah," "Jesus, Mary, and Joseph," and "Poor old Ireland."

"And did you try to stop the battle, Patrick?" I said.

"Oh, Mam," said Jamesy.

"I would have if I could, Honora," Patrick said. "I'd have thrown the cloak of invisibility around the whole lot." He stopped, sipping his punch.

"Well, you couldn't do *that*, of course. So what did you do?"

"I rode through the mountain pass to their position."

"And then, the luck!" Jamesy said. "The pipes saved us. Uncle Patrick saw the silver bits on my pipes shine in the light of the setting sun, right, Uncle Patrick?"

"I did, Jamesy."

"And came up behind us."

"A miracle," Molly said. "A certain miracle. Thanks be to God."

"A mearbhaill," I said to Máire.

"Thanks be to God," Lizzie echoed. "Saved." Rejoicing with us, though no one had appeared to rescue her own son. Killed six months ago.

A great murmur of gratitude then in our parlor.

"When do you go back, boys?" Barney asked.

"Go back?" I said. "They've come home. Surely the army doesn't expect—"

"The army does, Mam," Jamesy said. "Lucky enough to be here now. Without Uncle Patrick we'd be in camp with the rest of them. After Uncle Patrick got Daniel and me and James Mulloy away from the battlefield—"

"James Mulloy, too?" Gracie said.

"Of course," Daniel said. "Couldn't let my brother-in-law-to-be stumble around in the dark."

"Though the dark was a good thing—let us get up through the ravine, and then, well . . ." Jamesy stopped.

"Then what?" I said. "Where have you been for a month, and why couldn't you send a letter or telegram? Didn't you know how worried I'd be? You—"

"Wasn't possible, Honora," Patrick Kelly cut me off.

"Later, Mam," Jamesy whispered to me.

❖   ❖   ❖

Hours later, after more toasts and singing and even a round of jigs and reels, with Jamesy piping on the instrument he'd somehow managed to bring home, our guests left.

"A real hooley," Máire said.

"It was," I agreed, but there were questions to be answered before we slept. Only Patrick, our two soldiers, Máire, and I were left sitting before the fire. I'd sent Stephen and Michael to see Molly and the McKennas home. Gracie and Bridget were downstairs, reading a very long letter from James Mulloy.

"So," I said. "Tell me, Patrick. Why couldn't you let us know our sons were alive?"

"Don't blame Uncle Patrick," Jamesy said.

"I'm only asking Uncle Patrick," I said.

Patrick started laughing. At least he'd sat down in the chair across from us. "Uncle Patrick, the old man of the mountain, will tell you. Here we were: two Union soldiers, one Johnny Reb, and a fellow in buckskins with some very dodgy paperwork—behind the lines, both lines, and one of us with a rifle ball in his leg."

"What? Who?" Máire said. "Are you all right, Daniel?"

"Wasn't me, Mam."

"Jamesy?" I said. My God. Wounded.

"I'm fine, Mam. But the closest doctor Uncle Patrick knew was across the Tennessee border in Georgia. Confederate territory. Not a bad wound, Mam. Only in my calf. Of course, if the rifle ball had stayed in there . . . But getting me better took a week or so, and we had to kind of hide. There's these Home Guard fellows around—James Mulloy stayed with us, said he claimed us as his prisoners, just in case. But then I was better and Uncle Patrick got his pass from the Reb general."

"Pass?"

"That general was a Fenian, too," Daniel told me.

"So we could start back north. Slow enough going, though we had a horse for some of it, because of stopping for the meetings."

"What is Jamesy talking about, Patrick?" I said.

"We've Fenian Circles in both armies, and our numbers are growing," Patrick said. "Often the camps of the two sides aren't that far, and I can arrange joint meetings. The men pledge not to discuss the present war, and I can give news of the Brotherhood to both and remind them that when this conflict ends we will unite to free Ireland."

"Fifty thousand have taken the oath, Mam. Imagine, fifty thousand!" Jamesy said.

"What's this oath, Daniel?" Máire asked.

"A secret, Mam."

"I'll secret *you*. Tell me," Máire said.

"I can't. Explain, Uncle Patrick," Daniel said.

"Not such a secret anymore," Patrick said. "In March we'll convene an Irish National Fair, here in Chicago. The Fenians will be the sponsors, but we're inviting all Irish organizations throughout the country to deliberate, raise money. And I've met with your colonel Mulligan. He'll be one of our main supports, Honora."

"You can help us get ready for the Fenian Fair, Mam," Jamesy said. "We're on the organizing committee—official delegates from the Legion. Uncle Patrick fixed it—he's the senior delegate for the Brigade and the Legion and a lot of other regiments. General Sweeny ordered him that special uniform."

"Very nice," Máire said. "Now I want to hear that oath."

"Nothing you wouldn't promise yourself, Honora," Patrick said, and smiled at me. "Go on, Jamesy, Danny O."

The two stood up very straight. "I pledge my secret word of honor," they began, "as a truthful and honest man . . ." Deep, strong voices.

"That I will labor with earnest zeal for the liberation of Ireland from the yoke of England," they said together, "and for the establishment of a free and independent government on Irish soil."

They looked at Máire and me.

"Uncle Patrick says we are the first sons of Ireland able to make our ancient dream come true," Jamesy said.

"My dream is to have the war over and all of you alive and well and giving me grandchildren," I said.

"That will come, too, Mam."

So confident, as if living to father children is ordained. Jamesy had come close to death. I looked over at Patrick. He's proud of them, I thought, proud of that confidence. They're battle-tested now. The Fenian Fair in March, and Jamesy wants my help. Jamesy. Sitting here next to me. Alive. And Patrick Kelly had saved him. Thank you, Lord. Thank you, Blessed Mother. My son's alive.

Chapter 33

*I*F THE FENIANS can do *this*," Máire said to me as we joined the crowd surging into Bryant Hall, "surely freeing Ireland should be no bother to them."

Here it was, opening day, March 28, and the Irish National Fair was a success already. And no question as to who was behind it. Everyone— including the newspapers, even the *Chicago Tribune*—called the week-long convention Chicago's Fenian Fair.

"The biggest, most elegant hall in Chicago, and we've filled it," Máire said.

There hadn't been an assembly of free, proud, prosperous Irish people since the ancient gatherings held at Tara. No British soldiers to intimidate us. The men in uniform were our own Irishmen representing the fifty thousand members of the Fenian Brotherhood serving in both the Confederate and Union armies. They would become the force that would liberate Ireland. The fair would raise the money they needed.

Máire and I strolled past booths displaying Waterford crystal, Parian china, Connemara marble crosses, silver tea sets, gold watches, fine linen tablecloths, yes, but hand-knit sweaters and socks, too, blackthorn walking sticks and lengths of tweed—all donated, to be sold for the Cause. Illegal to do such fund-raising in Ireland.

There'd been a grand parade this morning. Máire and I cheered our sons. Daniel, Jamesy, Michael, and Stephen strode alongside Patrick

Kelly, who carried Grellan's crozier. "Kellys Abu!" Thousands marched with them—governors, congressmen, city officials, every Irish organization, all the workingmen's clubs, the police, firemen. It took hours for the parade to move by us.

And now here was the same con-glom-er-a-tion, as Owen Mulloy would say, trying to get a look at the prizes for the lottery that had been advertised in the papers for weeks. Some items filled one whole section of the hall: five magnificent rosewood pianos, seven "richly appointed" billiard tables—worth one thousand dollars each—and a six-foot-wide oil painting: "The Arrest of Sir Edward Fitzgerald," given by the Mooneys of Belfast.

"I bought one hundred chances on that," a man said to us.

We knew him—John Kelly, who owned a big saloon called the Parlour on Archer. A generous fellow.

Colonel Mulligan had donated a gold rifle mounted in a glass case. In a printed statement behind the glass, Colonel Mulligan promised to "devote all my heart and all my strength to the cause of Irish Nationality."

"Look," Máire said. She pointed to the list of contributions by military units: three hundred dollars from the Irish Brigade and five hundred dollars from the Irish Legion and big sums from all the Irish regiments in Ohio, Michigan, Massachusetts, New York, Kentucky, Tennessee, Louisiana, South Carolina.

"It's Patrick Kelly got all those," I said. Each theater in Chicago had donated a night's box office to the Cause. "Patrick arranged that, too," I said.

"Well, here comes our host now," Máire said. "Captain Kelly, looking very handsome, and smiling to boot."

"Why not? The fair's a great success," I said.

Patrick had Jamesy and Daniel, Stephen and Michael, and Bridget and Gracie with him.

"Mam, look what Uncle Patrick bought for us," Bridget said. She and Gracie both held up knitted shawls.

"And for us," said Stephen. He and Michael showed me frieze jackets.

"They'll fit right in," Patrick said, "when Ireland's a republic and we can all go home."

Máire laughed.

"Nothing to laugh at, Mam," Daniel said.

Máire took the shawl from Gracie and wrapped it around her. "I'll go back to Ireland anytime," she said, "as long as I have a return ticket in my pocket."

I looked at Patrick. And that's the answer you'd get from most people here, I wanted to say to him.

"The Irish won't really be respected in America until we have a nation of our own," Jamesy said.

"We're fighting for the Irish nationality," Daniel said, "to be who we are."

"What I am right now is hungry," Máire said.

"I've arranged a table in the gallery for you during the banquet," Patrick said. "No ladies are allowed at the dinner, I'm afraid, but you'll see everything and hear the toasts and music and speeches.

"And eat the food?" Máire said.

"The very best," Patrick answered.

A grand evening altogether. So much enthusiasm was generated for heading off to free Ireland that the lieutenant governor of Illinois (not Irish) stood up to plead "You can't all go back. We need you."

"No worries," Máire said to me.

✤ ✤ ✤

But now we were home, sitting by the fire. "The fair was a good job of work," Patrick said. "We raised fifty thousand dollars in the week." Máire and I were on the sofa. Patrick, in his shirtsleeves, leaned back in what had become "his chair" after three months. He'd be gone tomorrow, and Jamesy and Daniel with him, going south to join the last big campaigns of the war, he said.

The Irish Legion would march with General Sherman to capture Atlanta and then on to the sea, while Colonel Mulligan and the Irish Brigade would advance with the army attacking Richmond.

"Thank you, Honora, for all your help," Patrick said, "and you, Máire, for your hospitality. Longest I've ever lived in one place."

"Glad to have you, Uncle Patrick," Máire said.

Firelight flashed against the crystal glasses we'd won at the fair and turned the whiskey gold. The boys were at McKenna's, the girls downstairs. Only the three of us.

Patrick lifted his glass. "To you," he said, "the Keeley sisters and to all the gallant women of Ireland—our real heroes."

"I'll drink to that," Máire said, and did.

I raised the glass to my lips. Water in mine.

Patrick drained his glass, then stood up. He rolled down his sleeves and put on his uniform jacket. A bit more heft to him—probably never eaten well and regular in his life.

After he'd gone, Máire turned to me. "You'll miss him," she said.

"Of course. We all will. Michael and Stephen and Bridget have learned so much about their da from Patrick's stories. And Daniel and Jamesy—"

"*You*, Honora," Máire interrupted me. "You'll miss him."

"I have enjoyed helping with the fair."

My conscience hadn't bothered me too much over the letter writing or even the long discussions with Patrick by the fire. Arguments, really. Couldn't the Fenians use all this money and support and clout to fight the Sassenach Daniel O'Connell's way, with political pressure, agitation—not physical force? I'd say to Patrick. The mere threat of fifty thousand Fenians invading might convince the British to withdraw from Ireland, I said. Patrick said he didn't hold out much hope for a bloodless revolution. We'd fling history at each other late into the night. So, yes, I would miss Patrick Kelly, but I didn't like the way Máire was shaking her head at me, that half-smile.

"You're in love with Patrick Kelly."

"Máire, I'm not."

"Spare me, Honora. I'd say he's a grá for you, too, though he's careful not to let on. I bet he has a woman somewhere."

"He does not."

"Why wouldn't he? A fine-looking man, especially now he's tamed himself. And why are you so upset with me suggesting it?" She got the jug and poured whiskey into each of our crystal glasses. "Tell me," Máire said. "A bit of whiskey might help. Medicinal."

I took a long drink. The words poured out of me—how guilty I felt when I realized I did have feelings for Patrick, such a betrayal of Michael, and a forbidden relationship anyway.

"Forbidden? Who says?"

"The Church. There's an impediment to a widow marrying her husband's brother. I mean, it's possible to get a dispensation from the bishop, but still . . ."

"Dispensation? Impediment? And what are they when they're at home? One more stick to beat us with. Whose Church is it, anyway? I'd say the women at the Holy Hour have as good a claim as any bishop. Ask any one of them about impediments—she'd say, 'Patrick Kelly needs a wife and doesn't have one, and you need a husband and don't have one. Why not?'"

"I had a husband. The best man in the world."

"Who's been dead sixteen years," Máire said. "Honora, you've made your heart into a shrine to Michael Kelly, but isn't it yourself you're lighting candles to? Honora, the good mother; Honora, the faithful widow; Honora, the righteous woman. Michael would be ashamed of you."

"You don't understand," I said.

"I do understand. You think yourself into knots, torture yourself. Maybe Patrick's a mearbhaill. . . . Take a closer look."

"What's the use, Máire? I'm forty-one years old. Patrick's fifty-three."

"And I'm forty-three and doing nicely," said Máire. "You've years and years ahead of you." She stopped. "Feck it, Honora. Hide. What do I care? I saved you once. Well, I'm not doing it again. You're always saying we Irish rescued ourselves, saved each other. Well, save yourself. Rescue Patrick Kelly. At least tell him how you feel. There's a lovely room at the Tremont House—"

"Máire! I could never sleep with a man I wasn't married to."

"And I never sleep with a man married to anybody else. You're a coward, Honora. What about Maeve and the Brehon laws? Patrick Kelly's going back to war. He could die or disappear back to Ireland. Gone and never knowing—"

"All right, all right. Maybe it'd be no harm to talk to him."

"A nice long good-bye, and then who knows? I'll send Patrick up to you when he gets back from McKenna's."

⟡　⟡　⟡

Midnight had passed and dawn was close when Jamesy, Stephen, and Michael came in, all of them singing "Ireland Boys Hurrah" and well jarred, but then so am I, arranging words in my head for hours. Patrick will be at the door any minute.

"Go to bed, boys. Get some sleep."

But Jamesy dropped into Patrick's chair.

"It's late, Jamesy," I said.

"We wanted to give Uncle Patrick a good send-off, Mam," he said.

"Send-off?"

"He's gone, Mam," Jamesy said.

"Off with that James Stephens fellow," Michael said.

"An early start," Jamesy said. "Uncle Patrick's taking Stephens to visit Fenian Circles in the army on his way south. Michael and I wanted to go along, but Uncle Patrick said we had plenty to do here . . . Mam, are you all right?"

I must have slumped forward. The boys were standing over me. Jamesy held my shoulders.

"Some water," I said.

After all that, Patrick's gone. I looked at the faces of my sons, concerned about *me* when it's Jamesy going to the war, and the other two will follow if the fighting goes on much longer—in danger, all of them. Forgive me, Lord. I'd never flaunt the laws of the Church. Protect them, please, dear God. Keep them safe.

I stood up. "Come into the kitchen. I'll cook you some eggs. And Jamesy, there's extra socks on the bed, to take with you."

"Thanks, Mam. Oh, I wanted to tell you—I'm leaving the pipes with Michael. He's already got a good few tunes and, well, it's hot weather in Georgia—not good for the wood."

"I'll take great care of them," Michael said, sitting down at the table.

Afraid to risk the pipes with the battles that awaited them. I'll be making my Stations. Máire can mind her own business. And no whiskey.

❖   ❖   ❖

Nine candles to light every day—Paddy, Thomas, Jamesy, Daniel, James Mulloy, James Nugent, Colonel Mulligan, Patrick Kelly, and the final candle for Johnny Og. Eight of them in danger. One gone.

The flames ducked and dove, enclosed in the blue glass votive lights lined up before Our Lady's altar, my troops standing watch through the night. Keep them safe.

But young Michael's schoolmate was correct. The mathematics of battle prevailed. All eight could not survive. It was the Irish Brigade fell to the odds. Kernstown, July 23, 1864.

❖   ❖   ❖

Only a few months before the battle, the whole regiment had come to Chicago on furlough. April 1864. Paddy's three-year enlistment was done and dusted. He was home, courting Bridey Kelly from Roscommon. Safe. But then the call went out. Men were needed—even conscription couldn't fill the ranks. Alderman Comiskey told me the secretary to the British consul was making nice money declaring men who were drafted British citizens and exempt. "Traitors," Paddy had called them. But I couldn't blame the fellows, not with the number of casualties listed in the paper every day.

"I have to go back," Paddy had told me. "Plenty of the fellows haven't served their three years. My friends will need me."

"Thomas found a way to get out."

"And none of us soldiers have much time for him because of it. He as much as deserted, going off with that photographer fellow O'Sullivan. He's lucky Uncle Patrick fixed it when he brought James Stephens to meet Colonel Mulligan. Photography officer . . . How can he live with himself?"

Paddy had handed me a broadside. It invited men to reenlist in "Mulligan's Brigade." A bounty of four hundred and two dollars would be paid to veterans.

"I want to marry Bridey," Paddy said. "Reenlisting's the only way I can get the money we'll need."

"If Slattery would advance you some—"

"I can't go back to work for Slattery," he said.

"There are jobs galore, Paddy—the railroad and . . ." I stopped.

"The packinghouse? I tried it, don't you remember? Though now I'm well used to blood and muck all over me and the smell of death. I can't take orders anymore, Mam. I've had enough. I want to be my own boss. I'd like to buy the forge from Slattery. He wants to retire. Michael and I can run it, but I need money. See how veterans can get a four-hundred-and-two-dollar bonus if they reenlist? That's more than I can make in a year. Added to that is a month's pay. So, five hundred dollars, Mam, and my monthly pay until the war's over. I can save seven or eight hundred dollars. Bridey and I will get married while I'm home now, and then if I die, she'll get the money."

"Alanna," I said.

He let me hug him, my sturdy lad, but stayed straight and stiff in my arms.

"Aren't you afraid at all?"

"Mam, I was afraid when I stole the bishop's egg, but I did it. I still remember the jaws of that old slobbering hound."

"It was a lovely egg, Paddy, still the best I've ever tasted."

"Because we were starving. And that's why life for me and Bridey will be so good, because I know now what luck it is to be alive."

"It is, Paddy. A miracle."

"And to have children," he said.

"Yes."

"My firstborn will be a son," he said. "Michael Joseph Kelly."

"You've so much to live for, Paddy. Take care of yourself. Promise me that after the war's over you'll stay home, no matter what your uncle Patrick—"

"I won't be joining the Fenians, Mam," Paddy said. "I don't know how any fellows who've been in one war would want to be in another. No one wants peace more than a soldier who's been in combat—that's what my friend Marty Berndt in the Pennsylvania Volunteers says. And it's true, Mam. But *this* is *my* war. I have to finish it. But then, no more."

✧ ✧ ✧

Colonel Mulligan and Marion came to Paddy and Bridey's wedding, and James Nugent and Bridget managed a dance and a walk along the river that spring evening.

"He's asked me to marry him," Bridget whispered to me later, "and I said yes, I would. Yes."

Eyes shining. So happy. A reward for all her years of goodness, helping me raise her brothers.

"A lot of weddings when the war is over and they march back," Máire had said when the Brigade left in July.

As we stood on the platform waving good-bye, the train moved slowly from the station. "Don't cry, Mam," they'd told us. And we didn't. Smiling, all of us, and the men the same. Colonel Mulligan gave a little salute as he passed us. James Nugent held his hand on the glass of the window. Paddy nodded. And Marion Mulligan held her three-year-old up to us. She and her babies were going with the Brigade. She'd stay near headquarters in Virginia—"James wants us to be there for the victory." Then Kernstown. A good omen to stop the Confederates' last thrust there, because General Shields defeated a Confederate force at that very place at the start of the war.

But Colonel Mulligan, who had been named general that very day, wasn't allowed to follow Shields's battle plan. Disaster.

Colonel Mulligan was hit and badly wounded. James Nugent had been one of those carrying him to safety when the colonel saw the Brigade's flag fall onto the battlefield. "Lay me down," he'd told James. "Save the flag!" But when James Nugent picked up the banner, he too was shot. Enemy soldiers attacked the group and captured the colonel. He died two days later. Marion reached him two hours after his death. He was thirty-four. General Mulligan, but never Senator Mulligan or President Mulligan. James Nugent was missing, presumed dead, his body never found. Paddy had survived—just—knocked unconscious, he said, but able to escape with a number of the Brigade, more determined than ever to fight.

Bridget often stayed with Marion Mulligan now, helping her with the babies and trying to console Mrs. Nugent, who was determined to find her son's grave. The Confederates had recruited townspeople to bury the bodies left on the battlefield, and there was a chance someone in the area might remember James Nugent. A thousand broadsides were posted around Kernstown and the vicinity with this description: "Lt. Nugent was 18 years and six months old; six feet in height; rather slender; fair coloring, blue eyes, golden hair, regular features, white even teeth, smooth-shaved face, was dressed in dark blue jacket, with first lieutenant shoulder straps, black pants. Had on a plain gold ring with his own and other initials on the inside. Any person or persons knowing anything about his burial or grave, would be doing a great act of kindness to his mother and sisters by giving information."

It was her initials, Bridget told me, with James Nugent's, engraved inside that ring—J.H.N. and B.K. "A pledge to me," she said. "That's why he pressed his hand against the window—to show me his ring finger."

No one came forward. We waited. Would the war never end?

❖ ❖ ❖

With a big *whoosh*, the huge bonfire blazed up against the night sky. The South had surrendered! Palm Sunday, April 9, 1865. Michael and the Hickory Gang threw packing cases onto the tower they'd built as soon as word came. Peace. The neighbors came out. Such singing and dancing and hugging. Molly and Lizzie, James McKenna and Barney McGurk—the tavern emptied. All of Bridgeport celebrated together.

Stephen stood to the side with the firemen—keeping an eye on the flames. Máire and Gracie clapped along with John Joe's fiddle, but Bridget and I stood quiet. Peace had not come soon enough.

Now the victory bonfire illuminated Bridget's face. Peace never comes soon enough. The *Tribune* had estimated that six hundred thousand men had died in four years, the combined total for both armies. Some perished immediately on the battlefield, some from their wounds later, many from disease. Only a guess. Hard to know for sure. So many.

Bridget, Máire, Gracie, and I left the celebration and slipped into St. Bridget's. Quiet, lit only by the tabernacle lamp and the votive candles. One by one, the Holy Hour women came in—Lizzie, Molly, and the others—and we thanked God and His Blessed Mother that the killing was over. But it wasn't.

President Lincoln was assassinated April 14, 1865, Good Friday. Not even a week since we celebrated around the bonfire, and now Bridgeport stood together, watching the flag-draped caisson bear his body from the train station to the courthouse. Lines of girls in white dresses led the procession, followed by soldiers—companies, brigades, divisions. Yet these were the fellows who had left the fighting before the war was over. The rest were still making their own way home. Máire and Bridget and I watched the sad parade.

"Any information?" I asked Bridget.

"None," Bridget said. "Marion paid for more broadsides to be posted. Next month we're going down to Virginia. Maybe if we're there, we can find James, or his grave."

Find James? Was Bridget pretending to herself that somewhere in Virginia James Nugent was alive? Imagining that he'd lost his memory but would see the poster, read, "Six feet tall, slender, golden hair, gold ring," and say, "Why, that's me! I'm him, I'm James Nugent!"

For years after Johnny Leahy drowned, Máire had wondered if maybe he'd been saved at sea and was strolling the streets of New York—not sure of who he was, but whole and alive. Hard for me to believe Michael was dead, even though I'd seen his spirit leave his body. But when there is no body . . . Would Bridget wait and wait, nursing this hopeless love, keeping an image in her mind that had no reality?

The cortege passed us. A grand funeral, a solemn tribute. See how we revered our great president? We've done our best for him in these grand ceremonies. Now he can come back. But the dead don't return. Not to this world. James Nugent would not read his poster.

It was June 1865 before all the boys were finally home. Paddy and the Irish Brigade had returned the first of May. And now Irish families from all over Chicago assembled in front of St. Patrick's Church to welcome back the Irish Legion. Nine hundred had left three years ago. Only three hundred returned. Jamesy and Daniel, safe. Only Thomas missed the grand family reunion, off somewhere in the West with Timothy O'Sullivan, taking photographs, sending us a line or two now and then. And no Patrick Kelly.

"Uncle Patrick's fine, Mam," Jamesy was telling us. We were all gathered in our parlor the afternoon of the welcome home celebration. "He was with us at the end, General Sweeny's scout," Jamesy said. "He's a colonel now, colonel brevet—commissioned in the field. While the rest of the boys in the Legion were hanging around waiting to be sent home, Uncle Patrick got General Sweeny to issue orders for us"—Jamesy put on a military tone—"to be assigned to Colonel Kelly's staff for the purpose of accompanying him to New Orleans." Patrick was meeting with the Irish Fenians there, he said.

"You went back to New Orleans," Máire said. "Wonderful."

"Here's the best news. I found Lorenzo and Christophe!"

"Jamesy, how did you ever find them? I can't believe it!" I said.

"Believe it! You see, there was this big parade down Rampart Street, and here came the Corps d'Afrique, a colored unit in the Union army made up of free people from New Orleans and emancipated slaves. The soldiers had a brass band. Lorenzo was playing the trumpet!"

"Is M'am Jacques alive?" Máire asked.

"She is. Lorenzo and Christophe took us to see her. She lives in the convent with Sister Henriette's order, the Sisters of the Holy Family. Sister Henriette herself died ten years ago, but there's quite a number of sisters now. They have a big house on Royal Street."

"Ah, New Orleans," said Máire. "What a future I could have had there."

Daniel looked at her. "What do you mean, Mam?"

"I'll tell you when you grow up," she said.

"Grow up, Mam? I'm a soldier. I fought a war, and I'm about to fight another!"

"What do you mean?" Máire asked him.

I knew. Canada. "Jamesy," I started.

But Jamesy continued talking about New Orleans, with Maggie Nolan—the first girl he'd invited to our parlor—taking in every word. A match there, I hope. Paddy was very quiet. I saw Bridey lean over and whisper to him. He smiled.

Paddy had told no stories. The time I'd asked him about Kernstown, his own injury, the colonel's death, he only said, "Mam, I'm not talking about the war, no more than I would talk about the Great Starvation. Jamesy and Daniel might want to go back to Ireland, but not me. Bad memories."

"But what about the before times, Paddy?"

"I can't let myself remember even the good things, or the night-mares come back."

"Still, Paddy?" I'd asked him.

When we first came to Bridgeport, he'd cry out in his sleep. I'd find him covered in sweat. "A great rat's chewing on my hand, Mam, and I can't move because I'm dead."

I'd hold him and say, "You're not dead, a stór. You're alive."

"Not the old nightmares, Mam. New ones."

"Oh, Paddy . . ."

"But Bridey wakes me and tells me, 'You're alive, Paddy.' As you did, Mam."

Now, Máire put an arm around Daniel. "You're going nowhere, Daniel O'Connell Leahy."

❖ ❖ ❖

Summer came, but no lineup of weddings at St. Bridget's as Máire and I'd expected. Why wouldn't Jamesy marry Maggie, or Daniel his girl, Sadie Healy? All the other veterans in Bridgeport were making a mad rush to marry and have children.

Bridey was pregnant and Paddy over the moon—and me up there with him. Máire gave them her apartment, and she and Gracie moved up with us. "You've generous heart, Máire," I'd told her, but she'd said, "Why not?"

Daniel kept his room, and Jamesy moved down with him. Paddy insisted and Bridey agreed. "They'll be off on their own soon enough, and you'd be very crowded upstairs," Bridey said.

"Daniel and Jamesy are tired of us nagging them," Máire said.

"Nagging? They're twenty-three and twenty-two. The war took many years from them. Time to get a job, marry those girls."

But instead they'd disappear for days at a time. "Traveling," they'd say. When they were home, they'd stay out until all hours and sleep the day through. "Fenian business, Mam," Jamesy would say.

Máire didn't take much notice. She was working long hours at the Shop. Peace brought a boom in business. But I was worried.

One late summer's day, I'd found Jamesy sitting behind the house, looking out toward where the prairie had been, playing his pipes.

"Your father would pipe to himself like that, Jamesy," I'd said.

"I've been thinking a lot of Da lately," he'd said, "trying to remember his voice. I can see his face and picture the games—playing we were Irish warriors, swinging the chestnuts. But I can't hear him singing."

"Your brother Michael sounds a bit like him," I'd said.

"You know, Mam, we talk a lot about Ireland at the Brotherhood meetings, but so many of the fellows born here ask me if the country-side could really be as beautiful, as green, as their people tell them."

"And what do you say, Jamesy?"

"I say yes, but my memories are all jumbled. Ah well, I'll know soon enough," he'd said, and he'd gone back to his music.

Jamesy and Daniel had always been close to their sisters, and I'd thought the girls could talk to them, but Bridget and Gracie spent much of their time over at Marion Mulligan's, which worried me. "You've made your heart a shrine to Michael Kelly," Máire'd said to me. But Michael was my husband, my children's father, my fated love. For Bridget to spend her life mourning James Nugent . . . But when I said something like that to Bridget, in the gentlest way, she only looked surprised. "*You* must understand, Mam. You could never care for another man, nor could I." At least she'd be teaching in the fall. Twenty years old now, she had graduated with honors in May. Her additional two years of study had earned her a teaching certificate from the Sisters of Mercy and the offer of a job on the faculty of St. Xavier's. As Bridget received her diploma, Máire had whispered to me, "Miss Lynch should see us now."

Michael hadn't gone back to school. "Time for me to start earning a wage, and Paddy needs me." They were doing well now, at Kelly Brothers' Blacksmiths.

At eighteen, Stephen was the youngest fireman in Chicago, saving half of his wages, planning his future with Nelly Lang.

If only Jamesy . . .

One evening, Jamesy and Daniel had sat down Máire and me at the kitchen table. They laid out the last of their army pay, a good lump of money. "Take it," they'd said.

"Take it yourselves," I'd said. "Use it like Paddy did, set up a business, you and Daniel."

"You need real money to open a business," Jamesy had said.

Daniel had stood up and started pacing. "Oh, the capitalists will let us start little businesses in our own neighborhoods," he'd said, "grocery stores or forges like Paddy's and, of course, taverns. But they want Irishmen as laborers, full stop, not owners. Though they'll be getting a few surprises from the boys who saved the Union for them, who fought as substitutes for rich men's sons who bought their way out of serving! We're not going to work twelve hours for insulting wages. No more 'lie down, croppies, lie down.'"

"Jesus Christ, Daniel, are you a Fenian or a radical?" Máire'd said.

"A man can be both, Mam," Daniel had said. "Look at the Molly Maguires. They're Irish patriots who fight for justice for working men."

"And get bashed in the head by Pinkertons," I'd said.

"And then hanged," Máire had added.

"Be careful, Daniel," I'd said. "A man's tongue can get his nose broken. Start talking about justice at McCormick's factory, or out where Pullman's building railcars, or at the stockyards, you'll both be in jail."

Later, Jamesy had reassured me that Daniel wouldn't do anything to jeopardize the Fenian mission and that both of them were only waiting for the word to come—to move on Ireland or Canada.

"Jamesy, no," I'd said.

"But don't you want me to free Ireland? Plant the banner of freedom on the shores of Galway Bay?"

"Not if you get killed in the process!" I'd said.

But Máire'd told me to calm myself. "Nothing will come of it. According to Daniel, there's a lot of disagreement between the top fellows. Watch—they'll argue themselves out of the whole shebang. My Danny O will fall to Sadie Healy soon enough, and then we'll hear no more of all this."

"I hope you're right."

As we came up to our first peacetime Christmas, nothing had happened. Good.

Chapter 34

*Y*OU'RE NOT MARRYING James Mulloy now, and that's the end of it."
Máire, angrier than I'd ever seen her, pounded her fist on the kitchen
table.

But Gracie, sitting across from her, did not flinch. She leaned toward her mother, thumped the table herself, and said, "I am, too—if I
have to run away to do it."

I looked at Bridget, who shrugged, as surprised as I was at Gracie's
revolt.

Máire was flummoxed. "And we were having such a nice Christmas," she said.

We were indeed. It was St. Stephen's Day night, and we were still
celebrating full out, the boys and Patrick gone to McKenna's.

An almost frantic joy had been running through our boys from
the moment Patrick and James Mulloy had arrived on the afternoon
of Christmas Eve. Such backslapping and laughing from Jamesy and
Daniel, Stephen and Michael. Paddy'd been more reserved. I'd heard
Jamesy and Daniel and Patrick whispering on the stairs as they carried
Patrick's things down to Paddy's, where he was staying. Bridey was very
good to make a fuss over "the famous Uncle Patrick"—and her eight
months along.

❖   ❖   ❖

On Christmas morning, Patrick Kelly had led us all into St. Patrick's for Mass. He'd gone right up to the front and set St. Grellan's crozier on the side altar.

After Mass, I understood why Patrick had insisted we go to St. Patrick's. Men from different parishes, but all veterans of the Irish Legion and the Irish Brigade, came to the side altar to touch St. Grellan's crozier and shake hands with Patrick. Solemn, not a word said. The Fenian Brotherhood, keeping faith.

Afterward, the men had stood on the church steps, speaking to Patrick in low voices, Jamesy and Daniel next to him.

"Disturbing," I'd said to Máire.

But she'd said, "The more they talk, the less they do. What harm?"

She'd been more interested in her conversation with Joe and Margaret McCauley—St. Bridget parishioners, and the very couple whose request to marry had revealed the impediment to me. "Husband and wife, Honora. Dispensed," she'd told me. "Father Dunne's the vicar general now and can act for the bishop when he's away or sick, so when Bishop Duggan was in Rome, Father Dunne fixed them up. He dispensed them and married them. Only a minor impediment anyway, Margaret McCauley told me. Father Dunne would get you and Patrick Kelly dispensed in the snap of his fingers," she'd said, snapping her own. "We could have the wedding in Saint Bridget's before the Christmas flowers die, or maybe better, right here at Saint Patrick's."

"Enough, Máire," I said.

"The poor fellow, coming Christmas after Christmas. Home from the war now and—"

"Máire, please. I've myself sorted. And besides, Patrick Kelly's hatching plans. He'll not be here long."

Patrick Kelly would never consider a regular happy life to be worth living, I'd thought on Christmas night during our annual visit to the Langs. I only hope Patrick doesn't set Jamesy and Daniel on his path.

As I sat watching the dancing, Patrick walked over and sat on the chair next to me. "I don't waltz, Honora," he said.

"I know that, Patrick," I answered.

✦ ✦ ✦

A nice Christmas, as Máire said, but now here we were on St. Stephen's Day night with Máire and Gracie railing at each other. "I forbid you to marry James Mulloy," Máire said for what must have been the tenth time.

"Máire, you know Gracie fell in love with James Mulloy years ago. Why shouldn't they marry?" I said.

"Love? Please, how long will love last when she's shoveling shite on some godforsaken hill farm in Tennessee?"

"Not godforsaken! We'll breed champion racehorses," Gracie said.

"That was Owen and Michael's dream at Knocnacuradh—a line of great horses," I said to Máire.

"Mad," Máire said. "Gracie, you've no notion of the work, and what money do you have? You're staying here, finishing school, marrying a gentleman, living on Michigan Avenue like the ladies who come into the Shop!"

"But, Máire," I said, "if that's not what Gracie wants—"

"She doesn't know what she wants. She's eighteen."

"The same age you were when you got married," I said.

Gracie had grown into a beautiful woman, with the Keeley height and Máire's curves. Máire certainly understood what attracted men. She probably could manage Gracie into a wealthy marriage. Máire'd introduce Gracie to the clerk she'd worked with all these years who now owned the Shop, Marshall Field. Or she might find a husband for Gracie among the sons of the Board of Trade fellows she knew.

"I want Gracie to have an easier life than we had. I want her near me, and my grandchildren rich and respected, not . . ."

"Bastards like we are, Mam?" said Gracie. "Whose fault is that?"

Máire's mouth opened, but no words came.

"Gracie," I said, "you don't understand. She went with your father to save me."

We'd never told the girls the whole story, but I did now—Johnny Leahy's death, Father Gilley's refusal to let Máire wed, the Pykes appearing at my wedding, the *droit du seigneur.*

"That's horrible," Bridget said.

"It is, but that's the past," I said. "The Pykes weren't the *only* Irish landlords claiming the bride's first night. Plenty of children in America now were born because of . . . Well, let's thank God that *here* the mothers can start again. You're called Leahy. In Chicago it doesn't matter who your real father was. Or what country you come from or—"

"Don't you believe that, Honora," Máire said. "Now that the war is over and they don't need the Irish to fight for them anymore, it's back to twelve-hour days at the packinghouse for the paddys. . . . Grab a shovel or a miner's pick, or waste yourself on a mucky piece of land. I don't want that for Gracie." She started crying.

Gracie moved toward her, but I was there first. I put my arm around her. "It's not like Gracie's crossing the ocean," I started, but Máire shook free of my arm.

"With Thomas gone and Daniel up to who knows what, I want Gracie near me," she said.

"Máire, I'm surprised at you. The children have to make their own lives. You're the one always said that."

"Shut your gob, Honora! What do you know? You'll always have Bridget. She'll spend her life suffering for a dead man and enjoying every minute of it, just like her mother!"

"Máire, please," I said. I took her by the shoulders. "Don't say such things."

She reared up out of the chair, turned, put her hands on my chest, and pushed, hard. "Don't you tell me what to say!" She pushed me again.

I lost my balance and had to take a few steps backward. Then I went for her. But before I got to Máire, I was grabbed from behind. Stopped.

"Mam!" Bridget held me against her.

Gracie had Máire pinned down in the chair. Gracie looked up at Bridget. Silence.

I don't know if Bridget started first or Gracie, but in seconds they were bent over with the laughing, and there was nothing for it but that Máire and I join in.

"It's past midnight," Bridget said. "The fellows will be coming in from McKenna's. Wouldn't do to see their mothers wrestling like a pair of ejits."

The girls sat us down and made tea. We four sat, sipping from the new china cups.

After a bit, I said, "Sorry, Máire. But really . . . I don't mind what you say about me, but to insult Bridget . . ."

"Not an insult, Mam," Bridget said. "I admire you for staying true to my da. I love James Nugent. Him being gone doesn't change anything. No other man could replace him."

"Not replace him, Bridget," I said. "You'll never have a *first* love again, but love's deeper and wider than you think." I remembered

Granny's voice: *You've made God very small, Honora.* Had I reduced love to a memory I could control and taught Bridget to do the same? I have to make her understand. "You wouldn't be disloyal to James Nugent if some other young man—"

"Edward Cuneen," Gracie, who'd gone quiet, suddenly said.

"Gracie, don't," Bridget said.

But Gracie went on, "He was an officer in the Irish Brigade, a good friend of James Nugent. We see him at Mulligan's. He likes Bridget, I know. Comes to see her, but she'll hardly talk to him, though she wants to. And he's a nice fellow—good-looking, too."

"What about him, Bridget?" I asked.

"He understands that I can't . . ." She stopped.

"Can't what?" Máire said. "Don't you want a husband? Children?"

"I'll have my teaching, and you, Mam," Bridget said. "And my brothers and their children. I'll visit Gracie."

"But your whole life's ahead of you," I said to her.

"I'll get through it as you did, Mam. Left foot, right foot."

"No, Bridget, no," I started.

We heard the boys pounding up the stairs, singing.

"Listen to them," Gracie said.

We are the Fenian Brotherhood . . .

They were through the door for the last bit of the song.

Many battles we have won
Along with the boys in blue,
And we'll go and capture Canada
For we've nothing else to do!

"See, Mam?" said Gracie to Máire. "See? I have to marry James Mulloy right now or he'll go off again into another war, and I just can't bear it!"

Drunk as lords, all of them—Jamesy, Daniel, and James Mulloy, even Stephen and Michael. Only Paddy was anywhere near sober, and Patrick Kelly nowhere to be seen.

The boys settled themselves in the parlor, ready for an all-night singsong.

"Don't get too comfortable," Máire said. We four women stood at the door of the parlor. "You should be in your beds."

These are grown men she's talking to, I thought, but we're still their mothers. I took a breath, then said, "We forbid any of you to get involved in a war in Canada."

"That's right," Máire said. "Do you hear me, Daniel?"

"Paddy, talk some sense to them," I said.

"I can't stop them. But I won't go. Not with the baby coming."

"Then James Mulloy can't fight either. I'm going to have a baby," Gracie said.

"What?" Daniel stood up and grabbed James Mulloy off the sofa. "To do that to my sister!"

"But I didn't!" James Mulloy shouted, struggling with Daniel.

Gracie went over to them. "Stop! I didn't say I'm expecting a baby now. But I plan to. We're getting married this week, James Mulloy." She shook her finger in his face. "You promised if we did, you wouldn't go."

"She made me promise," James Mulloy said to the boys. "But I never thought her mother would let her."

"My mother's delighted," Gracie said. She turned to Máire.

The looks on the boys' faces . . . nothing Máire could do but laugh.

❖ ❖ ❖

Gracie married James Mulloy at St. Bridget's on New Year's Eve. She'd continued to surprise us by arranging with Sister Mary Francis de Sales at St. Xavier's to take her exams during Christmas week. Gracie left for Nashville with her diploma.

"Though what good it will do her on a horse farm, I don't know," Máire grumbled.

I told her she'd be singing another tune when she was watching a Mulloy horse named Askeeboy win a great race. "You were right to give them your blessing, Máire."

"You heard her. She was going to marry him anyway. Didn't know Gracie was so much like me. What about Bridget?"

Gracie had invited Edward Cuneen to the wedding and back to our parlor. She'd refused to have a big party. "The family's enough," she'd said.

I liked Edward—a farmer's son from Summit, down the canal. He'd studied at St. Mary's, as Colonel Mulligan had. He planned to teach at the public school in Summit while helping his father on the farm. He'd made a point of telling me Bridget could teach there, too, or if she preferred, stay at St. Xavier's. There was great transportation between Chicago and Summit—a horsecar, the train, even the canal boat. Very close to Bridgeport, too.

"I don't know, Máire," I said. "Edward's in love with her, no question, and I think she'd feel the same if she could let herself."

"Let herself," Máire repeated. "If only Daniel and Jamesy would have the sense to marry."

Not a chance.

"At least Patrick Kelly's not around, drilling them for battle."

Patrick had taken his bag from Paddy's and left the night that we were up in our parlor arguing. He'd heard all the ruckus and decided not to come in to say good-bye, I thought. He'd left an order for Jamesy and Daniel. They were to collect the name, address, and record of military service of every member of the Brotherhood in the area. General Sweeny had been named secretary of war of the Fenian Brotherhood. He was now commanding general of the Armies of Ireland, and Patrick Kelly had been made colonel in this Irish army. Patrick was joining General Sweeny on a tour of the East, organizing the troops. He'd be back in the spring.

Jamesy and Daniel spent the winter going to Fenian meetings all over Chicago and in places like Belvidere, Illinois, and Anderson, Indiana.

"It's been two years since the Fenian Fair. So much support, all that money raised. We've got to do something!" Jamesy said to me.

Then very bad news came from Ireland. The government, using information from informers, arrested hundreds of men for taking the Fenian oath. Some were Americans. No charges, just off to jail. Forget appealing to the United States. The British didn't recognize naturalized citizens. The attempted uprising was put down brutally.

❖ ❖ ❖

Then in February, we celebrated our own victory: A tiny baby defeated the Sassenach, starvation, landlords, gombeen men, and all who'd tried to destroy us. On February 11, 1866, Paddy's son—Michael

Joseph Kelly—was born and named for his grandfather. The great line of Kellys, stretching through the Piper and Murty Mor, the blacksmith, to William Boy of the great party and back as far as Maine Mor himself, would go on.

"The baby's gained a good bit of weight," I said to Bridey in March.

He was a month old now and flourishing. Máire and I watched Bridey feed the baby. She's nice plump breasts, I thought, not flat and falling like mine when Stephen was born during the Great Starvation. Michael, a stór, our grandson! We're alive. We wouldn't die to please them. Not mere survival, either. A bit of comfort. Nice things around us. How Mam would have liked to see Máire and me sitting in Bridey and Paddy's tidy parlor with its flowered carpet and lace curtains.

Doing all right for ourselves in America. Plenty of work for Kelly Brothers' Blacksmiths. Máire'd gotten another raise, and my letter writing was bringing in a good few dollars. With so much work around, everyone in Bridgeport seemed to be sending money back to Ireland and wanted a flowery American letter to go with it.

"Ah, Mike," Bridey said to the baby, "plenty there. Slow down."

"Mike?" I said to Bridey as I leaned over and stroked the baby's forehead lightly.

"Paddy calls him that," she said. "Michael Joseph Kelly is his name, of course. But Paddy says 'Mike' is short and sharp and good for shouting. 'I'm Mike Kelly,'" she said in a deep voice, "'and I can lick any man in the house!'"

Máire and I laughed. Mike. American. Ah well, if they like it . . .

We settled down for a good gossip. James McKenna's son doing so well at the tavern, Molly Flanigan looking to sell the boardinghouse—she'd get a good price. Newcomers were looking for places to live. Germans and Lithuanians were building their own churches in Bridgeport. Irish families were moving out to other neighborhoods, renting bigger places, even buying their own homes.

Funny, I said, how our neighbors settle farther south, while the Irish on the West Side move west and the North Siders go up the lakeshore. But no one hopscotched. A South Side family would never move north or west.

"Paddy wants to buy a piano," Bridey said. She looked down at the baby. "Mike's asleep. I'll put him in his cradle."

"A piano," said Máire. "Even the Pykes never had a piano."

A few minutes later, the boys came racketing in. They were all busy during the week, but they made a point of meeting at McKenna's on a Saturday night.

"If they wake the baby . . . ," said Bridey.

Nothing would do but for Paddy to bring his son out to his brothers and Daniel. The baby looked so small in his arms as these big men clustered around him. Jamesy touched the baby's face.

"See these fellows, Mike?" Paddy said, tilting his son up toward the boys. "Jamesy, Stephen, Michael, and Danny O? They'll stand with you against the world." Then to me, "Remember Da—the fingers and the fist?"

"I do, Paddy."

Mike smiled up at them—a real smile, not just gas bubbling up.

Michael reached out his finger, and the baby Mike took it.

"Some grip on this fellow," Michael said. "He'll strike the mighty blow! Here's a partner in the forge for us, Paddy."

"Ah, Mike," Paddy said to his baby son, "you'll not work away in a forge all your life. You'll be a banker and wear linen suits and a straw boater hat and be a grand fellow entirely."

Victory.

✧　✧　✧

Patrick Kelly arrived in mid-April. Chicago'd finally shaken off the winter, and the scraps of prairie left near Bridgeport bloomed into crab apple blossoms and buttercups. Why does America not have snowdrops? "Saint Bridget's flower," I'd told Bridget. "We need them."

"No matter, spring's here," Bridget had said.

Edward Cuneen had taken to coming in from Summit and meeting her at St. Xavier's after school. They took long walks along the Lake, she said, talking about James Nugent. Slowly, slowly, with a word here and there, I tried to nudge Bridget into choosing her own happiness.

She didn't understand me and my life, I'd told her. I'd suffered, of course, and I missed her da, but I didn't see myself as the noble Widow Kelly, my face set against adversity. I took great joy in her and the boys, and now Mike, found comfort and fun with my Bridgeport friends and satisfaction, too, from working in the office, at church, and doing my letters. "And Bridget, I had the before times. Your da and I"—how to say it without embarrassing her—"found such delight in each other, something you can't grasp unless you experience it. Didn't God Himself make the bodies of men and women this way?" She'd only nodded. I'd explained the Brehon laws to her, mentioned Queen Maeve. "Irishwomen enjoyed taking and giving pleasure," I'd said, "but the Great Starvation brought such overwhelming sorrow." And then I'd told her that certain priests tried to scare women into guilt and denial. James Nugent had been a generous fellow who would be glad to see her married to Edward Cuneen.

"So why don't you marry Uncle Patrick?" she'd said.

"Jesus Christ, what has Máire been telling you?" Everything, it seemed. A conspiracy. "I just might, if it keeps him from leading the boys into Canada and gets you to see sense."

"So do it," she'd said. "Prove your argument."

⊕ ⊕ ⊕

Patrick Kelly had been in Chicago a week now. Busy, staying downtown at the Tremont House. Better for meetings and such, he'd said. He hadn't even come to see the baby, so I was surprised when he walked into Paddy's parlor.

I was minding Mike. Bridey was out shopping. Late afternoon. Máire still at the Shop. Quiet.

Patrick leaned over, and I held the baby up to him. Mike, not a bit afraid, grabbed one of the brass buttons on the dark green tunic of the new uniform Patrick wore as an officer in the Army of Ireland. I eased Mike's little hand free.

"I didn't know I'd be so besotted," I said to Patrick as I rocked Mike, comfortable in Bridey's big chair, the coal fire warming the place.

Patrick sat in the chair across from me.

"Being a grandmother's a great thing altogether," I said. Mike yelped. "Whist, whist," I said. "Nana's here." Now I understood Granny Keeley giving her food to Dennis's girls. The next generation. Their turn.

"A young-looking nana," Patrick said to me.

"Forty-three," I said.

"Not old," he said. "I'm fifty-six."

"Only numbers," I said. "You don't change. You're the same fellow came walking into Knocnacuradh that night. It was three months before Paddy was born, and here's his son."

"I remember thinking Michael was a lucky man," Patrick said, "never knowing how few years he had left."

"He was only twenty-seven, Patrick. Now I realize how young that is."

"Yet his son has a son. Something."

"A great deal," I said. "Didn't you ever want a family of your own?" All these years, I'd never dared ask him.

"I thought I did have a family," he said.

"Yes, yes, of course you do," I said, and looked down at the baby, sound asleep now, a solid, strong little body. I stood up. "I'll put him in his cradle."

I carried Mike into Paddy and Bridey's bedroom. Patrick followed me. I bent over, easing Mike into the wooden cradle that Paddy'd made for him.

"There, there." Mike stirred. I knelt down and rocked the cradle. "*Siúil, siúil, siúil a rún . . .*"

I looked up at Patrick. He smiled. I stood up. Patrick took my hand. We watched Mike sleep, his chest rising and falling, easy breathing.

"Healthy," I whispered. Patrick and I stood very still. "We could be happy, Patrick," I said softly.

"Happy?" he said, making it sound like some strange outlandish word.

"Patrick . . . ," I started. Mustn't wake the baby.

I kept hold of Patrick's hand, led him back to the fire, and then sat the two of us down. Now or never. "Happy, Patrick," I said. "Happy *together*." I took his other hand, looked him straight in the eye. I started a whole rigmarole about how seeing Bridget deny herself made me realize that Michael would want Patrick and me to . . . I couldn't go on.

Patrick covered my two hands with his. Warm but rough, his palms were callused.

I tried again. "Patrick, I have feelings for you and think you might have, well, feelings for me."

He laughed. Threw back his head and laughed.

"Funny, is it?" I tried to pull my hands away, stand up, but he held on to me.

"It's only that 'feelings' seems such a puny word for what's between us, Honora."

"All right, I'll say it plain, once and once only. I love you, Patrick Kelly, and not as a brother, in spite of the canon laws and impediments and what the neighbors will think. Stay here with me. We could have years and years of happiness."

No response. Taking his ease, legs stretched out.

"For Jesus' sake, Patrick, say something. Stop me floundering around. Tell me if I'm making a fool of myself." I jerked my hands free, folded them in my lap, and looked down.

Patrick sat up, leaned over to me, took my chin in his hand, and turned my face toward him. "I love you right enough, Honora. You know that." His face was very close to mine.

Dear God, Patrick Kelly's going to kiss me. I lifted my shoulder, moving forward, but he only gripped my chin tighter and then let go. He stood up. Pacing. Then he stood over me, pointing his finger.

"Listen to me, Honora Keeley. If we put shape on this, utter the words, there's no going back. No more Uncle Patrick, the Christmas visitor. I'd want us to live together, as husband and wife. Do you understand?"

"I understand," I said.

"And?"

"I do want us to be together, married, but canon law is between us." I explained to him about the impediment, then told him a bishop could give us a dispensation and what Máire'd said about Father Dunne's having the power. And if Patrick were willing . . .

Patrick didn't seem to be listening. He was pacing as I talked. Then he stopped. "Bother the impediment and the dispensation," he said.

"Don't say that. We need a dispensation. I don't want to go against the Church, especially when there's a way around it."

"All right, we'll get the dispensation. But Honora, I want to know if you're willing to leave Chicago, follow me to the Republic of Ireland." He knelt beside me, stroked my cheek. Not guarded—a light in those hazel eyes. "By the end of the summer we will have established the Republic of Ireland on what was Canadian soil. We'll be a government-in-exile with a senate, an army, a navy. We'll be a nation with revenue, assets. And from this base we can liberate Ireland, drive the British out. America, France, and Spain will be with us as allies, at best, or friendly neutrals, at least. After seven hundred years of waiting, the moment is now. And I'm one of the leaders."

"But, Patrick, how?"

Patrick had an answer for everything. The Fenians had the men and money. They would invade Canada. As I listened to him, I could see it all happening—the Fenians crossing into Canada, the United States supporting them, the British relinquishing first Canada and then Ireland. Patrick explained that the Fenians already had a promise from the U.S. government. He'd been at the meetings. The British would raise holy hell when the Fenians crossed the border, but President Johnson himself had assured the Fenians they'd be given time to claim a piece of territory, then the United States would recognize the Republic, start negotiating with Britain. Many in Congress wanted to annex Canada anyway. The British owed the United States billions of dollars as reparations for the assistance they gave to the South in the Civil War. Canada was mostly wilderness, and there was no real unity among the provinces. Much of the population was French or Irish. They had no love for the British or their empire. Plenty of Fenians in Canada already. "The people want to be part of the United States. They will welcome us," Patrick said. "There'll be very little fighting. Jamesy and Daniel will be safe, I promise."

France had agreed to recognize the new Republic as soon as the flag was raised in return for exclusive timber rights. "Worth a fortune," Patrick said. While America would take most of the territory of Canada, the Republic of Ireland would have land enough for a settlement and government buildings. "We've been offered Montreal and Quebec City," Patrick said, "but we'll build our own capital—a grand meitheal—temporary, after all." He said that with the Irish privateers harassing British shipping on the one hand and international pressure being applied on the other, Britain might pack up and leave Ireland before the Fenians had a chance to invade. "Your bloodless revolution, Honora," he said.

Then Patrick led me over to Bridey's kitchen table. From inside his green tunic he took out a packet of papers and spread them out before me. "The battle plan," he said as he smoothed out the large square sheets with care. A military operation unlike any undertaken before by the Irish, he said. In past uprisings, ill-equipped and desperate men had flung themselves against a superior force. Now hardened soldiers, veterans of the toughest battles of the Civil War, men who longed to avenge the Great Starvation, would march against a few civilian militias in Canada. Four armies advancing from separate directions.

Patrick himself had purchased muskets at the government arsenal in Philadelphia and ammunition in Troy, New York. "The men selling me the arms wished us good luck," he said. "At one place, they wouldn't take my money." One hundred thousand dollars spent to buy ten thousand stands of arms and two and a half million ball cartridges, Patrick told me.

"Tom Sweeny wanted to wait until winter so we could move across the lakes on the ice, but the Brotherhood decided if we didn't act now, we'd lose our soldiers. Once the veterans marry and settle down, it's hard to call them back."

"Yes," I said.

Patrick showed me the declaration General Sweeny had written, to be read to the Canadian people:

> *We are an Irish Army of liberation. In the name of seven centuries of British iniquity and Irish misery, of our millions of famine graves, of our insulted name and race, we stretch forth the hand of brotherhood to you. Join us in smiting the tyrant.*

"Marvelous, isn't it?" he said, and now he did kiss me—but on the cheek, with the excitement of a comrade-in-arms, not the passion of a lover. "And I know all this country along the border," he said, putting his hand on a section of the map covered with quick sketches of pine trees. "The Ojibwa hunt and fish on both sides of it. They'll be with us as guides, warriors even. I feel as if all parts of me are coming together in this great campaign." He turned to me. "Are you with me, Honora?"

"You want me to come along, the way Marion Mulligan followed the colonel?"

He laughed now. Boyish. "No, no. This will be a very short war. I mean come up north when we build the capital. I'll have some title—secretary of this or that—a position. Something to offer you, Honora. Wonderful to have you by my side while we make history. The work you could do with your knowledge and skill! We need to create a whole new structure of government, write a constitution. So much to organize. In our Republic, women's voices will be heard."

"Patrick, it all sounds glorious."

"And you'll come with me?"

How could I? Leave my children? Mike? Máire? Bridgeport? Impossible. I'm settled now—Nana. I started to say all that to Patrick, but then that young Honora leapt up from somewhere inside me. I'd be only two days' journey away. My boys were men. Michael, the youngest, considered himself grown at seventeen. He planned to become engaged to Mary Ann Chambers, the girl he'd been courting. All of them had lives of their own. Wouldn't they be surprised to see their mam out on such an adventure! If I say no to Patrick, he'll be too proud to ever come back. He's right. We've gone too far. He can't be the visiting bachelor uncle anymore. What is it that I want? I wasn't sure what I was going to say until I spoke the words.

"I will," I said to him.

And then Patrick Kelly *did* kiss me.

⊕ ⊕ ⊕

Patrick left that night. He asked me to wait to tell the family until he returned. He wanted to speak to Paddy first. "Ask for my hand?" I'd said. But Patrick wanted to reassure Paddy he meant no disrespect to his father—a man talking to a man. I agreed and said nothing.

I'd stopped opposing Jamesy and Daniel, which confused Máire even after I'd explained there'd be no real fighting. "They'll be welcomed," I said.

On the last day of May, nearly two thousand Chicago Irishmen headed north. Michael and Stephen weren't with them. They blamed me for the letter they received from Colonel Kelly, ordering them to stay home.

Trouble began for the Fenians before they even left the city. Three railroads refused to carry them, and only by taking off their green caps and pretending to be laborers did they get any passage out of Chicago.

It seemed all would go as Patrick said. A Fenian troop captured Fort Erie, defeated the Queen's Own—the best of the militias. We all—men and women—celebrated in McKenna's. Fellows were planning to leave for Canada immediately, join the Fenians, be there for the victory.

But the army General Sweeny and Colonel Kelly meant to lead into Canada did not cross the border. Instead, at midnight on the sixth of June, Sweeny was arrested—not by the British, but by his own Union army comrade General George Meade. Betrayed. Most of the seven thousand Fenian soldiers were allowed to disperse, but during the evacuation one American officer allowed a British force to pursue some Fenians across the border into U.S. territory and stood by while the British sabered the unarmed men. A hundred were captured and held by the Canadians. Federal officials arrested Fenian leaders in

St. Louis, Buffalo, Cleveland, Chicago, and New York. So much for the support of the U.S. government.

Jamesy came home alone. Daniel had traveled west to Montana because General Thomas Meagher, the Young Ireland hero who'd led his own Irish Brigade during the Civil War, was now the acting governor of Montana. Daniel had joined the U.S. Cavalry. "He likes being a soldier," Jamesy told me. "And Montana's on the Canadian border. They might try again."

Jamesy didn't know what had happened to Patrick. With his record, there'd be little hope for him if he was captured. The Canadians were threatening to hang their Fenian prisoners without trials. A raid to rescue the prisoners was planned, Jamesy said.

"I won't be going," he said. "I'm laying *my* burden down, Mam. Christophe taught me a song while I was in New Orleans. The words go through my head." Jamesy sang softly.

I'm going to lay my sword and shield
Down by the riverside
Ain't gonna study war no more.

"Jamesy," I said, and hugged him close. Alive.

❖ ❖ ❖

"Uncle Patrick's getting hanged." Michael brought the news. The Canadians, angry that ten soldiers of the Queen's Own had been killed, wanted vengeance. Irish traitors had dared invade British soil. Execute them. No trials.

"They can't get away with *that*!" James McKenna said when I went to the tavern for news. "Any candidate wants an Irish vote better do something to get our Fenian prisoners a fair trial."

Máire and I went to see Alderman Comiskey. Could he intervene for Patrick? Huge pressure was being applied to help the prisoners, he told us. "Thank God there's an election on," Alderman Comiskey said. President Johnson wrote to Congress, saying that the invasion was designed to redress political grievances the Irish suffered at the hands of the British. There should be no death penalty for persons engaged in revolutionary attempts, the President said. "That should help," Alderman Comiskey told us. "Make the British think twice."

It did. "Reprieved for now," was the word in November.

"You'd think Patrick would have escaped by now," I said to Máire. We were alone by the fire, the first week in December.

All the Fenians arrested in the United States had been freed. And now, one by one the fellows held in Canada were returning home. But not Patrick.

Had they discovered his record? I'd hoped that because Patrick Kelly was such a common name, the connection had been missed. But if they found out who he is, five acts of Congress won't save him.

"I was thinking," Máire said, "could that greedy fellow at the British consulate be any use to us?"

"Máire, that's an idea. We could bring letters to him attesting to Patrick Kelly's good character."

"From important men who could return a favor," Máire said, "like Marshall Field . . ."

"Alderman Comiskey and Mr. Onahan . . ."

"Long John Wentworth and Father Dunne . . ."

That's it! Testimonials.

We found the secretary plumper and more prosperous but still ready to deal.

"Testimonials," he said as he leafed through the letters.

"And this." Máire passed over the pouch of silver dollars. "And this, too"—a statement listing the names of conscripted soldiers he'd claimed as citizens and the fees he'd charged, signed by the fellows. "A good story for the *Times*, what with all the interest in, uhm, U.S.-British relations."

He said a lot of rude things to us, but in the end he agreed to have the consul intervene for Patrick.

A week later, we got the wire: "Have been released—Patrick Kelly."

Chapter 35

$\mathcal{P}$ATRICK DIDN'T come at Christmas, nor was he at Jamesy's wedding to Maggie Nolan on St. Stephen's Day. He missed a very happy day. Bridget and Edward Cuneen told me they planned an Easter wedding. Stephen and Nelly Lang announced they'd marry next Christmas; my sons, starting their lives. Thank you, Lord.

Hard on Máire to be away from her sons and Gracie, especially with Gracie and James Mulloy expecting their first child. But Máire would go to Nashville for the birth.

"The joy of being a grandmother will astound you," I'd told Máire.

"That's good," Máire'd said, "and I'll enjoy the trip on the riverboat, too."

She'd received Christmas letters from Thomas and Daniel, full of the wonders of the West, and she talked about visiting them, too, someday.

"Doesn't seem like Christmas without Uncle Patrick," Michael had said.

"Probably in Ireland," Jamesy had said. "Some of the brothers are being smuggled across. Fighting on."

I'll never see Patrick Kelly again if that's true.

I remember Granny's story of "Queen Maeve and the Cattle Raid." Maeve needed a bull for her herd so she could remain equal to her husband, Ailil, the one who paid the bride price. She tried to buy the Brown Bull of Cooley and offered her own friendly thighs to the owner as part of the bargain. He'd refused her. "I'd rather go to war," the fellow told Maeve.

"Men," Granny'd said. Fighting on.

❖ ❖ ❖

January 6, 1867, the Feast of the Epiphany—Nollaig na mBan—Christmas of the Women. On this day in the before times, Mam and Granny Keeley and the women of Bearna gathered to smoke their clay pipes and sip some poitín. "Our own quiet celebration after the work of Christmas," Mam had explained.

"I'm sure the Blessed Mother took a bit of a rest after the shepherds left," Granny Keeley'd said. "Herself and Saint Bridget taking time to sit down for a chat."

I lay awake remembering that circle of women and our hearth. Bridget slept on beside me. I heard Máire's newest clock strike three times. A long time until dawn. Don't want to wake Bridget with my tossing and turning. Christmas recess at St. Xavier's, so she can sleep in. I'll get up and have a cup of tea.

No sound came from Máire's room. Michael and Stephen snored away in theirs as I walked into the kitchen.

I lit the kerosene lamp and stirred the fire in the brand-new iron stove, a Christmas gift from the boys. I filled a pot with water from the barrel and placed it on the stovetop, then drew a chair close to the open grate and sat down, glad for the warmth of the fire.

And then it descended upon me. The great sadness I always held so carefully away came over me in waves. Tears began falling. The weeping was for Michael, Mam and Da, and Granny Keeley, for my brothers and infant Grellan in the cillín. I was crying for white snowdrops and yellow whin bushes, for the sun on the green fields of Knocnacuradh and the warm sand of the Silver Strand under my feet, for the smell of turf fires and for stories told on winter nights, for songs and reels and making the Stations at St. Enda's well, for the back-and-forth of selling fish under the Spanish Arch, and for the wind filling the red sails of Da's púcán as he joined the great Claddagh fleet on their way to the sea. For Galway Bay.

Gone, gone, gone. A whole world lost to me and to millions more, the living as well as the dead. I'm here in Bridgeport, but I'm there, too. I'm Nana, but I'm that same young girl going off to wash her hair in the Tobar Geal stream. Irish and American, here and there. But I would never see Ireland again. Nor would my children or their children, either. I thought of our new neighbors, the Bigus family from Vilnius, the Prussian Oldakhs, of M'am Jacques and the millions stolen from Africa. All of us gone from our home places, never to return.

My shoulders dropped forward. My head fell into my hands. The sobs twisted through me, shaking my body.

After what seemed a very long time, the sobs eased and I took in some hiccuping breaths. I went to the water barrel to splash my face. I won't be surprised into grief like that again anytime soon.

The water for my tea was boiling over. I wrapped a corner of my dressing gown around the handle of the pot and lifted it up. I poured the steaming water into the teapot—another gift from my boys. Bridget had given me this wool dressing gown.

In a few hours, the sun will rise. I'll sip my tea and wait.

❂   ❂   ❂

It was Bridget came into the kitchen and woke me. Still dark. "Mam, someone's been pounding on the downstairs door."

Bridget carried the lantern down the stairs, with me behind her.

"What is it?" I spoke through the door.

"It's Patrick, Honora. Open up."

I did. Him, really him.

"Uncle Patrick!" Bridget grabbed his hand and pulled him inside.

"I've two friends with me."

"Bring them in," I said.

How weary Patrick looks, I thought as Bridget urged the two young men behind Patrick to come into the hallway. Patrick wore a heavy sheepskin jacket over leather fringed pants—the North Woods trapper clothes. What happened to his fine green uniform?

"I saw the light in the kitchen window and I knew you were up," Patrick said to me.

One young man spoke to the other in French.

"*Parlez-vous anglais?*" Bridget asked him.

"We speak English," said the taller of the two with a bit of a Galway accent. Had Patrick taught him?

"Up the stairs now," I said. "Be quiet as we pass this door. Don't want to wake the baby."

We settled the three at the kitchen table. I poured them tea and Bridget brought out the whiskey jug, adding a bit to each man's cup.

"I'll get the boys. They'll want to see Uncle Patrick," Bridget said.

I sat next to Patrick. "I'm only sorry it didn't work out for you, Patrick."

He sipped his tea, looking at me over the rim of the heavy china cup. "I appreciate your sympathy. And thank you for the letter from the British consul. My lawyer said it helped."

"Good."

"I've not given up, Honora. Only moving the battlefield."

I looked at the young French fellows. Do they understand? Probably only had the few words Patrick taught them. Something about them. I looked more closely at their faces, visible now in the light from the stove and lantern. Familiar-looking.

"Patrick, these fellows . . . ," I said. "I know them, but it's not possible. They'd be old."

"See, boys? I told you she'd recognize you." He smiled at me. "Honora, meet Joseph's son, Etienne, and Hughie's son, Jean. Boys, this is your auntie Honora."

Bridget, Stephen, and Michael came into the kitchen just then, and what a grand clamor of laughing and crying we had as my children met their Keeley cousins and welcomed Uncle Patrick.

"And my brothers?" I asked Patrick when the ruckus receded a bit.

"Alive, Honora," he said, "but being sensible men, they left a fifteen-hundred-mile winter journey to the young and foolish and those who don't know any better."

"And where's our aunt Máire, the Snowy-Breasted Pearl?" asked Jean.

"Here." Máire stood in the doorway. The boys rose. She looked at them for a long minute. "The Keeleys always were fine big men," she said, and moved to embrace each of them.

"Patrick, thank you. Thank you," I said.

Michael ran down for Paddy and Bridey and baby Mike. Stephen wanted to go over to get Jamesy and Maggie and the Langs.

"Later," I said. "Etienne and Jean aren't going anywhere. Neither is Patrick. Let them eat."

✦ ✦ ✦

Patrick told the story as we sat at the table after breakfast. He didn't speak about the invasion or prison or nearly hanging, but he told us how he'd found the Keeleys. "A French fellow was in prison with me. He said some Irishmen lived on the Saint Lawrence River—two brothers, married to French girls—with a whole load of boys—and the fellow said they were called Kelly or Keeley. After I was released, I thought I'd go see if there really were Keeleys living there on the Saint Lawrence. The town was across from Grosse Île, and I thought, It could be. It could be."

"Now I will tell," said Etienne. "So into Berthier comes this buck-skinned fellow."

"Berthier? Is that your townland?" I asked.

"Our village, Berthier-sur-Mer, though our *mer* is the Saint Lawrence River."

"Is there a strand?" I asked.

"There is. We're fishermen in our village."

"You would be. And your fathers?"

"The best, *les meilleurs.*"

"They would be," Máire said.

"Well, this buckskinned one came to our church, Notre Dame-de-l'Assomption, and spoke to the *curé*, Abbé Bonnenfaant."

"*Tried* to speak," Patrick said. "My French, his English?" He shrugged.

"The *curé* knew *les irelandais* had married Cecilé Peltier and Eloise Gaumand, and even knew they were raising the children of a brother who died at Grosse Île."

"Grosse Ile," repeated Jean, and blessed himself.

"What's Grosse Île, Mam?" Michael asked.

"A very sad place. Go on," I said.

"So," Etienne said, "he brought this fellow to our family."

"I knew your brothers at once," Patrick said to me. "Hughie's the image of your da. Joseph looks more like your mother."

"And you told them Mam and Da had died?"

"They knew," Patrick said. "A Connemara fellow came through about ten years ago."

If only Mam could have known her sons were alive with wives and children. I blinked my eyes against the tears.

Máire shook her head and sighed. "God rest them," she said.

"So, a reunion," Etienne said. "Our fathers cried, our mothers cried, our sisters cried, and we said we wanted to come to Chicago with Patrick."

"So, you were coming to Chicago?" I asked Patrick.

"I was," he said.

The sun was full up now. Etienne yawned and Jean's eyes were closed.

"These boys are exhausted," I said. "Stephen, put them in your room. Can Patrick go down with you, Paddy? Bridey?"

"He's welcome," Bridey said. She stood, the baby in her arms. Patrick started to say something, but Mike woke up and let out a yell.

"Great lungs on that fellow," said Patrick. "That's Michael's grandson all right—how he looked at that age."

"Really? He's like my da?" Paddy said.

"He is," said Patrick.

"Do you hear that, Mam?" Paddy said to me.

"Your uncle Patrick would know," I said.

"I would," he said.

"Now," I said, "time to sleep, because, boys, you have twenty years to tell us about."

"But I'm only seventeen," said Jean.

"Even more reason for you to rest up."

"We have letters for you," Etienne said.

"Good. We'll read them while you're asleep. When you wake up, you'll have boiled bacon and cabbage and pratties. You do eat Irish food, don't you?"

"Yes," said Etienne. "Our fathers taught our mothers. They tried to add spices, but our fathers preferred the plain."

"They would," Máire said.

Patrick went down with Paddy, Bridey, and the baby. Etienne and Jean went into Stephen and Michael's room, while Stephen left to get Jamesy and Maggie.

Máire and I sat in the kitchen, marveling together. No words needed. Sitting over our tea, smiling.

After a while, she said, "Patrick Kelly, Honora. I think he's come home. If you want him to stay, he will."

"Too late, Máire. He's hardly said a word to me. He brought our nephews to us as a kind of farewell. Patrick will be heading off soon. You'll see. He'll never settle. He can't."

"Michael Kelly was on his way somewhere, too. He stopped for you, Honora."

"But we were young."

"Be young again."

"I tried."

"Try again."

✧ ✧ ✧

So. We had a feast true to the spirit of William Boy O'Kelly himself, an abundance of food, laughter, stories, and dancing to the reels Jamesy played on the pipes. All of my children here, so happy to welcome Hughie's and Joseph's sons. Their cousins knew a few good steps themselves.

Máire and I jigged together. Then Máire stopped. She went very quiet. She's missing her sons and Gracie, thinking of Johnny Og. I squeezed her hand. She smiled and shook her head. "Ah well, I'll be with Gracie soon."

Patrick sat in his chair, the still point in the flow of family, not saying much and barely looking at me. Patrick had said he wouldn't be able to go back to being the bachelor uncle visiting at Christmas if we put words on our feelings. He was right. And now he will leave.

Bridey came in from the bedroom carrying the baby. Paddy went over and took Mike from her. "I'll go with you, Bridey."

She touched his face. "Stay for a while. You're enjoying yourself."

He is. Years since I'd seen Paddy chatting and laughing, singing even. Is the war finally letting go of him?

"I'll carry Mike down and come back," Paddy said, laying the baby against his shoulder, bringing him over to me.

Mike opened his eyes—the same blue as his father and grandfather—and regarded this noisy family of his. He straightened in Paddy's arms, big, nearly a year old now—a sturdy lad.

"Sleep well, Mike," I said, and kissed his forehead.

"Say good night," Bridey said.

Mike waved at us as Paddy carried him over to Patrick, who stretched out his finger to the baby. Mike grabbed it.

"His grandfather's grip," Patrick said.

Mike reached down and took a handful of the fringe on Patrick's leather tunic. Mike let out a string of grunts and gasps at Patrick, struggling to tell him something.

"Speaking in code," Patrick said. "A Fenian already." A rush of laughter. Patrick had been so dour all night. Now he stood up. "I'll be going, too," he said.

"Where are you going?" Máire asked.

"I'm stopping at McKenna's. James will want to refight the battle of Ridgeway and the invasion of Canada, and tell me the state of the Brotherhood."

"I can tell you in one word," Jamesy said. "Discouraged."

"We've been laid low before," Patrick said, "and always got up again." Then his first words directly to me: "My coat, Honora, please, and the crozier."

I got the sheepskin jacket and the leather case that held the crozier from my bedroom and brought them to him.

"Show us Saint Grellan's crozier, Uncle Patrick," Michael asked him. "Please."

Patrick hesitated, then drew the crozier from its case.

"Is it really gold?" Etienne asked, leaning closer to see.

"It is," Jamesy said. "Look at the designs on the shaft, the animal on the hilt. Great artistry in Ireland all those years ago."

"It looks like a shepherd's crook," Etienne said.

"Yes," I said. "A bishop's crozier's meant to symbolize the staff carried by the Good Shepherd."

Patrick nodded. "I know mine," he quoted, "and mine know me."

"It's been the Kelly battle standard, the cathach, for over a thousand years," Jamesy said.

"And a lot of good it's done them," Máire said.

None of the boys heard her. They were looking at Patrick Kelly.

Patrick handed the crozier to Jamesy. He held it for a moment, then passed it to Stephen, who handed the crozier to Michael. He held it out to Edward Cuneen. Bridget, standing near him, whispered, "No," but Edward didn't seem to hear her. He took the staff, then passed it to Etienne, who gave it to Jean. Jean extended the crozier to Paddy. Paddy kept his left arm around Mike and took the crozier in his right hand. Mike reached for the glittering stick, but Paddy held it far away from him. Bridey took Mike. He cried. He wanted this shiny toy.

"Shhh . . ." Bridey rocked him.

"A nation once again . . . ," Michael sang, and the other men joined him. Etienne and Jean knew all the words.

We women didn't sing with the men. This was their ritual.

No one spoke when the song finished.

Then Mary Ann Chambers, Michael's American-born girlfriend, spoke. "Can I see the staff, please?" she said to Paddy.

But Patrick took the crozier back. "There's a geis against women holding the crozier."

"A what?"

"A taboo," Patrick said to her, "unless the woman is taking the truth test."

"The truth test?" She turned to Maggie and Nelly.

Then the girls looked at me. For a moment, we left our Bridgeport parlor and stood together on a hillside in Ireland. Even Mike kept quiet, his eyes on Patrick.

"Anyone who takes hold of Grellan's crozier and swears falsely will be burned by the fire of justice." Patrick almost chanted the words.

"And have you seen it happen?" Mary Ann asked Patrick. "Fellows' hands getting burnt, I mean?"

"Never. The men who take an oath on Grellan's staff mean what they promise," Patrick said.

"At the time," Jamesy said. "Too bad they didn't all remember when the call went out to form up for the invasion of Canada." Jamesy said that during the war, Fenians from both armies had come together in caves or ravines at night to pledge themselves to Ireland on the crozier, fellows passing it one to another, all the time knowing they'd face one another as enemies on the battlefield the next day. "We forgot everything, except that we were Irishmen," he said, "and yet those same men stayed home."

They didn't want to fight anymore, I thought.

"*Our* fellows were ready, Jamesy," Stephen said.

"It was the other faction let us down," said Michael.

"I don't understand," Etienne said.

"Why would you?" I said.

Jamesy started to explain the ins and outs of Fenian feuds and how they still would have won if the U.S. Army hadn't confiscated their guns before the invasion. "American soldiers acted as spies for the British, didn't they, Uncle Patrick?"

Now Patrick spoke. "We were done in by the deceit of the U.S. government and the dishonesty of subordinate officers who promised General Sweeny more than they could deliver," he said. "Even our own turned against us. D'Arcy McGee, the very fellow who brought my letter to you in Galway, Honora, is an important man in Canada now. Yet he denounced us."

"Can't change the past," Máire said. "What's done is done."

Jamesy was ready to argue, but his wife, Maggie, picked up his pipes and handed them to him. "Enough politics," she said. "Play a reel."

Jamesy smiled at her. In a few minutes his fingers were racing along the chanter. Music filled the room.

"Come on, Etienne." Máire took his hands and whirled him around, and the dancing started up again.

Paddy took Mike from Bridey, hoisted him onto his shoulder, and he and Bridey left.

Patrick got ready to leave. He fastened the ties on his sheepskin coat, then settled the strap of the crozier across his back.

"How did you manage to keep the crozier safe in prison?" I asked him.

"The warden was Irish," he said.

"Uncle Patrick's going!" I shouted into the dancers.

"Good-bye!" and, "See you tomorrow!" as they moved forward and back.

"I'll walk you out," I said, wrapping my shawl around me. "A lot of Christmases," I said to him as we walked down the stairs.

"Remember the first one?" Patrick asked. "You, wrapped in a bear skin, sitting on these steps, putting manners on me."

"And you not listening to a word I said. Some things don't change."

We came to the bottom step.

"Good-bye, Honora," he said, and took my hand. "I'm leaving for Ireland in the morning."

Then he turned and walked away. The abruptness of the man.

"No!" I shouted at Patrick. "Wait, wait!"

But he kept moving, disappearing down the dark, empty street.

I started running, calling out, "Patrick, for God's sake, stop!"

Finally he did.

We'd reached the edge of Bubbly Creek where a row of gas

streetlamps shone down on the water. Sheets of ice floated on the surface, but Bubbly Creek never froze over completely.

"What is it?" Patrick asked. Enough light to see the irritation in his face, those hazel eyes drilling me. Impatient. Colonel Kelly. "What is it?" he asked again. "What?"

I took a breath. "You know well and good *what.* And you're not going anywhere until you give me some explanation." I looked up at him, straight into those military eyes. I can't waver. Now or never.

"Explanation?" He took a few steps toward the Bridgeport pumping station, shuttered and still now, its giant machine silent with the canal closed for the winter.

I kept pace with Patrick. "Yes," I said, "an explanation. The night before you left for Canada, you said you cared for me, asked me to marry you, to go with you."

"Honora, please. We failed in Canada. All that's over."

"And does 'all that' include me? You said—"

"What was said is better forgotten."

"Forgotten? Patrick, I—"

"Honora, I told you. I'm going to Ireland," he said. "There's a group of men, veterans of the war, trained. They are ready to go back to Ireland, set up in the Connemara mountains, harry the British soldiers. They want me to lead them. Action there would hearten fellows here."

"Patrick, if you get arrested, the British will hang you straight away."

"My death might be of some use."

"Martyrs help the Cause?"

"I'd be following some brave men to the gallows. I started on this road a long time ago. Even if this is the end for me, I won't turn back. I can't change."

"Can't change? This is America! People change themselves all the time. None of us are who we'd be if we'd stayed in Ireland. We probably wouldn't be alive at all, and no songs are written about the glory of starving to death, I can tell you that. You could do just as much for the Cause in Chicago as you can in the Connemara mountains. More, probably, but you'd rather die for Ireland than live for it."

"That's not true."

"It is. I understand that men sometimes have to go to war. Even in Mam's lullaby, the girl promises to sell her spinning wheel to buy her love a sword of steel, but that's so he can defend himself and come home."

"Victorious," Patrick said.

"Alive. Win or lose. Alive."

"I don't agree, Honora."

The wind had picked up. I started to shiver. "All right for you to spout opinions, warm in that big coat of yours," I said. "I have more to say, but I'm perishing in the cold."

"Well then, here."

Patrick undid his coat and began to shrug it off, but I stepped forward into his open arms. He closed the coat around us both. My arms went around him of their own accord. Patrick pulled me closer. I felt his chest pressed against me and then his lips on my hair. I lifted my face to him. He kissed me hard and quick.

"There," he said. Angry. "There. Satisfied?" He stabbed me with the word, and a run of fierce kisses. "There. There."

But I met each thrust, holding him tighter and tighter, returning each kiss. Then his lips softened. Our kisses turned easy and slow, and it was me whispering, "There, there," soothing him, loving him. "There."

Patrick had braced his back against the door of the pumping station and I was leaning full on him, under his coat. He straightened up. He dropped his arms to his sides.

"What's the matter?" I said. "Don't tell me you don't care . . ."

"I still have to leave," he said.

"Leave? You can't. We love each other."

"It doesn't matter. I won't let *this* make me weak. I won't desert—"

"Patrick, could you be lying to yourself? It's easy done, I know. But love *does* matter to you. Didn't I feel the desire pushing out of you?"

"I can lock it away again."

"That's not true."

"It is."

"All right, then. Take the truth test. Here, give me the crozier." I reached over his shoulder for the case.

He tried to twist away from me, but I caught hold of the leather case and tugged on it.

"Be careful, for God's sake! It's a thousand years old."

"Take the crozier out."

"You're acting like a mad woman."

"Do it," I said, not loosening my grip.

"All right." He took the strap off his shoulder, opened the flap, and eased the crozier from its case.

"Give it to me," I said. The crozier felt lighter than I'd expected, but then the staff wasn't solid gold but hollow inside, made to protect Grellan's hazel rod—that's the precious relic, the gold was only a shell around it.

"Take it!" I shouted at him.

"I will!" he shouted back. "You're unbalanced."

"Swear that in your heart of hearts, you want to leave me," I said.

He took the crozier, then leaned close to me so I could see how carefully he formed every word. "I want to leave this place and this woman and not return, so that I may serve the cause to which I have pledged my life. I refuse to love her. That is the truth." He lifted the crozier over his head.

I saw his eyes, lit by the streetlamp. He's gone for a soldier. Lost to me forever.

"The crozier's cold," he said. "A warrior's weapon, after all."

"And you're glad," I said, giving up. A hard man. I remembered Patrick digging boulders from our field, piling them into a stone wall—no chinks nor cracks, unyielding. I thought of how our Irish word for fate, dán, became dána, daring, and then danaid, grief. Patrick was accustomed to duty and grief, able to endure them. Let love take him over and happiness might undo him.

"Good-bye, Patrick," I said.

"I told you, I do know myself," Patrick said. But then he gave a yelp. "The heat—my hand. It must be friction. Jesus." He tried to open the fist he'd clamped around the crozier. "It's burning me," he said. He shook the crozier. "Damn, it's getting hotter!"

"Let go, Patrick! Let go!"

"I can't," he said. He tried to pry his fingers apart with his other hand. "Help me," he said, stretching his arm out toward me.

"Tell the truth."

He drew back, furious, then hurled the words at me:

"I love you. I want to be with you." His hand and arm started shaking, then went still. "Jesus, it's gone cold." He opened his hand and balanced the crozier on his palm. His fingers were neither burned nor blistered.

I looked up at him. A miracle.

Patrick stared down at his hand. "I never really thought it worked." He carefully put away the crozier. "Now what?" he said, so softly that I hardly heard him.

"Up to you," I said.

"I could never give up the struggle," he said.

"I know that. But couldn't you do more for Ireland alive in Bridgeport than dead in the Connemara mountains?"

"It could be," he said. A sliver of moonlight found his hazel eyes. He took my face in his hands. "I do so want you, Honora. I'd like to break into the station and make love to you right now."

"Why not?" I said.

He laughed—a boy for a moment. "I suppose we'd better marry first," he said.

"Wouldn't want to shock the children," I said.

"And Michael would expect me to show you the proper respect."

"He would," I said.

"I just don't know," he said. "I think I may be frightened."

"Oh, Patrick, look!" I said. The moon had turned Bubbly Creek silver. "A mearbhall."

"What's that?"

"Unexpected light," I said. "A gift."

For a long moment, Patrick looked at Bubbly Creek. "A gift," he repeated.

He put his arm around me, sheltering me with his coat. As we turned onto Hickory Street, we heard the pipes and saw the glow from the kerosene lamp. Our family was dancing in the parlor. And we would join them.

PART FIVE

Chicago Irish — 1893

Chapter 36

Morning, St. John's Night—June 23, 1893

"WHERE'S THE STUBBORN fellow?" Máire came through the front door, ready for battle.

"Patrick's in the kitchen, having his breakfast."

"I can't believe he's refusing to go to the Fair with us."

"A matter of principle, so he says."

"Principle? When we've arranged for the whole family to spend the day there together? Let me at him."

Since the Chicago World's Fair—or, more properly, the World's Columbian Exposition of 1893—had opened in May, millions of visitors had poured in from all over to marvel at its wonders. Today, June 23, I'd asked that our whole clan go to the Fair together.

Paddy's oldest son, Mike, had organized fifty-seven tickets for my twenty-seven grandchildren, two great-grandchildren, their parents, and Patrick and Máire's family.

A master plumber at twenty-seven, Mike'd helped transform the six hundred acres of swampland along Lake Michigan into the fabulous White City that contained, as he'd told me, "the grandest buildings ever constructed in the history of the world. The Manufactures and Liberal Arts Building alone covers thirty acres and has room for three hundred thousand people. Imagine that!"

Stephen's oldest boy, Ed, sixteen and the only redhead in the bunch, had worked with Mike. "I'm going to be a civil engineer," he'd told me, "and build bridges and tunnels and skyscrapers."

"But your father—" I'd started.

"Wants me to be mayor of Chicago," he'd finished my sentence. "I know. I'll do that, too."

Real goers, my grandchildren.

Mike and Ed had shown Patrick and me photographs of these brand-new Greek temples, Italian palaces, and Roman amphitheaters that had risen up along the lakeshore. We were impressed with what the boys called "architectural wonders" and admired the pictures of the buildings that each state in the Union had constructed: California's Spanish mission with its tower of oranges—"They give the fruit away every day!" Ed said; Iowa's pavilion made from corn; Washington's giant log cabin. And France, Spain, Austria, the countries of South and Central America, India, Japan, Russia, and Turkey all created massive pavilions to display their products, they told us.

We could see the most popular attraction right from the parlor window—the Ferris wheel.

"Two hundred and sixty-four feet tall," Ed said as we'd looked at the huge wheel, visible across the distance of four miles that separated Bridgeport from Jackson Park and the Fair.

"It's the centerpiece of the Midway," Mike had said.

"I've heard about the Midway," I'd told them.

They'd laughed. The Midway Plaisance provided the fun of the Fair. Algerian snake charmers, acrobats from Java, Hungarian Gypsy bands, and every manner of dancer and musician entertained in the villages set up along the mile-long strip where thousands of people from dozens of exotic places lived and displayed their cultures to the crowds.

And there, right next to the Cairo street where the famous Little Egypt performed her belly dance, stood not one but two Irish villages, each with its own complement of "native" performers and craftsmen.

That's where I wanted to take the family—to Ireland. But there was a problem.

"I'm boycotting both Irish villages," Patrick said to Máire, sipping his tea and looking up at her from his place at the kitchen table.

"Boycott? What's that?" she said.

As Patrick explained to her how a village in Ireland got rid of an agent called Captain Boycott, I sat Máire down and gave her a cup of tea.

"Refused to serve him in the shops, work on his estate, wouldn't speak to him or even look at him. He finally left."

"The Land League did it," I put in, sitting at the table. "They stand up to the landlords without violence."

"But what does that have to do with going to the Fair?" she asked.

Patrick pointed his finger at Máire. "Who built the so-called Irish villages? Who's collecting the admission fee, pocketing every cent spent there? The English!"

True enough. A Lady Aberdeen was sponsoring the Blarney Castle Irish village, while two British women had put together the Donegal version.

"An insult!" Patrick said, pounding his fist on the table. "As if Irish people couldn't organize ourselves. Remember the Fenian Fair? The neck of them . . . You can capitulate, but I won't."

"Listen, Patrick," Máire said, "the Sassenach don't give a fiddler's fart if you go to the Fair or not, but the kids do. You haven't seen Daniel since Canada. He's coming all the way from California with his wife and three children. My grandchildren will finally meet their cousins and Aunt Honey."

Colonel Daniel O'Connell Leahy commanded a cavalry company in San Francisco—not fighting the Indian Wars anymore, thank God.

Silken Thomas owned a share in a saloon in San Francisco. Máire was hoping he'd come with Daniel today. But with Thomas, you never knew.

Gracie and James Mulloy were definitely bringing their four from Nashville—all grown up now, and their oldest girl, Molly, had two children. "She's called her boy Johnny," Máire'd told me, "and really, he's the image of Johnny Og." Máire visited the Mulloys often, and she'd been there cheering in the stands when Askeeboy won the Kentucky Derby.

Máire had traveled to California soon after Patrick and I were married. (When I think of the way I tortured myself over that dispensation—and there'd been nothing to it.) She might have stayed in San Francisco except for the Great Chicago Fire. "I have to help Marshall start again," she'd said. She's still there—a great treat for all my granddaughters when I take them downtown to have lunch with Aunt Máire in the Walnut Room.

It was Máire who suggested placing stationery in the ladies' restrooms, and it was her idea to have a bargain basement so all the typists and office girls could shop at Field's, too.

The Shop took up a whole block on State Street. All the trolley cars met and turned around there, at the place we called "the Loop."

Máire'd found herself an apartment in one of the new skyscrapers rising twenty stories into the air. Amazing. Mike had explained to Patrick and me how steel could now be forged into frames that bore enormous weights. "Chicago's the pioneer," he said. A forest of these giants filled the streets of downtown.

"Thrilling!" Máire'd said. "And see how the windows are set back to let in the light without throwing shadows down on the street?" she'd added.

"Louis Sullivan's the fellow designing the best of them," Mike had said. Mike had gotten a lot of work from Louis after Máire and I'd introduced them. We knew his father, Paddy Sullivan, a great fiddler and dance teacher.

Good to know people in Chicago. Mr. Onahan was still going strong, and John Comiskey, too. But James and Lizzie McKenna were gone. And Molly Flanigan. Barney McGurk, too.

I sipped my cup of tea and looked from Patrick to Máire. "You won't convince him, Máire," I said.

"You're a pain, Patrick Kelly, no question. I don't know how you put up with him, Honora."

"He has his moments. Besides, it was you urged me to marry him," I said.

"Jesus, God forgive me," Máire said, and made such a face at Patrick that he laughed.

Máire had been right. Michael wouldn't have wanted me to lock myself away in a prison of my own righteousness. Michael had paid the bride price: no jealousy, never a begrudger, no meanness, no fear. I've had two fine men to love, two Kellys, I thought, and I'm very grateful.

Patrick and I often talked of Michael to each other and to the grandchildren. Sharing these memories made Michael real for them. Michael had stepped out of the sea to me fifty-four years ago this very day. My young hero, who would never grow old. A ghrá mo chroí.

Yet Patrick and I had built a strong, steady love, deep and satisfying. He'd sustained us in the hard times, all through those terrible days after the Great Fire, with Chicago burning and Stephen, a fireman, missing in the midst of the fury.

Patrick had stood with me, Paddy and Bridey, and their little ones on our roof, watching fireballs shoot across the sky and stone and steel buildings explode, all the while knowing Stephen and his fellow firemen were trapped in the center of that hell.

Paddy had wanted to run out and find Stephen, but Patrick kept him home. "Stephen's a smart, brave fellow. He will survive," Patrick had said.

For three days, the fire raged. Embers reignited, carried by the wind. Only for a drizzling rain, the whole city would have been ashes. As it was, the flames didn't reach Bridgeport or the South Side, but the North Side and downtown had been destroyed completely.

It was a week before Stephen came home.

"You've seen battle now," Paddy had said to him.

And I remembered the tiny baby born into Black '47 who'd sucked a rag soaked with Champion's milk in order to live. Stephen's been fighting since he first drew breath.

Three hundred people had died in the Fire. A miracle it wasn't many more, Stephen said. Buildings burned or were saved based on a shift in the wind. So many churches gone. Stephen had seen Father Conway standing on the steps of St. Patrick's, holding high St. Grellan's crozier, the flames rushing toward him. But the winds changed and the church was saved. "I'd say they were very glad Uncle Patrick had given Father Dunne the crozier," Stephen said.

Stephen had moved up his wedding date and married Nelly Lang that summer.

During the Fire, I'd thought of Billy Caldwell and that last Potawatomi war dance. The Indian campfires had blazed up again. Getting a bit of their own back? Chicago's wild heart still beating.

And then we'd gone to work, building a better city.

I'd always been grateful to Amerikay, to Chicago, for taking us in. I'd desperately needed Chicago, but now Chicago needed me. We hadn't spared ourselves. Still battles to be fought. Strikes. The Great Depression in '77 struck us hard, but now Chicago and my family were prospering.

The Fair proclaimed that triumph. Only twenty-two years since the Great Fire and we'd invited the world over to see what we'd accomplished. And how had Chicago opened this grand celebration? With what the newspapers called "the Greatest Display of Pyrotechnics in the History of the World." *Fireworks.* Very Chicago.

I'd said all this to Patrick and now listened while Máire set out the same argument. It wasn't the Fair he objected to, Patrick told her, only the Irish villages.

"But I've asked the whole family to assemble, so we can go to Ireland together," I said to him.

"No mean feat, gathering them all," Máire said.

"They're coming here first, aren't they?" Patrick asked. "I'll see them then."

He was dressed in his best suit, looking well, his face brown from working in his potato patch. He grows five different varieties, still experimenting, trying to find a prattie that would resist the blight. The grandchildren delighted in helping him, and in eating the potatoes they dug from the ground. Patrick still had a feeling for the land after all these years of city living. We'd our one great trip to the country, to remember.

❖　❖　❖

Right after the July day Michael married Mary Ann Chambers, Patrick and I had left Chicago and spent that summer wandering through the Great North Woods.

We'd gone by train and canoe to Medicine Lake in northern Wisconsin to stay with his friend Migizi, Bald Eagle. Night after night, we sat up with him and his family by their fire and heard the Ojibwa tales. I felt as though I were in Mam's cottage listening to Granny's stories.

Then Patrick and I had gone on alone, canoeing along rivers, across lakes, following Indian trails through the forests. We ate sweet, plump berries and wild apples and caught more different kinds of fish than I'd have thought existed.

We slept under a night sky crowded with stars. One time, Patrick woke me to watch streaks of red and green and purple light up in the darkness. "A mearbhaill," we told each other.

I'd worn leather pants and a tunic Migizi's wife had given me and became sixteen again, washing my hair in the cold, clear lake water. Patrick, always fit, carried the canoe and chopped wood. The Ojibwa don't mark ages. Numbers aren't important to them—every season brings gifts, they believe.

The Fianna lived like this, I thought. Queen Maeve had ridden in her chariot through just such wild country when Ireland still was clad with towering oak trees.

We'd reached Canada and had a reunion with Joseph and Hughie and their families. I'd met Dennis's girls—grown-up women now—one was the image of Josie, and the other had a son the spit of Dennis. A part of the two of them, going on, something saved from the suffering Dennis and Josie had endured.

I'd been worried about Patrick's being in Canada. After all, he'd invaded the place and was a wanted man. Patrick said there was little danger as long as we stayed in the French villages along the St. Lawrence. He rather enjoys the thought of being an outlaw, still, I'd thought. Keeps him young. We shared a moment of regret for the Republic of Ireland that might have risen on Canadian soil.

"We will be a nation once again," I'd said.

"We will," he'd answered.

"And no more lives lost in the process, please God," I'd said.

On the way home, we stopped to see the mysterious dolmens in the forest and the stones with ogham writing.

"We were a wandering people," I'd said, amazed.

❖   ❖   ❖

We never left Chicago again. And Patrick seemed content, busy with Irish politics and Chicago politics and the wide place where both came together. We'd made our own Ireland of the mind and spirit. Patrick told me about places I'd never known—the little lakes of Cavan, the Speerin mountains of Tyrone, the cliffs of Donegal and Dublin town—all places where he'd worked and wandered. Now I could imagine John Comiskey's Cavan and see the McKennas in Donegal, Barney McGurk in Tyrone. "At home," I'd said to Patrick one night, "I knew only Galway people and my Connemara cousins. I had to come to Chicago to meet the Irish."

And really it was easier being Irish in Chicago. In Ireland families were still being evicted, still struggling and starving, a steady stream of them coming to Chicago. Paddy's wife Bridey's brothers, Luke and Dominick, had survived the Great Starvation, held on to their land, paid their rent, but the blight had struck again and they'd lost everything. Paddy and Bridey had sent them their fares.

❖ ❖ ❖

"Well, I'm not sitting here arguing," Máire said. "I'm going to the station. The train from California comes in an hour, and after that Gracie and James are due." She stood up from the table.

"I'll ask Mike to go with you."

So handy to have Mike still living at home with Bridey and his brothers and sisters. Though it was time he got married. Still, what would his mother do when he left? She needed his wages, even with young Jimmy and Martin helping.

"No," Máire said. "But I will stop to get my ticket to the Fair from Mike, and ask him to come up and talk to Patrick." She settled her new hat on her head and stood up.

"You look lovely," I told her.

Máire pulled down the sleeves of her pink-and-white-striped dress and twirled so I could see the flounce of the skirt. "You'll wear the dress I gave you?" she asked.

"Putting it on now." Mine had green stripes and a pin-tucked bodice, Máire still trying to increase my bosom.

Máire turned to Patrick. "Any man would count himself lucky to escort two such beautiful women to the Fair. Catch yourself on! Honora, I'll see you in the Irish village. Any delays, we'll meet in the Medieval Banquet Hall for dinner."

Máire went out the door.

"So, Honora," Patrick said to me, "you understand why I can't be part of the Sassenach stealing from us one more time? Medieval Banquet Hall, is it?"

I put my hand on his. "Declare a cease-fire and come with us," I said. "I haven't told you the real reason I wanted all the family to go together today. I've failed them, Patrick, and going to the Irish village may be my one chance to make amends."

"Failed them? Honora, you and Máire saved your children. And their children exist because of you. . . . A huge number of people."

"Twenty-seven grandchildren, and two great-grandchildren," I said.

"And all of their fathers doing well," Patrick said. "Think of that."

"I know."

Jamesy, fifty now, had never lost the sweet face and disposition he had as a child. He still worked in the railroad office and played the pipes at céilis in grand parish halls all over the city. And Stephen, at forty-six, had been a fireman and a policeman and was now a tavern owner, as he'd planned. Michael, at forty-four, was a blacksmith, as his da had been, and he looked so like him. He'd learned his trade with Paddy at the forge, but what he cared most about was base ball and his team, the Chicago White Stockings. He'd become great friends with Charlie Comiskey, Alderman Comiskey's son, who played the game for a job. A pitcher, you call him. Edward Cuneen, Bridget's husband, farmed in Summit, eight miles south of here. She'd taught at St. Xavier's and raised four children. A young-looking forty-eight. And I've been very lucky in my daughters-in-law. Grand girls they are. They've made my sons happy and raised a fine new generation of Kellys.

Every one of my grandchildren said with great pride, "I'm Irish," but they had no real notion of Ireland. Each of them went to Mass every Sunday, attended Catholic schools, danced at St. Bridget's Hall, enjoyed Clan Na Gael picnics, and would grow up to support the Democratic Party. Chicago Irish, and happy to be. But they knew nothing of Maeve and Macha, St. Enda and Mac Dara.

I tried to tell them Granny's tales, as I'd promised her, but there never seemed to be time. All the grandchildren were so busy with school and then work. The young ones didn't gather around the fire through long winter nights as we had, in the before times. Out and about, all of them.

What did I expect? Even though I'd encouraged my own children to hold on to their Irish, not one of them remembered more than a smattering of the language. The grandchildren found even the simple phrases I taught them too difficult. An inheritance lost to them, though a friend of Patrick's called Dan Cassidy told me Irish words were slipping into American slang. " 'So long' is from 'slán,' " he'd said. "And when a fellow's told to say 'uncle' it's 'anacal'—mercy—he's asking for."

The grandchildren had no interest in Irish history. Too confusing, they told me. "Why burden them with all that?" Jamesy had asked me. Why indeed?

I certainly would never talk to them about the Great Starvation. I didn't want those pictures in their minds. I'd longed to connect them to the deep down Ireland that was their heritage. I hadn't.

I explained all this to Patrick as best I could, then told him that

I believed seeing the exhibits in the Irish villages might make the grandsons and granddaughters curious, start them asking questions. A once-in-a-lifetime chance.

"Come with me, Patrick. Please."

"It's us!" Agnella, four years old, Paddy's daughter's little girl and my first great-grandchild, came running into the kitchen. "Here comes everybody!" she said.

And in minutes, Kellys came marching in, laughing and talking, the older girls wearing flower-brimmed hats and long dresses, the little ones in skirts and middy blouses. As many boys in long pants now as in knickers, all with shining hair and polished shoes, giggling and talking, anxious to get to the Fair.

"Let's go!" Agnella said, making Jamesy and Maggie laugh.

"Here's Mike!" someone shouted.

"And Ed!"

The leaders.

Bridget had sat down next to me, her four children part of the melee somewhere. "Mine want to see Hagenback's Trained Wild Animals," she said.

Stephen's wife, Nelly, standing near, said, "I swear, every one of my eight want to see something different—Bedouins, horsemen, sword fights, or—"

"The moving pictures!" said Michael's wife, Mary Ann. "That's where mine want to go. Their friends say you'd think it was real life."

"That's all well and good," Patrick said, "but we're going to the Irish villages." And he covered my hand with his.

"So we all will be together," I said, smiling at him.

But now Mike leaned over to whisper into my ear, "My mother says she can't go."

I looked at him. How handsome he was and dressed so well in his white linen suit and straw boater hat. Paddy's wish come true.

Except Paddy . . .

"I'll go to her," I said.

Bridget stood up to go with me, but I told her to stay. I walked through the crowd of excited children and started down the stairs.

❖ ❖ ❖

If only Paddy hadn't been forced to go to work in the Stockyards after he lost the forge in the Depression. And then to have to take Mike out of school at thirteen and bring him into that horrible blood-soaked place. Even little Jimmy took a job in the foundry, and him only eleven. But what could Paddy do? They needed the wages. Paddy's poor body finally gave out—hard labor since a child and who knows what toll the years of starvation took on him, not to mention the war. His heart failed, the doctor said, sad in a man only forty-two years old. Not failed, I wanted to shout. It broke. Broke. When he saw his son Mike—who'd been studying at St. Ignatius High School with the Jesuits, who was meant to be a banker and wear a suit and a straw boater—hacking away at cattle carcasses and knew little Jimmy was sweeping floors instead of going to elementary school, his heart broke and his body followed.

"Why do hard times hit us over and over, Mam?" Paddy had asked me not long before he died. "Why did the blight have to return *three* times?"

"I don't know, a stór," I'd said.

"We come to Chicago and start doing well, and then it's the war. No sooner are we back from the war than the city burns. What is it, Mam?"

I was sitting up with him while Bridey slept. She was exhausted from nursing him and taking care of the children. Máire and I helped, but it was Bridey who spent herself. "If he would only eat," she'd say, and would cook all his favorites.

"I want to, Bridey," he'd say to her, "but I can't."

This night, Paddy had awakened and wanted to talk. "Am I dying, Mam?"

"You're very weak, Paddy."

"I've been lying here thinking," he'd said, "wondering why God lets these things happen."

And I saw again my sturdy lad clutching the candle at St. Enda's well, determined to keep trouble away.

"It's not God, Paddy," I'd said.

"Uncle Patrick would blame the Sassenach," he'd said.

"Well, they didn't help matters much," I had said. "But there's greed and badness everywhere. Think of the good people, Paddy, the ones who helped us on the *Superior* and in New Orleans."

"Imagine! Jamesy found Lorenzo and Christophe."

"That was a kind of miracle, Paddy. So was James Mulloy's coming to us. Uncle Patrick bringing your Keeley cousins, lost but found again. And you, Paddy, my firstborn. You're a wonder, too. Such a fine man. I'm so proud of you."

But he'd interrupted me. "I killed men in the war, Mam," he'd said. "Of course, they were trying to kill me. To think I lived through so much and here's my own heart, doing me in." He took my hand and looked at me, very serious—my sturdy lad, a boy turning to his mother. "Is there going to be a life hereafter, Mam?"

"I believe there will be, Paddy."

"Will I go to heaven?"

"Father Grogan heard your confession," I'd said, "and gave you the last rites. Didn't he say you had the greatest gift a man could have—the grace of a happy death?"

"I'd rather a few more years of happy life, Mam," Paddy had said.

"I know, a stór, but, well, priests, they talk like that."

"And God will forgive me?"

"Of course. You've been a good son, a good husband, a good father. You love your family. God judges us by how much we love."

"I do love Bridey and my children—Mike and Jimmy, Mary, Martin and Ed, Anne and little Honora. And you, Mam. I love you very much. And Da, of course. My brothers and Bridget, her husband, their wives. And Uncle Patrick and Aunt Máire and Thomas and Daniel and Gracie and Johnny Og, and all belonging to them. I love all my nieces and nephews," he'd said.

"That's a lot of loving. I'd say you're going straight to heaven, Paddy."

"I want my heaven to be with Da and Champion at Knocnacuradh in the before times, with Galway Bay shining below us in the sun."

"Then it will be. That would be my heaven, too. Keep a place by the fire for me, Paddy."

I'd kissed him and he slept. He died the next day.

❖ ❖ ❖

Three years now, and Bridey had been very brave. Another young widow, and she had seven children to care for, though Mike and Jimmy were grown and working and Mary had married a good fellow named Pat Kelly two years ago.

Bridey and Mary were sitting together in the parlor. Mary was feeding her two-year-old, Willie.

"I'll stay home with Mam," Mary said to me.

"I can't go, Honora," Bridey said as I sat next to her on the sofa that had been Máire's.

I remembered Máire sitting here, mourning Johnny Og.

"Very sore on you, Bridey," I said.

She nodded.

"Today's the day I met Paddy's father."

She smiled. "I know. On Saint John's Night. Paddy told me, every year."

"He loved you so much, Bridey. After the war, it was you taught him how to be happy again."

"We were happy. Great joy in that fellow," Bridey said.

"It might be good for you to go, Mam," Mary said.

"If you're able, Bridey, you'd be doing me a great favor."

I told her why I wanted the family to go to the Irish villages together.

Bridey didn't answer. We sat in silence.

Little Willie looked at us, not used to such quiet. He reached out and took the spoon away from Mary. "I feed me," he said, and started scraping at the bowl.

Paddy's grandson.

We laughed.

"Yes, Honora," Bridey said. "Let's go to the Fair."

Chapter 37

"Straight to the Irish village?" Mike asked me as we arrived at the Fair.

"Right to it, Mike," I answered.

Mike led the bunch of us through the entrance and down the Midway until we came to an arched gateway.

"Ireland," I said to Agnella. "See the sign? Céad Mille Fáilte. That's Irish. That's our language. It means 'A Hundred Thousand Welcomes.'"

Patrick held one of Agnella's hands while I had the other. "There's an even bigger welcome," he told her. "Fáilte Uí Cheallaigh—the Welcome of the Kellys."

"So many Kellys," Agnella said.

And all of them here because Michael Kelly stepped out of Galway Bay on that summer morning so many years ago.

Now Mike was speaking to Patrick and me. "Will you two do the honors and lead us into the Irish village?"

"We will indeed," Patrick said, and smiled at me.

"We're the first ones in Ireland!" Agnella said as we stepped under the arch.

Patrick laughed. "She sounds like Michael when we ran imaginary races on the course at Gallagh, with him on my shoulders," he said.

Then everyone else followed us into what a huge sign said was "Lady Aberdeen's Irish Village."

"Had to put her name right on it," Patrick said. "They never lack for cheek. Oh well, signs can be changed," he said to Jamesy, who'd come up to stand next to us.

"Faugh-a-Ballagh," Jamesy shouted.

And didn't his two small sons echo the battle cry.

"Now," Mike said to me, "where should we go first?"

"I'm not sure," I said. I looked around.

Rows of cottages lined a cobbled street that led to a grassy square and a castle. In the distance I saw the other village, a Donegal version. But both were only stage sets, I thought, like the scenery put up for Irish Night at McVicker's Theatre. Nothing real. Phony.

All these faces turned toward me, the whole family waiting for directions from me.

Then Nora, Paddy's youngest, named for me, spoke. "Aunt Máire says Marshall Field's has a store here, selling genuine reproductions of Celtic jewelry."

Genuine reproductions. That's all this is—a genuine reproduction. How could this phony place teach them anything about the real Ireland? Patrick was right. It was all a cod, with Lady Aberdeen collecting the quarter admission fee from people homesick for a place they'd never seen, could never know.

I looked at Patrick and shook my head. No, not this. No, we can't take them here.

But we couldn't leave. Máire and her family were waiting for us. I know what she'd say to me: What did you expect? Nothing's perfect. We'll have a good time. A day devoted to fun, and all of us together. Enjoy yourself.

And she'd be right. The children practically vibrated with energy, eager to explore whatever the village offered. Laughing. Teasing one another. Alive. My children's children. Our joy. Our triumph. We've won, Máire.

"Should we start with the Blarney Stone?" Mike asked.

"I heard the Blarney Stone was a fake," said Paddy's Martin. "Just some paving stone."

"We can pretend it's real," Jamesy said.

"We can indeed," I said to Mike. "Perhaps the young ones would like to tour the Irish villages on their own and then visit some of the other attractions on the Midway. We could meet them in the afternoon and then have dinner together."

Mike agreed, relieved, I thought.

"All right, everyone, get going," he said. "We'll meet at the Blarney Stone, and I've a table reserved for dinner at Mrs. Hart's Donegal Castle. Then we'll watch the fireworks."

Patrick and I saw a bench under a tall oak tree across from a row of neat cottages and settled ourselves down as the rest scattered. Agnella chose to stay with us.

"What does that say?" she asked, pointing to a sign stuck into the grass.

"'This sod comes from Ireland,'" I read.

"It's very green," she said.

"'Tis," Patrick agreed.

After a bit, Patrick and Agnella and I walked over to a building that advertised "Irish antiquities": The standing stone marked with ogham symbols was made from papier-mâché, but an authentic page from an illuminated manuscript was displayed under glass.

"Look at this, Agnella. See the animals around the letter? The Irish monks drew those almost fifteen hundred years ago."

"Nice," she said. "Makes the words pretty."

Patrick and I laughed.

We wandered along the cobbled street until the grown-ups—Jamesy and Maggie, Stephen and Nelly, Bridget and Ed, Michael and Mary Ann and Bridey—found us.

"The children made short work of the villages and now they're all at the Blarney Stone," Nelly said. "Let's go watch."

Mike had rented a Kodak camera. One after another, the children leaned out the window of the castle and kissed that hunk of rock, then waved at Mike as he snapped their pictures.

"A great souvenir of this happy day," said Jamesy's wife, Maggie.

"Aren't we lucky with the weather," Mary Ann said.

"The sun shining just for us," Bridget said.

"Listen, Mam!" Jamesy took my arm. "Pipes!"

We followed the sound to a crossroads in the center of the village. And there he was—a piper—seated under an oak tree, a tall, dark-haired fellow dressed in a kilt and a cloak, the uilleann pipes under his arm. We surrounded him.

"Charles McSweeney, at your service," the piper said.

"Our da was a piper," Jamesy said to him. "And our grandda, too."

"And where were these pipers from?" McSweeney asked.

"Kelly Country," said Patrick. "Gallagh of the Kellys."

"Ah," said McSweeney. "Where William Boy O'Kelly gave his famous party. One of the greatest pipers of all time was a Kelly from that area. Long before me, but I'm sure some of the tunes he played, I'm playing. Probably was your great-grandda."

"My son plays," I said, pointing to Jamesy.

"And where are your pipes?" the piper said to him. "We could play together."

"I'm afraid I'm past piping now," Jamesy said.

McSweeney looked around our circle. "A load of Kellys here to carry on the tradition."

And yet not one of the young generation could fiddle or pipe. Still, when he piped the tune, the younger children started dancing, leaping, and whirling, with Agnella in the center, jumping up and down.

Patrick gestured me over to him. "I found a blacksmith," he said.

We walked to the far side of the green and stood together, looking over the half door into the dark forge. The smith was a big man, and silent.

"Very like Murty Mor," Patrick said. "How could we ever explain a man like him to the young ones? I don't know if even your sons would be able to understand who he was."

"I wish I'd known him," I said.

The smith put a glowing horseshoe on the anvil and brought the hammer down on it.

"A mighty blow," I said to Patrick. "How I miss Paddy, my sturdy lad."

Patrick put his arm around my shoulders.

"Paddy and Michael," I said to Patrick. "I hope it's true that they're together."

"They are, Honora," he said. "And waiting for us."

"Paddy's telling his da what a fine man Mike is, supporting his mother, brothers, and sister with his wages, helping us."

And now Mike walked over to us.

"The forge," I said to him.

"My da," he said. "I wish . . ." He stopped.

"He sees us, Mike. He does," I said. "He's looking at you right now in your linen suit and boater hat. He's very pleased, Mike. I know it."

I hugged him. Tall like Paddy and my Michael, broad, that same black hair and those blue-sky eyes rimmed in violet. Michael Joseph Kelly.

"Now," he said, stepping back. "Dinner in Donegal. Aunt Máire will be wondering where we are."

The banquet hall at Donegal Castle called corned beef and cabbage "Ye Olde Medieval Fare." But there were good smells in the air and a slew of happy people.

And there Máire was—heading toward us.

Then as Agnella had said, here came everyone: Daniel and his family, Thomas, Gracie and James Mulloy and their two sons and two daughters—and Gracie holding her baby grandchild, Máire's great-grandson.

All the cousins together, for the first time ever.

An old man stood next to James Mulloy. He was leaning on a black-thorn stick.

"Jesus, Mary, and Holy Saint Joseph," I said, running toward him. "Owen Mulloy."

"Eugene," he said as we embraced.

✦   ✦   ✦

So. We talked and laughed and ate; second helpings were free. Portraits of Irish heroes surrounded us: Robert Emmet, Henry Gratton, Charles Stewart Parnell.

"They like their heroes of the Protestant persuasion," Patrick said to Owen.

"Poor Parnell," said Owen. "The uncrowned king of Ireland."

"And we can do without that giant statue of Gladstone in the corner," Patrick said.

"A stick of dynamite would take care of that," said Owen.

Patrick and Owen were off, talking Irish politics, two men in the know. "In-dis-pu-ta-ble in-con-sis-ten-cies!" I heard Owen say to Patrick as the talk raced up and down the long table.

A grand reunion, surely.

"What a crowd," Máire said to me. "Impressive what two sisters can accomplish."

Charles McSweeney, the piper, walked out on a platform at the front of the hall. "Quiet down now, the lot of you. We've some fine entertainment."

A clutch of fiddlers performed, tin whistles played, and young girls danced, their curls bouncing.

"And now, the tenor!" McSweeney announced.

"Gorgeous-looking," said Máire as the tenor took the stage.

"I know the fellow," Stephen said. "He's a Chicago police captain. Frank O'Neill, you call him. He made a book of Irish songs, collecting them."

"Sing 'I'll Take You Home, Kathleen,' " someone shouted from the crowd.

"That's not really an Irish song," O'Neill said. "It wasn't even an Irish person who wrote it."

"Well, whoever wrote it, wrote it for us," said the man in the audience.

"Sing it, sing it!" the crowd shouted.

"It's a good song," Owen said. "I used to sing it to Katie before . . . Thank God she died peacefully, in her own bed, with all of her children and grandchildren attending her. But what she desired more than anything, I couldn't give her. Katie wanted to go home. Ah well, she's there now, watching the sun go down on Galway Bay."

More shouting from the crowd. O'Neill said, "You win!" and began to sing. When he reached the chorus—"Oh! I will take you back, Kathleen"—the whole audience joined him: "To where your heart will feel no pain." We sang together: "And when the fields are fresh and green, I'll take you to your home again!"

He hit the high note and held it beautifully. There were sighs all around, loud applause. O'Neill raised his hands to quiet the crowd.

"Could we have a Galway song, Frank?" Stephen called out.

"Surely there's one among you Kellys could sing it!" he said.

"Michael!" his brothers shouted. "Michael! Michael! Michael! He's our singer!"

"All right, all right!" Michael said.

"Clear the way for the Galway man!" said McSweeney.

Michael stepped onto the stage. "I would like to dedicate this song to my aunt Máire, my uncle Patrick, to the memory of my da, and with great love and thanks to my mam, Honora Kelly. Up Galway!"

Cheers at this.

"Hoo-rah!" Patrick shouted.

Michael sang.

> It's far away I am today
> From scenes I roamed a boy
> And long ago the hour, I know
> I first saw Illinois.

I had never heard the song, but I understood the sentiment. An old man, gone for many decades, longs for home, friendship, and the "sweeter green" of Irish ground. And how beautiful Michael sang of this place he could ever only know through our memories. Connected. Somehow, someway, he *was* connected. Perhaps they all were, more strongly than seemed possible. More strongly than I knew.

He began the final verse. I clasped each word to myself.

> 'Tis all the Heaven I'd ask of God
> Upon my dying day
> My soul to soar forevermore
> Above you, Galway Bay.

Please God. This. All of us together, hereafter and forevermore, beside Galway Bay. Great applause. Michael hugged me. "Thank you," I said to my youngest son.

We left the dining room to find the sun setting. Darkness dropped over the Fair.

Ed caught me by the arm. "Wait until you see!" he said to me.

And Mike took my other arm. "Here now, any moment . . ."

Mike and Ed counted together, "One, two, three, there!"

In the snap of a finger, there was brightness everywhere. Light outlined every building: white bulbs, red ones, blue, green, yellow—Chicago making its own rainbow. . . . Glorious.

"Fairyland," I said to Patrick. "Tír na nOg."

"A mearbhall," Máire said to me. She'd come up beside us. "And I don't mean only the electricity."

"I know," I said. "We are very lucky. Amerikay saved us."

The crowd grew bigger and happier. More and more groups of young men and women went by, singing and laughing.

Stephen introduced us to a policeman friend of his named Phil McGuire and Phil's cousin from Philadelphia, Honora Kennedy.

I nodded and smiled, but I must have looked weary because Stephen asked me if I was all right.

"I'm fine for a woman who's been around the world in one day. Ed told me there are forty-eight countries and two thousand seven hundred fifty-four languages on the Midway."

"Ed would know," said Stephen.

"C'mon, everyone," Mike said. "I've reserved a gondola on the Ferris wheel just for the family."

"And will we fit?" I asked.

"There's room for forty-five people. They're as big as Pullman cars!"

"But there's more than fifty of us, with Máire and her family."

"I'll fix it," he said.

"Look up," Ed said to me. "The Ferris wheel isn't just tall. It moves. It takes a one-thousand-horsepower motor to keep it going. The Eiffel Tower can only stand still."

"Much better to move," I said.

Chicago will always be the best for Ed.

So, fifty-seven of us crammed into the gondola after Mike slipped a folded bill to the attendant.

"It's very safe," Mike said. "Don't worry."

"We're riding through the air in the world's most beautiful railroad car," I said to Patrick, next to me. Completely enclosed, glass windows, mahogany paneling.

"It would put you in mind of the canal boats," I called out to Máire.

"It would," she said.

Agnella had climbed onto my lap. I held her close as the huge wheel swung into motion. We went up and up and up, higher and higher until we could see all of the lit-up White City spread out below us.

"If I lifted Grellan's crozier," Patrick said, "it would touch the stars." He raised his arm. "Kellys Abu!" he shouted, and Agnella clapped her hands.

"This must be the way God sees the world," I said to Patrick. "Before and after flowing together. And look, look, the moon!"

High above the electric display, the full moon shone a strong, steady light. Moonlight slipped along the river, skimmed the top of the lagoon. A gleaming path rippled across the waters of Lake Michigan. Michael . . . marking the way home.

"Where's Bridgeport?" Agnella asked me.

"There, a rún. There, see the moon on the water?" I pointed. "That's the river."

"I see, I see," she said. "And where's Ireland?"

"Back there, in the Fair."

"No, no, not that Ireland. Not the village. The real Ireland. Where?"

"Well," I said, "you could follow the canal to the river and go south to New Orleans, then get on a boat to go across the ocean."

"Or," said Patrick, "you could travel up Lake Michigan to Canada and leave through the Saint Lawrence River."

"Or, take a train to New York and sail away on a big steamship," Máire said.

"Or even go west," said Daniel, who'd been listening, "past China and all around the world to Ireland."

"Do you have to go over water?" Agnella asked.

"You do," I said. "You see, Agnella, Ireland is an island surrounded by the sea."

"Could we ride the Ferris wheel to Ireland?"

"Fly over the water, you mean? The Children of Lir did," I said.

"Who are they?"

"The sons and daughter of a king, they were turned into swans."

"I'd like to be a swan," Agnella said.

"You know, Agnella," I said, holding her closer, whispering into her ear, "you can go to Ireland in an instant. Close your eyes and imagine—Ireland will be there."

"But what will it look like? Are there birds and flowers? Tell me, please."

"I'll tell you, alanna. I'll tell you everything."

Our moment at the very top passed. The wheel turned. We faced west as we started slowly going down. Beyond the lights of Chicago, away from the moon, the dark prairie stretched out, no limit to it. Irish people are scattered over the length and breadth of you, Amerikay. Have you swallowed us up whole and entire?

"Are you sad?" Agnella asked me as we stepped off the Ferris wheel.

We stood together for a moment, looking up. I bent down to her. "Why would I be sad?"

"That the ride is over," she said.

"Oh, but it's not, a stór. The wheel will keep moving. Circles and spirals," I said. "Life is circles and spirals. That's why the great stones of Ireland are carved with circles and spirals, to show us nothing ever really ends."

"Was it the Children of Lir put them on the stones?"

"They may have." I took her two small hands in mine. "Fadó," I said to Agnella.

"What?" she asked.

"Fadó," I repeated. "It's an Irish word. It means 'a long time ago' or 'once upon a time,' where stories begin."

"Fadó," she said. "Will you tell me the stories?"

"I will."

Máire and Patrick and the others had started along the Midway. I straightened up and, still holding Agnella's hand, walked on after them.

"My granny told me a lot of stories," I said to Agnella. "I must think of where to start."

"Begin where we're from. Name me *that* place."

"Galway Bay, a rún, Galway Bay."

Afterword

Galway Bay, though fiction, is rooted in research done over a period of thirty-five years in Ireland and the United States. The novel draws on family history, especially the memories of Honora Kelly, that my cousin Agnella Kelly, Sister Mary Erigina, who lived to be 107, shared with me. Honora was her great-grandmother, my great-great-grandmother. The two million who escaped the Great Starvation became forty-four million—completely American, but always Irish. *Galway Bay* is meant to echo their story, as well as the stories of all other groups who, forced to leave their homes, turn the tragedy of exile into triumph by simply surviving.

GLOSSARY

Most of the characters in *Galway Bay* would have been native Irish speakers at a time when the deliberate eradication of the language, a branch of Gaelic, was in full force in Ireland. Bearna and Connemara retained the language, and immigrants from those areas were bilingual well into the twentieth century. I think any Irish-American who gets the least glimpse of the rich, evocative language spoken by our ancestors for thousands of years and lost in a generation feels a kind of despair and a yearning for even the smallest crumbs of knowledge. In Ireland, efforts to restore Irish have been ongoing, and now there are schools where instruction takes place in Irish. A hopeful sign. I used some Irish words, many familiar from Irish songs and expressions, to at least nod in appreciation and sorrow at this heritage. This glossary is meant to be helpful, not definitive.

a ghrá (ah graw)—to call someone "love"
a ghrá mo chroí (ah graw muh [ch]ree)—the love of my heart
alanna (ah-lah-nah)—from the Irish leanbh (child)
amadán (ah-muh-daun)—fool
ard (ord)—top, a height; used in many townland names
a rún—my dear
Askeeboy (AS-kee-buoy)—townland name; from uisce (water) and bui (yellow); marshy land

a stór (ah sthor)—darling

bachall (BAW-kull)—staff, crozier

Bearna (BAR-nah)—gap

Beltaine (BYOWL-thine)—May Day

bogdeal (BOG-dall)—petrified wood

cairn (kern)—a pile of stones; a prehistoric burial mound

cathach (KAH-ha[ch])—battle standard

céili (KAY-lee)—social evening; dance

cillín (kill-een)—little church; cell; sometimes refers to an unconsecrated graveyard

colleen bawn (kah-leen bawn)—a term for a fair-haired girl

corn—the term for grain in England and Ireland

croppie—a negative word applied to Irish farmers

crozier (CROH-zher)—staff of a bishop or abbot

Cuchulain (Koo-[CH]UL-lan)—hero of the Ulster cycle of old Irish tales

curragh (CUR-ra[ch])—light canvas or hide boat with oars

Deirdre (DEER-druh)—legendary heroine who defied the king to elope with her lover, Naois

dubh (duv)—dark; black

fadó (fah-doe)—long ago; once upon a time

Fenian (FEE-nee-un)—revolutionary group established in 1855; named from the Fianna (band of warriors of Finn)

flaithiúlacht (flah-who-lu[ch])—very generous (from flaith: prince)

geis (gyas)—taboo, charm, spell

gombeen man—moneylender (from gaimbin: exorbitant interest)

grá (graw)—love

guilpin (gyil-peen)—a lout

Indian corn—dried American corn

Knocnacuradh (NOK-nuh-COOR-ruh)—from cnoc (hill); na (of the); curadh (champions)

Lughnasa (LOO-nuh-suh)—August 1; feast at the start of the harvest

lumper—a variety of potato

Macha (MAH-[ch]uh)—the Horse Goddess

Máire (MAH-ree)—Mary (Honora's sister)

mathair (MAW-hur)—mother

mearbhall (MEOW-rull)—literal: bewilderment; context: a strange light at sea, perhaps phosphorescent

meascán (mass-kawn)—a muddle

meitheal (MEE-hall)—communal work party

mhic (vic)—son

mo buachaill (muh WOO-[ch]ul)—my boy

mo ghrá (muh graw)—my love

na bi ag caint (maw-bee-egg-kaint)—don't talk nonsense; don't talk

ná habair tada (naw HAH-bur TAH-dah)—say nothing

Naois (NYUY-sheh)—Irish warrior; Deirdre's lover

Oisin (uh-sheen)—grandson of Finn; pre-Christian Irish king of legend

Grace O'Malley—sixteenth-century chieftain; the Pirate Queen of Connaught

pátrún (pat-run)—religious observance made at holy sites

poitín (pah-cheen)—illicit whiskey

piseog (PEE-sog)—evil spell

prattie (PRAY-tee)—a potato

púcán (pooh-kawn)—fishing boat with sail

Queen Maeve (Mave)—prehistoric queen of Ireland, heroine of the epic "The Cattle Raid of Cooley"

ráth (rah)—a prehistoric ring fort common in Ireland

rua (ROO-ah)—red

Samhain (SAU-en)—Halloween

Sassenach (SOSS-uh-na[ch])—the English (from Saxon)

scalpeen—a makeshift shelter

scraw—a clod of earth (from scraithin)

seachaint (SHOH-[ch]ant)—shun, avoid

siúil (shool)—walk

sláinte (slawn-cheh)—health; a drinking toast

slán (slawn)—health, safe, farewell

slán abhaile (slawn ah-wal-ya)—safe home

sliveen—slang for a low person

taoiseach (TYOY-shu[ch])—a chieftain

tobar (TUB-bur)—well, fountain, source

tobar geal (TUB-bur gyal)—pure water

uisce beatha (ISH-keh BAH-hah)—the water of life; whiskey

whist (weest)—like "shhh"; used in Ireland; probably derived from Irish

Acknowledgments

The process of writing *Galway Bay* really began in 1969, my first time in Ireland. When I think of all the people I met on my subsequent trips who said, "Welcome home," to me, I want to thank every single person. I wish I could name each one of you. Thank you.

I do want to express special gratitude to my own family: my father, Michael Joseph Kelly; my mother, Mariann Williams Kelly; my brother, Michael; my sisters, Randy, Mickey, Susie, and Nancy; and family members Martha Hall Kelly, Ernest Strapazon, Ed Panian, and Bruce Jarchow. Each made unique contributions to this book, as did my nieces and nephews. My great-niece Aidan and great-nephew Edward have begun Honora's seventh generation, an occasion for thanksgiving.

I'm grateful to my aunts and uncles and all my cousins, branches of the same tree, and express particular gratitude to Sister Mary Erigina, BVM, Agnella Kelly, who introduced me to Honora.

In Galway, Ireland, my research benefited greatly from Mary Qualter of the Galway County Library, who helped me solve many mysteries and introduced me to excellent local histories, especially the works on Bearna by Padraig Faherty and artist Geraldine Folan, who captures Galway Bay and the lost fishing hamlet of Freeport in her paintings.

Siobhan McGuinness and Jean Gormley of the Galway History Center were very helpful to me, and I thank them. I'm grateful to Sister Máire Mac Niallais, who located both Askeeboy and Eugene Mulloy of Nashville, connecting neighbors separated for a hundred and sixty years.

I want to thank the National University of Ireland, Galway, and the University of Ulster at Derry as well as the Royal Irish Academy and the National Library of Ireland for giving me access to their collections.

I very much appreciate the chance to use the resources of Delargy Centre for Irish Folklore and the National Folklore Collection, University College Dublin, Ireland, and thank Emer Ni'Cheallaigh and Jonny Dillon. Jonny translated the Irish material and kept me right on my own references to the language.

I learned much in visiting various heritage centers, especially those at Castle Blakeney and the Ulster American Folk Park.

I'm grateful to John and Pat Hume, Daithi and Antoinette O'Ceallaigh, Patsy O'Kane and all at Beech Hill House Hotel; Sharon Quinn, Roisin Nevin, Mary Mullan, and the staff of Ballynahinch House; Maeve Kelly, Gerard Kelly-O'Brien, Padraig Keeley, and the other families of Carna; and taxi drivers beyond counting.

I wish to thank my friends in Dublin: Mary Sheerin, Mary Maher, Mary Cummins, Maeve Binchy, Sharon Plunkett, and Philip Nolan.

In Chicago, I thank the skilled and generous research staff of the Chicago History Museum, the librarians at the Newberry Library, and the Harold Washington Branch of the Chicago Public Library. Bonnie Rowan guided me at the Library of Congress and the National Archives in Washington, D.C. Thank you.

I'm grateful to my own CUNY Graduate Center Library. Quinnipiac University's Great Hunger Room, The Lender Family Special Collection of the Arnold Bernhard Library, receives my thanks and my admiration for their unique contribution in bringing together a rich archive and ensuring that the Great Starvation will not be forgotten. This includes the wonderful bronze statue "Irish Mother and Child" by sculptor Glenna Goodacre, who did the Vietnam Nurses' Memorial. In this figure the artist captures the determination and resilience of the Irish women who saved us. (The statue also resembles in a startling way my sister Susie, both in spirit and appearance.) Goodacre also uses "Irish Mother and Child" as one of the thirty-five life-size figures that depict the Great Starvation and the Journey to America in the powerful Irish Memorial in Philadelphia. Thank you to the government of Canada for the Grosse Île Irish Memorial National Historic Site. I was also touched and inspired by the New York

Irish Hunger Memorial in Battery Park City. To stand by the authentic nineteenth-century cottage on a hillside covered with native Irish plants is an emotional experience. I thank artist Brian Tollo, and former governor George Pataki (his mother, Margaret, whose mother was born in Ireland, was on the executive committee). I would like to thank historian Maureen O'Rourke Murphy, PhD, who has raised awareness of the Great Starvation through this memorial, her work in developing a curriculum for the New York State schools, and her own scholarship and her leadership in the American Conference for Irish Studies. I am grateful, too, for the encouragement she's given me. Many collections of letters, documents, diaries, and newspapers, as well as books on a whole range of subjects, enriched *Galway Bay*. I've listed some of them on MaryPatKelly.com.

In the last few years, studies of the Great Starvation have multiplied. I have found Cormac O'Grada's work especially helpful, as well as Thomas Keneally's *The Great Shame,* and I kept coming back to *The Great Hunger* by Cecil Woodham Smith.

I want to thank my teachers, professors Sam Levin and Marvin Magdalaner of the CUNY Graduate Center; John Kelly of the Parlour, the Kelly Gang, and Roberta Aria Sorvino, Mary Anne Kelly DeFuccio, Monique and Danielle Inzinna, Bruce and Carole Hart, Mary Bringle, Laura Aversano, and Maria Frisa. I'm grateful to Bill Pindar and all at the Stony Point Center. Thanks to Meredith Meagher and Betty Martinez.

Thank you very much to the outstanding team at Grand Central Publishing, Hachette Book Group. I'm very proud that Maureen Egen, so revered in publishing during her tenure at Warner Books, made *Galway Bay* possible. Thank you for that, Maureen, and for giving me editor Frances Jalet-Miller. Her intelligence, sensitivity, and honesty contributed greatly to this book. I appreciate the encouragement I received from Jamie Raab, executive vice president of Hachette Book Group and publisher of Grand Central Publishing. Thank you to senior editor Karen Kosztolnyik for championing *Galway Bay*. At Hachette Book Group I'm also grateful to executive managing editor Harvey-Jane Kowal and to copy editor Sona Vogel for taming the hefty manuscript, to the art department for the beautiful cover, and to senior publicist Elly Weisenberg Kelly for her enthusiasm.

And then there's Kathy Danzer. Her incomparable computer skills transformed hundreds of legal pads into a manuscript. I thank her, as my first reader, for her judgment, kindness, and rock hard belief in the process. Because she's a woman of the theater, she insisted that the show must go on. We had to be ready for opening night. And we were.

I'm grateful to Barbara Leahy Sutton, the friend of a lifetime and a distinguished editor of the *Chicago Tribune*. She guided me personally and professionally.

Thank you, Martin Sheerin, my husband and most precious connection to Ireland, for letting me read to you when I got stuck. You always know how to help me out.

About the Author

As an author and filmmaker, Mary Pat Kelly has told various stories connected to Ireland. Her award-winning PBS documentaries and accompanying books include *To Live for Ireland*, a portrait of Nobel Peace Prize winner John Hume and the political party he led; *Home Away from Home: The Yanks in Ireland*, a history of U.S. forces in Northern Ireland during World War II; and *Proudly We Served: The Men of the USS Mason*, about the only African-American sailors to take a World War II warship into combat, whose first foreign port was Belfast. She wrote and directed the dramatic feature film *Proud*, starring Ossie Davis and Stephen Rea, based on the USS *Mason* story.

She's written *Martin Scorsese: The First Decade* and *Martin Scorsese: A Journey; Good to Go: The Rescue of Scott O'Grady from Bosnia;* and a novel, *Special Intentions*, inspired by her experience as a nun.

Mary Pat Kelly worked in Hollywood as a screenwriter for Paramount and Columbia Pictures and in New York City as an associate producer with *Good Morning America* and *Saturday Night Live*. She received her PhD from the City University of New York.

Born and raised in Chicago, she lives on Manhattan's Upper West Side with her husband, Web designer Martin Sheerin from County Tyrone.

MaryPatKelly.com
GalwayBayTheBook.com

READING GROUP GUIDE

Discussion Questions

1. "We wouldn't die," Honora tells her great-granddaughter. The theme of survival as victory informs *Galway Bay*. What qualities allow a person to triumph over horrific circumstances? Do Honora, Michael, Máire, Granny, and others show such characteristics? What motivates them, gives them strength? Have you faced difficulties in your own life that demanded such determination? Have your ancestors struggled through historic calamities? Do you think knowing their stories enhances your life, or do you think the past is past and should be forgotten? Have you looked into your genealogy? If so, how does what you discovered affect you?

2. The novel opens in the "before times," when despite hardship and oppression the characters have created a place for themselves where songs, stories, communal celebration, faith, and family life can bring happiness. Did you find this portrayal believable? How does the way the Keeley family, Honora and Michael Kelly, Máire, and Owen Mulloy see themselves contrast with the way the landlords and British government regarded them? Do you think there are present-day communities judged differently by the larger society?

3. Many couples in literature fall in love at first sight, as do Honora and Michael. Do you believe in such instant attraction? Can it lead to long-lasting love? What do you think of the relationship between

Honora and Patrick? How would you characterize Máire's attitude toward men and marriage?

4. The two main women characters, Honora and Máire, do not conform to the usual stereotype of a nineteenth-century Irish woman. Do you think this is a strength or weakness of the novel? The two sisters have quite different characteristics and beliefs. Do you think they complement each other or do the differences bring mostly conflict? Honora's and Máire's biggest disagreement comes when their sons enlist in the Civil War. What do you think of each mother's reaction and the way each chooses to cope with having her sons in combat?

5. Prayer and ritual play an important part in *Galway Bay*. What do you think of Honora's beliefs, of Máire's? Are there issues raised between them that have relevance to the practice of religion now?

6. Children have a central role in *Galway Bay*. What does each one—Paddy, Jamesy, Bridget, Stephen, Michael, Johnny Og, Thomas, Daniel, and Gracie—reveal about the effect horrific circumstances have on a child? How do these early experiences mark the children as they become adults?

7. *Galway Bay* incorporates characters and incidents from Irish-American history that are not widely known. Were you surprised by people such as James Mulligan and Billy Caldwell, and events such as the Irish units fighting each other in the Civil War and the Fenian invasion of Canada? Was anything else new to you?

8. Honora argues against the use of physical force to liberate Ireland. "I want my sons to live for Ireland, not to die for it," she tells Patrick. He maintains that freedom must be won by armed struggle. What do you think of each one's position? How are the same issues debated today?

9. One million Irish people died from starvation and related diseases while food was being exported from the country. How does the novel explore this situation? What do you make of the relief efforts attempted? Do any contemporary situations come to mind? Honora calls the escape of her family and two million more Irish from the

Great Starvation "one of the greatest rescues in human history" and says, "We saved ourselves." What do you think she means? What effect do you think those immigrants and their descendants—now forty-four million—have had on the United States? How does their story resonate for other immigrants and exiles, past and present?

10. Honora takes her grandchildren and great-grandchildren to the Irish villages at the World's Columbian Exhibition to connect them to a heritage she hasn't been able to pass down to them. Do you understand her disappointment at the display? Do you think it is possible to connect with the true culture of our ancestors? Is it desirable? Little Agnella's interest encourages Honora. All will be well. Do you believe one child's understanding can really make such a difference?